Praise for

THE HEART'S INVISIBLE FURIES

"A picaresque, lolloping odyssey for the individual characters and for the nation that confines them. The book blazes with anger as it commemorates lives wrecked by social contempt and self-loathing . . . a substantial achievement."
—THE GUARDIAN

"An epic full of verve, humour and heart . . . sure to be read by the bucketload . . . deeply cinematic [and] extremely funny."
—THE IRISH TIMES

"This is nothing less than the story of Ireland over the past seventy years, expressed in the life of one man . . . highly entertaining and often very funny. . . . Big and clever."
—THE TIMES SUNDAY REVIEW

"Bleak, bittersweet, and Irish to the bone . . . explore[s] the relationship between Catholicism and patriarchy in midcentury Ireland and beyond."
—O, THE OPRAH MAGAZINE

"The most inviting and completely spellbinding book this author has ever written . . . an outstandingly memorable achievement."
—CHRISTIAN SCIENCE MONITOR

"More than a coming-of-age story, *The Heart's Invisible Furies* is one man's journey from persecution to toleration."
—BOOKPAGE

"Enchanting . . . With evocative descriptions of each city and fateful plot turns that twist the narrative in surprising ways, Boyne adroitly captures Cyril's shifting identity as he grapples with nationality, class, and sexuality. . . . The life of Cyril Avery is one to be relished."
—PUBLISHERS WEEKLY

"Boyne, who has a wonderful gift for characterization, does a splendid job of weaving these various lives together in ways that are richly dramatic, sometimes surprising, and always compelling. . . . Utterly captivating and not to be missed."
**—BOOKLIST
(STARRED REVIEW)**

"With quick strokes and bitter humor, Boyne's opening scene encapsulates the Irish Church's hypocrisy. . . . Boyne continues his crusading ways with the quiet keening of this painful, affecting novel."
**—KIRKUS REVIEWS
(STARRED REVIEW)**

JOHN BOYNE

The Heart's Invisible Furies

HOGARTH

London   New York

For John Irving

Copyright © 2017 by John Boyne

Reading Group Guide © 2018 by Penguin Random House LLC

All rights reserved.
Published in the United States by Hogarth, an imprint of the Crown Publishing Group, a division of Penguin Random House LLC, New York.
crownpublishing.com

HOGARTH is a trademark of the Random House Group Limited, and the H colophon is a registered trademarks of Penguin Random House LLC.

Reading Group Guide and the accompanying colophon are trademarks of Penguin Random House LLC.

Originally published in hardcover in the United States by Hogarth, an imprint of the Crown Publishing Group, a division of Penguin Random House LLC, New York, in 2017.

Library of Congress Cataloging-in-Publication Data is available.

ISBN 978-1-5247-6079-3
Ebook ISBN 978-1-5247-6080-9

Printed in the United States of America

Cover design: Evan Gaffney
Cover photograph: © Mary Evans/HENRY GRANT/The Image Works

10 9 8

First Paperback Edition

"Am I alone in thinking that the world becomes a more repulsive place every day?" asked Marigold, glancing across
the breakfast table toward her husband, Christopher.

"Actually," he replied, "I find that—"

"The question was rhetorical," said Marigold, lighting
a cigarette, her sixth of the day. "Please don't embarrass
yourself by offering an opinion."

—Maude Avery, *Like to the Lark* (The Vico Press, 1950)

PART I
SHAME

1945 The Cuckoo in the Nest

The Good People of Goleen

Long before we discovered that he had fathered two children by two different women, one in Drimoleague and one in Clonakilty, Father James Monroe stood on the altar of the Church of Our Lady, Star of the Sea, in the parish of Goleen, West Cork, and denounced my mother as a whore.

The family was seated together in the second pew, my grandfather on the aisle using his handkerchief to polish the bronze plaque engraved to the memory of his parents that was nailed to the back of the woodwork before him. He wore his Sunday suit, pressed the night before by my grandmother, who twisted her jasper rosary beads around her crooked fingers and moved her lips silently until he placed his hand atop hers and ordered her to be still. My six uncles, their dark hair glistening with rose-scented lacquer, sat next to her in ascending order of age and stupidity. Each was an inch shorter than the next and the disparity showed from behind. The boys did their best to stay awake that morning; there had been a dance the night before in Skull and they'd come home moldy with the drink, sleeping only a few hours before being roused by their father for Mass.

At the end of the row, beneath a wooden carving of the tenth station of the cross, sat my mother, her stomach fluttering in terror at what was to come. She hardly dared to look up.

The Mass began in the typical fashion, she told me, with the priest's wearied discharge of the Introductory Rites and the congregation's discordant singing of the Kyrie. William Finney, a neighbor of my mother's from Ballydevlin, made his way in all his pomposity to the pulpit for the first and second liturgical readings, clearing his throat into the heart of the microphone before pronouncing every word with such dramatic intensity that he might have been performing on the stage of the Abbey Theater. Father Monroe, perspiring noticeably under the weight of his vestments and the intensity of his anger,

followed with the Acclamation and the Gospel before inviting everyone to be seated, and three red-cheeked altar boys scurried to their
side-bench, exchanging excited glances. Perhaps they had read the
priest's notes in the sacristy beforehand or overheard him rehearse his
words as he pulled the cassock down over his head. Or maybe they just
knew how much cruelty the man was capable of and were happy that
on this occasion it was not being directed toward them.

"My family are all Goleen as far back as records go," he began, looking out at one hundred and fifty raised heads and a single bowed one.
"I heard a terrible rumor once that my great-grandfather had family in
Bantry but I never saw any evidence to justify it." An appreciative
laugh from the congregation; a bit of local bigotry never hurt anyone.
"My mother," he continued, "a good woman, loved this parish. She
went to her grave having never left a few square miles of West Cork
and didn't regret it for a moment. *Good people live here*, she always told
me. *Good, honest, Catholic people.* And do you know something, I never
had cause to doubt her. Until today."

There was a ripple around the church.

"Until today," repeated Father Monroe slowly, shaking his head in
sorrow. "Is Catherine Goggin in attendance this morning?" He looked
around as if he had no idea where he might find her, even though she
had been seated in the same pew every Sunday morning for the past
sixteen years. In a moment, the head of every man, woman and child
present turned in her direction. Every head, that is, except for those of
my grandfather and six uncles, who stared resolutely forward, and my
grandmother, who lowered hers now just as my mother raised her
own in a see-saw of shame.

"Catherine Goggin, there you are," said the priest, smiling at her and
beckoning her forward. "Come on up here to me now like a good girl."

My mother stood up slowly and made her way toward the altar, a
place she had only ever been before to take Communion. Her face was
not scarlet, she would tell me years later, but pale. The church was hot
that day, hot with the sticky summer and the breath of excited parishioners, and she felt unsteady on her feet, worrying that she might faint
and be left on the marble floor to wither and rot as an example to other
girls her age. She glanced at Father Monroe nervously, meeting his
rancorous eyes for only a moment before turning away.

"As if butter wouldn't melt," said Father Monroe, looking out at his flock and offering a half-smile. "How old are you now, Catherine?" he asked.

"Sixteen, Father," said my mother.

"Say it louder. So the good people at the back of the church can hear you."

"Sixteen, Father."

"Sixteen. Now lift your head and look out at your neighbors. At your own mother and father who have lived decent, Christian lives and been credits to the parents who went before them. At your brothers, whom we all know to be fine upstanding young men, hard workers who have led no girl astray. Do you see them, Catherine Goggin?"

"I do, Father."

"If I have to tell you to speak up again, I'll hit you a slap across this altar and there's not a soul in the church that would blame me for it."

"I do, Father," she repeated, louder now.

"'I do.' That will be the only time you ever utter those words in a church, do you realize that, little girl? There'll never be a wedding day for you. Your hands are going to your fat belly, I see. Is there a secret that you're hiding?"

A gasp from the pews now. This was what the congregation had suspected, of course—what else could it have been?—but they had waited for confirmation. Eyes flitted back and forth between friends and enemies alike, conversations already being prepared in their heads. *The Goggins*, they would say. *I would expect nothing less from that family. He can barely write his name on a scrap of paper and she's a peculiar article.*

"I don't know, Father," said my mother.

"You don't know. Of course you don't know. Sure aren't you just an ignorant wee slut who has no more sense than a rabbit in a hutch? And the morals to match, I might add. All you young girls out there," he said now, raising his voice as he turned to look out at the people of Goleen, who sat still in their seats as he pointed at them. "All you young girls are to take a look at Catherine Goggin here and learn what happens to girls who play fast and loose with their virtue. They find themselves with a child in their belly and no husband to take care of them."

A roar went around the church. There had been a girl who got herself pregnant on Sherkin Island the previous year. It was a wonderful scandal. The same had happened in Skibbereen the Christmas before last. Was Goleen to earn the same mark of shame? If so, the news would be all around West Cork by teatime.

"Now, Catherine Goggin," continued Father Monroe, placing a hand on her shoulder and squeezing the bone tightly between his fingers. "Before God and your family and all the good people of this parish, you're to name the pup who lay down with you. You're to name him now so he can be made to give his confession and be forgiven in the eyes of the Lord. And after that you're to get out of this church and this parish and blacken the name of Goleen no more, do you hear me?"

She looked up and turned to my grandfather, whose face was set like granite as he stared at the statue of the crucified Jesus hanging behind the altar.

"Your poor daddy can't help you now," said the priest, following the direction of her gaze. "Sure he wants nothing more to do with you. He told me so himself last night when he came to the presbytery to report the shameful news. And let no one here blame Bosco Goggin for any of this, for he brought up his children right, he brought them up with Catholic values, and how can he be held to account for one rotten apple in a barrel of good ones? Give me the pup's name right now, Catherine Goggin, give me his name so we can cast you out and not have to look at your filthy face anymore. Or do you not know his name, is that it? Were there too many of them for you to be certain?"

A low murmur of discontent could be heard around the pews. Even in the midst of gossip, the congregation felt this might be going a step too far, for it implicated all of their sons in the immorality. Father Monroe, who had given hundreds of sermons in that church over the course of two decades and who knew well how to read a room, pulled back a little.

"No," he said. "No, I can tell that there's still a shred of decency inside you and there was only one lad. But you'll give me his name right now, Catherine Goggin, or I'll know the reason why."

"I won't say," said my mother, shaking her head.

"What's that?"

"I won't say," she repeated.

"You won't say? The time for timidity is long since past; do you not realize that, no? The name, little girl, or I swear before the cross that I will whip you from this house of God in shame."

She looked up now and glanced around the church. It was like a film, she would later tell me, with everyone holding their breath as they wondered to whom she might point the finger of blame, each mother praying that it would not be her son. Or worse, her husband.

She opened her mouth and seemed to be on the verge of an answer but changed her mind and shook her head.

"I won't say," she repeated quietly.

"Get on with you so," said Father Monroe, stepping behind her and giving her an almighty kick in the back with his boot that sent her stumbling down the altar steps, her hands outstretched before her, for even at that early stage of my development she was ready to protect me at all costs. "Get on out of here, you floozy, and out of Goleen, and take your infamy to another place. There's houses in London that have been built for the likes of you and beds there where you can throw yourself on your back and spread your legs for all and sundry to satisfy your wanton ways."

The congregation gasped in horrified delight at his words, the teenage boys thrilled by such notions, and as she picked herself up off the ground the priest stepped forward again and dragged her by the arm through the nave of the church, spittle dribbling down his mouth and chin, his face red with indignation, and perhaps his excitement was even visible to those who knew where to look for it. My grandmother looked around but my grandfather gave her a puck on the arm and she turned back. My Uncle Eddie, the youngest of the six and the closest in age to my mother, stood up and shouted, "Ah come on, that's enough now," and at those words my grandfather stood too and laid his son out with one punch to the jaw. My mother saw no more after that, as Father Monroe discarded her into the graveyard beyond and told her that she was to leave the village within the hour and from that day forward the name of Catherine Goggin would no more be heard or spoken of in the parish of Goleen.

She lay on the ground, she told me, for a few minutes, knowing that the Mass had a good half hour to run yet, before slowly picking herself up and turning in the direction of home, where, she guessed, a packed bag would be waiting for her by the front door.

"Kitty."

A voice from behind made her turn around and she was surprised to see my father walking toward her nervously. She'd noticed him in the back row, of course, as the priest dragged her toward the doors, and to his credit he'd had a look of shame upon his face.

"Haven't you done enough?" she asked, putting a hand to her mouth and drawing it away to examine the blood that had seeped into her untrimmed nails.

"This wasn't what I wanted at all," he told her. "I'm sorry for your trouble, truly I am."

"For my trouble?" she asked. "In a different world, this would be our trouble."

"Ah come on now, Kitty," he said, using the name he'd called her by from the time she was a child. "Don't be like that. Here's a couple of pounds," he added, handing her two green Irish punts. "This should help you get started somewhere else."

She looked at them for a few moments before holding them up in the air and slowly tearing them down the center.

"Ah, Kitty, there's no need for—"

"No matter what that man in there says, I'm no whore," she told him, crumpling the pieces up into a ball and throwing them at him. "Take your money. A bit of sticking tape will put them back together and you can buy my Auntie Jean a nice dress for her birthday instead."

"Jesus, Kitty, will you keep your voice down, for God's sake?"

"You'll not hear it again," she told him, turning away and heading for home and then the late-afternoon bus to Dublin. "Good luck to you now."

And with that she took her leave of Goleen, the place of her birth, which she would not see again for more than sixty years, when she would stand in that same graveyard with me and search among the gravestones for the remains of the family that had cast her out.

A One-Way Ticket

She had her savings, of course: a few pounds that she'd squirreled away in a sock in her dresser drawer over the last few years. An elderly aunt, three years dead by the time of my mother's disgrace, had given her the occasional few pennies when she ran errands for her and these had accumulated over time. And there was still something left over from her Communion money and a little more from her Confirmation. She'd never been a spender. There wasn't much that she needed and the things that she might have liked, she didn't know existed in the first place.

As expected, the bag was waiting for her when she got home, neatly packed and propped up next to the front door, her coat and hat thrown on top of it. She discarded these over the arm of the sofa, for they were hand-me-downs and she guessed that the Sunday clothes on her back would be more valuable to her in Dublin. Opening it now, she checked for the sock-purse and there it was, its secret as carefully concealed as her own had been until the previous evening when her mother had walked into her bedroom without knocking and discovered her standing before the mirror with her blouse undone, one hand stroking her convex belly with a mixture of fear and fascination.

The old dog looked up at her from his place in front of the fire and offered a lengthy yawn but didn't trot over with his tail wagging like he usually did, hoping for a pat or a compliment.

She went to her bedroom and took one last look around for anything she might want to take with her. There were books, of course, but she had read them all and there would be books at the other end of her journey too. A small porcelain statue of St. Bernadette stood on her bedside table and for no sensible reason that she could think of, other than causing irritation to her parents, she turned its face to the wall. There was a small music box too, her mother's originally, where she stored her keepsakes and treasures, and she began to sort through it as the ballerina turned and the melody sounded a tune from Pugni's *La Esmeralda* before deciding that these things belonged to a different life and she closed it firmly, the dancer bending forward at the waist before disappearing from sight altogether.

And *grand*, she thought as she left the house for the final time before making her way along the road to the post office, where she sat on the dry grass until a bus arrived, taking a backseat by an open window and breathing steadily throughout the journey to stop her from getting sick as it took her over rocky terrain into Ballydehob and the front of Leap, onward to Bandon and Innishannon before twisting north into Cork City itself, a place she had never visited but that her father had always said was filled with gamblers, Protestants and drunkards.

For two pence, she drank a bowl of tomato soup and a cup of tea in a café on Lavitt's Quay and then walked along the banks of the River Lee to Parnell Place, where she bought a ticket for Dublin.

"Do you want a return?" the driver asked her, shuffling his satchel as he rooted around for change. "You'll save money if you're coming back again."

"I won't be coming back," she replied, taking the ticket from his hands and placing it carefully in her purse, for she had a sense that this might be an item that would be worth holding on to, a paper memory with the date of the beginning of her new life stamped across it in heavy black ink.

From Out Near Ballincollig

A lesser person might have felt frightened or upset as the bus pulled away from the quays to begin its journey north but not my mother, who held a staunch conviction that the sixteen years she had spent in Goleen being spoken down to, ignored or treated as somehow less important than any of her six brothers had led her toward this moment of independence. Young as she was, she'd already made an uneasy peace with her condition, which, she told me later, she had discovered for the first time in Davy Talbot's grocery shop on the main street, standing next to ten piled-up boxes of fresh oranges, when she felt my unformed foot give a little kick into her bladder, just a spasm of discomfort that might have been anything at all but that she knew would eventually be me. She didn't consider any back-room terminations, even though there was gossip among some of the girls in the village regarding a widow-woman in Tralee who did terrible things with Epsom salts, rubber vacuum bags and a pair of forceps. For six shillings, they said, you could be in and out of her house in a couple of hours, three or four pounds the lighter. No, she knew exactly what she was going to do when I was born. She simply had to wait until I arrived in order to put her Great Plan into place.

The bus to Dublin was busy and at the first stop a young man climbed on board carrying an old brown suitcase and glanced around at the few remaining empty seats. As he paused next to my mother for a moment, she could feel his eyes burning into her but didn't dare turn to look at him in case he was someone familiar with her family who had already heard the news of her shame and would only need to see her face to make some cutting remark. Nothing was said, though, and after a moment he walked on. Only when the bus had traveled another five miles along the road did he make his way back to where she was sitting and point at the empty place beside her.

"Do you mind?" he asked.

"Do you not have a seat down the back?" she asked, glancing toward the rear of the bus.

"The fella next to me is eating egg sandwiches and the smell of them is knockin' me sick."

She shrugged and moved her coat to let him sit down, taking him in with a quick glance as she did so. He was wearing a tweed suit with a tie loosened at the neck and a cap that he took off and held between his hands. A couple of years older than her, she decided, eighteen or nineteen perhaps, and although my mother was what in those days was called "a looker," the combination of her pregnancy and the dramatic events of the morning left her in no mood for flirtation. Boys in the village had often tried to initiate romances with her, of course, but she had never been interested, earning a reputation for virtue that had now been shattered. There were a few girls of whom it was said that it only took a little encouragement for them to do something or show something or kiss something, but Catherine Goggin had never been one of them. It would come as a shock to those boys, she realized, when they learned of her disgrace and there would be some among them who would regret never having tried a little harder to seduce her. In her absence they would say that she had always been a floozy and this mattered a great deal to my mother, for she and the person they would fashion from their sordid imaginations would have little in common except for a name.

"Soft day all the same," said the boy next to her.

"What was that?" she asked, turning to look at him.

"I said it was a soft day," he repeated. "Not bad for this time of year."

"I suppose so."

"Yesterday it was raining and the sky this morning looked heavy with showers. But look, there's been no spillage at all. It's grand out."

"You take an interest in the weather, do you?" she asked, hearing the sarcastic tone in her voice but not caring.

"I grew up on a farm," he told her. "It's second nature to me."

"I did too," she said. "My father spent half his life staring at the sky or sniffing the late-afternoon air for rumors of what was to come the following day. They say it always rains in Dublin. Do you believe that?"

"We'll find out soon enough, I suppose. Do you go all the way, you do?"

"I beg your pardon?"

His face went scarlet, from the base of his neck to the tips of his ears, and the speed of the transformation fascinated her. "To Dublin," he said quickly. "Do you go all the way to Dublin or will you be getting off at one of the stops?"

"Do you want my window seat?" she asked. "Is that it? Because you can have it if you want. I'm not particular."

"No, not at all," he said. "I was only asking. I'm happy where I am. Unless you're going to start in on the egg sandwiches too, that is."

"I've no food at all," she told him. "I only wish I did."

"I have half a baked ham in my case," he told her. "I could slice you off a rasher if that would help."

"I couldn't eat on a bus. I'd be sick."

"Can I ask you your name?" asked the boy, and my mother hesitated.

"Is there a reason you want to know it?"

"So I can call you by it," he said.

She looked into his face and for the first time noticed how handsome he was. A face like a girl's, she told me afterward. Clear skin that had never known the pull of a razor. Long eyelashes. Blond hair that tumbled over his forehead and into his eyes no matter how hard he tried to tame it. There was something in his manner that made her believe that he wasn't a threat to her in any way and so she relented, letting down her guard at last.

"It's Catherine," she said. "Catherine Goggin."

"Pleased to meet you," he replied. "I'm Seán MacIntyre."

"Are you from the city, Seán?"

"No, I'm from out near Ballincollig. Do you know it there?"

"I've heard of it but I've never been there. I've never been anywhere, really."

"Well, you're going somewhere now," he said. "Up to the big smoke."

"I am, yes," she said, turning to look out the window at the fields as they passed and the children working in the haystacks, who jumped up and down to wave when they saw the bus coming along the road in their direction.

"Do you go up and down a lot?" asked Seán a moment later.

"Do I what?" she asked, frowning at him.

"To Dublin," he said, putting a hand to his face, and perhaps he was wondering why everything he said seemed to come out the wrong way. "Do you go up and down the road a fair amount? Maybe you have family up there?"

"I don't know a soul outside West Cork," she told him. "The place will be a mystery to me. What about yourself?"

"I've never been there but a friend of mine went up over a month ago and got a job quick-smart in the Guinness Brewery and he said there's one waiting for me there too if I want it."

"Do them lads not spend all their time drinking the profits?" she asked.

"Ah no, sure there'd be rules, like. Bosses and so on. Fellas going round making sure that no one's supping the porter. My friend, though, he tells me that the smell of the place would drive you half wild. The hops and the barley and the yeast and what have you. He says you can smell it on the streets all around and the people who live nearby go around with daft expressions on their faces all day long."

"They're probably all drunk," said my mother. "And it didn't cost them a penny."

"My friend says it takes a few days for a new worker to get used to the smell of the place and until you do you can feel queer sick."

"My daddy likes a Guinness," said my mother, recalling the bitter taste of the yellow-labeled bottles that my grandfather occasionally brought into the house and that she had tried herself once when his back was turned. "He goes down to the pub every Wednesday and Friday night, as regular as clockwork. On Wednesdays he limits himself to three pints with his pals and comes home at a respectable time but on Friday nights he gets polluted. He'll often come in at two o'clock in the morning and rouse my mother from her bed to cook him a plate of sausages and a ring of black pudding and if she says no, then he raises his fists to her."

"Every night was a Friday night with my daddy," said Seán.

"Is that why you want to get away?"

He shrugged. "Partly," he said after a long pause. "There was a bit of trouble at home, if I'm honest. It was for the best that I leave."

"What kind of trouble?" she asked, intrigued now.

"Do you know, I think I'd rather just put it all behind me if it's all the same to you."

"Of course," she said. "It's none of my business anyway."

"I didn't mean it like that."

"I know you didn't. It's fine."

He opened his mouth to say something more but their attention was distracted by a little boy running up and down the aisle. He wore the headdress of a Red Indian and was making the sounds to match, a terrible howling that would have given a deaf man a headache. The bus driver let out an almighty roar and said that if someone didn't take control of that child, then he'd turn the bus around and take them all back to Cork City and there would be no refunds for anyone.

"So what about you, Catherine?" asked Seán when peace was restored. "What takes you up to the capital?"

"If I tell you," said my mother, who somehow already felt that she could trust this stranger, "will you promise not to say anything cruel to me? I've heard a lot of unkind words today and, truth be told, I don't have the strength for anymore of them."

"I try never to say unkind words," replied Seán.

"I'm to have a baby," said my mother, looking him full square in the eye and without an ounce of shame. "I'm to have a baby and I don't have a husband to help me rear him. And there's war over it, needless to say. My mammy and daddy threw me out of the house and the priest said I was to leave Goleen and never darken the place again."

Seán nodded but this time, despite the indelicacy of the subject, he didn't blush. "Sure these things happen, I suppose," he said. "We're none of us perfect."

"This one is," said my mother, pointing toward her belly. "For now anyway."

Seán smiled and looked ahead, and they said nothing to each other for a long while after that and perhaps they both dozed off or perhaps one of them shut their eyes to give that impression so they could be left alone with their thoughts. Either way, it was more than an hour later when, awake again, my mother turned to her companion and touched him lightly on the forearm.

"Do you know anything about Dublin?" she asked. Perhaps it had finally struck her that she had no idea what she would do or where she would go when they arrived.

"I know that it's where Dáil Éireann sits and that the River Liffey runs through the heart of it and Clerys department store stands on a big, long street named after Daniel O'Connell."

"Sure there's one of those in every county of Ireland."

"True enough. Just like there's a Shop Street. And a Main Street."

"And a Bridge Street."

"And a Church Street."

"God preserve us from the Church Streets," said my mother with a laugh, and Seán laughed too, a pair of kids giggling at their irreverence. "I'll go to hell for that," she added when the laughter stopped.

"Sure we're all going to hell," said Seán. "Me worst of all."

"Why you worst of all?"

"'Cause I'm a bad lad," he said with a wink, and she laughed again and felt a need to go to the toilet, wondering how long it would be before they might stop somewhere. She told me afterward that this was the only moment during their acquaintance when she felt anything close to an attraction for Seán. In her mind she entertained a brief fantasy that they would leave the bus as sweethearts, marry within the month and bring me up as their own. A nice dream, I suppose, but it was never going to be.

"You don't strike me as a bad lad," she told him.

"Ah, you should see me when I get going."

"I'll bear that in mind. So tell me about this friend of yours. How long did you say he's been up in Dublin?"

"Just over a month now," said Seán.

"And do you know him well?"

"I do, yes. We got to know each other a couple of years back when his father bought the farm next to ours and we've been great pals ever since."

"You must be if he's setting you up with a job. Most people just look out for themselves."

He nodded and looked down at the floor, then at his fingernails, then out the window. "Portlaoise," he said, noticing a passing sign. "We're getting closer anyway."

"Do you have brothers or sisters who'll miss you?" she asked.

"No," said Seán. "There was just me. After I was born, my mammy couldn't have anymore and Daddy never forgave her for it. He plays around, like. He has a few different fancy-women and no one ever says a thing about it because the priest says that a man expects a houseful of children from his wife and a barren field takes no planting."

"They're sweethearts, aren't they?" asked my mother, and now Seán frowned. For all his mischief, he wasn't accustomed to mocking the clergy. "I have six brothers," she told him after a moment. "Five of them have straw in their heads where their brains should be. The only one I have any time for, my youngest brother Eddie, wants to be a priest himself."

"How old is he?"

"A year older than me. Seventeen. He goes into the seminary in September. I don't think he'll be happy, because I know for a fact that he's mad for the girls. But he's the youngest, you see, and the farm has already been parceled off for the first two, and the next two are to be teachers, and the fifth wouldn't be capable of work on account of a softness in his head, so that just leaves Eddie and so he must be the priest. There's great excitement over it, of course. I suppose I'll miss all that now," she added with a sigh. "The visits and the clothes and the ordination by the bishop. Do you think they let fallen women write letters to their seminarian brothers?"

"I know nothing of that life," said Seán, shaking his head. "Can I ask you a question, Catherine, and you can tell me to go and whistle if you don't want to answer it."

"Go ahead so."

"Does the daddy not want to take some responsibility for . . . you know . . . for the baby?"

"He does on his eye," said my mother. "Sure he's happy as Larry that I've got out of the place. There'd be murder if anyone found out who it was."

"And are you not worried at all?"

"About what?"

"About how you're going to cope?"

She smiled. He was innocent and kind and perhaps a little naïve, and there was a part of her that wondered whether a big city like Dublin was the right place for a fella like him. "Of course I'm worried," she said. "I'm worried out of my head. But I'm excited too. I hated living in Goleen. It suits me to get away."

"I know that feeling. West Cork does funny things to you if you stay there too long."

"What's your friend's name anyway? The one at Guinness's?"

"Jack Smoot."

"Smoot?"

"Yes."

"That's a fierce odd name."

"There's Dutch people in his family, I think. Going back, like."

"Do you think he'd be able to find a job for me too? I could work in the office maybe."

Seán looked past her and bit his lip. "I don't know," he said slowly. "I'll be honest with you and say that I wouldn't like to ask him as he's already put himself out to find a place for me and him only in the door a wet week."

"Of course," said my mother. "I shouldn't have asked. Sure I can take a stroll up there myself one day if nothing else shows up. I'll have a sign made and wear it around my neck. *Honest Girl Seeks Work. Will*

Need Some Time Off in About Four Months. I shouldn't joke about it, should I?"

"You've nothing to lose, I suppose."

"Would you say there are lots of jobs in Dublin?"

"I'd say that you wouldn't be too long looking anyway. You're a . . . you know . . . you're a—"

"I'm a what?"

"You're pretty," said Seán with a shrug. "And employers like that, don't they? You could always be a shop girl."

"A shop girl," said my mother, nodding slowly, considering it.

"Yes, a shop girl."

"I suppose I could."

Three Ducklings

In my mother's opinion, Jack Smoot and Seán MacIntyre were as different as chalk and cheese, so it surprised her that they were such good friends. Where Seán was outgoing and affable to the point of innocence, Smoot was a darker and more reticent figure, given, she would discover, to prolonged periods of brooding and introspection that occasionally veered toward despair.

"The world," he would remark to her a few weeks into their acquaintance, "is a terrible place and it was our misfortune to be have been born into it."

"Still, the sun is out," she would reply then, smiling at him. "So there's that at least."

As the bus arrived in to Dublin, Seán grew more animated in the seat next to her as he looked out the window, his eyes opening wide as he took in the unfamiliar streets and buildings that marked their approach, larger and more tightly packed together than any in Ballincollig. When the driver pulled in to Aston Quay, he was first up to collect his case from above and seemed agitated to be left waiting as the passengers ahead of him gathered their belongings. When he finally disembarked, he looked around anxiously until, with a glance across to the opposite side of the quay, he saw a man walking toward him from the direction of the small waiting room next to McBirney's department store, at which point he broke into a relieved smile.

"Jack!" he roared, his voice almost choking in happiness as the man, about a year or two older than him, approached. They stood before each other for a moment, grinning, before shaking hands heartily and Smoot, in a rare moment of playfulness, pulled Seán's cap off his head and threw it in the air in delight.

"You made it then," he said.

"Did you doubt me?"

"I wasn't sure. I thought I might be left standing here like O'Donovan's donkey."

My mother walked toward them, as happy as anyone to be out in the fresh air again. Unaware, of course, that a plan had been hatched somewhere between Newbridge and Rathcoole, Smoot didn't pay any attention to her and focused entirely on his friend. "What about your father?" he asked. "Did you—"

"Jack, this is Catherine Goggin," said Seán as she stopped next to him, doing her best to appear inconspicuous. Smoot stared at her, uncertain why the introduction was being made.

"Hello," he said after a brief pause.

"We met on the bus," said Seán. "We were sitting next to each other."

"Is that so?" said Smoot. "Are you visiting family up here?"

"Not exactly," said my mother.

"Catherine has found herself in a bit of bother," explained Seán. "Her mammy and daddy threw her out of the house and they won't have her back, so she's come up to Dublin to try her luck."

Smoot nodded, his tongue bulging in his cheek as he considered this. He was dark-haired, as dark as Seán was fair, and his cheeks were pockmarked with tiny scars. His broad shoulders gave my mother the immediate image of him carrying wooden barrels of Guinness around the forecourt of the brewery, swaying beneath the air-polluted stench of hops and barley. "There's many who try that," he said finally. "There's chances, of course. Some don't make it and they take the boat across the water instead."

"I've had a recurring dream since I was a child that if I ever set foot on a boat, then it would sink and I would drown," said my mother, inventing this bit of nonsense on the spot, for she'd never had any such dream and only said it now so that the plan that she and Seán had concocted on the bus would come to fruition. She hadn't been scared before, she told me, but once she arrived in the city the idea of being left alone frightened her.

Smoot had no answer to this and simply stared at her with disdain before turning back to his friend.

"Sure we'll get along then, will we?" he asked, putting his hands in his coat pockets and nodding at my mother to dismiss her. "We'll go to our lodgings and then for a bite to eat. I've had nothing but a sandwich all day and I could devour a small Protestant if someone was to pour a little gravy over his head."

"Grand job," said Seán, and as Smoot turned to lead the way, Seán followed two steps behind with his suitcase in one hand, while Catherine trailed a few feet behind him. Smoot, glancing around, frowned and they both stopped, placed their bags on the ground. He stared at them as if they were both mad before walking on and once again they both followed. Finally, he turned to the pair of them, his hands on his hips in bewilderment.

"Is there something going on here that I don't understand?" he asked.

"Listen, Jack," said Seán. "Poor Catherine here is all alone in the world. She hasn't a job or much money to find one. I said that maybe she could stay with us for a few days, just until she gets herself sorted. You don't mind, do you?"

Smoot didn't reply for a moment and my mother recognized the mixture of disappointment and resentment on his face. She wondered whether she should simply say that it was all right, that she didn't want to be any bother to either of them and that she would leave them in peace, but then Seán had been so kind to her on the bus and if she didn't go with him now, then where would she go?

"Do you two know each other from back home, is that it?" asked Smoot. "Is this some game you're playing on me?"

"No, Jack, we only just met, I promise you."

"Hold on a minute," said Smoot, his eyes narrowing as he looked at my mother's stomach, which, five months into my development, was becoming round. "Are you . . . ? Is that . . . ?"

My mother rolled her eyes. "I should take an ad out in the paper," she said, "for the amount of interest there is in my belly today."

"Ah here," said Smoot, his face growing darker than ever. "Seán, has this got something to do with you? Are you bringing this problem to my door?"

"Of course not," said Seán. "I told you, we only just met. We were sitting next to each other on the bus, that's all."

"And sure I was already five months gone by then," added my mother.

"If that's the case," said Smoot, "then why does she become our responsibility? You've no ring on your finger, I see," he added, nodding toward my mother's left hand.

"No," said my mother. "And little chance of getting one now."

"Are you after Seán, is that it?"

My mother's mouth fell open in a mixture of laughter and offense. "I am not," she said. "Sure how many times do we have to tell you that we only just met? I'd hardly be setting my cap for anyone after a single bus journey."

"No, but you're happy to ask them for favors."

"Jack, please, she's alone," said Seán quietly. "We both know what that's like, don't we? I thought a little bit of Christian charity wouldn't do us any harm."

"You and your fucking God," said Smoot, shaking his head, and my mother, strong woman though she was, blanched at the obscenity, for people, as a rule, did not use such words in Goleen.

"It'll be only for a few days," repeated Seán. "Just until she finds her way."

"But there's very little room," said Smoot in a defeated tone. "It was just meant to be for the two of us." There was a long silence and finally he shrugged his shoulders and gave in. "Come along so," he said. "It looks as if I'm to have no say in the matter, so I'll make the best of things. A couple of days, you say?"

"A couple of days," agreed my mother.

"Just until you get yourself sorted?"

"Just until then."

"Hmm," he said, striding ahead, leaving Seán and my mother to follow.

The Flat on Chatham Street

As they walked toward the bridge, my mother looked over the side of the railings into the River Liffey, a filthy determination of brown and green making its way urgently toward the Irish Sea as if it wanted out of the city as quickly as possible, leaving the priests, the pubs and the politics far behind it. Inhaling, she pulled a face and declared that it was nowhere near as clean as the water of West Cork.

"You could wash your hair in the streams down there," she declared. "And there's many that do, of course. My brothers go to a little creek at the back of our farm every Saturday morning for their wash with a single stick of Lifebuoy Soap between them and they come back shining like the sun on a summer's day. Maisie Hartwell was caught watching them one time and her daddy leathered her for it, the filthy article. She was after their mickeys."

"The buses," declared Smoot, turning around and plucking the butt of a cigarette from his mouth before grinding it out beneath his boot, "go both ways."

"Ah now, Jack," said Seán, and the disappointment in his voice was so touching that my mother knew immediately that she would not want to be on the receiving end of such a tone.

"That's what we call a joke," said Smoot, quietly chastised.

"Ha," replied my mother, "ha."

Smoot shook his head and continued on, and she was free to look around at the city, a place she had heard of all her life that was supposedly full of whores and atheists but that seemed much like home, only with more cars, bigger buildings and better clothes. In Goleen, there was only the working man, his wife and their children. No one was rich, no one was poor and the world maintained its stability by allowing the same few hundred pounds to pass back and forth from business to business, from farm to grocery store and from wage packet to public house on a regular basis. Here, though, she could see toffs in dark pinstriped suits sporting carefully constructed mustaches, ladies in their finery, dockers and boatmen, shop girls and railway workers. A barrister walked by on his way to the Four Courts in full regalia, his black poplin gown inflating in the air behind him like a cape, his white bobbed wig threatening to blow off in the breeze. From the opposite direction, a pair of young seminarians, weaving on the pavement with drink, were followed quickly by a small boy with a coal-blackened face and a man dressed as a woman, which was a creature she had never seen before. *Oh, for a camera!* she thought. *That'd soften their cough in West Cork!* As they came to the crossroads, she turned to look down the length of O'Connell Street and saw the tall Doric column that stood halfway along with the statue standing proudly on the plinth, its nose in the air so it didn't have to inhale the stink of the people it lorded over.

"Is that Nelson's Pillar?" she asked, pointing toward it, and both Smoot and Seán looked around.

"It is," said Smoot. "How did you know that?"

"It wasn't a hedgerow school I went to," she told him. "I can spell my own name too, you know. And count to ten. It's a fine thing all the same, isn't it?"

"It's a load of old stones thrown up to celebrate the Brits winning another battle," said Smoot, ignoring her sarcasm. "They should send the bastard back to where he came from, if you ask me. It's been more than twenty years since we achieved independence and still we have a dead man from Norfolk looking down over us, watching our every move."

"I think he adds a certain splendor to the place," she said, more to annoy him than anything else.

"Do you now?"

"I do."

"Good luck to you so."

She would get no closer to Horatio on this occasion, however, for they were walking in the opposite direction, making their way along Westmoreland Street and past the front gates of Trinity College, where my mother stared at the handsome young men gathered beneath the arch in their smart clothes and felt a twitch of envy in the pit of her stomach. What right did they have to such a place, she wondered, when it would forever be denied to her?

"They'd be a right stuck-up bunch in there, I'd say," said Seán, following the direction of her eyes. "And all Protestants, of course. Jack, do you know any of the students in there at all?"

"Oh, I know every one of them," said Smoot. "Sure don't we all go out for dinner together every night and toast the King and say what a great fella Churchill is."

My mother could feel a flame of irritation begin to burn inside her. It hadn't been her idea to share lodgings for a few nights with them, it had been Seán's, and an act of Christian charity on his part at that, but the plan made, she couldn't see why Smoot had to be so rude about it. Along up Grafton Street they went anyway before turning right on to Chatham Street and finally to a little red door next to a pub where Smoot removed a brass key from his pocket and turned to look at them.

"There's no landlord on the premises, thank Christ," he said. "Mr. Hogan stops by on a Saturday morning for his rent money and I meet him outside and all he ever talks about is the bloody war. He's up for the Germans. Wants them to make it one-all. The feckin' eejit thinks that it'd be great justice if the Brits had their backs broken but what would happen next, I say to him, *What's the next country along? We are*. We'd all be saluting Hitler by Christmas and goose-stepping down Henry Street with our arms in the air. Not that it'll come to that though, sure the bloody thing is almost over. Anyway, I pay rent here of three shillings a week," he added, looking at Catherine, and she took his point without saying anything to acknowledge it. Seven days in a week, that meant five pence a day. Two or three days: fifteen pence. That was only fair, she decided.

"Penny pictures!" called a boy walking down the street with a camera hanging around his neck. "Penny pictures!"

"Seán!" cried my mother, tugging at his arm. "Look at that. A friend of my father's in Goleen had a camera. Have you ever had your picture taken?"

"I haven't," he said.

"Let's have one now," she said enthusiastically. "To mark our first day in Dublin."

"Waste of a penny," said Smoot.

"I suppose it would be a nice memory," said Seán, waving the boy over and handing him a penny. "Come on, Jack. You get in it too."

My mother stood next to Seán but when Smoot came over he elbowed her out of the way and the shutter clicked just as she turned to him in irritation.

"You'll have it in three days," said the boy. "What's the address?"

"Right here," said Smoot. "You can throw it through the letter box."

"Do we only get one?" asked my mother.

"They're a penny each," said the boy. "If you want a second, it'll cost you more."

"One's grand," she said, turning away from him as Smoot used the key to let them in.

The staircase was narrow, allowing only one person to ascend at a time, the wallpaper yellow and peeling from the walls on both sides. There was no handrail and as my mother reached for her bag, Seán picked it up and ushered her forward after Smoot.

"Go along between us," he said. "We couldn't have you fall and injure the baby."

She smiled at him gratefully and when she reached the top she entered a small room with a tin bathtub in one corner, a sink and, running along the far wall, the most enormous sofa that my mother had ever seen in her life. How on earth anyone had ever got it up the stairs was a mystery to her. It looked so plump and comfortable that it was all she could do not to collapse into its embrace and pretend that all her adventures of the last twenty-four hours had never happened.

"Well, this is all there is," said Smoot, looking around with a mixture of pride and awkwardness. "The sink works when it takes the notion but the water is cold and it's a bitch to fill the bucket and drag it over to the tub anytime you need a wash. If you need the toilet, you may use one of the pubs nearby. Only look as if you're intending to meet someone in there or they put you out on the street."

"Are we to have *fucks* and *bastards* and *bitches* all the time, Mr. Smoot?" asked my mother, smiling at him. "I don't really mind, you understand, but just so that I know what to expect."

Smoot stared at her. "Do you not like my language, Kitty?" he asked, and her smile faded quickly now.

"Don't call me that," she said. "It's Catherine, if you don't mind."

"Well, I'll try to be more of a gentleman around you if it offends you so much, Kitty. I'll watch my fucking p's and q's now that we have a . . ." He stopped and made a deliberate nod toward my mother's belly. "A lady in the house."

She swallowed, ready to pounce, but what could she do when he was providing a roof over her head?

"It's a grand place," said Seán finally, to break the tension. "Very cozy."

"It is," said Smoot, smiling at him, and my mother wondered whether there was anything she could do to earn his friendship in the way that Seán obviously had but nothing came to mind.

"Perhaps," she said eventually, glancing at a half open door in the corner, through which she could see a single bed in the adjoining room, "perhaps this was a mistake. There's not room for three of us here, is there? Mr. Smoot has his bedroom, and the sofa, Seán, was intended for you, I suppose. It wouldn't be right for me to deprive you of it."

Seán stared at the ground and said nothing.

"You can top and tail with me," said Smoot, looking at Seán, whose face had turned scarlet with embarrassment. "Kitty here can take the sofa."

The atmosphere in the room became so awkward and uncomfortable that my mother didn't know what to think. Minutes went by, she told me, and the three of them just standing there in the center of the room, not uttering a word.

"Well then," she said finally, relieved to have found a sentence lurking somewhere in the back of her mind. "Is anyone hungry at all? I think I have the price of three dinners to say thank you."

A Journalist, Perhaps

Two weeks later, on the day that news reached Dublin that Adolf Hitler had put a bullet in his head, my mother wandered into a cheap jewelry shop on Coppinger Row and bought herself a wedding ring, a small golden band with a tiny gemstone to ornament it. She still hadn't moved out of the flat on Chatham Street but had reached a discreet understanding with Jack Smoot, who made his peace with her presence by rarely acknowledging it. To make herself useful, she kept the place clean and used what little money she had to ensure a meal was on the table when they came home from work, for Seán had found a place at Guinness's after all, although he wasn't particularly enjoying it.

"I carry bags of hops around the place half the day," he told her as he lay in the bath one evening soothing his muscles while my mother sat on the bed in the next room, her back turned to him but the door half open so they could talk. It was a peculiar room, she thought. Nothing on the walls except a St. Brigid's cross and a photograph of Pope Pius XII. Next to that was the photograph that had been taken on the day they arrived in Dublin. The boy had done a poor job of it, for although Seán was smiling and Smoot looked half human, her body was split down the middle by the frame, her head turned to her right in annoyance at the way Smoot had pushed her. A single dresser stood against one wall, in which the clothes of both lads were mixed up together as if it didn't matter who owned what. And the bed itself was hardly big enough for one, let alone the pair of them sleeping top-to-tail. It was no wonder, she told herself, that she heard the most peculiar sounds emerging from there during the nights. The poor boys must have had a terrible time trying to sleep.

"My shoulders are bruised," continued Seán, "my back is sore and I'm suffering terrible headaches from the smell of the brewery. I may look out for something else soon because I don't know how long I can stand it there."

"Jack seems to enjoy it all the same," said my mother.

"He's made of stronger stuff than me so."

"What else would you do?"

Seán took a long time to reply and she listened as he splashed around in the tub. I wonder was there any part of her that wanted to turn around at that moment and let her eyes rest on the body of the young lad in his bath, whether she might have ever considered walking over without an ounce of shame and offering to share it with him? He'd been kind to her and was a handsome devil, or so she told me. It would have been difficult for her not to develop something along the lines of an attachment.

"I don't know," he said eventually.

"There's something in your voice that tells me that you do know."

"There's one idea I have," he said, sounding a little embarrassed. "But I don't know if I'd be fit for it."

"Tell me so."

"You won't laugh?"

"I might," she said. "I could do with a good laugh as it happens."

"Well, there's the newspapers," he said after a brief pause. "The *Irish Times*, of course, and the *Irish Press*. I have a notion that I could write things for them."

"What kind of things?"

"Bits of news, you know. I did a bit of writing back home in Ballincollig. Stories and what have you. A few poems. No good, most of them, but still and all. I think I could get better if I was given a chance."

"Do you mean a journalist?" she asked.

"I suppose so, yes. Am I daft?"

"What's daft about it? Sure someone has to do it, don't they?"

"Jack doesn't think it's a good idea."

"And what does that matter? He's not your wife, is he? You can make your own decisions."

"I don't know if they'd even take me on. But Jack doesn't want to stay on at Guinness's forever either. He has an idea for his own pub."

"That's just what Dublin needs. Another pub."

"Not here. In Amsterdam."

"What?" asked my mother, raising her voice in surprise. "Sure why would he want to go there?"

"I suppose it's the Dutch side of him," said Seán. "He's never been but he's heard great things about the place."

"What kind of things?"

"That it's different from Ireland."

"Well, that can hardly come as a great revelation. There's canals and the like there, isn't there?"

"Different in other ways than that."

He said nothing more and my mother began to worry that he'd fallen asleep and slipped beneath the surface of the water.

"I have a bit of news myself," she told him, hoping that he'd answer quickly or she'd have no choice but to turn around.

"Go on so."

"I have an interview for a job tomorrow morning."

"You do not!"

"I do," she said as he splashed away again, using the small bit of soap that she'd picked up from a market stall a few days earlier and pre-

sented to Smoot, partly as a gift for allowing her to stay and partly as
encouragement for him to have a wash.

"Good girl yourself," said Seán. "Where is it anyway?"

"The Dáil."

"The what?"

"The Dáil. On Kildare Street. You know, the parliament building."

"I know what the Dáil is," replied Seán, laughing. "I'm just surprised, that's all. What class of a job is it at all? Are you to be a TD? Are
we to have our first female Taoiseach?"

"I'd be serving in the tearoom. I'm to meet a Mrs. Hennessy at
eleven o'clock and she's going to give me the once-over."

"Well, that's a bit of good news anyway. Do you think you'll—"

A key in the lock, it stuck for a moment, was taken out and rein-
serted, and when my mother heard Smoot walking into the other
room she moved over a little on the bed so that he wouldn't notice her
sitting there, her eyes resting on the crack in the wall that looked like
the journey of the River Shannon through the Midlands.

"There you are," he said, using a tender sort of voice that she had
never heard him employ before. "Now, there's a fine sight to return
home to."

"Jack," snapped Seán immediately, his tone different too, quick to
silence him. "Catherine's inside."

My mother turned around on the bed and glanced toward the front
room at the same moment that Smoot looked across, and her glance,
she told me afterward, was torn between the fine bare chest on Seán,
muscled and hairless as he lay in the dirty water, and the face on
Smoot, which was growing more annoyed by the second. Confused,
uncertain what mistake she had made exactly, she turned back around,
glad to hide her blushing face.

"Hello, Jack," she cried cheerfully.

"Kitty."

"Back from the slog?"

He said nothing and there was a long silence from the living room
and my mother longed to turn around to see what was going on. The
two boys weren't talking aloud but even in the silence she could tell
there was some class of a conversation going on between them, even

if it was only through the way that they looked at each other. Finally, Seán spoke.

"Catherine was just telling me that she has a job interview in the morning. In the tearoom of the Dáil, if you can believe it."

"I'd believe anything she tells me," said Smoot. "Is this right, Kitty? Will you be joining the ranks of the working women at last? Christ alive, there'll be a united Ireland next."

"If I give a good account of myself," said Catherine, ignoring his sarcasm. "If I impress the manageress, then hopefully the job will be mine."

"Catherine," said Seán, raising his voice. "I'm getting out now, so don't turn around."

"Sure I'll close the door altogether and leave you to dry yourself. Do you need fresh clothes?"

"I'll get them," said Smoot, walking into the bedroom and taking Seán's trousers from the back of a chair and a fresh shirt, underwear and socks from the dresser drawer, which he held in his hands for half a minute while staring down at Catherine, daring her to look up at him, which, eventually, she did.

"Will they not have a problem, do you think?" he asked. "The lads in the Dáil?"

"With what?" she asked, noticing how he held Seán's clothes protectively in his arms, the boy's smalls to the fore as if he wanted to intimidate her with them.

"With that," he said, pointing toward my mother's stomach.

"I bought a ring," she replied, holding out her left hand and showing it to him.

"It's well for those with money. And what about when the child is born?"

"I have a Great Plan for that," she said.

"So you keep saying. Will you ever tell us what it is or do we have to guess?"

My mother said nothing and Smoot walked away.

"I hope you get it," he muttered as he passed her, quiet enough so only the two of them could hear. "I hope you get the bloody job and then you can get the fuck out of here and leave us both in peace."

An Interview at Dáil Éireann

When my mother arrived at the Dáil the following morning, the wedding ring was clearly visible on the fourth finger of her left hand. She gave her name to the Garda standing on duty at the front door, a sturdy-looking individual whose expression suggested there were a hundred places he would rather be than there, and he consulted a clipboard of the day's visitors before shaking his head and declaring that she wasn't on the list.

"I am," said my mother, leaning forward and pointing at a name next to 11:00—*for Mrs. C. Hennessy.*

"That says Gogan," said the Garda. "Catherine Gogan."

"Well, that's just a mistake," said my mother. "My name is Goggin, not Gogan."

"If you don't have an appointment, I can't let you in."

"Garda," said my mother, smiling sweetly at him. "I assure you that I am the Catherine Gogan whom Mrs. Hennessy is expecting. Someone has merely written my name down incorrectly, that's all."

"And how am I to know that?"

"Well, what if I wait here and if no Catherine Gogan shows up, then can you let me in instead of her? She'll have missed her chance and I might be in luck for the job instead."

The Garda sighed. "Ah here," he said. "I get enough of this at home."

"Enough of what?"

"I come to work to get away from this type of thing," he said.

"Away from what type of thing?"

"Go along in and don't be annoying me," he said, practically pushing her through the doors. "The waiting room is on the left there. Don't even think of going anywhere else or I'll be after you faster than green grass through a goose."

"Charming," said my mother, slipping past him and walking toward the room he'd indicated. Stepping inside and sitting down, she looked around at the grandeur of the place and found that her heart was beating hard within her chest.

A few minutes later, the door opened and a woman of about fifty entered, slender as a willow tree with dark-black hair that she wore cropped close to her head.

"Miss Goggin?" she said, stepping forward. "I'm Charlotte Hennessy."

"It's Mrs. Goggin, actually," said my mother quickly, standing up, and in a moment the expression on the older lady's face changed from friendly to disconcerted.

"Oh," she said, noticing my mother's belly. "Oh dear."

"It's a pleasure to meet you," said my mother. "Thank you for taking the time. I hope the position is still available?"

Mrs. Hennessy's mouth opened and shut several times like a fish twisting back and forth on the deck of a boat until the life drained out of it. "Mrs. Goggin," she said, her smile reasserting itself as she indicated that they should both sit down. "It is still available, yes, but I'm afraid there's been a misunderstanding."

"Oh?" said my mother.

"I was looking for a girl for the tearoom, do you see? Not a married woman with a child on the way. We can't have married women here in Dáil Éireann. A married woman must be at home with her husband. Does your husband not work, no?"

"My husband did work," said my mother, looking her full in the face and allowing her lower lip to tremble a little, a performance that she'd been practicing in the bathroom mirror all morning.

"And he's lost his position? I'm sorry, but there's still nothing that I can do for you. All our girls are single girls. Young girls like you, naturally, but unmarried. That's how the gentlemen members prefer things."

"He didn't lose his position, Mrs. Hennessy," said my mother, removing her handkerchief from her pocket and dabbing at her eyes. "He lost his life."

"Oh, my dear, I'm so sorry," said Mrs. Hennessy, a hand to her throat now in shock. "The poor man. What happened to him, if you don't mind my asking?"

"The war happened to him, Mrs. Hennessy."

"The war?"

"The war. He went over to fight just as his father had fought before him and his grandfather before that. The Germans got him. Less than a month ago now. A grenade ripped him to shreds. All I have left of him is his wristwatch and his false teeth. The lower set."

This was the story that she had concocted and even in her own mind she knew it was a risky one, for there were those, many of whom worked in that very House, who thought poorly of Irishmen who went to fight for the British. But there was a heroic sound to the tale and, for whatever reason, she had decided this was the way to go.

"You poor unfortunate creature," said Mrs. Hennessy, and when she reached out to squeeze my mother's hand, she knew that she was halfway home. "And you in the family way. That is a tragedy."

"If I had time to think of tragedies, it would be," said my mother. "But I can't afford to, that's the truth of it. I've this little one to think of," she added, placing a hand across her belly protectively.

"You'll not believe this," said Mrs. Hennessy, "but the same thing happened to my Auntie Jocelyn during the First War. She'd been married to my Uncle Albert for only a year and didn't he only sign up with the Brits and get himself killed at Passchendaele? The day she heard the news was the same day she found out that she was to have a child."

"Do you mind if I ask, Mrs. Hennessy," asked my mother, leaning forward, "how did your Auntie Jocelyn cope? Was she all right in the end?"

"Oh not a bother on her," declared Mrs. Hennessy. "You never met a woman like her for positivity. She just got on with things, didn't she? But then that's what people did in those days. Great women, every one of them."

"Magnificent women, Mrs. Hennessy. I could probably learn a thing or two from your Auntie Jocelyn."

The older woman beamed in pleasure but then her smile faded a little again. "Still and all," she said. "I don't know if this could work. Do you mind if I ask how long you have to go?"

"Three months," said my mother.

"Three months. The job is full time. I'd expect you'd have to leave after the baby is born."

My mother nodded. Of course she had her Great Plan so knew that this wouldn't be the case but here was her moment and she was determined to seize it.

"Mrs. Hennessy," she said. "You seem like a kind woman. You remind me of my late mother, who took care of me every day of her life until she succumbed to the cancer last year—"

"Oh, my dear, your trials!"

"You have her kindness in your face, Mrs. Hennessy. Let me cast aside all dignity now and throw myself on your mercy and make a suggestion. I need a job, Mrs. Hennessy, I need one badly so I can put money away for the child when he or she arrives and I have almost nothing as it is. If you could find it in your heart to take me on for these next three months, then I will work like a cart horse for you and give you no cause to regret your decision, and when my time comes, perhaps you can advertise again and find a young girl who needs a chance then just like I need a chance right now."

Mrs. Hennessy sat back, the tears forming in her eyes. I think of it now and wonder why my mother was applying for a job in the Dáil at all when she should have been across the Liffey giving an audition for Ernest Blythe.

"Your health," asked Mrs. Hennessy finally. "Do you mind if I ask how your health is in general?"

"Tip-top," said my mother. "I haven't had a day's illness in my life. Not even during these last six months."

Mrs. Hennessy sighed and looked around the walls, as if all the men represented there in gilt-edged frames could give her guidance. A portrait of W. T. Cosgrave hung over her shoulder and he seemed to be glaring at my mother as if to say that he could see through every one of her lies and if he could only wrench himself away from that canvas he'd chase her out of the place with a stick.

"And the war's almost over," said my mother after a moment, a bit of a non sequitur considering the conversation they were having. "Did you hear that Hitler's killed himself? The future looks bright for us all."

Mrs. Hennessy nodded. "I did hear, yes," she said with a shrug. "And good riddance to him, if God will forgive me for saying so. We'll all have better times ahead of us now, I hope."

A Longer Stay

"So it's up to the pair of you," my mother told Seán and Smoot that night as they sat together in the Brazen Head eating a good stew that they shared out between them from a ceramic tureen. "I can go next week when I get my first week's pay or I can stay in the flat on Chatham Street until after the baby's born and give you a third of what I earn in the meantime to cover my rent. I'd like to stay, as it's comfortable and you're the only two people I know in Dublin, but you've been very good to me since I got here and I don't want to out-stay my welcome."

"I don't mind," said Seán, smiling at her. "I'm happy as things are. But of course, it's Jack's place really, so it's up to him."

Smoot took a piece of bread from a plate in the center of the table and dragged it around the rim of his bowl, not letting a single morsel of the stew go to waste. He put it in his mouth and chewed it carefully before swallowing and then reached for his pint to wash it down.

"Sure we've put up with you this long, Kitty," he said. "A few more months won't make much difference, I suppose."

The Tearoom

The job in the Dáil tearoom was a lot more difficult than my mother had anticipated and, perhaps appropriately considering the setting, each girl had to learn to be diplomatic in her dealings with the elected members. All day long, the TDs marched in and out in a fug of body odor and cigarette smoke, demanding a cream cake or an éclair to go with their cup of coffee and rarely displaying any familiarity with manners. Some flirted with the girls but didn't intend their teasing to lead anywhere; others hoped that it would and could become aggressive if they were thwarted. There were stories of girls who'd been seduced and then fired when the man grew weary of her; stories of others who'd turned down an indecent proposal and been fired for that too. Once you caught the eye of a TD, it seemed that it could only lead in one direction and that was toward the dole queue. There were just four women elected to the Dáil at the time and my mother referred to them as the MayBes—Mary Reynolds from Sligo-Leitrim and Mary Ryan from Tipperary, Bridget Redmond from Waterford and Bridget Rice from Monaghan—and they were the worst of all, she said, for they didn't want to be seen speaking to the working girls in case one of the men came over and asked them to warm their pot or help to sew a button back on to their shirt sleeve.

Mr. de Valera didn't come in very often, she told me, as the tea was generally brought to him in his office by Mrs. Hennessy herself, but from time to time he might pop his head in the door if he was looking for someone and take a seat with some of the backbenchers, gauging the mood of the party. Tall and skinny, a bit gormless looking, she said he was never anything but polite and once reprimanded one of his own junior ministers for clicking his fingers at her, an action that earned him her eternal gratitude.

The girls she worked alongside were full of concern for my mother's situation. Seventeen years old by now, with a fictitious husband dead in a war that had finally come to an end and an all too real child ready to push its way out into the world, they regarded her with a mixture of fascination and pity.

"And your poor mammy died too, I heard?" asked an older girl, Lizzie, as they stood by the sink one afternoon washing dishes.

"She did," said my mother. "A terrible accident."

"I heard it was the cancer."

"Oh yes," she replied. "I meant a terrible misfortune. That she got the cancer at all."

"They say it carries down the family line," said Lizzie, who must have been the life and soul of any party. "Would you not worry that you'd get it yourself one day?"

"Well, I hadn't thought about it before," said my mother, stopping what she was doing and considering it. "But I'll think of nothing else now that you've said it." For a moment, she told me, she wondered whether she might, in fact, be in danger of developing the disease until she remembered that her mother, my grandmother, was alive and well and living with her husband and six straw-brained sons two hundred and thirty miles away in Goleen, West Cork. She relaxed again after that.

The Great Plan

In mid August, Mrs. Hennessy called her into her office and said that she thought the time had come for my mother to leave the job.

"Is it because I was late this morning?" asked my mother. "It's the first time that's ever happened. But there was a man standing outside my front door as I was leaving and he had a look on his face that said he wanted to murder me. I didn't want to go out alone while he was still there. I went upstairs and looked out the window and it was another twenty minutes before he turned on his heel and disappeared down Grafton Street."

"It's not because you were late," said Mrs. Hennessy, shaking her head. "You've always been punctual, Catherine, unlike some of them. No, I just think the time has come, that's all."

"But I still need the money," she protested. "I have my rent to think of and the child and—"

"I know, and I feel for you, but would you take a look at yourself, you're as big as a house. You can't have more than a couple of days to go. Is there nothing stirring, no?"

"No," she said. "Not yet."

"The thing is," said Mrs. Hennessy. "I've had . . . would you sit down, Catherine, for God's sake, and take the weight off. You shouldn't be standing in your condition anyway. The thing is, I've had complaints from some of the TDs."

"About me?"

"About you."

"But sure I'm never anything other than polite. Other than to that gombeen-man from Donegal who presses against me every time he passes and calls me his cushion."

"Oh I know that well enough," said Mrs. Hennessy. "Haven't I been watching you myself over these last three months? You'd have a job for life here if it wasn't for, you know, the fact that you will have other responsibilities soon. You're everything I look for in a tea girl. You were born to the role."

My mother smiled, deciding to take this as a compliment even though she wasn't entirely sure that it was one.

"No, it's not your manners they're complaining about. It's your condition. They say that seeing a woman so far along in her pregnancy puts them off their custard slices."

"Are you having me on?"

"This is what they've told me."

My mother laughed and shook her head. "Who said these things?" she asked. "Will you name names, Mrs. Hennessy?"

"I won't, no."

"Was it one of the MayBes?"

"I won't say, Catherine."

"Party affiliation then?"

"A little bit of both. A few more of the Fianna Fáil crowd, though, if I'm honest. But you know what they're like. The Blueshirts don't seem so bothered."

"Is it that little weasel that calls himself a Minister for—"

"Catherine, I'm not going to get into specifics with you," insisted Mrs. Hennessy, holding a hand in the air to silence her. "The fact is that you've only got days left anyway, a week at most, and it's in your best interests to stay off your feet. Would you not just do me the favor of calling it a day without any trouble about it? You've been wonderful, you have, and—"

"Of course," said my mother, realizing that she would be better off not begging for more time. "You've been very kind to me, Mrs. Hennessy. You gave me a job when I needed one and I know it wasn't the easiest decision to make. I'll see out the day and leave with a special place in my heart for you."

Mrs. Hennessy breathed a sigh of relief and sat back in her chair. "Thank you," she said. "You're a good girl, Catherine. You'll make a wonderful mother, you know. And if you ever need anything—"

"Well, there is something, actually," she replied. "After the baby's born, could I come back, do you think?"

"Come back where? Come back here to the Dáil? Oh no, that wouldn't be possible. Sure who'd look after the baby for one thing?"

My mother glanced out the window and took a deep breath. This would be the first time she had spoken aloud of her Great Plan. "His mother will look after him," she said. "Or her. Whichever it is."

"His mother?" asked Mrs. Hennessy, baffled. "But—"

"I won't be keeping the baby, Mrs. Hennessy," said my mother. "It's all arranged. After I give birth, there's a little hunchbacked Redemptorist nun who's going to come to the hospital to take the child away. A couple on Dartmouth Square are going to adopt it."

"Heavens above!" said Mrs. Hennessy. "And when was all this decided, if you don't mind my asking?"

"I decided on the day I found out that I was pregnant. I'm too young, I have no money and there's no chance that I can provide for the child. I'm not heartless, I promise you that, but the baby will be better off if I give it up to a family who can actually give it a good home."

"Well," replied Mrs. Hennessy, considering this. "I suppose these things do happen. But are you sure you'll be able to live with your decision?"

"No, but I think it's for the best nevertheless. The child stands a better chance with them than it would with me. They have money, Mrs. Hennessy. And I haven't a bean."

"And your husband? Is it what he would have wanted?"

My mother couldn't bring herself to lie anymore to this good woman and perhaps the shame showed in her face.

"Would I be right in thinking that there was no Mr. Goggin?" Mrs. Hennessy asked finally.

"You would," said my mother quietly.

"And the wedding ring?"

"I bought it myself. In a shop on Coppinger Row."

"I thought as much. No man would ever have the sense to choose something so elegant."

My mother looked up and smiled a little and was surprised to see that Mrs. Hennessy was starting to cry, and she reached into her pocket for a handkerchief to pass across to her.

"Are you all right?" she asked, surprised by this unexpected surge of emotion.

"I'm fine," said Mrs. Hennessy. "Not a bother on me."

"But you're crying."

"Only a little bit."

"Is it something I said?"

Mrs. Hennessy looked up and swallowed hard. "Can we think of this room as akin to the confessional?" she asked. "And that what we say between each other stays in here?"

"Of course," said my mother. "You've been very kind to me. I hope you know that I have great affection and respect for you."

"That's sweet of you to say. But I always guessed that the story you gave me wasn't quite true and I wanted to show you the compassion that was never shown to me when I was in your position. Maybe you won't be surprised if I say that there was never a Mr. Hennessy either." She extended her left hand and they both looked at her wedding ring. "I bought that for four shillings in a shop on Henry Street in 1913," she said. "I haven't taken it off my finger since."

"Did you have a child too?" asked my mother. "Did you have to bring it up alone?"

"Not quite," said Mrs. Hennessy hesitantly. "I'm from Westmeath, did you know that, Catherine?"

"I did, yes. You told me once."

"I haven't set foot in the place since I left. But I didn't come to Dublin to have my baby. I had it at home. In the bedroom I'd slept in every night of my life until then, the same room where the poor child was conceived."

"And what happened to him?" asked my mother. "Was it a him?"

"No, it was a her. A little girl. A beautiful little thing. She didn't last long. Mammy cut the cord once she was out of me and Daddy took her out the back where a bucket of water was waiting and he held her under for a minute or two, long enough to drown her. Then he threw her in a grave that he'd dug a few days earlier and covered her over and that was the end of that. No one ever knew. Not the neighbors, not the priest, not the Gardaí."

"Jesus, Mary and Joseph," said my mother, sitting back in horror.

"I never even got a chance to hold her," said Mrs. Hennessy. "Mammy cleaned me up and I was put onto the road later that same day. They said I was never to return."

"I was denounced from the pulpit," said my mother. "The parish priest called me a whore."

"Those fellas have no more sense than a wooden spoon," said Mrs. Hennessy. "I've never known cruelty like the cruelty of the priests. This country . . ." She closed her eyes and shook her head, and my mother said that it looked like she wanted to scream.

"That's a terrible story," said my mother eventually. "I suppose the baby's daddy didn't offer to marry you?"

Mrs. Hennessy gave a bitter laugh. "He wouldn't have been able anyway," she said. "He was already married."

"Did his wife find out?"

Mrs. Hennessy stared at her and when she spoke her voice was low and mixed with shame and loathing. "She knew well enough," she said. "Didn't I tell you that she cut the cord?"

My mother said nothing for a moment and when she finally realized what Mrs. Hennessy meant she put a hand to her mouth and felt that she might be sick.

"As I said, these things happen," said Mrs. Hennessy. "Your decision is made, Catherine? You're going to give the child up?"

My mother couldn't find her voice but nodded.

"Then give yourself a couple of weeks afterward to get better and then come back to me. We'll tell people that the baby died and soon enough they'll forget all about it."

"Will that work?" asked my mother.

"It will work for them," she replied, reaching over and taking my mother's hand in hers. "But I'm sorry to say, Catherine, it will never work for you."

Violence

It was growing dark as my mother made her way home that evening. Turning the corner onto Chatham Street, she was annoyed to notice a figure emerging unsteadily from Clarendon's pub, the same man whose presence outside her door that morning had made her late for work. He was wildly overweight with a wrinkled face gone red with the drink and two or three days' growth of beard that gave him the appearance of a vagrant.

"There you are now," he said as she walked toward her front door, the stench of whiskey on his breath so strong that she was forced to pull back from him. "Large as life and twice as ugly."

She said nothing but took the key from her pocket and in her anxiety she struggled to insert it correctly.

"There's rooms up above, isn't there?" asked the man, glancing up toward the window. "A rake of them or just the one?"

"Just the one," she said. "So if you're looking for lodgings, I'm afraid you've come to the wrong place."

"The accent on you. You sound Cork-born to me. Where are you from? Bantry? Drimoleague? I knew a lass once from Drimoleague. A worthless creature who went with any man who asked her."

My mother looked away and tried the key again, cursing beneath her breath as it jammed in the lock, causing her to twist the metal violently to release it.

"If you could just step out of the light," she asked, turning to look him in the eye.

"Just the one flat," he said, scratching his chin as he considered this. "So you live with them, do you?"

"With who?"

"That's a curious arrangement altogether."

"With *who*?" she insisted.

"With the queer fellas, of course. But what would they want with you anyway? They've no use for a woman, either of them." He stared at her belly and shook his head. "Did one of them do this? No, sure they wouldn't have it in them. You probably don't even know who's responsible, do ya, ya dirty little slut."

My mother turned back to the door and this time the key slid in easily and the lock released. Before she could step inside, however, he pushed past her and marched into the hallway, leaving her standing on the street, uncertain what to do. It was only when he began to make his way up the staircase that she regained control of her senses and grew angry at the intrusion.

"Get down here, you," she called up to him. "This is a private residence, do you hear me? I'll call the Gardaí!"

"Call whoever the fuck you like!" he roared back, and she looked up and down the street but there wasn't a sinner in sight. Gathering all her courage, she followed him up the staircase, where he was rattling ineffectively at the door handle.

"Open this now," he said, pointing a fat finger at her, and she couldn't help but notice the dirt that lived beneath his long fingernails. A farmer, she decided. And his accent was Cork too, but not West Cork or she would have been able to identify it quickly. "Open it now, little girl, or I'll put my foot right through it."

"I will not," she said. "And you'll leave these premises or I'll—"

He turned his back on her, waving her away, and as good as his word lifted his right boot, gave the door an almighty kick and it burst open, slamming against the wall and causing a pot to fall from a shelf into the bathtub with a terrific clatter. The living room was empty but even as he stumbled inside with my mother in hot pursuit the sound of anxious voices could be heard from the bedroom beyond.

"Get out here, Seán MacIntyre!" roared the man, reeling in his drunkenness. "Get out here now till I beat some decency into you. I warned you what I'd do if I ever caught the pair of you together again."

He lifted his stick—my mother hadn't even noticed the stick until that moment—and brought it down solidly against the table a few times, hard enough to make her jump at the noise of it. Her own father had a stick just like this one and many was the time she had observed him set upon one of her brothers with it in a fury. He had tried to use it on her on the night that her secret was revealed but, mercifully, my grandmother had held him back.

"You have the wrong place," cried my mother. "This is madness!"

"Get out here!" roared the man again. "Get out here or I'll come in there and get you myself. Come on now!"

"Leave," said my mother, pulling at his sleeve, but he pushed her away violently, causing her to fall against the armchair whereupon a swift pain coursed through her back and ran along the length of her spine, like a mouse scurrying for cover. The man reached for the bedroom door, flinging it wide open, and there, to my mother's astonishment, were Seán and Smoot, naked as the day they were born, sitting up against the headboard of the bed, expressions of utter terror on their faces.

"Jesus Christ," said the man, turning away in disgust. "Get out here now, you dirty little bastard."

"Daddy," said Seán, jumping from the bed, and my mother couldn't help but stare at his naked body as he rushed to cover himself with trousers and shirt. "Daddy, please, let's just go downstairs and—"

He stepped into the living room but before he could say another word the man, his own father, grabbed him by the scruff of the neck and smashed his head hard against the one shelf that stood affixed to the wall and carried only three books, a Bible, a copy of *Ulysses* and a biography of Queen Victoria. There was a terrible sound and Seán let out a groan that seemed to emerge from the very depths of his being, and when he turned around his face was pale and a black mark stood out on his forehead, pulsating for a moment as if uncertain what was expected of it, before turning red as the blood began to pour. His legs gave way beneath him and, as he collapsed to the ground, the man reached down and dragged him with one hand toward the doorway, where he began to kick him repeatedly, beating him with his stick and issuing blasphemies with every fresh assault.

"Get off him!" cried my mother, throwing herself on the man as Smoot emerged from the bedroom with a hurley stick, a red and white sticker affixed to it showing two towers and a ship sailing between them, and charged toward their attacker. He hadn't put a stitch of clothes on and even in the drama of the moment my mother was shocked by the hair that covered his torso, so unlike the chests of Seán, my father or any of her brothers, and the long, still-glistening manhood that shook between his legs as he advanced on them.

The man roared as the hurley hit him in the back but it was an ineffective blow and he pushed Smoot away with such force that the younger man fell backward over the sofa and into the doorway of the bedroom beyond, where, she realized now, the boys had been lovers since the day the bus had arrived in Dublin from Cork. She had heard of such people. The boys in school made fun of them all the time. Was it any wonder, she asked herself, that Smoot had never wanted her there? It was to be their love-place, that was it. And she was the cuckoo in their nest.

"Jack!" cried my mother, as Peadar MacIntyre—for that was the man's name—took his son by the head once more and kicked his body with such barbarous force that she could hear the sounds of ribs cracking. "Seán!" she screamed, but when the boy's head twisted toward her his eyes were wide open and she knew that he had already departed this world for the next. Still and all, she would not allow more injury to come to him and ran back across the room, determined to pull the man away, but with her first attempt he took her by an arm and, in a quick movement, gave her a mighty kick that sent her through the open doorway and tumbling down the staircase, each step, she told me later, making her feel an inch closer to death herself.

Landing with a crash on the ground below, she lay on her back for a moment, staring up at the ceiling, gasping for breath. Inside her belly, I protested strongly at the insult and decided that my time had come, and my mother let out a ferocious scream as I broke free of the womb and began my first journey.

Pulling herself to her feet, she looked around. Another woman in her position might have opened the front door and thrown herself out onto Chatham Street, roaring for help. But not Catherine Goggin. Seán was dead, she was certain of that, but Smoot was still up there and she could hear him pleading for his life and then the sounds of violence, the screams of pain, the curses that lashed down on the boy's head as Seán's father attacked him too.

Crying out with every movement, she dragged herself up the first step, up another and another until she had ascended halfway. She screamed as I made my presence felt and there was something in her mind, she told me later, that said I had waited nine months, I could wait another nine minutes. She continued her climb, entering the flat with perspiration running down her face, water and blood seeping down her legs, frightened by the image of the madwoman in the mirror opposite with the bedraggled hair, split lip and torn dress. From the room beyond, Smoot's cries were growing less pronounced as the kicks and the whips of the stick continued, and she stepped over Seán's body, glancing quickly at the open eyes on his once-beautiful face, and had to stop herself from crying out in grief.

I'm on my way, I thought as she moved forward purposefully, looking around the room for a weapon before her eyes landed on the hurley that Smoot had dropped on the floor. *Are you ready for me?*

One swift swing was all it took, God love her, and Peadar MacIntyre lay knocked out. Not dead—he would live for eight more years, in fact, eventually choking on a fishbone in his local pub, the jury having set him free, finding that his crime had been committed under the extreme provocation of having a mentally disordered son—but unconscious, and my mother and I threw ourselves down on Smoot's body, the poor lad's face muddled with the beating, his breath disordered, close enough to death now too.

"Jack," she cried, cradling his face in her lap and then letting out a blood-curdling shriek as everything in her being told her to push, to push now, and my head began to emerge from between her legs. "Jack, stay with me. Don't die; do you hear me, Jack? Don't die!"

"Kitty," said Smoot, the word muffled as it emerged from his mouth along with a couple of broken teeth.

"And don't fucking call me Kitty!" she roared, screaming once again as more of my body squeezed itself out into the August night.

"Kitty," he whispered, his eyes beginning to close, and she shook him as the pain racked through her body.

"You have to live, Jack," she cried. "You have to live!"

And then she must have passed out, for silence was restored to the room until a minute later, when I took advantage of the peace and quiet to push the rest of my tiny body onto the filthy carpet of the upstairs flat on Chatham Street in a bundle of blood and placenta and slime. I waited a few moments to gather my thoughts before opening my lungs for the first time and with an almighty roar, one that must have been heard by the men in the pub below who came running up the staircase to discover the cause of such a racket, announced to the world that I had arrived, that I was born, that I was part of it all at last.

1952 The Vulgarity of Popularity

One Little Girl in a Pale-Pink Coat

I first met Julian Woodbead when his father called to the house on Dartmouth Square to discuss ways to keep his most valuable client out of prison. Max Woodbead was a solicitor, a very good one by all accounts, with an insatiable desire to mix in the highest echelons of Dublin society and an office on Ormond Quay, close to the Four Courts. From his window, he enjoyed a view across the Liffey toward Christ Church Cathedral and liked to claim, somewhat unconvincingly, that whenever he heard the bells ring he would fall to his knees and say a prayer to the late Pope Benedict XV, who had ascended to the throne of St. Peter on that same September day in 1914 that he was born. My adoptive father had hired him after a series of misadventures concerning (but not limited to) gambling, women, fraud, tax evasion and an assault on a journalist from the *Dublin Evening Mail*. The Bank of Ireland, where my father held a prominent position as Director of Investments and Client Portfolios, had no particular rules about how its employees spent their time when they were not at their desks, but they took a dim view of the bad publicity that he was bringing their way. In recent months, he had been seen gambling thousands of pounds at Leopardstown Races, been photographed coming out of the Shelbourne Hotel with a prostitute at four o'clock in the morning, fined for urinating over the side of the Ha'penny Bridge while he was in his cups, and given an interview on Radio Éireann in which he said that the country's finances would be in a better position if the Brits had shot the Minister for Finance, Seán MacEntee, after the Easter Rising, as they'd originally planned to do. He'd also been castigated for attempting to kidnap a seven-year-old boy on Grafton Street, a trumped-up charge as he had simply taken him by the hand and dragged him across to Trinity College under the impression that the frightened child, who shared my height and hair color but was unfortunately a mute, was me. An affair with an actress of some renown was suggested by the *Irish Press*, who made their disapproval clear by reprimanding him for "extra-marital shenanigans with a lady of the theater when his own wife, who our more literary readers might know has some small celebrity of her own, is recovering from a distressing bout of cancer of the ear canal." The upshot was that the Department of Revenue launched a formal investigation into my father's accounts and, to no one's surprise, discovered that he had been cheating on his tax returns for years to the tune of more than thirty thousand pounds. Immediate suspension from the bank followed and The Man from the Revenue announced that he intended to use the full power of the judicial system to make an example of him, at which point Max Woodbead, inevitably, was called.

Of course, when I say "my father," I don't mean the man who handed two green pound notes to my mother outside the Church of Our Lady, Star of the Sea, in Goleen seven years earlier to soothe his conscience. No, I mean Charles Avery, who, along with his wife, Maude, opened their home to me after signing a sizable check to the Redemptorist convent for all their help in the matter of finding a suitable child. From the start, they never pretended to be anything other than my adoptive parents and, in fact, schooled me in this detail from the time I could first understand the meaning of the words. Maude claimed that this was because she didn't want the truth to come out at a later date and for me then to accuse her of deceit, while Charles insisted that it was because he wanted to be clear that, while he was happy to go through with the adoption for his wife's sake, I was not a real Avery and would not be looked after financially in adulthood in the manner that a real Avery would have been.

"Think of this more as a tenancy, Cyril," he told me—they had named me Cyril for a spaniel they'd once owned and loved—"an eighteen-year tenancy. But during that time there's no reason why we shouldn't all get along, is there? Although if I had a son of my own, I'd like to think he would have been taller than you. And shown a little more skill on the rugby field. But I suppose you're not the worst. God only knows whom we might have got. Do you know, at one point there was even a suggestion that we take in an African baby?"

The relationship between Charles and Maude was cordial and business-like. They had little to do with each other most days, exchanging no more than a few cursory sentences necessary to the efficient running of the household. Charles left every morning at eight o'clock and rarely returned before midnight, when he invariably spent a minute or two on the porch, trying to fit his key into the lock and not caring if he reeked of drink or cheap perfume. They didn't sleep in the same room or even on the same floor, nor had they ever done so since my arrival. I never once saw them hold hands, or kiss, or say that they loved each other. But for all that, they never fought. Maude's way of dealing with Charles was to treat him like an ottoman, of no use to anyone but worth having around, while Charles showed scant interest in his wife but found her presence both reassuring and unsettling, much like Mr. Rochester must have felt toward Bertha Mason as she rattled around the attic of Thornfield Hall, a relic from his past that remained an inexorable part of his daily life.

They had no children of their own, of course. An early and vivid memory is of Maude confiding in me that there had been a little girl once, a year after she and Charles were married, but she had endured a difficult labor and not only had the child, Lucy, died, but a subsequent operation meant that she would not be able to get pregnant again.

"A blessed relief in so many ways, Cyril," she remarked, lighting a cigarette and staring out into the fenced park at the center of Dartmouth Square, on the lookout for intruders. (She loathed non-residents appearing in the gardens, despite the fact that they were, strictly speaking, public property, and was known for rapping on the windowpanes and shooing them away like dogs.) "There is simply nothing more disgusting than the naked body of a man. All that hair and such terrible smells, because men don't know how to wash themselves properly unless they've been in the army. And their secretions, which seep forth from their appendages when aroused, are repellent. You're lucky that you will never have to endure the indignity of relations with the male member. The vagina is a much purer instrument. I feel an admiration for the vagina that I simply have never felt toward the penis." If I recall correctly, I was around five years old when she passed this piece of wisdom on to me. Perhaps it was because both Charles and Maude spoke to me in such an adult manner, apparently forgetting (or failing to notice) that I was just a child, that my own vocabulary grew quicker than other children's my age.

Maude had a career of her own, for she was the author of a number of literary novels, published by a small press in Dalkey. A new one appeared every few years to positive reviews but minuscule sales, something that pleased her enormously, for she considered popularity in the bookshops to be vulgar. In this endeavor, Charles was never anything but supportive and rather enjoyed introducing her as "my wife, the lady novelist Maude Avery. Never read a word of her work myself but, God bless her, she keeps on churning them out." She wrote all day, every day, even Christmas Day, and rarely emerged from her study except to prowl around the house in a haze of cigarette smoke, looking for boxes of matches.

Why she wanted to adopt a child at all is a mystery to me, as she showed no interest whatsoever in my well-being, although she was never actively unkind or cruel. However, I couldn't help but feel deprived of affection and once, when I came home in tears to tell her that one of my school friends, the boy who sat next to me in Latin class and with whom I often ate my lunch, had been run over and killed by a bus on Parnell Square, she simply remarked that it would be ghastly if anything like that happened to me, as they had gone to so much trouble to find me in the first place.

"You weren't the first one, you know," she said, lighting another cigarette and taking a long drag as she counted off the babies on her left hand. "There was a girl in Wicklow to whom we paid a sizable amount of money but when the baby was born it had a peculiar-shaped head and I simply hadn't the energy. And then there was another in Rathmines who we took on approval for a few days but the baby just cried all the time and I couldn't bear it so we sent her back. And then Charles said he would accept no more girls, only a boy, and so I was stuck with you, darling."

I was never hurt by these types of remarks, for she didn't mean them maliciously; it was simply her way of speaking and, having never known anything different, I accepted that I was just a living creature who shared a house with two adults who rarely acknowledged each other. I was fed, clothed and schooled, and to complain would have shown a level of ingratitude that probably would have baffled them both.

Only when I reached an age where I was old enough to understand fully the concept of natural and adoptive parents did I break one of our home's golden rules and enter Maude's study uninvited to inquire as to the identities of my real mother and father. When I located her through the miasma and managed to clear my throat enough to speak, she simply shook her head in bewilderment, as if I had asked her to tell me the distance to the nearest mile between the Jamia Mosque in Nairobi and the Todgha Gorge in Morocco.

"For heaven's sake, Cyril," she said, "that was seven years ago. How on earth would I recall? Your mother was a girl, I know that much."

"And what happened to her?" I asked. "Is she alive?"

"How should I know?"

"Don't you even remember her name?"

"It was probably Mary. Aren't most Irish country girls called Mary?"

"So she wasn't from Dublin?" I asked, seizing on this piece of information like a tiny nugget of gold discovered at the heart of a placer deposit.

"I really couldn't tell you. I never met her, never communicated with her and never knew the first thing about her other than the fact that she had allowed a man to engage in carnal relations with her, resulting in a child. That child being you. Now look, Cyril, can't you see that I'm writing? You know you're not supposed to come in here when I'm at work. I lose my train of thought if I'm interrupted."

I always called them Charles and Maude, never "Father" and "Mother." This was on Charles's insistence as I wasn't a real Avery. It didn't bother me particularly but I know it made other people uncomfortable and once, in school, when I referred to them thus, a priest punched me around the ears and told me off for being modern.

I faced two problems at an early age, one of which might have been the natural result of the other. I was cursed with a stutter that seemed to have a mind of its own—it would be there some days and disappear on others—and it had the ability to drive both my adoptive parents to distraction. It stayed with me until the age of seven when, on the same day that I met Julian Woodbead, it vanished forever. How these two events are connected remains a mystery to me but the damage to my confidence was already done and I found myself painfully shy, nervous of most of my classmates, with the exception of that one child who had been squashed beneath the wheels of the number 16 bus, horrified by the prospect of speaking in public and simply incapable of conversing with anyone lest my affliction rear its head and cause people to laugh at me. It bothered me greatly, for I was not by nature a solitary person and I longed for a friend, someone to play games with or share my secrets. Occasionally, Charles and Maude would host a dinner party where they would come together as Husband and Wife, and on such occasions I would be brought down and passed around from couple to couple like a Fabergé egg they'd purchased from a descendant of the last Russian Tsar.

"His mother was a fallen woman," Charles liked to say. "And we, in an act of Christian charity, took him in and gave him a home. A little hunchbacked Redemptorist nun brought him to us. If you ever want a child, the nuns are the people to call, that's what I say. They have plenty of them. I don't know where they keep them all or how they get them in the first place but there's never a shortage. Introduce yourself to our guests, Cyril."

And I would look around the room, at six or seven couples dressed in the most extraordinary clothes, bedecked with jewelry, each of whom stared at me as if they expected me to sing a song, perform a dance, or pull a rabbit out of my ear. *Entertain us*, their expressions said. *If you can't entertain us, then what is the point of you anyway?* But in my anxiety I would be unable to utter a word and I would simply look down at the ground and perhaps start crying, and then Charles would wave me away and remind the room that I wasn't his son at all, not really.

When the scandal broke, I was seven years old and became aware of it due to the comments of my classmates, most of whose fathers worked in similar environments to Charles and who took great pleasure in telling me that he was for the high jump and would surely be jailed before the year was out.

"He's not my father," I would point out, unable to look any of them in the eye and clenching and unclenching my fists in anger. "He's my adoptive father." I had been trained well.

Intrigued by the things that were being said about him, however, I began to scour the newspapers for information and, although they were careful not to publish a libel, it was clear that Charles, like the Archbishop of Dublin, was a man much feared, much admired and much hated. And, of course, there was no shortage of rumors. He was regularly to be found in the company of both the Anglo-Irish aristocracy and the ne'er-do-wells of the city. On any given night, he could be discovered throwing ten-pound notes down on the tables of illicit gambling halls. He had murdered his first wife, Emily. (*Was there a first wife?* I asked once of Maude. *Oh yes, now that you mention it, I think there was*, she replied.) He had made and lost his fortune thrice over. He was an alcoholic and had cigars sent on a cargo ship from Cuba by Fidel Castro himself. He had six toes on his left foot. He had once had an affair with Princess Margaret. There was an endless supply of stories regarding Charles and there may even have been truth to some of them.

So perhaps it was inevitable that one day the services of Max Woodbead would be required. Things had to be in a bad way for that to happen and even Maude had begun to emerge from her study occasionally to wander around the house muttering dark asides about The Man from the Revenue as if he might be found hiding under the stairs or stealing her emergency supply of cigarettes from the bread bin in the kitchen. On the day that Max showed up, I hadn't spoken to a single person in eight days. I'd kept note of it in a diary. I hadn't raised my hand in class, hadn't said a word to anyone in school, had eaten my meals in perfect silence, which was how Maude preferred it anyway, and generally hid away in my bedroom, wondering what was wrong with me, for even at that tender age I knew that there was *something* about me that was different and that would be impossible ever to put right.

I would have stayed in my bedroom that day—I was reading *Kidnapped* by Robert Louis Stevenson—had it not been for the scream. It came from the second floor, where Maude's study was located, and echoed around the house in such a fashion that I assumed someone was dead. Running out to the landing, I peered over the bannister and saw a little girl of about five in a pale-pink coat standing on the floor below me, her hands pressed to her cheeks as the most horrific sound emerged from her mouth. I had never seen her before and within a few seconds she turned on her heel and ran like an Olympic athlete down the stairs toward the first floor, down once again to the ground floor, along the hallway and out onto the street beyond, slamming the heavy wooden door behind her so hard that the knocker rattled against the plate several times. I went back into my room and looked out the window and there she was, charging into the heart of Dartmouth Square, at which point I lost sight of her. My heart was beating wildly in my chest and I went back out to the landing, hoping for an explanation, but there was no one there and the house had returned to silence.

Disturbed now from my reading, I realized that I was thirsty and made my way downstairs in search of something to drink and to my surprise found another child—a boy of my own age—sitting in a chair in our hallway, a chair that existed for ornamental reasons and was not supposed to be used, turning the pages of a comic.

"Hello," I said, and he glanced up at me and smiled. He had blond hair and piercing blue eyes that captivated me immediately. Perhaps it was because I had been silent for more than a week that my words tumbled out of me like water overflowing a neglected bath. "My name's Cyril Avery and I'm seven years old. Charles and Maude are my parents, although they're not my real parents, they're my adoptive parents, I'm not sure who my real parents are, but I've lived here forever and I have a room on the top floor. No one ever goes up there, except the maid to clean it, so I have things just as I like them. What's your name anyway?"

"Julian Woodbead," said Julian. And a moment later I realized that I didn't feel shy around him at all. And that my stutter had gone.

Julian

There is no denying the privilege in which Julian and I were brought up. Our families had money and status. They moved in elegant circles, with friends who held important positions in government or the arts. We lived in large houses where the menial work was undertaken by middle-aged women who arrived on early-morning buses, making their way from room to room under the weight of dusters, mops and brooms, and who were discouraged from speaking to us.

Our housekeeper was named Brenda, and Maude insisted that she wear slippers around the house as the sound of Brenda's shoes on the wooden floors disturbed her writing. Her study was the only room in the house that the housekeeper was not permitted to clean, which accounted for the fact that there were always dust mites floating in the air alongside the cigarette smoke, creating a heavy atmosphere that was at its most overpowering in the late afternoon when the sun poured through the windows as it continued its journey westward. While Brenda was a constant of my childhood, Julian's family employed a series of maids, none of whom lasted more than a year, and whether it was the difficulty of the work or the unkindness of the Woodbeads that drove them away I never knew. But for all that we had, for all the luxury to which we were accustomed, we were both denied love, and this deficiency would be scorched into our future lives like an ill-considered tattoo inscribed on the buttocks after a drunken night out, leading each of us inevitably toward isolation and disaster.

We attended different schools. I walked down to Ranelagh every morning, where I had a place at a small junior preparatory, while Julian was in a similar establishment a few miles north on a quiet street close to St. Stephen's Green. Neither of us knew where we would be going after sixth class but as Charles and Max had both been Belvedere College boys in their youth—this was where they had met, in fact, becoming friends as stalwarts of the rugby team that had lost to Castleknock College in the final of the 1931 Leinster Schools Cup—we assumed that there was a good chance that we would end up there too. Julian was not as unhappy in the education system as I was but then he was much more of an extrovert by nature and found it easier to fit in with others.

On the afternoon that we met we exchanged only a few pleasantries in the hallway before I invited him upstairs, as children do, to see my room, and he followed me cheerfully and without question to the top of the house. As he stood beside my unmade bed, examining the books on my shelves and the toys that lay scattered on the floor, it occurred to me that he was the first child, other than myself, ever to set foot in there.

"You're lucky to have so much space," he said, balancing on the tips of his toes as he looked out the window into the square beyond. "And you have it all to yourself?"

"Yes," I said, for my domain consisted of three rooms: a bedroom, a small bathroom and a living area, which, I suppose, made it more of a self-contained apartment than anything else, not something that most seven-year-olds could lay claim to. "Charles has the first floor, Maude has the second and we all share the ground."

"You mean your parents don't sleep together?" he asked.

"Oh no," I said. "Why, do yours?"

"Of course they do."

"But why? Don't you have enough bedrooms?"

"We have four," he said. "My bedroom is next door to my sister's," he added, pulling a face.

"Was that the little girl who ran screaming from here earlier?" I asked.

"Yes."

"Why was she screaming? What upset her?"

"I haven't the foggiest," said Julian with a shrug. "She's always becoming hysterical over something. Girls are strange creatures, don't you think?"

"I don't know any," I admitted.

"I know lots. I love girls, even though they're crazy and mentally unbalanced, according to my father. Have you ever seen a pair of breasts?"

I stared at him in surprise. I was only seven years old; such thoughts had not yet occurred to me but even then Julian's sexually precocious mind was already turning toward women. "No," I said.

"I have," he told me proudly. "At a beach on the Algarve last summer. All the girls were going around topless. I got sunburned I stayed out so long. Second-degree burns! I can't wait to have sex with a girl, can you?"

I frowned. The word was a new one to me. "What's sex?" I asked.

"You really don't know?" he asked.

"No," I said, and he took great delight in describing in detail actions that to me seemed not just unpleasant and unsanitary but possibly criminal.

"Oh that," I said when he was finished, pretending that I had known all along, for I didn't want him to look down on me and think me too innocent for his friendship. "I thought you were talking about something else. I know all about that."

"Do you have any dirty magazines?" he asked me then.

"No," I said, shaking my head.

"I have. I found one in my father's study. It was full of naked girls. It was an American magazine, of course, because naked girls are still illegal in Ireland."

"Are they?" I asked, wondering how they bathed if that was the case.

"Yes, the Church doesn't let girls be naked until they're married. But the Americans do and they take their clothes off all the time and let their pictures go into magazines and then men go into shops and buy them with copies of *History Today* or *Stamps Monthly* so they don't look like perverts."

"What's a pervert?" I asked.

"It's someone who's a sex maniac," he explained.

"Oh."

"I'm going to be a pervert when I grow up," he continued.

"So am I," I said, eager to please. "Perhaps we could be perverts together."

Even as the words came out of my mouth I could tell there was something not quite right about them and the expression on his face, one of disdain combined with mistrust, embarrassed me.

"I don't think so," he said quickly. "That's not how it works at all. Boys can only be perverts with girls."

"Oh," I said, disappointed.

"Do you have a big thing?" he asked a few moments later, after picking up all the keepsakes on my desk, examining them and putting them back down again in the wrong places.

"Do I what?" I asked.

"A big thing," he repeated. "You need a big thing if you want to be a pervert. Shall we see whose is the biggest? I bet mine is."

My mouth dropped open in surprise and I felt a curious stirring at the pit of my stomach, an entirely new sensation that I couldn't quite understand but that I felt happy to encourage.

"All right," I said.

"You first," said Julian.

"Why me first?"

"Because I said so, that's why."

I hesitated but, not wanting him to change his mind and move on to a different game, I undid my belt buckle and pulled my trousers and underwear down to my knees and he leaned forward, an interested expression on his face as he stared at it. "I think that's what they call average," he said after a moment. "Although even that might be generous of me."

"I'm only seven," I said, feeling offended as I pulled my pants back up.

"I'm only seven too but I'm bigger," he said, pulling his trousers down now in order to show me, and this time I could feel the room spin a little as I stared at it. I knew there was danger to this, that to be caught would be to invite trouble and disgrace, but the risk excited me. His was definitely bigger and it fascinated me, for it was the first penis outside of my own that I had ever seen and, as he was circumcised and I was not, it intrigued me.

"Where's the rest of it?" I asked.

"What do you mean?" he said, pulling his pants up and refastening his belt without an ounce of self-consciousness.

"The rest of your thing," I said.

"They cut it off," he said. "When I was a baby."

I felt a stab of pain run through me. "Why did they do that?" I asked.

"I'm not sure," he said. "It happens to lots of boys when they're young. It's a Jewish thing."

"Are you Jewish?"

"No, why? Are you?"

"No."

"Well then."

"It won't happen to me," I said, horrified by the notion of anyone coming at my nether regions with a knife.

"It might. Anyway, have you ever been to France?"

"To France?" I asked, uncertain why he was asking. "No. Why?"

"We're going there on our summer holidays this year, that's all."

"Oh," I said, disappointed that we had moved away from talking about sex, perverts and things, as I would have liked to continue discussing them for a little while longer but he seemed to have grown bored with them now. I wondered if I brought the conversation back to girls whether he might indulge me a little longer.

"Do you just have one sister?" I asked.

"Yes," he said. "Alice. She's five."

"Any brothers?"

He shook his head. "No. You?"

"I'm an only child." At that age, of course, it didn't even occur to me that my birth mother might have gone on to have more children. Or that my natural father had most likely sired a brood of them before or since my conception.

"Why do you call your parents Charles and Maude?" he asked.

"They prefer it that way," I said. "I'm adopted, you see, and it's to show that I'm not a real Avery."

He laughed and shook his head and said something that made me laugh: "Bizarro."

A tap on the door disturbed us and I turned around cautiously, like a character in a scary film that thinks there's a murderer waiting outside. No one ever visited the top floor except Brenda and even she only dared to enter when I was at school.

"What's the matter?" asked Julian.

"Nothing."

"You look nervous."

"I'm not nervous."

"I said you *look* nervous."

"It's just that no one ever comes up here," I said.

I watched as the door handle slowly turned, then took a step back and Julian, infected by my anxiety, moved toward the window. A moment later, a cloud of smoke entered the room followed, inevitably, by Maude. I hadn't seen her in days and was surprised that her hair was not quite as blonde as usual and she was looking painfully thin. Her recent illness had left her with a weak appetite and she rarely ate anymore. "I can't keep anything down," she had told me on the last occasion that we had spoken. "Anything except nicotine, that is."

"Maude," I said, surprised to see her there.

"Cyril," she replied, glancing around, surprised to see another boy in my room. "There you are. But who is this?"

"Julian Woodbead," said Julian in a confident tone. "My father is Max Woodbead, the famous solicitor."

He extended a hand and she stared at it for a moment as if baffled by its appearance. "What do you want?" she asked. "Money?"

"No," said Julian, starting to laugh. "My father says it's good manners to shake hands upon making a new acquaintance."

"Oh, I see," she said, leaning over and examining his fingers. "Is it clean? Have you been to the bathroom lately? Did you wash your hands afterward?"

"It's perfectly clean, Mrs. Avery," said Julian.

She sighed, reached out her own hand and shook his for about a tenth of a second. "You have very soft skin," she said, purring a little. "Little boys generally do, of course. They're not used to hard work. How old are you, if you don't mind my asking?"

"I'm seven," said Julian.

"No, Cyril is seven," she replied, shaking her head. "I was asking how old *you* are."

"Well, I'm seven too," he said. "We both are."

"Both seven," she said almost in a whisper. "Isn't that a bit of a coincidence?"

"I don't think it is really," he said, considering it. "Everyone in my class at school is seven. And everyone in Cyril's too, I imagine. There's probably the same number of seven-year-olds in Dublin as there are people of any age."

"Perhaps," replied Maude, unconvinced. "Might I ask what you're doing in Cyril's bedroom? Did he know that you were coming? You're not being unpleasant to him, are you? He does seem to attract bullies."

"Julian was sitting in the hallway," I told her. "On the ornamental chair that isn't supposed to be used."

"Oh no," said Maude, appalled. "That was my mother's."

"I didn't damage it," said Julian.

"My mother was Eveline Hartford," said Maude, as if this would mean something to one or the other of us. "So as you know, she simply adored chairs."

"They are terribly useful," replied Julian, catching my eye and winking at me. "If one wants to sit down, I mean."

"Well, yes," said Maude in a distant tone. "I mean that's what they're for, isn't it?"

"But not the ornamental chair," I pointed out. "You told me never to sit on that one."

"That's because you have a habit of collecting dirt," she said.

"Julian, on the other hand, looks rather clean. Did you have a bath this morning?"

"I did, actually," said Julian. "But then I have a bath most mornings."

"Good for you. I find it almost impossible to persuade Cyril to wash."

"That's not true," I said, insulted, in part because I was meticulous about my personal hygiene but also because even at that age I hated when people attributed characteristics to me that had no basis in truth.

"I would, however, ask you not to sit in it again if you don't mind," continued Maude, ignoring my interruption.

"You have my word, Mrs. Avery," said Julian, performing a little bow at the waist that made her smile, an event almost as rare as a solar eclipse. "You write novels, don't you?" he asked then.

"That's right," she said. "How did you know that?"

"My father told me. He said he hasn't read any himself because you mostly write about women."

"I do," she admitted.

"Might I ask why?"

"Because the male writers never do. They don't have the talent, you see. Or the wisdom."

"Julian's father is here to see Charles," I said, keen to turn the conversation away from chairs and books. "When I discovered him downstairs, I thought he might like to come up to see my room."

"And did you?" asked Maude, sounding astonished by the concept. "Did you want to see Cyril's room?"

"Yes, very much so. He has a lot of space up here, doesn't he? I envy him that. And that skylight is wonderful. Imagine being able to lie in bed at night and look up at the stars!"

"Someone died up here once, you know," said Maude, sniffing the air, which was already filled with carcinogens from her cigarettes, as if hoping for the last olfactory vestiges of death.

"What?" I asked, appalled. "Who?" This was the first time I had heard this.

"Oh I can't remember. Some . . . man, I think. Or possibly a woman. A *person*, shall we say. It was all such a long time ago."

"Was it natural causes, Mrs. Avery?" asked Julian.

"No, I don't think so. If memory serves, he, she or it was murdered. I'm not sure if the killer was ever caught. It was in all the papers at the time." She waved her hand in the air and some ash fell on my head. "I can't remember the details very well," she said. "Was there a *knife* involved? For some reason, I have the word *knife* in my head."

"A stabbing!" said Julian, rubbing his hands together in glee.

"Do you mind if I sit down, Cyril?" asked Maude, pointing at the bed.

"If you must."

She sat and smoothed down her skirt, fishing another cigarette from her silver case. Her fingers were long and bony, the skin almost translucent. I would have only needed to look a little closer to make out the joints between the phalanges.

"Do you have a light?" she asked me, holding a fresh cigarette in my direction.

"No, of course not," I said.

"I bet *you* do," she said, turning to Julian and allowing her tongue to move slowly across her upper lip. Had I been a little older I would have realized that she was flirting with him and he was flirting right back. Which, of course, is a little disturbing in retrospect considering the fact that he was just a child and she was thirty-four by then.

"I might have some matches," he replied, turning out the contents of his pockets onto my bedspread: a piece of string, a yo-yo, a florin, the Ace of Spades and, indeed, a match. "I knew it," he said, smiling at her.

"Aren't you a useful little thing?" she replied. "I should lock you up and never let you go."

Julian struck the match off the sole of his shoe and when it lit first time I found it hard to conceal my admiration. He held it out to Maude, who leaned forward, keeping her eyes locked on his as the cigarette began to spark, and then she sat back again, her left hand poised on the mattress behind her. She continued to stare at him before turning her face toward the ceiling and blowing a great cloud of white smoke in the air, as if she was preparing to announce the election of a new Pope.

"I was writing, you see," she declared after a moment, apropos of nothing. "I was writing my new novel and I could hear voices up here.

It was simply too distracting. My train of thought derailed. And so I thought I would come up to see what all the fuss was about."

I raised an eyebrow skeptically. It seemed unlikely to me that Maude had heard us talking from the floor below, particularly when we had scarcely been making any noise at all, but perhaps her hearing was more finely attuned than I realized, despite her now-resolved cancer of the ear canal.

"Do you enjoy being a writer, Mrs. Avery?" asked Julian.

"No, of course not," she said. "It's a hideous profession. Entered into by narcissists who think their pathetic little imaginations will be of interest to people they've never met."

"But are you successful?"

"It depends on how you define the word *success*."

"Well, do you have a lot of readers?"

"Oh no. Heaven forefend. There's something terribly crude about a popular book, don't you think?"

"I don't know," said Julian. "I'm afraid I don't read very much."

"Neither do I," said Maude. "I can't remember the last time I read a novel. They're all so tedious and writers do go on at such length. Brevity is the key, if you ask me. What was the last book you read?"

"*Five Have a Wonderful Time*," said Julian.

"Who wrote that?"

"Enid Blyton."

She shook her head as if the name meant nothing to her.

"Why don't you want people to read your books, Maude?" I asked, a question that I had never put to her before.

"For the same reason that I don't walk into strangers' houses and tell them how many bowel movements I've enjoyed since breakfast," she said. "It's none of their business."

"Then why do you publish them?"

"One has to do something with them, Cyril, doesn't one?" she said with a shrug. "Otherwise what's the point of writing them at all?"

I frowned. This didn't make sense to me but I didn't want to pursue the subject. I wanted her to go back downstairs and leave Julian and me to our incipient friendship. Perhaps he'd ask to see my thing again and take his out for a second viewing.

"Your father is here to save the day, isn't he?" asked Maude, turning to Julian again and patting the space on the bed beside her.

"I'm not sure," said Julian, taking the hint and sitting down. I was surprised and annoyed to see him staring at her legs. *Everyone has legs*, I thought. What was so special about Maude's? "Does it need saving?"

"The Man from the Revenue is after us," she replied, her tone suggesting that she was confiding in one of her closest friends. "My husband, Cyril's adoptive father, has not always been as diligent with his finances as he might have been and it seems that his misdemeanors have finally caught up with him. I keep a separate accountant myself, of course, to look after the tax issues with my books. Fortunately, as I sell so few I don't have to pay anything. It's a blessing in some ways. As it happens, I give my accountant more than I give The Man from the Revenue. Has he been to your house at all?"

"Who?" asked Julian.

"The Man from the Revenue. What do you suppose he looks like?"

He frowned, uncertain what she meant. I thought about it too and despite my youth I felt sure that there were *many* men employed by the Department of Finance, and possibly even the occasional woman.

"Wouldn't there be a group of them?" I asked. "Each of whom looks after different cases?"

"Oh no," said Maude, shaking her head. "No, as far as I know there's only one. Busy fellow, I imagine. Anyway, the point is your father is here to keep my husband out of jail, isn't he? I'm not saying a spell inside wouldn't do Charles the world of good but I'd be obliged to visit, for form's sake if nothing else, and I don't think I could do that. I imagine they're rather unpleasant places, prisons. And I don't think you can smoke in there."

"I think you can," I said. "Don't prisoners use cigarettes as currency?"

"And to fend off potential attacks by homosexuals," said Julian.

"Well, quite," agreed Maude, who didn't seem in the least shocked by Julian's choice of words. "But I don't think Charles need worry too much about that, do you? His best days are behind him."

"Homosexuals in prison aren't picky, Mrs. Avery," said Julian. "They'll take whatever they can get."

"No, but they're not blind either."

"What's a homosexual?" I asked.

"A man who's afraid of women," said Maude.

"Every man is afraid of women as far as I can see," said Julian, displaying an understanding of the universe far beyond his years.

"That's true," she said. "But only because most men are not as smart as women and yet they continue to hold all the power. They fear a change of the world order."

"Is Charles going to jail?" I asked, and even though I had no great affection for the man the idea made me uneasy.

"That's up to Julian's father," said Maude. "On how good he is at his job."

"I don't know much about my father and your husband's business," said Julian. "He only brought me with him today because I set fire to a curtain last week and I'm not allowed to be in the house on my own anymore."

"Why did you do that?"

"It was an accident."

"Oh." She seemed satisfied by this response and stood up now, pressing the cigarette out on my bedside table, leaving a scorch mark in the wood that would never disappear. Glancing around she seemed astonished by the very existence of the room and I wondered where she thought I'd been sleeping for the past seven years. "So this is where you hide away, Cyril, is it?" she asked dreamily. "I often wondered." She turned and pointed at the bed. "And I suppose this is where you sleep."

"It is," I admitted.

"Unless it's ornamental," said Julian. "Like your mother's chair."

Maude smiled at both of us and made her way toward the door. "Do try to keep it down, boys, if you can. I intend to return to my writing now. I believe the train is reapproaching the station. I might get a few hundred words down if I'm lucky."

And with that, to my great relief, she left us alone.

"What a peculiar lady," remarked Julian, taking his shoes and socks off now and, for no explicable reason, jumping up and down on my bed. I looked at his feet and noticed how neatly trimmed his toenails were. "My mother's nothing like yours."

"She's my adoptive mother," I pointed out.

"Oh yes. Did you ever meet your real mother?"

"No."

"Do you think your adoptive mother is secretly your real mother?"

"No," I said. "What sense would that make?"

"How about your adoptive father then?"

"No," I repeated. "Definitely not."

He reached over and took Maude's discarded cigarette from the table and drew noisily on the filter, pulling a face as he held it dangerously close to the curtain. Now that I knew he had form when it came to burning draperies, I watched him warily.

"Do you think your father is going to jail?" he asked me.

"My adoptive father," I said. "And I don't know. I suppose he might do. I don't know much about what's going on except that he's in a spot of bother. That's how he refers to it anyway."

"I was in jail once," said Julian casually, falling down on the bed now and stretching out as if he owned the place. His shirt had come loose from his trousers, revealing his navel and stomach, and I stared at them, rather fascinated by his pale skin.

"You were not," I said.

"I was," he said. "I swear."

"When? What did you do?"

"Not as a prisoner, of course."

"Oh," I said, laughing. "I thought that's what you meant."

"No, that would be ridiculous. I went with my father. He was representing a man who murdered his wife and he brought me with him to the 'Joy."

My eyes opened wide now in fascination. I had a peculiar obsession at that age with murder stories and a visit to *the 'Joy*, the colloquial term for Mountjoy Prison, was a common threat that teachers used to admonish us. Our every misdeed, from forgetting our homework to yawning in class, resulted in the promise that we were likely to end our days there at the end of a hangman's noose, despite the fact that capital punishment wasn't actually legal in Ireland anymore.

"What was it like?" I asked.

"It smelled of toilets," he said, grinning, and I giggled in appreciation. "And I had to sit in the corner of a cell when they brought the man in and my father started asking him questions and making notes

and saying that he needed to clarify a few things so he could explain
them to the man's barrister, and the man asked does it matter that my
wife was a dirty slut who put it about with every Tom, Dick and Harry
in Ballyfermot, and my father told him that they would be doing
everything they could to impugn the victim's character, as there was a
good chance that a jury would forgive a man a murder if the victim
was a whore."

I gasped. I'd never heard such words spoken aloud before and they
filled me with horror and excitement. I could have sat there all afternoon listening to Julian, so great an impression was he making on me,
and would have asked many more questions about his experience at
the prison only at that moment the door opened again and a tall man
with ludicrously bushy eyebrows poked his head inside.

"We're going," said the man, and Julian jumped up immediately.
"Why are you not wearing your shoes or socks?"

"I was trampolining on Cyril's bed."

"Who's Cyril?"

"I'm Cyril," I said, and the man looked me up and down as if I was
a piece of furniture he was considering acquiring.

"Oh, you're the charity case," he said, sounding uninterested. I
didn't have any answer to this and by the time I thought of something
clever to say they had both left the room and were making their way
downstairs.

A Great Love Affair

The question of how Charles and Maude met, fell in love and got married was one that fascinated me throughout my childhood. Two people who could not have been more ill-suited to each other's company
had somehow managed to find each other and sustain something re-
sembling a relationship while apparently feeling no interest or affection for the other whatsoever. Had it always been that way, I wondered?
Had there ever been a time when they looked at each other and felt
desire, respect or love? Was there a moment when they realized that
this was the person they wanted to be with over all others? And, if not,
why on earth had they committed to a shared life? It was a question

that I asked each of them at different times during our acquaintance and the answers I received could not have been more different:

Charles:

"I was twenty-six years old when I met Maude and there wasn't any part of me that was looking for either a girlfriend or a wife. I'd been down that road before and the whole thing had proved insufferable. You probably don't know this, Cyril, but I was married when I was only twenty-two and widowed a couple of years later. Oh, you did know? Well, there are all sorts of rumors going around about how Emily died but let me make one thing very clear: I did *not* murder her. And no charges were ever brought to suggest that I did, despite the best efforts of a certain Sergeant Henry O'Flynn of Pearse Street Garda Station. There was never a shred of evidence to suggest anything untoward took place but the engines that power Dublin are lubricated by exactly this kind of irresponsible tittle-tattle and a man's reputation can be destroyed overnight if you're not willing to fight back. The truth is, Emily was a lovely girl, very personable if you like that sort of thing, but she was also my first girlfriend, the girl to whom I lost my virginity, and no man with any sense should marry the girl to whom he loses his virginity. It's like learning to drive in some clapped-out old banger and then holding on to it for the rest of your life when you've developed the skill to handle a BMW in rush-hour traffic on a busy Autobahn. A few months after the wedding, I realized that I couldn't possibly be satisfied with one woman for the rest of my life and started to cast my net a little wider. Look at me, Cyril; I'm a ridiculously good-looking man now, so you can only imagine what I looked like in my twenties. Women fell over themselves to get to me. And I was generous enough to let them approach. But Emily caught wind of my extra-marital shenanigans and completely overreacted, threatening to call the parish priest in, as if that was something that would concern me, and I said, *Darling, take a lover if you want, it makes no difference to me. If you need cock, there's plenty of it out there. Big ones, small ones, perfectly formed ones, misshapen ones. Bent ones, curved ones, straight ones. Young men are basically walking erections and any one of them would be happy to stick it in someone as beautiful as you. Try a teenager if you like. They'd be only too delighted and you know they could go five or six times a night without even stopping to take a breath.* I meant this as a compliment but, for whatever reason, that's not how she took it and she fell into a spiral of recrimination and depression. Maybe she had always suffered some sort of psychological affliction, so many women do, but within months she was taking medication to stop her going completely doolally. And then one day she swallowed a few too many pills just before she took a bath and down she went under the water, bubble bubble, goodnight and good luck to all. And, yes, it's true that I inherited a lot of money from her, which is why all that gossip began in the first place, but I assure you that I had *nothing* to do with what happened that day and her death saddened me a great deal. I didn't have sex for almost two weeks afterward out of respect for her memory. You see, here's the thing, Cyril, and if I'd had a real son I would have ensured that he understood this: monogamy is simply not the natural state for man, and when I say man I mean man or woman. It just doesn't make sense to manacle yourself sexually to the same person for fifty or sixty years when your relationship with that person can be so much happier if you give each other the freedom to enter and be entered by people of the opposite sex whom you find attractive. A marriage should be about friendship and companionship, not about sex. I mean what man in his right mind wants to have sex with his own wife? However, despite all that, when I laid eyes on your adoptive mother for the first time I knew immediately that I wanted her to be the second Mrs. Avery. She was standing in the lingerie section of Switzer's department store when I saw her, running her hand along a railing of bras and panties, a cigarette hanging perilously close to the silk, and I walked up to her and asked her whether she needed any help choosing the right pair. My God, that woman had perfect tits! She still does. Have you ever taken a good look at your adoptive mother's tits, Cyril? No? Don't look so embarrassed; it's the most natural thing in the world. We suckle them as babies and long to suckle them as adults. She slapped my face when I said that but that slap remains one of the most erotic moments of my life. I grabbed her hand and kissed the underside of her wrist. It smelled of Chanel No. 5 and Marie-Rose sauce. I suppose she'd just come from lunch and as you know she's always been partial to a prawn cocktail. I told her that if she didn't come to the Gresham Hotel with me that afternoon for a glass of champagne I would throw myself into the Liffey and she said, *Drown for all I care* and that she had no intention of spending a Wednesday afternoon getting drunk in a hotel bar with a strange man. And yet somehow I talked her around and we ended up taking a taxi to O'Connell Street and drinking not one but six bottles of champagne over the course of not one but six hours. Can you believe it? We were practically paralytic by the time we were finished. But not so paralytic that we couldn't take a room in the hotel and make love for forty-eight hours with scarcely a break. My God, that woman did things to me that no woman before or since has ever done. Until you've been fellated by your adoptive mother, Cyril, you will not know what a quality blowjob really is. We were married within months. But once again time took its toll. Maude became more obsessed with her writing and I with my career. I grew bored of her body and I daresay she grew bored of mine. But whereas I sought comfort elsewhere it seemed that she had no interest in taking a lover and because of that she's remained celibate for years now, which probably accounts for her moods. It's true, we're not the ideal couple but I loved her once and she loved me and somewhere inside us both lingers the shadow of two twenty-something sexual beings drinking Veuve Clicquot in the Gresham, laughing our backsides off and wondering whether we could ask the receptionist for a bedroom key or whether the police or the Archbishop of Dublin might be called if we did."

Maude:

"I really can't remember. It might have been a Wednesday, if that's any use to you. Or possibly a Thursday."

When My Enemies Pursue Me

The relationship between my adoptive parents simply wasn't engaged enough for them to generate the kind of passion required for an argument, which meant that Dartmouth Square was for the most part a harmonious place to live. In fact, the only serious fight I ever witnessed between them took place on the night the jurors came to dinner, a plan so ill-advised in its conception that it baffles me to this day.

It was one of those rare evenings when Charles returned home early from work. I had just left the kitchen with a glass of milk in my hand and was astonished to see him walking through the door, his tie not loosened around his neck, his hair not disheveled upon his head, his gait not unsteady, a series of *nots* that suggested something terrible had taken place.

"Charles," I said. "Are you all right?"

"Yes, I'm fine," he replied. "Why shouldn't I be?"

I glanced at the grandfather clock in the corner of the hallway and, as if it was in cahoots with me, it struck six o'clock with half a dozen long and echoing chimes. As we waited for it to finish, Charles and I stayed exactly where we were, not saying a word, although we smiled awkwardly and acknowledged each other's presence with the occasional nod of the head. Finally, the ringing came to an end.

"It's just that you never come home at this hour," I said, picking up where I'd left off. "You realize that it's still daylight out and the pubs are still open?"

"Don't be cheeky," he said.

"I'm not being cheeky," I told him. "I'm concerned, that's all."

"Oh. In that case, thank you. Your concern is noted. You know, it's remarkable how much easier it is to unlock the door when it's bright outside," he added. "Usually I'm stuck on the porch for a few minutes at least before I can get in. I always thought it was a problem with the key but perhaps it was me all along."

"Charles," I said, putting my glass down on an occasional table and walking toward him. "You're completely sober, aren't you?"

"Yes, Cyril," he replied. "I haven't had a drink all day."

"But why? Are you ill?"

"I have been known to get through the day without lubrication, you know. I'm not a complete alcoholic."

"Not a complete one, no," I said. "But you are quite good at it."

He smiled and for a moment I thought I saw something approaching tenderness in his eyes. "It's kind of you to care," he said. "But I'm perfectly fine."

I wasn't so sure. In recent weeks, his usual exuberance had diminished noticeably and I often passed his study to find him seated behind his desk with a faraway expression on his face, as if he couldn't quite understand how things had got this far. He had bought a copy of *One Day in the Life of Ivan Denisovich* in Hodges Figgis and could be found engrossed in it at every spare moment, showing more interest in Solzhenitsyn's novel than he ever had in any of Maude's, even *Like to the Lark*, which she had practically disowned when sales figures soared toward triple figures. That he was comparing his own trials to that of a prisoner in a Soviet labor camp says something of his sense of personal injustice. Of course, he'd never expected his case to go all the way to trial, assuming that a man in his position and with his wide network of influential contacts would be able to prevent such an injustice taking place. And even when it became clear that there was nothing he could do to stop the trial going ahead, he was certain that he would be found innocent of any wrongdoing, despite his obvious guilt. Prison, he believed, was something that happened to other people.

Max Woodbead was a regular visitor to Dartmouth Square during those weeks, and Charles and he would veer from drunken caterwauling to the singing of old Belvedere College songs—*Only in God is found safety when my enemies pursue me / Only in God is found glory when I am found meek and lowly*—to roaring at each other in furious rages, storms that echoed around the house and caused even Maude to open the door of her study and stare out in bewilderment as she escaped the festering twilight of her writing room.

"Is that you, Brenda?" she asked me on one of those occasions when, for some forgotten reason, I was found loitering around the second floor.

"No, it's me, Cyril," I said.

"Oh, Cyril, yes," she said. "Of course, the child. What on earth is going on downstairs? Has there been a break-in?"

"Mr. Woodbead is here," I said. "He came over to discuss the case with Charles. I think they might be raiding the drinks cabinet."

"It's no good, of course. He's going to jail. Everyone knows it. All the whiskey in the world won't change that."

"And what will become of us?" I asked anxiously. I was only seven years old; I wasn't prepared for a life on the streets.

"I'll be all right," she said. "I have a little money of my own."

"But what about me?" I asked.

"Why must they be so loud?" she asked, ignoring my question. "Really, it's too much. How is a person supposed to get any work done? By the way, since you're here, can you think of another word for *fluorescent*?" she asked.

"Glowing?" I suggested. "Luminous? Incandescent?"

"Incandescent, that's the one," she said. "You're a clever boy for eleven, aren't you?"

"I'm seven," I told her, struck once again by the question of whether my adoptive parents even realized that I was a child and not some sort of small adult who had been foisted upon them.

"Well then. Even more impressive," she said, closing the door behind her and returning to her smoke-filled cave.

The case were the two words that echoed around our home throughout most of 1952. They were never far from any of our minds and always on the tip of Charles's tongue. He seemed to be genuinely insulted that he was being made to suffer such public indignity and hated seeing his name in the papers for any reason other than a celebratory one. Indeed, when the *Evening Press* published an article stating that his wealth had been much exaggerated over the years and that should he lose and face not only a period of imprisonment but a hefty pecuniary punishment he would most likely go bankrupt and be forced to sell the house on Dartmouth Square, he spiraled into a blustering hurricane of rage, like King Lear in the badlands, calling forth to the winds and the cataracts and the all-shaking thunder to drench the steeples, drown the cocks and singe his fine head of dark hair until the thick rotundity o' the world had been struck flat. Max, instructed to issue legal proceedings against the newspaper, wisely ignored the directive.

The dinner party was arranged for a Thursday night, four evenings into a trial that was expected to last two weeks. Max had selected a single juror whom he believed to be particularly susceptible to influence and run into him accidentally on purpose as he walked along

Aston Quay one night, inviting him into a pub for a drink. While there, Max informed the man, one Denis Wilbert of Dorset Street, who taught mathematics, Latin and geography at a school near Clanbrassil Street, that the close relationship he had formed with twelve-year-old Conor Llewellyn, his star pupil who received top marks in every examination despite the emptiness of his deeply attractive head, was one that could be misconstrued by both the newspapers and the Gardaí alike and that if he didn't want this information to appear in the public domain he might want to give serious thought to his verdict in *Department of Finance v. Avery.*

"And of course," he added, "anything you can do to persuade the other jurors would be most welcome too."

With one in his pocket he hired his favorite disgraced Garda to gather dirt on the rest of the panel. To his disappointment, former Superintendent Lavery came back with precious little. Three had secrets, he was told: one man had been accused of exposing himself to a girl on the Milltown Road but the charges had been dismissed as the girl had been a Protestant; one had a subscription with an agency in Paris who sent him a selection of postcards every month featuring naked women wearing jodhpurs; and a third (one of only two female jurors) had given birth to a child outside of marriage and failed to inform her employers, who would undoubtedly have sacked her as they were the supposed guardians of public morality: the parliament of Ireland, Dáil Éireann.

Rather than track each person down and make veiled threats to expose their secrets, Max did something far more gentlemanly: he invited them to dinner. Using Mr. Wilbert, the pedophile teacher, as his middleman, he made it clear that should they refuse the invitation, the information that he had gathered on them would be leaked to the papers. What he didn't mention, of course, was that he would neither be the host of the dinner nor a guest around the table; instead, that honor would fall to the man in the dock, my adoptive father, Charles Avery.

Charles invited me and Maude into his study that evening, shortly before the guests arrived, and we settled into the wing-backed armchairs that stood opposite his desk while he laid out his plans for the night ahead.

"The most important thing," he told us, "is that we put on a united front. We need to give the impression that we are a happy, loving family."

"We *are* a happy, loving family," said Maude, sounding offended by any suggestion to the contrary.

"That's the spirit," said Charles. "As much as it won't be in any of their interests to bring in a guilty verdict, we need to soothe their consciences by making them believe that tearing the three of us apart would be a reprehensible act akin to introducing divorce in Ireland."

"Who are they anyway?" asked Maude, lighting a fresh cigarette as the one she was smoking was coming perilously close to the end. "Are they our sort of people?"

"I'm afraid not," replied Charles. "A teacher, a dockworker, a bus driver and a woman who works in the tearoom at Dáil Éireann."

"Good Lord," she said. "They let anyone on to juries these days, don't they?"

"I think that's always been the case, my love."

"But was it really necessary to invite them into our home?" she asked. "Could we not have simply taken them out for a meal in town? There are any number of restaurants that people of that type would never get the chance to enjoy."

"Darling," replied Charles, smiling. "O sweet-natured wife of mine, remember this dinner is a secret. If it were to get out, well, there would naturally be a lot of trouble over it. No one must know."

"Of course, but they sound so mundane," said Maude, rubbing her arm as if a cold wind had just entered the room. "Will they have washed?"

"They seem clean in court," said Charles. "Actually, they make a real effort. Best suits and so on. As if they're going to Mass."

Maude opened her mouth in horror. "Are they papists?" she asked.

"I have no idea," said Charles in exasperation. "Does it matter?"

"As long as they don't want to pray before we eat," she muttered, looking around the study, a room in the house that she almost never entered. "Oh look," she said, pointing at a copy of Marcus Aurelius's *Meditations* that was lying on a side table. "I have that same edition upstairs. How funny."

"Now, Cyril," said my adoptive father, turning to me. "Strict house rules are in play tonight, understand? Only speak when you're spoken to. Don't make jokes. Don't break wind. Look at me with as much ad-oration in your eyes as you can possibly muster. I left a list of things that we do as father and son on your bed. Did you memorize it?"

"I did," I said.

"Repeat them back to me."

"We fish the great lakes of Connemara together. We attend GAA matches in Croke Park. We have an ongoing game of chess where we only make one move per day. We braid each other's hair."

"I told you, no jokes."

"Sorry."

"And don't call us 'Charles' and 'Maude,' all right? For tonight, you must address us as 'Father' and 'Mother.' It will sound peculiar to our guests if you say anything else."

I frowned. I wasn't sure I could bring myself to say those words anymore than a different child might be able to bring themselves to call their parents by their Christian names.

"I'll try my best . . . Father," I said.

"You don't need to start now," instructed Charles. "Wait until the guests have arrived."

"Yes, Charles," I said.

"You're not a real Avery, after all."

"What exactly is the point of all this anyway?" asked Maude. "Why must we debase ourselves for these people?"

"So that I can stay out of prison, sweet one," replied Charles cheer-fully. "We must flatter and cajole and if all else fails I will take them in here one by one later in the evening and write them each a check. Ei-ther way, I intend to end this evening confident in a verdict of *not guilty*."

"Will Mr. Woodbead be coming to dinner?" I asked, and Charles shook his head.

"No," he said. "If it all goes tits-up, he can't afford to be seen to have had anything to do with this."

"Charles, your language, please," said Maude with a sigh.

"So Julian won't be coming either?" I asked.

"Who is Julian?" asked Charles.

"Mr. Woodbead's son."

"Why on earth would he?"

I looked down at the carpet and felt my heart sink. I had only seen Julian on one other occasion since his initial visit and that was almost a month before, when we had got on even better than we had the first time, although, to my great disappointment, an opportunity had not presented itself for either of us to pull our pants down and expose ourselves to each other. I had been intoxicated by the notion of a friendship with him and the fact that he seemed to enjoy my company too was such a startling concept that it had started to dominate my thoughts. But of course we were not schooled together and therefore we were unlikely to meet again unless Max brought him to Dartmouth Square. It was a source of the deepest frustration to me.

"I just thought he might," I said.

"Sorry to disappoint you," said Charles. "I had thought about inviting a bunch of seven-year-olds to dinner but then I remembered that tonight was really rather important and our future happiness might depend on the outcome."

"So he's not coming?" I said, just to clarify.

"No," said Charles. "He's not."

"So Elizabeth won't be coming either?" asked Maude.

"Elizabeth?" asked Charles, sitting upright as if startled, his face flushing a little.

"Max's wife."

"I didn't know that you knew Elizabeth."

"I don't. Not very well anyway. But we've met at a couple of charity events. She's rather lovely in an obvious sort of way."

"No, Elizabeth won't be coming," said Charles, looking down at the desk again and drumming his fingers on his ink blotter.

"Just the working-class people," said Maude.

"Yes, just them."

"What fun."

"It's only for a few hours, my darling. I'm sure you can get through it."

"Will they understand which knives and forks to use?" she asked.

"Oh for pity's sake," said Charles, shaking his head. "They're not animals. What do you think they're going to do? Stab the beef with a toothpick, hold it in the air and start chewing around the sides?"

"Are we having beef?" she asked. "I was rather in the mood for fish tonight."

"There's a fish starter," said Charles.

"Scallops," I said. "I saw them in the kitchen."

"I'm not being a snob," insisted Maude. "I only ask because if these people are unaccustomed to fine dining they might feel intimidated by the prospect. Faced with competing sets of cutlery they might think that we're mocking them and react to their humiliation by despising you even more. You forget that I'm a novelist, Charles. I have a keen understanding of human nature."

My adoptive father's tongue bulged in his cheek as he considered this. She had a point. "Well, what do you suggest I do?" he asked eventually. "It's a five-course meal. There's a dozen pieces of cutlery at each table setting. I can hardly stick labels on each one, saying, *this is the fish knife, this is the bread knife, this is the pudding fork*, can I?"

"No," said Maude. "And it would be impossible to find labels that small anyway. Particularly at such short notice. We'd need to order them in."

Charles stared at her and seemed on the verge of laughing, which would surely have shocked both of us, as it was a sound with which we were entirely unfamiliar.

"Is there anything else we need to know?" asked Maude, glancing at her watch. "Or can we leave now?"

"Am I holding you up?" asked Charles. "Is there some place you need to be? Is the local tobacconist having a one-hour sale on cigarettes, perhaps?"

"You know I don't care for jokes," she said, standing up and smoothing down her skirt. I glanced at Charles and was surprised to see how he stared at her, his eyes looking her up and down with unfiltered desire, for she was still a very beautiful woman. Also, she knew how to dress. "What time are they arriving anyway? I haven't put my face on yet."

"Another half hour," said Charles, and she nodded and slipped out of the room.

"Wouldn't the judge mind if he found out?" I asked a few moments later, after Charles had returned to his papers and seemed to have forgotten that I was still there. In fact, he jumped a little in the seat when I spoke.

"Wouldn't the judge mind what?" he asked.

"The fact that you're inviting four of the jurors to dinner. Wouldn't
he think there was something dishonest about that?"

Charles smiled and looked at me with something approaching tenderness in his eyes. "Oh, my dear boy," he said. "You really aren't an
Avery, are you? It was the judge's idea."

The Perfect Family

"Might I say, Mr. Avery—"

"Please, let's not stand on ceremony. Call me Charles."

"Might I say, Charles, that I've long maintained an interest in the
law," said Denis Wilbert, the pedophile schoolteacher from Dorset
Street, who had shaken my hand upon arriving and held on to it, sand-
wiched between his two sweaty paws, for much longer than necessary, causing me to run to the bathroom immediately to wash it. "I
follow it in the papers, you see. The work of An Garda Síochána. The
various trials, the barristers, the solicitors and what have you. The
High Court appeals and the constitutional challenges. I actually considered reading law in university until I realized that my true calling
lay with children. I'm never truly happy unless I'm in the company of
a little boy. As many little boys as possible, in fact! But I'm ashamed to
say that there have been times when I've believed that if a man stands
accused in the dock, then he's probably guilty of the crime—"

"Or the woman," interrupted Jacob Turpin, the pervert dockworker
who liked to spend his evenings lurking around the Milltown Road,
waiting for little girls to cross his path so that he could treat them to a
quick flash of his shortcomings.

"Please, Mr. Turpin," said Wilbert, who seemed to consider himself
a cut above due to his superior education. "If you don't mind, I might
just finish what I was saying to Charles and then, if you have something pertinent to add, you can—"

"I only meant that you find women in the dock too," said Turpin,
whose bright-red hair, almost luminous in its hue, was strangely hypnotic. "There was this lassie who worked in the offices at CIÉ and she
was running a scam with the invoices and got five years for it. Sure
you wouldn't be up to them, would you? The women, I mean."

"As I was saying," continued Wilbert, raising his voice now so as not to be interrupted again, "I thought that if a man stood accused in the dock, then not only was he probably guilty but that he was also a disreputable sort, the type that society should banish to the wilderness, like a leper or an Australian. But this evening, sitting in this wonderful home, eating this fine dinner in the company of such a respectable family, it puts a lie to that notion and I disavow myself of it. I disavow myself of it wholeheartedly and without prejudice! And if I may, I'd like to raise my glass to you, Charles, and wish you well over the days to come as you endure this difficult and unjust ordeal."

"I'll drink to that," said Joe Masterson, the bus driver from Templeogue with a prurient interest in horsewear-related pornography, who had scarcely stopped drinking since arriving in Dartmouth Square. He downed his glass of wine and looked expectantly at the bottle in the center of the table; when no one offered him a refill, he helped himself, which even I knew went against dinner-party etiquette.

"You're very kind," said Charles, smiling benevolently at his guests. "All of you. However, I hope you don't think for a moment that my invitation for you to join me and Maude for dinner tonight was made out of anything other than a desire to get to know you better."

"But of course it wasn't your invitation at all, was it?" asked Charlotte Hennessy, the fourth juror present and the only lady. "It was Mr. Woodbead's. And none of us knew that we were coming to your house. We were under the impression that we were going to his."

"As I explained earlier, dear lady," said Charles, "Max was called away on urgent business and, having no way of contacting you, he asked me to step in as your host."

"You're a gentleman and a scholar," said Masterson.

"But then why did he invite us here?" asked Mrs. Hennessy.

"He's having some renovations done to his own home," explained Charles. "And so he's been staying with us for a little while. Of course, I hadn't planned on staying in tonight. It's my regular evening with the local chapter of St. Vincent de Paul. And to be honest, I thought my presence might be misconstrued as prejudicial. But I couldn't have allowed you to show up and be turned away without your dinner. That's not how we do things in Dartmouth Square."

"So many unusual circumstances," replied Mrs. Hennessy. "And so many coincidences. It's almost unbelievable."

"Sometimes the truth is," Charles replied smoothly. "But I'm glad things have worked out in the way they have. Sitting in the dock every day and looking across at your honest faces I've been struck time and again by how deeply I would like to know you all in private life, away from the rancid atmosphere of the courtroom."

"I've always said," announced Turpin, reaching down to scratch himself and doing a thoroughly good job of it, "that the man with the most class is the man who doesn't recognize the class system. There's many in your position who wouldn't have the likes of us in their house."

"With respect, Mr. Turpin," said Wilbert, taking off his spectacles, which I noticed he did every time that he wanted to appear serious. "I am a master at a prestigious boarding school. I hold a Bachelor's degree in Mathematics. My father was a pharmacist and my mother once gave an interview on Radio Éireann regarding the best type of flour to use in the baking of a traditional Irish barmbrack. I would consider myself to be the equal of any man."

"Oh right enough," said Turpin, chastised. "Where do you live then, Denis? Do you have a big house like this one?"

"I happen to live with my mother," replied Wilbert, sitting up straight, prepared to fend off any attacks on his character. "She's not getting any younger and needs me to care for her. Of course," he added, staring directly at me and speaking in a very deliberate fashion, "I have my own room and there are many nights when she's out at bingo and I can do as I please."

"Do you not have a wife, Mr. Wilbert?" asked Maude from the other end of the table, her voice carrying so sharply that I jumped. "Is there not a Mrs. Wilbert lurking in the undergrowth somewhere?"

"Sadly not," he replied, blushing slightly. "I have not been blessed with good fortune in that department."

"The happiest day of my life," remarked Charles, putting down his knife and fork, and I swear that I could see tears forming in his eyes as he spoke, "was the day that Maude agreed to marry me. I didn't think I had a chance. But I also knew that I could achieve anything with her by my side and that our love would somehow sustain us through good times and bad."

We all, as one, turned to Maude in anticipation of her reaction; had I known at the time who Joan Crawford was, I would have said that she was giving us her very best Joan Crawford, an expression that mixed contempt and vulnerability as she took a long drag of her cigarette and blew the smoke from her lips so steadily that it created a miasma behind which her true feelings could hide.

"I'm on to my second wife," said Masterson. "My first died when she was thrown from her horse. She was a show jumper, you see. Four-year-old event horses. I still keep her outfits in the wardrobe in the spare room and sometimes I like to go in there and just rub my hand along the velvet or give them an old sniff to remember her. I asked my current wife to model them for me but she's fierce peculiar about things like that. To be honest, and I only say this because I feel that I'm among friends, I wish I'd never married again. My first wife was a lovely girl. The new one . . . well, she has a mouth on her, that's all I'm saying."

"A mouth on her?" asked Mrs. Hennessy. "Isn't that a normal thing? How would the poor woman breathe without a mouth?"

"Ah now, you know what I mean," said Masterson, laughing and looking around at the other men while jerking his thumb in her direction as if to say, *And here's another one, wha*'? "She gives me the backchat all the time. I've told her I'll get the priest in one of these days to her if she doesn't buck up her ideas."

"What a lucky woman," said Mrs. Hennessy, turning away from him. "Did I read somewhere that you were married once before too, Mr. Avery?" she asked, looking at Charles.

"I don't know," he replied. "Did you?"

"Tell us about you, Cyril," said Wilbert, winking at me in such a lascivious way that I squirmed in my seat. "Do you enjoy school? Are you attentive to your studies?"

"It's all right," I said.

"And what's your favorite subject?"

I thought about it. "Probably history," I said.

"Not mathematics?"

"No, I'm not very good at mathematics."

"Did I mention that I have a Bachelor's degree in Mathematics?" he asked.

"Yes," said Charles, Maude, Mrs. Hennessy, Turpin, Masterson and I in unison.

"Perhaps I could help you out sometime," he suggested. "A little private tuition can go a long way. You could come around some evening when Mother is at bingo and—"

"No, thank you," I said, taking a mouthful of steak and hoping that he would turn his attentions elsewhere.

"And you own a tea shop, Mrs. Hennessy?" roared Maude unexpectedly, and Masterson put a hand to his chest in fright as if he was about to have a heart attack. "That's right, isn't it?"

"Not quite," she replied. "I'm manageress of the tearoom in Dáil Éireann."

"How interesting. Have you been there a long time?"

"Since 1922, when the Oireachtas held their first meeting in Leinster House."

"Fascinating," said Charles, and, in fairness to him, he did sound rather interested. "So you were present for the foundation of the state?"

"I was, yes."

"That must have been some day."

"It was," agreed Mrs. Hennessy, her voice softening a little now. "It was very exciting. I'll never forget how happy we all were. And Mr. Cosgrave, of course, was cheered by all sides of the House when he stood up to make his first speech as President of the Executive Council."

"Christ alive, that's thirty years ago," said Turpin, shaking his head. "How old are you anyway? You must be getting on a bit, are you?"

"I'm sixty-four, Mr. Turpin," she replied sweetly. "Thank you for asking."

"I would have guessed somewhere around that," he said, nodding. "You have that look that a lot of women your age get. All jowly, do you know what I mean? With dark bags under your eyes. And as for the veins on your legs, you must have got them from standing in the tearoom all day long. No offense meant, of course."

"How could I possibly be offended by such a gallant speech?" she asked with a smile.

"An intriguing place to work all the same, wouldn't you say?" said Charles. "All those important men going to and fro every day. You must hear a lot of secrets there, am I right?"

"If I did, Mr. Avery, do you think I'd let any of them escape my lips? I haven't kept my position for three decades by being indiscreet."

"But you're to retire soon, or so I heard," he continued. "And please, no more Mr. Avery. I've told you, it's Charles."

"I am indeed planning on retiring toward the end of the year," she admitted, narrowing her eyes. "Do you mind if I ask how you knew that?"

"Well now, I haven't built this house by being indiscreet either," he said, winking at her. "Let's just say that a little bird told me. How's the pension fund anyway? I hope you've been careful. You could have a good many years ahead of you yet and you'll want to be well looked after."

"I believe I've been prudent," she said coldly.

"I'm glad to hear it. Money matters when one is getting older. You never know when you might fall ill. You hear some terrible things about what happens in hospitals. If you ever need advice, feel free to ask me."

"I think we'll wait to see how the trial works out first, don't you?" she said. "Before I consider coming to you for financial advice."

"Do you want to be a banker too, Cyril?" asked Masterson. "Like your daddy there?"

I looked toward Charles, waiting for him to point out that I was not a real Avery, just an adopted son, but he said nothing, simply picked at his food and threw me a look that said *You can answer.*

"I don't think so," I said, staring at my plate and pulling my foot away when I felt Wilbert's shoe touching mine beneath the table. "I haven't really thought about it. I'm only seven."

"A wonderful age," said Wilbert. "My favorite of all the ages between six and ten."

"He's a fine-looking lad all the same," said Turpin, turning to Maude. "He's the image of yourself."

"He looks nothing like me," said Maude, which was reasonable enough.

"Ah he does now," insisted Turpin. "You can see it around his eyes. And in his nose. He's his mammy's son."

"You're a very perceptive man, Mr. Turpin," she replied, lighting another cigarette as the ashtray next to her began to spill over onto the linen. "The justice system will certainly benefit from your being on the jury."

"I'm not sure if you're aware of it," said Charles, "but my dear wife here is one of Ireland's foremost lady novelists."

"Oh, Charles, please don't," she said, waving her hand in the air to shush him but only succeeding in sending more smoke down the table, causing Mrs. Hennessy to turn her face away and clear her throat.

"I'm sorry, my dear, but I must tell our guests. I'm so proud of Maude, you see. How many novels have you written now, darling?"

A long pause. I started to count the seconds in my head and I reached twenty-two before she spoke again.

"Six," she said finally, "and I'm working on my seventh."

"Isn't that great all the same?" said Turpin. "It's great to have a hobby. My wife knits."

"Mine plays the accordion," said Masterson. "An awful bloody racket. My first wife, though, could ride a horse like Elizabeth Taylor in *National Velvet*. She was the spit of her too, everybody said so."

"You'll be on the tea towel one of these days," said Turpin.

"The tea towel?" asked Maude, frowning.

"You know, the one that all the tourists buy," he explained. "With the pictures of the Irish writers on them."

"That will never happen," said Maude. "They don't put women on that. Only men. Although they do let us use it to dry the dishes."

"Who was that lady novelist who pretended she was a man?" asked Turpin.

"George Eliot," said Wilbert, taking off his glasses and wiping them with his handkerchief.

"No, he *was* a man," said Masterson. "But there was one who was really a woman but *said* she was a man."

"Yes, George Eliot," he repeated.

"Whoever heard of a girl called George?"

"George Eliot was her pseudonym," said Wilbert patiently, as if he was speaking to a backward but attractive boy in his schoolroom.

"Then what was her real name?"

Wilbert opened his mouth but no words emerged.

"Mary Ann Evans," said Mrs. Hennessy before things could get too embarrassing. "Actually, I've read one of your novels, Mrs. Avery," she added. "By pure chance. Nothing connected with your husband's trial. One of the girls at the tearoom gave it to me as a birthday present last year."

"Oh dear," replied Maude, looking like she might be ill. "I hope you didn't read it."

"Of course I did. What else would I do with it, use it as a coaster? I thought it was very beautifully written."

"Which one was it?"

"*The Quality of the Light.*"

Maude pulled a disgusted face and shook her head dismissively. "I should have burned the manuscript of that one," she said. "I don't know what I was thinking when I wrote it."

"Well, I liked it," said Mrs. Hennessy. "But you're the author and if you say it's terrible, then I suppose I'll have to take your word for it. I must have misunderstood it."

"You should dismiss the girl who gave it to you," remarked Maude. "She obviously has very poor taste."

"Oh no, she's my right-hand woman," replied Mrs. Hennessy. "I'd be lost without her. She's been with me seven years now. In fact, she's due to take over the management of the tearoom when, as Mr. Avery so rightly pointed out, I retire later in the year."

"Well, better a tearoom than a library, I suppose," said Maude. "Now look, are we going to sit here all evening making small talk or are we going to get to the heart of the matter?"

We all looked at her in surprise and I could see Charles open his eyes anxiously, hoping that she wasn't going to destroy his plans by saying something untoward.

"The heart of the matter being what exactly?" asked Wilbert.

Maude put her cigarette out despite not having another one ready to go, took a long drink from her glass of wine and looked around the table at her guests before settling her expression into one of pure sorrow. "I know I shouldn't say this," she began, using a tone I had never heard her employ before, "I know I shouldn't speak of this issue while we are gathered here enjoying this wonderful meal and this fantastically spirited conversation but I must speak. I must! I need to let you know, lady and gentlemen of the jury, that my husband Charles is entirely innocent of all the things of which he has been accused and—"

"Maude, dear," said Charles, but she held up a hand to silence him.

"No, Charles, I will have my say. He has been accused in the wrong and I worry that he will be found guilty and taken off to prison and what is to become of us then? My every day, my every moment, is enriched by the love that we share, and as for our son, as for our poor dear Cyril—"

I looked up and swallowed, wishing for all the world that she wouldn't drag me into this.

"Cyril has taken to coming into our bed every night, bereft, weeping inconsolably, dreading the fate that might lie in store for his beloved father. Twice now he's soiled the sheets but we don't hold him accountable, although it's costing us a fortune in dry-cleaning bills. It's heartbreaking for a mother to witness such pain in one so young. Particularly now, when he's so ill."

All heads turned to me now and my eyebrows raised. Was I ill? I hadn't realized that I was. It was true that I'd had a bit of a runny nose lately but it was nothing to knock me off my feet.

"I know this is neither here nor there," continued Maude, "and you all have your own families to think about, but I am just in awe of how brave Cyril has been, dealing with his cancer in such a brave and uncomplaining way while all this unpleasantness has been building around us."

"Good Lord," cried Mrs. Hennessy.

"Cancer, is it?" asked Turpin, turning to me in delight.

"Oh," said Wilbert, sitting back in his seat as if it might be catching.

"Terminal, I'm afraid," said Maude. "He'll be lucky if he's still here by Christmas. Realistically, I think he's more likely to be gone by Halloween. And if Cyril were to die without his beloved father by his side and I were to be left alone in this house without the two people I cherish the most in the world . . ." She shook her head and the tears started to flow down her cheeks, drawing pathways through her makeup. Her left hand began to shake but that might have been because it was unaccustomed to going this long without a cigarette resting between the second and third fingers. "Well, I already know what I would do in that eventuality," she said quietly. "However, I will not say the words aloud for the act itself is a mortal sin but I believe it would be the only recourse open to me."

There was absolute silence in the room. Charles was a loving family man, Maude was making plans for her own suicide and I only had a few months to live. All of this was news to me. For a moment, I wondered whether any of it might actually be true but then I recalled that I hadn't been near a doctor in a long time and it was unlikely that such a fatal diagnosis would be made without someone at least taking my temperature or checking my blood pressure.

"No one should be left in such solitude," said Turpin.

"A man needs to be with his family at such a painful time," said Masterson.

"Do you need a hug, Cyril?" asked Wilbert.

"What type of cancer do you have?" asked Mrs. Hennessy, turning to me. "Because I have to say you look as if you're bristling with good health."

I opened my mouth, trying to conceive an answer. I didn't know anything about cancer, other than it was a scare word that adults employed to suggest the imminent deaths of friends and enemies alike, and I racked my brain for what might be the best response. Cancer of the fingernails? Of the eyelashes? Of the feet? Was foot cancer even a thing? Or maybe I could appropriate Maude's own recent illness and claim that I had cancer of the ear canal? Fortunately, I didn't have to say anything, for before I could select a tumor-ridden body part the doorbell rang and we heard Brenda walking through the hallway to answer it, followed by a roar from whoever was standing on the doorstep and the sound of our housekeeper trying to keep him out of the living room, and then the door burst open and there stood Max Woodbead, his hair askew, his face purple with anger, looking from one of us to the other until his eyes landed on Charles. He glared at him, his eyes wide with fury, but chose not to speak, leaping across the room, toppling him from his chair and punching him with a ferocity that would have made a man half his age proud. And even in the chaos of the moment, I couldn't help but glance out into the hallway, hoping that Julian might have accompanied him, but there was no one there except Brenda, who was watching the beating taking place with something akin to pleasure on her face.

The Island of Lesbos

"Of all the women in Ireland, you had to fuck the wife of the one man who's trying to keep you out of prison," said Maude after the guests had left. She was drinking whiskey with Charles in the front parlor while I eavesdropped from the staircase in the hallway, a toxic fusion of anger, disbelief and exasperation evident in her tone. From my vantage point, I could see my adoptive father pressing a fingertip tenderly to the developing bruise on his cheek, his tongue occasionally flicking out, lizard-like, to investigate the split lip and broken front tooth that had caused the bloodlines on his chin. Clouds of smoke moved aggressively toward him and as he turned his head away he noticed me sitting outside and offered an apologetic wave, four of his fingers dancing despondently in the air like an imprisoned pianist forced to play one of Chopin's more depressing sonatas from memory. He didn't seem perturbed by my presence nor did he seem unduly upset by the farcical events of the evening. "Max might have saved you," continued Maude, raising her voice now. "And more importantly, he might have saved this house. What's going to happen to us now?"

"There's really nothing to worry about," said Charles. "My barrister will take care of everything. If you ignore the spectacular floor show, I felt that the night went rather well."

"Then you're an idiot."

"Let's not descend into name-calling."

"If we lose Dartmouth Square—"

"That will never happen," insisted Charles. "Just leave it to Godfrey, all right? You haven't seen him in action. The jury laps up every word he says."

"He might have a very different view of you when he hears that you seduced Elizabeth Woodbead. Aren't he and Max close friends after all?"

"Don't be ridiculous, Maude. Whoever heard of a barrister and a solicitor who felt any emotion other than mutual loathing? And Elizabeth didn't need seducing. If anything, she was the predator when it came to our little *affaire de coeur*. She pursued me like a lion on the trail of an impala."

"I find that hard to believe," said Maude.

"I'm a handsome, powerful man, with a well-earned reputation in this town as a formidable lover. Women love that sort of thing."

"What you know about women," replied Maude, "could be written in large font on the back of a postage stamp and there'd still be room for the Lord's Prayer. For all your great flirtations and seductions, for all your tarts, whores, girlfriends and wives, you've really learned nothing about us over the years, have you?"

"What is there to learn?" he asked, possibly just trying to annoy her now that she was pouring scorn on his masculinity. "It's not as if these are particularly complex creatures that we're talking about. Unlike dolphins, for example. Or St. Bernard dogs."

"My God, you're insufferable."

"And yet you married me and have remained my steadfast companion and helpmate throughout the years," he replied, a rare touch of irritation in his voice. Usually he laughed off any slights that came his way, so assured was he in his superior status, but not tonight. Perhaps he too was becoming nervous about what lay ahead. "The qualities that you claim to find insufferable are the very ones that have kept you with me for ten years."

"Max will be around at Godfrey's right now," she said, choosing to ignore this observation, "telling him the whole story. And if he has a wife of his own, he will most likely take Max's side."

"Godfrey doesn't have a wife," said Charles, shaking his head. "He's not the marrying kind."

"What do you mean?"

"Well, he's one of them, isn't he?" he replied. "A queer. A Nancy-boy. But he's damn good at his job all the same, despite all that. One thinks that these fellows can only be useful as hairdressers or flower arrangers but I've never seen a more dedicated or hard-nosed advocate than Godfrey. He almost never loses, which is why I hired him."

There was a long silence before Maude spoke again. "Does anyone know?" she asked.

"Know what?"

"About Godfrey. That he's a friend of Mrs. King's?"

"It's an open secret around the law library. Obviously he can't do anything about it, poor fellow. It is a criminal offense after all."

"Disgusting," said Maude.

"What's disgusting?"

"The idea of it."

Charles laughed. "Don't be such a prude," he said.

"It's not prudish to know what's natural and what isn't."

"Natural?" asked Charles. "Didn't you tell me once that you'd developed similar feelings for some girl you knew from one of your literary societies?"

"Nonsense," said Maude. "You're fantasizing now."

"No, I'm not. I remember it distinctly. You told me that you'd had a dream about her where you were picnicking together by a river and the sun was out and she suggested that you both take your clothes off and go for a swim and afterward, as you lay naked on the bank together, you turned to her and—"

"Oh do shut up, Charles," she snapped.

"Sapphic love," he said cheerfully.

"Absolutely ridiculous."

"A trip across the water to the island of Lesbos."

"You're making this up," she said, raising her voice.

"I am not," he replied. "And you know very well that I'm not."

"What do dreams mean anyway? They're just a lot of silly nonsense."

"Or wish fulfillment. The subconscious representation of our true desires."

"You're a fool to say that."

"I didn't say it. Sigmund Freud did."

"Yes, well he also said that the Irish were the one race of people for whom psychoanalysis is of no use whatsoever. So please don't try to uncover my inner thoughts. You won't be able. What are you trying to suggest anyway?"

"Nothing at all, my dear. Only that if I have gone looking for physical affection elsewhere, you can't really blame me for it, can you? It's not as if it's something you've shown much interest in since that afternoon at the Gresham all those years ago."

"If I haven't, perhaps it's because I know the kind of man you are. You've always had an affinity for deviants, haven't you? And for peculiar sexual practices. I mean that thing you wanted to do with the tires and the garden hose that time. I still shudder when I think of it."

"You might have enjoyed it if you'd given it a go. Anyway, I think it's a little hypocritical of Max to be so outraged. It's not as if he's been faithful to Elizabeth himself. The man is even worse than I am. The only difference is that he can't help but feel jealous, whereas that's an emotion that holds no interest for me at all. He can stick it wherever he likes, as far as he's concerned, but God forbid that Elizabeth should seek a little variety."

"That's hardly the point," said Maude. "Elizabeth's a friend of mine."

"My dear, don't be ridiculous. You don't have any friends."

"An acquaintance then."

"You're worrying over nothing, I promise you. Max will wake up tomorrow and feel like an ass for behaving in such a boorish fashion. He'll be over here first thing in the morning, apologizing before court is even in session."

"If you think that, then you're more of a fool than I took you for."

I couldn't listen to anymore of the argument and went up to my bedroom at the top of the house, closing the door behind me, and opened my mouth wide as I looked in the mirror, shining a torch into my throat to assure myself that I didn't actually have cancer. Nothing in there seemed any different from usual.

It was hard to know how the four jurors would respond to the scene they had witnessed. Once the fight had begun, Masterson and Turpin had jumped to their feet to cheer Charles and Max on, like children excited by a playground brawl, shouting advice to the combatants regarding how they should take their man down. Wilbert had taken his glasses off and made a half-hearted attempt to separate the two men, receiving a bloody nose for his troubles that caused him to burst into tears and retire to a corner of the room where he sat with his head in his hands declaring that his mother would *not* be happy when he returned home. Mrs. Hennessy had risen from the table and left the room with quiet dignity. I had run out after her, wondering whether she was going to call the police, but instead she had simply reached for her hat and coat from the hallstand before turning around and noticing me standing there.

"You shouldn't have to witness a scene like that, Cyril," she said, her face filled with concern. From beyond the door, I could hear the sound of chairs being knocked over and Maude asking everyone to be careful of an ornamental cigarette stand that had come all the way from St. Petersburg. "It's disgraceful that grown men should carry on in that way in front of you."

"Is Charles going to go to prison?" I asked, and she glanced toward the dining room to ensure that the fight was not about to spill out into the hallway.

"That's not something that's been decided yet," she said, kneeling down before me and brushing the hair away from my forehead, the way adults often do with children. "There are twelve of us on the jury. We need to hear all the evidence before reaching a verdict. I have no idea why Mr. Woodbead invited us here tonight for this elaborate deception. It's bad enough having to listen to those jackasses every day in the Four Courts without having to dine with them too. The truth is, I only came because he implied that . . . well, it doesn't matter what he implied. I'm sure he won't go through with his threat. I should have simply told him to go ahead and do his worst. Now go on up to bed, there's a good boy." She tilted her head a little to the side and smiled, her expression thoughtful now. "It's the strangest thing," she said. "You remind me of someone but I can't think who." She pondered for a few moments and shrugged. "No," she said. "It's gone. Anyway, I better be going. I have to be back in court by nine o'clock in the morning. Goodnight, Cyril."

And with that she shook my hand, put a sixpence into my palm, and slipped out into the darkness of Dartmouth Square where, by a stroke of good luck, a taxi happened to be passing. It pulled up and she disappeared into the night while I stood on the doorstep, looked out toward the city and wondered whether anyone would even notice if I went missing.

The Man from the Revenue

The days that followed were a whirlwind of activity and perhaps there was an inevitability to how the case would be concluded. My adoptive father, with the optimism of an author working on the sixth volume of a series that no one seems to be reading, believed that his friendship with Max Woodbead would survive their little contretemps but he could scarcely have been more wrong, and when Max took his revenge some months later, it was swift and directly on target. In the meantime, however, he continued to act as Charles's solicitor while making it clear that he would behave in a professional manner until the trial was over but after that their relationship would be terminated forever.

Maude and I traveled to the Four Courts together on the final day to hear the verdict and, as I had not been allowed to attend during the trial itself, I was fascinated and a little frightened by the majesty of the Round Hall, where the families of victims and criminals alike mixed in a curious mélange of quarry and miscreant while barristers marched to and fro in black gowns and white wigs, laden down with folders and trailed by anxious-looking juniors. My adoptive mother was seething with rage, for the case had received so much publicity over recent weeks that her latest novel, *Amongst Angels*, had found its way to the front table of the Hodges Figgis Bookshop on Dawson Street, a location that none of her previous work had ever come close to troubling in the past. Alerted to the fact that morning over breakfast by our housekeeper, Brenda, who had been shopping in town the afternoon before, she extinguished her cigarette in the center of an egg yolk and started to tremble in fury, her face pale with humiliation.

"The vulgarity of it all," she said. "Popularity. Readers. I can't bear it. I knew Charles would destroy my career in the end."

Worse was to come, however, when, shortly after we sat down, a lady seated a few rows behind us approached with a copy of that same book and hovered beside our pew, smiling eagerly as she waited to be acknowledged.

"Can I help you?" asked Maude, turning to her with all the warmth of Lizzie Borden dropping in to say goodnight to her parents.

"You're Maude Avery, aren't you?" asked the woman, who was in her sixties and had a helmet of blue hair whose color was not one that could be found anywhere in nature. Had I been a little older I would have recognized her as one of those people who attended court on a regular basis, the building being warm and the entertainment free, and who knew the names of all the barristers, judges and ushers and probably had a better understanding of the law than most of them.

"I am," said Maude.

"I hoped that you'd be here today," said the woman with a broad and excited smile. "I've been watching out for you throughout the trial but you never appeared. I expect you've been writing. Where do you get your ideas from anyway? You've a great imagination altogether. And do you write by hand or on a typewriter? I have a story that would sell millions but I don't have the talent to write it down. I should tell you it and then you could write it for me and we could share the money. It's about the olden days, of course. People love stories about the olden days. And it has a dog in it. And doesn't the poor dog only go and die?"

"Could you leave me alone, please?" asked Maude, trying hard to control her temper.

"Oh," said the woman, her smile fading a little. "You're all upset, I can see. You're worried about your husband. I've been here every day and I can tell you that you're right to be worried. He hasn't a hope. He's a very handsome man all the same, isn't he? Well, if you could just sign this book for me I'll leave you in peace. Here's a pen. I want you to write *For Mary-Ann, best of luck with the operation on your varicose veins, lots of love,* and then your signature and the date."

Maude stared at the book as if she had never seen such a repulsive object in her life and for a moment I thought she was going to take it from the woman and fling it across the courtroom, but before she could do so, the bailiff opened one of the side doors, the jury and the court officials entered and she waved the woman away, like a tourist scattering pigeons in Trafalgar Square.

I watched Charles as he took his place in the dock and for the first time I could see real anxiety in his face. I don't think he had ever believed that things would get this far and yet there he was, his future about to be determined by twelve complete strangers, none of whom, as far as he was concerned, had any business judging him at all.

I looked for Turpin the dockworker and found him in the second row, wearing the same suit that he'd worn on the evening he came to dinner in Dartmouth Square. When he caught my eye, he blushed a little and looked away, which I took as a bad sign. Seated next to him was Masterson, who imitated the moves of a boxer with his fists. In the front row, looking considerably irritated not to have been appointed the foreman of the jury, was Wilbert, and something told me that he had probably brought his Bachelor's degree in Mathematics with him in a bid to secure that position. It hadn't worked, however, for the foreman was not a man at all, but a woman, and Wilbert looked as if he'd swallowed a wasp when the bailiff asked her to stand.

Just before Mrs. Hennessy opened her mouth to speak, however, I realized that I had no idea what I wanted her to say. Other boys in my position might have offered a silent prayer that their father would be released, for the notion of prison and the prospect of a family being torn apart was one that, particularly in those unenlightened days of the early 1950s, was shameful. What would happen to me and Maude if we were left alone, I asked myself. How would I get through a day at school with such a scandal hanging over my head? And yet somehow, to my surprise, I found that I didn't particularly care how things turned out. Maude struck a match loudly to light a fresh cigarette, the noise startling the silenced chamber as everyone, including my adoptive father, turned to stare at her in disapproval. She looked back at them shamelessly, placing the cigarette between her lips in a provocative fashion and inhaling deeply before blowing a cloud of smoke into the heart of the courtroom, tapping ash onto the floor between us with her index finger. I noticed a smile pass across Charles's face, some element of fascinated adoration which might have explained how these two mismatched people had stayed together for so long, and was that a wink that Maude gave him just before Mrs. Hennessy declared him guilty as charged? It was. It most certainly was.

But what of Max Woodbead? Did he smile at the moment of condemnation? He had his back to me so I couldn't tell, but I did notice that he leaned over his papers and covered his mouth with one hand so either he was masking his delight or another of his teeth had come loose after the fisticuffs of a few nights earlier.

The press gallery emptied quickly as its occupants ran from the courtroom to the line of telephone boxes that stood like sentinels along the quays in order to phone the result in to their editors. The judge made a few comments to the effect that Charles could expect a custodial sentence and my adoptive father immediately stood up and asked in a proud tone whether he might be given a moment to address the court.

"If you must," said the judge with a sigh.

"Would it be possible," asked Charles, "for me to begin my sentence today? As soon as I leave the dock?"

"But I haven't decided the length of your term yet," replied the judge. "And you're eligible for bail until the date of sentencing. You could go home for a couple of weeks, Mr. Avery, to get your affairs in order."

"My affairs are what got me into this mess in the first place, Your Honor. I'd just as soon take a break from them. No, if I'm going down, I might as well start now," said Charles, a pragmatist to the last. "The sooner I get in, the sooner I get out, am I right?"

"I suppose so," said the judge.

"Grand so," replied Charles. "I'll start today then if it's all the same to you."

The judge scribbled something down on a legal pad before him and glanced toward Godfrey, Charles's barrister, who gave a shrug as if to say that he respected his client's wishes and would make no appeal.

"Is there anything else you'd like to say," asked the judge, "before you're taken down?"

"Only that I humbly accept the decision of the court," he replied. "And I will serve my time without complaint. I'm just glad that I don't have any children to witness this moment of degradation. That, at least, is a mercy." An assertion that left at least four members of the jury with utterly baffled expressions on their faces.

As we left the courtroom to a hungry pack of journalists and photographers, Maude ignored their questions and flashbulbs, marching forward purposefully without even a cigarette as her armor, and I did my best to keep up with her, aware that the slightest stumble on my part would result in me being squashed beneath the boots of the press.

"Him!" cried Maude unexpectedly, her voice echoing around the Four Courts, and as she pulled to a screeching halt, so did the media scrum around us. As it had inside the courtroom when she struck the match, every head turned in her direction. "The nerve of him!"

I followed the direction of her gaze to see a middle-aged man of indistinctive appearance, wearing a dark suit and sporting a small mustache that to my mind was a little too Hitler-like for comfort, standing in the center of a group of similarly attired men, accepting their congratulations.

"Who is he?" I asked. "Do you know him?"

"It's The Man from the Revenue," she declared, striding toward him as one hand reached into her bag. The accountant turned and observed her approach with fear in his eyes, glancing toward the hand as it emerged. Perhaps in that moment he thought that she was going to pull a gun on him and shoot a bullet through his heart; perhaps he wondered why he had devoted his life to the investigation and prosecution of improper financial transactions within the Irish banking sector when his first love had always been performance art. Or perhaps he didn't have a clue who she was. Either way, he didn't say a word and when she stopped in front of him, her face red with rage, he was surely bewildered by the fact that she was waving a copy of *Amongst Angels* in his face, which, quite quickly, she brought down on his head.

"Are you happy now?" she screamed. "Are you pleased with yourself? Goddamn it, but you've made me popular!"

1959 The Seal of the Confessional

1019 The Seal of the Confessional

A New Roommate

Although it would be another seven years before I laid eyes on Julian Woodbead again, he remained a constant in my mind throughout that time, an almost mythological figure who had walked into my life one day to overwhelm me with confidence and charm before disappearing just as quickly. When I woke in the morning, I would often think of him waking too, his hand, like mine, slipping inside his pajamas to encourage the cascade of endless pleasure that our youthful tumescence had begun to offer. Throughout the day he was there in one form or another, commenting on my actions, a wiser, more self-assured twin who knew how I should act, when I should speak and what I should say better than I did. Despite the fact that we had only been in each other's company twice and briefly on both occasions, I never questioned why he had become a figure of such importance to me. Of course, I was still too young to recognize my fascination for what it was and put it down to a sort of hero worship, the type I had read about in books, and this awe seemed characteristic of boys like me, quiet boys who spent too much time alone and were uncomfortable in the presence of people their own age. So when we were unexpectedly thrown into each other's company again, it unsettled as much as delighted me but I was determined that we should become firm friends. Of course, I never expected that by the year's end Julian would have become the most famous teenager in the country but then who could have predicted such an unexpected turn of events? Violence and political unrest were not the everyday considerations of fourteen-year-old boys in 1959; as with most generations we were solely concerned with when we would next eat, how we could improve our social standing among our peers and whether anyone might do to us the things that we were doing to ourselves several times a day.

I had entered Belvedere College as a boarder a year earlier and, to my surprise, I didn't hate it as much as I had expected to. The anxiety that had marked my childhood had begun to lessen and, while I was still not the most outgoing of pupils, I didn't walk down populated corridors in fear of assault or insult. I was one of that fortunate cadre of boys who, for the most part, is left to his own devices, neither popular nor disliked, not interesting enough to befriend but not fragile enough to bully.

The dormitories contained what were called "paired rooms," furnished with two beds, a large wardrobe and a single dresser. My roommate during my first year was a boy named Dennis Caine, whose father was that rarest of creatures in the 1950s: a critic of the Catholic Church who wrote inflammatory articles in newspapers and was regularly given airtime by excitable producers at Radio Éireann. A pal of Noël Browne's, whose Mother and Child Scheme had brought down a government when Archbishop McQuaid realized that his proposal meant that Irish women might be allowed an opinion of their own without having to run it past their husbands first, it was said that he was on a mission to extract the clerical poison from the secular body, and he was regularly portrayed in pro-Catholic newspaper cartoons as a snake, which made no sense whatsoever considering the analogy. Dennis, who had been admitted to the school before the Jesuits realized who his father was, was accused of cheating in an exam and, with absolutely no evidence whatsoever to support the allegation, expelled after a farcical inquiry and cast into the wilderness of a nondenominational education.

Of course, everyone knew that the entire thing had been a setup and that the priests, acting upon the orders of some superior power, had simply planted evidence to show his father what happened to those who went against the authority of the Church. Dennis protested his innocence but perhaps he didn't mind too much, for the guilty verdict meant that he could leave Belvedere and the tender embrace of the school forever. He disappeared with scarcely a goodbye.

And then Julian arrived.

A rumor had gone around that a new boy would be joining us, which was unusual in itself, as it was already the middle of the school year. The rumor escalated into speculation that it was the son of someone in a public position, a boy who, like Dennis, had been expelled from his previous school for some egregious crime. Charlie Chaplin's son Michael was mentioned, as was one of Gregory Peck's children. A bizarre rumor took hold for a few hours that the former French President Georges Pompidou had chosen Belvedere for his son, Alain, when one of the sixth-form prefects swore that he had overheard the geography and history teachers discussing security arrangements. And so, when the headmaster, Father Squires, stood up at assembly on the day before Julian's arrival to announce the name of our new alumnus, most of my classmates were disappointed that his surname was not one that suggested a more illustrious heritage.

"Woodbead?" asked Matthew Willoughby, the obnoxious captain of the rugby team. "Is he one of us?"

"One of us in what way?" asked Father Squires. "He's a human being if that's what you mean."

"He's not a scholarship boy, is he? We've got two of them already."

"Actually, his father is one of Ireland's most prominent solicitors and a former Belvedere boy himself. Those of you who read the newspapers might be familiar with Max Woodbead. He's represented most of Ireland's top criminals in recent years, including many of your own fathers. You're all to welcome Julian and treat him with courtesy. Cyril Avery, you'll be his roommate since you have an available bed in your room, and let's hope that he doesn't turn out to be as dishonest as his predecessor."

Of course, I knew more than my classmates about Max Woodbead but I told no one of our past encounters. My interest in Julian meant that I had followed his father's career and growing celebrity closely over the seven years since Charles's trial and watched as his practice had grown considerably, to the point where only the very wealthiest defendants could afford to hire him. There were reports that he was worth over a million pounds, an enormous amount of money in those days. He owned a country home on the Dingle Peninsula, a flat in Knightsbridge where his lover, a famous actress, lived, but his main residence was a house on Dartmouth Square in Dublin that he shared with his wife Elizabeth and their children Julian and Alice, the same house that had once belonged to Charles and Maude and which he had purchased in an act of revenge within six months of my adoptive father's incarceration in Mountjoy Prison. Moving his family in and forcing Elizabeth to sleep next to him in the room that had once been Charles's was his idea of punishment.

Max's other claim to fame was his growing public profile. He appeared regularly in the newspapers and on the radio criticizing the government, every government regardless of its colors, and pining for a restoration of Ireland's place within the Empire. He was engaged in a rhapsodic love affair with the young Queen, whom he adored, and considered Harold Macmillan to be simply the finest politician who had ever lived. He longed for a return to the days of the Anglo-Irish aristocracy with a governor-general on Kildare Street and Prince Philip roaming the Phoenix Park, shooting every unfortunate animal that had the temerity to cross his path. Of course, he engendered the animosity of an entire nation for his anti-Republican views but that only made him more popular with the media, who broadcast his every wild utterance and sat back rubbing their collective hands in glee as they waited for the outrage to begin. Max was living proof that it doesn't matter if people love you or loathe you; as long as they know who you are, you can make a good living.

And so when I returned from Latin class the following afternoon and saw the door to my room standing ajar and heard the sound of someone shuffling around inside, I felt a mixture of excitement and queasiness, guessing that Julian had arrived. I turned around and ran back along the corridor toward the bathroom, where a full-length mirror was pinned to one of the walls with the express intention of intimidating us after our morning showers, and examined myself quickly, taking a comb from my pocket and running it through my hair before checking there were no lunch remnants stuck between my teeth. I was desperate to make a good first impression but felt so sick with nerves that I worried I would end up embarrassing myself.

I knocked on the door and when no answer came pushed it open and stepped inside. Julian was standing by Dennis's old bed, removing his clothes from his suitcase and placing them in the lower section of our shared chest of drawers. Turning around, he looked at me without any particular interest and although it had been a long time since we'd last seen each other I would have known him anywhere. He was around the same height as me but had a more muscular frame, with blond hair that fell over his forehead with as much languor as it had when he was a child. And he was ridiculously handsome, with clear blue eyes and skin that, unlike most of our classmates, had not been tarnished by acne.

"Hello," he said, unfolding a coat and brushing it carefully with a clothes brush before hanging it in the wardrobe. "And who might you be?"

"Cyril Avery," I said, extending my hand, which he stared at for a moment before shaking it. "This is my room. Well, our room now, I suppose. It was Dennis Caine's and mine until a few weeks ago. But he got sacked for cheating in an exam even though everyone knows he didn't do it. Now it's our room. Yours and mine."

"If this is your room," he said, "then why did you knock?"

"I didn't want to startle you," I replied.

"I don't startle easily." He closed the drawers and looked me up and down before raising his right hand in simulation of a pistol and using his index finger to point to a spot just to the right of my heart. "You've missed a button on your shirt," he said.

I looked down and, sure enough, one of the buttons was undone, the two sides of my shirt falling open like the mouth of a tiny hatchling, exposing the pale skin beneath. How had I missed that during my rigorous preparations? "Sorry," I said, fastening it quickly.

"Cyril Avery," he said, frowning a little. "Why do I know that name?"

"We've met before," I told him.

"When?"

"When we were children. At my adoptive father's house on Dartmouth Square."

"Oh," he said. "Are we neighbors? My father owns a house on Dartmouth Square too."

"Actually, it's the same house," I said. "He bought it from mine."

"I see." Some memory trickled down into his consciousness and he clicked his fingers as he remembered, pointing at me once again. "Didn't your father go to prison?" he asked.

"He did," I admitted. "But only for a couple of years. He's out now."

"Where was he?"

"The 'Joy."

"Exciting. Did you visit?"

"Not often, no. It's no place for a child, or at least that's what he always said."

"I was there myself once," he said. "When I was a boy. My father was representing a man who murdered his wife. The place smelled of—"

"Toilets," I said. "I remember. You told me before."

"Did I?"

"Yes."

"And you remembered? Even all these years later?"

"Well," I said, feeling my face begin to redden slightly, not wanting my fascination with him to reveal itself too quickly. "I have been there myself since, as I said, and I thought the same thing."

"Great minds and all that. So what happened when he got out, did he leave the country?"

"No, the bank took him back."

"Really?" he said, bursting out laughing.

"Yes. Actually, he's doing very well again. But they changed his job title. He used to be Director of Investments and Client Portfolios."

"And what is he now?"

"Director of Client Investments and Portfolios."

"Forgiving sort, aren't they? Still, a spell in prison is probably a badge of honor for people in that field."

I looked down at his feet and noticed that he was wearing runners, a fashion statement that was new to Ireland at the time.

"My father brought them back from London," he said, following the direction of my eyes. "They're my second pair, actually. I had them in a six but my feet grew. I'm an eight now."

"Don't let the priests see them," I said. "They say runners are only worn by Protestants and socialists. They'll confiscate them."

"They'd have a hard job," he said, but all the same he used the tip of his right foot to kick the left shoe off at the heel before using his stockinged toes to remove the right and kick the pair under his bed. "Not a snorer, are you?" he asked.

"Not that I know of," I said.

"Good. I am, I'm told. Hope I don't keep you awake."

"I don't mind. I'm a heavy sleeper. I probably won't hear you."

"You might. My sister says that when I get started I'm like a fog-horn."

I smiled; already, I longed for bedtime. I wondered whether he was one of those boys who went to a toilet cubicle to change or whether he would simply strip off in the room. I suspected the latter. I doubted he had any self-consciousness at all.

"What's it like here anyway?" he asked. "Is there any fun to be had?"

"It's all right," I said. "The boys are fine, the priests are vicious, of course, but—"

"Well, that's to be expected. Have you ever met a priest who didn't want to beat six shades of shit out of you? They get off on it, of course."

My eyes and mouth opened wide in scandalized delight. "No," I admitted. "Not so far anyway. I think it's something they teach them in the seminary."

"It's because they're all so sexually frustrated, of course," he told me. "They can't have sex, you see, so they beat up little boys and it gives them stiffies when they do it. It's the closest they get to orgasms during the day. It's ridiculous, really. I mean *I'm* sexually frustrated but I don't think beating up children will solve the problem."

"What would?" I asked.

"Well, fucking, of course," he said, as if it was the most natural thing in the world.

"Right," I said.

"Haven't you ever noticed, though? The next time one of the priests hits you, take a look downstairs and you'll see that he's flying at full mast. And afterward they go back to their rooms and wank themselves silly thinking about us. Do they come into the shower rooms here?"

"Well, yes," I said. "To make sure that everyone is washing themselves correctly."

"Bless your pure heart," he said, looking at me as if I was an innocent child. "It's not our personal hygiene that they're interested in, Cyril. In my last school, there was a priest named Father Cremins who tried to kiss me and I punched him in the nose. It broke. There was blood everywhere. But of course there was nothing he could do about it because he could hardly report me in case I said what had provoked the attack. He told everyone that he'd walked into a door instead."

"Boys kissing boys!" I said, laughing nervously and scratching my head. "I didn't know that . . . I mean it seems strange that . . . after all, when there are—"

"Are you all right, Cyril?" he asked. "Your face has gone all red and you're waffling."

"I think I'm getting a cold," I said, my voice choosing that exact moment to slip between registers. "I think I'm getting a cold," I repeated, adopting my deepest tone now.

"Well, don't give it to me," he said, turning away to place his toothbrush and facecloth on his bedside table along with a copy of *Howards End*. "I can't stand being ill."

"Where were you before here anyway?" I asked after a lengthy pause, when it seemed as if he'd forgotten that I was even in the room.

"Blackrock College."

"I thought your father was a Belvedere boy."

"He is," he replied. "But he's one of those past pupils who likes to revel in memories of his glory days on the rugby field but probably remembers enough bad things about the place to make him send his own son somewhere else. He took me out of Blackrock when he found out that my Irish-language teacher had written a poem and published it in the *Irish Times*, casting doubt on the virtue of Princess Margaret. He won't hear a word said against the Royal Family, you see. Although they do say that Princess Margaret is a bit of a slut. Apparently she puts it about with half the men in London and some of the women too. I wouldn't say no, though, would you? She's a looker. A lot more fun than the Queen, I imagine. Can you imagine the Queen going down on Prince Philip's cock? It's the kind of image that would give you nightmares."

"I remember your father," I told him, startled by the frankness of his conversation and wishing to steer it back to safer territory. "He interrupted a dinner party in my house once and had a fight with my adoptive father."

"Did your old man fight back?"

"He did. But it didn't do him any good. He took a pasting."

"Well, old Max was a prizefighter when he was younger," said Julian proudly. "He's still pretty handy with his fists, actually," he added. "I should know."

"Do you remember meeting me back then?" I asked.

"There's a tiny bell ringing somewhere in my head," said Julian. "Maybe I remember you *slightly*."

"My room was the one on the top floor of the house."

"My sister Alice uses that room now. I never go up there. It reeks of perfume."

"Well, what about you?" I asked, feeling a little sad that he didn't use my old room; I rather liked the idea of us having that in common. "Where do you sleep?"

"A room on the second floor. Why, does it matter?"

"Is it the room overlooking the square or the garden at the rear of the house?"

"The square."

"That was my adoptive mother's study. Charles had the first floor and Maude had the second."

"Of course," he said, brightening up now. "Your mother was Maude Avery, wasn't she?"

"That's right," I said. "Well, my adoptive mother."

"Why do you keep saying that?"

"It's the way I was brought up," I told him. "I'm not a real Avery, you see."

"What an odd thing to say."

"My adoptive father insists that I make it clear to people."

"So I'm sleeping in the room where Maude Avery wrote all her books?"

"If you have the room that overlooks the square, then yes."

"Gosh," he said, impressed. "Now, that is something. A real claim to fame, wouldn't you say?"

"Is it?" I asked.

"Of course it is. It was Maude Avery's writing room! *The* Maude Avery! Your father must be rolling in it now," he added. "Wasn't there a point last year where she had six books in the top-ten-bestsellers chart at the same time? I read that it was the first time this had ever happened."

"I think it was seven, actually," I said. "But, yes, I suppose he is. He makes more money from her work than he does from his own."

"And how many languages is she translated into now?"

"I don't know," I said. "A lot. It seems to grow all the time."

"It's a pity she died before she knew real success," said Julian. "She would have been gratified to know how respected she's become. There are so many artists who have to wait until they're dead to be fully appreciated. You know Van Gogh only sold one painting during his lifetime? And that Herman Melville was an absolute unknown while he was alive and was only discovered, so to speak, when he was already in the ground? He was worm food before anyone even took a second glance at *Moby-Dick*. He idolized Hawthorne, of course, and was always popping over there for his tea but who can name one of Hawthorne's novels now?"

"*The Scarlet Letter*," I said.

"Oh yes. The one about the girl who puts it about while her husband's at sea. I haven't read it. Is it dirty? I love dirty books. Have you read *Lady Chatterley's Lover*? My father got a copy in England and I snuck it out of his library to read it. It's pure filth. There's a wonderful bit where—"

"I don't think fame was what Maude was looking for," I said, interrupting him. "Actually, I think the idea of literary approbation would have appalled her."

"Why? What's the point of writing if no one reads you?"

"Well, if the work has some value, then there's merit in that alone, surely?"

"Don't be ridiculous. It's like having a wonderful voice but only singing to an audience of deaf people."

"I don't think that's the way she viewed art," I said. "Popularity didn't interest her. She had no desire for her novels to be read. She loved language, you see. She loved words. I think she only felt truly happy when she was staring at a paragraph for hours at a time and trying to refine it into a thing of beauty. She only published her books because she didn't like the idea of all that hard work going to waste."

"What a load of old nonsense," he said, dismissing what I had said as if it was scarcely worth his consideration. "If I was a writer, I would want people to read my books. And if they didn't, I would feel that I had failed."

"I'm not sure that I would agree," I said, surprised to find myself contradicting him but I wanted to defend Maude's beliefs. "To be honest, I think there's more to literature than that."

"Have you read any of them?" he asked me. "Your mother's novels, I mean?"

"My adoptive mother," I said. "And, no, I haven't. Not yet."

"None of them?"

"No."

He laughed and shook his head. "But that's appalling. She was your mother, after all."

"My adoptive mother."

"Stop saying that. You should try *Like to the Lark*. It's wonderful. Or *The Codicil of Agnès Fontaine*. There's an extraordinary scene in that book where two girls bathe together in a lake and they're totally naked and there's so much sexual tension between them that I guarantee you won't get to the end of the chapter without pulling Percy out for the old five-finger shuffle. I adore lesbians, don't you? If I were a woman, I would absolutely be a lesbian. London is full of lesbians, or so I hear. And New York. When I'm older, I'm going to go over there, become friends with a few of them and ask can I watch them when they're doing it. What do you suppose they do exactly? I've never been quite sure."

I stared at him and felt myself growing a little unsteady on my feet. I had no answer to any of this and, truth be told, I wasn't entirely sure that I knew what a lesbian was. As excited as I had been about Julian's arrival at Belvedere, I began to think that perhaps we were operating on completely different levels of consciousness. The last book I had read was a *Secret Seven*.

"Do you miss her?" he asked me, closing his emptied suitcase now and pushing it under the bed next to his runners.

"What's that?" I asked, my mind on other things.

"Your mother. Your *adoptive* mother. Do you miss her?"

"A little, I suppose," I admitted. "We weren't very close, to be honest. And she died only a few weeks before Charles got out of prison, which was almost five years ago now. I don't think about her very much anymore."

"And what about your real mother?"

"I don't know anything about her," I said. "Charles and Maude said they had no idea who she was. They got me from a little hunchbacked Redemptorist nun when I was only a few days old."

"What killed her? Maude, I mean."

"Cancer," I said. "She'd had it a few years before in her ear canal. But then it started again in her throat and tongue. She smoked like a chimney. I almost never saw her without a cigarette in her hand."

"Well, that might do it. Do you smoke, Cyril?"

"No."

"I don't like the idea of smoking. Have you ever kissed a girl who smoked?"

I opened my mouth to reply but language escaped me and to my horror I could feel the blood rushing toward my penis in response to such candid conversation. I let my hands drop before my crotch, hoping that Julian wouldn't be as conscious of my excitement as he was of the priests who had beaten him in Blackrock.

"No," I said.

"It's awful," he said, pulling a disgusted face. "You don't get the taste of the girl at all, just that foul nicotine." He paused for a moment and stared at me, half-amused. "You have kissed a girl, though, haven't you?"

"Of course," I said, laughing with the insouciance of one who's been asked whether he has ever seen the ocean or traveled on an airplane. "Dozens of them."

"Dozens?" he said, frowning. "Well, that's a lot. I've only kissed three so far. But one of them let me put my hand down her brassiere to touch her breast. Dozens, you say! Really?"

"Well, maybe not dozens," I said, looking away.

"You haven't kissed anyone at all, have you?"

"I have," I said.

"No, you haven't. But that's all right. We're only fourteen, after all. It's all in front of us. I intend to live a long and healthy life and fuck as many girls as I can. I'd like to die in my bed, aged one hundred and five, with a twenty-two-year-old bouncing up and down on top of me. And what are the chances of kissing anyone in here anyway? It's all boys. I'd rather kiss my granny and she's been dead for nine years. But look, do you want to help me unload my books? They're in that box over there. Can I mix them in with yours or would you rather I put them on a separate shelf?"

"Let's mix them in together," I said.

"All right." He stood back and looked me up and down again and I wondered whether perhaps another button had come undone. "Do you know, I think I do remember you now," he said. "Didn't you ask me whether you could see my thing?"

"No!" I said, appalled by the accusation, which, after all, was entirely false considering it was him who had asked to see mine. "No, I didn't."

"Are you sure?"

"Quite sure," I said. "Why would I want to see your thing? I have one of my own, after all. I can see it whenever I want."

"Well, there was definitely a boy who asked me around that time. I'm sure it was you. I remember the room and it's Alice's room now."

"You couldn't be more wrong," I insisted. "I have absolutely no interest in your thing and never have had."

"If you say so. It's a very nice thing anyway. I can't wait to start using it in the way that God intended, can you? You've gone quite red, Cyril," he added. "Not frightened of girls, are you?"

"No," I said. "Not at all. If anything, they should be frightened of me. Because I want to, you know . . . have lots of sex with them. And stuff."

"Good. Because I suppose we'll have to be friends, you and I, since we're sharing a room. We could go on the hunt together sometimes. You're not a bad-looking fellow, after all. There might be a few girls who could be persuaded to let you do it with them. And of course, they're all crazy about me."

The TD from Dublin Central

The teachers were crazy about him too and awarded him the gold medal for *Most Improved Pupil* at the Easter prize-giving ceremony, which was greeted with derision by those students who did not hold Julian in the same high esteem as I did. Since he hadn't even been enrolled at Belvedere College during the previous term, it was a mystery to them how he had managed to improve at all and the rumor went around that Max had granted a scholarship to the school on the condition that his son's résumé would be padded with glory over the coming years. I was delighted, of course, for it meant that as part of his reward he would be joining me and four others—the gold-medal winners in English, Irish, mathematics, history and art—on a trip to Dáil Éireann to witness the workings of the Irish parliament.

I had won the English prize for an essay I'd written entitled "Seven Ways to Better Myself," in which I listed various qualities that I knew would impress the priests but that I had absolutely no intention of pursuing in real life (except for the last one, whose addendum wasn't a problem to me at all). They were, in order of appearance:

1 Study the life of St. Francis Xavier and recognize aspects of his Christian behavior that I could emulate.

2 Identify those boys in my class who were struggling at subjects in which I excelled and offer to help them.

3 Learn a musical instrument, preferably the piano but definitely not the guitar.

4 Read the novels of Walter Macken.

5 Begin a novena dedicated to the repose of the soul of the late Pope Pius XII.

6 Find a Protestant and make him see the errors of his ways.

7 Banish all impure thoughts from my mind, particularly those that focused on the intimate parts of people of the opposite gender.

It wasn't the gold medal that I craved so much as the day out, the destination of which changed every year and had previously included such exhilarating venues as Dublin Zoo, Howth Head and Dun Laoghaire pier. This year, however, things had taken a more exciting turn with the announcement of a visit to the city center, a place that, despite its proximity to our school, was out of bounds to us at all times with no exceptions according to the student handbook. As boarders we could leave Belvedere on weekends as long as we were in the custody of a parent, a guardian or a priest, none of which particularly appealed to us. However, it was absolutely forbidden to spend any time in O'Connell Street or Henry Street, which, we were told, were havens for vice and iniquity, or Grafton Street and its environs, which were the domain of writers, artists and other deviants.

"I know the city center quite well," Julian told me on the short bus journey from Parnell Square to Kildare Street. "My father brings me and Alice there for lunch occasionally but he always refuses to take me to the places that I really want to go."

"Which ones are they?" I asked.

"Harcourt Street," he replied knowingly. "That's where all the girls hang out. And the nightclubs on Leeson Street. But of course they're not open till nighttime. I hear that the women there will do it with anyone if you buy them a Snowball."

I said nothing and looked out the window at the posters advertising *Ben-Hur* that hung from the front of the Savoy Cinema. As infatuated as I was with Julian, I found his tendency to talk constantly about girls frustrating. It was an obsession for him, as much as it is for most fourteen-year-old boys I suppose, but he seemed excessively preoccupied with sex and wasn't shy about telling me all the things that he would do to any girl who would let him have his way with her, fantasies that both aroused and distressed me with the certain knowledge that he would never want to do any of those things with me.

Did I spend much time examining my feelings for Julian in those days? Probably not. If anything, I deliberately avoided analyzing them. It was 1959, after all. I knew almost nothing of homosexuality, except for the fact that to act on such urges was a criminal act in Ireland that could result in a jail sentence, unless of course you were a priest, in which case it was a perk of the job. I had a crush on him, I recognized that much at least, but I didn't think any harm could come from it and assumed that in time those feelings would pass and my attentions would shift toward girls. I thought I was just a slow developer; the notion that I could have what was then considered to be a mental disorder was one that would have horrified me.

"The seat of government," said Father Squires, rubbing his hands together in glee as we disembarked the bus on Kildare Street and made our way past the pair of Gardaí standing by the gates to the courtyard, who waved us in without even a word when they saw the collar around our principal's neck. "Think, lads, of all the great men who have passed through these doors. Éamon de Valera, Seán Lemass, Seán T. O'Kelly. The Countess Markievicz who, strictly speaking, was not a man at all but had the heart and guts of one. We'll not speak of Michael Collins and the Blueshirts. If you see any of them renegades inside, look the other way as you would a Medusa. They're the sort of West Brit good-for-nothings that your daddy would have great time for, am I right, Julian Woodbead?"

All heads turned in Julian's direction and he shrugged his shoulders. The Jesuits, of course, were ideologically opposed to Max Woodbead's veneration for the British Empire and would have considered his love affair with Queen Elizabeth II to be heretical, although it didn't prevent them from taking his money.

"Probably," said Julian, who believed that taking offense at anything a priest said was beneath his dignity. "We've had James Dillon over to the house a few times for dinner if that's what you mean. Nice enough fellow, I suppose. Could do with a little advice on the personal hygiene front, of course."

Father Squires shook his head in scorn and led the way through the doors, where we were met by an usher who bowed and scraped before the priest before giving us a tour of the ground floor of the House and leading us up a narrow staircase toward the Visitors' Gallery, where we took our seats in the colonnade. The chamber, that green horseshoe of independence that represented everything that the Irish people had fought for over the years, lay before us and there was the Taoiseach, the great Éamon de Valera himself, who we scarcely believed existed outside of newspaper reports and our history lessons, holding forth on some topic to do with taxation and agriculture, and there wasn't a boy among our number who didn't feel they were in the presence of greatness. How often had we had read about his role at Boland's Mill during the Easter Rising of 1916 or how he had raised millions of American dollars to assist in the establishment of an Irish Republic three years later? He was the stuff of legend and there he was, in full sight of us, reading from a sheaf of papers in an uninterested voice as if none of these grand events were anything to do with him at all.

"Keep quiet now, lads," said Father Squires, his eyes growing moist with adoration. "Listen to the great man speak."

I did as I was told but it wasn't long before I grew bored. He may well have been a great man but he didn't seem to know when he'd made his point and should sit down again. Leaning over the railing, I glanced around at the half-empty seats of the chamber and counted how many of the Teachtaí Dála were asleep. The number was seventeen. I searched for women TDs but there were none to be found. Matthew Willoughby, who had won the history medal, had brought a notebook with him and was busy scribbling down every word that was said and as time went on and Father Squires showed no sign of wanting to leave, my eyes started to close and only when Julian tapped me on the arm and nodded toward the door behind us did I come back to life.

"What?" I said, stifling a yawn.

"Let's go outside and take a look around," he said.

"We'll get in trouble."

"And what if we do? Does it matter?"

I looked over toward Father Squires. He was seated in the front row, practically dribbling with Republican zeal. The chances of him noticing that we had abandoned our posts were nonexistent.

"Let's go," I said.

We stood up and snuck out the same way that we had come in, ignoring the ushers standing on duty at the doors of the gallery lest they challenge us on our departure, and made our way down the staircase where another Garda was sitting on an ornamental chair—the very replica of the one that had once sat on the ground floor of the house on Dartmouth Square—reading a newspaper.

"Where do you lads think you're going?" he asked, looking as if he didn't particularly care about the answer but felt duty-bound to ask anyway.

"Toilet," said Julian, grabbing his crotch with one hand while doing a little dance on the spot as the man rolled his eyes.

"Along down the corridor there," he said, pointing the way as he dismissed us.

We walked past him and past the toilets too, staring up at the oil portraits of the unknown dignitaries that glared down at us from the walls as if they knew that we were up to no good, and felt the excitement of being young, alive and unsupervised by adults. I had no idea where we were going, neither of us did, but it felt great to be on our own and having an adventure.

"Do you have any money on you, Cyril?" Julian asked after we had run out of corridors to investigate.

"Some," I said. "Not much. Why?"

"There's a tearoom over there. We could get something to drink."

"Right enough," I said and we made our way inside, holding our heads high as if we had every right to be there. It was a large room, about thirty feet wide and four times as long, and a woman was seated behind a desk on the nearest wall, a cash register next to her, watching people come to and fro as she counted her receipts. To my surprise, a pair of yellow phone boxes, the like of which I had only ever seen on street corners, stood on either side of her desk. One was occupied by a TD whose photograph I had seen in the papers but the other was empty. The tables ran in three long rows and despite the fact that there were plenty of empty seats the men were gathered like moths around the few tables where the flame of seniority burned bright. I recognized a group of junior Fianna Fáil TDs sitting on the floor near a couple of ministers, waiting for a seat at the top table to open up and doing their best not to acknowledge the sheer indignity of their position.

Naturally, Julian and I avoided the occupied tables and made our way to an empty one by a window, where we sat down with all the confidence of a couple of young dauphins until a young waitress, not much older than either of us, noticed us and came over. She was wearing a tight-fitting black and white uniform with the two top buttons of her blouse undone and I could see Julian staring at her in hunger, his pupils dilating as he took her in. She was a looker, there was no denying it, with shoulder-length blonde hair and pale clear skin.

"Let me wipe that clean for you," she said, leaning over and running a damp dishcloth across the top of the table while she glanced from one of us to the other. I noticed her gaze settle on Julian, who was so much more handsome than me, and envied the ease with which she could take him in and appreciate his beauty. As she turned away to clear some napkins from the table's previous occupants, he sat up straight, craned his neck forward and it was obvious that he was doing everything he could to look down her open blouse to capture every square inch of breast that was on display, to record it like a still photograph and develop it whenever he felt the urge. "What can I get you?" she asked finally, standing up again.

"Two pints of Guinness," said Julian, casual as you like. "And do you have any of that walnut cake that you had in here last Tuesday?"

She stared at him with an expression that mingled amusement with attraction. He was only fourteen but behaved in such an adult and confident fashion that I could tell that she didn't want to dismiss him out of hand.

"We're out of walnut cake," she said. "There was a run on it earlier. We have a bit of almond, though, if you'd like that."

"Oh Christ no," said Julian, shaking his head. "Almond gives me terrible gas. I have a group of constituents coming in to see me later this afternoon and the last thing I need is to be burping all over them. They'll never vote for me again and that'll be me out of a job. I'll have to go back to teaching. What's your name anyway, sweetheart?" he asked, and I looked down at my fingers, counting them one by one and wishing that she would just bring a pot of tea to the table and leave us in peace. "I haven't seen you in here before, have I?"

"Bridget," said the waitress. "I'm new."

"How new?"

"This is my fourth day."

"The virgin waitress," said Julian, breaking into a broad grin, and I glanced across at him, scandalized by his choice of words, but Bridget seemed pleased with the flirtation and was ready to give back as good as she got.

"That's as much as you know," she said. "They say Elizabeth I was a Virgin Queen but she was putting it about to every man left, right and center. I saw a film about her with Bette Davis."

"I'm more of a Rita Hayworth man myself," he said. "Have you seen *Gilda*? Do you go to the pictures much?"

"I'm only saying," she said, ignoring his question. "Don't judge a book by its cover. Who are you anyway? Do you have a name?"

"Julian," said Julian. "Julian Woodbead. TD for Dublin Central. When you've been here a few weeks, you'll get to know all our names. The other girls do."

She stared at him and I could see that she was balancing in her mind the sheer impossibility of a boy his age being an elected representative while, at the same time, considering how ludicrous it would be for him to be making such a story up. In the right light, he could have passed for older than fourteen—not enough that any sensible person would believe he was a TD but enough that a new girl in the tearoom might be anxious enough about challenging him.

"Is that right?" she said suspiciously.

"It is for the moment," he replied. "But there'll be an election in a year or two and I think my days might be numbered. The Blueshirts are giving me an awful run for my money on the social welfare benefits. You're not a Blueshirt, are you, Bridget?"

"I am not," she snapped. "Would you give me some credit? My family has always stood with Dev. My grandfather was in the GPO on Easter Sunday and two of my uncles fought in the War of Independence."

"It must have been fierce busy in the GPO that day," I said, looking up and speaking for the first time. "There's barely a man, woman or child in Ireland who doesn't claim that their father or grandfather was at one of the windows standing his post. It must have been near impossible to buy a stamp."

"Who's this fella then?" asked Bridget of Julian, looking at me as if I was something that had been dragged in by the cat on a cold winter's night.

"My sister's eldest lad," said Julian. "Don't mind him, sure he doesn't know what he's talking about. His hormones are all over the place at the moment. Now, about those pints of Guinness, darling, is there any risk of getting them before I pass out with the thirst?"

She looked around as if uncertain what she should do. "I don't know what Mrs. Goggin would say."

"And who's Mrs. Goggin?" asked Julian.

"The manageress. My boss. She says I'm on trial for six weeks and we'll see after that."

"She sounds like a difficult article."

"No, she's very nice, actually," said Bridget, shaking her head. "She gave me a chance here when no one else would."

"Well, if she's all that nice, then I don't think she'd object to you taking an order from an elected TD from Dublin South, do you?"

"I thought you were Dublin Central?"

"You're misremembering. I'm Dublin South."

"You're a bit of a laugh but I don't believe a word you say."

"Ah, Bridget," said Julian, looking at her mournfully. "Don't be like that. If you think I'm a laugh now, I promise you that I'm even more fun when I have a drink in me. Two pints of Guinness, that's all we want. Come on now, we've a thirst on us like Lawrence of Arabia."

She issued a deep sigh, as if she couldn't be bothered debating anymore, before walking away and, to my astonishment, returning a few minutes later with two full dark pints of Guinness Stout, which she placed before us, the yellow foam at the top spilling lazily over the head, leaving a snail's trail along the side of the glass.

"Enjoy them now," she said. "Mr. TD for wherever you're from now."

"We will," said Julian. He lifted his pint and took a long gulp and I watched his face grimace a little as he tried to swallow. His eyes closed briefly as he fought the urge to spit it back up. "Christ, that tastes good," he said with all the credibility of a Parisian complimenting a meal in Central London. "I needed that."

I took a sip from mine and, as it happens, didn't mind the taste at all. It was warmer than I had expected and had a bitter flavor to it but, somehow, it didn't make me gag. I gave it a sniff, then took another mouthful and breathed out through my nose. *All good*, I thought. *I could get used to this.*

"What do you think, Cyril?" he asked me. "Do I have a chance?"

"A chance at what?"

"A chance at Bridget."

"She's old," I said.

"Don't be ridiculous. She's only about seventeen. Three years older than me. That's a great age for a girl."

I shook my head, feeling a rare irritation with him. "What do you know about girls anyway?" I asked. "You're all talk."

"I know that if you say the right things to one you can get her to do whatever you want."

"Like what?"

"Well, most of them won't let you go all the way but they'll give you a blowie if you ask nicely."

I said nothing for a moment and considered this. I didn't want to display my ignorance before him but was eager to know. "What's a blowie?" I asked.

"Ah come on, Cyril. You're not that innocent."

"I'm *joking*," I said.

"No, you're not. You don't know."

"I do," I said.

"Well, go on then. What is it?"

"It's when a girl kisses you," I said. "And then she blows into your mouth."

He stared at me in bewilderment before starting to laugh. "Why would any sane person do such a thing?" he asked me. "Unless you'd drowned, of course, and she was trying to bring you back to life. A blowie, Cyril, is where they put your thing in their mouth and give it an old suck."

My eyes opened wide and I felt the familiar stirring in the crotch of my pants, attacking me faster than usual, my whole body alive with the idea of someone doing this to me. Or me doing it to someone else.

"That's not true," I said, blushing a little, for as exciting as it sounded I found it hard to imagine that anyone would actually do such a bizarre thing.

"Of course it is," he said. "You're so naïve, Cyril. We'll have to knock that out of you one day. You need a woman, that's what you need."

I turned away and my mind flitted to an image of Julian in our room every night, undressing for bed. The casual way he discarded his clothes, the complete lack of inhibition he showed as he stripped naked and slowly, casually, provocatively put on his pajamas while I pretended to read and tried not to make it obvious that I was watching from over the top of my book to capture another part of his body in my memory. A vision of him coming over to my bed to give me a blowie filled my mind and I struggled not to whimper in longing.

"Excuse me," said a voice from halfway down the tearoom, and I turned to see a woman of about thirty marching toward us. Her hair was tied up on her head and she was wearing a different uniform to the one that the waitresses wore, a more professional outfit. I glanced at the metal badge pinned above her right breast that bore the words: *Catherine Goggin, Manageress.* "Are those pints of Guinness that you boys are drinking?"

"They are," said Julian, barely looking up at her. His interest in girls did not extend this far up the age ladder. She might have been his great-grandmother for all the interest he had in her.

"And how old are you both?"

"Sorry," said Julian, standing and picking up his jacket from behind the chair. "No time to chat. I have a meeting of the parliamentary party to attend. Are you right there, Cyril?"

I stood up too but the woman pressed a hand firmly down on both our shoulders, pushing us back into our seats.

"Who served you these drinks? Sure you're only children."

"I'll have you know that I'm the TD for Wicklow," said Julian, who seemed to be working his way slowly down the east coast of the country.

"And I'm Eleanor Roosevelt," said the woman.

"So why does your name badge say Catherine Goggin?" asked Julian.

"You're with the school party that came in this morning, aren't you?" she asked, ignoring his question. "Where's your teacher? You shouldn't be wandering the corridors of Dáil Éireann alone, let alone drinking alcohol."

Before we could answer, I saw Bridget running over to our table, her face red and flustered, and behind her in hot pursuit was the irate face of Father Squires, followed by our four award-winning classmates.

"I'm sorry, Mrs. Goggin," said Bridget quickly. "He said he was a TD."

"And how could you possibly believe that?" asked Mrs. Goggin.

"Sure would you take a look at them, aren't they only children? Do you have no more sense than a sweeping brush? I'm away on my holidays to Amsterdam next week, Bridget; do I have to spend all my time there worrying that you're serving alcohol to minors?"

"Get up, the pair of you," said Father Squires, pushing his way between the two women. "Get up and shame me no more. We'll have a conversation about this when we're back at Belvedere, so we will."

We stood up again, both a little embarrassed by how things had turned out, and the manageress turned on the priest furiously. "Don't be blaming them," she said. "Sure aren't they just causing trouble the way any kids will? You're the one who's supposed to be looking after them. Letting them loose in Leinster House," she added, shaking her head in disgust, "where the business of the nation is conducted. I don't think their parents would be too happy to know they were down here supping pints of Guinness when they should have been learning, do you? Well, Father, do you?"

Father Squires stared at her in utter astonishment, as did we all. It's unlikely that anyone had ever spoken to him like this since the moment the collar first went around his neck, and for his accuser to be a woman was the worst insult of all. I could hear Julian chuckling beside me and knew that he was impressed by her audacity. I was impressed myself.

"You'll keep a civil tongue in your head, Missy," said Father Squires, poking a finger into her left shoulder. "You're addressing a man of the cloth, you know, not one of your boyfriends from Kehoe's public house."

"My boyfriends, if I had any, would surely have more sense than to let underage boys wander the corridors unsupervised," she said, refusing to be intimidated by him. "And I won't be poked and prodded by priests, do you hear me? Those days are long behind me. So take care not to touch me again. Now, this is my tearoom, Father, I'm in charge of it and you're to take this pair out of here right now and leave the rest of us to get on with our work."

Father Squires, looking as if he was about to have a series of heart attacks, a nervous breakdown and a stroke all at the same time, turned on his heel and marched away in full dudgeon. He could barely speak, the poor man, and I don't think he did until we were safely back on the grounds of Belvedere College, when, of course, he let rip at me and Julian. As I stood to leave the tearoom, however, I glanced back at Catherine Goggin and couldn't help but smile at her. I had never seen anyone put a priest in his place in the way that she had just done and thought the whole thing had been better than the pictures.

"Whatever punishment is coming my way," I told her, "it was worth it just to see that."

She stared at me for a moment before bursting out laughing.

"Go along now, you little demon," she said, reaching forward and ruffling my hair.

"You're in there," whispered Julian in my ear as we left the tearoom. "And there's nothing better than an oul' one for teaching a young dog a few tricks."

Max's Right Ear

In the early autumn of 1959, Max Woodbead wrote an article in the *Irish Times* condemning Éamon de Valera—a man he despised—and his government for relaxing its policy on the internment without trial of suspected IRA members. *End their imprisonment by all means*, he wrote, his words appearing next to a particularly obnoxious photograph of him sitting in the garden of what had once been my home, wearing a three-piece suit, a luxurious white rose spilling out from his buttonhole while he studied a plate of cucumber sandwiches that lay before him, *but rather than letting an assortment of misguided patriots and uneducated thugs roam the streets to cause carnage with their guns and bombs, it might be more beneficial to simply line them up against a wall and shoot them, just as our erstwhile overseers did to the leaders of the Easter Rising when they dared to challenge the divine authority of His Imperial Majesty, King George V.* The piece received extensive coverage across the media and as levels of outrage increased he was invited onto Radio Éireann to defend his position. Butting heads with a rabidly Republican interviewer, he claimed that it had been a dark day for Ireland when the country had severed its ties with England. The brightest minds in Dáil Éireann, he claimed, would never be as sharp as the dimmest eggheads in Westminster. Those who were taking part in the Border Campaign he condemned as cowards and murderers and, in one of his more self-satisfied moments (and one that he had surely rehearsed in advance to ensure maximum provocation), suggested that a sustained Luftwaffe-style blitzkrieg of the border along the counties of Armagh, Tyrone and Fermanagh would put an end to the terrorist activities of the Irish people once and for all. Asked why he possessed such fervently pro-English views when he had been born in Rathmines, he almost burst into song as he pointed out that his family had been one of the most prominent in Oxford for centuries. He seemed truly proud to admit that two of his ancestors had been be-headed by Henry VIII for opposing the king's marriage to Anne Boleyn and that another had been burned at the stake by Queen Mary herself—unlikely—for tearing down signs of Roman idolatry at Ox-ford Cathedral.

"I was the first of my family to be born in Ireland," he said, "and this was only because my father moved here to practice law after the end of the Great War. And as the Duke of Wellington, who I think we would all agree was a magnificent man, said: *Just because a man is born in a stable, this does not make him a horse.*"

"Maybe not a horse, but an ass for certain," declared Father Squires the following day in class, haranguing Julian for Max's treasonous sen-timents. "Which makes you a hinny or a mule."

"I've been called worse," said Julian, not looking in the least af-fronted. "The thing is, there's no point trying to equate my father's political opinions with my own. He has so many, you see, while I have absolutely none."

"That's because your head is empty."

"Oh I don't know," he muttered under his breath. "There's a few idle thoughts in there somewhere."

"Would you, as a proud Irishman, at least condemn him for the things he said?"

"No," replied Julian. "I don't even know what you're so incensed over. I never read the papers and I don't own a radio, so I have no idea what he said to cause all of this fuss. Was it something to do with la-dies being allowed to swim at the Forty Foot? He does grow enraged whenever that subject comes up."

"Ladies being . . ." Father Squires stared at him in disbelief, and I wondered how long it would be before his stick appeared to make mincemeat of my friend. "This has nothing to do with ladies being allowed to swim at the Forty Foot!" he roared. "Although it'll be a cold day in hell when that is allowed to happen. That's nothing more than a bunch of shameless hussies getting their kicks by parading around half naked."

"Sounds all right to me," said Julian with a half-smile.

"Have you not been listening to a word I've been saying? Your father is a traitor to his own people! Do you feel no shame for that, no?"

"No, I don't. Isn't there something in the Bible about sons not being put to death for the sins of their fathers?"

"Don't quote the Bible at me, you bloody West Brit brat," said Father Squires, storming down to our table and standing over us so I could smell the sweat that followed him around like a guilty secret. "And what it says is that they shall *both* be put to death for their *own* sins."

"That sounds a bit harsh. And I didn't quote it anyway. I paraphrased it. And obviously got it hopelessly wrong too."

This was the type of back-and-forth which seemed to annoy most of our classmates, turning Julian into a rather unpopular figure, but the way he challenged Father Squires delighted me. He was arrogant, certainly, and had no respect for authority but he made his pronouncements with such insouciance that I found it impossible not to be charmed by him.

So vocal was Max, however, on his condemnation of the IRA that perhaps no one should have been too surprised when, a few weeks later while leaving Dartmouth Square one morning for an appointment at the Four Courts, an attempt was made on his life. A gunman, hiding in the center of the gardens—Maude would *not* have been happy—fired two bullets in his direction, one lodging in the woodwork of the front door, the other skimming past the right side of his head, tearing his ear off and coming perilously close to what I suppose would be considered his brain. Max ran back inside screaming, blood pouring down the side of his face, and barricaded himself in his study until the Gardaí and the ambulance arrived. At the hospital, it became quite clear that no one had any sympathy for him whatsoever and even less interest in tracking down his intended assassin and so, when he was released, half deaf and with an inflamed red scar where his right ear used to be, he hired a bodyguard, a burly man with the look of a more muscular Charles Laughton and who went by the name of Ruairí O'Shaughnessy, a surprisingly Gaelic title for one in whose hands Max was placing his life. Wherever Julian's father went, O'Shaughnessy went too, and they became quite a familiar pair around Inn's Quay. Unbeknownst to any of us, however, was that, having failed to kill him for his verbal insults, the IRA had decided to try something a little more imaginative next time to punish him. A far more daring project was in the works, where Max was not the target at all.

Borstal Boy

Having enjoyed our brief escape from the clutches of Belvedere College during Julian's short-lived career as a TD, we decided to try our luck on the outside more often. Soon we were visiting city-center cinemas for afternoon matinées or strolling through the grounds of Trinity College to gawp at the Protestants, who seemed to have been dehorned by some benevolent shearer upon admission. We were drawn to the record and clothes shops along Henry Street, despite the fact that we could afford very little, and when Julian stole a copy of Frank Sinatra's *Songs for Swingin' Lovers!* from a market stall, we ran all the way back to school, delirious with the exhilaration of youth.

A few weeks after our visit to the Dáil, we were walking along O'Connell Street one afternoon, having fled Parnell Square after a particularly tedious geography class, and I felt a spontaneous burst of joy that I had never quite known before. The sun was out, Julian was wearing a short-sleeved shirt that accentuated his biceps, and my pubic hair had finally kicked in. Our friendship had never been closer and hours stretched before us where we could talk and exchange confidences, excluding anyone and anything from our tiny universe that didn't interest us. For once, the world seemed to be a place filled with possibilities.

"What shall we do today?" I asked, pausing by Nelson's Pillar and using the shade from the pedestal to keep the sun from my eyes.

"Well, actually—hold on," said Julian, stopping abruptly by a staircase that led beneath the street to a public urinal. "Two minutes. Call of nature."

I waited where I was, kicking my heels against the base of the statue and looking around. To my right, I could see the General Post Office, where Max Woodbead's nemeses, the leaders of the 1916 Rising, had exhorted Irishmen and Irishwomen, in the name of God and of the dead generations, to answer a summons to the flag and strike for their freedom.

"*You're a good-looking lad,*" growled a voice from behind me and I turned to see Julian grinning madly and starting to laugh when he saw the expression on my face. "I was down in the jacks," he said, nodding back toward the Pillar, "and this man comes up to me while I'm taking a piss and says that to me."

"Oh," I said.

"I forgot that's where all the queers hang out," he said, shuddering. "In underground lavatories waiting for innocent young boys like me to come along."

"You're hardly an innocent young boy," I said, glancing back toward the staircase, wondering who or what might ascend from there to drag Julian or me down into that dark underworld.

"No, but that's what they look for. Guess what I did?"

"What?" I asked.

"I turned around and pissed all over his trousers. He got a good look at my thing but it was worth it. It'll be hours before his pants are dry enough for him to come back up. You should have heard the names he called me! Imagine, Cyril! A dirty queer calling *me* names!"

"You should have hit him," I said.

"No need for that," he replied, frowning. "Violence never solved anything."

I said nothing. Whenever I tried to agree with him on subjects of this nature, he always seemed to backtrack on me, leaving me baffled as to how I had got things so wrong.

"So," I said, and we walked on, keen to put as much distance between us and the public toilet as possible while trying not to think about how awful it must be to have to go to such places to find anything approaching affection. "What shall we do today?"

"Let's have a think," he said cheerfully. "Any suggestions?"

"We could go take a look at the ducks in St. Stephen's Green," I suggested. "If we picked up a loaf of bread, we could feed it to them."

Julian laughed and shook his head. "We won't be doing that," he said.

"Well, what if we walked down toward the Ha'penny Bridge? They say that if you jump up and down on it, it starts to rock. We could frighten the life out of the old women as they're crossing it."

"No," said Julian. "Not that either."

"Well, what then?" I said. "You suggest something."

"Did you ever hear of the Palace Bar?" he asked, and I knew at once that he'd already planned our afternoon for us and I would have no choice but to fall in line.

"No," I said.

"It's just off Westmoreland Street. All the students from Trinity College go there. And the oul' fellas because they serve the best porter. Let's go there."

"A pub?" I said dubiously.

"Yes, Cyril, a pub," he replied, brushing his hair back from his forehead and grinning. "We want an adventure, don't we? And you never know who we might run into. How much money have you got on you?"

I fished around in my pockets and pulled out my change. Although I almost never saw him, Charles was fairly generous in my allowance, fifty pence arriving in my school bank account every Monday morning without fail. A real Avery, of course, would probably have got a pound.

"Not bad," said Julian, totting it up in his head. "I've got about the same. We've the makings of a good afternoon there if we use it sensibly."

"They won't serve us," I said.

"Of course they will. We look old enough. Well, I do anyway. And we have money, which is all that these places really care about. We'll be fine."

"Can we go see the ducks first?" I asked.

"*No*, Cyril," he said, torn between frustration and amusement. "Fuck the ducks. We're going to the pub."

I said nothing—it was rare that the F word was employed by any of us and when it was, it signaled absolute authority. There was simply no going against the F word.

Just before we entered the pub, Julian stopped outside a pharmacy and dug around in his pockets, pulling out a piece of paper. "Give me two minutes," he said. "I have to pick something up."

"What?" I asked.

"A prescription."

"A prescription for what? Are you sick?"

"No, I'm grand. I had to see a doctor the other day, that's all. It's nothing serious."

I frowned and watched him as he walked inside and, a moment later, followed him in.

"I told you to wait outside," he said when he saw me.

"No, you didn't. What's wrong with you anyway?"

He rolled his eyes. "It's nothing," he said. "Just a rash."

"What sort of a rash? Where is it?"

"Never you mind where it is."

The pharmacist appeared from the dispensary behind him and handed something across. "Use it lavishly on the affected area twice a day," he said, taking Julian's money.

"Will it sting?"

"Not as much as it will if you don't use it."

"Thank you," said Julian, putting the packet in his pocket, handing across the money and marching off, leaving me to follow in his wake.

"Julian," I said when we were back on the street. "What was all that—"

"Cyril," he said. "It's none of your business, all right? Just leave it. Come on, here's the pub."

I said nothing more, not wanting to incur his wrath, but I was hurt and disappointed that he wouldn't let me into his secret. There were two doors at the entrance, set out into the street like two sides of an equilateral triangle, and Julian chose the left-hand one, holding it open just long enough for me to follow him inside. A narrow corridor faced a long and colorful bar where a half-dozen men were seated at stools, smoking and staring at their pints of Guinness as if within that dark liquid the meaning of life could be discovered. Past the bar were a couple of empty tables and beyond them, a snug. The barman, a tetchy-looking character with pumpkin-orange hair and eyebrows to match, slung a towel over his shoulder and eyed us warily as we made our way toward the nearest table.

"The snug is for women and kids," whispered Julian to me. "Or for men hiding on their wives. We'll stay out here. I've a terrible thirst on me!" he roared, making me jump as every head in the place turned in our direction. "But after a long day's work at the docks there's nothing I enjoy more than a pint. You're the same, aren't you, Cyril? Landlord, will you bring a couple of pints of the black stuff over here?" he shouted, smiling at the ginger behind the counter.

"I will on my nelly," he said. "How old are you pair anyway? Yous look like children."

"I'm nineteen," said Julian. "And my friend here is eighteen." He pulled all his money out of his pocket and nodded at me to do the same so the man could see that we could pay for what we ordered. "Why do you ask?"

"Just making conversation," he said, reaching for one of the taps. "You realize that I might have to charge lads your age a little more than usual? I call it the Youth Tax."

"Whatever you think is fair," said Julian.

"Ah fuck off," said the barman, but he said it more from amusement than annoyance. A few minutes later, he brought over the drinks, set them down before us and returned to his station.

"What time is it now?" asked Julian, and I nodded toward the clock on the wall.

"Almost six," I said.

"Grand job. How do I look?"

"You look like a Greek god sent down by the immortal Zeus from Mount Olympus to taunt the rest of us inferior beings with your aston-ishing beauty," I said, which somehow, in translation, came out as "You look fine, why?"

"No reason," he said. "Just checking. You're a good man, Cyril," he added, reaching over and resting his hand on top of mine for a mo-ment, and a current of electricity ran through me, as exhilarating as I imagined it would feel were he to lean forward and press his lips against my own. He looked into my eyes and held them briefly before frowning a little; perhaps he could sense an emotion that even he was not yet mature enough to understand.

"You are too, Julian," I began, and perhaps in the heat of the moment I might have been ready to become more rapturous in my praise and give myself away entirely but before I could say another word the door to the pub swung open and I looked across as two girls entered, one of whom, to my surprise, seemed familiar to me. They glanced around nervously, for they were the only women in the place, before catching sight of me and Julian, at which point the girl in front smiled and strode toward us.

"Bridget," said Julian, turning now, taking his hand from mine quickly and breaking into a wide smile. "There you are. I knew you'd come."

"You knew nothing of the sort," she said, winking at him. "I bet you probably said a few novenas to make your wishes come true, though."

Of course, I realized then, it was the waitress from the Dáil tearoom, dressed to the nines in a tight-fitting red dress that drew attention to her breasts, her face a clown's visage of makeup. Next to her was another girl, perhaps a year younger, shorter, no makeup, the very definition of mousey, with mud-brown hair, beer-bottle glasses and an expression that suggested she had recently eaten something that didn't agree with her. The Cyril to Bridget's Julian, so to speak. My heart sank as I realized that this was exactly why she was here and I turned to stare at Julian, who at least felt enough shame to avoid my eye.

"What'll you have, ladies?" he asked, clapping his hands together as they sat down.

"Are these seats clean?" asked the second girl, taking a handkerchief from the sleeve of her blouse and wiping it against the fabric.

"The arses of some of the best men and women in Dublin have sat in them," he told her. "Sit yourself down there, sweetheart, and if you catch any diseases I promise to pay the vet bill myself."

"Charming," she said. "You're a real gentleman."

"We'll have two Snowballs," said Bridget. "This is my pal Mary-Margaret."

"You remember Cyril, don't you?"

"How could I forget him? Cyril the Squirrel."

"Cyril the Squirrel!" repeated Julian, bursting out laughing at her hilarious joke.

"You have an angelic look about you, did anyone ever tell you that?" she asked, leaning forward and examining my face. "He looks as if he's never been kissed," she added to Julian, and I felt like a specimen under a microscope that two doctors were studying closely.

"I'll just have an orange juice," said Mary-Margaret, raising her voice a little.

"Two Snowballs," repeated Bridget.

"Two Snowballs!" shouted Julian to the barman, pointing at our glasses, which were perilously close to empty. "And two more pints of plain!"

"I'll be on my ear," said Mary-Margaret. "And I have to be up for six o'clock Mass in the morning. Father Dwyer is on tomorrow and he says a lovely Mass."

"Sure you haven't had a drop yet," said Bridget. "One is hardly going to tip you over the edge into alcoholism."

"One," she insisted. "But one is all I'll have. I'm not a drinker, Bridget, as you know."

"Howaya, Mary-Margaret?" said Julian, winking at her and nodding toward me. "This is my pal Cyril."

"You already said that. Do you think I have the memory of a goldfish?"

"What do you think?"

"What do I think of what?"

"Of Cyril? Cyril the Squirrel?"

"What am I supposed to think of him?" she asked, looking me up and down like I was the creature from the black lagoon and she'd had the bad luck of standing close to the water while I crawled onshore.

"A queer fella in a public toilet asked could he give him a blowie earlier."

My mouth fell open in horror, Mary-Margaret's in disbelief, and Bridget's in delight.

"That never happened," I said, and my vocal cords chose that unfortunate moment to crack a little. "He's making it up."

"This isn't my standard of conversation at all," said Mary-Margaret, turning to Bridget. The Snowballs arrived at the same moment and she took a sniff of hers before swallowing almost all of it in one go without showing any particular reaction. "Are these going to be vulgar boys? Because I don't care for vulgar boys, as you know. I'll have another one of these if they're going."

"Two more Snowballs!" roared Julian.

In the silence that followed, Mary-Margaret turned to look at me again and if anything she seemed even less impressed by me now than she had before, which was something that I hadn't thought possible.

"Cecil, is it?" she asked.

"Cyril," I said.

"Cyril what?"

"Cyril Avery."

"Well," she said with a little sniff. "It's not the worst name I've ever heard."

"Thank you."

"I only came because Bridget asked me to. I didn't know that we were making up a foursome."

"Neither did I," I said.

"That's not my standard at all," she said.

"How was the tearoom today?" asked Julian. "Did President Eisenhower stop by to say hello?"

"Mr. Eisenhower is the American President," said Mary-Margaret, turning to him contemptuously. "Our President is Mr. O'Kelly. You can't be that ignorant, surely?"

"I was making a joke, Mary-Margaret," said Julian, rolling his eyes. "Have you ever heard of one of those?"

"I don't care for jokes," she replied.

"I've never even heard of President Eisaflower," said Bridget with a shrug.

"Eisenhower," I said.

"Eisaflower," she repeated.

"That's it," I said.

"Do you work in the tearoom too, Mary-Margaret?" asked Julian.

"I do not," she said, insulted by the very suggestion, despite the fact that her friend was sitting next to her. "I'm a junior cash assistant on the foreign exchange desk at the Bank of Ireland, College Green."

"You are not," said Julian.

"I am," she said.

"You are not. You're making it up."

"Why would I do such a thing?" she asked.

"Right then, say something in Norwegian."

Mary-Margaret stared at him as if she didn't quite understand what he was getting at before turning to Bridget, who leaned forward and slapped Julian's forearm playfully, leaving her hand there afterward, which made me want to pick up a stray knife from the next table and cut it off.

"Don't mind him," said Bridget, full of fun. "He thinks he's the bee's knees."

"And the cat's pajamas," said Julian with a wink.

"You're the cat's something."

"That doesn't even mean anything," I said quietly.

"The Norwegians use Norwegian kroner," announced Mary-Margaret, pulling a face and looking away. "I don't care for it very much, if I'm honest. When you count it out, it leaves an ink stain on your hands and that's not my standard at all. I prefer international currency that leaves no residue. Australian banknotes are very clean. As are those of their nearest neighbors, the New Zealanders."

"Christ alive, you're a fascinating creature," said Julian, and by now we'd finished another round and more had just arrived, on my orders after Julian had looked at the near-empty glasses and given me a nudge.

"Actually, that's a common misconception," I said. "New Zealand isn't Australia's nearest neighbor at all."

"Of course it is," said Mary-Margaret. "Don't be ridiculous."

"I'm not being ridiculous. Papua New Guinea is closer. We studied it in geography class."

"There's no such place," she said.

"Well," I said, uncertain how I could go about proving it, "there is."

"Stop flirting with the poor girl, Cyril," said Julian. "She'll be on you like a bear on a beehive if you keep this dirty talk up."

"I work on the foreign exchange desk at the Bank of Ireland, College Green," she repeated, in case we had forgotten her telling us this a few minutes before. "I think I know a little more about world geography than you."

"Not if you've never heard of Papua New Guinea," I muttered, burying myself in my pint.

"I bought a new pair of nylons," said Bridget, apropos of nothing. "I'm debuting them tonight. What do you think?" And she swung around to the left of the stool so her legs could stretch out before us. I had little to compare them against but I could tell that they were impressive enough, if you liked that sort of thing. From the top of her head to the soles of her feet, Bridget was a stunner and there was no point denying it. All I had to do was look at Julian to see how infatuated he was. I recognized the expression on his face only too well, for I wore it myself most of the time.

"They're absolutely gorgeous," said Julian, winking at her. "But I bet I could talk you out of them."

"Cheek," she said, slapping his arm again and laughing before turning her attention back to me. "Howaya anyway, Cyril?" she asked. "Do you have any news for me?"

"Not too much," I said. "I got a Highly Regarded for my essay on Pope Benedict XV and his efforts to pursue a peace settlement during the First World War."

"And you're only telling me now?" said Bridget.

"You never asked," I said.

"Jesus, there's a pair of them in it," said Julian, looking back and forth between Mary-Margaret and myself.

"Is it just me or does this place smell?" asked Mary-Margaret, pulling a face.

"It might be just you," said Julian. "Have you had a bath this week?"

"I *meant*, is it just me who thinks that there's a smell?" she asked, snarling at him.

"It does smell a bit like piss," said Bridget.

"Bridget!" said Mary-Margaret, scandalized.

"That's because we're sitting at the top of the stairs," said Julian. "And the men's jacks are down there. All you need to do, Mary-Magdalen, is turn your head around that corner and you'll be able to see all the oul' lads with their things out."

"It's Mary-Margaret," said Mary-Margaret. "Not Mary-Magdalen."

"My mistake."

"And I'd rather you didn't talk about things, if you please."

"Nothing wrong with things," said Julian. "None of us would be here without them. I'd be lost without my thing. It's my best friend, after Cyril here. Although I'll leave you to figure out which one I have more fun with."

I smiled, the drink beginning to affect me a little, considering it quite a compliment to be higher ranked in his estimation than his penis.

"Bridget," said Mary-Margaret, turning to her friend. "I don't care for this type of dirty talk. It isn't my standard."

"Boys are obsessed with their things," said Bridget, shaking her head. "It's all they ever talk about."

"Not true," said Julian. "Only last week I had a conversation with a lad from my mathematics class about quadratic equations. Although now that I think of it, we were taking a piss side by side at the time and I have to admit I took a quick look at his to see how I measured up."

"Who was it?" I asked, feeling a stirring in my crotch at the thought of it.

"Peter Trefontaine."

"And how was it?"

"Small," said Julian. "And it curved to the left a little in a weird way."

"Would you please stop?" asked Mary-Margaret. "I have to be up for Mass in the morning."

"With Father Dwyer, yes, you mentioned. I bet he's got a tiny thing."

"Bridget, I will leave if this boy continues to—"

"Stop it, Julian," said Bridget. "You're embarrassing Mary-Margaret."

"I'm not embarrassed," she insisted, her face turning puce now. "I'm repulsed. There's a difference."

"No more talk of things so," said Julian, taking a long drink from his pint. "Although it might interest you to know that many years ago, when Cyril here and I were only children, he asked whether he could see my thing."

"I did not!" I cried, horrified. "He asked me!"

"There's no shame in it, Cyril," he said, smiling. "It was just youthful high jinks, that's all. It's not like you're a queer or anything."

"I did not ask to see his thing," I repeated, and Bridget spat a little of her Snowball on the table as she started laughing.

"If this is the sort of conversation we're going to have—" said Mary-Margaret.

"I didn't!" I insisted.

"In fairness, I have a very nice thing," said Julian. "Cyril will tell you."

"How would I know?" I said, blushing furiously.

"Because we share a room," he replied. "Don't pretend you haven't looked. I've looked at yours. You have quite a nice one yourself. Although it's not as big as mine. But it's bigger than Peter Trefontaine's even when you don't have a stiffie, which, let's face it, isn't very often. You'd be the first to admit that, wouldn't you, Cyril?"

"Oh my stars," said Mary-Margaret, looking as if she was about to faint. "Bridget, I want to go home."

"Actually, Mary-Margaret, you're the only one around this table who hasn't seen my thing," said Julian. "Which I suppose makes you the odd one out."

There was silence as we all took in what he had said. I felt my stomach slowly dip and realized that for all of our escapes from Belvedere College together, sometimes Julian escaped alone, or—worse by far—escaped with someone who was his sexual peer and with whom he could go in search of girls. The notion that he had a life outside our life, outside our friendship, was deeply hurtful to me. And the realization, as it slowly dawned, that Bridget had seen his thing, whether this meant she had simply touched it or looked at it or given him a blowie or gone all the way with him was almost too much for me to bear. For the first time since I was a child, I felt like a child.

"You've an awful mouth on you," said Bridget, half-embarrassed, half-aroused by his words.

"Well, you have a great one on you," he replied, leaning forward and smiling, and before any of us knew what was happening they were kissing. I glanced down at my drink, trembling a little before lifting it to my lips and finishing it off in one go, then stared around the room as if nothing at all was happening.

"Isn't the ceiling work very intricate?" I asked, looking up so I didn't have to watch the pair of them pawing away at each other.

"My mother is in the Legion of Mary," declared Mary-Margaret. "I don't know what she'd say to this kind of carry-on."

"Relax," said Julian, as they separated and he sat back with a contented look on his face. A look that said *I'm young, I'm good-looking, I like girls and they like me; there is no end to the amount of fun I'm going to have once I leave the shackles of a secondary education behind me.*

"Do you like the tearoom, Bridget?" I asked, desperate to change the subject.

"What?" she said, looking at me in bewilderment. She seemed unsettled by the passionate kiss and had a look on her face that suggested she wanted nothing more than for me and Mary-Margaret to leave her and Julian alone so they could go wherever they had gone in the past to do whatever they had done. "What tearoom?"

"The tearoom you work in," I said. "What other tearoom would I be talking about? The tearoom in Dáil Éireann."

"Oh right," she said. "Sure we're splitting our sides all day, Cyril, with laughter. Ah no, I'm only teasing you, it's all right. The TDs are a smarmy bunch and most of them can't resist slapping your arse when you walk past them but they tip well because they know that if they don't, Mrs. Goggin will sit them at a rotten table the next day and they'll never get to ingratiate themselves with a minister."

"Was she the one who had the go at us in the Dáil that day?" asked Julian.

"It was, yeah."

"Christ, she was some piece of material."

"Ah no," said Bridget, shaking her head. "Mrs. Goggin is one of the good ones. She demands a lot from her staff but works harder than any of us at the same time. And she never asks anyone to do anything that she won't do herself. She has no airs and graces, unlike some in that building. No, I won't hear a word said against her."

"Fair enough," said Julian, chastised. "To Mrs. Goggin," he said, raising his pint.

"To Mrs. Goggin," said Bridget, raising hers too, and what choice did Mary-Margaret and I have but to join in.

"Do you have a Mrs. Goggin in the Bank of Ireland?" asked Julian.

"No, we have a Mr. Fellowes."

"And do you like him?"

"It's not my place to have an opinion on my superiors."

"Is she always this cheerful?" asked Julian of Bridget.

"The smell of piss is getting worse in here," she said in reply. "Should we sit somewhere else, do you think?"

We looked around but the Palace had grown busy with the work crowd and we were lucky to have a seat at all.

"There's nowhere else," said Julian, yawning a little as he made way into his next pint. "Christ, we're lucky enough to have kept this table for so long. The regulars would have every right to tip us off it."

"Do you mind?" said Mary-Margaret.

"Do I mind what?"

"Not taking the name of the Lord our God in vain."

"I don't mind in the slightest. Why, did he drop in to your desk on the foreign exchange at the Bank of Ireland, College Green, after his lunch to tell you that he doesn't like it?"

"Have you not read the Ten Commandments?" she asked.

"No, but I've seen the film."

"Bridget, this is beyond the beyonds. Are we to sit here all evening and listen to this gibberish?"

"For what it's worth," I said, feeling the room begin to spin a little, "the capital of Papua New Guinea is Port Moresby."

"What?" said Mary-Margaret, looking at me as if I was an imbecile before turning to Julian. "Is this fella soft in the head or what?" she asked.

"Do you suppose Yul Brynner has a baldie head or does he shave it for the films?" he said in reply.

"Bridget!"

"He's only having a laugh, Mary-Margaret," said Bridget. "Don't mind him."

"I don't like jokes about Yul Brynner," said Mary-Margaret. "Not when he gave such an impassioned performance as the Pharaoh Ramses. I'd prefer that we show him a little more respect, if you don't mind."

"Is he a friend of yours then?" asked Julian. "You have friends in high places all the same. God, Yul Brynner, Mr. Fellowes."

"The Lord giveth and the Lord taketh away," said Mary-Margaret, which didn't seem to me to have any bearing on what we'd just been talking about.

"But I'm the Lord," said Julian.

"What?" asked Mary-Margaret, confused now.

"I said I'm the Lord. I've been sent down by my father, who's also the Lord, to set people on the right path. What we want, the daddy and me, is for everyone to take their clothes off and just leap on each other like wild dogs in heat. Adam and Eve were naked, as you'll know if you've read the Book of The Beginnings of It All, chapter one, verse one: *And lo there was man and lo there was woman and neither of them had a stitch on and lo and lo the woman did lie down and lo, the man did do all kinds of mad stuff with the woman, who had big tits and was gagging for it.*"

"That's not in the Bible," insisted Mary-Margaret, leaning over the table, her hands clenching into fists as she prepared to rip Julian's throat from his neck.

"Well, maybe not the bit about the big tits but the rest of it is spot on, I think."

"Squirrel," she said, appealing to me. "Are you really friends with this person? Is he leading you astray?"

"It's *Cyril*," I barked.

"Sorry, what are we talking about?" asked Bridget, on whom the Snowballs were beginning to have an effect. "I was off in a world of my own. I was thinking about Cary Grant. Is it just me or is Cary Grant the most handsome man alive?"

"Present company excepted," said Julian. "Only a blind man could deny Cyril the Squirrel's charms. But while we're on the subject of ridiculously handsome man, has anyone seen who's over there at the bar?"

We all turned our heads to look and my eyes ran along the six or seven statues seated on their stools, staring at their reflections in the mirror behind the bar.

"Who?" asked Bridget, reaching forward and grabbing Julian's hand. "Who is it? I heard Bing Crosby is over for a golf championship. Is it him?"

"Look over there toward the end," said Julian, nodding in the direction of a portly man with a jowly face and dark hair who was seated on the last stool before the stained-glass division. "You don't recognize him, no?"

"He looks like Father Dwyer," said Mary-Margaret. "But a man like that wouldn't be caught dead in a place like this."

"He reminds me a bit of my Uncle Diarmuid," said Bridget. "But he died two years ago, so it can't be him either."

"It's Brendan Behan," said Julian, sounding amazed that we didn't recognize him.

"Who?" asked Bridget.

"Brendan Behan," he repeated.

"The writer?" I asked, the first time I had spoken in a long time, and Julian turned to me with an expression that suggested he'd forgotten I was even there.

"Of course the writer," he said. "Who else could I mean, Brendan Behan the milkman?"

"Is he the man who wrote that *Borstal Boy* thing?" asked Mary-Margaret.

"And *The Quare Fellow*," said Julian. "A great Dubliner."

"Is he not a terrible drunk?" she asked.

"Says the girl on her fourth Snowball."

"Father Dwyer said that was an awful play. And the book he wrote about the prison, Daddy wouldn't have it in the house."

"Mr. Behan! Mr. Behan!" cried Julian, turning around and waving his arms in the air, and, sure enough, the man turned around and looked at us, a disdainful expression dissolving into a cheerful one, perhaps on account of our youth.

"*Anseo*," he said. "Do I know you?"

"No, but we know you," said Julian. "My pal and I here are Belvedere boys and we value the written word even if the Jesuits don't. Would you join us at all? I'd consider it an honor to buy you a pint. Cyril, buy Mr. Behan a pint."

"Sold," said Behan, shuffling off his seat and walking over, taking a smaller stool from a nearby table to join our group and settling in between Mary-Margaret and myself, leaving Julian and Bridget next to each other. The moment he sat down he turned to Mary-Margaret and looked into her eyes before slowly glancing down to focus on her breasts.

"A fine pair," he said, looking around the table as a fresh round arrived and Julian took the money from my hand before handing it to the barman. "Small but not excessively so. Just right for the palm of a man's hand. I've always believed there's a direct correlation between the size of a man's hand, the circumference of his wife's tits and the happiness of their marriage."

"Saints alive!" said Mary-Margaret, looking as if she was about to faint.

"I read your book, Mr. Behan," said Julian before she could hit him.

"Please," said Behan, raising a hand while he smiled beatifically at us all. "No formalities, please. Call me Mr. Behan."

"Mr. Behan it is so," said Julian, laughing a little.

"And why did you read it? Did you have nothing better to do with your time? How old are you anyway?"

"Fifteen," said Julian.

"Fifteen?" asked Bridget, feigning shock. "You told me you were nineteen."

"I am nineteen," said Julian cheerfully.

"When I was fifteen," said Behan, "I was too busy pulling my mickey to be worrying about reading books. Fair play to you now, young fella."

"This is not my standard," said Mary-Margaret, making good headway through her fifth Snowball and being so appalled by the turn the conversation had taken that she had little choice but to order another.

"My father tried to get it banned," continued Julian. "He hates anything to do with Republicanism, so I had to see what all the fuss was about."

"Who's your father?"

"Max Woodbead."

"The solicitor?"

"That's the one."

"Who got his ear shot off by the IRA?"

"Yes," nodded Julian.

"Jayzuz," said Behan, shaking his head and laughing as he lifted the pint that Mary-Margaret had ordered and drank a good quarter of it without batting an eyelid. "You must have a few quid so. We'll keep you on call here all night."

"Can I ask you a question, Mr. Behan?" asked Bridget, leaning forward with a look on her face that suggested she was either going to ask where he got his ideas or whether he wrote by hand or on a typewriter.

"If it's will you marry me, the answer's no, but if it's will I take you out the alley for a quick ride, then it's yes," said Behan, and there was a long silence before he started laughing and took another mouthful of his Guinness. "I'm only pulling your leg, darling. Let's have a look at your legs anyway. Swing 'em out there. Come on, all the way; let the dog see the rabbit. Jayzuz, they're not bad all the same. You've two of them, which always helps. And they go up a fair way."

"They meet in the middle too," said Bridget, a line that made me, Julian and Mary-Margaret sit back in a mixture of admiration and disbelief. Julian looked as if he was about to rise off the seat in lust at the very idea.

"Is this your fella, it is?" Behan asked, nodding at Julian.

"I don't know yet," said Bridget, shooting Julian a sidelong glance. "I haven't made up my mind yet."

"I'm buttering her up," said Julian. "I'm giving her the old Woodbead charm."

"She'll be getting the old Behan charm if you're not careful. And what about you, young fella?" he asked, turning to me. "You look like you'd rather be anywhere else but here right now."

"Not at all," I said, not wanting to let Julian down. "I'm having a great time."

"You are not."

"I am."

"I am what?"

"I am, Mr. Behan?" I said, uncertain what he meant.

"I can see right through you," he said, leaning forward and looking me directly in the eyes. "You're like a wall of glass. I can see right into the depths of your soul and it is a dark cave filled with indecent thoughts and immoral fantasies. Good man yourself."

A long silence followed, during which everyone at the table, with the exception of Behan himself, felt awkward.

"Bridget," said Mary-Margaret finally, breaking the silence but slurring her words. "I think it's time I went home. I don't want to stay here any longer."

"Have another Snowball," said Bridget, who was getting as drunk as any of us, and she waved her finger over the table without even looking around and, to my astonishment, within about two minutes, a fresh round arrived.

"Was everything you said in your book true?" asked Julian. "In *Borstal Boy*, I mean."

"Christ, I hope not," said Behan, shaking his head as he lifted his next pint. "A book would be terrible boring if everything in it was true, don't you think? Especially an autobiography. I can't remember half of it anyway, so I presume I've slandered a few people along the way. Was that why your daddy wanted to have it banned?"

"He doesn't approve of your past."

"Do you have a sensational past, Mr. Behan?" asked Bridget.

"I have a few of them. Which part is it that he didn't like?"

"When you tried to blow up the Liverpool docks," said Julian. "The bit that landed you in Borstal in the first place."

"Your daddy isn't a sympathizer then?"

"He wants the Brits to come back in and take control," said Julian. "He's born and bred in Dublin but he's ashamed of the fact."

"Well, sure it takes all sorts to make a world. And what about you, young fella?" he asked, turning his attention to me.

"I don't care," I said. "I have no interest in politics."

"Tell him who your mother is," said Julian, nudging me in the arm.

"I don't know who my mother is," I replied.

"How can you not know who your mother is?" asked Behan.

"He's adopted," said Julian.

"And you don't know who your mother is?" he asked.

"No," I said.

"Then why did he—"

"Tell him who your *adoptive* mother is," said Julian, and I looked down at the table, focusing on a stain that I was trying to scrub clean with my thumb.

"Maude Avery," I said quietly.

"Maude Avery?" asked Behan, putting his pint down and staring at me with a mixture of disbelief and humor. *"Like to the Lark* Maude Avery?"

"That's the one," I said.

"One of the best writers Ireland has ever produced," he said, slapping his hand down on the table a few times. "Do you know, I think I remember you now. You were at the funeral. I was there myself."

"Of course I was at the funeral," I said. "She was my adoptive mother."

"She'll find her peace with the Lord," said Mary-Margaret in an evangelical tone that made me turn to her with a contemptuous expression on my face.

"I can see you still in the front row in a little dark suit," said Behan. "Sitting right there next to your father."

"His adoptive father," said Julian.

"Shut up, Julian," I said, a rare moment of displeasure from me to him.

"You gave one of the readings."

"I did," I said.

"And sang a song."

"No, that wasn't me."

"It was a beautiful tune. You had us all in tears."

"Again, not me. I can't sing."

"Yeats said it was like listening to a choir of angels. O'Casey said it was the first time he'd cried in his entire life."

"I didn't sing anything," I insisted.

"Are you aware of the esteem in which we all held your mother?"

"I didn't know her very well," I said, wishing that Julian hadn't brought this topic up.

"How could you not know her well?" asked Behan. "If she was your mother?"

"My adoptive mother," I insisted for the umpteenth time.

"When did she adopt you?"

"When I was three days old."

"Three years old?"

"Three *days* old."

"Three days old? Sure then she was your real mother, for all intents and purposes."

"We weren't close," I said.

"Have you read her books?"

"No," I said.

"None of them?"

"None of them."

"I've told him," said Julian, perhaps feeling a little excluded from the conversation.

"Not even *Like to the Lark*?"

"Why do people keep telling me to read that? No, not even *Like to the Lark*."

"Right so," said Behan. "Well, you should if you have even a small interest in Irish literature."

"That's exactly what I have," I said.

"Christ," he said, looking from Julian to me and back again. "Your father is Max Woodbead, your mother is Maude Avery. What about you girls? Who are your parents? The Pope? Alma Cogan? Doris Day?"

"I'm going downstairs to the jacks," I said, standing up and looking around the table. "I need a piss."

"We don't need to know," said Mary-Margaret.

"Fuck you," I said, before giggling uncontrollably.

"Do you know something," said Behan, smiling at her sweetly, "if you want to loosen yourself up a little, maybe you should go down there with him. I bet he'd find a way to sort you out. You've got to lose it sometime, Missy, and so does he. This pair on the other hand," he added, nodding toward Julian and Bridget. "They're well into it already, I'd say. Sure he's only short of dragging her under the table and sticking it to her right here."

I stepped over the back of the chairs before I could hear her response and stumbled downstairs, urinating long and furiously against the back wall and wishing that we had never come to the Palace Bar to begin with. How long was Behan going to sit with us? And why hadn't Julian told me that he had planned a foursome for the evening? Was he afraid that, had I known, I would never have come? The fact was, I would have anyway. It was easier to sit in front of him, watching him get up to all sorts, than it was to be left alone in our room at Belvedere College, imagining it.

When I came back upstairs, Behan was back on his barstool and

Bridget was rubbing Mary-Magdalen's arm while she dabbed at her eyes with a handkerchief.

"It's just such a vulgar question," she was saying. "What kind of a woman would do such a thing?"

"Don't upset yourself, Mary-Margaret," said Bridget. "It's an American thing, that's all. He probably heard about it over there."

"Cyril, your round I think," said Julian, nodding in the direction of the girls and rolling his eyes.

"We're not going to stay here all night, are we?" asked Bridget.

"I'm not staying another minute," said Mary-Margaret. "To be spoken to like that in public by a man such as him. My private parts are my own business and no one else's." She swung around and, showing a bit of life for the first time since she'd arrived, roared over toward the bar-stool, "They should send you back to Borstal and let you rot there, you filthy article!"

Behan's shoulders heaved with laughter and he raised his pint in salute while the rest of the men hooted and shouted lines like *That's you told now, Brendan* and *Fair fucks to the little bitch* and Mary-Margaret looked like she might burst out crying again or simply go on a rampage and tear the Palace Bar apart brick by brick.

"Dublin's a big place," said Julian, trying to hold the evening together. "We could go sit out on the grass at Trinity College and watch all the queers play cricket."

"Let's do that," said Bridget. "It's a nice evening out after all. And they always look so handsome in their all-whites."

"If the grass gets too cold, you can rely on me to keep you warm," he said, and she giggled again as we all stood up.

Finishing our drinks and making our way toward the door, I pushed ahead, trying to get closer to Julian, anxious to ask him whether we might be able to go somewhere, just the two of us, but as I did so I brushed Mary-Margaret's arm by mistake.

"Do you mind?" she snapped. "Manners cost nothing."

"Sorry," I said, frightened of looking at her in case she turned me to stone.

We stood on the street, Mary-Margaret and myself weighed down with our miserable faces while Julian and Bridget practically used each other as scaffolding.

"What was that you said, Cyril?" asked Julian, looking over at me while Bridget buried herself deep in his neck and, inexplicably as far as I could see, appeared to be biting him like some sort of drunken vampire.

"I said nothing."

"Oh right. I thought you said you were going to walk Mary-Margaret to her bus stop and then take the bus back to school yourself and you'd see me tomorrow."

"No," I said, shaking my head in bewilderment. "I didn't even open my mouth."

"I think you're trying to lead me into temptation," said Bridget, winking at him, and she pressed even closer to his body as I turned away and caught sight of a car streaking its way around the corner of Dame Street at an unnatural speed before turning in our direction, racing along Westmoreland Street and pulling in next to us with a screech of its brakes as the back doors were flung open.

"What the hell?" asked Julian, as two men in balaclavas leaped from the backseat, grabbed him roughly and dragged him to the rear of the car, where a third man had already opened the boot. Before anyone could protest, they pushed him inside, slammed it shut and jumped back into the car before speeding off again. The whole thing had taken no more than half a minute and as the car raced down O'Connell Street out of sight, all I could do was stand there and stare at it as it disappeared into the distance, uncertain what madness had just taken place before my eyes. It was only quickness of thought on my part that made me grab Mary-Margaret as she bent over and started vomiting on the pavement, half a dozen Snowballs making their way back into the world, but then she dragged me to the ground on top of her where we lay in a suspicious position until an old woman passing by hit me with her umbrella, saying that we weren't animals and if we didn't stop what we were doing that moment, she'd call the Gardaí and have us both locked up for public indecency.

Ransom

While the number of spelling and punctuation errors in the ransom note suggested a degree of illiteracy on the part of Julian's kidnappers, it was to their credit that it was unfailingly polite:

> **Hello. We have the boy. And we know his daddies a rich man and a traytor to the cause of a united Ireland so we want £100,000 or well put a bullet in his head.**
> **Await further instructions.**
> **Thank you & best wishes.**

Within hours, every news report in the country was leading with the kidnap, and a terrible photograph of Julian, looking angelic in his school uniform, was circulating throughout the media. Upon the instructions of the Garda Commissioner, little information was given out other than to confirm the identity of the fifteen-year-old boy, to admit that he was the son of one of Ireland's most prominent solicitors, and to confirm that he had been abducted in broad daylight in the middle of the city center. At a hastily arranged press conference, the Commissioner avoided any questions referring to the Irish Republican Army or the Border Campaign and simply said that no member of the Gardaí would rest until the boy was found, although as it was quite late in the day already they wouldn't start the search in earnest until the following morning at nine o'clock.

Bridget, Mary-Margaret and I were brought to Pearse Street Garda Station and when I asked why they were left sitting in the corridor while I was brought into a private room, I was told that this was to ensure that I didn't molest either of them on Garda premises. I'm not sure what it was about my appearance that made me seem like a pubescent rapist but for some peculiar reason I took this as a compliment. They gave me a cup of warm tea, heavily sweetened, and half a packet of Marietta biscuits, and only as my trembling began to diminish did I realize that I'd been shaking ever since the car had pulled away from Westmoreland Street with Julian in the boot. I was left alone for the best part of an hour and when the door finally opened, to my astonishment, my adoptive father marched in.

"Charles," I said, standing up and offering him my hand, which was his preferred form of greeting. I had tried to hug him only once, at Maude's funeral, and he had recoiled from me as if I had leprosy. It had been several months since I had seen him and his complexion was darker than before, as if he had just come back from a foreign holiday. Also, his hair, which had been turning a rather dignified shade of gray, had undergone a volte-face, for it was entirely black again. "What are you doing here?"

"I'm not quite sure," he said, looking round the room with the curiosity of someone who had never been in a police cell before, despite the fact that he had spent a couple of years brooding over his fraudulent tax activities in the 'Joy. "I was in the bank when the Gardaí arrived and, I must admit, when they walked into my office I got a bit of a fright. I thought I was in trouble again! But, no, it was just to tell me that you were being held here and they needed a parent or guardian to be present while they questioned you and I suppose I'm the closest thing to either one of those. How are you anyway, Cyril?"

"Not very good," I told him. "My best friend got kidnapped by the IRA a few hours ago and bundled away to God knows where. I don't even know if he's alive or dead."

"That's desperate," he said, shaking his head. "And did you hear that Seán Lemass is the new Taoiseach? What do you make of him anyway? I don't like the amount of oil he puts in his hair. It gives him an air of malevolence." He turned around as the door opened and an older Garda stepped inside, carrying a folder and a cup of tea, and introduced himself as Sergeant Cunnane.

"You're the boy's father?" he asked Charles as we all sat down.

"His adoptive father," he replied. "Cyril isn't a real Avery, as you can probably tell just by looking at him. My wife and I took him into our home when he was just a baby in an act of Christian charity."

"And is your wife on her way in to us too?"

"I'd be shocked if she was," he said. "Maude died a few years ago. Cancer. She beat it when it was in the ear canal but once it spread to her throat and tongue that was it. Curtains."

"I'm very sorry," said the sergeant, but Charles waved his sympathy away.

"Don't be, don't be," he said. "Time has been a great healer. And it's not as if I didn't have other options. Now, tell me, Sergeant, what's going on here exactly? I heard a little bit on the radio on the way in but I'm mostly in the dark."

"It seems that your son—"

"Adoptive son."

"It seems that Cyril here and his friend Julian left the grounds of Belvedere College earlier today in contravention of school rules for a rendezvous with two older girls in the Palace Bar, Westmoreland Street."

"Are those the two girls I saw sitting out there in the corridor? One of them was in floods of tears and the other looked bored out of her tits."

"Yes, that was them," said Sergeant Cunnane as I looked away in embarrassment.

"Which one was yours, Cyril?" he asked, turning to me. "Tears or tits?"

I bit my lip, unsure how to answer. Strictly speaking, neither of them was mine but if we had to be paired in any specific way, there could only be one accurate answer.

"Tears," I said.

He made a *tsk* sound and his face registered his disappointment. "Do you know," he said, turning to the sergeant again, "if I'd had to put money on it, I would have guessed that he'd say *tears*, but I really hoped for his own sake that he would say *tits*. Sometimes I wonder where I went wrong. It's not as if I brought him up to *respect* women."

"Mr. Avery," said the sergeant, doing well to keep his composure. "We have to ask your son . . . your Cyril . . . *Cyril*, a few questions. Can you just remain quiet while we get through this?"

"Of course, of course," he said. "Terrible business all the same. Who's this Julian fellow anyway? The one who got kidnapped?"

"My roommate," I told him. "Julian Woodbead."

He shot forward in his seat like a bullet. "Not Max Woodbead's young lad?"

"That's right, sir," said the sergeant.

"Ha!" he cried, bursting into an unexpected round of applause. "Funny story, Sergeant. So this fellow, Max Woodbead, was my solicitor a few years back. He wasn't as well known then as he is now, of course. He made his name off me, you might say. There was a time when we were the best of friends but I hold my hands up and admit that I made a few wrong decisions on the marital front and let's just say that I laid the old garden hose down on someone else's front lawn, Max's front lawn to be precise, and when he found out he gave me a right seeing-to." Charles slammed his fist down on the table, making us both jump and causing the sergeant's tea to spill over the side of his cup. "And do you know something, I never held it against him. Not for a moment. He was quite within his rights. But then after I went to prison, he bought my house at a knock-down price and threw my wife and adoptive son out on the street, and Maude was not a well woman. That was a terrible thing to do and I'll never forgive him for it. But having said that, it's an awful thing to lose a son. A parent should never have to bury a child. I had a daughter once but she only lived a few days and—"

"Mr. Avery, please," insisted the sergeant, rubbing his temples as if he had a headache coming on. "No one has lost anyone yet."

"Well, misplaced a son then, if you prefer. There's a quote coming back to me. Oscar Wilde, I think. Do you know it?"

"If you could just remain silent, sir, while I talk to Cyril?"

Charles looked baffled, as if he couldn't quite understand what the problem was. "But sure he's sitting right there," he said, pointing at me. "Ask him anything you like; I'm not stopping you."

"Thank you," said Sergeant Cunnane. "Now, Cyril, you're not in any trouble. But I need you to be honest with me, all right?"

"Yes, sir," I said, anxious to please. "But can I just ask you, do you think Julian is dead?"

"No, I don't," he said. "It's early days and we haven't even received details of where the kidnappers want the money to be sent. They'll hold on to him for a bit yet. He's their collateral, you see. There's no reason for them to harm him."

I exhaled in relief. The idea of Julian being murdered made me dizzy with terror; I wasn't sure that I'd be able to survive such an outcome.

"Now, Cyril, tell me why you went into town this afternoon?"

"It was Julian's idea," I said. "I thought we were going in to look at the shops or maybe go to the pictures but really he'd arranged to meet

Bridget and wanted me with him because she was bringing another girl to make up a foursome. I would have been happy to have gone to Stephen's Green to feed the ducks."

"Oh for God's sake," said Charles, rolling his eyes.

The sergeant ignored him as he wrote all this down. "And how did he know Miss Simpson?" he asked me.

"Who's Miss Simpson?"

"Bridget."

"Oh."

"Where did they meet?"

"In the tearoom at Leinster House," I said. "We went there on a school trip a couple of weeks ago."

"And they hit it off, did they?"

I shrugged. I wasn't sure how to answer this.

"Did this Bridget creature ever come to your school?" he asked. "Did she stay with Julian in your room at all?"

"She did not," I said, blushing. "I didn't even know that Julian had stayed in touch with her. They must have been writing to each other but he never said a word about it to me."

"We'll know about that soon enough," said Sergeant Cunnane. "We have an officer over there now doing a search. He should be back any time now."

I opened my eyes wide in panic and felt my stomach drop. "A search of what?" I asked.

"Of your room. In case there's anything there that might help us find Julian."

"Will you just be searching his side of the room?" I asked.

"No," he said, frowning. "Sure we don't know which side is his, do we? And things can get mixed up anyway. Sorry, Cyril, but we'll be looking through your things too. You've nothing to hide, have you?"

I glanced around for a bin; there was a possibility that I might be sick.

"Are you all right?" he asked me. "You've gone a bit pale."

"I'm grand," I said, my voice catching in my throat. "I'm just worried about him, that's all. He's my best friend."

"Ah Jesus, Cyril," said Charles, looking a bit disgusted. "Would you stop talking like that? It makes you sound like a right Nancy-boy."

"Have you ever seen Julian associating with strangers?" the sergeant asked me, ignoring my adoptive father's latest interruption.

"No," I said.

"Any strange men on the school grounds at all?"

"Only the priests."

"You mustn't lie to me, Cyril," he said, pointing a finger at me. "Because I'll know if you're lying."

"If that's true, then you must know that I'm not," I said. "I haven't
seen anyone."

"All right. The thing is we have reason to believe that the men who
seized Julian have been planning this for sometime. His father received death threats from the IRA after the piece he wrote in the *Sunday Press* a couple of months ago, saying that the supreme musical
composition of all time is 'God Save the Queen.'"

"I have something to admit," said Charles, leaning forward, a serious expression on his face now.

"What's that, Mr. Avery?" asked Sergeant Cunnane, turning to him
doubtfully.

"It's not something I've ever told anyone before but in this room,
which is a sort of confessional I suppose, I feel I can say it, particularly
since I'm among friends. The thing is, I think the Queen is a very attractive woman. I mean she's thirty-three now, I think, and that's
about five years older than I usually go for but I would make an exception in her case. There's something quite frisky about her, don't you
think? I'd say she takes a bit of warming up but once you've loosened
the corsets—"

"Mr. Avery," said the sergeant. "This is a serious business. Could I
ask you to stop talking, please?"

"Oh be my guest," said Charles, sitting back again and folding his
arms. "Cyril, answer the man before he has us all locked up."

"But he hasn't asked me anything," I protested.

"I don't care. Answer him."

I turned to the sergeant with a bewildered look on my face.

"Cyril, has anyone ever approached you to ask you where you and
Julian might be discovered at any particular time?"

"No, Sergeant," I said.

"And who would have known that you were going to the Palace Bar today?"

"I didn't even know myself until we got there."

"But Julian knew?"

"Yes, he had it planned."

"Maybe he tipped off the IRA," suggested Charles.

"Why would he do that?" asked Sergeant Cunnane, staring at him as if he was a complete moron.

"You're right. Makes no sense. Move on."

"And Miss Simpson, Bridget," continued the sergeant. "She must have known too?"

"I presume so."

"And what about her friend, Miss Muffet?"

"Miss Muffet?" I said, staring at him. "Mary-Margaret's surname is Muffet?"

"Yes."

I tried not to laugh. It didn't seem like her standard at all. "I don't know what she knew or didn't know," I said.

There was a tap on the door, a young Garda looked inside and the sergeant excused himself, leaving Charles and me alone together.

"So," he said, breaking the silence after a minute or two. "How have you been anyway?"

"Grand," I said.

"And school is going well?"

"Yes."

"Work is hell. I'm in there all day and half of the night. Did I tell you that I'm getting married again?"

"No," I said, surprised. "When?"

"Next week, actually. To a very nice girl named Angela Man-ningtree. A chest out to here and legs that go all the way down to the floor. Twenty-six years old, works in the civil service, Department of Education, or does until the wedding anyway. Quite intelligent too, which, actually, I rather like in a woman. You must meet her sometime."

"Will I be invited to the wedding?" I asked.

"Oh no," he said, shaking his head. "It will be quite a small affair.

Just friends and family. But I'll make sure to introduce you to her the next time you're on school holidays. I'm not quite sure what Angela's actual relationship to you will be. She won't be your stepmother or your adoptive stepmother. It's a mystery. I might consult someone in the legal profession for the actual term. Max is the best lawyer I know but I suppose now wouldn't be the right time. You have a cut above your eye, by the way. Were you aware of that?"

"I was, yes."

"Did one of the kidnappers do that to you as you battled valiantly to save your friend from their clutches?"

"No," I said. "An old woman hit me with her umbrella."

"Of course she did."

The door opened again and Sergeant Cunnane came back in, flicking through some pages that he held in his hand.

"Cyril," he said. "Did Julian have a paramour apart from this Bridget girl?"

"A what?" I asked.

"A girlfriend."

"No," I said. "Not that I know of anyway."

"The thing is, we've discovered a number of letters in your room, addressed to Julian. They're quite . . . suggestive in their way. Erotic, you know? Dirty stuff. About the way this girl feels about him and the things she wants to do to him. But the problem is they're unsigned."

I stared at the table and tried to think of anything that would stop my face from bursting into flames. "I don't know anything about them," I said.

"I tell you what," he said. "If Mrs. Cunnane had half the imagination that this girl has, I'd be taking early retirement."

Both he and Charles burst out laughing at this and I looked down at my shoes, praying that the interview would come to an end soon.

"Anyway, this all looks harmless enough," he said. "It probably has nothing to do with the kidnapping. Still, we have to follow up every lead." He turned the pages and read some more, his lips moving as his eyes flickered across the words and finally he frowned when he reached something he didn't understand.

"What does that mean, do you think?" he asked, showing the letter to Charles and pointing something out, and my adoptive father whispered something in his ear. "Christ alive," said the sergeant, shaking his head in disbelief. "I never heard of such a thing. What type of a woman would do something like that?"

"The very best type," said Charles.

"Mrs. Cunnane certainly wouldn't but then she's from Roscommon. Well, whoever this lassie is she wants to do it to Julian Woodbead."

"Ah to be young again," said Charles with a sigh.

"Can I go now?" I asked.

"You can," said Sergeant Cunnane, gathering his papers. "I'll be back in touch if I have anymore questions. And don't worry, young Cyril, we're doing everything we can to find your friend."

I left the room and looked up and down the hallway for Bridget and Mary-Margaret but they were nowhere to be seen and so I waited for Charles, who seemed surprised to see me still standing there, and we walked out onto Pearse Street together.

"Well, goodbye," he said, shaking my hand. "Until next time!"

"Have a good wedding," I told him.

"Very kind of you! And I hope they find your friend. I feel for Max, really I do. If I'd had a son and the IRA had kidnapped him, I'd be desperately upset. Goodbye for now, Cyril."

"Goodbye, Charles."

And with that I turned right and made my way across the road and over O'Connell Street Bridge, back in the direction of Belvedere College, where, I felt certain, further punishment would await me.

Ordinary Decent Sins

Having issued instructions as to where the £100,000 was to be left, the kidnappers signaled their disappointment at not receiving it by sending the little toe from Julian's left foot to the house on Dartmouth Square the following Tuesday. In an unnecessarily cruel gesture, they addressed the package to his younger sister Alice, who, upon opening the blood-soaked wrapping paper, probably ran screaming from the house with the same degree of hysteria as she had during that unexplained incident seven years earlier.

> We want our money,
> or next time it'll be something worse.
> Best regards.

In response, Max issued a statement to the effect that he couldn't raise the amount required in such a short space of time, an assertion that was flatly contradicted by the *Dublin Evening Mail*, who claimed that he had liquid assets worth more than half a million pounds that could be withdrawn from the bank with only twenty-four hours' notice. Elizabeth Woodbead, Julian's mother and my adoptive father's erstwhile lover, appeared on the television news with tears rolling down her face, begging for her son's release. She wore a chunky locket around her neck and some of the boys in my class speculated that it contained Julian's detached toe, a possibility that seemed too disgusting to contemplate.

Three days later, a second parcel arrived, left overnight outside the Woodbeads' front door, and this time they waited for the police to arrive before opening it. Inside was the thumb from Julian's right hand. Still Max refused to pay and at Belvedere College a group of us gathered in my room, the official place of pilgrimage for those with an interest in the case, to debate why he was being so callous.

"He's obviously a skinflint," said James Hogan, an uncommonly tall boy who was known to have a serious crush on the actress Joanne Woodward, with whom he had been conducting a one-way relationship by post for more than a year. "Imagine not caring that your own son has been mutilated!"

"It's hardly mutilation," said Jasper Timson, a keen piano-accordion player who had the room next to ours and who was constantly annoying me by finding reasons to talk to Julian on his own. On one occasion I had come into our room to discover the two of them sitting side by side on Julian's bed with a bottle of vodka between them, laughing so uproariously that my jealousy had nearly exploded into a fight. "And I think Julian can survive with nine toes and nine fingers."

"Whether he can survive or not is hardly the point, Jasper," I said, ready to attack him if he continued to speak in so thoughtless a fashion. "It must have been terrifying for him. Not to mention painful."

"Julian's a tough cookie."

"You barely know him."

"I know him quite well, as it happens."

"No, you don't. You're not his roommate."

"I know he's the kind of guy who if he was giving someone the kiss of life, he'd use tongue."

"Take that back, Timson!"

"Oh shut up, Cyril! You're not his bloody wife, so stop carrying on as if you are."

"Have you noticed that the body parts are getting bigger?" asked James. "I wonder is his thing bigger than his thumb."

"It's *much* bigger," I said, without thinking, and they all stared at me, uncertain how to react to this intimate announcement. "Well, we share a room," I said, blushing a little. "And anyway, things are always bigger than thumbs."

"Peter's isn't," said Jasper, referring to his own roommate, Peter Trefontaine, the curious curvature of whose thing Julian had remarked upon on that fateful afternoon in the Palace Bar. "It's tiny. And yet he's always flashing it around our room as if he's got something to be proud of."

The third delivery came exactly a week after the kidnapping and, in their cruelest gesture yet, the box contained Julian's right ear.

He looks just like his daddie now,

said a note written on the back of a John Hinde postcard, the one with the two redheaded children standing on either side of a donkey laden down with turf in the bog lands of Connemara.

But this is our last warning.
If we don't get our money, next time it'll be his head.
So pay heed to us now and have a pleasant weekend.

A second press conference was held, this time in the Shelbourne Hotel, and any sympathy that the gathered media had previously felt for Max had clearly vanished now that Julian had been deprived of three body parts. The general feeling, reflected in the country at large, was that here was a man who valued money over his own child and so angry was the nation that an account had been set up in the Bank of Ireland where people could donate their own money to help fund the ransom. Apparently it already stood at almost half the requested amount. I only hoped that Charles hadn't been put in charge of it.

"I have heard many criticisms of late regarding my actions in this affair," declared Max, sitting upright at the press conference and wearing a Union Jack tie for added provocation. "But it will be a cold day in hell when I give a penny of my hard-earned money to a group of vicious Republicans who believe their cause can be furthered by the kidnapping and torture of a teenage boy. If I was to give them what they want, it would only be used to buy guns and bombs which in turn would be employed against the British forces that quite rightly occupy the land north of the border and should be reinstated in the south. You can chop my son up into little bits," he added, somewhat unwisely, "and post him back to me in a hundred Jiffy bags and I still won't give in to your demands." There was a long pause as he shuffled a few papers on the desk before him—he had obviously veered away from the prepared script—before piping up again. "Obviously I don't want you to actually do that," he said. "I was speaking metaphorically."

While all this was going on, the greatest manhunt in the history of the state was being led by Sergeant Cunnane, and Julian had, within the space of a week, become perhaps the most famous person in Ireland. Gardaí in every county were following leads, checking farmhouses and deserted barns for anything that might give them a clue as to the whereabouts of the kidnappers but without success.

School continued as normal and the priests insisted that we pray for our missing classmate before each lesson, which meant eight prayers a day, not including our regular morning and evening benedictions, but it seemed as if God was either not listening or was on the side of the IRA. Bridget gave an interview to the *Evening Press* in which she said that she and Julian were on *the most intimate terms* and that she had never had a boyfriend who was so polite or so respectful as him. *Not once did he ever try to take advantage of me*, she said between sobs, and I expected her nose to start growing, so outrageous were her lies. *I don't think such impure thoughts ever crossed his mind.*

On the nights when I was left alone in our room, one hand behind my head, the other down the front of my pajamas bottoms, as I lay in

Julian's bed staring up at the ceiling, I began to come to terms with who I was. I had known from as far back as I could recall that I was different from other boys. There was something inside me that longed for the intimate friendship and approval of my peers in ways that others never did. It was a disease that the priests referred to from time to time as one of the most venal of all sins and they told us that any boy wicked enough to have lustful thoughts about another boy would surely go straight to hell and spend eternity there, burning in the raging fires as the Devil sat alongside him laughing and poking him with his trident. There were so many times that I had fallen asleep in that room, my mind filled with lurid fantasies about Julian, whose head lay on a pillow not ten feet from my own, his mouth half open as he dreamed, but now my fantasies were not sexual but gruesome. I thought of what his kidnappers might be doing to him at that moment, which body part they would sever next and how awful it must have been for him every time they took a saw or a pair of pliers to his body. I had always known Julian as a brave soul, a happy-go-lucky fellow who never let the world weigh him down, but what fifteen-year-old boy could possibly go through such an ordeal and come out the same person?

After much soul-searching, I decided to go to confession. I thought that perhaps if I prayed for his release and confessed my sins then God might see fit to take pity on my friend. I didn't go to the church at Belvedere, where the priests would have recognized me and probably broken the seal of the confessional to have me expelled. Instead, I waited until the weekend and made my way into town alone, heading toward Pearse Street and the large church that stood next to the train station.

I had never been there before and was a little overawed by the grandeur of the place. The altar was laid for the following day's Masses and candles were lit in rows of a dozen or more on brass stands. It cost a penny to light one and I threw two ha'pennies into the box before selecting one and placing it in the front row center, watching as the flame flickered for a few moments before settling. Kneeling on the hard floor, I said a prayer, a thing I had never done with any solemnity before. *Please don't let Julian die,* I asked God. *And please stop me from being a homosexual.* Only when I stood up and walked away did I realize that that had been two prayers, so I went back and lit a second candle, which cost me another penny.

There were a couple of dozen people scattered around the pews and staring into space, all of them old, and I walked past them looking for a confession box with a light on. When I found one, I stepped inside, closing the door behind me, and waited in the darkness for the grille to slide open.

"Bless me, Father, for I have sinned," I said quietly when it did, a gust of body odor rushing toward me with such force that I reared back and hit my head against the wall. "It has been three weeks since my last confession."

"What age are you, son?" asked the voice from the other side, which sounded quite elderly.

"Fourteen," I said. "I'll be fifteen next month."

"Fourteen-year-old boys need to go to confession more than once every three weeks," he said. "I know what you lads are like. Up to no good every minute of the day. Will you promise me that you'll go more often in the future?"

"I will, Father."

"Good lad. Now, what sins do you have to confess to the Lord?"

I swallowed hard. I had been going to confession fairly regularly since my first communion seven years earlier but not once had I ever told the truth. Like everyone else, I simply made up a collection of ordinary decent sins and rattled them off with little thought before accepting the obligatory penance of ten Hail Marys and an Our Father afterward. Today, however, I had promised myself that I would be honest. I would confess everything and if God was on my side, if God really existed and forgave people who were truly contrite, then he would recognize my guilt and set Julian free without any further harm.

"Father, over the last month I have stolen sweets from a local shop on six occasions."

"Holy God," said the priest, appalled. "Why did you do that?"

"Because I like sweets," I said. "And I can't afford them."

"Well, there's some logic to that, I suppose. And tell me, how did you do it?"

"There's an old woman who works behind the counter," I said. "And all she does is sit and read the newspaper. It's easy to take things without her noticing."

"That's a terrible sin," said the priest. "You know that's probably that good woman's livelihood?"

"I do, Father."

"Will you promise me never to do such a thing again?"

"I will, Father."

"All right then. Good lad. Anything else?"

"Yes, Father," I said. "There's a priest in our school who I don't like very much and in my head I call him The Prick."

"The what?"

"The Prick."

"And what in God's name does that mean?"

"Do you not know, Father?" I asked.

"If I knew, would I be asking you?"

I swallowed hard. "It's another word for a . . . you know, for a thing."

"A thing? What do you mean, a thing? What class of a thing?"

"A thing, Father," I said.

"I don't know what you're talking about."

I leaned in and whispered through the grille. "A penis, Father."

"Holy God," he repeated. "Did I hear you right?"

"If you thought I said a penis, then, yes, you did, Father."

"Well, that is what I thought you said. Why in God's name would you call a priest in your school a penis? How could he possibly be a penis? A man can't be a penis; he can only be a man. This makes no sense to me at all."

"I'm sorry, Father. That's why I'm confessing it."

"Well, whatever it is, just stop doing it. Call him by his proper name and show a bit of respect to the man. I'm sure he treats all the lads in your school well."

"He doesn't, Father. He's vicious and he's always beating us up. Last year he put a boy in the hospital for sneezing too loud in class."

"I don't care. You'll call him by his proper name or there'll be no forgiveness for you, do you understand me?"

"Yes, Father."

"Right then. I'm almost afraid to ask but is there anything else?"

"There is, Father."

"Go on so. I'll hold on to my chair."

"It's a bit delicate, Father," I said.

"That's what the confessional is for, son," he said. "Don't worry, you're not talking to me, you're talking to God. He sees everything and he hears everything. You can have no secrets from him."

"Do I have to say it then, Father?" I asked. "Will he not know anyway?"

"He will. But he wants you to say it out loud. Just for clarification purposes."

I took a deep breath. This had been a long time coming but here it was. "I think I'm a bit funny, Father," I told him. "The other boys in my class are always talking about girls but I never think about girls at all, I just think about boys, and I think about doing all sorts of dirty stuff to them like taking their clothes off and kissing them all over and playing with their things and there's this one boy and he's my best friend and he sleeps in the bed next to mine and I can't stop thinking about him all the time and sometimes when he's asleep I pull my pajamas down and I have a right go at myself and I create an unholy mess in the bed and even after I do it and think that I might be able to go to sleep I start thinking about other lads and all the things I want to do to them and do you know what a blowjob is, Father, because I started writing stories about the lads I like and particularly about my friend Julian and I started using words like that and—"

There was an almighty crashing sound from opposite me and I looked up, startled. The shadow of the priest in the darkness had vanished and in its place a beam of light was streaming in from up above.

"Is that you, God?" I said, looking up toward its source. "It's me, Cyril."

From outside the confessional, I heard shouts and opened the door to peep outside. The priest had fallen out of his box and was lying on the floor, clutching his chest. He must have been at least eighty years old and the parishioners were leaning over him, crying out for help as his face began to turn blue. One of the floor tiles had broken in two next to his head.

I looked down at him, my mouth open in bewilderment, and he slowly raised a gnarly finger and pointed it at me. His lips parted and I saw how yellow his teeth were as he began to dribble down his chin.

"Am I forgiven, Father?" I asked, leaning over him, trying to ignore the stench of his breath. "Are my sins forgiven?"

His eyes rolled in his head, his entire body gave one great convulsion, he let out a roar and that was it, he was gone.

"God bless us, Father's dead," said an elderly man who had been kneeling on the floor, supporting the priest's head.

"Do you think he forgave me?" I asked. "Before he croaked, I mean?"

"He did, I'm sure of it," said the man, taking my hand now and letting the priest's head fall rather hard against the marble floor, a tinny sound echoing around the church. "And he'd be happy to know that his last act on this earth was to spread God's forgiveness."

"Thank you," I said, feeling cheered by this. I left the church as the ambulance men made their way inside. It was an unusually sunny day and, truth be told, I did feel absolved, even if I knew that the feelings that I had hidden inside myself wouldn't be going away anytime soon.

The next morning, I awoke to the news that Julian had been found. A group of Special Branch officers had followed leads that led them to a farmhouse in Cavan and he was discovered locked in a bathroom while his three captors slept outside. One was killed in the ensuing fracas and the other two were under arrest. Missing a toe, a thumb and an ear, the rest of him was still intact and he had been taken to hospital to begin his recovery.

Had I been a person of more religious scruple, I might have believed that God had answered my prayers, but the fact was, before going to sleep that night I'd already committed a few more sins, so instead I put it down to good detective work on the part of An Garda Síochána. It seemed like the most convenient explanation to me.

1966 In the Reptile House

Like Soft Pillows

Although the strict routine was drearily repetitive at times, I found its familiarity strangely comforting. Every morning my alarm would sound at six o'clock precisely and I would engage in a little light onanism before rising at a quarter past. Being first in line to the shared bathroom meant there was no risk of the water turning cold and when I emerged, bare-chested and with a towel wrapped around my waist, there was Albert Thatcher, the young accountant who had the room next to mine, wearing a pair of Y-front briefs and a sleepy expression, which was not an entirely disagreeable way to start the day. Albert and I had been lodgers at the home of an elderly widow, Mrs. Hogan, on Chatham Street for more than a year, moving in only weeks apart, and we generally got along quite well. The building itself boasted a rather odd design. One flat had been purchased by Mrs. Hogan's late husband some thirty years earlier as a rental property and after his death a dividing wall had been removed to create two upstairs bedrooms. Mrs. Hogan and her son, Henry, however, lived in the house next door—the former entirely mute, the latter completely blind—and yet between them they monitored our comings and goings with all the efficiency of a government intelligence agency. Like conjoined twins, the two were never seen apart, Henry's arm permanently attached to his mother's as she led him to and from Mass every morning and up and down the street for his evening constitutional.

On the rare occasions when they ventured upstairs, looking for overdue rent, perhaps, or returning shirts that Mrs. Hogan ironed at a rate of tuppence for five, we would hear their four feet slowly ascending the staircase, the mute leading the blind, and Henry, who seemed to have no interest in anything, would ask the questions that his mother, an inveterate busybody, wanted answered.

"Mammy says there were strange noises coming from upstairs a week last Tuesday," he said once in a typical exchange while Mrs. Hogan nodded furiously, craning her neck to see whether we had marijuana plants growing in the living room or prostitutes asleep in one of our beds. "Mammy doesn't like strange noises. They unsettle her something awful."

"It can't have been us," I replied. "A week last Tuesday, I went to the pictures to see Steve McQueen in *The Sand Pebbles* and Albert was out dancing at the Astor Ballroom in Dundrum."

"Mammy says the noises kept her awake," Henry insisted, his eyes rolling in his head as they tried to latch onto something that might restore his view on the world. "Mammy doesn't like being kept awake. Mammy needs her sleep."

"Were you kept awake yourself, Henry?" asked Albert from where he was lying on the sofa reading *One Flew Over the Cuckoo's Nest*, and the unfortunate young man jumped in surprise, turning his head in the direction of the voice. Perhaps he'd been unaware that someone else was even in the room.

"When Mammy is awake, I am awake," he replied, offended now, as if we had accused him of being a bad son. "She's a martyr to the hemorrhoids. When they're acting up, neither of us can get a wink."

The noises in question were, most likely, not of my making at all but of Albert's, who was something of a lady's man and rarely went a week without bringing a girl home for what he called a bit of "slap and tickle, how's your father, say no more," which was torturous for me because his headboard was loosely fitted on the other side of the wall to my own and this meant that when he was riding a girl the endless banging would keep me awake, just as Mrs. Hogan's piles prevented her from sleeping. I had a bit of a crush on Albert too, which didn't help, but this was more a consequence of our daily proximity than anything else, for he wasn't particularly good-looking.

I left the flat every morning at half past seven to make my way toward the Department of Education on Marlborough Street, stopping only for a cup of tea and a fruit scone along the way, and was usually at my desk on the first floor by a quarter past eight. I had been working there for almost three years by now—ever since leaving Belvedere College in a blaze of mediocrity—thanks in part to the good offices of my adoptive father's third and now-estranged wife—this was how we determined I should refer to her in conversation—Angela, who had been a popular figure at the department until her marriage to Charles when, as the law dictated, she was forced into retirement.

Things had ended badly between the pair less than a year after their wedding when, in an act of uncharacteristic generosity, Charles had invited me to accompany them to the South of France for two weeks' holiday. I had met Angela only once in advance of the trip but from the moment we arrived in Nice we got along famously; so well, in fact, that I woke one morning to find her climbing into bed next to me, naked as the day she was born, and as I was naked too the entire scene turned into something of a West End farce. I cried out in surprise and, upon hearing the door open, ran headlong to the comfort of the wardrobe until Charles wrenched the doors open to find me cowering inside.

"The funny thing is, Cyril," he said in his most withering tone as I sat curled in the corner, my hands modestly covering my groin, "I'd have a lot more respect for you if I came in here and you were taking her up the Khyber Pass. But no, that's just never going to be you, is it? You just run and hide. A real Avery would never do that."

I said nothing, which seemed to disappoint him even more, and he turned his fury on Angela, who was still lying in bed, the sheet fallen to her waist exposing her breasts. She seemed bored with the whole scenario and was rotating one finger around her left nipple in an insouciant manner while whistling "You've Got to Hide Your Love Away" discordantly. An argument ensued, too tedious to recount, and the upshot was that on their return to Dublin they went their separate ways and an application was made in the London courts for a speedy divorce. (Charles had had the foresight to marry in England in anticipation of such an eventuality. His track record with marriage, after all, was not exemplary.) In the meantime, however, as I was lazing around and not doing very much with my time, Angela tried to make amends for embarrassing me by putting in a word on my behalf with her former employers. I received a phone call inviting me in for an interview, which came as something of a surprise as she had neglected to tell me, and without ever thinking for a moment that I would like to be a civil servant, I woke up one morning and that's exactly what I was.

The work itself was incredibly boring and my colleagues a little irritating, the engines of their days fueled by personal and political gossip. The office I worked in was large with a high ceiling, an old stone fireplace in the center of one wall and a portrait of the Minister, relieved of two of his chins, hanging above it. A desk was positioned in each of the four corners, their occupants facing the center of the floor, where a single table stood, supposedly for departmental meetings but, in reality, rarely used.

Our supposed leader was Miss Joyce, who had been working as a civil servant in the department since its foundation forty-five years earlier in 1921. She was sixty-three years old and, like my late adoptive mother Maude, was a compulsive smoker, favoring Chesterfield Regulars (Red), which she imported from the United States in boxes of one hundred at a time and stored in an elegantly carved wooden box on her desk with an illustration of the King of Siam on the lid. Although our office was not much given to personal memorabilia, she kept two posters pinned to the wall beside her in defense of her addiction. The first showed Rita Hayworth in a pinstriped blazer and white blouse, her voluminous red hair tumbling down around her shoulders, professing that "**ALL MY FRIENDS KNOW THAT CHESTERFIELD IS MY BRAND**" while holding an unlit cigarette in her left hand and staring off into the distance, where Frank Sinatra or Dean Martin were presumably pleasuring themselves in anticipation of erotic adventures to come. The second, slightly peeling at the edges and with a noticeable lipstick stain on the subject's face, portrayed Ronald Reagan seated behind a desk that was covered in cigarette boxes, a Chesterfield hanging jauntily from the Gipper's mouth. "**I'M SENDING CHESTERFIELDS TO ALL MY FRIENDS. THAT'S THE MERRIEST CHRISTMAS ANY SMOKER CAN HAVE— CHESTERFIELD MILDNESS PLUS NO UNPLEASANT AFTER-TASTE**" it said, and sure enough he appeared to be wrapping boxes in festive paper for the likes of Barry Goldwater and Richard Nixon, who, I'm sure, were only thrilled to receive them.

Miss Joyce sat in the corner to my right, the section of the room that got the best light, while in the corner to my left sat Miss Ambrosia, an incredibly vacuous and highly unfocused young woman of about twenty-five who liked to shock me by flirting outrageously and regularly recounting her multitudinous sexual exploits. She generally had at least five men on the go, everyone from barmen to dance-hall entrepreneurs, show jumpers to pretenders to the Russian throne, and had no shame in juggling them like some nymphomaniacal circus act. Every month without fail there would be a day where she would be found weeping at her desk, claiming that she had "spoiled herself" and that no man would ever want her now, but usually by teatime she would sit up suddenly, make a rush to the Ladies' toilets and return wearing a relieved expression, informing us that her Auntie Jemima had come to visit for a few days and she'd never been so happy to see her. This baffled me and on one occasion I inquired as to where her Auntie Jemima lived, for she seemed to make it her business to be in Dublin every month for a few days. My colleagues burst out laughing and Miss Joyce remarked that she too had once had an Auntie Jemima but that she had last visited during the Second World War and she didn't miss her one little bit.

The final member of our group, Mr. Denby-Denby, sat directly across from me and more often than not, when I looked up, I found him watching me with the intensity of a serial killer deciding how best to disembowel his victim. He was a rather flamboyant fellow in his mid fifties who wore colorful waistcoats and matching bow ties and, in speech and manner, conformed to the traditional stereotype of the homosexual, although, of course, he would never have admitted to such an orientation. He wore his hair in a bouffant style and it was a curious shade of sickly yellow, more a chartreuse than anything else, although his eyebrows were closer to maize. Every so often, with the same regularity as the visits of Miss Ambrosia's Auntie Jemima, he would come into work with his hair brighter than ever, practically luminescent, and we three would stare at it, trying not to laugh, and he would look back defiantly, daring us to say a word. I almost fell off my seat in amazement one afternoon when he mentioned the existence of a Mrs. Denby-Denby in Blackrock and a gaggle of little Denby-Denbys—nine of them! *Nine!*—whom he and his wife had produced with astonishing regularity from the mid 1930s into the late 1940s. The possibility of him engaging in coitus with a woman took me by surprise but the fact that he had done it on at least nine occasions—*nine!*—was almost too much for my mind to take in. It gave me hope for my own future.

"Here he comes," said Mr. Denby-Denby, sitting erect in his chair as

I strolled through the door that fine spring morning debuting a new jacket I had recently purchased in anticipation of the good weather. "Twenty-one years old and never been kissed. Do you know who you remind me of, Mr. Avery? Botticelli's *St. Sebastian*, that's who. Have you ever seen it? You must have. Have you, Miss Joyce? Hangs in the State Museum in Berlin. Stripped down to his skivvies and with half a dozen arrows poking out of his body. Absolutely divine. There's a lesser version by Il Sodoma but we won't speak of that."

I threw him an irritated look, my first of the day, and sat at my desk, unspooling the copy of the *Irish Times* that awaited me every morning and turning the pages for anything that might have relevance to our work. From the first day I had arrived in the department, I had resented Mr. Denby-Denby's presence, for although he was even more deeply closeted than I, his willingness to make little secret of his true sexual orientation both embarrassed and confused me.

"Look at those lips, Miss Joyce," he continued, putting a hand to his heart and fluttering it above his fuchsia waistcoat as if he was about to pass out in the throes of desire. "Like soft pillows. The type you, Miss Ambrosia, probably dream of buying in Switzer's if you can save up enough money."

"Why would I need to buy pillows, Mr. Denby-Denby?" asked Miss Ambrosia. "Sure as often as not my head's lying on someone else's."

"Oh, get her!" cried Mr. Denby-Denby, and I rolled my eyes. In the office next door there were three quiet gentlemen, Mr. Westlicott Sr., his son Mr. Westlicott, and his grandson Mr. Westlicott Jr., a family triumvirate who observed the same formality of address as we did, calling each other "Mr. Westlicott" at all times, and I rather hoped that someone in there would retire or get run over by a bus so I could transfer into their company. And perhaps one or other of them might adopt me and I could be a Mr. Westlicott too; I was sure to have more success with adoption the second time around than I'd had the first.

"Less tittle-tattle, please, and more work," said Miss Joyce, lighting up a Chesterfield (Red), but no one paid any attention.

"So tell us, Mr. Avery," said Mr. Denby-Denby, leaning forward now, his elbows on the table, his head balanced on his hands. "What mischief did you get up to over the weekend? Where does a handsome young puppy go these days when he's straining at the leash?"

"Actually, I went to a rugby match with my friend Julian," I replied, doing my best to assert my rugged masculinity. "And on Sunday I stayed home and read *A Portrait of the Artist as a Young Man.*"

"Oh, I don't read books," said Mr. Denby-Denby, waving this remark away as if I had expressed an eccentric interest in Middle Eastern symbolism or the origins of trigonometry.

"I'm reading Edna O'Brien," said Miss Ambrosia, lowering her voice lest any of the Mr. Westlicotts overheard her and reported her for vulgarity. "She's pure filth."

"Don't let the Minister hear you say that," said Miss Joyce, blowing a perfect O of smoke from her lips. It was impossible not to stare as it rose toward the light fitting and slowly evaporated into the air before sneaking its way in to pollute our lungs. "You know what he thinks about women who write. He won't have them on the curriculum."

"He doesn't like women who read either," said Miss Ambrosia. "He told me that reading gives women ideas."

"It does," said Miss Joyce, nodding her head fiercely. "I'm in full agreement with the Minister on that. My life would have been a lot easier if I had been allowed to stay illiterate but Daddy insisted that I learn to read. He was a very modern man, was Daddy."

"I absolutely *adore* Edna O'Brien," declared Mr. Denby-Denby, throwing his hands in the air in excitement. "If I wasn't a happily married man, I could get lost in that woman's body for years at a time. I declare before God and all that is good and holy that a more handsome woman was never bred from these shores."

"She left her husband, you know," said Miss Joyce, pulling a face. "What class of a person does something like that?"

"Good enough for him," said Miss Ambrosia. "I'm going to leave a husband one day too. I've always felt that my second marriage will be much more successful than my first."

"Well, I think it's shocking," said Miss Joyce. "And her with two children to look after."

"Whenever I look at Edna O'Brien," continued Mr. Denby-Denby, "I get the impression that she wants to put every man she meets across her knee and give them a good spanking until they show her the proper respect. Oh, to be the bare bottom beneath that alabaster palm!"

Miss Ambrosia spat a little of her tea out and even Miss Joyce allowed herself something approaching a smile.

"But *anyway*," he said after a moment, shaking his head to dismiss these ideas. "You were telling us about your weekend, Mr. Avery. Please tell me that it wasn't all rugby and James Joyce."

"I could make something up if you like," I told him, putting down my newspaper and looking across at him.

"Go on so. I'd love to know what sordid little fantasies come to life in that mind of yours. I bet they'd make a Gypsy blush."

He had me there. If I had actually told him any of the fantasies that kept me awake at nights, the two women might have fainted and he might have leaped across the room in lust. I'd killed a priest, after all, the last time I recounted the things that I wanted to do, and had no desire to have anymore blood on my hands.

"When I was twenty-one," continued the ridiculous popinjay, looking toward the fireplace and attempting what can only be called a faraway look, "I was out on the town every night of the week. There wasn't a girl in Dublin who was safe when I was nearby."

"Really?" asked Miss Ambrosia, turning to him with an expression that mirrored my own.

"Oh I know what you're thinking, Missy," said Mr. Denby-Denby. "You look at me now and you think how could that slightly plump man in the autumn of his years, albeit with a magnificent head of blond hair, ever have been attractive to girls of my age but I promise you, if you could have seen me in my youth I was quite the gallant. There was many a girl who threw her cap in the ring for me. *Lock up your daughters*, that's what the people of Dublin used to say when they saw Desmond Denby-Denby coming. But those days are gone now, of course. For every aging butterfly, there's a young caterpillar. You, Mr. Avery, are that young caterpillar. And you must enjoy your larval period, for it will come to an end all too soon."

"What time does the Minister have to be in the Dáil today?" I asked Miss Joyce, hoping to bring this conversation to an end, and she opened her diary, running a finger down the left-hand side of the page as she tapped the ash from her cigarette into her Princess Grace of Monaco ashtray.

"Eleven o'clock," she said. "But I have Miss Ambrosia down to accompany him this morning."

"I can't," said Miss Ambrosia, shaking her head.

"Why ever not?" asked Miss Joyce.

"Auntie Jemima."

"Ah," said Miss Joyce, and Mr. Denby-Denby rolled his eyes.

"I'll do it," I said. "It's a sunny day. I'd be happy to get out of the office."

She shrugged. "Well, if you're certain," she said. "I'd go myself only I don't actually want to."

"Perfect," I said, smiling. The advantage of accompanying the Minister to the Dáil was a trip in the ministerial car to Leinster House, where I could leave him alone with his cronies and wait until the minute he entered the chamber for his afternoon nap, when I could be out the door and straight to the pictures, followed by a pint or two with Julian in the Palace Bar or Kehoe's. The perfect day.

"I think I should mention," said Miss Ambrosia after a rare few minutes of silence when some actual work might have been getting done, "I'm giving serious consideration to having relations with a Jew."

I was taking a sip from my mug of tea when she said this and nearly spat it across my desk. Miss Joyce raised her eyes to heaven, shook her head and said, "Saints preserve us," while Mr. Denby-Denby simply clapped his hands and said, "Wonderful news, Miss Ambrosia, there's nothing more delicious than a little Jew boy. What's his name anyway? Anshel? Daniel? Eli?"

"Peadar," said Miss Ambrosia. "Peadar O'Múrchú."

"Jesus wept," replied Mr. Denby-Denby. "That's about as Jewish as Adolf Hitler."

"Oh for shame!" cried Miss Joyce, slapping a hand down on her desk. "For shame, Mr. Denby-Denby!"

"Well, it's true, isn't it?" he said, not looking the least bit guilty before turning back to Miss Ambrosia. "Tell us all about him, ducky. What does he do, where does he live, what does he look like, who are his people?"

"He's an accountant," said Miss Ambrosia.

"Well of course he is," said Mr. Denby-Denby, waving this away. "I could have guessed that. They're *all* accountants. Or jewelers. Or pawnbrokers."

"He lives with his mother off Dorset Street. He's neither tall nor short but he has a lovely head of curly black hair and he's a great kisser."

"Sounds divine. I think you should do it, Miss Ambrosia. And I think you should take photographs and bring them in for us all to see. Is he big in the downstairs department, do you think? Cut, of course, but that's not his fault. That's parents mutilating a boy before he even has a say in the matter."

"Ah now, this is getting beyond the beyonds," said Miss Joyce, raising her voice. "We need to tame the conversation in this office, we really do. If the Minister came in and heard us—"

"He'd see that we were just concerned for Miss Ambrosia and hoping to steer her in the right direction," said Mr. Denby-Denby. "What do you think, Mr. Avery, should Miss Ambrosia have carnal relations with her curly-haired Jew? A big cock makes all the difference, don't you think?"

"I really don't care," I said, standing up and making my way to the door so no one could see how red my face had gone. "Now, if you'll excuse me, I'll be back in a moment."

"Where do you think you're going?" asked Miss Joyce. "You've only been here ten minutes."

"Call of nature," I said, disappearing down the corridor and into the Gents, which was mercifully empty, and I stepped into a cubicle to pull down my pants and examine myself carefully. The rash had just about cleared up, thankfully. The redness had dissipated and the itching had gone away at last. The cream the doctor had given me had worked a treat. (*You must be wary of dirty girls*, he had told me as he buried his face in my crotch, using a pencil to lift my flaccid penis from where it hung in disgrace. *Dublin is full of dirty girls. Find yourself a nice clean Catholic wife if you can't control your lust.*) I flushed and stepped outside again to wash my hands and there was Mr. Denby-Denby standing by one of the sinks, arms folded, giving me one of those smiles that suggested he could see right through to the depths of my soul, a place even I did not like to visit very often. I glanced at him for a moment, said nothing, and turned on the taps so forcefully that they splashed up on us both.

"Did I see you out and about on Saturday night?" he asked me without any preamble.

"I beg your pardon?" I said.

"Saturday night," he repeated. "I was taking a walk along the banks of the Grand Canal and happened to pass a little establishment that I've heard rumors about over the years. Rumors to the effect that it is a place frequented by gentlemen of a certain perverted disposition."

"I don't know what you mean by that," I said, not looking up at the mirror.

"Mrs. Denby-Denby's older sister lives on Baggot Street, you see," he continued. "And I was on my way over to drop off her pension. The poor dear can't get out anymore. *Arthritis*," he added, mouthing the word for no discernible reason. "We'll say nothing."

"Well, I don't know who you think you saw but it certainly wasn't me. I was out with my friend Julian on Saturday night. I already told you that."

"No, you said you went to a rugby match with him in the afternoon but that you spent the evening at home reading. I know next to nothing about sporting events but I know that they don't take place under cover of dark. It's other things that happen then."

"Sorry, yes," I said, growing flustered now. "That's what I meant. I was at home reading *Finnegans Wake*."

"It was *Portrait of the Artist* earlier. If you're going to make up a book, Cyril, don't make one up that no one with even an ounce of sense would bother reading. No, this was almost midnight and—"

"You were bringing your sister-in-law's pension over at midnight?" I asked.

"She stays up very late. She's a martyr to the insomnia."

"Well, you must be mixing me up with someone else," I said, trying to get past him, but he swept to the left and right like Fred Astaire as he blocked my path.

"What do you want from me, Mr. Denby-Denby?" I asked. "Julian and I went to the game in the afternoon, then we went for a few drinks. Afterward, I went home and spent an hour or two reading." I hesitated and wondered whether I could get the next phrase out. I'd never said it aloud before. "And then, if you must know, I went out for dinner with my girlfriend."

"Your wha'?" he asked, raising an eyebrow in amusement. "Your girlfriend, is it? This is the first we're hearing about that."

"I don't like to bring my private life into work," I replied.

"So what's her name, this girlfriend of yours?" he asked.

"Mary-Margaret Muffet," I said.

"Is she a nun?"

"Why would I be dating a nun?" I asked, bewildered.

"I'm joking," he said, holding his palms out before me and the scent of lavender wafted in my face. "And what does Little Miss Muffet do, if you don't mind me asking? When she's not sitting on her tuffet. Or yours."

"She's an assistant on the foreign exchange desk at the Bank of Ireland, College Green."

"Oh, the glamour. Mrs. Denby-Denby worked in the office at Arnott's when I first met her. I thought that was the height of it but it looks as if you've set your sights on banking over trade. You're like one of those spinsters straight out of Mrs. Gaskell. It won't make it any easier though, you know."

"It won't make *what* any easier?" I asked.

"Life," he said with a shrug. "Your life."

"Can't you just let me pass?" I asked, looking him in the eye now.

"I only say it because, believe it or not, I care about your welfare," he said, moving to the side now and following me out the door. "I know it was you that I saw, Cyril. You have a very distinctive gait. And I'm just saying that you need to be very careful, that's all. The Gardaí have a habit of raiding that establishment when they're in the mood for a little mindless persecution and if you were to get yourself into trouble, well I don't need to tell you that your position here at the department would be in the most serious jeopardy. And just think what your mother would say!"

"I don't have a mother," I told him, slipping out the side door to the car pool, where I saw the Minister approaching and raised a hand to greet him. As we drove off, I looked back toward the front door of the building and saw Mr. Denby-Denby watching me go with a pitiful expression on his face. From a distance, his hair looked brighter than ever, like a beacon leading a sinking ship to safety.

The Great Shriveling

The circumstances of my reacquaintance with Mary-Margaret Muffet were neither romantic nor propitious. A journalist from the *Sunday Press* by the name of Terwilliger was writing a weekly series on crimes that had shocked Ireland since the foundation of the State and he wanted to include an article on the kidnapping and mutilation of Julian Woodbead, perhaps the most infamous of all offenses in recent years since it had involved a minor. He found contact details for the four main participants in the drama, excluding the two remaining kidnappers themselves, of course, who had been incarcerated in the 'Joy since 1959, but only Mary-Margaret and I were available to talk to him.

At the time, Julian was traveling through Europe with his latest girlfriend, Suzi, a ghastly piece of high-class ornamentation whom he'd picked up while walking along Carnaby Street in search of a Homburg similar to the one that Al Capone had favored. I had met her only once, when they had come back to Dublin for a weekend to visit Max and Elizabeth. She bit her nails constantly and chewed on pieces of roast beef before spitting the gnarled remains into a see-through bag that she carried with her for just that purpose. She didn't swallow, she told me, as she was far too committed to her modeling career to risk anything entering her stomach.

"That's not strictly speaking true," said Julian with a predictable smirk, and I pretended not to have heard him. Instead, I asked her whether she knew Twiggy and she rolled her eyes.

"Her *name*," she said, as if I was the most ignorant creature on the face of the planet, "is Lesley."

"But do you know her?"

"Of course I know her. We've worked together a few times."

"What's she like?"

"Pleasant enough, I suppose. Too nice to have any lasting career in this industry. Believe me, Cecil, this time next year no one will remember her name."

"It's Cyril," I said. "And what about the Beatles? Do you know them?"

"John's a friend," she replied with a shrug. "Paul isn't, not anymore, and he knows why. George was my last before Julian."

"Your last what?" I asked.

"Her last fuck," said Julian, taking the grisly remains of his girl-friend's dinner and placing it on the table behind us. "Can you believe it? George Harrison walked in the door just before me!"

I tried not to throw up.

"No, there was someone else," said Suzi nonchalantly.

"What? Who? I thought I came next."

"No, you couldn't do it, remember?"

"Oh yes," he said, grinning a little. "I forgot."

"Couldn't do it?" I asked, intrigued. "Why not?"

"Crabs," he said with a shrug. "Picked them up from God knows who. Suzi wouldn't come anywhere near me until I had a clean bill of health."

"Well of course I wouldn't," she said. "What do you take me for?"

"And what about Ringo?" I asked, wanting to move away from Ju-lian's crabs. "Where do you stand on him?"

"I don't stand anywhere on him," she said, waving his name away like an insolent fly that was buzzing around her face. "I'm not sure he's worth standing on. I mean all he does is play the drums. A trained monkey could do that."

The conversation continued in this way for sometime—Suzi had strong views on Cilla Black, Mick Jagger, Terence Stamp, Kingsley Amis and the Archbishop of Canterbury, four of whom were former lovers of hers—and by the end of our night out, I disliked her even more than I had disliked the idea of her, which previous to that evening had not even seemed possible to me.

Naturally, I didn't tell Mr. Terwilliger any of this when he phoned, simply mentioning that Julian was out of the country and uncontacta-ble. He was very disappointed—Julian was the star turn after all—and said that this was the second piece of bad news he'd received, for Ju-lian's former paramour, Bridget Simpson, wasn't available either.

"She's probably forgotten all about him anyway," I said. "I daresay she's been through quite a few Julians since then."

"Actually, no," said the journalist. "Miss Simpson is dead."

"Dead?" I repeated, sitting up abruptly in my office chair in the same way that Miss Ambrosia did whenever she realized that her Auntie Jemima had come to visit. "How dead? I mean how did she die?"

"She was murdered by her driving instructor. Apparently she wouldn't play with his gear stick, so he drove the pair of them into a wall out near Clontarf. She died on impact."

"Jesus," I said, uncertain how to respond to this. I hadn't liked her very much but that had been years ago. It seemed like a nasty end.

"So that just leaves you and Miss Muffet," he said.

"Who?" I asked.

"Mary-Margaret Muffet," he said, and I could tell that he was reading the name from a piece of paper. "She was your girlfriend at the time, am I right?"

"She was not!" I cried, even more shocked by this insinuation than I had been by the news of Bridget's death. "I barely knew the girl. She was a friend of Bridget's, that's all. I don't even know how they knew each other. She came along to make up a foursome."

"Ah right," he said. "Well, she's agreed to meet with me. Do you think you'd be able to come along at the same time? It would make more sense if I could get a conversation going between the pair of you, a reminiscence of what happened on the day in question, you know how it is. Otherwise she'll tell me one thing when I'm talking to her and you'll say something completely different and the reader won't know who to believe."

I wasn't sure that I wanted to have any part of it but didn't like the idea of Mary-Margaret, of whom I had only a vague memory, having the spotlight all to herself and making potentially slanderous remarks about Julian to the national press, so I agreed to meet with them. When I arrived on the appointed afternoon, I shook hands with her warily but, to my relief, our joint recollections of that day in 1959 did not differ very much. We told Terwilliger everything we remembered, although Mary-Margaret made it clear that she was unwilling to discuss the surprise involvement of Brendan Behan in the incident for the simple reason that the man was a vulgarian and she wouldn't like his words to be repeated in a newspaper where impressionable children might stumble upon them.

Afterward, it seemed polite to ask whether she wanted to join me for a cup of coffee and we made our way toward Bewley's Café on Grafton Street, taking one of the booths by the wall as we tried our best to make conversation.

"I generally don't like Bewley's," said Mary-Margaret, pulling a handful of napkins from the dispenser on the table and placing them on the seat beneath her bottom to avoid any contamination. She wore her hair in a bun at the back of her head and, although she was dressed like a representative from the Legion of Mary, there was no denying that she was pretty enough if you liked that sort of thing. "The seats can be terrible sticky. I don't think the girls clean them after people drop their crumbs. That wouldn't be my standard at all."

"But they do make a good cup of coffee," I said.

"I don't drink coffee," she said, taking a sip from her tea. "Coffee is for Americans and Protestants. Irish people should drink tea. That's how we were brought up after all. Give me a nice cup of Lyons and I'm content."

"I don't mind the occasional cup of Barry's myself."

"No, that's from Cork. I only drink Dublin tea. I wouldn't risk something that's made the journey up on the train. They do a lovely cup of tea in Switzer's café. Have you ever been there, Cyril?"

"No," I admitted. "Why, is that somewhere you go a lot?"

"Every day," she said, beaming with pride. "It's very convenient for those of us employed by the Bank of Ireland on College Green and it has a more elite clientele, which seems only right and proper. I don't think the bank directors would be at all happy if they saw me in any old street café."

"Right," I said. "Well, you're looking great anyway. That was a mad day all the same, wasn't it? The day Julian got kidnapped."

"It was very disturbing," she replied, shivering a little, as if someone had just walked over her grave. "I had nightmares about it for months afterward. And when they started delivering his body parts—"

"That was terrible," I agreed.

"How is he anyway?" she asked me. "Are you still in touch?"

"Oh yes," I said, quick to assert our ongoing alliance. "He's still my best friend. And he's very well, thanks for asking. He's in Europe at the moment but he sends me the occasional postcard. I'll see him when he gets back. We phone each other sometimes too. I have his parents' phone number here, look." I took out my address book and flicked through to the Ws, displaying the Dartmouth Square address that had once been mine. "He has my number too. And if he can't get me he always leaves a message with my flatmate and he passes it on."

"Settle down, Cyril," she said, frowning a little. "It was just a question."

"Sorry," I replied, feeling a little embarrassed by my enthusiasm.

"He got over it then?" she asked.

"Got over what?"

"The kidnapping, of course."

"Oh yes. He's never been the type to let something like that get him down."

"And the loss of a toe, finger and ear?"

"He still has nine of each. Well, not nine ears obviously. He only has one ear left but it's more than some people have, I suppose."

"Who?" she asked, frowning at me. "Who has less ears than that?"

I thought about it. No one sprang to mind. "His father only has one ear too," I said. "They have that in common at least. The IRA shot one of them off a few months before the kidnapping,"

"They're a terrible shower, the IRA," she said. "I hope you don't have anything to do with them, Cyril Avery?"

"I do not," I said, shaking my head quickly. "I don't have any interest in things like that. I'm not political at all."

"I suppose he walks with a limp, does he?"

"Who?"

"Julian. And him with only nine toes. I suppose he walks with a limp?"

"I don't think so," I said, uncertain whether he did or not. "If he does, I've never spotted it. To be honest, the only thing that really bothers him is the ear. Obviously his hearing is only half as good as it could be and he looks a bit odd without it, but he grew his hair long and it covers the right-hand side of his head, so no one really notices. He still looks amazing."

Mary-Margaret gave a little shudder. "The directors of the Bank of Ireland don't allow any of their male employees to wear their hair long," she said. "And I don't blame them. It looks a bit too Nancy-boy for me. And I prefer a man with two ears. One ear wouldn't be my standard at all."

I nodded and glanced around the café for the nearest fire exit and to my horror caught the eye of a student priest sitting with two older priests a few seats away from us, drinking a Coca-Cola and eating an Eccles cake. I recognized him from the back row of the Metropole Cinema where I had sat next to him during a screening of *A Man for All Seasons* a few nights earlier. He'd placed his overcoat on his lap and I'd given him a hand-job in the dark. The smell of it after he came was only rancid and people had started to turn around and stare at us, so we had no choice but to make a run for it just as Richard Rich was taking the stand to betray Thomas More. We both flushed red as we saw each other and turned away.

"What's the matter with you?" asked Mary-Margaret. "All the blood has rushed to your face."

"I have a bit of a cold," I told her. "The fever comes and goes."

"Don't be giving me any of your germs," she said. "I don't want to come down with anything. I have my job to think of."

"I don't think it's catching," I said, taking a sip from my coffee. "I was very sorry to hear about Bridget, by the way," I told her. "You must have been very upset."

"Well," she said in a firm voice, putting her cup down and looking directly at me. "Naturally, I was very sorry to hear that she had died and the circumstances were, of course, appalling but the truth is that I had cut my ties with her sometime before."

"Oh right," I said. "Did you have a falling-out of some sort?"

"Let's just say that we were very different types." She hesitated for a moment but then seemed to throw caution to the wind. "The truth is, Cyril, Bridget Simpson was a tarty piece and I didn't care to be around that sort of element anymore. I lost track of the number of men with whom she had relations. I said to her, *Bridget*, I said, *if you don't clean up your act, you'll meet a terrible end*, but she didn't listen to me. She said that life was for living and that I was too uptight. Me! Uptight! Can you imagine it? Sure I only live for a good laugh. Anyway, it was when she started involving herself with married men that I said enough was enough. I put my foot down and told her that I would have nothing more to do with her if she carried on with that sort of malarkey. The next thing I heard she'd been killed in a car crash in Clonmel."

"I heard it was Clontarf," I said.

"Well, one of the Clons. I went to her funeral, of course, and lit a candle for her. I told her poor mother that she should take comfort in the fact that Bridget had taught us all a great lesson. That if you live a dissolute life, then you can expect to meet a horrible death."

"And how did she take that?"

"The poor woman was so grief-stricken she couldn't say a word. She just stared at me in shock. She probably blamed herself for bringing her daughter up without any sense of decency."

"Or maybe she thought you were being a little insensitive?" I suggested.

"No, I don't think it was that at all," she said, appearing baffled by this remark. "Read your Bible, Cyril Avery. It's all in there."

We sat in silence for a few minutes and I noticed the student priest standing up and making his way toward the doors, throwing an anxious look in my direction as he fled. For a moment, I felt a certain sympathy for him and, just as quickly, I felt it for myself too. Then I wondered whether he was signaling that he was off to the pictures and if he was, how quickly I could escape Bewley's Café and follow him.

"Can I ask you a question, Cyril?" asked Mary-Margaret, and I looked back at her, trying to stifle a yawn. I wondered why I hadn't just gone back to the office after the interview and avoided all of this.

"You can," I said.

"Where do you go to Mass?"

"Where do I go to Mass?"

"Well, you have two ears on you anyway even if your pal doesn't. Yes, where do you go to Mass?"

I opened my mouth in surprise, searched for an answer, couldn't find one and so closed it again. The truth was that I never went to Mass. The last time I had been in a church was seven years earlier when I'd killed a priest by telling him all the perverted thoughts that went through my head.

"Mass," I repeated, hedging for time. "Are you a big Mass-goer yourself then?"

"Of course I am," she said, frowning so hard that her forehead divided into five distinct lines, like the staff on a piece of sheet music. "What do you take me for? I go to Baggot Street every day. They do a lovely Mass there. Have you ever been to the church on Baggot Street?"

"No," I said. "Not that I can recall."

"Oh you must go sometime. There's a wonderful atmosphere to the place for one thing. The scent of incense mixed with the smell of dead bodies is only breath-taking."

"Sounds lovely."

"It is. And Father gives a wonderful sermon. He's a real fire-and-brimstone type, which I think is just what Ireland needs right now. There's all sorts out there these days. I see them in the bank all the time. Students coming in from Trinity College wearing next to nothing, their hands in the backs of their boyfriends' denim jeans. You don't own any denim jeans, do you, Cyril?"

"I have one pair," I said. "But they're a bit long on me. I don't wear them very often."

"Throw them away. No man should be seen in a pair of denim jeans. Of course, I see the whole world from my position on the foreign exchange desk at the Bank of Ireland, College Green. I had a divorced woman from England in last week, would you believe? I made my disapproval clear, I don't mind telling you. And there was a young man in only yesterday going around more like a girl than a boy. Oh, the way he spoke! He was one of those, of course," she added, bending her right hand at the wrist. "I refused to serve him. I told him he could go to the Allied Irish Bank if he wanted his money changed. They cater to that class of person there. He caused such a fuss. Do you want to know what he called me?"

"Not really," I said.

"A b-i-t-c-h," she said, leaning forward and spelling the word out quietly. She shook her head then and looked away. "I'm still not the better of it," she added after a moment. "Anyway, I asked the security guard to throw him out. And do you know what he did then?"

"No," I said. "Since I wasn't there."

"He started crying! He said his money was as good as anyone's and he was sick of being treated like some second-class citizen. I told him that if I had my way he wouldn't be a citizen at all. Of course, we all started laughing at him then, the customers too, and he sat down on one of the benches with a miserable look on his face as if *we* were in the wrong! They should lock all the Nancy-boys up, if you ask me. Put them out on one of the islands off the west coast where they can do no harm to anyone but each other. But anyway, Cyril, what we were talking about? Oh yes, where do you go to Mass?"

"Westland Row," I told her, for want of a better answer. It was hard enough to keep up with her list of prejudices without trying to think of a Dublin church of which she might approve.

"Oh, that's a beautiful building," she said, surprising me by not dismissing it for being too tall, too wide or having too many letters in its name. "A lovely bit of stonework in there. It's on my list every year on Holy Thursday when I do my *Visita Iglesia*. I wonder if I've ever seen you in there?"

"Anything is possible," I said. "But most things are unlikely."

"And tell me this and tell me no more," she added, taking another sip from her tea and pulling a face. It seemed that even the tea was conspiring against her now. "What do you do with yourself?"

"I'm sorry?"

"I'm assuming that you have a good job somewhere?"

"Oh right, yes," I said, telling her about my work at the Department of Education, and her eyes lit up immediately.

"Now, that's a great career to have," she said. "Almost as good as working in a bank. You simply can't go wrong with the civil service. They can't fire you for one thing, even if times are hard and you're completely incompetent. Daddy always wanted me to join the civil service but I said, *Daddy, I'm an independent young woman and I'll find my own position*, and find it I did on the foreign exchange desk at the Bank of Ireland, College Green. But I always think the great thing about the civil service is that you can go in there at twenty years old, spend every day of your life behind one desk and before you know it you're an old man and it's all behind you and the only thing left to do is die. There must be great security in that."

"I hadn't really thought about it that way," I said, feeling a curious mélange of mortality and misery at the idea. "But I suppose you're right."

"Did I ever tell you that my Uncle Martin was a civil servant?"

"Well, no," I said. "But then we've only just met again."

"He was a wonderful civil servant. And a lovely man. Although he had a twitch in his cheek and I don't like a man with a twitch. It makes me uncomfortable."

"Does he still work there?" I asked. "Maybe I might know him?"

"No," she said, tapping her temple. "He got the dementia," she told me, lowering her voice almost to a whisper. "He can't remember who he is half the time. The last time I saw him he thought I was Dorothy Lamour!" She barked a laugh and looked around, shaking her head in delight before her face turned stony with disgust once again. "Would you take a look at her?" she said.

I turned to glance in the direction in which she was staring and saw a young girl making her way down the center aisle of Bewley's, a young stunner who was defying the weather by wearing as few clothes as possible. The eyes of every man in the place were on her behind as she passed. Almost every man anyway.

"Mutton dressed as lamb," said Mary-Margaret, curling her lip. "That wouldn't be my standard now at all."

"Would you like a cream cake to go with your tea?" I asked.

"No, thank you, Cyril. Cream doesn't agree with me."

"Right." I checked my watch and saw that we had already been in the café for seven minutes, which I thought was long enough. "Well, I suppose I better be getting back," I said.

"Getting back where?"

"Back to work," I said.

"Oh listen to you," she said. "Mr. Hoity-Toity."

I had no idea what she meant by this. It didn't seem like such a bizarre idea that I should return to work, since it was only three o'clock in the afternoon.

"It was nice to see you again, Mary-Margaret," I said, extending my hand

"Hold on there now, you, till I give you my phone number," she said, reaching into her bag for a pen and paper.

"Why?" I asked.

"But sure how else would you be able to call me if you didn't know what my number was?"

I frowned, uncertain what she was getting at. "I'm sorry," I said. "Did you want me to call you? Was there something you needed to ask me? Because I can stay a little longer if there is."

"No, we'll save something to talk about for next time." She scribbled down a number and handed it across to me. "It'll be better if you call me than the other way around. I wouldn't be the type to phone a boy. But I won't be waiting by the telephone for you either, so don't get any notions on that score. And if Daddy answers, tell him that you're a civil servant from the Department of Education, because he'll approve of that. Otherwise he'll give you short shrift."

I stared at the piece of paper in my hand and didn't know what to say. This was entirely outside of my realm of experience.

"Call me on Saturday afternoon," she said. "And we'll make plans for Saturday night."

"All right," I said, uncertain what I was getting myself into but confident that I had no choice in the matter.

"There's a picture that I want to see," she told me. "It's playing in the Metropole. *A Man for All Seasons.*"

"I've seen that one," I said, not adding that I'd had to leave just as Richard Rich was betraying his mentor for Wales because I needed to wash the smell of ejaculate off my hands.

"Well I haven't," she said. "And I want to."

"There's lots of other pictures on," I said. "I'll have a look in the paper later and see what's what."

"I want to see *A Man for All Seasons,*" she insisted, leaning forward and glaring at me.

"Right so," I said, standing up before she could pick up a knife and do to me what the IRA had done to Julian. "I'll call you on Saturday so."

"At four o'clock. Not a minute earlier."

"Four o'clock," I said, turning around and making my way out of the café, the perspiration already starting to cause my shirt to stick to my back. Walking back to work in the sunshine, I considered the situation. Without ever having intended to, and without even wanting such a thing, it seemed that I had a girlfriend. And my girlfriend was Mary-Margaret Muffet. Apparently I was her standard. On one hand the idea terrified me, for I had no knowledge of how to behave with a girl and even less interest in finding out, but on the other this was a great development in my life, for it meant that there was a chance I could be just like everyone else and no one would be suspicious of me. And thank God, I wouldn't have to join a seminary, which I'd been vaguely considering as an answer to all my problems for about a year now.

Back in the office, I ignored an endless conversation that my colleagues were having about Jacqueline Kennedy and sat down to write a long letter to Julian, telling him that I'd fallen in love with a beautiful girl I'd met in Bewley's Café. I described her in the most complimentary way I could and implied that we'd been having relations every which way for the last few months. I did everything I could to sound as sexually promiscuous as him and signed off by saying that the only problem with having a girlfriend was not being able to take advantage of all the other girls that were out there. *I couldn't do that*, I told him. *I love her too much. Still*, I added, *just because I'm on a diet doesn't mean I can't take a look at the menu*. I sent the letter care of the Western Union office in Salzburg, where he and that Suzi harpy had gone skiing, and hoped that his curiosity might bring him back to Dublin soon so we could go on double dates together and then maybe the girls would strike up a friendship and tell us to go out for drinks on our own so they could talk about knitting and recipes and so on and it would just be Julian and me left alone together, like it was supposed to be.

Within a few weeks, Mary-Margaret and I were an established couple and every Sunday she gave me a list of the things we would be doing during the week ahead. I had Tuesdays and Thursdays off but had to be with her every other evening, most of which were spent sitting together on the sofa in her front room while her daddy watched television and ate chocolate-covered Brazil nuts, all the time proclaiming that he was sick of chocolate-covered Brazil nuts.

After about a month, it occurred to me that nothing sexual had occurred between us yet and decided that it might be worth a try. After all, I had never enjoyed any intimacy with a girl and there was always the possibility that if I tried it, I might actually enjoy it. And so, after her daddy went up to bed one night, I leaned over and without any warning pressed my lips against hers.

"Excuse me," she said, rearing back on the sofa with an appalled expression on her face. "What do you think you're doing, Cyril Avery?"

"I was trying to kiss you," I said.

She shook her head slowly and looked at me as if I'd just admitted that I was Jack the Ripper or a member of the Labor party. "I thought you had a little bit more respect for me than that," she said. "I had no idea that all this time I was going out with a sex pervert."

"I don't think that's quite accurate," I said.

"Well, how else would you describe yourself? Here I am trying to watch *Perry Mason*, little knowing that all the time you were planning on raping me."

"I wasn't planning anything of the sort," I protested. "It was just a kiss, that's all. Shouldn't we be kissing if we're doing a line together? There's nothing wrong with that, Mary-Margaret, is there?"

"Well, maybe," she said, considering it. "But you could at least have the decency to ask in future. There's nothing less romantic than spontaneity."

"All right," I said. "Well, can I kiss you then?"

She thought about it and finally nodded her head. "You can," she said. "But make sure to keep your eyes closed and your mouth too. And I don't want your hands anywhere near me. I can't stand to be touched."

I did as instructed, pressing my lips against hers again and mumbling her name as if I was lost in the passion of a great love affair. She remained rigid on the sofa and I could tell that she was still watching the television, where Perry Mason was getting tough with a man in the witness box. After about thirty seconds of this uncontrollable eroticism, I pulled away.

"You're a great kisser," I told her.

"I hope you're not suggesting that I have a past," she said.

"No, I only meant that you have very nice lips."

She narrowed her eyes, uncertain whether that too might be the sort of thing a sex pervert would say. "Well, that'll be enough for one night," she said. "We don't want to get carried away, do we?"

"Fair enough." I glanced down at the crotch of my pants. There had been no movement whatsoever. If anything, there had been what could only be called A Great Shriveling.

"And don't think that one thing will lead to another, Cyril Avery," she warned me. "I know there are girls out there who will do anything to hold on to a man but that's not my standard. That's not my standard at all."

"No problem," I said, meaning every word of it.

Everywhere, People Stare

It was a difficult time to be Irish, a difficult time to be twenty-one years of age and a difficult time to be a man who was attracted to other men. To be all three simultaneously required a level of subterfuge and guile that felt contrary to my nature. I had never considered myself to be a dishonest person, hating the idea that I was capable of such mendacity and deceit, but the more I examined the architecture of my life, the more I realized how fraudulent were its foundations. The belief that I would spend the rest of my time on earth lying to people weighed heavily on me and at such times I gave serious consideration to taking my own life. Knives frightened me, nooses horrified me and guns alarmed me, but I knew that I was not a strong swimmer. Were I to head out to Howth, for example, and throw myself into the sea, the current would quickly pull me under and there would be nothing I could do to save myself. It was an option that was always at the back of my mind.

I had few friends and even when I considered my relationship with Julian I had to admit that our bond was built on little more than my obsessive and undeclared love. I had guarded and nurtured that alliance jealously over the years, ignoring the fact that were it not for my determination to stay in touch he might have moved on years ago. I had no family to speak of, no siblings, no cousins, no idea as to the identities of my birth parents. I had very little money and had grown to hate the flat on Chatham Street, for Albert Thatcher had acquired a serious girlfriend and when she stayed over the sound of their lovemaking was as ghastly as it was arousing. I longed for a place of my own, a door with only one key.

In desperation I turned to Charles, asking for a loan of one hundred pounds so that I could set myself up in a better situation. I had seen a flat above a shop on Nassau Street with a view over the lawns of Trinity College but I could never have afforded it on the pitiful salary that I earned. The loan, I told him, would allow me to live there for two years while I saved money and tried to build a better life for myself. We were sitting in the yacht club at Dun Laoghaire when I broached the idea, eating lobster and drinking Moët and Chandon, but he refused me instantly, declaring that he didn't loan money to friends, as such acts of philanthropy always ended badly.

"But we're more than friends, surely," I said, throwing myself on his mercy. "You're my adoptive father, after all."

"Oh come along, Cyril," he replied, laughing as if I was making a joke. "You're twenty-five years old now—"

"I'm twenty-one."

"Twenty-one then. Naturally, I care about you, we've known each other a long time, but you're not—"

"I know," I said, holding up a hand before he could finish that sentence. "It doesn't matter."

Of most concern to me, however, was my overwhelming, insatiable and uncontrollable lust, a yearning that was as intense as my need for food and water but that, unlike those other basic human needs, was always countered by the fear of discovery. There were nighttime excursions to the banks of the Grand Canal or the clustered forests at the heart of the Phoenix Park, furtive explorations of the narrow laneways off Baggot Street and the hidden passages that zigzagged from the Ha'penny Bridge toward Christ Church Cathedral. The darkness concealed my crimes but convinced me that I was a degenerate, a pervert, a Mr. Hyde who left my benevolent Dr. Jekyll skin behind on Chatham Street as soon as the sun went down and the clouds passed slowly to cover the moon.

Satisfying my lust was not the problem. In the city center, it wasn't difficult to find a young man with similar predilections and a simple exchange of looks could create an instant contract as we made our way wordlessly to a hiding place with little chance of discovery, fumbling behind bushes, careful not to look into each other's eyes as our hands pulled and caressed while our lips moved hungrily as we stood with our backs against trees, lay together on the grass or knelt before each other in attitudes of supplication. We would paw at each other's bodies until one of us could take no more, then gush forth into the earth beneath our feet, and although the urge was always to leave as quickly as possible afterward, good etiquette meant that you could not go until the other boy had reached his climax too. A quick *thank you* would be followed by our turning in opposite directions and walking quickly away, making for home with a silent prayer that the Gardaí were not following us as we swore in our heads that this was the last time, that we would never do such a thing again, that we were done with it forever, but then the hours would pass, the urges would return and by the following night our curtains would be twitching as we looked outside to see what the weather was like.

I didn't like going to the parks because they were usually populated by older men with cars looking for someone young to fuck in the back-seat, the stench of their Guinness and sweat enough to sublimate any desire that I might feel. But I went when I was desperate, fearing for the day when I too might find myself driving past Áras an Uachtaráin in search of young skin. I stopped going when the old men began to offer me money. They would pull up next to me and if I refused them would say that there was a pound note in it for me if I did what I was asked. And once or twice, when times were hard, I accepted their pound but sex without desire was not something that turned me on. I could not commit the act for money. I needed to want it.

Only once did I dare to bring someone home to Chatham Street and that was because I was drunk, dizzy with lust, and the boy I had met, a few years older than me at twenty-three or twenty-four, put me so much in mind of Julian that I thought I could spend a night with him and imagine that my friend had somehow succumbed to my desires. The boy's name was Ciarán, or at least that was the name he gave me, and we met in a downstairs bar off Harcourt Street, a place whose blacked-out windows encouraged its clientele to feel that they, like the Beatles, had to hide their love away. I went there occasionally, for it was a good place to meet someone as shy and anxious as me under cover of simply stopping in for a pint. I saw him as he returned from the bathroom and we exchanged a look of mutual appreciation. A few minutes later, he came over to ask whether he could join me.

"Of course," I said, nodding toward the empty chair. "I'm on my own."

"Sure we're all on our own," he replied with a wry smile. "What's your name anyway?"

"Julian," I said, the name out of my mouth before I could even consider the wisdom of the choice. "And you?"

"Ciarán."

I nodded and took a drink from my Smithwick's, trying not to stare at him too intensely. He was ridiculously handsome, much better looking than the type I normally ended up with, and of course it was he who had made the decision to approach me, which meant that he was interested. We said nothing for a while. I racked my brain for some sensible conversation starter but my mind was a blank and I was relieved when he took the lead.

"I've never been here before," he said, looking around, and the familiar way in which he nodded at the barman made me know that this wasn't true. "I heard it was a bit of craic."

"Me neither," I said. "I was just passing by and stopped in for a drink. I didn't even know there was a bar here."

"Do you mind if I ask what you do?" he asked.

"I work in Dublin Zoo," I told him, which was my standard reply to this question. "In the reptile house."

"I'm frightened of spiders," said Ciarán.

"Actually, spiders are arachnids," I said, as if I knew what I was talking about. "Reptiles are lizards and iguanas and so on."

"Oh right," he said. I glanced behind him to where an old man, his belly hanging over the belt of his trousers, was sitting at the bar looking longingly in our direction. I could tell from his expression that he wished he could join us, that he had some natural place in our company, but we were forty years younger than him, so of course he didn't and he stayed where he was, perhaps contemplating the random unkindness of the universe.

"I'll probably not stay long," said Ciarán eventually.

"Nor me," I said. "I have work in the morning."

"Do you live nearby?"

I hesitated, having never brought anyone home to Chatham Street. But this was different. He was just too good to let go of. And then there was the Julian-lookalike thing. I knew I wanted more than some illicit fumble in an alleyway that stank of piss and chips and the previous night's washed-away vomit. I wanted to know what it would be like to hold him, to really hold him, and to be held by him, to be really held.

"Not too far," I said slowly. "Near Grafton Street. But it's a bit difficult there. What about you?"

"Not possible, I'm afraid," he said. It occurred to me how quickly we understood each other, how little discussion it took to make it clear that we wanted to go to bed with each other. For all they said, I was sure that the heterosexual lads would have loved it if women had behaved like us.

"Well, maybe we could take a walk," I said, willing to settle for the usual if that was all that was on offer. "It's not a bad night out."

He considered this only briefly before shaking his head. "Sorry," he said, placing a hand on my knee beneath the table, which set off sparks of electricity around my body. "I'm not really the outdoors type, to be honest. Sure never mind. Nothing ventured, nothing gained, am I right? Another time, perhaps."

He stood up and I knew that I was on the verge of losing him and made a quick decision. "We could try mine," I said. "But we'd have to be quiet."

"Are you sure?" he asked, looking hopeful.

"We'd have to be *very* quiet," I repeated. "I have a flatmate and the landlady and her son live downstairs. I don't know what would happen if they found us."

"I can be quiet," he said. "Or I can try to be anyway," he added with a smile, which made me laugh, despite my unease.

We left the bar and made our way back toward St. Stephen's Green. There were any number of good reasons not to allow him to cross the threshold but none was strong enough to fight the fact that every atom in my body longed for his and soon enough we were standing outside the bright-red door where there was nothing left to do but slide the key into the lock. In my anxiety, I struggled to insert it correctly.

"Just wait here a minute," I whispered, leaning so close to him that our lips were almost touching. "Let me see whether the coast is clear."

The lights were out in the hallway and the door to Albert's room was closed, which meant that he was probably asleep. I turned back and waved Ciarán inside and we made our way upstairs. When I opened my own door, I pushed him inside, locked it behind us and within a minute we were on the bed, tearing at each other's clothes like a pair of teenagers and all notions of being quiet went out of my head as we did what we had come here to do, what we had been born to do.

It was an entirely new experience to me. Usually the temptation was to get it over with as quickly as possible and run away but for once I wanted to take things slowly. I had never had sex in a bed before and the sensation of the sheets against my bare skin was incredibly arousing. I had never run my hands along a man's leg, never felt the ripple of the hairs beneath my palm, never known what it was like for my bare feet to touch his or to turn him over and run my tongue along his spinal cord as his back arched in pleasure. In the dull light that trickled through the curtains from the streetlamp outside we felt the sincerity of what we were doing and soon I forgot about Julian altogether and thought only of Ciarán.

As night turned toward morning, I felt something that I had never felt during sex before. Something more than lust or the frantic urgency for an orgasm. I felt warmth and friendship and happiness, and all this for a stranger, all this for a man whose real name I probably didn't even know.

Finally, he turned to me and smiled, shaking his head with that familiar expression of regret. "I better go," he said.

"You could stay," I suggested, surprised to hear such words emerge from my mouth. "You could leave when my flatmate is having his bath in the morning. No one would know."

"I can't," he said, climbing out of bed, and I watched as he reached for his clothes, which were scattered among my own on the floor. "My wife will be expecting me back soon. She thinks I'm on a night shift."

My heart sank inside my chest and I realized that I had felt the gold band on his left hand against my back as he had held me and thought nothing of it. He was married. Of course he was. And, as he buttoned his shirt and searched for his shoes, I saw that the revelation meant nothing to him.

"Have you lived here long?" he asked as he dressed, for silence was worse than anything.

"A while," I said.

"It's nice enough," he said, before stopping and looking around the walls. "Is it just me or does this crack look like the journey the River Shannon takes through the Midlands?"

"That's what I've always thought," I said. "I've asked the landlady to fix it but she says that it will cost too much and it's been there forever, so no harm."

I lay back down, pulling the sheets up to my neck to cover my nakedness, and wanted him to stop talking and just leave.

"Listen, we could do this again sometime if you like?" he suggested as he made his way toward the door.

"I can't," I said, repeating his own phrase. "Sorry."

"No problem," he replied with a shrug. It had been nothing more than a fuck for him, one of many probably. There would be another tomorrow night, and another at the weekend, and another during the week after that. A moment later, he was gone and a part of me didn't care if Albert, Mrs. Hogan or her blind son opened their doors to find him leaving but there was no uproar from downstairs and it seemed that he had escaped without notice.

There Are No Homosexuals in Ireland

A few days later, I made an appointment with a doctor. His name was Dr. Dourish, his practice located in a row of red-bricked houses in Dundrum, a part of the city that I did not know well. There were a number of doctors that had some association with the civil service and from whom we could receive favorable rates, but not trusting the rules of their profession within Catholic Ireland I was nervous of exposing myself—either literally or metaphorically—to anyone who might reveal my secret to my employers. I had hoped that he might be young and sympathetic toward my situation and was disappointed to find that he was well into his sixties, close to retirement age and looked about as friendly as a teenage boy woken for school on Monday morning. He smoked a pipe throughout our consultation, picking tiny shreds of tobacco from his yellow teeth that he deposited in an ashtray on the desk that he did not seem to have emptied in sometime. A

St. Brigid's cross on the wall made my heart sink a little, not to mention the statue of the Sacred Heart behind his desk containing a flickering bulb that gave it a rather ghostly aspect.

"Mr. Sadler, is that right?" he asked, picking up the file his secretary had given him and for which, naturally, I had provided a false name.

"That's right," I said. "Tristan Sadler. That's my name. Always has been since the day I was born."

"And what can I do for you today?"

I looked away, glancing toward the bed that stood against one of the walls and on which I wished that I could lie, like a psychiatric patient, while he stood behind me. I wanted to recount my woes without having to see the expression on his face. The inevitable disgust.

"Do you think I could lie down?" I asked.

"Why?"

"I'd prefer it."

"No," he said, shaking his head. "That's not for patients. It's where I have my afternoon nap."

"Right. I'll stay where I am so."

"If you would."

"I wanted to talk to you," I said. "I think there's something wrong with me."

"Well of course there's something wrong with you. Sure why else would you be here? What is it?"

"It's a little delicate."

"Ah," he said, smiling a little and nodding his head. "Do you mind if I ask how old you are, Tristan?"

"I'm twenty-one."

"Would it be a matter of an intimate nature?"

"Yes."

"I guessed as much," he said. "You've caught something, am I right? The women in this city have gone to hell, if you ask me. Dirty little pups, all of them. We should never have given them the vote, if you ask me. It gave them ideas."

"No," I replied. I had, of course, caught one or two things in recent times but I had another doctor, one on the Northside, that I used during those moments and he always prescribed me something that sorted the problem out quickly. "No, it's nothing like that."

"All right then," he said with a sigh. "So what is it then? Spit it out, man."

"I think . . . the thing is, Doctor, I haven't quite developed in the way that I'm supposed to."

"I don't follow you."

"I suppose I mean that I'm not as interested in girls as I should be. As other lads my age are."

"I see," he said, his smile fading now. "Well, that's not as abnormal as you might think either. Some boys are late developers. Is it not a big priority for you then? The old sex, I mean."

"It's a very big priority," I told him. "It's probably my biggest priority. I think about it all day long from the minute I wake up in the morning until the minute I go to bed. And then I dream about it. Sometimes I even have dreams where I go to bed and I have dreams in my dreams about it."

"Then what's the problem?" he asked, and I could tell that he was growing frustrated by my obfuscation. "Can you not get a girlfriend, is that it? You're not a bad-looking fellow. I'm sure there's lots of girls who'd be happy to do a line with you. Are you shy, is that it? Do you not know how to talk to them?"

"I'm not shy," I said, finding my voice now and determined to get it out and damn the consequences. "And as it happens I have a girlfriend, thank you very much. But I don't really want one is the thing. It's not girls that I think about, you see. It's boys."

There was a long silence during which I didn't dare to look up at him, focusing instead on the carpet beneath my feet and where it had worn thin from the amount of people who had sat in that same seat over the years, dragging their shoes back and forth in anxiety, grief or depression. The silence continued for so long that I feared Dr. Dourish had died of shock and that I had another corpse on my conscience. Finally, however, I heard him push his seat back and I glanced up as he walked over to a cabinet, unlocked it and removed a small packet from the top shelf. He closed the door again, relocked it and sat down, placing the mysterious package on the desk between us.

"First," said Dr. Dourish, "you mustn't think that you're alone in your affliction. There have been plenty of boys who have had similar feelings over the years, from the Ancient Greeks to the present day. Perverts, degenerates and sickos have existed since the dawn of time, so don't for a minute think that you're anything special. There are even some places where you can get away with it and no one bats an eyelid. But the important thing for you to remember, Tristan, is that you must never act on these disgusting urges. You're a good, decent Irish Catholic boy and . . . you are a Catholic, aren't you?"

"Yes," I said, even though I had no allegiance to any religion.

"Good lad. Well, unfortunately you've been cursed with a terrible sickness. Something that falls on random people for no apparent reason. But you must not think for a moment that you are a homosexual, because you aren't."

I flushed a little at the utterance of that dreaded and proscribed word, which was almost never spoken in polite society.

"Yes, it's true," he continued, "that there are homosexuals all over the world. England has lots of them. France is full of them. And I've never been to America but I imagine they have more than their share too. I wouldn't think it's all that common in Russia or Australia but they probably have some other repulsive thing to compensate. But here's what you have to remember: *There are no homosexuals in Ireland.* You might have got it into your head that you are one but you're just wrong, it's as simple as that. You're wrong."

"It doesn't feel as simple as that, Doctor," I said carefully. "I really think that I might be."

"But were you not listening to me?" he asked, smiling at me as if I was a complete ignoramus. "Amn't I after telling you that there are no homosexuals in Ireland? And if there are no homosexuals in Ireland, then how on earth could you be one?"

I thought about it, trying my best to locate the logic in his argument.

"Now," he continued. "What makes you think that you're one of them anyway? A dirty queer, I mean."

"It's pretty simple," I said. "I'm both physically and sexually attracted to men."

"Well, sure that doesn't make you a homosexual," he said, opening his hands wide in a gesture of acceptance.

"Doesn't it?" I asked, a little baffled by this. "I thought it did."

"Not at all, not at all," he said, shaking his head. "You've just been watching too much television, that's all."

"But I don't own a television," I said.

"Do you go to the pictures?"

"I do."

"How often?"

"Once a week usually."

"Well, that will do it. What was the last picture you saw?"

"*Alfie.*"

"I don't know that one. Was it any good?"

"I liked it," I said. "Mary-Margaret said it was disgusting and that Michael Caine ought to be ashamed of himself. She said he was a filthy article with no respect for himself."

"Who's Mary-Margaret?"

"My girlfriend."

He burst out laughing again and sat forward, refilling his pipe and lighting it with a series of stop-start puffs as the tobacco flamed from red to black and back again. "Would you listen to yourself, Tristan," he said. "If you have a girlfriend, then you're definitely not a homosexual."

"But I don't like my girlfriend," I pointed out. "She's judgmental and critical of everything and everyone. She's always telling me what to do and orders me about like I'm a dog. And I never look at her and think she's pretty. I can't even imagine wanting to see her with her clothes off. Whenever I kiss her, I feel like throwing up afterward. And sometimes I look at her and just wish she'd meet someone else and drop me so I wouldn't have to be the one to do it. Also, she has this weird smell. She says washing too often is a sign of pride."

"But sure we all feel that way about the women," said Dr. Dourish with a shrug. "I've lost track of the number of times I've wanted to slip something into Mrs. Dourish's hot chocolate at night so that she wouldn't wake up in the morning. And I have access to everything I'd need too. I could write a prescription for poison and there's not a jury in the land would question it. But that doesn't make *me* a homosexual, does it? How could it be? I love Judy Garland and Joan Crawford and Bette Davis. I never miss any of their pictures."

"I just want it to stop," I said, raising my voice in frustration. "I want to stop thinking about men and be just like everyone else."

"Which is why you came to see me," he replied. "And I'm glad to say that you've come to the right place, because I can help you."

My heart lifted a little and I looked across at him hopefully. "Really?" I asked.

"Oh yes," he said, nodding his head in the direction of the small package he'd placed on the desk between us. "Pick that up like a good man and open it."

I did as instructed and a small syringe with a long, pointed needle, about the size of my index finger, fell out.

"Do you know what that is?" asked Dr. Dourish.

"I do," I said. "It's a syringe."

"Good lad. Now, I want you to trust me, all right? Give the syringe to me." I handed it across and he nodded toward the bed. "Go over there and sit on the edge."

"I thought that wasn't for patients?"

"I make an exception for degenerates. And take your trousers off first."

I felt anxious about what was going to happen next but did as I was told, letting my trousers fall around my ankles and sitting where he had told me. Dr. Dourish approached me, holding the syringe in his right hand in a rather threatening way.

"Now take your underpants off," he said.

"I'd rather not," I said.

"Do as you're told," he said, "or I won't be able to help you."

I hesitated, embarrassed and nervous, but finally did as instructed and tried not to look at him as I sat there, naked from the waist down.

"Now," said the doctor. "I'm going to call out some names to you and I want you to react to them in whatever way feels natural to you, all right?"

"All right," I said.

"Bing Crosby," he said, and I didn't move, just looked at the wall ahead, thinking of the night I'd gone to see a re-release of *High Society* with Mary-Margaret in the Adelphi Cinema on Abbey Street. She'd been disgusted by the whole thing, asking what kind of dirty tramp would divorce one man for another and then go back to the first one on the day of her second wedding. It showed a lack of moral conviction, she claimed. Which was not her standard at all.

"Richard Nixon," said Dr. Dourish then, and I grimaced. There was talk that Nixon was going to be running for President again in 1968 and I hoped that he wouldn't. There was something about seeing that face in the newspapers every morning that put me off my breakfast.

"Warren Beatty," he said, and this time my face lit up. I had loved Warren Beatty ever since I'd seen him opposite Natalie Wood in *Splendor in the Grass* a few years earlier and had been first in line for *Promise Her Anything* when it had opened in the Carlton the year before. Before I could contemplate his beauty any further, however, I found myself leaping off the bed in unexpected agony, tripping over my feet as my trousers conspired to take me down, and I fell to the floor, writhing in agony and clutching my groin. When I finally dared to take my hands away, there was a tiny red mark on my scrotum that had not been there five minutes earlier.

"You stabbed me!" I cried out, looking across at Dr. Dourish as if he was insane. "You stabbed me in the balls with your syringe!"

"I did indeed," he said, bowing a little as if he was accepting words of gratitude. "Now get up here, Tristan, so I can do it again."

"I'll do no such thing," I said, struggling to my feet and weighing up whether I should punch him in the face or just make a run for it. I must have been a comical sight standing there in the middle of his surgery with my cock hanging out, my trousers hanging off me and my face red with fury.

"You want to be cured, don't you?" he asked in a benevolent, avuncular tone, ignoring my obvious distress.

"I do, yes," I said. "But not like this. It hurts!"

"But this is the *only* way," he said. "We will train your brain to associate feelings of lust toward men with the most intense pain. That way you will not allow yourself to feel these disgusting thoughts. Think of Pavlov's dog. It's a similar principle."

"I don't know Pavlov and I don't know his dog," I said, "but unless either of them has been stabbed in the balls with a syringe I don't think they can have any idea what I'm feeling right now."

"Fine," said Dr. Dourish with a shrug. "Continue with your sordid fantasies. Live a life that is dominated by disgusting and immoral thoughts. Be an outcast from society for the rest of your days. It's your choice. But remember, you came here for help and I am offering help. It's up to you whether or not you accept it."

I thought about this and as the pain subsided I slowly—very, very slowly—made my way back toward the bed and sat down, trembling and close to tears. I gripped the side of the bed and closed my eyes.

"Very good," he said. "Now, let's try again. Pope Paul VI."

Nothing.

"Charles Laughton."

Nothing.

"George Harrison."

And if there were any patients awaiting their turn outside I daresay they turned on their heels and ran when they heard the sounds of my screams piercing the plasterwork and threatening to tear down the walls. When I stumbled out, half an hour later, barely able to walk and with tears rolling down my cheeks, the surgery was empty except for Dr. Dourish's secretary, who was seated behind her desk, writing a receipt.

"That'll be fifteen pence," she said, handing the docket across, and I reached carefully—very, very carefully—into my pocket for the money. Before I could retrieve it, however, the door to the doctor's office opened and, worried that he was going to come at me crying "Harold Macmillan! Adolf Hitler! Tony Curtis!" I wondered whether I should make for a run for it.

"An extra three pence for a syringe, Annie," said Dr. Dourish. "Mr. Sadler is taking one with him."

"Eighteen pence then," she said, and I put the money on the table and limped out, glad to breathe the fresh air of Dundrum. Making my way down the street toward the shopping center I stopped at a bench and sat down, adjusting myself to find a comfortable position, and put my head in my hands. A young couple, the wife showing early signs of pregnancy, stopped when they saw me and asked whether I was all right, whether there was anything they could do for me.

"I'm fine," I said. "Thank you, though."

"You don't look all right," said the woman.

"That's because I'm not. I've just had a man stab a needle into my scrotum about twenty times over the course of an hour. And it hurts like hell."

"I'd imagine it would," said the man nonchalantly. "I hope you didn't pay for that kind of treatment."

"I paid eighteen pence," I said.

"You could get a good night out on that if you were careful," said the woman. "Do you need a doctor? There's one down the road if—"

"It was the doctor who did it," I said. "I just need a taxi, that's all. I want to go home."

"Helen," said the man. "Keep an eye out for a taxi. The poor man can hardly stand." And no sooner had she turned around and raised her hand in the air than one came our way and pulled in.

"Nothing is worth this kind of upset," said the woman as I climbed into the backseat. She had a kindly face and there was a part of me that wanted to weep on her shoulder and tell her all my woes. "Whatever's wrong with you, don't worry. It'll all come good in the end."

"I wish I had your confidence," I said, closing the door as the car pulled away.

Before the Whole Car Could Go Up in Flames

A few weeks later, the Minister was caught with his pants down.

A supposedly happily married man who dragged his wife and children to Mass with him every Sunday morning, he could usually be found standing in the church grounds afterward, regardless of the weather, shaking hands with his constituents and promising to see them all at the GAA match the following weekend. A country TD, he'd stayed in his Dublin flat at the weekend only to be discovered in the early hours of Sunday morning being sucked off in his car by a sixteen-year-old drug addict who had only been released from serving six months for public order offenses in the Finglas Child and Adolescent Center earlier that day. The Minister was arrested and brought to Pearse Street Garda Station, where he refused to give his name and did the usual routine of demanding all their badge numbers, insisting that none of them would have a job by the end of the day. When he tried to leave, he was bundled into a cell and left to stew.

It only took about an hour for someone to identify him. A junior Garda, tasked with bringing cups of tea to the residents of the drunk tank, took one look at the Minister's fat, sweaty face, recognized him from the evening news and went outside to inform his sergeant who, no fan of the government of the day, made a couple of discreet phone calls to a journalist friend of his. By the time he had been processed, bailed and released, the scrum had formed outside and he emerged into the daylight to a barrage of questions, accusations and the endless click-clack of camera shutters.

When I arrived at the department the following morning, the media were parked outside on Marlborough Street and I made my way up to the office to find Miss Joyce, Miss Ambrosia and Mr. Denby-Denby at the heart of the drama.

"There you are, Mr. Avery," said Miss Joyce as I put my bag down. "What kept you until this time?"

"It's only just gone nine," I said, glancing up at the clock. "Why, what's happened?"

"Have you not heard?"

I shook my head and Miss Joyce did her best to explain, using every euphemism known to man to avoid saying the necessary words, but the more flustered she grew, the less sense she made and finally Mr. Denby-Denby threw his hands in the air in frustration and stepped in to make things clear.

"The Garda knocked on the window of his car," he said, raising his voice so there could be no confusion over what had taken place, "and found the pair of them inside with their trousers around their ankles and the boy with the Minister's cock in his mouth. There'll be no way out of this one for him. It's going to make a hell of a splash. No pun intended."

I opened my mouth wide in a mixture of disbelief and amusement, and perhaps it was unfortunate that it was still open in the shape of an O when the Minister himself walked in, pale, perspiring and petulant. He pointed a finger at me and let out a roar.

"You!" he said. "What's your name again?"

"Avery," I told him. "Cyril Avery."

"Are you trying to be funny, Avery?"

"No," I said. "Sorry, sir."

"Because I'll tell you this, I've had enough jokes for one morning and I'm likely to punch the nose off the next man who makes any kind of crack. Do you understand me?"

"Yes, sir," I said, looking down at my shoes and trying not to laugh.

"Miss Joyce," he said, turning to our supposed leader. "Where are we on this now? Have you put anything out yet? We have to get in front of this thing before it spirals out of control."

"I've drafted something," she said, reaching for a piece of paper on her desk. "But I wasn't sure what line you wanted to take. And Miss Ambrosia has finished your wife's statement."

"Read it to me," he said.

Miss Ambrosia stood up and cleared her throat, as if she was preparing for an audition, and read aloud from her notebook.

"The Minister and I have been married for more than thirty years and in all that time I have never had any occasion to question his loyalty, his deeply felt Catholicism or his abiding love for women. The Minister has always been in thrall to the female form."

"Ah for Christ's sake," he said, storming over to the window, noticing the gathered crowd below on the street and stepping away again before they could spot him. "You can't say that, you stupid bitch. You make me sound like I'm a philanderer. Like I can't keep it in my pants."

"Well, you can't," said Mr. Denby-Denby. "And don't call Miss Ambrosia names, do you hear me? I won't put up with it."

"Shut up, you," said the Minister.

"In all that time," continued Miss Ambrosia, editing herself as she read, *"I have never had occasion to question his loyalty or his manhood."*

"Jesus, that's even worse. Do you even know what a manhood is? I'd say you do by the cut of you."

"Well, that's a bit rich," said Miss Ambrosia, sitting down again. "At least I don't blow little boys in motorcars."

"I didn't blow anyone!" he roared. "If anyone was getting blown it was me. Although, of course, it wasn't me anyway, as it never happened."

"That's a great quote," said Mr. Denby-Denby. "We should definitely put that into the press release. *I don't blow teenage boys. They blow me.*"

"Is there anyone around here who can write?" asked the Minister, looking from one of us to the other and ignoring this last remark. "This is supposed to be the Department of Education, isn't it? Does anyone in here actually *have* one?"

"Minister," said Miss Joyce, using the tone she always employed when she was trying to calm a situation. I suspected it had been used many times over the decades that she had worked there. "Tell us what you want us to do and we will do it. That's our job, after all. But we need you to provide guidance. That, after all, is *your* job."

"Right," he said, momentarily appeased and sitting down at the table in the center of the room before standing up again like a man with a bad case of piles. "First things first. I want the Garda who arrested me to be arrested and fired immediately from the force. No appeals, no holidays owing, no pension. Get on to Lenihan in Justice and tell him I want it done before lunchtime."

"But on what charge?" she asked.

"The unlawful detainment of a cabinet minister," he said, his face red now with fury. "And I want everyone who works in Pearse Street Garda Station to be put on suspension until we find out who leaked it to the press."

"Minister, the Minister for Justice doesn't answer to the Minister for Education," she said quietly. "You can't tell him to do anything."

"Brian will do whatever I ask him to do. We go back a long way, the pair of us. He'll stand by me, no problem."

"I'm not sure that's true," she said. "In fact, the first communication I received this morning was from my opposite number in Justice who made it clear that Mr. Lenihan would not be available to take any of your calls."

"That bloody bastard!" he shouted, knocking a file off my desk and sending about three hundred pages of departmental memos flying across the floor. "Then you're to go over there and do it in person, do you hear me? Tell him that I have enough dirt to bury him if he doesn't do as I ask."

"I can't do that, sir," she insisted. "It's against all protocol. And as a member of the civil service I certainly cannot be party to any suggestions of blackmail from one cabinet member to another."

"I don't give a fuck about your bloody protocol, do you hear me? You'll do what I tell you or you'll be gone by the end of the day too. And this is the line that I want put out there: the boy in the car was simply the son of an old friend who had fallen on some difficult times. I ran into him by chance, offered him a lift home and pulled over onto Winetavern Street to discuss the possibility of his getting a job here as a waiter in Leinster House. While we were talking, he dropped his cigarette, it fell to the floor and he simply bent over to retrieve it before the whole car could go up in flames. If anything, he was performing a heroic action and should be commended for it."

"And as he did so," said Mr. Denby-Denby, "your belt fell open, your trousers fell down, his did too, and somehow your cock landed halfway down his throat. Makes perfect sense. I can't see how anyone would question an explanation like that."

"You. Out," said the Minister, pointing at Mr. Denby-Denby and clicking his fingers. "Get out, do you hear me? You're fired."

"You can't fire me," replied Mr. Denby-Denby, standing up with great dignity and folding his newspaper under his arm. "I'm a civil servant. I'm here for life, God help me. But I'll go for a cup of tea and a slice and leave you to figure out how to get away with it, because I honestly can't be bothered to listen to anymore of this nonsense. But let's face it, lovey, of the two of us I'm the only one who'll still have a job at the end of the day."

The Minister watched him leave and I thought there was a chance that he might leap on top of him and bash his head against the floor but he had been struck speechless. I guessed that it had been a long time since anyone had spoken to him in this fashion. Miss Ambrosia and I looked at each other and we couldn't help it, we bit our lips, trying not to laugh out loud.

"One word from either of you," said the Minister, pointing at us now, and we scampered back behind our desks and kept our heads down.

"Minister," said Miss Joyce calmly, ushering him back toward the table at the center of the room. "We can issue any press release that you like, we can say anything that you want us to say, but the key thing right now is that you come across to the electorate as contrite and don't make yourself seem anymore ridiculous than you already have. It's your political advisor who should be telling you this anyway, not me."

"I beg your pardon?" he said, astonished by her impudence.

"You heard me, sir. No one is going to believe the preposterous tale that you just told. No one with any brains in their head anyway, so I suppose some of your colleagues might fall for it. But I promise you the Taoiseach will have you horsewhipped out of the chamber if you even try to take that line in there. And is that what you want? To ruin your political career forever? The public will forgive and forget, in time, but Mr. Lemass never will. If you're to have any hope of a come-back in the future, then the trick is to go now before you're pushed. Believe me, you'll thank me for this in the long run."

"Listen to you," he said, his voice filled with contempt. "You think you can say anything you want to me now, don't you? You think you know it all."

"I don't know it all, Minister, no," she said. "But I know enough not to pay for oral sex with an underage and probably deeply disadvantaged boy on a public street in the middle of the night. I know that much at least." She stood up and returned to her own desk, looking back at him as if she was surprised that he was still there. "Now, if there's nothing else, Minister, I suggest you get yourself over to the Taoiseach's office before another minute has passed. We're busy here. We have to prepare for the arrival of your successor later today."

He looked around in dismay, his face white, his nose pulsating red, and perhaps he knew then that the jig was up. Out he went and a few minutes later Mr. Denby-Denby returned with a cream slice and a cup of coffee. "Who do you think we'll get next?" he asked, the events of the last hour already just a footnote for his memoirs. "It won't be Haughey, will it? That man gives me the willies. He always looks like he's just come back from burying bodies up the Dublin mountains."

"Mr. Avery," said Miss Joyce, ignoring him and turning to me. "Would you mind going over to Leinster House and keeping an eye on developments for me? If you hear anything, give me a call. I'll be at my desk all day."

"Yes, Miss Joyce," I said, gathering up my coat and bag, happy at first to be able to head over to the Dáil, where the real action would be found. However, after my initial amusement, I found myself in two minds as I made my way down O'Connell Street and around the walls of Trinity College. On one hand I had never liked the Minister, who had always treated me with utter disdain, but on the other, I knew as well as anyone how difficult it must have been for him to keep his true proclivities to himself. How long had he been lying to his wife, to his friends and family, to himself? He was well into his sixties, so that meant an entire lifetime.

In Leinster House, the TDs and their advisors were gathered on every corridor and in every alcove, whispering away, gossiping like fishwives. Everywhere I turned, I could hear people using words like *faggot*, *shirt-lifter* and *dirty queer*. The atmosphere was one of vicious animosity, with each man disassociating themselves from their colleague by making clear that they had never been friends with a pervert like that in the first place and that they had been planning on putting his name forward for deselection at the next election anyway. Making my way down a corridor where portraits of William T. Cosgrave, Éamon de Valera and John Costello looked down at me with sanctimonious contempt, I saw the Taoiseach's Press Officer marching toward me, incandescent with rage after what had presumably been a morning spent fending off the media. He passed me by before stopping and turning around and looking directly at me.

"You," he said, snarling at me. "I know you, don't I?"

"I don't think so," I replied, even though we'd met on at least a dozen occasions.

"Yes, I do. You're from the Department of Education, aren't you? Avery, isn't it?"

"That's right, sir," I said.

"Where's himself? Is he with you?"

"He's back at Marlborough Street," I said, presuming that he meant the Minister.

"With his trousers down around his ankles, I suppose?"

"No," I said, shaking my head. "At least they were around his waist when I saw him an hour ago. They could be anywhere now, I suppose."

"Are you trying to be funny, Avery?" he asked, leaning so close to me that I could smell the stale cigarette smoke and whiskey on his breath and a rancid stink of cheese and onion crisps. A group had gathered to watch us, sensing a potential drama. *This is a great day*, their expressions read. *Lots going on!* "Would you look at the cut of you anyway," he continued. "What kind of coat is that you're wearing? What color is it, pink?"

"It's maroon, actually," I said. "I got it at Clerys. It was half price in the sales."

"Oh you got it at Clerys, did you?" looking around at the spectators for encouragement as he grinned at them to show me up.

"I did, yes," I said.

"I suppose he hired you himself, did he? The Minister? An interview on his sofa with the door locked? The pair of you playing hide the sausage?"

"No, sir," I said, growing red at the insinuation. "I got the job through a contact of mine. My adoptive father's third and now-estranged wife. She used to work here and—"

"Your what?"

"My adoptive—"

"You're one too, aren't you?" he asked. "I can always tell."

"One of what, sir?" I asked, frowning.

"A dirty queer. Just like your boss."

I swallowed hard and looked around at the forty or so people watching us now, parliamentary secretaries, TDs, ministers and then, stopping as he passed to see what the commotion was, the Taoiseach himself, Seán Lemass. "No, sir," I whispered. "Actually, I have a girlfriend. Mary-Margaret Muffet. She works on the foreign exchange desk at the Bank of Ireland, College Green, and goes to Switzer's café every morning for a cup of tea."

"Sure even Oscar Wilde had a wife. They all do so no one will suspect. It must be high jinks all the time at the Department of Education, is it? Do you know what I'd do with all the queers if I could catch them? I'd do what Hitler did. You can say what you like about the man but he had a few good ideas. Round them up, arrest them, then gas the lot of them."

I could feel a mixture of anger and humiliation forming at the pit of my stomach. "That's a terrible thing to say," I said. "You should be ashamed of yourself."

"Oh should I?"

"Yes. You should."

"Ah go fuck yourself."

"You go fuck yourself," I shouted, unwilling to take anymore of his abuse. "And clean your teeth, for God's sake, if you're going to stand this close to someone, you fat old bollix. I'm about to pass out with the stench of your breath."

"What did you just say?" asked the Press Officer, staring at me in astonishment.

"I said," I replied, raising my voice now, encouraged by what I thought was the approval of the crowd. "Clean your teeth if you're going to—"

I didn't reach the end of my sentence, having been felled by one swift punch to the head, and years of anger built up inside me as I picked myself up, my right hand clenching into a fist as I swung at him. He moved just in time, however, and rather than connecting with his chin, which had been my intended target, my knuckles smashed against a pillar behind me and I let out a yelp of pain. As I massaged them and spun around for a second try, he hit me again, just above my right eye, and I could see money starting to change hands among the TDs.

"I'll give you three to one on the young lad," said one.

"Ten to one would be more fair. Sure look at him, he's already almost out for the count."

"Get away from him!" came a voice out of nowhere, a woman's voice, as the manageress from the tearoom appeared, parting the crowd like Moses parting the Red Sea. "What's going on here?" she cried with all the authority of someone who had been there longer than any of them and who knew she'd be there long after they were all voted out of office. "You, Charles Haughey," she said, pointing to the Minister of Agriculture, who was standing on the sidelines, a pound note hovering in the air that he quickly returned to his wallet. "What are you all doing to this poor boy?"

"Don't be worrying, Mrs. Goggin," purred Haughey, stepping

forward and placing a hand on her arm that she quickly shook off. "It's only a bit of high spirits, that's all."

"High spirits?" she asked, raising her voice. "Look at him! There's blood pouring from his eyebrow. And here, in the seat of parliamentary democracy. Have you no shame, any of you?"

"Calm yourself, dear lady," said Haughey.

"I'll calm myself when you and your thugs get off this corridor, do you hear me? Go on now or I swear to God that I'll call the Gardaí on the lot of you."

I looked up and saw the smile fade from Haughey's face. He looked as if he wanted to do to her what the Press Officer had done to me but then he closed his eyes for a moment, waited until he had control of his temper, and when he opened them again he was perfectly composed.

"Come along, men," he said, turning to the scrum, who seemed willing to take their orders from him. "Leave the lad alone. We'll leave the bitch from the tearoom to clean up the mess. And the next time you see me, sweetheart," he added, reaching out and taking Mrs. Goggin's chin in his hand and holding it tightly, spitting a little as he spoke to her, "you'll keep a civil tongue in your head. I'm a patient man but I don't put up with backchat from whores. I know who you are and I know what you're like."

"You don't know anything about me," she said as she pulled away from him, trying to sound brave but I could hear the anxiety in her voice.

"I know everything about everyone," he said, smiling. "That's my job. Good day to you now. Have a pleasant afternoon."

I sat up slowly, my back against the wall as they moved away, and put a hand to my mouth where I could taste blood. When I took it away again, my palm was red, the result of a cut on my upper lip.

"Come along with me," said Mrs. Goggin, helping me to my feet. "Come into the tearoom till I get you sorted out. You've no need to worry. What's your name anyway?"

"Cyril," I said.

"Well, don't be worrying, Cyril. We'll have the place to ourselves, so no one will be looking at you. Everyone's going to the chamber to hear the Minister's speech."

I nodded and followed her inside as I remembered the afternoon that Julian and I had walked through these same doors seven years earlier during our school trip, drinking pints of Guinness while he passed himself off as a TD for whichever Dublin constituency he was pretending to represent at the time. And I was certain that this was the same woman who had come over to chastise us for underage drinking but ended up attacking Father Squires for leaving us with the run of the place instead. Fearless in the face of authority, she had proved her worth to me twice now.

I sat down at a table by the window and she returned a moment later with a glass of brandy, a bowl of water and a damp facecloth that she used to wipe the blood off my face. "You've no need to worry," she said, smiling at me. "It's just a scratch."

"No one has ever hit me before," I said.

"Drink that down now. It'll do you the power of good." As she took the cloth away, she looked into my eyes and frowned for a moment, sitting back as if she saw some expression there that she recognized, before shaking her head and dipping the cloth into the bowl again. "How did it start anyway?"

"It's this business with the Minister for Education," I told her. "The Press Officer has probably had a rotten morning and was looking for someone to take it out on. He thought I was one of them, you know."

"One of who?"

"A queer."

"And are you?" she asked in so casual a tone that she might have been asking me what the weather was like outside.

"Yes," I said, the first time I had ever admitted this aloud to another person, the word out of my mouth before I could even try to drag it back.

"Well, it happens," she said.

"I've never told anyone that before."

"Really? So why did you tell me?"

"I don't know," I said. "I just felt like I could, that's all. That you wouldn't mind."

"Why would I mind?" she asked. "It's nothing to do with me."

"Why do they hate us so much anyway?" I asked after a lengthy pause. "If they're not queer themselves, then what does it matter to them if someone else is?"

"I remember a friend of mine once telling me that we hate what we fear in ourselves," she said with a shrug. "Perhaps that has something to do with it."

I said nothing and sipped on my brandy, wondering whether it was even worth my while returning to the office that afternoon. It probably wouldn't be long before news of what had taken place reached Miss Joyce and although no member of the government could technically fire a member of the civil service, there were ways around these things and my position was probably even more tenuous than either Mr. Denby-Denby's or the Minister's. When I looked up, I saw that Mrs. Goggin's eyes had filled with tears and she had taken her handkerchief from her pocket to wipe them away.

"Don't mind me," she said, attempting a smile. "It's just that I find this kind of violence very upsetting. I've seen it before and I know where it can lead."

"You won't tell anyone, will you?" I asked.

"Tell them what?"

"What I just told you. That I'm not normal."

"Ah Jesus," she said, laughing as she stood up. "Don't be ridiculous. We're none of us normal. Not in this fucking country."

The Muffets

I didn't tell Mary-Margaret that I had lost my job—that wouldn't have been her standard at all—but with so little money in my bank account, I began to worry how I would pay my rent when the first of the month came around. Not wanting Albert to ask me any awkward questions or for either of the Hogans to wonder why I was still at home during daylight hours, I left the Chatham Street flat at the usual time every morning and wandered aimlessly around the city until the cinemas opened. A few pence could gain me access to an early show and if I hid in the toilets afterward, I could go back in once the lights went down and stay for the rest of the afternoon.

"There's something not quite right with you at the moment, Cyril," said Mary-Margaret on the night of her birthday, when I used what little funds I had to take her out to dinner. I had brought her to a new

Italian restaurant on Merrion Square that had got excellent reviews but after examining the menu she said that she had more respect for her stomach than to eat foreign food and stuck to pork chops, potatoes and a glass of tap water. "Are you not feeling yourself?"

"I am," I said. "Quite regularly, actually."

"What does that mean?"

"Nothing," I said, shaking my head. "No, I'm fine. There's nothing for you to worry about."

"But sure what kind of person would I be if I didn't worry?" she asked in a rare moment of empathy. "I'm very fond of you, Cyril. You should know that by now."

"I do," I said. "And I'm very fond of you too."

"You're supposed to say that you love me."

"All right," I replied. "I love you. How are your chops?"

"Undercooked. And the potatoes are very salty."

"You put the salt on yourself. I saw you."

"I know, but still. I'd say something to the waiter but, as you know, I don't like to cause a fuss." She put her knife and fork down and looked around, lowering her voice. "Actually, there's something that I want to discuss with you. I hate to bring it up when we're having such a lovely night out but you're going to find out sooner or later anyway."

"I'm listening," I said. To my surprise, I could see that she was close to tears, a condition to which she never succumbed, and something in me softened as I reached across to take her hand.

"Don't, Cyril," she said, pulling away from me. "Have a little decorum."

"What did you want to say?" I asked with a sigh.

"I'm a bit upset," she told me. "But if I tell you, you have to promise that nothing will change between us."

"I'm pretty certain that nothing will ever change between us," I said.

"Good. Well, you know my cousin Sarah-Anne?"

"Not personally," I said, wondering why her family felt the need to double-barrel all their daughters' names. "I think you've mentioned her once or twice but I'm not sure if we've ever met. Is she the one who wants to be a nun?"

"No, of course not, Cyril," she said. "That's Josephine-Shauna. Do you know what your problem is?"

"That I never listen?"

"Yes."

"So which one is Sarah-Anne?" I asked.

"The one who lives out in Foxrock. She's a primary-school teacher, which always struck me as a bit odd as she can't do long division and is practically illiterate."

"Oh yes," I said, recalling a girl I'd encountered at a garden party once who had flirted shamelessly with me. "A very pretty girl, am I right?"

"Pretty is as pretty does," said Mary-Margaret with a sniff.

"What does that even mean?" I asked. "I've never understood the phrase."

"It means what it means," she said.

"Fair enough."

"Well, we've had a bit of bad news about Sarah-Anne," she continued.

She had my attention now. This wasn't the type of conversation that Mary-Margaret usually entertained over dinner. She generally preferred to discuss how little decorum the young people had in their standards of dress or how that loud rock 'n' roll music was like the Devil screaming in her ears.

"Go on," I said.

She looked around again to make sure that she couldn't be overheard and then leaned in. "Sarah-Anne has fallen," she said.

"Fallen?"

"Fallen," she confirmed, nodding her head.

"Did she hurt herself?"

"What?"

"When she fell? Did she break something? Was someone not there to help her up?"

She looked at me as if I had gone mad. "Are you trying to be funny, Cyril?" she asked.

"No," I said, baffled. "I just don't know what you mean, that's all."

"She's *fallen*!"

"Yes, you said, but—"

"Oh for pity's sake," she hissed. "She's going to have a baby."

"A baby?"

"Yes. Five months from now."

"Oh, is that all?" I asked, returning to my lasagne.

"What do you mean, is that all? Is that not enough?"

"But sure lots of people have babies," I said. "If there weren't any babies, there wouldn't be any adults."

"Don't be ridiculous, Cyril."

"I'm not being ridiculous."

"You are. Sarah-Anne isn't married."

"Ah, right," I said. "I suppose that puts a different complexion on things."

"Of course it does," said Mary-Margaret. "Her poor parents are beside themselves. Auntie Mary is under twenty-four-hour supervision because she threatened to stick a carving knife into her head."

"Into whose head? Hers or Sarah-Anne's?"

"Both, probably."

"Well, does she know who the father is?"

Her mouth fell open in disgust. "Of course she does," she said. "What kind of girl do you think she is anyway? You must have a very low opinion of the Muffet family."

"I don't even know her," I protested. "I don't have any opinion on her at all."

"The father is some buck from Rathmines, if you please. Works in a linen factory, which wouldn't be my standard at all. Of course, he's agreed to marry her, so that's one thing, but they can't get a church date for another six weeks and by then she'll be showing."

"Well, at least he's doing the right thing," I said.

"After he did the wrong thing. Poor Sarah-Anne, she was always such a good girl. I don't know what got into her. I hope you don't get any ideas, Cyril. You better not think that I'm going to indulge in that level of behavior."

"Believe me, I don't," I said, setting my knife and fork aside now, my appetite slipping away at the very idea. "The last thing in the world I want to do is seduce you."

"Well, you can put the seventeenth of next month into your diary. That's the wedding day."

"Right so," I said. "What are you going to give her?"

"What do you mean?"

"As a wedding present. I suppose something for the baby would be useful."

"Ha!" she said, shaking her head. "I will *not* be giving her a present."

"Why not?" I asked. "What kind of person shows up to someone's wedding and doesn't bring a gift?"

"If it was a normal wedding, then of course I'd get them something," she told me. "But it isn't, is it? I don't want to signal my approval. No, they made their bed. They may lie in it now."

I rolled my eyes and felt a prickle of perspiration at the back of my neck. "Do you always have to be so judgmental?" I asked.

She looked at me as if I'd just slapped her. "What did you just say to me, Cyril Avery?"

"I asked if you always have to be so judgmental. It's bad enough living in this country with the way people carry on and the hypocrisy we see all around us but isn't that kind of attitude for old people who don't realize that it's a new world we're living in? We're still young, Mary-Margaret. Can you not try to have a little sympathy for someone who's going through a difficult time?"

"Oh, you're fierce modern, aren't you, Cyril?" she said, sitting back and pursing her lips. "Is this your way of telling me that you want to have your way with me too, is that it? That you want to take me back to your flat and drag me into your bedroom, get your lad out, stick it in me and pump away until you've given me a good seeing-to?"

Now it was my turn to look astonished. I could scarcely believe that she would say something like this, let alone have the words for it.

"Because if that's what you think, Cyril," she continued, "you have another thing coming. I don't do that with anyone. And after we're married, don't expect it on any night other than a Saturday, with the lights off. I was brought up properly, you know."

I made a mental note to have plans for every Saturday night after we were married and then panicked at the idea of marrying at all.

When had this been decided? We'd never even discussed such a thing. Had I proposed and forgotten all about it?

"I'm just saying that this is 1966," I told her. "It's not the 1930s. Girls get pregnant all the time. Sure I don't even know what the story was with my own mother, do I?"

"What are you talking about?" she asked, pulling a face. "You know exactly what the story was with your mother. The whole country does. Sure don't they study her books in the university now?"

"My birth mother," I said, correcting myself.

"Your what?"

My mouth fell open in surprise as I realized that in all the time that we'd been together I had never mentioned the fact that I was adopted. I told her now and she paled visibly.

"You're what?" she asked.

"Adopted," I said. "Well, I mean I was adopted. A long time ago. When I was a child."

"And why have you never told me this before?"

"I didn't think it was particularly important," I said. "Believe me, there's worse things I could tell you."

"Not particularly important? So who are your real mother and father?"

"I haven't a clue," I said.

"And are you not interested? Do you not want to find out?"

I shrugged. "Not really," I said. "Charles and Maude were my parents for all intents and purposes."

"Saints alive," she said. "So your mother might have been fallen too?"

I stared at her and felt a burst of anger within my chest. "Realistically speaking," I said, "almost certainly."

"Oh my God. Wait till I tell Daddy. No, I won't tell Daddy. And you're not to tell him either, do you hear me?"

"I hadn't planned on it," I said.

"He'd be shocked. It could bring on one of his hearts."

"I won't say a thing," I told her. "Although I really don't think it's all that important. There's lots of people who are adopted."

"Yes, but to come from stock like that. It's a bad strain in the family."

"The same thing that's happened to your cousin," I said.

"That's different," she snapped. "Sarah-Anne made a mistake, that's all."

"Well, maybe my mother just made a mistake too," I pointed out. "Would you not consider that?"

She shook her head, entirely dissatisfied. "There's something going on with you, Cyril Avery," she insisted. "Something you're not telling me. But I'll get to the bottom of it. I promise I will."

The Fall of Horatio

My flatmate Albert became engaged to be married to his girlfriend Dolores on a Monday night in early March and I joined him, his fiancée and an assortment of their hard-drinking brothers and sisters in Neary's pub to celebrate. A few hours later, unable to sleep as his headboard banged rhythmically against my wall, it was all that I could do to stop myself from marching in and throwing a bucket of water over the pair of them. The sound of their relentless passion had an unsettling effect on me, however, making me desperate for human contact, and, giving in to my frustrations, I threw on the same clothes that I'd been wearing earlier in the day and made my way down the stairs to emerge into the darkness of Chatham Street, already half-aroused by the excitement of what I hoped was to come. Stepping outside, I heard what I thought was the sound of footsteps behind me and looked around nervously but to my relief the street appeared to be empty.

Sometimes a few boys my own age could be found around the narrow, cobblestoned streets by the Stag's Head and I went there only to find them deserted. Crossing Dame Street and turning right for Crown Alley, I saw two young men standing by a wall, their heads held close in conversation, and I hid in a doorway, prepared to be a voyeur if that was all that was available to me. But instead of the sound of zips and anxious kissing, they were speaking to each other in Northern accents, and such was the urgency of their tone that I wished I had walked on instead of staying to eavesdrop.

"I just want to watch," said the taller of the two, a young man who sounded excitable and dangerous. "How often in our lives will we get to see something like this?"

"I don't care," said the other. "If we're too close when it happens, we could get caught."

"We won't get caught."

"How do you know that? And do you want to be the one explaining it to the boss if we do?"

My shoe slipped a little on the pavement and they turned in my direction, leaving me with no choice but to step out of the doorway and stride past them, hoping that they would not turn aggressive.

"What were you doing there?" asked the younger man, marching over. "Were you listening to us?"

"Leave it, Tommy," said his friend, and I took the opportunity to walk on, faster now, and to my relief they didn't follow me. Crossing over the Ha'penny Bridge, I aimed for one of the hidden corridors off Abbey Street where I had enjoyed a few clandestine encounters in the past and sure enough there was someone waiting there, smoking a cigarette as he leaned against a lamp post, and he signaled, tipping a finger to his cap as he saw me. When I got closer, however, I could see that he was old enough to be my grandfather and turned on my heel, cursing my luck. I began to resign myself to the idea of returning home unsatisfied when I remembered the public toilets toward the north end of O'Connell Street, the same place in which Julian had been propositioned some seven years earlier.

I had only ever had sex in a public toilet twice before, the first by accident—if one can have sex by accident—when I was seventeen and had been caught short walking past Trinity College and ran inside to the second-floor bathroom of the arts block for a piss. Standing at a urinal while one of the students washed his hands nearby, I grew conscious of the fact that he was staring at me. I looked around nervously but when he smiled I got an instant erection, the urine splashing off the wall and back against the crotch of my trousers. He laughed, then nodded in the direction of one of the cubicles, and I had followed him inside for my official deflowering. The second time was on a night as disappointing as this one, when I had been forced into a public convenience on Baggot Street for a deeply unsatisfying session with a boy my own age who burst forth like Vesuvius into my palm the moment I touched him. The seedy nature of these places meant that I preferred to stay away from them but I was desperate and so walked in the direction of Nelson's Pillar, wanting nothing more than to get the act over with so I could go home to bed.

Again, I had the distinct impression that I was being followed so I stopped, looking around anxiously, but could see no one behind me, save for a few drunks settling themselves against the walls of the GPO with blankets and cardboard boxes. Still, I kept my wits about me as I got closer to the toilet and saw the gate leading from the street lying open, its seductive light beckoning me inside.

I made my way down the steps and as I turned the corner into the black-and-white tiled room, I glanced around, disappointed to find there was no one there. I sighed and shook my head, ready to admit defeat, and was about to leave when a lock turned cautiously in one of the cubicles and a door opened to reveal a frightened-looking lad of around eighteen, wearing spectacles and a hat pulled down over his forehead. He peeped out like a nervous puppy growing accustomed to new surroundings and I looked back at him, waiting for some signal that we were there for the same reason. It was possible, of course, that he had simply been using the facilities and was about to wash his hands and leave. To say anything and be proven wrong could lead to disaster.

I gave him about thirty seconds and he didn't move at all, just stared at me, but when I saw his eyes move up and down my body I knew there was nothing to worry about.

"I don't have much time," I said, and to my surprise, after all I'd been through tonight, I found that I was no longer in the mood. I was standing in an underground cellar, surrounded by the stench of piss and shit, and condemned to finding some desperate form of affection with a complete stranger. My shoulders slumped in defeat and I pressed my thumb and forefingers to the corners of my eyes. "It's not fair, is it?" I said quietly after a moment, uncertain whether I was saying it to him, to myself or to the universe.

"I'm frightened," said the boy, and I pulled myself together, feeling pity for him. He was trembling; it was obvious that he was new at this.

"Do you ever just want to kill yourself?" I asked, looking him directly in the eyes.

"What?" he said, looking confused.

"There are times," I told him, "when I feel like taking a bread knife and just driving it into my heart."

He said nothing, looking around in bewilderment, before finally turning back to me and nodding.

"I tried it last year," he said. "Not a bread knife. It was a different way. Tablets. But it didn't work. I had to have my stomach pumped."

"Let's just go home," I said.

"I can't go home," he told me. "They threw me out."

"Who did?"

"My parents."

"Why?" I asked.

He looked down at the ground, embarrassed. "They found something," he said. "A magazine. I had it sent over from England."

"Then let's just go for a walk," I said. "We can walk and talk. Do you fancy that? Do you want to just go somewhere and have a chat?"

"All right," he said, smiling at me, and I felt an immediate affection for him, not desire, not lust, just affection.

"What's your name?" I asked.

He thought about it. *Peter* was what he came up with.

"I'm James," I said, reaching out a hand, and he took it and smiled again. It was at this moment that I realized that in all the encounters that I had ever had with strangers I had never looked into anyone's eyes before. I could remember some faces, some haircuts, some shoes, but the color of their eyes?

And that was the moment when I heard footsteps coming down the stairs. I turned around, my hand still holding his, as a uniformed member of An Garda Síochána appeared before me, the self-congratulatory smile on his fat, smug face mixing with the contempt that he felt for me and my kind.

"Well, what do we have here?" he asked. "A couple of Nancy-boys, is it?"

"Garda," I said, releasing the boy's hand. "This isn't what it looks like. We were just talking, that's all."

"Do you know how many times I've heard that line, you dirty queer?" he asked, spitting on the floor at my feet. "Now turn around there till I put the cuffs on you and don't try anything or I'll beat the living shit out of you and there's not a soul in the land who would blame me for it."

Before I could move I heard more footsteps and then, to my horror, a familiar face appeared in the doorway and I knew that I hadn't been wrong when I left Chatham Street. Someone *had* been following me all the way here. Someone who knew that I wasn't being completely honest with her.

"Mary-Margaret," I said, staring at her as she put her hands to her mouth, looking from one of us to the other in disbelief.

"This is the Gents' toilets," said Peter, rather pointlessly considering the situation. "There shouldn't be any women in here."

"I'm not a woman," she snapped, raising her voice as she turned on him with a fury that I had never seen before. "I'm his fiancée!"

"You know this fella, do you?" asked the Garda, turning to her now, and the boy saw his opportunity and ran forward, pushing the older man aside and almost knocking Mary-Margaret off her feet as he made a break for it. He was up the stairs and gone before any of us could move.

"Come back here, you!" called the Garda, looking up the stairs, but he knew it was pointless to follow. He was well over fifty and in bad shape; the boy would be halfway down O'Connell Street by now and gone forever.

"Well, I've got one of you anyway," said the Garda, turning back to me. "Are you ready for three years inside, son? Because that's what your type gets."

"Cyril!" cried Mary-Margaret, bursting into tears. "I knew there was something wrong. I knew it. But not this. I didn't think it would be this. I never suspected you were a pervert."

I barely heard her as the future passed quickly before my eyes: the newspaper reports, the court case, the inevitable guilty verdict, the indignities I would be subjected to in Mountjoy Prison. The possibility that I could even be murdered in there. Stories like that circulated all the time.

"Oh, Cyril, Cyril!" cried Mary-Margaret, her face in her hands. "What will Daddy say?"

"Please," I said, turning to the Garda, ready to throw myself on his mercy. "Let me go. I swear I won't do anything like this again."

"Not a chance in the world," he replied, pulling back and hitting me across the face.

"Hit him again, Garda," cried Mary-Margaret, her face red with humiliation and anger. "The filthy article."

And he did as he was asked, punching me so hard that I fell against the wall, my cheek colliding with the top of one of the urinals, and I heard the sound of something cracking within, followed by an instant numbness on the left-hand side of my face. When I turned back, a tooth fell from my mouth and we all watched as it bounced across the floor before settling on the edge of an open drain, hovering there with the impertinence of a golf ball that has reached the very edge of the hole but decided not to fall in.

I turned to look at my attacker, who was nursing the knuckles of one hand with the fingers of the other, and I stepped back, fearing that he would hit me again. I weighed up the possibility of punching him instead and making my escape but even in my distress I knew that this would be pointless. I might be able to overcome him but Mary-Margaret would surely report me and then they would come for me eventually. And so I gave in.

"Fine," I said, defeated, and the Garda reached out, taking me by the shoulder, and we ascended the steps together toward the street. Breathing in the cool night air I glanced toward the clock that hung outside Clerys department store from which every Dubliner set his or her watch. It had just turned one thirty in the morning. Three hours earlier I had been in the pub with my newly engaged friends. An hour before I had been in bed. I looked toward Mary-Margaret, who was staring at me with utter hatred on her face, and shrugged.

"I'm sorry," I said. "I can't help what I am. It's the way I was born."

"Fuck you!" she roared.

Before I could register my surprise at her words, an extraordinary noise burst from overhead, as if the heavens had opened and transformed themselves into a cacophonous thunder, and all three of us looked up in fright.

"Jesus, Mary and Joseph!" cried Mary-Margaret. "What in God's name was that?"

The noise seemed to diminish for a moment but then it grew louder and as I stared up I saw the statue of Admiral Lord Nelson teetering on his pillar, his expression more furious than ever, and it seemed to me that he had come to life as he leaped from his pedestal, his arms and head exploding from his body as the stone shattered above us.

"Look out!" cried the Garda. "The pillar's coming down."

He let go of me as we scattered, the stones began to fall, and I heard the noise of the great sculpture exploding into fragments and starting to rain down onto O'Connell Street.

This is it, I thought. *This is the moment of my death.*

I ran as fast as I could, somehow escaping the blocks of stone as they crashed to the ground, breaking into hundreds of pieces, shrapnel raining down on my back and head. I waited for unconsciousness, sure that it would bring my tormented life to an end at any moment. When I stopped running and turned around to look back, the street was at peace once again but the area where the three of us had been standing was invisible now under a cloud of smoke. In the heat of the moment, all I could think about was those moments when, as a child, I had entered Maude's study uninvited and been unable to find her in the fog.

"Mary-Margaret!" I cried, my voice turning into a roar as I ran back.

As I got closer to where we had been standing, I stumbled over a body and looked down and there was the Garda who had arrested me, flat on his back now, his eyes wide open, dead to the world. I did my best to feel sorry for him but in my selfishness I couldn't. He was gone and it wasn't my fault, there was no more to it. There would be no arrest. No public humiliation.

I heard a sound to my left and there was Mary-Margaret lying under a great boulder, Nelson's nose pressed to her cheek as if he was having a good sniff of her perfume, one of his eyes lying on the ground staring at her. She was still breathing but I could tell from the gasping in her throat that she hadn't long left.

"Mary-Margaret," I said, taking her hand. "I'm sorry. I'm so sorry."

"You're a filthy article," she hissed, blood seeping from her mouth as she struggled to get the words out. "Not my standard at all."

"I know," I said. "I know."

And then, a moment later, she was gone. And so was I, running down O'Connell Street for home. There was no point staying there. I knew one thing for sure: that this was the end of it. There would be no more men, no more boys. It would just be women from now on. I would be like everyone else.

I would be normal if it killed me.

1973 Keeping the Devil at Bay

Some Mothers Do 'Ave 'Em

Julian arrived at my flat just before eight o'clock wearing a tie-dyed shirt open halfway down his chest, a pair of hip-hugger jeans and a purple Nehru jacket. Although his hair was cut into a close crop, reminiscent of Steve McQueen in *Papillon*, he eschewed the requisite sideburns, which only brought attention to his missing right ear. Around his neck he wore a chain of mixed shells and beads which, he told me, he'd purchased from a centenarian stall holder in Rishikesh when he and a former girlfriend had traveled there to meet the Maharishi Mahesh Yogi. The colors picked up the sparkle from a psychedelic ring on his right hand that he had stolen from Brian Jones when they were coming down from an LSD high in Arthur's nightclub on East 54th Street two weeks earlier.

"Other than that, it's been a quiet few months," he said, looking me up and down with a frown. "But why aren't you dressed yet? We're going to be late."

"I am dressed," I replied. "Look at me."

"Well, you're wearing clothes," he agreed. "But not the type that a twenty-eight-year-old man with any sense of style would wear on a night out, especially when they're going to a stag party. Who did you get them from anyway, your dad?"

"I've never met my dad," I said.

"Your *adoptive* father then," he replied with a sigh. "Honestly, Cyril, must you say that every single—"

"Charles and I don't share clothes," I said, interrupting him. "We're completely different sizes for one thing."

"Well, you're not going out looking like that. Or rather, I'm not going out with you looking like that. Come on, you must have something in there that doesn't make you look like Richard Nixon's less fashionable younger brother."

He marched past me and when he opened the door to my bedroom

I felt panic course through my body, such as one might feel while in-
serting a faulty plug into a damaged socket. My mind scrambled as I
tried to recall whether I had left anything incriminating on display in
there. I prayed that my autumn 1972 edition of *Modern Male*, featuring
a swarthy boxer on its cover wearing nothing but a pair of bright-red
gloves, was safely locked away in the second drawer of my bedside
locker, accompanied by the issue of *Hombre* that I'd ordered from a
carefully worded advertisement on the back page of the *Sunday World*
just after Christmas. I'd spent two weeks panicking over its arrival,
fearing that some religious zealot with X-ray eyes from Dublin Airport Customs would seize the package and rip the degenerate publica-
tion from its wrapping before making an outraged phone call and
sending the Gardaí to my door. And then there was the issue of *Vim*
that I'd stolen from an adult shop masquerading as a Unionist meeting-
place on a day trip to Belfast six months earlier. On the journey home,
stopped at border control, I'd stuffed it down the back of my trousers
but, luckily for me, the inspectors seemed content to confiscate two
gross of condoms from an elderly grandmother who was disguising
her bad intentions in a Legion of Mary outfit.

I'd planned on putting all these magazines into a paper bag the following morning and disposing of them in a dustbin a few streets from
my flat, a final farewell to a way of life that I was leaving behind.
Standing there now, afraid to move as my friend rummaged around
my bedroom, I reasoned with myself that Julian would have no cause
to open the locker, so I was probably safe. It was shirts and jeans he
was looking for, after all, not the type of knick-knacks and trifles that
were generally kept in such places. But still, there was something lingering at the back of my mind, some slight disquiet that I had not been
as careful as I should have been, and it came back to me at the same
moment that he appeared before me in the doorway, holding a magazine with such distaste that it might have been a soiled handkerchief
or a used prophylactic.

"What the fuck is this, Cyril?" he asked, staring at me in bewilderment.

"What's what?" I said, trying my best to sound innocent of all
wrongdoing.

"*Tomorrow's Man*," he said, reciting the words printed across the cover. "*The International Magazine of Body-Building*. Don't tell me you've taken that up, have you? Everyone knows that's just for queers."

I gave an enormous stretch, simulating fatigue in the hope that this might explain the pulsating redness that had come into my cheeks.

"I've been putting on a bit of weight lately," I said. "I thought it might help me to lose it."

"Where? On your eyebrows? Sure there's not a pick on you, Cyril. If anything, you look malnourished."

"Sorry, yes, that's what I meant," I told him. "I want to put weight on, that's it. Some muscle. Lots of muscle. Lots and lots of muscle."

"You just said that you wanted to lose it."

"I got confused," I said, shaking my head. "I can't think clearly today at all."

"Well, I suppose that's understandable considering what's happening tomorrow. Jesus, would you take a look at this fella," he said, pointing to the muscle-bound youth adorning the front of the magazine wearing nothing but a green posing pouch, his hands behind his head as he flexed his muscles and stared off into the distance, apparently lost in thought. "Some mothers do 'ave 'em, am I right?"

I nodded, hoping that he would put the blasted thing away and return to the question of what I was going to wear, but he flicked through the pages instead, shaking his head and bursting out laughing at the specimens of masculinity that, if I was honest, were not entirely to my taste but who I appreciated for their willingness to disrobe for a camera.

"Do you remember Jasper Timson?" he asked.

"From school?" I asked, recalling the annoying boy from our year at school who played the piano accordion, was constantly trying to steal Julian away from me and over whom I'd nevertheless had the occasional wank.

"Yes. Well, he's one of them."

"One of what?" I asked innocently. "A swimmer?"

"No, a queer."

"Get out of town," I said, employing a line I'd heard recently in *The French Connection*.

"It's true," he told me. "He's even got a boyfriend. They live together in Canada."

"Christ," I said, shaking my head in disbelief. What, he just "had" a boyfriend and they just "lived together"? Could it really be that simple?

"Actually, I always knew that he was of them but I never told a soul," said Julian.

"How did you know? Did he tell you?"

"Not in so many words. But he made a pass at me once."

My eyes opened wide in disbelief. "Get. Out. Of. Town," I repeated, pausing for effect between each word. "When? How? Why?"

"It was back when we were in third or fourth year, I can't remember which. Someone had snuck a bottle of vodka into school and a few of us knocked it back after a maths exam. Do you not remember?"

"No," I said, frowning. "I don't think I was there."

"Maybe you weren't invited."

"So what happened?" I asked, trying not to allow the semi-insult to wound me too deeply.

"Well, the pair of us were sitting on my bed," he said. "Backs to the wall. We were pretty drunk and talking a load of old nonsense and the next thing I knew he'd leaned over and had his tongue halfway down my throat."

"You are fucking *kidding* me," I cried, appalled and excited all at once, the room spinning slightly as I tried to take this in. "And what did you do? Did you hit him?"

"Of course I didn't hit him," he said, frowning. "Why would I do that? I'm a peaceful guy, Cyril. You know that."

"No, but—"

"I kissed him back, that's what I did. It seemed like the polite thing to do at the time."

"You did *what*?" I asked, wondering whether my head was about to spin around my shoulders in three-hundred-and-sixty-degree turns while my eyes popped from my head, like that little girl in *The Exorcist*.

"I kissed him back," repeated Julian with a shrug. "I'd never done that before. With a boy, I mean. So I thought what the hell. Let's see what it's like. I'll try anything once. When I was in Africa, I ate a crocodile steak."

I stared at him, astonished and devastated at the same time. Julian Woodbead, the one boy with whom I'd been in love all my life and who had never shown the slightest romantic interest in me, had gone lips to lips with Jasper Timson, a boy whose greatest passion in life was playing the piano fucking accordion! In fact, I could remember walking in once to find the pair of them giggling away. It must have happened only a few minutes earlier. I sat down, anxious to hide the massive erection that had built in my trousers.

"I don't believe it," I said.

"Hey, don't bug out," said Julian nonchalantly. "It's 1973 for Christ's sake. Get with the program. Anyway, it didn't last very long and did nothing for me, so that was the end of that. Nothing ventured, nothing gained. Jasper wanted more, of course, but I said no. I told him that I wasn't a dirty queer and he said he didn't care if I was or wasn't, he still wanted to suck my cock."

"Jesus Christ!" I said, sitting up now, practically trembling in a mixture of rage and desire. "You didn't let him, did you?"

"Of course I didn't let him, Cyril. Give me some credit. Anyway, he didn't seem too bothered, because he didn't try again. Although one good thing came out of it: he said that if I was going to go around kissing people then I should clean my teeth first because my breath smelled of Tayto crisps. That was sound advice. I've stuck with it over the years and it's got me far."

"But you were friends with Jasper until the end of school," I said, recalling how I had always felt a twinge of jealousy whenever I saw them together.

"Of course I was," said Julian, looking at me as if I was mad. "Why wouldn't I be? He was a right laugh, was Jasper. I looked him up when I was in Toronto last year but he and his fella had gone off on a dirty weekend somewhere. He'd love this though," he added, tossing the copy of *Tomorrow's Man* on an armchair and returning to the bedroom, where he pulled open my wardrobe and looked inside judgmentally. "But you should get rid of it, Cyril. People could get the wrong idea. Now, let's have a look at what you've got in here. This maybe?" He held up a purple, wide-collared shirt that I'd bought in the Dandelion Market a few months earlier and had never got around to wearing.

"Do you think?" I asked.

"Well, it's better than that granddad gear. Come on, put it on and let's get the night started. Those pints won't drink themselves."

I felt slightly self-conscious as I took my shirt off, and the fact that he continued to watch me as I dressed filled me with anxiety.

"How's that?" I asked.

"Well, it's an improvement. If I'd had a couple of extra hours, I could have taken you into town and got you some proper gear. Doesn't matter." He threw his arm around me and I carefully inhaled the scent of his cologne, my lips unbearably close to his jawline. "How are you feeling anyway? Ready for the big day?"

"I suppose," I said, not the most confident of replies, as we left the flat and made our way toward Baggot Street. I'd been living alone on Waterloo Road for a few years by now, employed as a researcher at RTÉ, where my workload was divided equally between religious programing and farming shows. I knew next to nothing about either but found out quickly enough that all you had to do was hold a microphone in someone's face and he'd talk till the cows came home.

We'd arranged to go to Doheny & Nesbitt's, where some of my colleagues were gathered for the stag party, and I was a little anxious about introducing them to Julian. I'd spoken about him often, describing the many milestones of our friendship, but this would be the first time that these two important elements of my life had come into contact with each other. Over the years, I had created two fundamentally dishonest portraits of myself, one for my oldest friend and another for my newest ones, and they had only a few brushstrokes in common. Revelations from either side could see the whole artifice fall apart and with it the plans I had made for my future.

"I was sorry to hear about you and Rebecca," I said as we crossed the Grand Canal, trying hard to conceal my delight that Julian had broken up with his latest squeeze. "I thought you and her were well suited."

"Oh that's old news," he said with a wave of his hand. "Anyway, there's been an Emily since then, a Jessica, and now I'm on to a new Rebecca. Rebecca mark two. Smaller tits but, fuck me, she's a spitfire in the sack. Not that it will last very long, of course. Another week or two, I'd say, at most."

"How do you get bored with people so quickly?" I asked, for the concept was one that I simply couldn't grasp. Had I been lucky enough to find a person with whom I wanted to have regular sex while still being able to walk hand in hand with him on the streets of Dublin without being arrested, I would never have let him go.

"It's not exactly *boredom*," he said, shaking his head. "But there's a whole world of women out there and I'm not interested in being stuck with the same one for the rest of my life. There's been a few along the way, of course, that I wouldn't have minded a longer relationship with but they insist on monogamy and I'm not built for that. This might surprise you, Cyril, but I've never once cheated on a girlfriend."

"No, you just dump them instead."

"Exactly. And isn't that a more honest way to behave? But here's the thing, and I think everyone secretly believes this if they'd just let themselves admit it: the world would be a much healthier place if we allowed each other to do exactly what we wanted, when we wanted, with who we wanted, and didn't lay down puritanical rules for how to conduct our sex lives. We could live with the person we love the most, for companionship and affection, but we could go out and have sex with willing partners and perhaps even talk about it when we got home."

"By that logic," I said, "you and I could get married and live together forever."

"Well, yes," he replied, laughing. "I suppose we could."

"Just imagine it!"

"Yes."

"Anyway, these things are easy to say," I told him, trying not to linger on that idea too deeply. "But you wouldn't like it if your girlfriend slept with someone else."

"If you think that," he said, "then you don't know me at all. I genuinely couldn't care less. Jealousy is an utterly futile emotion."

We passed Toners on our left-hand side and he marched across the road, the traffic coming to a halt to let him pass; when I followed in his wake a moment later, every car honked their horn at me. Pushing open the door to the pub I could hear the buzz of the crowd within and looked around for my colleagues. I was expecting three of them: Martin Horan and Stephen Kilduff, two fellow researchers who shared an office with me, and Jimmy Byrnes, an on-air reporter who thought he was one of Ireland's biggest celebrities just because he'd appeared on a few episodes of *7 Days*. When I found them seated together at a corner table, I raised a hand in greeting but my smile faded when I saw that they'd been joined by a fourth person, Nick Carlton, a cameraman who worked on *Wanderly Wagon* and whom I had gone to great pains to ensure heard nothing about this gathering.

"Cyril!" they shouted, and I wondered how it would look if I bolted for the door and made a run for it down Baggot Street. Bizarre, I assumed, and so I introduced Julian to each of them in turn and he took orders for a fresh round of drinks, striding over to the bar where the crowd parted like Moses before the Red Sea to let him through.

"Nick," I said, glancing at him as I sat down. "I didn't expect to see you here tonight."

"Well, it's not my usual sort of establishment, I grant you," he said, lighting a Superking and holding it in his left hand, which he held at a right angle to his arm, his elbow resting on the table before him. "But I thought I'd come out and see how the other half lives."

The truth was, I envied Nick Carlton. He was the only homosexual I knew who not only embraced his sexuality but sang it proudly from the rooftops. But such was his good humor and his resolute lack of shame that no one seemed to mind. The other lads made jokes about him behind his back, of course, in order to emphasize their own rigid heterosexuality, but nevertheless they usually included him in their outings and seemed to have adopted him as something of a mascot.

"And I'm very glad I did now," he continued, glancing toward Julian, who was returning with a tray of pints. "Nobody said you were bringing Ryan O'Neal with you."

"Ryan O'Neal was on *The Late Late Show* a few weeks back," said Jimmy. "I'm surprised you didn't come down and stake out his dressing room, Nick."

"I was under strict instructions from the powers that be to leave him in peace," said Nick. "Spoilsports. Anyway, it was Miss O'Mahoney's birthday that night and she'd never have forgiven me if I hadn't shown up."

The lads guffawed and I laid into my Guinness, downing about a third of it in one go.

"Have I seen you on *7 Days*?" Julian asked Jimmy, who beamed with delight at being recognized. "It's all showbiz here, I'd say, is it? You must get to see all the stars out at RTÉ."

"I've met Princess Grace of Monaco," said Stephen.

"I've met Tommy Docherty," said Martin.

"Occasionally, I write the script for Mr. Crow," said Nick.

Perhaps it was his clothes, or the way he talked, or the way he looked. Perhaps it was the aura of sex that always emanated from him, as if he'd just risen from the bed of a model and left the house without even bothering to take a shower. Whatever it was, men, women, straight or gay, everyone wanted Julian to like them.

"Mr. Crow," said Julian, considering this for a moment. "He's the lad that pops out of the clock on *Wanderly Wagon*, is that right?"

"Yes," said Nick, flushing a little in glory.

"Get out of town!"

"That's my line," I said irritably, to no avail.

"Why, do you watch it?" asked Nick, ignoring me.

"I've seen it."

"It's a kids' show," I said.

"Yeah, but it's mad stuff. Are you all on drugs when you're making it or what?"

"I couldn't possibly comment," said Nick, winking at him. "But let's just say it's always a good idea to knock before entering anyone's dressing room."

"What is it you do yourself, Julian?" asked Stephen, offering him a cigarette, which he refused. Julian didn't smoke. He had a phobia about it and always told girls that they would have to quit if they wanted a relationship with him.

"I don't do very much at all, to be honest," he said. "My old man's ridiculously rich and he gives me a monthly allowance, so I just go off and do a bit of traveling. Once in a while I write an article for *Travel & Leisure* or *Holiday*. Last year I visited Mauritius with Princess Margaret and Noël Coward and wrote a piece about the wildlife there."

"Did you fuck her?" asked Nick casually.

"I did, yes," replied Julian, as if it was neither here nor there. "Only once but, trust me, once was enough. I'm not keen on being ordered around."

"Did you fuck him?"

"No, but he was polite enough to ask. She didn't. She just seemed to assume that's what I was there for."

"Jesus Christ!" said Jimmy, utterly enthralled.

"That must be why you have such a good color," said Nick. "All that time spent on private islands populated by Old Money whores and nouveau riche chi-chi men. Any chance you'd take me with you next time?"

Julian burst out laughing and shrugged his shoulders. "Why not?" he said. "There's always room in my suitcase for a little one."

"Who says I'm a little one?" asked Nick, faking offense.

"Get me drunk enough and maybe I'll find out," said Julian, and the whole table, with the exception of me, exploded in laughter.

"I don't want to point out the obvious," said Nick when the merriment died down. "But are you aware that you're missing an ear?"

"I am," said Julian. "And look." He held up his right hand to display the four fingers that remained there. "I'm down a thumb too. And the little toe from my left foot."

"I remember when you were kidnapped," said Martin, for I had told them all before about the most famous incident of Julian's (and my own) life so far. "We had bets in class on which body part would arrive in the post next."

"And let me guess," said Julian. "You all hoped it would be my dick."

"Yeah," said Martin with a shrug. "Sorry."

"It's OK. Everyone wanted that. Fortunately, it's still where it should be."

"Prove it," said Nick, which made Stephen spit a mouthful of Guinness across the table, narrowly missing me.

"Sorry," he said, grabbing a napkin to clean up the mess.

"Actually, they said they were going to pop an eye out next," said Julian. "But I was found before that could happen. I asked Damien last year whether he thought they would have gone through with it and he said they would."

"Who's Damien?" I asked, having not heard him mention any friend by this name before.

"One of the kidnappers," he replied. "Do you remember the guy who threw me in the boot of the car? Him."

We were all silent for a few moments and I stared at him in bewilderment. "Wait a minute," I said finally. "Are you telling me that you've been in touch with one of those IRA guys?"

"Yes," he said with a shrug. "Did you not know that? We've been pen pals for quite a while now. I go in to visit him in jail occasionally too."

"But why?" I asked, raising my voice. "Why would you do that?"

"Well, it was a very intense experience," he said casually. "I spent a week living with those guys under very trying circumstances. And you must remember that they weren't very much older than we were back then. They were almost as frightened as I was. Their overlords, or whatever you call them, had tasked them with kidnapping me and they wanted to do it right. To get promoted up the ranks, so to speak. Actually, we got along quite well most of the time."

"Even when they were cutting parts of you off?" I asked.

"Well, no. Not then. Although Damien never did that. In fact, he threw up when they cut my ear off. We get along very well now as it happens. He's due for release in about ten years. I daresay I'll take him out for a pint. Forgive and forget, that's my motto."

"Well, good for you," said Nick. "No point holding a grudge, is there?"

I felt utterly uncomfortable sitting next to him, because, although we didn't know each other well, he had seen a side of me that the others hadn't. Shortly after I'd started working at RTÉ, a party had been organized for the spurious reason of celebrating Dana winning the Eurovision Song Contest and a large group of us had ended up in a city-center pub in the small hours of the morning. I was already three sheets to the wind when I found myself out in a back alley taking a piss and a moment later Nick appeared in the laneway too. I had never even fancied the man but, depressed and horny, I took a chance and made a lunge for him before he could even start what he'd come out there to do, pressing him back against the wall and kissing him while grabbing his hand and pushing it down toward my cock. He went with it for about half a minute before shaking his head and pushing me away.

"Sorry, Cyril," he said, looking at me with something approaching pity. "You seem like a nice fella but you're just not my type."

I sobered up almost immediately. I had never, ever been rejected and was dumbfounded that my advances should be rebuffed. In those days, homosexuals took what they could, where they could and were glad of it. Attraction was considered a bonus but never a requirement. When I woke late the next afternoon, the memory slowly returning to me like a ghastly nightmare that wouldn't go away, I was horrified by what I had done. I considered handing in my notice immediately at RTÉ but it had taken too long for me to find a job that paid enough to allow me to live alone and the idea of going back to sharing with someone was unbearable. And so I pretended that it had never happened and in the three years since then had done my best to avoid him. But it was impossible to shake the knowledge that whenever he looked at me he understood me better than anyone else alive.

"So let me get this straight," said Martin, looking toward me and Julian. "You two have known each other since your school days, is that right?"

"We shared a room for six years," said Julian.

"I bet Cyril loved that," said Nick, and I threw him a filthy glance.

"Although, actually, we first met when we were seven," I pointed out, wanting to stress just how long we had been in each other's lives. "His father came to my house to meet with my adoptive father and I found Julian lurking in the hallway."

"Cyril always tells me that," said Julian. "I don't remember it."

"Well I do," I said quietly.

"I remember some lad when I was that age asking whether we could show each other our cocks but Cyril claims that wasn't him."

The three lads spluttered over their pints and Nick put a hand to his face. I could see his shoulders shuddering with laughter. I didn't bother to repudiate it again.

"And you're the best man?" asked Stephen, when the teasing died down.

"I am," said Julian.

"How's the speech coming along?"

"It's almost there. I hope no one's too sensitive. It's a bit blue at times."

"Ah, Julian," I said, pulling a face. "I asked you to keep it clean."

"Don't worry, it's mild enough," he said, grinning at me. "Alice would kill me if I said anything out of order. So here's to Cyril anyway," he added, lifting his pint, and the others did too. "A lifelong friend and, twenty-four hours from now, my brother-in-law. My sister's a very lucky woman."

"She must have done something wonderful in a previous life," added Nick as he clinked his glass against mine.

Alice

Although Alice's and my paths had crossed occasionally over the years, our romantic relationship had only begun some eighteen months earlier at a party to mark Julian's departure to South America for a six-month trek across the Andes. This was probably his most infamous escapade, as it involved traveling with his girlfriends at the time, a pair of Finnish twins by the names of Emmi and Peppi who, he claimed, had been conjoined at birth and were only separated by an American surgeon when they were four years old. It was true that whenever I looked at them they seemed to be leaning toward each other at a slightly unnatural angle.

Only two years my junior, Alice had matured from a somewhat awkward adolescence into an incredibly beautiful young woman, a female version of Julian himself, sharing the fine cheekbones and deep-blue eyes that had first drawn my adoptive father Charles to their mother Elizabeth, rather than the bulbous nose and amphibian-like eyes that they might have inherited from Max. She did not, however, share her brother's promiscuous ways, having spent seven years dating a young medical student named Fergus, a relationship that had come to an end on the morning of their wedding when he telephoned just as she and Max were leaving Dartmouth Square for the church to tell her that he couldn't go through with it. *Cold feet* was his predictable and boring explanation and within a few days he had disappeared off to Madagascar where, it was said, he was still working as a junior doctor in a leprosy clinic. I remember running into Julian by chance a few days later on Grafton Street and can still recall the distressed expression on his face as he told me what had happened. He loved his sister deeply and the notion of someone hurting her was unbearable for him.

"Don't feel you have to sit with me, Cyril," said Alice as we looked over toward the corner of the bar where Julian was seated like the meat in a Finnish sandwich while a group of his friends ogled them enviously, longing for a bite. "If you'd rather go over there with the boys, I'm perfectly content with my book."

"They're all strangers to me," I said. "Where did he find them anyway? They look like the cast of *Hair*."

"I think they're what are commonly referred to as socialites," she said, her voice dripping with disdain. "The dictionary definition would be a bunch of self-regarding, narcissistic, physically attractive but intellectually hollow individuals whose parents have so much money that they don't need to do a day's work themselves. Instead, they go from party to party, desperate to be seen, while gradually corroding from the inside out, like a spent battery, due to their lack of ambition, insight or wit."

"You're not a fan then?" I asked, and she just shrugged. "Still, it sounds like more fun than getting up at seven o'clock every morning and traipsing across the city to sit behind a desk for eight hours. What are you reading anyway?" I asked, noticing the corner of a book poking out from her bag, and she reached down to retrieve a copy of John McGahern's *The Dark*. "Isn't that banned?"

"I believe it is, yes," she said. "What's your point?"

"I don't have one, really. What's it about?"

"A boy and his abusive father. I should give it to Julian to read."

I said nothing. If there was any serious tension between her brother and father, I had never heard about it before.

"So tell me, Cyril," she said. "Are you still working in the civil service?"

"Oh no," I said. "I left there a long time ago. It wasn't for me. I work for RTÉ now."

"That must be exciting."

"It has its moments," I lied. "And what about you? Do you work?"

"I believe I do but Max would say differently." As I waited for her to continue, it struck me that she, like me, called her father by his Christian name. "I've been researching and writing a PhD in English Literature at UCD for the last few years. I wanted to go to Trinity but the Archbishop wouldn't let me."

"Did you ask him?"

"I did," she said. "I went all the way to the palace in Drumcondra and knocked on the front door, bold as brass. His housekeeper wanted to kick me out into the gutter, of course, because I was wearing a dress that exposed my shoulders, but he invited me in and I made my request in person. He seemed to think that I was a bit odd for wanting a career at all. He told me that if I put as much effort into finding a husband as I did into my studies I'd have a home, a family and three children by now."

"What a charmer," I said, laughing despite myself. "And what did you say?"

"I told him that when your fiancé leaves you on the morning of your wedding while two hundred of your friends and family are waiting for you in a church half a mile away, then marriage isn't necessarily the first thing on your mind."

"Ah," I said, looking down at my shoes uneasily. "I suppose not."

"He said I was a lovely girl, though," she added with a smile, "so I have that going in my favor at least. Anyway, as it turns out I'm glad that I ended up in UCD. I've made some good friends there. I'll finish my degree in about a year's time and the department has already offered me a teaching position for the following semester. I could be a professor in about five years if I keep my head down and don't lose my focus."

"And is that what you want?" I asked her. "To spend your life in academia?"

"It is," she said, looking around and wincing at the raucous noise coming from Julian's friends. "I sometimes feel as if I wasn't supposed to live among people at all. As if I would be happier on a little island somewhere, all alone with my books and some writing material for company. I could grow my own food and never have to speak to a soul. I look at him sometimes," she added, nodding toward her brother, "and it's as if we were born with two life-forces between us but he got all of his share and half of mine too."

She didn't say this with any resentment or self-pity—it was clear to me from the look on her face that she adored him as much as I did—and I felt an instant kinship with her. Her idea of a safe haven appealed to me too. A place I could go, simply to be left alone.

"Do you think that's because of . . . well, what happened?" I asked. "Your desire to remove yourself from the world, I mean."

"Because of what Fergus did to me?"

"Yes."

She shook her head. "No, I don't think so," she said. "I was a rather solitary child and that didn't change much as I grew older. Although it didn't help, of course. That kind of humiliation is almost never visited upon a person. Did you know that Max insisted on the reception going ahead afterward?"

"What?" I said, uncertain whether she was joking or not.

"It's true," she continued. "He said that the wedding had cost him a fortune already and he wasn't going to allow that amount of money to go to waste. So he dragged me off to the hotel in the Daimler that he'd booked for me and Fergus, and when we got out, the staff were all lined up along the red carpet. I could see some of them looking at us wondering why has that young woman married a man old enough to be her father and the rest thinking that was the reason I had such a miserable expression on my face. There was a champagne reception, where I had to go from person to person, thanking them for coming and apologizing on Fergus's behalf, and then I was made to sit at the head table while the guests ate and drank to their hearts' content. Max even made a speech, if you can believe it. He read it from a piece of paper and didn't change a word, because apparently he'd spent days on it. *This is the happiest day of my life*, he said. *Alice deserves this. I've never seen a happier bride.* It went on and on like that. It was almost comical."

"But why on earth did you go through with it?" I asked. "Why didn't you just go home? Or, you know, jump on a flight to Mars or someplace?"

"Well, I was a bit shell-shocked, I suppose. I didn't know what else to do. I loved Fergus, you see. Very much. And of course, I'd never been jilted on my wedding day before," she added, smiling a little, "which meant I wasn't sure what the etiquette of the situation was. So I just did what I was told."

"Fucking Max," I said, surprising both of us by my use of a word that I rarely employed.

"Fucking Fergus," replied Alice.

"Fucking both of them. What do you think, should we have a couple more of these fucking drinks?"

"Fuck yes," she said, and I grinned as I stood up to make my way to the bar.

"You'll miss him, I suppose?" said Alice when I returned with two large glasses of wine. "Six months is a long time."

"I will," I said. "He's my best friend."

"Mine too," she said. "So what does that make us?"

"Rivals?" I suggested, and she laughed. I was drawn to her; there was no question about that. Not physically but emotionally. Temperamentally. For the first time in my life, I felt content to be seated in the company of a girl while Julian was somewhere else in the room. My eyes were not being constantly pulled in his direction, nor was I feeling jealous that others were dominating his time. It was an entirely new sensation for me and one that I rather enjoyed.

"Have you seen anyone famous out at RTÉ?" she asked me after a brief silence, during which I had racked my brain for something witty to say and come up short.

"Paul McCartney was there once," I said.

"Oh I love Paul McCartney! I saw the Beatles when they played the Adelphi in 1963. I even went to the Gresham Hotel afterward and pretended I was a guest so that I could get in to see them."

"Did it work?"

"No. Biggest disappointment of my life." She hesitated and then smiled at me. "Well, you know, that is until the obvious. Can I tell you something, Cyril?"

"Of course," I said.

"It's about my PhD," she said. "The thing is, I'm writing it on your mother's books."

"Really?" I said, raising an eyebrow.

"Yes. Does that make you uncomfortable?"

"No," I said. "But you should probably know, Maude was my adoptive mother, not my birth mother."

"Yes, I know that," she said. "Where did they get you from anyway? Were you found on the doorstep one day? Or did you just wash in on the tide at Dun Laoghaire pier?"

"The family legend has it that a little hunchbacked Redemptorist nun brought me to them," I told her. "They wanted a child, or they said that they did, and here was a child."

"And your birth parents? Have you ever tracked them down?"

"I've never even tried. I'm not that interested, to be honest."

"Why not?" she asked. "Are you angry at them?"

"No, not at all," I told her. "I had a reasonably happy childhood, which is rather strange in retrospect, as neither Charles nor Maude showed any particular interest in me at all. But they didn't beat me or starve me or anything like that. I wasn't a Dickensian orphan, if you know what I mean. And as for my birth mother, well I daresay she did what she had to do. I assume she was unmarried, that's where adopted babies usually come from, isn't it? No, I don't feel any anger at all. What's the point?"

"That's good to hear. There's nothing more tedious than a grown man blaming his parents, birth or otherwise, for all the things that have gone wrong in his life."

"You're assuming that things have gone wrong in my life."

"There's something in your face that tells me that you're not happy. Oh I'm sorry, that's a very personal remark. I shouldn't have said that."

"No, it's fine," I said, although I felt a little crestfallen that she could read me so well.

"Anyway, Fergus was quite like that. Always blaming other people for issues that were his own to solve. It was one of the few things that I didn't like about him, if I'm honest."

"So are you still angry at him?" I asked, conscious that this too was a deeply personal question but it balanced out what she had said to me.

"Oh I hate him," she said, and I noticed a flush of color come into her cheeks and the manner in which the fingers of her left hand dug into her palm, as if she wanted something to take away her pain. "I absolutely detest him. Afterward, I didn't feel very much at all for a week or two. I suppose I was in shock. But then the fury rose and it hasn't subsided since. Sometimes I find it difficult to control. I think it was around the time that everyone stopped asking me whether I was all right, when lives went back to how they had been before. Had he been in Dublin I might well have gone over there, broken down his door and stabbed him as he slept. Fortunately for him, he was in Madagascar with his lepers."

I snorted some of my drink through my nose and had to retrieve my handkerchief from my pocket to wipe my face. "Sorry," I said, unable to stop laughing. "It's just the way you put it. I'm not mocking you."

"It's fine," she said, laughing now too, and I could see that it did her good to make light of it. "It *is* quite comical when you think of it. I mean if he'd left me for Jane Fonda then that would be one thing. But for a bunch of lepers? I didn't even know that there *were* lepers anymore. I only knew what they were because Max's favorite film is *Ben-Hur* and I've been forced to watch it with him numerous times."

"Well, it was his loss," I said.

"Oh don't patronize me," she snapped, turning serious again. "People always say that, you see, but they're wrong. It wasn't his loss. It was mine. I loved him." She hesitated for a moment and then repeated the phrase, with added emphasis on the crucial word. "And I still miss him, despite everything. I just wish he'd been honest with me, that's all. If he'd told me a few days before that he didn't love me enough to marry me, if we could have just sat down and discussed things, then even if he'd still wanted to call it all off, it would have been difficult but at least I could have been part of the decision. I wouldn't have had to suffer such deep humiliation. But the manner in which he left me? Simply telephoning when I was already in my dress to tell me about his ridiculous 'cold feet'? What sort of man does that? And what sort of woman does it make me that if he walked in here right now I'd probably throw myself into his arms?"

"I'm sorry that happened to you, Alice," I said. "No one should have to endure such cruelty."

"Fortunately for me," she said, looking down and wiping her eyes, where the tears were threatening to break over the banks of her eyelids, "I had your mother to console me. Your *adoptive* mother, that is. I simply threw myself into my work. Her work. I've lived and breathed Maude Avery since then and in her books I've found great solace. She was a wonderful writer."

"She was," I said. I had at least read most of her novels by then.

"It's as if she understood completely the condition of loneliness and how it undermines us all, forcing us to make choices that we know are wrong for us. With each successive novel, she explores the theme even more deeply. It's extraordinary. Did you read Malleson's biography of her?"

"I glanced at it," I said. "I didn't read it cover to cover. The woman he presented seemed very different from the woman I knew. As if she was a fictional character, not a real person. Or one of them was. The Maude I knew or the Maude who comes through from the pages of her books. Or both of them, who knows?"

"You feature in it, you know."

"Yes, I know."

We were silent for a few moments until Alice spoke again. "I still find it astonishing that I live in the house that was once hers," she said. "And yours, I suppose. It was a nasty thing that Max did, buying it out from under Maude's feet when your father went to jail. And at such a knock-down price."

"Well, Charles had it coming," I said with a shrug. "If he hadn't seduced your mother, then Max wouldn't have wanted revenge."

"My mother likes to play the innocent victim in that story," she told me. "But she was equally culpable. No woman is ever truly seduced. It's a mutual decision on the part of the seducer and the seduced. Ironically, the only person who really suffered was the one who had done nothing wrong."

"Maude."

"Exactly. Maude. She lost her home. She lost her writing room. She lost her sanctuary. To have a place where you feel safe, where you can work, is more important than anyone can realize until it's gone. Especially for a woman. And of course, she died not long afterward."

"Yes, but that was the smoking," I said, beginning to feel a little upset by the turn the conversation was taking. The grief and pity that Alice felt for my adoptive mother had never been equaled by me in the twenty years since her death and it shamed me that this was the case. "It wasn't as if she died of a broken heart or anything."

"But it couldn't have helped. Don't you think the two things were connected? That the cancer took over completely because of all the things she'd lost?"

"No, I think she died because she spent all her adult life puffing on cigarettes non-stop from the moment she woke up in the morning until the moment she went to sleep at night."

"Well, perhaps you're right," said Alice in a conciliatory tone. "Of course, you knew her and I didn't. Perhaps you're right," she repeated. Another long silence followed and I thought we were finished talking about Maude but, no, she had one more thing to tell me.

"I met her once, you know," she said. "When I was just a child. I was about five or six years old and Max had taken me and Julian over to Dartmouth Square for a meeting with your father. I think it was around the time of the court case. Anyway, I needed the bathroom and went upstairs in search of it but, of course, the house is so large and there are so many floors that I got lost and wandered into what I suppose was her office. At first I thought the house was on fire because the room was simply filled with smoke—"

"Yes, that was her office," I said.

"I could barely see through it to the other side. But gradually my eyes grew accustomed to it and I saw a woman seated at a desk wearing a yellow dress staring at me and trembling slightly. She didn't move but just raised her hand like the Ghost of Christmas-Yet-to-Come, pointed in my direction and then she uttered a single word, a question—*Lucy?*—and I froze, terrified and uncertain what to do. She stood up and walked slowly toward me and although she was pale as a ghost she stared at me as if *I* was the ghost and when she reached out to touch me I became so utterly terrified that I ran from the room and went screaming down the stairs before charging out the front door. I didn't stop running until I got to the other side of Dartmouth Square, where I hid behind a tree waiting for my father and brother to reappear. I'm pretty sure I wet my pants in fright."

I stared at her, astonished and delighted by the story. I had always remembered the strange little girl in the pale-pink coat running through the house as if the Hound of the Baskervilles was after her but had never known what had happened to frighten her so badly. Now, at last, I knew. There was something comforting in laying that story to rest.

"Lucy was her daughter," I said. "She must have thought that you were her."

"Her *daughter*? There's no mention of a daughter anywhere in Malleson's biography."

"She was stillborn," I explained. "Maude had a terrible pregnancy, I believe. Which is why she couldn't have children afterward."

"Right," said Alice, and I could see that this information was something that might be useful to her in her thesis. "Anyway, that was my only encounter with her," she continued. "Until I decided to make a study of her work, that is, two decades later."

"She'd be dismayed if she knew that you had," I said. "She hated any form of publicity."

"Well, if it wasn't me it would be someone else," she replied with a shrug. "And there will be others. She's simply too important *not* to write about, don't you think? What was she like anyway? Sorry, I'm not fishing for my thesis. I'm genuinely interested."

"It's hard to say," I replied, wanting to move on to other subjects. "I lived with her for the first eight years of my life but our relationship was never what you would call close. She wanted a child, which was why she and Charles adopted me, but I think she wanted one in the same way that she wanted a Persian rug or a light fitting from the Palace of Versailles. Just to have, you know? She wasn't a bad woman, not really, but I can't say I ever got to know her. After Charles went to prison, it was just the two of us for a few months but she was already dying by then so we never had a chance to talk as parents and children should."

"Do you miss her?" asked Alice.

"Sometimes," I said. "I almost never think of her, if I'm honest. Except when people mention her books. They've become so highly thought of that I occasionally get letters from students asking for help with their theses."

"And do you offer it?"

"No. It's all there in the books themselves. There's nothing much I can add that would be of any use to anyone."

"You're right," said Alice. "So why any of them feel the need to talk about their work in public or give interviews is beyond me. If you didn't say what you wanted to say in the pages themselves, then surely you should have done another draft."

I smiled. The truth was that I wasn't a big reader and knew next to nothing about contemporary literature but I liked the fact that Alice did. Maude without the coldness.

"Do you write yourself?" I asked, and she shook her head.

"No, I wouldn't be able," she said. "I don't have the imagination. I'm a reader, pure and simple. I wonder how long I have to stay here anyway. There's nothing I'd like more than to go home and curl up with John McGahern. Metaphorically speaking, of course." She blushed almost immediately and reached out to touch my arm. "I'm so sorry, Cyril," she said. "That was rude of me. I don't mean I'm not enjoying your company—I am."

"It's all right," I said, laughing. "I know what you meant."

"You're very different from Julian's other friends," she remarked. "They're all so boring and vulgar and whenever I'm around them they say things to try to shock me. They think because I'm bookish and mousy that I will squeal at their vulgarities but they're wrong. I'm actually quite unshockable."

"I'm glad to hear it," I said.

"Have you spoken to the Finnish twins?"

"No," I said. "What's the point? They'll be gone by the next time I see Julian."

"True. Life's too short to make the effort. And what about you, Cyril? Do you have a set of Finnish twins of your own hidden away somewhere? Swedes? Norwegians? Or just one girl if you want to be old-fashioned about things?"

"No," I said, feeling a little uncomfortable that the conversation was turning toward my romantic life, or lack thereof. "No, I've never had very much luck in that department, I'm afraid."

"I don't believe that for a moment. You're nice looking and you have a good job. You could probably get any girl you want."

I glanced around. The music was so loud that no one could overhear us. And something inside me felt suddenly tired of subterfuge.

"Can I tell you something?" I said.

"Is it something scandalous?" she asked, smiling at me.

"I suppose so," I said. "It's something I've never told Julian. But somehow . . . I don't know why, I just feel I can trust you with it."

The expression on her face changed a little, from amused to intrigued. "All right," she said. "What is it?"

"Promise you won't tell your brother?"

"Promise she won't tell her brother *what*?" asked Julian, appearing behind our seat suddenly, and I jumped as he leaned between us, planting a quick kiss on his sister's cheek and then a quick kiss on mine.

"Nothing," I said, the moment lost, pulling away from him and feeling my heart rate elevating dramatically within my chest.

"No, go on, tell me!"

"Just that I'm going to miss you when you're gone, that's all."

"Well, I should think so too! Best friends are hard to come by, after all. Now, who's for another drink?"

Alice raised her empty glass at him and he scampered off back to the bar as I looked down at my shoes.

"So?" she asked. "What was it?"

"What was what?"

"You were about to tell me something."

I shook my head. Another time, maybe. "It was what I said," I told her. "That I'll miss him, that's all."

"Well, what's so scandalous about that? I was hoping for something far more juicy."

"Sorry," I said with a shrug. "I suppose it's not the sort of thing men generally say about their friends, is it? We're supposed to be stoical and keep our feelings to ourselves."

"Who says so?"

"Everyone," I told her.

A few days later, after Julian had departed for South America, I was at home one evening when the telephone rang.

"Cyril Avery," I said when I lifted the receiver.

"Oh good," said a voice. A female voice. "I was hoping I had the right number."

I frowned. "Who's this?" I asked.

"It's the voice of your conscience. You and I need to have a little talk. You've been a very bad boy, haven't you?"

I said nothing but pulled the receiver away from my ear for a moment and stared at it in bewilderment before slowly bringing it back. "Who is this?" I repeated.

"It's me, silly. Alice. Alice Woodbead."

I hesitated for a moment, uncertain why on earth she was calling me.

"What's the matter?" I asked, panicking slightly. "It's not Julian, is it? He's all right, isn't he?"

"Yes, he's fine. Why shouldn't he be?"

"No reason. I'm just surprised to hear from you, that's all."

"You mean you weren't waiting by the phone for me to call?"

"No. Why, should I have been?"

"You really know how to flatter a girl, don't you?"

My mouth opened and shut a few times. "Sorry," I said. "That came out wrong."

"I'm starting to feel a little foolish now."

"No, no," I said quickly, aware that I was behaving quite rudely. "I'm sorry. You caught me unawares."

"Why, what were you doing?"

Not much, just sitting around flicking through some pornography and wondering whether I had time for a quick wank before dinner, would have been the truthful answer.

"I was reading *Crime and Punishment*," I said.

"Never read it. Always meant to. Any good?"

"It's OK. There isn't a lot of crime but rather a lot of punishment."

"Story of my life. Look, Cyril, say no if you want to—"

"No," I said.

"What?"

"You told me to say no if I wanted to."

"Yes, but let me ask the question first. Good God, you don't make this easy on a girl, do you?"

"Sorry. What did you want to ask?"

"I wondered . . ." She trailed off and coughed for a moment, and for the first time she began to sound less confident. "Well, I wondered whether you might like to join me for dinner some evening?"

"Dinner?" I asked.

"Yes. Dinner. You do eat, don't you?"

"I do," I said. "I have to. Otherwise I get hungry."

She paused. "Are you teasing me?"

"No," I said. "I'm just not used to this, that's all. So I'm probably saying stupid things."

"I don't mind. I say stupid things all the time. So we've established that you eat to fend off the hunger pangs. Would you care to eat with me? This weekend perhaps?"

"Just the two of us?"

"And the other people in the restaurant. I won't be cooking for you; I'm not that domesticated. But we don't have to talk to any of the other people there unless we run out of things to say."

I thought about it. "I suppose we could do that," I said.

"I think I need to sit down," she replied. "Your enthusiasm is overwhelming me."

"Sorry," I said again, laughing now. "Yes. Dinner. You and me. And a restaurant. This weekend. That sounds good."

"Excellent. I'm going to pretend that wasn't like pulling teeth and look forward to it. I'll drop you a line before Saturday with a time and place. All right?"

"All right."

"Goodbye, Cyril."

"Goodbye, Alice."

I hung up and looked around, uncertain how I was supposed to feel. Was this a date? Was she asking me out on a date? Were women even *allowed* to ask men out on dates? I shook my head and went back to my room. I didn't feel like a wank anymore. And I didn't feel like dinner either.

A few days later, however, I found myself sitting opposite Julian's sister in a restaurant talking about something inconsequential and she reached across, placed her hand atop mine and looked me directly in the eye.

"Can I just get something out in the open, Cyril?" she said, the scent of her lavender perfume a pleasant note in the air.

"Of course," I said, nervous about what she might be about to say.

"The thing is, I felt a strong connection with you at Julian's going-away party and hoped that you might call. Actually, I always liked you whenever we met in the past, but of course I was with Fergus then. But of course you didn't call, so I called you instead. I'm shameless, I know. Anyway, I don't know whether you're seeing anyone or not, I assume not or you probably wouldn't have agreed to come out tonight, but if you are, or if you're not interested in me in the slightest, could you just let me know, because I don't want any misunderstandings between us. Not after everything I've been through. I quite like you, you see."

I looked down at the plate before me, breathing deeply in and out. I knew immediately that this would be one of the defining moments of my life. I could tell her the truth, as I had intended the previous week, confide my secrets in her and ask for her friendship. If I did so, there was a good chance that she would be a better friend to me than her brother had ever been. But at that moment, lacking the courage to be honest, I simply didn't feel ready. A few dates wouldn't hurt anyone. I enjoyed her company. It wasn't as if we were getting married or anything.

"No, I'm not seeing anyone," I told her, looking up and smiling, despite myself. "And of course I'm interested in you. What normal man wouldn't be?"

Eight Words

I imagine that everyone around that table assumed that I was a virgin when the fact was I had probably had more sex than any of them, even Julian, albeit in far less romantic settings. But they had experienced things that I never had, pleasures that I felt certain were superior to the ephemeral thrill of a quickly forgotten climax.

I knew nothing, for example, of foreplay or seduction, of how it might feel to meet a stranger in a bar and strike up a conversation, mindful of the possibility that it might lead somewhere more interesting. The truth was, if I was not screwing within ten minutes of meeting a man, then it was probably never going to happen at all. My Pavlovian response to an orgasm was to pull up my pants and run away. I had never had sex during daytime; instead, it was a shameful activity to be conducted in haste, in hiding and in darkness. I associated sexual congress with the night air, with the outdoors, with my shirt on and my trousers around my ankles. I knew the sensation of tree bark imprinting itself against the palms of my hands as I fucked someone in a park and the smell of sap against my face as a stranger pushed against me from behind. Sex was not scored by sighs of pleasure but by the scurrying urgency of rodents in the undergrowth and the sound of cars rushing past in the distance, not to mention the associated fear that from those same roads might come the unforgiving scream of Garda sirens, responding to the outraged phone call of a traumatized dog-walker. I had no idea what it would be like to wrap my arms around a lover beneath the sheets as we fell asleep, whispering words of gentle affection that drifted carelessly into sleepy tenderness. I had never woken with another person or been able to satisfy my tenacious early-morning desire with an unapologetic partner. I could number more sexual partners in my history than anyone I knew but the difference between love and sex could be summed up for me in eight words:

I loved Julian; I had sex with strangers.

And so I wonder what would have surprised them more: to have known all that or to have learned that I *had*, in fact, had sex with a woman. Only once, granted, but the extraordinary moment had taken place three weeks earlier when, to my surprise, Alice insisted that we go to bed together and, even more surprisingly, I had agreed.

Intimacy was one of the things that I had managed to avoid over the eighteen months of our courtship and for once I found myself grateful to be living in Ireland, a country where a homosexual, like a student priest, could easily hide their preferences by disguising them beneath the murky robes of a committed Catholic. Naturally, as it was only 1973 and we were children of our time, it was a subject that Alice and I were shy of discussing aloud and so we used the person we had in common, Julian, as our conduit into the subject.

"He has sex with different people constantly," I whined a few weeks before the wedding as we sat in Doyle's on College Green, both of us a little excited from having watched Robert Redford and Paul Newman alternate between T-shirts, tuxedos and slicked-back hair for two hours in *The Sting*. I was in one of those moods where my resentment at her brother's sexual prowess and unyielding heterosexuality put me in the mood to belittle him. "He basically does it with anyone he wants, which is really disgusting when you think about it. But is he actually happy?"

"Are you kidding me, Cyril?" Alice replied, amused by the absurdity of my question. "I'd say he's ecstatic. Wouldn't you be?"

I knew she was teasing me but I didn't laugh. Sex hovered around the edges of our lives like an anxious guest at a party. It was obvious that sooner or later one of us would have to bite the bullet and go over to say hello. I just didn't particularly want it to be me.

"Did I mention," she said, not quite looking me in the eye, "that Max and Samantha are going to London next weekend?"

"No," I said. Samantha was Max's second wife. Much like my own adoptive father, who that year was engaged to the woman who would become, albeit briefly, the fourth Mrs. Avery, Alice's father had obtained a divorce from Elizabeth in the UK on the grounds of unreasonable behavior. In fairness to him, he had cited his *own* unreasonable behavior in the suit, not hers, for after all the most unreasonable thing that she'd ever done, aside from her brief affair with Charles, was stay with the bastard. Shortly after the decree nisi had come through, Max had married an aspiring actress who bore an uncanny and deeply disturbing resemblance to Alice herself. This was a subject that was absolutely off limits, although I was often keen to ask Julian whether he noticed the likeness and, if so, what he made of it.

"We should go to London sometime," she continued.

"I daresay we'll have plenty of holidays to look forward to after we're married," I said. "We could go to Spain someday. That's very popular. Or Portugal."

"Portugal?" she said, raising an eyebrow in mock-excitement. "Do you really think so? I never imagined I could be the kind of girl who would grow up and get to go to Portugal!"

"All right then, America," I said, laughing. "Or Australia. Anything's possible. We'd have to save for an awfully long time if we wanted to go that far but—"

"It's hard to believe that I'm twenty-six years old and have never set foot outside Ireland."

"Well, I'm twenty-eight," I pointed out, "and neither have I. What are they doing in London anyway?"

"Oh, Samantha has a meeting with Ken Russell."

"Who's Ken Russell?"

"Film director. You know, *The Devils. Women in Love.* Oliver Reed and Alan Bates wrestling with their bits hanging out."

"Oh yes," I said. "It's all soft porn, isn't it?"

"Well, I suppose it depends on how old you are," she said. "For our parents' generation, yes, it probably is. For us, they're art films."

"I wonder what our children will call them," I said. "Quaint but terribly passé, I suppose."

"Children?" she said, looking across at me hopefully. "It's funny we've never talked about children, isn't it? Considering we're getting married in a few weeks' time."

"Yes, I suppose so," I said, and for the first time in my life it occurred to me that I had never given any thought whatsoever to the idea of being a father. I paused to think about it and found that the idea quite appealed to me. Perhaps I had never allowed myself to consider it before because I knew how impossible it would be.

"Would you like to have a family, Cyril?" she asked me.

"Well, yes," I said. "Yes, I think I probably would. I'd quite like to have a daughter. Or many daughters."

"Like a gentleman from a Jane Austen novel. You could settle a thousand pounds and a hundred acres in Hertfordshire on each one after your death."

"And if they quarreled, their punishment would be an afternoon in the company of the local Miss Bates."

"I think I'd prefer a son," said Alice, looking away, and I noticed her eyes drift to an incredibly handsome young man who had just walked into the pub. Her eyes lingered over his body as he leaned over the bar, glancing at the beer pumps as he made his choice. She swallowed suddenly and for the first time I saw real lust in her eyes. I didn't blame her—I would have climbed over the dead bodies of my closest friends to get to him myself—but when she looked back the smile she wore was one of resignation, as if she wanted *that* but had to settle for *this*, and *this* wasn't even much good to her so far in the department that really mattered. I felt a stab of guilt and found myself locked into pained silence. Suddenly, the Austen jokes seemed absurd and embarrassing.

"What were we talking about?" she asked eventually, her train of thought having not only derailed but jumped the tracks entirely, driven over a cliff and crashed one hundred feet into a ravine below, killing everyone on board.

"Children," I said. "You'd like a little boy. I'd like a little girl."

I may not have known much about pregnancies but I knew that you couldn't have a son or a daughter without actually doing it first. The priests at school had once muttered something to the effect that when a mummy and a daddy loved each other very much, they lay close together and the Holy Spirit descended upon them to create the miracle of new life. (Charles, in his one attempt at a man-to-man talk with me, had put it rather differently. "Get her kit off," he said. "Play with her tits a bit, because the ladies love that. Then just stick your cock in her pussy and ram it in and out a bit. Don't hang around too long in there—it's not a bloody train station. Just do your business and get on with your day." It's no wonder he managed to secure so many wives, the old romantic.)

I tried to imagine what it would be like to undress Alice, for her to undress me, for us to be lying in a bed together, naked. For her to look down at my penis and stroke it or suck it and then guide it inside her.

"What's wrong?" asked Alice.

"Nothing, why?"

"You've gone a funny color. You look like you're about to be sick."

"Do I?"

"Seriously, Cyril. You're practically green."

"I am a little lightheaded, now you mention it," I said, reaching for my pint.

"Then you probably shouldn't drink that. Would you like some water?"

"Yes, I'll get some."

"No," she practically shouted, standing up and pushing me back into my seat. "No, I'll get it."

She made her way over to the bar and I followed her with my eyes, wondering why she was so keen, and then I saw that the young man was still there and as she took her place at the bar next to him, she began throwing him oblique glances. The barman was busy and they stood patiently, side by side, for a few moments until he leaned over and said something to her and she gave a quick reply. Whatever she had said, he burst out laughing, and I knew that this wasn't just flirting on his part. Alice had a quick wit; it was one of the things I loved about her the most.

And yes, I *did* love her. In my way. In my own selfish and cowardly way.

I watched as they talked, and then the barman approached, took their orders and they talked about something else. He must have asked whether she was there alone, because she shook her head and nodded in my direction and when he saw me sitting there, waiting for her to return, he looked disappointed. When he turned back to Alice, I was able to focus on his face, for they were staring so intently at each other that they were utterly oblivious to me. The young man was not only extremely good-looking but there was warmth in his expression too. I knew nothing of him but I believed that he would treat the girl he loved with gentleness and affection. A moment later, she came back with my glass of water, sat down and I pretended that I hadn't observed anything of their exchange.

"There was something I wanted to talk to you about," she said suddenly, looking a little irritated now, a flush of color in her cheeks. "And I'm just going to spit it out since it doesn't feel as if you're going to take the lead no matter how much I hint. The reason I mentioned that Max and Samantha are going to London next weekend is because the house will therefore be empty. I think you should come over, Cyril. Come for dinner, we'll drink a couple of Max's best wines and, you know, go to bed together."

I said nothing but felt as if a great weight was being wrapped around my entire body, such as the good burghers of Amsterdam were wont to do during the seventeenth century when they tied millstones around the necks of convicted homosexuals before throwing them into the canals and leaving them to drown.

"Right," I said. "I see. Interesting idea."

"Look, I know how religious you are," she said. "But we're going to be married soon, after all."

Of course, I wasn't religious at all. I cared nothing for it and, aside from occasionally thinking that Jesus With Long Hair And A Beard was rather hot, I never gave any thought to an afterlife or the matter of mankind's creation. This was a deception—yet another—that I had propagated since Alice and I had first started dating and I had used it from our first date as an excuse to stop me from having to go to bed with her. The downside of this arrangement was that in order to appear consistent I had to go to Mass every Sunday morning. Fearing that she might pull a Mary-Margaret and follow me unawares—unlikely, given their very different dispositions, but nevertheless a possibility—I regularly attended eleven-thirty Mass at Westland Row, the same church where fourteen years earlier I had killed a priest by confessing my perversions to him. I never sat on that side of the church, of course. I had done so once, seen the broken tile that hadn't been mended since his fall, and it still gave me the creeps. Instead, I took my place near the back and generally had a little snooze until some old woman gave me a punch in the arm to wake me up, staring at me as if I alone was responsible for the downfall of Western Civilization.

"I don't know," I said after a lengthy pause. "I want to, I really do. But you know what the Pope says—"

"I don't care what the Pope says," snapped Alice. "I have no interest in fucking the Pope."

"Jesus, Alice!" I said, giggling a little at her choice of words. I might not have been religious but that sounded a little iniquitous, even to me.

"No, not him either. Look, Cyril, let's call a spade a spade. We're getting married soon. And all going well we'll have a very happy, very successful marriage over the next fifty years or so. That's what I want anyway, isn't it what you want?"

"Yes, of course it is," I said.

"Because," she added, lowering her voice a little, "if you have any doubts, any doubts at all, there's still time for you to say so."

"But I don't have any doubts, Alice," I said.

"The last thing I need is to get another phone call when I'm already in my dress. You understand that, Cyril, don't you? I don't know how I survived what Fergus did to me. I'm telling you right now that I couldn't go through that twice. It would be the end of me."

I stared at her, uncertain where all this had come from. Had she been thinking this for sometime? Did she *suspect* something? By the bar, I saw the handsome young man finishing his pint and reaching for his jacket.

Now is your chance, I told myself. *Tell her the truth. Trust her to understand, to forgive your deceit, to be your friend, to help you and love you still.*

And then tell her that we can discuss it some other time but right now she needs to go over to the bar and give that man her phone number before it's too late.

"Cyril?" said Alice, sounding suddenly concerned. "What's wrong?"

"Nothing," I said. "Why?"

"You're crying."

"I'm not crying," I said, but when I reached a hand to my cheeks, to my astonishment they were wet and the tears were rolling from my eyes. I hadn't even noticed. I wiped them away with my handkerchief and tried to pull myself together.

"Alice," I said, looking at her more intently than I had ever looked at anyone in my life as I reached forward to take her hand.

"Why were you crying?"

"I wasn't."

"You were!"

"I don't know. I must have a cold. Alice—"

"What?" she asked nervously. "Tell me, Cyril. Whatever it is, just tell me. I promise that it will be all right."

"Will it though?" I said, looking directly at her.

"You're frightening me now."

"I'm sorry, Alice. This is all my fault."

"What's your fault? Cyril, what have you done?"

"It's what I haven't done. What I haven't said."

"Why, what haven't you said? Cyril, you can tell me anything, I promise. You look so unhappy right now. Nothing can be that bad, surely?"

I looked down at the table and she remained silent, waiting for me to speak. "If I tell you," I said eventually, "then you'll hate me. And I don't want you to hate me."

"But I could never hate you! I love you!"

"I've made a terrible mistake," I said.

She sat up, her face growing darker now. "Is there someone else?" she asked. "Have you been seeing someone else?"

"No," I said, even though I had. Just not in public. "It's not that."

"Then what? Jesus, Cyril, just tell me!"

"All right," I said. "The thing is, ever since I was a boy . . ."

"Yes?"

"Ever since I was a boy, I've known that—"

"Excuse me."

We both looked up and standing over us was the handsome young man from the bar. I thought he'd left but, no, he was simply standing there with a wide smile on his face, looking slightly embarrassed.

"I'm sorry to interrupt," he said.

"What?" asked Alice, looking up at him irritably. "What is it?"

"It's just . . . look, I wouldn't normally do this type of thing," he said. "Only I thought there was a bit of a connection between us back there. I wondered whether you might give me your phone number, that's all. If you didn't mind. Maybe I could take you out some night?"

She stared at him in disbelief. "Are you joking me?" she asked.

"No," he said, frowning. "Sorry, did I get the wrong idea? Only it seemed as if—"

"I'm sitting here with my fiancé," she said, turning to me. "Can't you see that? Do you normally ask girls out when they're sitting with their fiancés? Are you that sure of yourself?"

"Oh," he said, turning and looking at me in shock. "I'm terribly sorry. I didn't think . . . actually, I assumed you were brother and sister."

"Why on earth would you assume that?" asked Alice.

"I don't know," he said, completely flustered now. "Something about the way you were both sitting. The way you were looking at each other. I didn't think you were *together* together."

"Well, we are. And that's an incredibly rude thing to say."

"Yes," he said. "I'm sorry. I apologize to you both."

And with that he turned around and made his way out of the bar as Alice watched after him, shaking her head. *Go after him*, I should have said. *Go after him before he disappears forever!*

"Can you believe that?" she asked, turning back to me.

"It was a mistake," I said. "He didn't mean anything by it."

"I'm surprised you didn't punch him."

I stared at her. "Did you want me to? I'm not really the punching type."

"No, of course not. Only . . . oh I don't know what I'm saying. This evening is going all wrong. Let's forget that ever happened and just tell me whatever you were going to tell me."

"I can't even remember now," I lied, wishing I could just leave.

"Of course you can. You said that ever since you were a little boy—"

"Ever since I was a little boy I wasn't sure that I could ever make someone happy," I said quickly, dismissing the entire thing. "That's all. It sounds stupid, all right? Can we just leave it at that?"

"But you make me happy all the time," she said.

"Do I?"

"I wouldn't be marrying you if you didn't."

"Right," I said.

"But look, while we're being honest with each other, there's something I want to tell you too. And I'm just going to spit it out, OK?"

"OK," I said, feeling utterly miserable.

"The thing is, I think we should have sex. With each other. *Before* we get married. Just to be sure."

"Be sure about *what*?"

"Can I ask you something?" she said.

"You can ask me anything."

"Will you tell me the truth?"

I wondered whether she noticed my hesitation. "Of course," I said.

"Have you ever been with a woman, Cyril?"

I knew that I could be honest with her about this at least.

"No," I said, looking down at the table and rubbing my finger against some invisible mark imprinted into the wood. "No, I haven't."

"I thought not," she said, and there was something approaching relief in her tone. "I felt certain that you were a virgin. It's the Church, you see. They've messed all you boys up. Not Julian, of course. Julian is different. Although I suppose he's got his own problems with his constant need for affirmation. They've made you think that sex is something dirty when it's not. It's perfectly natural. It's part of life. It's how we all got here in the first place. And it can be wonderful if it's done right. Even when it's done wrong it's still better than a poke in the eye with a rusty nail. Oh, I'm not suggesting that everyone should be going out and doing it left, right and center like Julian does but if you really like someone—"

"I suppose what you're saying is that *you've* had sex," I said.

"I have, yes," she said. "And I'm not ashamed to admit it. That's not going to be a problem, is it? You're not going to get all judgmental on me, are you?"

"No, of course not," I said. "It makes no difference to me how carelessly some people want to cast themselves into the fires of hell for all eternity."

"What?"

"I'm kidding."

"You better be."

"But have there been many?" I asked, intrigued.

"Does it matter?"

"I suppose not. But I'd like to know anyway."

"Well, let's put it this way," she said. "More than the Queen. Less than Elizabeth Taylor."

"How many?" I insisted.

"Do you really want to know or are you just being a pervert?"

"A little of both," I said.

"Three, if it matters that much to you," she said. "My first was with a friend of Julian's when I was eighteen. My second—"

"A friend of *Julian's*?" I said, interrupting her. "Who?"

"Well, maybe I shouldn't say. I suppose he might be a friend of yours too."

"*Who?*" I repeated.

"I actually don't remember his surname," she said. "I met him by chance, on a night out with Julian just after I got my Leaving Cert results. It was at a party in someone's house. His name was Jasper. He played the piano accordion. Of course, no one should play the piano accordion in public, they should be made to do it on some desert island somewhere, but as it turned out he played it rather well. I remember thinking that he had very sexy fingers."

"*Not Jasper Timson!*" I said, sitting forward in shock.

"That's the one," she said, clapping her hands in delight. "Well done, you! Oh, I suppose that means you *do* know him then."

"Of course I know him," I said. "We went to school together. Are you actually telling me that you lost your virginity to Jasper Timson?"

"Well, yes," she said with a shrug. "You have to lose it to someone, don't you? And he was sweet. And good-looking. And he was *there*, which somehow was enough for me at the time. Look, Cyril, you said you didn't mind."

"I don't mind. You know he lives in Toronto now, with his . . ." I paused and made quotation marks in the air with my fingers, "his *boyfriend*."

"Yes, Julian told me," said Alice, laughing as she sat back with a slight giggle.

"He tried to kiss him too once, you know." It was all I could do not to burst out laughing.

"Did he? Doesn't surprise me. It would only have surprised me if he *hadn't* tried to kiss him. Anyway, I knew he was a homosexual even then. He confided in me that he thought he was but he wasn't absolutely certain. Anyway, we were both young, we liked each other, I wanted to lose mine before another day passed, so I suggested we give it a go."

"And what did he say?" I asked, stunned by all of this.

"Oh he jumped at the offer. And so we both leaped into bed. And it was fine. We both got what we wanted out of it. I got to pop my cherry and he got to realize that he was definitely not interested in doing that ever again. At least not with a girl. We shook hands afterward and went our separate ways. Well, metaphorically speaking. We didn't *literally* shake hands. I mean, I suppose we might have done but I can't imagine it. We probably kissed each other on the cheek. Which I think he preferred to where he *had* been kissing me. Anyway," she continued, sounding as if she wanted to bring this conversation to a rapid end. "After Jasper, there was a boy who I dated for a few months, an aspiring actor who was most definitely *not* a homosexual, unless he was torturing himself by trying to have sex with every girl in Dublin. And then, finally, Fergus, of course."

"Of course," I said. "Good old Fergus."

"We only got onto this topic," she continued, "because I said that I want us to sleep together when Max and Samantha go to London."

"Christ, you're just mad for it, aren't you?" I said.

"Shut up, Cyril," she said, slapping my hand with her own. "You're only pretending to be annoyed. So what do you say?"

"What room do you sleep in?"

"What?"

"In Dartmouth Square. Don't forget, I grew up there."

"Oh yes, of course. Well, my room is on the second floor."

"Julian told me you had my old room. On the top floor."

"I moved down a flight. All those stairs!"

"Well I'm not doing it there," I said quickly. "That was Maude's bedroom. There's just . . . I couldn't. I really couldn't."

"Fine. We can go up to the top floor if you prefer. Into your old bedroom. How does that sound?"

I thought about it and nodded reluctantly. "All right," I said. "Yes, well I suppose so. If it's that important to you."

"It should be important to *both* of us."

"It is," I said, sitting up straight now and thinking, *Fuck it*; if Jasper Timson—who was even more of a homosexual than I was, considering he had an actual *boyfriend*—could do it, then so could I. "I'm in. I mean I will be in. No, that's all wrong, I don't mean I'll—"

"Relax, Cyril. It's fine. Shall we say Saturday? Around seven o'clock."

"Saturday," I agreed. "Around seven o'clock."

"And have a bath before you come over."

"Of course I'll have a bath," I snapped. "What do you take me for?"

"Sometimes boys don't."

"*You* have a bath," I said. "Remember, I know where you've been."

She smiled. "I knew you'd be willing when you saw how important it was to me. That's one of the things I love about you, Cyril. You're not like other boys. You're sensitive to my feelings."

"Yes, well . . ." I said, knowing that the days ahead would be long ones for me.

I kept my hands off myself for the rest of the week and didn't go anywhere near the side streets or parks that were my regular nighttime haunts, wanting to be as randy as possible come the big moment. I tried to put it out of my head that no matter what happened then, even if it all went well, there was still that fifty years that Alice had mentioned ahead of us to think about too. In my foolishness, I decided that was a bridge I'd cross when I got to it.

And as things turned out, Saturday night went better than I could ever have predicted. I felt a genuine warmth toward her anyway, an affection bordering on the romantic if not quite the sexual, and there had been many times when I had enjoyed the prolonged kissing sessions in which we engaged. I insisted on the lights staying off, of course, for I wanted to get to know her body first by touch before being confronted with the reality of it, and although it was not what I wanted—it was soft to the touch, not muscled and hard as I liked, and smoother than I had ever imagined skin could be—I somehow found myself lost in the novelty of it and performed in a way that I think could best have been described as "perfectly adequate."

"Well, that's a start, at least," said Alice when it was over.

She hadn't reached any sort of climax, of course, although I had. Which seemed rather ironic to me, all things considered.

A Sign

When I woke, the sun was being a total bollix, pouring through the window and scorching through my eyelids. I hadn't even bothered to draw the curtains on my return a few hours earlier, collapsing face-down and fully clothed on the sofa, where the combination of a hang-over with an awareness of my predicament now made me feel as if my last moments were upon me. I closed my eyes, desperate to return to sleep, but was quickly hauling my sorry carcass toward the bathroom, unsure whether I needed to piss or vomit. In the end I settled for both, concurrently, before making my way nervously to the mirror. Dracula would have felt less fear examining his own reflection.

Of course, I looked terrible, like the victim of some random act of overnight violence, mugged and left for dead before being inexplicably brought back to life by a malevolent physician.

I hoped that a long hot shower might help me to recover but an immediate and permanent end to world hunger would have been more likely. It was a quarter to eleven by now and I was due at the church by twelve. I imagined Alice in Dartmouth Square, putting her dress on, surrounded by bridesmaids, while they each tried not to make inappropriate references to what had happened the last time they'd gathered for such an event.

Suddenly, the realization of how to solve all my problems hit me. It would involve losing all my friends, including Julian—*especially* Julian—but in time they would see that it had been for the best and they would surely forgive me. Taking a handful of loose change from the bedside table I put on my dressing gown and dragged myself to the payphone in the corridor, dialing the number before I could change my mind. When Max answered, I pressed the A button, heard the coins tumble into the chamber and swallowed, racking my brain for the right words.

"Hello?" he said, sounding as if he'd already had a drink or two, despite the early hour. "Max Woodbead?" In the background I could hear laughter, the sounds of girls' voices and of glasses clinking together. "Hello?" he repeated. "Who's there? Speak up, for Christ's sake, I haven't got all day."

But I said nothing, hanging up and returning to my room, knowing that it was no good.

Twenty minutes later, I was making my way toward the church in Ranelagh, growling at anyone who happened to smile in my direction and the lads who shouted from their cars that I was beginning a life sentence. Feeling ill again, I paused and, realizing that I still had a good half hour to spare, took a detour into a teashop at the corner of Charlemont. It was busy but there was an empty table in the corner and I sat there, by the window, ordering a large, strong cup of coffee and two glasses of water, both filled with ice, and began to relax a little as I sipped them, watching the students making their way into town, the businessmen heading for their offices, the housewives wheeling shopping bags toward Quinnsworth, and wondered whether there had ever been a moment when my life might have taken a different turn. How had Jasper Timson, a fucking piano-accordion player for Christ's sake, ended up living with his boyfriend in Toronto, while I was preparing to marry a woman in whom I had no sexual interest whatsoever? When was the exact moment that I might have found some courage and for once in my life done the right thing?

Right now, I told myself. *This is it! This is the moment! There's still time!*

"Give me a sign," I muttered to the universe. "Just something to give me the courage to walk away."

I jumped as a hand touched my shoulder and looked around to see a woman and a small child standing next to me, glancing toward the empty seats at my table.

"You don't mind, do you?" she asked. "Only there isn't anywhere else."

"Be my guest," I said, although I would have preferred to have been left alone.

The child—a boy of about eight or nine—sat down opposite me and I glared at him as he took in my wedding suit and seemed amused by it. He was very neatly dressed, wearing a white shirt beneath a blue tank-top, and his hair was carefully combed with an immaculate side-parting. He looked like he could have been the kid brother of the young Nazi who sang "Tomorrow Belongs to Me" in *Cabaret*, the last film that Alice and I had gone to together. The boy was carrying four books in his hands and he laid them out on the table before him, apparently deciding which one merited his attentions the most.

"Can I ask you a favor?" asked the woman. "You wouldn't look after Jonathan for me for a few minutes, would you? I just need to use the facilities, then I have a phone call to make and then I'll be ordering some tea. Are you getting married today? You're dressed for it."

"In about an hour," I said, certain that I recognized her from somewhere but unable, just at that moment, to place her. "And who's Jonathan?"

"Naturally, I'm Jonathan," said the little boy, extending his hand to me. "Jonathan Edward Goggin. And who might you be?"

"Cyril Avery," I said, staring at the small hand that gave off a slight odor of soap before giving in and shaking it. "It's fine," I said to his mother. "I won't let anyone kidnap him. I know the signs for that."

It was obvious that she didn't understand what I meant by that but she turned away regardless and made her way toward the doors at the other corner of the room while I looked back at the boy and he concentrated on his books. "What are you reading?" I asked him eventually.

"*Well*," he declared with an enormous sigh, as if the weight of the world was upon his shoulders but he was trying to remain stoical about it. "I haven't *quite* decided yet. I was at the library this morning, you see; it's my regular day, and Mrs. Shipley the librarian recommended these three here, and she's usually an excellent advocate of good storytelling, so I took her advice. This one seems to be about a rabbit who takes a baby fox as a companion but I can't see how that could work because no matter how much kindness the rabbit shows the fox, eventually it will just grow up and eat him. This one here is about a group of children, distantly related I suspect, they usually are, who solve crimes on their summer holidays but I flicked through it on the way here and I found the word *nigger* in there and there's a black boy in my class at school and he says that word is a very bad word and he's an *extremely* good friend of mine, probably my third-best friend, so I might avoid it just to be on the safe side. And this one is some nonsense about the 1916 Rising and the thing is, I'm just not political. I never have been. So I might just go with this one here, which was the one I chose myself." He held up the book and I glanced at the cover, an image of a boy standing tall, legs parted, holding a cockerel under one arm and a mysterious box under the other while what looked like refugees walked past in the background. The words *The Silver Sword* were printed in the top right-hand corner.

"What's it about?" I asked.

"Well, I don't really know," he said. "As I haven't started it yet. But the back cover says it's about the war and children fleeing the Nazis. Do you know about the Nazis? I know all about them. They were the *worst*. Just awful, awful people without a *shred* of humanity between them. But here's the thing, Mr. Avery—"

"Call me Cyril," I said.

"No, I couldn't do that. You're really old and I'm just a child."

"I'm *twenty-eight*!" I said, appalled and insulted.

"Wow," he said, laughing. "That is *so* ancient. You're like a dinosaur. Anyway, here's the thing, as I was saying before you so rudely interrupted me, I prefer stories about things that really happened. And the war really happened, didn't it, so I want to know about it. Did you fight in the war, Mr. Avery?"

"No," I said. "On account of the fact that I was born a few months after it ended."

"I find that very hard to believe," said Jonathan, shaking his head. "You look so old that if you said you'd fought in the *First* World War, I wouldn't have fallen off my seat in surprise!"

And with that he burst out laughing and continued to laugh for so long and so hard that I had no choice but to laugh along.

"Shut up, you little prick," I said eventually, even though I was still laughing, and he switched to giggling now. "I have a hangover, that's all."

"You said a bad word," he told me.

"I did," I admitted. "I learned it in the trenches at Verdun."

"Verdun was a battle in the First World War," he announced. "It lasted eleven months and General von Hindenburg, who later became President of Germany, was in charge. I knew you were old. And what's a hangover?"

"It's when you pour so much drink down your throat that you wake up the next day feeling like the wreck of the *Hesperus*."

I glanced around in search of his mother but there was no sign of her as yet.

"So are you looking forward to getting married?" asked Jonathan. "Don't people usually do that when they're much younger? Could you not find someone to marry you until now?"

"I'm a late developer," I said.

"What's that mean?"

"Give it a few years. Something tells me you'll understand in time."

"And you're marrying a woman?"

"No, I'm marrying a train. The eleven-o-four from Castlebar."

He frowned. "How can you marry a train?" he asked.

"There's nothing in the constitution that says I can't."

"I suppose not. And if you love the train and the train loves you, then I suppose you should marry it."

"I'm not marrying a train, Jonathan," I said with a sigh, taking a long drink from my iced water. "I'm marrying a woman."

"I knew it. You're silly."

"I am silly," I admitted. "I'm about the silliest man you've ever met. I'm a complete fucking idiot, actually."

"You said another bad word. I bet you're going to have sex with your wife tonight, aren't you?"

"How do you know about sex?" I asked. "You're only about six."

"I'm eight. And I'll be nine in three weeks' time. And I know all about sex, actually," he added, not seeming the least embarrassed. "My mother told me all about it."

"Let me guess," I said. "When a mummy and a daddy love each other very much, they lie close together and the Holy Spirit descends upon them to create the miracle of new life."

"Don't be ridiculous," said Jonathan. "That's not what happens at all." At which point he proceeded to give me a very frank description of how a man and woman went about the business of fornicating, even telling me a few things that I had not known before.

"How on earth do you know all these things?" I asked him when he'd finished his rather graphic and stomach-churning lecture.

"My mother says that one of the problems in this country is that no one is willing to talk about sex because of the influence of the Catholic Church and she says that she wants me to grow up understanding that a woman's body is something to be cherished, not something to be afraid of."

"I wish she'd been *my* mother," I muttered.

"When I'm grown up, I intend to be a very considerate lover," said Jonathan, nodding his head fiercely.

"Good for you. And what does your father say about all this?"

"Oh I don't have a father," he said.

"Of course you have a father. You don't know anything about sex if you don't understand that everyone has a mother and a father."

"I mean I don't *know* my father," said Jonathan. "I'm illegitimate."

"I hate that word."

"I do too. But I wear it as a badge of honor. I find that if I say it to people, then they don't say it behind my back. They can't gossip in corners, saying, *Do you know that Jonathan Edward Goggin is illegitimate?* because I'll already have told them. One–nil to me. In fact, every time I meet someone new I make sure to tell them quite soon."

"Doesn't your mother mind?"

"She'd prefer that I didn't. But she says that I have to do whatever feels right and that she's not going to make my decisions for me. She says she's my mother, not my grandfather."

"What on earth does that mean?"

"I haven't the foggiest," said Jonathan. "But she says that she'll explain it to me some day."

"You're a bit of an oddball, Jonathan," I said. "Has anyone ever told you that?"

"Nineteen people this year alone," he said. "And it's only May."

I laughed and checked my watch. Five more minutes and I would have to go.

"What's the name of the girl you're marrying?" asked Jonathan.

"Alice," I said.

"There's a girl named Alice in my class," he replied, opening his eyes wide, apparently excited that we should have this in common. "She's really really really pretty. She has long blonde hair and eyes the color of opals."

"Is she your girlfriend?" I asked.

"No!" he screamed, making the other people in the café turn around and stare in our direction. He went bright red then. "No, she's not my girlfriend at all!"

"Sorry," I said, laughing. "I forgot, you're only eight."

"A girl called Melanie is my girlfriend," he said.

"Oh right. Fair enough."

"And I'm going to marry her one day."

"Really? Good for you."

"Thank you. Isn't it funny that you're getting married this morning and I'm telling you about the girl I'm going to marry when I'm all grown up?"

"It's hilarious," I said. "All you need is love; it's all any of us need."

"The Beatles," said Jonathan quickly. " 'All You Need Is Love,' a Lennon-McCartney composition, although it's actually written by John Lennon. *Magical Mystery Tour*, 1967. B-side, Song 5."

"You're a Beatles fan then?" I asked.

"Of course. Aren't you?"

"Of course."

"Who's your favorite Beatle?"

"George," I said.

"Interesting."

"Who's yours?"

"Pete Best."

"Interesting."

"I always root for the underdog," said Jonathan.

We sat and stared at each other and, all things considered, I felt a little disappointed when his mother returned.

"I'm so sorry," she said, looking a little flustered. "My phone call took longer than I expected. I'm trying to arrange a flight to Amsterdam and Aer Lingus doesn't make it easy. I have to go into their offices tomorrow and that will take up half my day."

"It's fine," I said, standing up. "But I better go now."

"He's marrying a girl called Alice," said Jonathan.

"Is he indeed?" she said. "Lucky Alice." She paused then and stared at me. "We know each other, don't we?" she asked. "You look terribly familiar."

"I think we do," I said. "Didn't you use to work in the tearoom at Dáil Éireann?"

"Yes, I still do, actually."

"I used to be a civil servant. Our paths occasionally crossed there. I once got punched in the face by the Taoiseach's Press Officer and you took care of me afterward."

She thought about this and shook her head. "I have a vague memory of that," she said. "But then again, punch-ups happen there all the time. Are you sure it was me?"

"Definite," I said, but pleased that she didn't recall it, as of course I had confided in her that day about my sexuality. "You were very kind to me."

"All right. It's just that you remind me of someone I once knew. A long time ago."

I shrugged and turned to Jonathan, offering him a half-bow as I prepared to leave.

"It's been a pleasure, young man," I said.

"Good luck with your forthcoming wedding to your fiancée Alice," he said.

"He's an interesting boy," I said to his mother as I stepped past her. "You're going to have your hands full with him."

"I know," she said, smiling. "But he's my darling. And I'm not letting this one go. Oh!"

"What?" I asked, for she had shivered suddenly. "Are you all right?"

"Yes," she said. "I just had one of those strange sensations, as if someone walked over my grave."

I smiled, said my goodbyes and made my way toward the door. *Fuck you,* I said to the universe. *All I asked for was a sign, something to give me the courage to walk away, and you couldn't even do that.* I had no choice.

It was time to get married.

Loving Someone Else

I entered the sacristy by the side door to find Julian seated at a table, looking over the Order of Service for the ceremony. For someone who must have had just as few hours of sleep as me, he seemed remarkably fresh-faced, having rid himself of the stubble that he'd been favoring lately and got a haircut. It was a surprise to see him wearing his reading glasses—he almost never wore them around people—but he took them off as soon as he saw me and placed them in his top pocket. It probably goes without saying that his new suit fitted him like a second skin.

"There you are," he said, grinning up at me. "The condemned man. How's the head?"

"Terrible," I told him. "How's yours?"

"Not too bad, all things considered. I got a couple of hours' sleep, then went for a swim in the Countess Markievicz pool before visiting my barber. He put hot towels over my face and hummed Simon and Garfunkel songs while he shaved me and the whole thing was incredibly relaxing."

"You did all that in the last nine hours?" I asked, baffled.

"Yes, why not?"

I shook my head. How could someone drink as much as him, be out as late as him and then get up, do all that and still look so attractive? Were some people just given everything?

"I feel like I'm going to be sick," I said. "I might be better off going back to bed."

His smile faded and he threw me an anxious look before bursting out laughing. "Jesus," he said. "Don't do that to me, Cyril. I thought you were serious for a minute."

"What makes you think I'm not?" I muttered. "Anyway, I'm here, amn't I?"

"You realize I'd have no choice but to kill you if you let my sister down, right? You were in some form last night all the same. I suppose the nerves were getting to you. Your friend Nick was pretty upset by the way you spoke to him."

"He's not my friend," I said. "And how do you know how he feels?"

"Oh, I ran into him earlier. Just by chance on Grafton Street. We went for a quick coffee."

I sat down and closed my eyes. Of course he had. And of course *they* had. I could have predicted it.

"What's the matter?" he asked, coming over and taking the seat next to me. "Do you need an aspirin?"

"I've had four already."

"How about some water?"

"Yes, please." He went over to the sink and when he couldn't find a glass, reached for a large golden chalice with silver inlay along the knop, filled it to the brim and covered it with a bronze paten before handing it to me. "Bless you, my son," he said.

"Thanks, Julian," I said.

"Are you sure you're going to be OK?"

"I'll be fine," I told him, trying to look cheerful. "Happiest day of my life."

"It's hard to believe that we're going to be brothers-in-law in an hour or so, isn't it? After all these years of friendship, I mean. I don't know if I've ever said it, Cyril, but I was really happy when you asked me to be your best man. And when you asked Alice to marry you."

"Who else would I ask?" I said.

"Well, there's a lot of girls out there."

"I meant who else would I ask but you?" I said. "You're my best friend, after all."

"And you're mine. She looked so happy when I was leaving the house this morning."

"Who did?"

"Alice, of course!"

"Oh yeah. Of course. Is she here yet anyway?"

"No, the priest said he'll give us the nod when she and Max arrive. I saw your father out there, though. And the new Mrs. Avery. She's a bit of a stunner, isn't she?"

"My adoptive father," I said. "And, yes, she's a model, as it happens."

"Get out of town!"

I rolled my eyes.

"Why?" I asked. "Were you thinking of having a crack at her yourself later?"

"It crossed my mind, but no. Models are hard work and they're all fucking crazy. I tried it on with Twiggy once and she was having none of it."

"I guess that means she's crazy," I said.

"I didn't mean it like that. But she looked at me like I was something she trod in. Even Princess Margaret wasn't that rude. Fair play to Charles all the same. He still manages to pull them, doesn't he? I hope I'm still having as much luck as he is when I'm that age."

I felt the water reacting badly inside my stomach and beads of perspiration beginning to break out across my forehead. What was I even doing here? Years of regret and shame began to overwhelm me. A lifetime of lying, of feeling that I was being forced to lie, had led me to a moment where I was not only preparing to destroy my own life but also that of a girl who had done nothing whatsoever to deserve it.

Sensing my despair, Julian came over and placed an arm around me, and it felt entirely natural when I allowed my head to rest on his shoulder. I wanted nothing more than to close my eyes and fall asleep while he held me. The scent of his cologne was subtle and beneath it I could smell the lingering odor of whatever cream the barber had used earlier. "What's the matter, Cyril?" he asked me quietly. "You don't seem like yourself at all. It's natural to be nervous on your wedding day but you do know how much Alice loves you, right?"

"I do," I said.

"And you love her too, don't you?" His tone hardened a little when I didn't reply immediately. "You love my sister, don't you, Cyril?"

I inclined my head a little to give the appearance of an affirmative answer.

"I wish my mother was here, that's all," I said, the sentiment surprising me, for I had not realized that I wished any such thing.

"Maude?"

"No, my real mother. The woman who gave birth to me."

"Oh right," he said. "Have you been in touch with her then? You never said."

"No," I replied. "I just wish she was here, that's all. To help me. To talk to me. When she made the decision to walk away from me, it must have been incredibly difficult. I just wonder how badly it affected her afterward, that's all. I'd like to ask her."

"Well, I'm here," said Julian. "So if there's anything you need to talk about, that's what a best man is for. Not to mention a best friend."

I looked up at him and quite unexpectedly began to cry.

"Jesus Christ, Cyril," said Julian, sounding truly worried. "You're starting to scare me now. What's the matter with you anyway? Come on, you can tell me anything, you know that. Is it just the drink? Do you need to be sick?"

"It's not the drink," I said, shaking my head. "But I can't . . . I can't tell you."

"Of course you can. Think of all the things I've told you over the years. Christ, if we were to write some of that down I wouldn't come out of it smelling like roses, would I? You haven't been with another girl, have you? Behind Alice's back? It's not something like that, is it?"

"No," I said. "No, there's been no other girl."

"Because if you had, well, I suppose you could just chalk it up to experience. Alice is no saint either, you know. A marriage only begins when you take your vows. After that, you have to stay faithful, I suppose, or what's the point? But if you've had a few slips along the way—"

"It's not that," I insisted, raising my voice.

"Then what? What is it, Cyril? Just tell me, for Christ's sake."

"I'm not in love with her," I said, looking down at the ground, noticing for the first time that Julian's shoes were a little scuffed at the sides. He'd forgotten to polish them. Maybe he wasn't perfect after all.

"What did you just say?" he asked me.

"I said I'm not in love with her," I repeated quietly. "I'm very fond of her. She's the kindest, most thoughtful, most decent girl I've ever known in my life. The truth is, she deserves better than me."

"You're not going to get all self-loathing on me, are you?"

"But I don't love her," I repeated.

"Of course you fucking love her," he said, taking his arm from my shoulder now.

"No," I said, feeling intense excitement to hear the words emerging from my mouth. "I know what love is, because I feel it for someone else. Just not for her." It was as if I had left my body and was floating in non-corporeal form a few feet above us, looking down, watching carefully, intrigued to know how this scene was going to play out. And still delusional enough to wonder if there was any chance of me going home with a different Woodbead than the one I was there to marry.

Julian took a long time to speak again. "But you just told me," he said slowly, sounding out every word carefully, "that there's been no other girl."

"The truth is I've been in love for as long as I can remember," I said, keeping my voice as steady as possible. "Since I was a child, in fact. I know it sounds stupid to believe in something as corny as love at first sight, but it's what happened to me. I fell in love years ago and I've never been able to let go of that person since."

"But who?" he asked, the words almost a whisper as I turned my head toward him. "Who is it? I don't understand."

Our eyes locked and I knew then that my entire life had led me toward that moment, to that sacristy, to the two of us sitting next to each other, and, without planning it, I leaned forward to kiss him. For a few seconds, no more than three or four, our lips pressed against each other and I felt that curious mix of tenderness and masculinity that defined him. They parted just a touch, almost automatically, and so did mine.

I moved my tongue forward.

And then it was over.

"What the fuck?" said Julian, leaping to his feet and stumbling back toward the wall, almost tripping over his own feet as he did so. He didn't sound so much angry as utterly bewildered.

"I can't marry her, Julian," I said, looking across at him and feeling braver now than I ever had before. "I'm not in love with her."

"What are you talking about? Is this a joke?"

"I'm not in love with her," I insisted. "I'm in love with you. I've been in love with you for as long as I can remember. Since that first moment I came downstairs in Dartmouth Square and saw you sitting in the hallway. All the way through our school days. And every day since."

He stared at me, the pieces starting to fall into place, and he turned away, looking out the sacristy window to the gardens beyond. I said nothing, my heart pounding so hard within my chest that it felt as if I might be having a heart attack. And yet I didn't feel frightened. I felt instead as if a great burden had finally been lifted from my shoulders. I felt excited. And free. Because there was no way that he would allow me to marry his sister now. Not knowing what he knew. Whatever happened next might be painful but at least I would not be condemning myself to a lifetime with a woman for whom I felt no desire.

"You're a queer," he said, turning back to me, his tone lost somewhere between a question and a statement.

"I suppose so, yes," I said. "If you want to put it like that."

"Since when?"

"Since always. I don't have any interest in women at all, that's the truth of it. I never have had. I've only ever . . . you know, done it with men. Well, except for once a few weeks ago, with Alice. She wanted to. I didn't. But I thought it was worth trying."

"Are you telling me that you've had *sex* with men?" he asked, and I was surprised to hear such disbelief in his voice. He who could scarcely get through twenty-four hours without fucking someone.

"Of course I have," I said. "I'm not a total eunuch, you know."

"How many? Four? Five?"

"Jesus, does it matter?" I asked, recalling a similar conversation I had had with Alice and how I had been uncertain whether I wanted to know her number out of interest or perversity.

"Yes, it matters. Maybe it's just a phase and—"

"Oh come on, Julian," I said. "I'm twenty-eight years old. I'm past phases."

"*How many then?*"

"I don't know. Two hundred maybe? Probably more."

"*TWO HUNDRED?*"

"Which is probably a lot less than you've slept with."

"Jesus fucking Christ," he said, panicking now, making perfect circles on the carpet as he marched around. "You can't be fucking serious. You've been lying to me for the last twenty years."

"I haven't been lying," I said, desperate for him to tell me that it was all right, that everything would be fine in the end. That he'd fix things. That Alice would understand and life could return to normal.

"Well, what else would you call it?"

"I didn't know how to tell you."

"So you thought you'd wait until *today*? Until *now*? When you're about ten minutes away from marrying my *sister*? Jesus Christ," he added, shaking his head. "And I thought that fucker Fergus was bad."

"I'm nothing like Fergus," I said.

"No, he's a fucking *saint* compared to you."

"Julian, you can't hate me because I'm gay. That's not fair. It's 1973, for God's sake."

"You think I hate you because you're *gay?*" he asked, looking at me as if he had never heard anything so stupid in his life. "I don't give a fuck that you're gay. I never would have cared. Not for a moment, if you had bothered to tell me. If you had treated me like an actual friend instead of someone you were just lusting over. I hate you because you've *lied* to me all these years, Cyril, and, worse still, you've lied to Alice. This is going to break her heart. Have you any idea what it was like for her after Fergus?"

"She'll understand," I said quietly.

"She'll what?"

"She'll understand," I repeated. "She's a very empathetic person."

Julian laughed in disbelief. "Stand up, Cyril," he said.

"What?"

"Stand up."

"Why?"

"Because I said so. And if you love me so much, then you must want to make me happy. And it would make me very happy if you stood up."

I frowned, uncertain what was going to happen next, but I did as he asked and stood.

"There," I said. "I'm standing."

But not for long. A moment later, I was on the floor, sprawled on my back, a little dazed and with a pain so sharp running through my jaw that I wondered whether he'd broken it. I put a hand to my face and could taste blood inside my cheek.

"Julian," I said, looking up at him, close to tears. "I'm sorry."

"I don't give a fuck if you're sorry," he said. "Do you know something, I've never felt more contempt for anyone in my whole life than I do for you right now. I swear to God if it wasn't for the fact that I have no intention of spending the rest of my life in jail I would break your fucking neck right now."

I swallowed, feeling pitiful inside. Everything was ruined. When he retreated to one of the side walls, rubbing his chin with one hand as he thought all of this through, I stumbled to my feet and sat down again, nursing my jaw.

"I should go," I said finally.

"Go?" he said, turning around and frowning. "Go where?"

"Go home," I said with a shrug. "There's no point in me staying here, is there? I've done enough damage. You'll have to tell her, though," I added. "I can't do it. I can't face her."

"Tell her? Tell who? Tell *Alice*?"

"Of course," I said.

"You think *I'm* going to tell her?"

"She loves you," I reasoned. "She'll want you with her today, not me."

"I'm not telling her anything," said Julian, raising his voice again and advancing on me with such ferocity that I shrank back in the seat. "Let me tell you what's going to happen here today, you stupid fucking prick, and what's not going to happen. If you think that I'm going to allow my sister to be humiliated for the second time in front of all her family and friends, you're completely fucking delusional."

I stared at him, uncertain what he was getting at. "So what do you want me to do?" I asked him.

"What you promised to do," he said. "We're going to go out there together, you and I. We're going to stand side by side at the altar while Max walks my sister up the aisle. And we're both going to wear the biggest shit-eating smiles that anyone ever wore in their entire lives, and when the priest tells you to say *I do*, you're going to say it as if your entire life depends on it. And afterward, you and Alice are going to walk back down the aisle as husband and wife, and you, my friend, are going to be a good and faithful husband to her and if I ever, if I *ever* hear of you going off with some queer behind her back, I will come after you and personally cut your balls off with the rustiest penknife I can find. Do I make myself clear, Cyril?"

I stared at him and swallowed hard. It was impossible to believe that he meant any of this.

"I can't," I said, trying to hold back the tears. "It's the rest of my life we're talking about."

"And it's the rest of Alice's. You're going to fucking marry her, Cyril, do you understand me?"

"You're saying that you want your sister to marry me? Knowing what you know?"

"Of course I don't *want* her to. And if she walked in here right now and said she didn't want to marry you, I'd lift her off the ground and carry her out on my shoulders. But she's come here to get married and that's what's going to happen. She fucking *loves* you, Cyril, if you can believe she would love someone so morally vacuous."

"And what about us?" I asked, his words hitting me like arrows.

"Us? What us? What are you talking about?"

"You and I. Will we still be friends?"

He stared at me and started laughing. "You're unbelievable," he said. "You are absolutely unbe-fucking-lievable. We're not friends, Cyril. We never have been friends. I never even *knew* you, that's the truth of it. The person I thought of as Cyril Avery never even existed. So, no, we won't be friends ever again. When we see each other at family functions, I'll be polite to you so no one finds out the truth. But don't ever think that I feel anything toward you other than total and utter loathing. And if you dropped dead on your honeymoon, I'd cry no tears over you."

"Don't say that, Julian," I said, starting to weep again. "Please, you can't mean it. I love you."

He ran at me then, lifting me off the chair and pinning me up against the wall, one hand holding me there by the collar while the other pulled back, clenched into a fist. It was trembling in rage. Had he hit me right at that moment, I know that he would have killed me.

"If you ever say that to me again," he hissed. "If you ever say *any-thing* like that to me again, I swear to God they will be the last words you ever speak. Do you understand me?" I let my body go slack and nodded as he stepped away from me. "What the fuck is wrong with you people?" he asked me. "Why do you have to lie about everything? Hide everything? Why not just tell the truth? What the fuck is wrong with simply being honest with people from the start?"

I laughed bitterly and looked away. "Don't even try going down that road, Julian," I said, ready to fight back now if I had to. "You don't have a clue what you're talking about. But then people like you never do."

There was a tap on the door and we both turned as the priest glanced inside, a cheerful smile on his face.

"Your bride awaits you, young man," he said, his grin fading only a little as he saw my slightly disheveled state. I looked at Julian, pleading with him to set me free, but he looked away and walked toward the door.

"Make sure you comb your hair before you come out here," he said, the last words he would speak to me for many years. "Remember where you are. And what you've come here to do."

Crazy Naked Man

Three hours later, a respectable married man at last, I found myself standing in the Horseshoe Bar of the Shelbourne Hotel making small talk with the President of Ireland, Éamon de Valera. His presence at the reception was an incredible coup for Max, whose obsession with social climbing had become even more pathological in recent years, although the great man had declined to attend the ceremony itself earlier in the day, citing an unmissable appointment with his chiropodist. The former Taoiseach, Jack Lynch, was there too, keeping a careful distance from Charles Haughey, who was standing by the bar giving an uncanny impression of one of those unsettling fairground figures, carved from porcelain, whose bodies remain still while their eyes move slowly around the room. Sport was represented by Tipperary's Jimmy Doyle, who had won six All-Ireland hurling medals for his county over recent years, literature by Ernest Gébler and J. P. Donleavy, while at a table in the corner my adoptive father's new wife, Rosalyn, was sucking up to Maureen O'Hara, who smiled politely but kept checking her watch, no doubt wondering when might be a good time to ask the concierge to hail her a taxi.

I found it impossible to concentrate on what Dev was saying, for my attention was focused almost exclusively on Julian, who was standing next to an anxious-looking Archbishop Ryan, while one of the bridesmaids did her best to engage him in conversation. Usually he would have been flirting away—Julian, that is, not the Archbishop— wondering whether he should take her back to his room for a quickie before dinner or wait until afterward when he could put a bit more time and effort into the seduction, but for once he appeared completely

uninterested. Whenever I caught his eye, he gave me a look that combined disappointment and murderous intent before turning away and
ordering another drink. There was a part of me that wanted to take
him aside to explain why I had done the things I had done, or indeed
hadn't done, but I knew there was no point. There was nothing I could
say that would make him forgive me, nothing that could possibly excuse my actions. Our friendship, such as it had been, was over.

When I finally managed to escape the President, who was holding
forth in quite graphic terms about the state of his bunions, I looked
around for a quiet corner where I might find a canapé fork to stick
through my heart. Whichever way I turned, however, I found myself
being leaped upon by another of our three hundred guests, most of
whom were complete strangers to me, each one wanting to shake my
hand but let me know that I had condemned myself to fifty years of
trying without success to satisfy the little woman.

"Tonight's the night, eh, boy?" said the old men whose leery smiles
I wanted to punch off their wrinkly old faces. "Getting a few pints into
you to build up the auld energy, wha'?"

"You'll be starting a family soon," said their wives, practically lac-
tating at the idea of my impregnating Alice at regular intervals over
the years ahead. "Have three in three years, that's my advice to you. A
boy, a girl and an either/or. A gentleman's family. And then let that be
an end to the whole filthy business." One even leaned forward and
whispered in my ear, *"After that, I would suggest separate bedrooms. To
keep the Devil at bay."*

I felt surrounded by people and noise, overwhelmed by the stench
of perfume and alcohol and suffocated by the haze of cigarette smoke.
I was like a child trapped at a carnival, unable to find my way to the
exit, my heart starting to beat faster as the crowds closed in around
me. Finally, battling forward in the direction of the lobby, I turned to
find Alice standing next to me, looking equally dazed and uncomfortable. She smiled but I noticed the shadow of some private anxiety
crossing her face.

"We should have kept the numbers down, shouldn't we?" I said,
leaning in and having to shout to make myself heard. "I don't know
who half these people are."

"Friends of Max's," she said, shaking her head. "It didn't look so bad on paper but I can barely find time to talk to my actual friends. The average age is sixty-plus. There's a man over there wearing an actual colostomy bag outside his trousers."

"Not anymore. A child ran into him and burst it."

"Oh Good Lord. It's a *wedding*!"

"We could sound the fire alarm," I suggested. "And then choose who we let back in afterward. They need to have all their own hair and teeth and a reasonable chance of looking good in the photographs later."

She gave me a half-smile but didn't seem pleased.

"I knew I shouldn't have given him free rein," she muttered. "I should have learned from—oh God, sorry, Cyril."

"What?" I asked.

"It doesn't matter."

"No, tell me."

She had the good grace to look embarrassed. "I was going to say that I should have learned from last time," she said. "Until I realized what an inappropriate thing that was to say, today of all days."

"Oh trust me," I said. "It's tame compared to some of the things I've said today."

"People keep giving me money too," she added. "In envelopes. I don't know what I'm supposed to do with it. So I gave them all to him," she added, nodding toward the bar.

"*Charlie Haughey?*" I said, raising my voice, appalled. "You gave all our money to *him*? We'll never see it again! It'll all be sent up North to the Provos!"

"*Julian,*" she said, shaking her head. "I gave it to Julian."

"Oh. All right. That's not so bad, I suppose."

"Actually, I have another one here," she said, pulling an envelope from one of the mysterious compartments of her dress. "You wouldn't bring it over to him, would you?"

"No," I said, quicker than I had intended. There was no chance that I was going anywhere near her brother. "Actually, I was just going out for some air."

"Are you all right? You look a little red in the face."

"It's just too stuffy in here, that's all. I'll be back."

I tried to leave but she put a hand out to stop me. "Wait," she said. "I need to talk to you."

"I'll be back in a few minutes. Promise."

"No, I need to talk to you *now*."

"Why?" I asked, surprised by the urgency in her tone. "Is something wrong? What's he said to you?"

"What's *who* said to me?"

"No one."

"What's no one said to me? What are you talking about, Cyril?"

I glanced across the room at Julian, who was watching us now while wearing a furious expression, and I started to feel annoyed by his attitude. *If you didn't want me to marry her,* I thought, *then you could have stopped me. But now that I've gone through with it, don't fucking look at me like that.*

She opened her mouth to speak but, before she could reply, her mother Elizabeth appeared arm in arm with a boyfriend young enough to be her grandson and I saw my chance to escape.

"Don't leave," Elizabeth purred, taking my hand and holding on to it. "You haven't met Ryan yet."

"I haven't," I agreed, reaching out and shaking the boy's hand. He was young, certainly, but if I had to be honest I didn't think he was all that special. He looked a bit like Mickey Rooney in the Andy Hardy films. Only not quite as tall. Halfway across the room I could see Charles watching the pair of them, perhaps recalling his and Elizabeth's infamous trysts of 1952 that had led to such trouble.

"Marriage is such an outdated institution, don't you think?" said Ryan, looking at me and Alice as if he had just been confronted by a pair of turds in human form.

"That's an odd thing to say," said Alice. "To a bride on her wedding day, I mean."

"Ryan is just joking," said Elizabeth, bursting out laughing. She'd clearly won the award for First Drunk At The Wedding. "He's from Vermont," she added, as if this explained everything.

"I was in Vermont once," said Charles, slipping in between the two of them and using his elbows to separate them. "I spent a few weeks in Newport. On business," he added, dramatically.

"Newport is in Rhode Island," said Ryan. "Different state."

"I'm aware of that," said Charles, humbled. "I was making a non sequitur. I was in Vermont once. And, in other news, I was in New-port, Rhode Island. On a different occasion."

"This is Charles Avery," said Elizabeth, thrilled beyond belief to have the chance to show off her little treasure. "And *this* is Ryan Wil-son."

"Hey," said Ryan.

"Good afternoon," said Charles.

"Charles is Cyril's father," said Elizabeth.

"Adoptive father," said Charles and I in unison.

"He's not a real Avery," added Charles after a short pause. "Anyway, what brings you here, young man? Are you engaged in some sort of student exchange?"

"No, I'm Elizabeth's lover," he replied without missing a beat and, to give him credit, even Charles was impressed by such un-Irish frank-ness.

"Fair enough," he said, for once looking a little deflated. I wasn't sure why he was bothering, to be honest. It wasn't as if he had any in-terest in re-igniting things with Elizabeth. He'd told me once, after all, that he thought it was a mistake for any man to marry a woman old enough to be his wife.

"I'll be right back," I whispered to Alice.

"Wait," she said, turning and gripping my arm. "I need to talk to you."

"When I'm back!"

"It's really important. Just give me—"

"Jesus Christ, Alice," I said irritably, shaking her off, the first time I had ever raised my voice to her.

"Woah, buddy!" said Ryan, and I shot him a contemptuous glance.

"Five minutes," I said to Alice. "Call of nature."

As I left the room, I found my head turning, as if independent of my will, toward Julian again but he had his back to me now and was lean-ing over the bar with his head in his hands. There was something about the way his shoulders were shuddering that made me think he was crying but I dismissed this as an impossibility. I had never seen Julian weep in his entire life, not even when he returned home from the loving embrace of his IRA kidnappers, short a thumb, a toe and an ear.

Once in the lobby I felt able to breathe again but when I saw Dana making her way toward me, arms outstretched for a hug and some form of unspeakable musical congratulation emerging from her ruby lips, I turned on my heels and ran toward the staircase, taking them two at a time and breaking into a run as I ascended to the fifth floor penthouses where the bridal suite held pride of place at the center of the corridor. I fumbled around for my key, then quickly closed the door behind me as I ripped off my tie, making my way to the bedroom, where a cool breeze was blowing through an open window, inhaling and exhaling deeply until I began to feel my heart rate return to normal. I sat down on the corner of the bed but it had been covered with such a delicate throw and handfuls of rose petals that it only served to deepen my despair and so I stood up almost immediately, moving over to the sofa.

I twisted the gold ring, newly placed on the fourth finger of my left hand. It came loose a little too easily and I held it in the palm of my hand, judging its weight, before laying it on a side table next to an unopened bottle of red wine. Alice and I had spent an entire Saturday afternoon shopping for the rings and it had been fun; we'd spent more money than we'd intended and by the end of the day, when we were having dinner, I felt such strong affection toward her that I had begun to wonder whether our friendship might ultimately blossom into love. But of course I was deluding myself, for love was one thing but desire was something else entirely.

A part of me regretted having told Julian anything; another part resented the fact that I had been forced to hide my true self for so long. He'd said in the church that if I'd told him the truth from the start he wouldn't have cared but I didn't believe that for a moment. Not for a single moment. When we'd first shared a room at Belvedere College, he would have asked for a transfer if I had explained my feelings for him. And even if he had shown any kindness or understanding toward me at the time, word would have soon got out and the other boys would have made my life a misery. The priests would have expelled me and I would have had no home to go to. If only Charles and Max had never met, I told myself. If only the lives of the Averys and the

Woodbeads had never intersected in the first place. My nature might not have turned out any different but at least I wouldn't have found myself in this terrible mess. Or would there have simply been another Julian; was there someone else like him out there somewhere under whose spell I would have fallen? Another Alice? It was impossible to know. Trying to understand it all was giving me a headache.

I walked toward the pair of French doors that opened onto the balcony, peering outside tentatively like a minor member of the Royal Family when the crowds have all gone home. Looking across the treetops into the parkland of St. Stephen's Green was a vantage point that I had never enjoyed before. But this was Dublin, the nation's capital. The place of my birth and a city I loved at the heart of a country I loathed. A town filled with good-hearted innocents, miserable bigots, adulterous husbands, conniving churchmen, paupers who received no help from the State, and millionaires who sucked the lifeblood from it. Glancing down, I watched as the cars drove around the Green, the horses and traps filled with tourists, and the taxis pulled up to the hotel. The trees were bursting into full verdure and I wished that I could simply spread my arms and take flight, soar above them and look down on the lake before ascending into the clouds like Icarus, happy to be scorched by the sun and disintegrate into nothingness.

The sun was out and I removed my jacket and waistcoat, throwing them back into the living room, where they landed on the side of a chair. My shoes felt tight on my feet and I kicked them off too, followed quickly by my socks, and the feeling of the stone balcony beneath my bare feet was curiously invigorating. I breathed in the fresh afternoon air and a sense of calm began to take me over.

Had the balcony extended farther across the street, I would have been able to walk out and turn my head to the left to see the corners of Dáil Éireann, where Julian and I had enjoyed one of our earliest adventures together. Farther ahead, farther than I could possibly see, I might have spotted Dartmouth Square and the house where I had been reared, the same one that Maude and I had been forced to quit in disgrace after Charles's incarceration and where I had laid eyes on Julian for the first time after watching in bewilderment as Alice ran screaming from my adoptive mother's second-floor office. Where I had fallen in love, before I even knew what those words meant.

As I dwelled on these memories and felt the breeze lift my sprits, it seemed entirely natural for me to take my shirt off and allow the wind to blow against my chest. In fact, it was so pleasurable, so hypnotic, that I undid my belt and removed my trousers, feeling neither shame nor self-consciousness, until I was standing there several hundred feet above the streets of Dublin wearing nothing but my underwear.

I glanced to my right but the buildings at the northern tip of the Green prevented me from enjoying a clear view of the flat on Chatham Street where I had once lived with Albert Thatcher and been forced to deal with the sound of his headboard banging against my wall night after night. To go back seven years, I thought, and do things differently.

I had gone this far, I told myself. What had I to lose? I reached down and removed my underwear, kicking them back inside the room, and felt a little giddy as I stood on the balcony, leaning over, and stared across the top of the city, naked as I had been on the day of my birth.

Had I been able to see forever, I could have looked out to the other side of Dublin itself, through Kildare and Tipperary and onward to Cork City, then into the toe of the country at Goleen itself where, although I did not know it at the time, my grandparents were being buried side by side that same afternoon, having being run over by a speeding car as they left the funeral Mass of Father James Monroe, the man who had banished my mother from the town some twenty-eight years earlier. I would have seen my six uncles standing next to each other at the gravesides as they ever did in ascending order of age and stupidity and my own father, the man who had planted me in my mother's womb, standing nearby, accepting the condolences of neighbors and wondering whether he would be expected to buy a round of drinks for everyone when they made their way to Flanavan's pub later.

I would have seen it all, had I been able to see, but I could see none of it because I had spent my entire life blind and deaf and mute and ignorant, devoid of any senses save the one that governed my sexual compulsions and that had brought me to this terrible place from which, I was certain, there could be no return.

It was easy to lift my body to the top of the barrier and swing my legs over the side. So easy that I wondered why I had not done it years before. I looked down at the street below, at my own nakedness hovering above it, not a soul looking up to the heavens to watch me. I rocked back and forth a little, allowing my center of gravity and the breeze to do their work. My hands gripped the ironwork and then, gradually, they started to loosen.

Let go, I told myself.

Let go.

Just fall . . .

I took a deep breath and the last thought that I allowed to pass through my mind was not about my mother, my adoptive parents, Julian or any of the strangers that I had been forced to fuck in darkness over the years. My last thought was directed toward Alice. In apology for what I had done to her. At how it would take this to set her free again. And somehow I felt entirely at peace as I took my hands away and allowed my body to lean forward.

And then a child's voice, calling from the street below:

"Look, Mammy, that man has no clothes on!"

I pulled back in fright. My hands gripped the ironwork once again. I heard shouts from the people on St. Stephen's Green, screams, excitement and delirium, hilarity and horror. I looked down as the crowd gathered and the vertigo that had eluded me before kicked in now, almost causing me to fall when I didn't want to, and it took all my strength and focus to swing around, to ignore the shrieks and laughter from below as the people of the city caught sight of me. I fell back into the room and lay gasping on the carpet and couldn't quite understand why I was naked. A moment later, the phone rang.

I lifted it, expecting either the voice of the hotel manager or a Garda Síochána, summoned in from the street beyond. But no, it was just Alice. Calm, completely unaware of what I had just tried to do, her tone filled with compassion and love.

"There you are," she said. "What are you doing up there? I thought you said you'd only be a few minutes."

"Sorry," I told her. "I left my wallet up here, that's all. I'm on my way back down now."

"No," she said. "Don't come down. I'm coming up. There's something I want to talk to you about. It's important."

This again, I thought. "What has Julian said?" I asked.

There was a long pause. "We'll talk upstairs," she said. "When we're alone."

"Let me come down to you."

"*No*, Cyril," she insisted. "Just stay where you are, all right? I'm on my way up."

And with that she was gone. I put the receiver down and looked down at my wedding suit, scattered on the floor now. It would only be a couple of minutes before she was walking through the door. And others would surely be here in less time than that when the crowd from the street reported what they had seen. So I did the only thing that I could think of. I reached for my suitcase, pulled out a change of clothes and threw them on. Pulling open the hand luggage I had brought with me for the honeymoon, I took out the only things I needed: my wallet and my passport. I put a hat on and pulled it down over my forehead, glancing at my wedding ring where I had left it but deciding not to pick it up. Leaving the room, I didn't go toward the staircase but to the other end of the corridor, to the elevator that the staff used when bringing room-service meals up and down between the floors.

Glancing back down the corridor as the doors sealed shut behind me, I felt certain that I saw a burst of white, a billowing cloud of wedding dress, as Alice appeared at the top of the staircase. But then I was locked into silence and transported down into the bowels of the building, where a private staff entrance led me out onto the corner of Kildare Street. A crowd had gathered. They were looking up toward the roof of the building, waiting for the crazy naked man to reappear, half of them hoping that he would be saved, half of them hoping that he would jump.

There was nothing left for me here, I knew that much. So what else could I do but follow my own advice and get out of town?

PART II

EXILE

1980 Into the Annex

By the River Amstel

I could see the argument taking place from halfway down the street. A giant of a man wearing a heavy overcoat with fur trim across the shoulders and, perversely, a tattered gray-tweed deerstalker hat. Next to him, a young boy, perhaps a third his size, in denim jeans and a dark-blue jacket with a white T-shirt underneath. They were arguing loudly, the boy shouting at the older man, his arms flailing in the air as he grew more and more enraged. When the man spoke, his tone was obviously controlled but indisputably more threatening. After a moment, the boy turned around to storm off but before he could get more than a few feet away the man reached out and grabbed him roughly by the collar, pinning him up against the wall and punching him hard in the stomach. The boy crumpled to the ground, his knees rising to protect himself from further assault when he fell to the wet pavement. He turned his head and his body jerked forward as he vomited into the gutter. When he was finished, the man reached down and dragged him back to his feet before whispering something in his ear and discarding him roughly, the boy's body falling back into the pool of sick as his attacker walked away into the darkness. Throughout all of this I had held back, having no desire to get involved in a street fight, but now that the boy was alone I made my way quickly toward him. He looked up in fear as I approached and I could see tears streaming down his face. He was young, fifteen at most.

"Are you all right?" I asked, reaching a hand out to help him up, but he flinched, as if I was intent on hurting him too, and pushed himself back toward the wall. "Can I help you?"

He shook his head, pulling himself painfully to his feet, and with one arm pressed against his wounded stomach shuffled away, turning the corner in the direction of the Amstel River. I watched him go before putting the key in my door and stepping inside. The whole incident had taken only a minute or two, and just as quickly I put it out of my mind, giving no further thought to what had caused the fight or where the boy might go next.

Pulling Myself out of the Shit

Incredibly, I never learned to ride a bicycle until I lived in Amsterdam.

For some, the sight of a man in his mid-thirties cycling unsteadily around the Vondelpark while another ran behind, ready to catch him should he fall, was like something out of a Chaplin film, but this was how I spent many weekend afternoons during the summer of 1980. After causing a multiple pile-up near the Rijksmuseum and almost sliding beneath the axles of a tram in Frederiksplein, I was advised to sit for my *Verkeersdiploma*, which most children passed by Grade Seven in school, and failed three times—a record, I was told, by the disbelieving instructor—receiving stitches in my right knee after a particularly nasty collision with a lamppost before finally passing and being given the uncertain freedom of the roads.

My first extended solo cycle took place a few weeks later when I left the city for Naarden, a journey of about ninety minutes, where I was to meet Bastiaan's parents, Arjan and Edda, for the first time. Bastiaan, who was taking the train from Utrecht after work, had promised to be there early in order to make the introductions, so I felt anxious when I arrived a little ahead of schedule. I had never met a boyfriend's parents before and wasn't sure about the etiquette of the situation. Even if I had been talking to the one member of my family who I presumed was still alive—Charles—I doubted that he would have even entertained the idea of such an encounter.

A long road, humped by unhelpful rocks and random potholes, led to the Van den Bergh farm and I found my unsteady cycling further threatened by a pair of dogs who came charging in my direction the moment they caught sight of me, barking loudly and offering no clue as to whether they were excited or enraged by my appearance. Although I generally liked dogs, I had never owned one and their ambiguous greeting, not to mention their determination to scamper around me, led to my falling off once again and landing in an enormous steaming pile of shit the scent and texture of which suggested that it had not long escaped the bowels of some aged incontinent cow. I looked down at my brand-new chinos and the *Parallel Lines* T-shirt that was my pride and joy and could have wept at the filthy brown streaks smeared across Debbie Harry's perfect face.

"You fucking fuckers," I muttered as the dogs came over and, feigning innocence, wagged their tails in acknowledgment of their small victory. The larger of the two cocked his leg and took a piss against my fallen bike, an indignity that I thought was a little much. Up ahead, I heard a voice call out a stream of words and narrowed my eyes to see a woman standing outside the farmhouse, hands on hips, waving toward me. From this distance, I couldn't make out what she was saying but guessed that this was Bastiaan's mother and had no choice but to pick myself up and, my attackers in tow, make my way toward her. As I got closer, I noticed her eyes were lingering in faint amusement on my soiled clothes.

"You must be the Irish boy," she said, nibbling at her lower lip as she sized me up.

"Cyril," I said, not bothering to extend my filthy hand. "And you must be Mrs. Van den Bergh."

"Call me Edda," she said. "You know that you're covered in cow shit, yes?"

"I do," I said. "I fell off my bike."

"What kind of person falls off a bike? Have you been drinking?"

"No. Well, not today anyway. I had a few beers last night but I'm pretty sure they're—"

"It doesn't matter," she said, interrupting me. "In Holland, even drunk people can cycle without falling off. I've been known to fall asleep with my head on my handlebars and still make it home safely. Come inside. Arjan is at the top field but he'll be down soon."

"I can't," I told her, looking down at my ruined clothes. "Not like this anyway. Maybe I should go home and come back another day?"

"This is a farm, Cyril," she said with a shrug. "It's nothing we're not used to. Come. Follow me."

We went inside the house and I kicked my boots off at the door, not wanting to cause any unnecessary mess. She took me through the living room and down a narrow corridor that led to a bathroom before opening a nearby cabinet and handing me a towel that felt to the touch as if it had been used, washed, dried and returned to its shelf ten thousand times. "You can take a shower in here," she said. "Next door is Bastiaan's old bedroom and he still keeps some clothes in the wardrobe. Change into something when you're finished."

"Thank you," I said, closing the door behind me before turning to my own reflection in the mirror and mouthing the word *Fuck* with as much quiet intensity as I could muster. I stripped quickly and stepped into the stall—the water pressure was abysmal and the temperature had only two settings, freezing and scalding, but somehow I managed to wash all the crap from my face and hands, dissolving the single bar of soap into nothingness as I scrubbed myself. I turned around at one point to allow the water to cascade down my back and legs and, to my astonishment, could make out the figure of Mrs. Van den Bergh in the bathroom, lifting my soiled clothes from the floor and throwing them over her arm. Before leaving, she turned and stared directly at my naked figure before nodding in satisfaction and exiting the bathroom. *Most odd*, I thought. When I was finished, I peeped outside to make sure the corridor was empty before darting into the next room and closing the door behind me.

There was something faintly erotic about being alone in Bastiaan's childhood bedroom and I couldn't stop myself from lying down on the single bed that had been his for eighteen years before he left for university. I tried to imagine him falling asleep there as a teenager, fantasizing about bare-chested swimmers or floppy-haired Dutch pop stars as he embraced his sexuality instead of running from it. It was in this bed that he had lost his virginity at the age of fifteen to a boy from his local football team when he spent the night there after a cup final match. When he told me that story, a softness in his expression, a dampness in his eyes at the blissful memory, I had been torn between grudging respect and overwhelming jealousy, for I simply couldn't compare my own early experiences with his. The fact that the boy, Gregor, remained a vague presence in his life still was astonishing to me, for until meeting Bastiaan himself I had never encountered a lover twice.

From the start, Bastiaan spoke freely about his love life. He hadn't slept with many people, no more than a dozen or so, but most of them had been boys with whom he had gone on to form some type of subsequent relationship, sometimes romantic, sometimes as nothing more than friends. A few still lived in Amsterdam and if they met by chance on the street, they would throw their arms around each other and exchange a kiss while I stood awkwardly by their side, still alarmed to witness such open public displays of affection between two men, always assuming that the people around us, who could not have cared less, might turn on us.

Despite how open he had been with me, for Bastiaan never lied or withheld anything, I found it much more difficult to be honest with him about my past. It wasn't that I was ashamed of the large number of sexual partners I had had over the years, but I had come to realize that there was something rather tragic about my pathological promiscuity. For, yes, I might have fucked countless boys but when it came to romance I was still a virgin. Slowly, as I grew to love and trust him, I unburdened myself of the story of my once-obsessive love for Julian Woodbead, sparing him some of the more pitiful stories out of fear that I might scare him away, and a month after we started dating, when it was becoming clear that this was no passing fancy on either of our parts, I told him the story of my ridiculous three-hour marriage. Listening in amazement, torn between horror and hilarity, he finally shook his head in disbelief, unable to understand why I would have put myself and Alice through such incredible deceit.

"What's wrong with you people?" he asked, looking at me as if I was clinically insane. "What's wrong with Ireland? Are you all just fucking nuts over there, is that it? Don't you want each other to be happy?"

"No," I said, finding my country a difficult one to explain. "No, I don't think we do."

Standing up now, I took a pair of jeans and a denim shirt from inside the bedroom wardrobe and put them on. They hung a little loose on me, for Bastiaan had a bigger build and was more muscular than I, but it felt exciting to wear his clothes. Once, on the second occasion that I had slept at his flat, I hadn't enough time to return home to change for work and he had offered me a pair of his own underwear; wearing them throughout that day had been such an erotic experience that I found myself masturbating in the toilets at work a couple of hours later to discharge my excitement, a shocking sacrilege considering where I was employed. Wearing his clothes now gave me a similar thrill, although I resisted any urge to lay hands on myself in case his mother marched in unannounced once again. We'd only known each other ten minutes, after all, and she'd already seen me naked. She didn't need to see me jerking off too.

Making my way back down the corridor, I stepped inside the kitchen, where a man with a gentle expression sat reading a newspaper. He had deep, furrowed lines on his face and wore his overcoat, despite being indoors, but took it off with a sigh when he saw me.

"Edda tells me that you fell in the shit," he said, folding the paper in half and placing it on the table before him. He wore his sleeves long, I noticed, despite the hot weather.

"I did," I admitted.

"It happens," he said with a shrug. "We all fall in the shit many times during our lives. The trick is pulling ourselves out again."

I nodded, unsure if he was being philosophical or simply stating facts.

"My son should be here," he said when I introduced myself. "I hope you don't think we brought him up with such bad manners."

"He must have been delayed," I said. "He's not a good timekeeper at the best of times."

"He never has been," said Arjan, asserting his primacy over me.

Edda came over and placed two mugs of coffee on the table, and I sat down, glancing around at the room. Although the Van den Bergh house was small, they had filled every nook and cranny with curiosities accumulated over the years. The walls might have been papered or painted, it was impossible to tell with the collection of family photographs that adorned them. The shelves were dipping with books while a stand next to a record player held an enormous pile of LP albums. It was no wonder, I told myself, that my boyfriend had left it such a calm and well-adjusted adult as opposed to the completely fucked-up creature that I had been when I started to make my way in Dublin. Nevertheless, it astonished me that a couple who had witnessed so much horror in the world could manage to find beauty in it ever again.

I knew their story, of course. On our fourth date, over pints of beer at our favorite bar, MacIntyre's on Herengracht, Bastiaan had told me how his parents had left their wedding ceremony in 1942 with the words of the Sheva Brachot still ringing in their ears and within the hour had been rounded up by the Nazis, along with some three hundred other Jews, before being sent to the Dutch transit camp at Westerbork. They remained there for almost a month, catching sight of each other only once, when their paths crossed during a work detail, before Arjan was dispatched to Bergen-Belsen and Edda to Auschwitz, journeys and experiences that they somehow survived before being liberated by the British and Russian armies respectively toward the end of the war. It was 1946 before they found each other again by chance in that same place, that same bar, when it had been called De Twee Paarden. Their families wiped out, Edda had found work there as a waitress and Arjan happened to stop in one evening with his first week's wages in search of oblivion. Almost exactly nine months later, their joyful and unexpected reunion had resulted in Bastiaan, their only child.

Although I'm sure that Bastiaan had told his parents where I had been working for the past two years, they feigned surprise when I mentioned it. I had rather dreaded the moment, being so conscious of their histories, but they seemed interested, despite claiming never to have visited the House itself, for reasons they did not explain. After moving on to completely different subjects for the next ten minutes, however, Arjan surprised me by returning to it, mentioning that he had been in the same class at school with Peter Van Pels during the late 1930s while Edda had once attended a birthday party with Margot Frank although she had never, to the best of her knowledge, met Anne.

"Peter and I played football on the same team," Arjan explained, looking out the window toward the fields beyond, where the dogs were chasing each other in another burst of energy. "He wanted to be a striker but our coach insisted on his playing in defense. He had no great skill but he was fit, so fit that he could run anyone off the pitch. My sister Edith came to watch the match every Saturday morning because she liked him, although she was too shy to say so. He was too old for her anyway. My father would never have allowed it. Peter was always late for training; it became frustrating to me. I decided one day to have it out with him but that, of course, was the day that he disappeared forever. Into the annex."

I felt both moved and startled by this information, to know that the

man seated opposite me had such a personal connection with someone whose picture I saw every day and whose story had become such
a part of my life. I glanced toward Edda but she kept her back to me.
Eventually, however, she turned around, clearing her throat but not
making eye contact with me as she spoke, as if she was an actress on a
stage reciting a monologue.

"Mr. Frank ran a spice company," she declared. "Mr. Frank was a
gentleman, a dear friend of my father's. Whenever we stopped in,
Mr. Frank always asked after my mother's health, for she was frequently ill; she suffered with asthmatic attacks, and he kept a jar of
toffees behind Miss Gies's desk for children such as I. Years later, after
the diary was published, I saw Mr. Frank once in Dam Square and
wanted to approach him, to remind him of Edda, who had been in his
office many times as a girl, but I hesitated. I watched as he passed
among the tourists, unseen, jostled by some of them. A man wearing
an Ajax T-shirt thrust a camera into his hands and asked him to take a
photograph of him and his wife, and afterward he took the camera
back without so much as a thank-you, as if Mr. Frank existed for no
other reason than to do his bidding. I wondered what any of the people
in the square that day would do if they knew that here was a man
among men. And then, his head bowed, he simply disappeared from
sight. It was the only time I ever saw Mr. Frank in the flesh after the
war."

There were so many questions that I wanted to ask but I was uncertain how intrusive my curiosity might be. In the four years that I'd
lived and worked in Amsterdam, I had met dozens of survivors of the
death camps and formed professional connections with many of them
due to my work at the museum but there was something more intimate to me about this moment, for here were two people who had
gone through the worst of all possible experiences and survived it, and
I was in love with their son and he, to my utter astonishment, appeared to be in love with me too.

"How can you bear it?" asked Edda, sitting down now and raising
her voice, partly in anger and partly in bewilderment. "Working there,
I mean? Spending every day in such a place? Does it not become painful? Or is it worse than that, have you simply become immune to it all?"

"No," I said, choosing my words carefully. "It fascinates me.

Growing up in Ireland I knew very little of what had taken place during the war. They didn't teach us about it. And now I learn more every day. At the museum, our education plan is always growing. We welcome school groups all the time. It's my job to help educate them about the things that happened there."

"And how can you do that?" she asked, sounding genuinely perplexed. "When you understand absolutely nothing about it yourself?"

I said nothing. It was true that I could not possibly understand as they understood, could not feel as they felt, but since arriving in Amsterdam and finding work as a junior curator at the museum, my life had begun to hold meaning for me for the first time. I was thirty-five years old and felt that I belonged somewhere at last. That I was of use. The House mattered to me more than I could possibly say. It was a place steeped in historical danger and yet, perversely, it was also a place where I felt utterly safe.

"Of course it's important," she continued with a sigh. "I don't dispute that. But to spend all day there with those ghosts." She shivered and Arjan reached across to place his hand atop hers; his sleeve rode up a little now and when my eyes glanced toward it, he pushed it back down. "And why are you interested anyway? Are there no Irish Jews who you can patronize?"

"Not many," I admitted, stung by her choice of verb.

"There are not many anywhere," said Arjan.

"I know all about your country," she said. "I've read about it. I've heard about it. It sounds like a backward place. A people with no empathy for anyone. Why do you let your priests decide everything for you?"

"Because they always have, I suppose."

"What a ridiculous answer," she said with an irritated laugh. "Still, at least you abandoned it. I think you were clever to do that."

"I didn't abandon it," I said, surprised to feel unexpected stirrings of patriotism in a soul that I had always thought devoid of such parochial bullshit. "I left it, that's all."

"Is there a difference?"

"I think so."

"You'll go back someday, I expect. All Irish boys go home to their mothers in the end, don't they?"

"If they know who their mothers are, perhaps."

"Well, I couldn't do what you do," she said. "I don't even like visiting Amsterdam anymore. I haven't been near the Westerkerk in years and I loved climbing to the summit when I was a girl. It's like . . ." and here she turned to her husband. "Elspeth's son. What's his name again?"

"Henrik," said Arjan.

"Yes, Henrik. The son of a friend of ours. A historian. And he has spent the last two years working in the museum at Auschwitz. How can he do such a thing? How can he bear it? It baffles me."

"Would you ever consider giving a talk at the House?" I asked, an idea coming half-formed into my head and translating itself into words before I had a chance to consider them properly. "Perhaps to some of the children who visit?"

"I don't think so, Cyril," said Arjan, shaking his head. "What could I say anyway? That Peter Van Pels was a good footballer? That my sister, like Anne Frank, had a crush on him? This is almost forty years ago, remember. I don't have anything to say that would be of interest to anyone."

"Then perhaps you could talk about your time at—"

He stood up, pushing his chair back with such force that it screeched across the tiled floor, making me wince at the sound. Looking up, it struck me how big he was, how hard he had worked to keep himself in shape. Physically, he had a similar build to the man who had beaten up the boy outside my apartment a few days earlier but his heft belied his gentle nature and I felt ashamed to make the comparison. No one spoke for a few moments until Arjan turned around and made his way slowly toward the sink, turning on the taps as he began to rinse out the teacups.

"You shouldn't lose touch with your home," said Edda finally, reaching out and taking my hand in hers, her tone softening now. "It's where all your memories were made. Perhaps you should bring Bastiaan sometime. Does he want to see it?"

"He says he does," I said, glancing at the clock and hoping that he would arrive soon. "Maybe someday. We'll see. The truth is, I'm happy in Amsterdam. Holland feels more like home to me than Ireland ever did. But I'm not sure if I could ever go back. The truth is, when I left—"

And then, to my relief, before I could reveal too much of myself, I heard footsteps ascending the steps outside to the front door. There was a quick triple tap on the woodwork before the sound of the latch being pulled and there was Bastiaan, red-faced from rushing to get there, marching in and hugging both his parents in a display of family love that was utterly foreign to me, before turning and smiling at me in a way that said there was no one else in the world he wanted to see more at that moment than me.

By Rokin

I was seated in the window of a bar on Rokin waiting for my friend Danique to arrive. The woman who had originally hired me as a junior curator, she had left her job at the Anne Frank House a year earlier for a position at the United States Holocaust Memorial Museum in Washington, D.C., but was back in Amsterdam for a week or two to attend a family wedding. I had forgotten to bring a book with me and was staring out the window, my eyes drawn to the bar across the street. It was a popular hangout for rent boys, a darkened hovel full of easy trade, lonely middle-aged men with wedding rings in their coat pockets, half-finished bottles of beer and instantaneous pick-ups. In my first months in the city, at my lowest depths following my exile from Dublin, I had found myself there once or twice, in search of the oblivion of uncomplicated sex. Looking across now out of prurient interest, I saw two men emerge through the front door, one who looked familiar to me, one who did not. The first was the man who had punched the boy on the street outside my apartment a few weeks earlier. I knew him from his girth, his fur-trimmed overcoat and his ridiculous deerstalker. He took a cigarette from his pocket and lit it quickly as the other man, a forty-something with sallow skin and a Manchester United T-shirt, returned a wallet to his back trouser pocket. A moment later, the door opened again and somehow it didn't surprise me at all to see that same boy emerge from inside, his hair bleached into some unnatural hybrid of brown and blond. Deerstalker laid his hand down on the boy's shoulder in a paternal gesture before shaking Man Utd's hand, and when he raised his arm in the air a taxi appeared immediately and the boy and his client climbed into the backseat before driving away. After they departed, he glanced across the street and our eyes met for a moment. He stared at me, cold and bellicose, and I turned away, happy to see my friend walking toward me now with a smile on her face.

The Anger of the Exile

When I first became familiar with Amsterdam, I found myself increasingly drawn to those parts of the city that offered art galleries and curiosity shops, book stalls and street artists. I attended concerts, bought tickets to plays and spent long afternoons in the Rijksmuseum, studying exhibition after exhibition in an attempt to broaden my mind. With almost no knowledge of the history of art, I didn't always understand what I was looking at, nor did I have the capacity to contextualize a particular painting or sculpture, but the work began to move me and any loneliness I felt soon became tempered by a developing interest in creativity.

It was one of the reasons, perhaps, why I found my work at the Anne Frank House so stimulating, for inside the museum lay the stories of others and the words of one, a combination that had an unpredictable effect on every visitor who walked through its doors. I had never led a particularly cultured life in Dublin, despite the fact that I had spent my formative years in the home of a novelist and her husband. Knowing how books had formed the bedrock of Maude's life, it began to strike me as strange that she had never shown any interest in encouraging my own interest in literature. There were books in Dartmouth Square, of course, books beyond number, but not once had Maude walked me around the shelves, pointing out the novels or story collections that had first inspired her, nor had she ever thrust any of these works into my hands, insisting that I read them so we could discuss them afterward. And once I left that house to begin the deeply private and depressingly fraudulent existence that would characterize my third decade I intentionally ignored anything that might draw me back to the complicated years of my childhood.

The canal area between Herengracht and the River Amstel was my favorite part of the city and I would often stop at MacIntyre's pub for dinner as I made my way home from work. During my nomadic years in Europe, I had studiously avoided Irish bars, but there was something about the blend of Dutch and Irish traditions there that appealed to me, the decor reminding me of home but the food and atmosphere being firmly rooted in the culture of somewhere entirely different.

The bar was frequented primarily by gay men but was not so much a pick-up joint as a casual hangout. Occasionally, a couple of rent boys would come in and attract the attention of the older men sitting alone at their tables reading *De Telegraaf* but unless they conducted their business quickly, the proprietor, Jack Smoot, would throw them out, directing them back toward Paardenstraat and Rembrandtplein with fiercely uttered warnings not to return.

"A little trade from time to time is fine," he told me one evening after ejecting a tall, dark-haired boy in a pair of tight denim shorts that did him no favors. "But I won't allow MacIntyre's to get a reputation for hustlers."

"None of them are Dutch, are they?" I asked, watching the boy as he stood outside staring into the canal, his shoulders slumped in defeat. "He looked Greek or Turkish to me."

"Most of them are Eastern European boys," said Smoot, barely glancing outside. "They come over here to make their fortunes but they don't have the same success as the girls. No one's interested in seeing boys posing in their underwear in a window in De Wallen. They have about five good years, if they're lucky, then they start to show their age and no one cares anymore. If you want him—"

"Jesus," I said, retreating in my seat, offended. "Of course I don't want him. He's just a child. But isn't there some other way he could make a living? He looked as if he's starving."

"He probably is."

"So why throw him out? At least he would have made enough to eat tonight."

"Because if I let one do it, then I have to let them all do it," said Smoot. "And I didn't set this place up to be a haven for rent boys. He wouldn't have approved of that."

"Who wouldn't?" I asked, but he ignored my question and returned behind the bar, washing his hands in the sink and ignoring me for the rest of the night.

I'd grown friendly with Jack Smoot ever since I'd started frequenting MacIntyre's. He was about twenty years older than me and an intimidating presence with his shaven head, eyepatch and a walking stick that supported a lame left leg. Once, when I stayed late on a Friday night with a girl I was friendly with from work, he invited me to spend the night with him in his flat upstairs, but I declined and he seemed more upset by my rejection than I had expected him to be, for I assumed that he hit on his regulars frequently, sometimes successfully, sometimes not. I made sure to return the next night, hoping that things would not be awkward between us, and to my relief he behaved as if nothing untoward had happened. Now, he usually left me alone to enjoy my dinner but would sometimes join me for a drink before I left for home and it was on one such occasion that he surprised me by revealing himself to be Irish.

"Well, half Irish," he said, correcting himself. "I was born there. But I got out of the place when I was twenty."

"You've no trace of an accent," I told him.

"I worked hard to get rid of it," he said, tapping on the table nervously with badly chewed nails.

"Where are you from?"

"Out near Ballincollig," he said, looking away, his tongue bulging in his cheek. I could feel his entire body tensing beside me.

"Where's that? Kerry?"

"Cork."

"Oh right," I said. "I've never been there."

"Well, you haven't missed much."

"And do you go back often?"

He laughed, as if I'd asked a ridiculous question, and shook his head. "I do not," he said. "I haven't set foot in Ireland in thirty-five years and it would take an army of mercenaries to drag me back there now. Awful country. Horrible people. Terrible memories."

"And yet," I said, a little unsettled by his bitterness, "you run an Irish bar."

"I run an Irish bar because it makes money," he told me. "This place is a little goldmine. I may hate the country, Cyril, but I don't mind her people coming over here and putting money in my till. And once in a while someone comes in and there's something in his voice or his expression that . . ." He trailed off and shook his head before closing his eyes, and I could tell that whatever scars lingered from his past, there was little chance of them ever healing.

"What?" I asked when he showed no signs of continuing. "Something that what?"

"Something that reminds me of a boy I used to know," he said, looking up with a half-smile, and I decided to ask no more questions. Whatever his memories were, they were private ones and no business of mine.

"Anyway, I admire people like you, Cyril," he said finally. "People who got away. It's the ones who've stayed that I despise. The tourists who come over here on Friday mornings on the first Aer Lingus flight with no plans other than to drink themselves stupid, then make their way to the Rosse Buurt to get laid, although by then they're usually too drunk to get it up anyway. Then they leave again on Sunday afternoon, back to their civil-service jobs with Monday-morning hangovers, convinced that the whores enjoyed the five minutes they spent with them just because they smiled through it all and gave them a kiss when they were leaving. I bet you never see a group of Irish tourists in the Anne Frank House."

"Not often," I admitted.

"That's because they're all in here. Or places like this."

"You know, I worked for the civil service when I was younger," I told him.

"I'm only half-surprised to hear you say it," he said. "But you left, so you mustn't have enjoyed it."

"It was all right. The truth is I might be still there today if . . . well, there was an incident and there was no staying on after that. I didn't care much, to be honest. I got a job in RTÉ and that was more interesting."

Smoot took a sip from his drink and glanced out the window, watching as the bicycles went past, an occasional bell ringing in the air to warn a careless pedestrian. "Funnily enough," he said, "I know someone who works in the Dáil."

"A TD?"

"No, a woman."

"There are women TDs," I said.

"Are there?"

"Of course there are, you sexist pig. Well, a few of them anyway. Not many."

"She isn't a TD. She works behind the scenes. I didn't like her very much when we first met. In fact, I hated her. I thought of her as a cuckoo in my nest. But then, as things worked out, she saved my life. I wouldn't be sitting here today talking to you if it wasn't for her."

The bar, which was busy, felt quiet around us. "How?" I asked. "What happened?"

He said nothing, simply shook his head, and then breathed in very deeply, as if he was fighting off tears. When he looked up at me, all I saw was pain on his face.

"Are you still friends?" I asked. "Does she come over to see you?"

"She's my best friend," he said, rubbing the edge of his thumb against the corners of both eyes. "And, yes, she comes every year or two. Saves her money and flies to Amsterdam, and the pair of us sit right here at this table, crying like babies as we talk about the past. Here's the thing you have to understand about Ireland," he said, leaning forward now and pointing a finger at me. "Nothing will ever change in that fucking place. Ireland is a backward hole of a country run by vicious, evil-minded, sadistic priests and a government so in thrall to the collar that it's practically led around on a leash. The Taoiseach does what the Archbishop of Dublin says and for his obeisance he's given a treat, like a good puppy. The best thing that could happen to Ireland would be for a tsunami to rise up in the Atlantic Ocean and drown the place with all the vengeance of a biblical flood and for every man, woman and child to disappear forever."

I sat back, startled by the vehemence in his tone. Smoot was generally a fairly benevolent presence; to hear such rage in his voice unsettled me. "Come on," I said. "That might be going a bit far, don't you think?"

"If anything, it's not going far enough," he said, betraying a little of the Cork accent in his voice now, and perhaps he heard it too, for he shuddered, as if the fact that it remained inside him somewhere, buried deep and inexorably within his soul, was upsetting to him. "Think yourself lucky, Cyril," he added. "You got out. And you don't ever have to go back."

Bastiaan

It was in MacIntyre's pub that I met Bastiaan for the first time. I noticed him when I arrived, sitting at a corner table with a glass of Jupiler, reading a Dutch edition of one of Maude's novels. Although I didn't keep track of the various languages into which her work had been translated, and certainly didn't benefit from any royalties, all of which went directly to Charles, I understood from the occasional retrospective newspaper article that they were widely available around the world and that her work was now being studied at many universities. I had seen copies of *Like to the Lark* at a train station in Madrid, watched a stage adaptation of *The Codicil of Agnès Fontaine* in an underground theater in Prague and sat near Ingmar Bergman in a café in Stockholm while he made notes in the margins of *My Daughter's Ghost*, three years before his triumphant adaptation of that novel at the Kungliga Operan. It seemed that her reputation was only growing as year followed year. Maude would have been mortified.

Bastiaan was utterly engrossed in the book when I noticed him and was only a few pages from the end. The closing pages, an epilogue, reunited a man and woman in a London hotel decades after the end of the Great War in a testy encounter that provided my favorite scene from any of my adoptive mother's books, and I sat at the bar, drinking a beer while trying not to appear too obvious in my interest. When he turned the last page, he put the book down on the table and stared at it for a few moments before taking his glasses off and rubbing the bridge of his nose. I was aware that I was ogling him but I couldn't help myself. He wore his dark hair shorter than the general style of the time, had about two days of stubble and was ridiculously good-looking. I guessed that he was around the same age as me, perhaps a year or two younger, and I felt the familiar pang that overcame me whenever I encountered someone so attractive that there seemed to be little possibility of our ever making a connection.

A moment later, however, he glanced over and smiled. I told myself to stand up, to go to his table, to sit down with him—God knows I had an obvious conversation starter with the book that he'd been reading—but for some reason I turned away. And then, before I could gather my courage, he stood up and to my frustration waved a hand toward the barman before leaving.

"Your timidity is going to be the death of you, Cyril," said Jack Smoot, placing a fresh drink before me.

"I'm not timid," I said timidly.

"Of course you are. You're nervous of being rejected. I can see it in your face. You don't have much experience of men, do you?"

"Not much," I admitted. *Sex, yes*, I stopped myself from saying, *but men, no.*

"This isn't Dublin, you know," he continued. "This is Amsterdam. If you see someone you like, you go over and say hello. You talk to them. Especially if it seems that they like you too. And Bastiaan likes you, I can tell."

"Who's Bastiaan?" I asked.

"The man you keep staring at."

"I don't think he even noticed me," I said, wishing that he would contradict me.

"Trust me, he noticed you."

I returned to MacIntyre's the following evening, hoping he might be there, but to my disappointment the table in the corner was empty and I sat down and carried on with *De wereld volgens Garp*, which I was reading for the second time—this time in Dutch—in an attempt to improve my language skills. About twenty minutes later, however, he arrived, glanced around the room and went to the bar to order two beers before sitting down opposite me.

"I came back hoping you might be here," he told me by way of introduction.

"I did too," I said.

"I thought if you weren't going to speak to me, then I should speak to you."

I looked directly into his eyes and somehow already knew that seated across from me was the most important man I would ever know in my life. More important than Charles Avery. More important than Julian Woodbead. The only one whom I would ever love and who would ever love me in return.

"I'm sorry," I said. "I'm a little shy, that's all."

"You can't be shy in Amsterdam," he said, echoing Smoot's words of the previous night. "It's against the law. You can get locked up for less."

"I'd spend a lot of time in prison if that was the case," I told him.

"What's your name?" he asked me.

"Cyril Avery."

"Your accent. You're Irish?" His face fell a little. "Are you just visiting?"

"No, I live here," I told him. "I'm here to stay."

"You work here?"

"At the Anne Frank House. I'm a curator there."

He hesitated briefly. "OK," he said.

"And you?" I asked. "What do you do?"

"I'm a doctor," he told me. "A research scientist, to be more precise. Communicable diseases."

"What, like smallpox and polio and things like that?"

He paused for a moment. "That sort of thing, yes. Although it's not quite the area I work in."

"What area do you work in?"

Before he could reply, Smoot appeared, pulling over a seat and grinning at us like some diligent matchmaker whose work was done.

"You found each other then?" he asked, grinning at us both. "I knew you would eventually."

"Jack here is always telling me that Ireland is a terrible place," said Bastiaan. "Can it be true? I've never been there."

"It's not that bad," I said, surprised at my willingness to defend my homeland. "Jack hasn't been home in a long time, that's all."

"It's not home," said Smoot. "And neither have you."

"When were you last there?" asked Bastiaan.

"Seven years ago."

"It's not a good place for people like us," said Smoot.

"People like us?" asked Bastiaan, turning to him. "What, bar owners, museum curators and doctors?"

"Take a look at this," said Smoot, ignoring the question as he lifted his eyepatch to reveal a clump of scar tissue across the skin where his eye should have been. "This is what Ireland does to people like us. And this too," he added, raising his cane and rapping it hard, three times, against the floor, making the other patrons turn their heads in our direction. "I haven't walked easily on two legs in thirty-five years. Fucking Ireland."

I gave a deep sigh; I wasn't in the mood for Smoot's bitterness that night. I glared at him, hoping he would take the hint to leave, but Bastiaan leaned over in interest and examined his wounds for a moment or two.

"Who did this to you, my friend?" he asked quietly.

"Some fat old bastard from Ballincollig," said Smoot, his face darkening at the memory. "He took exception to the fact that his son came up to Dublin to be with me and so he followed him up one day, waited outside our flat until he could get in and then bashed the boy's brains in against the wall before turning his fury on me. I would have bled to death if there hadn't been someone else there that night."

Bastiaan shook his head in disgust. "And what happened to him?" he asked. "Did he go to jail?"

"He did not," said Smoot, sitting up straight, and I could tell that the pain was almost too much for him, even from a distance of so many years. "The jury let him off, but no great surprises there. A jury of twelve other fat old Irish bastards who said that his son was mentally disordered and so he had the right to do what he did to him. And to me. If you want to know what he stole from me, just take a look at the wall there." He nodded toward a photograph nailed to the stonework next to us; I hadn't even noticed it until now. "Seán MacIntyre. The boy I loved. The boy he murdered." I stared at it, two men standing next to each other, one smiling at the camera, the other—a younger Smoot—glaring at it, while to their right, the figure of a woman was split down the middle by the frame. "A couple of months after that picture was taken, Seán was in his grave."

I glanced back toward the bar, wishing he would return there. To my relief, two tourists entered the bar and Smoot looked around and sighed.

"I better get back to it," he said, lifting his cane and hobbling back to serve them.

"Have you eaten?" I asked Bastiaan, wanting to get out of there quickly in case Smoot returned. "Would you like to grab some dinner with me?"

"Of course I would," he said, grinning at me as if there could be no doubt about the answer. "Did you think I came back here just to look at Jack Smoot's missing eye?"

Ignac

We discovered Ignac lying up against the doorway of our apartment in Weesperplein on a freezing cold Saturday night a few weeks before Christmas.

Bastiaan had moved in two months earlier and the simple pleasure of our cohabitation made me wonder why I had ever cared what other people might think. It had been seven years since I'd left Dublin and during that time I had neither gone back to my homeland nor communicated with anyone from my past. The truth was, I had no idea what had happened to any of them, whether they were even alive or dead. Nor, for that matter, did they have any clue what had happened to me. The notion that I might never return, however, saddened me, for as much as I loved Amsterdam, I still thought of Ireland as home and occasionally longed to be walking down Grafton Street while the carol singers were performing outside Switzer's or taking a stroll along the pier at Dun Laoghaire on a chilly Sunday morning before enjoying lunch in a local pub.

To my surprise, it was Charles I thought about the most. He might have been a hopeless adoptive father and I might never have been a real Avery but nevertheless I had grown up in his house and buried inside me were tender feelings toward him, feelings that seemed all the stronger for our estrangement. I thought of Julian less frequently and when I did it was no longer with desire or lust. Instead, I wondered whether he had forgiven me for the lies I had told him and for the terrible crime I had committed against his sister. For the most part, I tried not to think of Alice at all, pushing her out of my mind whenever she appeared, for while I did not blame myself for all the hardship I had caused others in my life, I certainly blamed myself for the pain I had caused her. Still, in my naïveté I assumed that enough time had passed for them both to have moved on and perhaps to have forgotten me. I couldn't possibly have guessed the things that were taking place in my absence.

There was something enchanted about walking along the river on cold nights like that, the lights on the Amstel Hotel illuminating the cyclists as they made their way up and down Sarphatistraat, the sight-seeing barges sailing past us with tourists taking photographs through misted-up windows. Bastiaan and I could hold hands as we made our way home and passing couples didn't bat an eyelid. In Dublin, of course, we would have been assaulted, beaten to within inches of our lives, and when the Gardaí finally arrived to scrape us off the pave-ment they would have laughed in our faces and told us that we had no one to blame but ourselves. In Amsterdam, we exchanged Christmas greetings with strangers, remarked on the cold weather and felt under no threat at all. Perhaps it was the fact that we lived in such peace that made the appearance of the wounded boy huddled on our doorstep in the snow such an incongruous sight.

I recognized him instantly from our two previous encounters. He was wearing the same clothes that I had seen him in on the night of the altercation with his deerstalker pimp and his hair was as haphaz-ardly bleached as it had been when I'd watched him stepping into the taxi with the Manchester Utd supporter. But his face was swollen above the right cheek now and a dark bruise beneath his eye was pre-paring to flower into a rainbow of colors over the days ahead. Dried blood ran from his lip to his chin and I could see that he had lost one of his lower teeth. Bastiaan moved toward him quickly, reaching for his wrist to check for a pulse, but it was obvious that the boy was still alive, just very badly beaten.

"Should we call an ambulance?" I asked.

"I can take care of him," said Bastiaan, shaking his head. "It's mostly superficial. But we'll have to take him upstairs."

I hesitated, uncertain whether I wanted to bring a stranger into our home.

"What?" he asked, looking toward me.

"Is it safe?" I said. "You realize he's a rent boy, right?"

"Yes, and one who's been badly assaulted. Do you want to just leave him out here to freeze to death? Come on, Cyril, help me pick him up."

I acquiesced grudgingly. It wasn't that I didn't feel for the boy but I had seen what his pimp was capable of and didn't particularly want to involve myself. But by now Bastiaan had already started to lift the boy and he turned to me with a frustrated expression that asked what was I waiting for and soon we were dragging him upstairs to our apartment, where we propped him up in an armchair as he opened one eye sleepily and looked back and forth between us, mumbling something indecipherable beneath his breath.

"Get me my bag," said Bastiaan, nodding toward the corridor. "It's in the wardrobe," he told me. "You'll see a black leather satchel above my suits."

I did as instructed and watched from the doorway as Bastiaan spoke quietly to the boy, trying to get some sense out of him. At one point, he roused himself and lashed out, shouting unintelligible words at us both, but Bastiaan held his arms until he collapsed back into a half-sleep.

"How old do you think he is?" I asked.

"Fifteen. Sixteen at most. He's so thin. He can't weigh more than sixty kilos. And look." He lifted the boy's right arm and showed me a series of pockmarks that ran along his arm, puncture wounds from hypodermic needles. He took a bottle from his bag and soaked a ball of cotton wool in liquid from it before applying it to the red marks. The boy winced a little as the coldness of the liquid touched his skin but didn't wake.

"Should we call the police?" I asked, and Bastiaan shook his head.

"There's no point," he said. "The police will only blame him. They'll take him to a cell to dry out but he won't get the help he needs."

"Does he need a doctor?"

Bastiaan turned to me with an expression that mingled amusement with irritation. "I am a doctor, Cyril," he said.

"I mean a real doctor."

"I *am* a real doctor!"

"I mean a GP," I said, correcting myself. "An emergency room. You know what I mean. You're a research scientist! When was the last time you did something like this?"

"He doesn't need anything more than what I've already done for him. It's best to let him sleep it off. He'll be sore when he wakes up, but I can write him a prescription for painkillers in the morning." He lifted the boy's T-shirt and felt his prominent ribs for cracks. I could make out dark-purple spheres from where his assailant's fist had struck.

Bastiaan checked the underside of his left arm but it was clear and then took off his shoes and socks to check his feet and between his toes but there were no more needle marks there either.

"He'll have to stay here tonight," said Bastiaan, standing up and walking to the bathroom to wash his hands. "We can't send him back out on the streets like this."

I bit my lip, uncertain whether I approved of this idea or not, but waited for him to come back out to say so.

"What if he wakes up in the middle of the night and he's completely confused about where he is or what's happened to him? He might think *we* beat him up. He could come into our room and kill us."

"You don't think you're being a little melodramatic?" asked Bastiaan.

"No, I don't. It's a possibility. You read about these kinds of things in the papers all the time. And what if his pimp comes back looking for him?"

"He's not going to come looking for this kid until his bruises have healed and he can rent him out again. Cyril, we'll be fine. Look at him; he's barely there. He wouldn't be able to hurt a fly."

"Still—"

"If it sets your mind at rest, we'll lock our bedroom door. And we can lock the living room door too. If he wakes up in the night and tries to get out, I'll hear him rattling the handle and come out to him."

"All right," I said, not entirely reassured. "But just for tonight, OK?"

"Just for tonight," he said, reaching over to kiss me. "He'll be sober in the morning and we can bring him somewhere better then."

I gave in. There was no arguing with Bastiaan when he wanted to help someone. It was in his nature. And so we laid him on the sofa with a couple of pillows beneath his head and threw some sheets over him. As Bastiaan turned out the light, I glanced down at the boy again. His breathing had become more regular and he'd brought his thumb to his lips as he slept. In the pale moonlight that seeped through the half open curtain, he looked just like a child.

The following morning, I woke up surprised that there had been no sounds in the night and even more surprised that there still weren't any. My first thought was that the boy was dead, that he'd woken up in the early hours, taken something else and overdosed. We hadn't checked for anything in his jacket pockets, after all, and who knew what he kept in there. I shook Bastiaan, who looked back at me sleepily and then sat up, scratching his head.

"We better go in there," he said.

He unlocked the door slowly and I held my breath, preparing myself for some horrendous scene, but to my relief the boy was alive, awake and sitting up on the couch with one of the blankets wrapped around him. He looked utterly furious, however, and breathed noisily through his nostrils as he glared at us.

"You locked me in," he said, and as he started to speak I could see that his jaw still hurt, for he put a hand to it to ease the pain.

"It was for our safety," said Bastiaan, stepping into the room and walking slowly over to sit by the window. "We had no choice. It was for your safety too."

"I should be gone by now. It costs more if I spend the night. You locked me in so you have to pay for it. Two hundred guilders."

"What?" I asked.

"Two hundred guilders!" he shouted. "I want my money."

"Shut the fuck up, we're not giving you any money," said Bastiaan, but in a completely calm tone. The boy looked across at him, startled, and Bastiaan smiled in reply. "How does your face feel?" he asked.

"Sore."

"And your ribs?"

"Even worse."

"It'll take a few days. Who did this to you?"

The boy said nothing, looking down at the pattern on the blanket and frowning deeply. I suspected that he was unsure how to deal with the situation in which he found himself.

"You have to pay me," he said after a lengthy silence, but this time in a more plaintive voice. "It's not fair if you don't pay me."

"Pay you for what?" I asked. "What do you think happened here last night anyway?"

He jumped to his feet and marched around the room in search of his shoes and socks and when he found them, sat back on the sofa, massaging his toes for a few moments before putting them on.

"You're bastards if you don't pay me," he said, and I could hear the emotion building in the back of his throat. Tears, I suspected, were not far away. "And there's two of you, so I want twice as much. Five hundred guilders!"

"It was only two hundred a minute ago," I said. "Wouldn't double be four hundred?"

"Interest!" shouted the boy. "And a tax for locking me in overnight! Every minute you don't pay, my price goes up."

"We're not going to give you any money," said Bastiaan, standing up and approaching him, but when the boy took a combative stance he held his hands in the air in a peaceful gesture and sat back down again.

"Six hundred," he said now, his voice rising in fury, and if the entire scene had not been so peculiar I would have laughed, for there was absolutely nothing threatening about this child. Bastiaan could have felled him with the side of his hand had he chosen to.

"We're not going to give you any money," repeated Bastiaan. "And whatever you might think, nothing happened here last night. We didn't bring you here for sex. We found you outside. At our front door. Lying in the snow. You'd been beaten."

"You're a liar," said the boy, looking away. "You both fucked me and I want my money. Seven hundred guilders!"

"We'll have to take out a mortgage if this goes on much longer," I said, throwing my hands in the air.

"I can help you, if you want me to," said Bastiaan. "I'm a doctor."

"A doctor who fucks little boys, yes?" shouted the boy. "You and your friend here?"

"We didn't lay a finger on you," I said, exhausted now by his petulance and wishing that he would just leave. "So one more line like that and you're back out on the street."

The boy jutted his tongue into the corner of his mouth and looked out the window. The light seemed to hurt his eyes and he turned back to me almost immediately. "Why did you bring me up here if you didn't want to fuck me?" he asked. "You only want to fuck this old man?"

"He's hardly old," I said. "He's only thirty-three."

"Why didn't you leave me out there?"

"Because it's the middle of winter," said Bastiaan. "You were injured and you were freezing. You think I would have left you on the streets? I told you, I'm a doctor. I do what I can to help people. The marks on your arms . . . what drugs are you taking?"

"I don't take drugs," said the boy peevishly.

"You do take drugs," said Bastiaan. "You inject yourself with them. It's obvious. We'll have to do something about that. And what about diseases?"

"What about them?"

"Do you have any? Gonorrhea, chlamydia—"

"Of course I don't," he said. "I don't fuck women. You only get diseases if you fuck the dirty bitches in the windows; everyone knows that. You can't get anything from men."

"The world is a cesspool," said Bastiaan. "Believe me, I know. It's my field. Anyway, I don't care how anyone makes a living, what you do is up to you, but if you need help, if you want help, then I can help you. It's your choice."

The boy considered this for a moment and then leaped from his seat and lashed out, aiming a punch at Bastiaan's jaw, but Bastiaan was too quick and strong for him and he caught his arm, holding it tightly behind the boy's back.

"Calm down," he said.

"You calm down," said the boy, bursting into tears.

Bastiaan pushed him away and sent him toppling back onto the couch, where he sat, head down, his face in his hands. "Please give me some money," he said finally, looking up at us.

"How about we buy you lunch instead?" asked Bastiaan. "Are you hungry?"

The boy gave a bitter laugh. "Of course I'm hungry," he said. "I'm always hungry."

"What's your name?" I asked him.

The boy thought about this for a long time before answering. It felt as if he was weighing up the question of whether or not he should be honest. "Ignac," he said finally, and I knew he was telling the truth.

"Where are you from?"

"Ljubljana."

"Where's that?" I asked.

"Slovenia," said the boy contemptuously. "Don't you know anything about geography?"

"Not really," I said with a shrug, and I could see Bastiaan hiding a smile. "How long have you been in Amsterdam?"

"Six months," he said.

"All right," said Bastiaan, standing up and nodding determinedly. "Let's go out, all of us. I'm hungry, Cyril's hungry. We'll get some lunch. You'll come with us, Ignac. All right?"

"If I come to lunch with you," said Ignac, "can I come back here afterward?"

"Absolutely not," I said.

"Where do you normally sleep?" asked Bastiaan.

"There are some rooms," said the boy, non-committally. "Near Dam Square. The boys from Music Box and Pinocchio go there during the day. When the men don't want us."

"Then that's where you should go," said Bastiaan.

"I can't," said Ignac.

"Why not? Was it a client who hit you or your pimp?"

The boy said nothing, just stared at the floor. He was starting to tremble a little and I went to the bedroom to fetch him a jumper. Bastiaan followed me in and sat on the bed as he put his shoes on. A moment later, I heard the sound of the front door slamming and, as we both ran out into the hallway, the clatter of footsteps running down the stairs. I looked at Bastiaan, who was leaning back against the wall, a disappointed expression on his face, shaking his head.

"Well," he said with a shrug. "We tried."

"My wallet," I said, looking over at the table by the door where I always left it when I came in at night, next to my keys. Of course it was gone. "The little fucker."

A Surprise Visitor

Three nights later we were home alone, watching television, and I found myself still thinking about the boy.

"What do you think he did with that money?" I asked.

"Who?" asked Bastiaan. "What money?"

"Ignac," I said. "The money he stole. Do you think he used it to feed himself?"

"It wouldn't have got him far," he said. "You only lost a couple of hundred guilders. Far less than he wanted. He probably spent it on drugs. And I'm sure he has debts to pay off. We're kidding ourselves if we think he bought fruit and vegetables."

I nodded. I loved Amsterdam but this experience had left a sour taste in my mouth.

"Do you think we should move?" I asked.

"Move where?" asked Bastiaan.

"I don't know. A quieter part of the city. Or Utrecht maybe. It's not so far away."

"But it's convenient here," said Bastiaan. "For the hospital, for the Anne Frank House. Why would you want to move?"

I stood up and walked over to the window and looked down toward the street where people were making their way up and down, alone, in pairs, in groups. Any one of them, I realized, might be preparing to rent someone, anyone, for an hour or for the night.

A knock on the door surprised me—we never had visitors—and I made my way out to the corridor to open it. Standing outside was Ignac, paler than he had been a few nights before, his bruises half-healed. He looked very frightened. In his hands he held my wallet and he trembled as he held it out to me.

"This is yours," he said. "I'm sorry."

"Right," I said, taking it off him, completely astonished to see him again.

"It's empty, though," he added. "I'm sorry about that too. I spent all the money."

"Yes," I said, looking inside. "So why did you bring it back to me?"

He shrugged and turned away, glancing down the staircase, and when he turned back, Bastiaan was standing beside me, equally surprised to see the boy at our door.

"Can I stay here tonight?" he asked us. "Please?"

A Time of Slaves

Despite having sat at that same table and looked at that same photograph dozens of times, it still came as a surprise when I finally realized why it looked so familiar to me.

"This picture," I said to Bastiaan as he sat down, placing a couple of fresh beers on the table, followed by Ignac, who was carrying our dinner from the kitchen area. "The one of Smoot and Seán MacIntyre. Do you see the building they're standing in front of?"

"Yes," he said, leaning in and peering at it. "What about it?"

"Look behind them," I told him. "I used to live in that building in the mid sixties. It's on Chatham Street. You can just about see my bedroom window up there if you squint."

Bastiaan and Ignac looked closer at it but neither seemed particularly impressed.

"Well, I thought it was interesting," I said, sitting back in my seat. "All this time that I've been sitting here looking at it and I never even noticed." Ignac was still standing there and I looked up at him. "What?" I said.

"Aren't you going to tip your waiter?" he asked.

"How about we tip you by not evicting you?" said Bastiaan, and he snorted as Ignac made his way back behind the bar and started to wipe down the counter. I watched him for a few moments before turning to my food. The bad bleach job was gone, he'd shaved his hair down to a buzz-cut and put on a little weight. All told, he looked a lot healthier than he had when we'd taken him in.

"So how long have you wanted to be a father?" I asked, and Bastiaan looked across at me in surprise.

"What do you mean?"

"Well, all the effort you've put in with him since he came to Weesperplein. You're good at it, you really are. Better than me."

"Neither of us are his father," said Bastiaan. "We mustn't forget that."

"I know. But it's starting to feel as if we are, isn't it? Or surrogate father figures anyway. It's been three months now, after all."

"Three months and two weeks."

"And look how much he's changed. No more drugs, no more selling himself to strangers, he's eating healthy food, he's got a job. And most of that is down to you. So tell me, how long have you wanted to be a father? Don't you think it's strange that we've never talked about this before?"

"Always, I suppose," he said after a lengthy pause. "I never minded being gay, it never really bothered me, even when I was a teenager."

"Well, that's because you were fucking all the local footballers," I said. "I wouldn't have minded it either if I'd been having your experiences."

"*One* footballer, Cyril," he said. "*One.* And he was the goalkeeper."

"That still counts. Quick with his hands."

"Well, anyway, I didn't mind being gay but it always bothered me that I probably wouldn't have kids. If I'd been a woman, I'm sure I would have had a few by now. What about you?"

"Honestly?" I said. "I've barely given it a thought my whole life. My childhood was fucked up. I had such peculiar experiences of parenthood when I was actually *being* parented that it put me off. And yet, the funny thing is, now that we have one, or are pretending to have one, I find that I'm quite enjoying it."

Of course, when the idea of Ignac moving in was first brought up I had been deeply uncertain about it. I was sure that he would either steal from us again or return some night in a drug-induced frenzy and commit some irrevocable act of violence against one or the other of us, but Bastiaan had persuaded me that we should help him for no other reason than he had asked for our help. That in itself seemed a logical equation to him. And then, what started out as an agreement that he might sleep in our spare room for a few days while he hid from his pimp turned into a few weeks and eventually the three of us sat down and decided to make things permanent. Jack Smoot agreed to give him a part-time job in MacIntyre's and the rest of the time he stayed home, reading and scribbling in a notebook that he kept locked away in his room.

"You don't want to be a writer, do you?" I asked him once.

"No," he said. "I just like writing stories, that's all."

"So that's a yes then," I said.

"It's a maybe."

"You know my adoptive mother was a writer," I told him.

"Was she any good?"

"She was very good. Maude Avery? Maybe you've heard of her?" He shook his head. "Well, you will if you go on reading at the rate you have been."

"Did she like it?" he asked me. "Did it make her happy?"

And that, I realized, was a question I found impossible to answer.

The more Bastiaan and I got to know Ignac, the more he revealed about his past. He was shy at first, uncertain whether or not he could trust us but, as with his writing, the words eventually came. He told us that he had arrived in Amsterdam from Slovenia a few weeks after his mother died, when his paternal grandmother, in whose care he had been left, handed him a train ticket and told him that she wasn't prepared to take care of him anymore. She had no money, she told him, and even less interest in bringing up another teenager, having failed spectacularly with her own son, Ignac's father. When we asked about him, he made it clear that was a subject closed to us. The train ticket took him to Amsterdam and he'd been in the city less than a week when he turned his first trick. He told us that he wasn't gay, that he was, in fact, attracted to girls, although he had never slept with one and didn't particularly want to, not after all the things he had done with his body since leaving Ljubljana. He didn't seem embarrassed by his experiences, nor did we make him feel there was anything wrong with them, but it was obvious that he hated the life that he had fallen into. We asked about his friends and he said that although he knew many boys in the city he did not think of them as friends; they were simply runaways, refugees or orphans from many different countries who'd come to Amsterdam in order to make money and in whose company he found himself on a daily basis.

"I needed to eat," he said with a shrug, avoiding our eyes as he explained it. "And I made money doing it."

He'd started to take drugs for no other reason than it helped to pass the long mornings and afternoons before the men came calling in the bars at night. With nothing to do, he spent his days in the coffee shops where the other rent boys gathered, sitting around talking rubbish and smoking weed before graduating on to more serious substances. Bastiaan took this in hand from the day he moved in, bringing him to one of his colleagues at the hospital, who helped him to wean his body back to health. Clean and sober now, his skin had begun to glow and his disposition had definitely improved.

I had only seen his deerstalker pimp once since Ignac had come to live with us and that was a week or two earlier when I'd arranged to meet the boy after leaving work for the evening. We were due to meet Bastiaan for dinner and as we made our way along Singel, it made me happy to see that the boy had a noticeable bounce in his step.

"Tell me about Ireland," he said, the first time he'd shown any interest in my home country.

"What do you want to know?"

"What's it like there? You're not going to go back anytime soon, are you?"

"Oh God no," I said, shivering at the idea, partly out of fear of confronting the mess I'd left behind, even if it had been seven years before. "I doubt I'll ever go back."

"When you do, will you take me with you? I'd like to see it."

"Ignac, I just said that I don't want to return. Ever."

"Yes, but you're lying. I can tell from your voice. You'd love to go back."

"There's nothing there for me anyway now," I said. "My friends, my family . . . none of them would have anything to do with me."

"Why? What did you do that was so terrible?"

I saw no reason not to come clean. "I lied to my best friend for twenty years, never telling him that I was in love with him, then married his sister and left her during the wedding reception without so much as saying goodbye."

"Shit," he said, biting his lip and trying not to laugh. "That's not good."

"No. And anyway, Bastiaan would never find a hospital interested in his kind of research in Dublin."

"Don't they have sex diseases in Ireland then?" he asked with a snigger, and despite his own past it was easy to see how young he really was.

"Lots," I told him. "But we pretend they don't exist and no one ever talks about them. That's how we do things in Ireland. If you catch something, you go to the doctor and he gives you a shot of penicillin, and on the way home you go to confession and tell the priest your sins."

"It can't be as bad as you say," he said, and I was about to give him more details when he stopped short in the street so abruptly that I had already walked on about fifteen feet before I noticed he wasn't there and had to double back to find him again.

"What?" I asked. "What's wrong?" I looked ahead and saw that familiar giant in his fur-trimmed overcoat walking toward us, deerstalker firmly in place on his head. I would have pulled Ignac into the nearest doorway but at that same moment the man looked up and saw us and broke into a wide smile. A moment later, he was standing in front of us, his arms open wide as he embraced his former charge, who froze in his master's arms.

"And there was me thinking that you'd drowned in the Amstel," said the man. "I thought you'd gotten so stoned you'd fallen in before I could push you. Either that or you'd run off with some Russian oil tycoon and forgotten who'd taken care of you all this time."

Ignac opened his mouth to answer, but I could tell that he was terrified. I took him by the arm and pulled him back a few steps.

"We have to go," I said.

"And who's this?" asked the man, looking me up and down, a mixture of good humor and menace. "I don't think we've met, have we? I'm Damir."

He extended an enormous hand toward me and despite myself I shook it briefly, so as not to cause any trouble.

"We have to be somewhere," I said.

"We all have to be somewhere," he replied with a smile. "Tell me your name. I told you mine. Have some manners, my friend."

"Cyril," I said. "Cyril Avery."

"Well, Cyril. Let me ask you a question. Are you a capitalist or a communist?"

I frowned, uncertain what he was getting at. "I don't think I'm either," I said.

"Then you're a capitalist," he replied. "Most people are if they're honest with themselves. And the nature of capitalism is that we look after ourselves first but when we buy a service or a product we pay money to the shopkeeper who provided the goods. You know this, yes?"

"I didn't buy Ignac," I said, not even bothering to pretend that I didn't understand where he was going with this. "And he's not yours to sell anyway. We don't live in a time of slaves."

"Don't we?" asked Damir, laughing. "I wish I could agree with you on that." He stared at me for a moment before turning back to the boy. "Where have you been these last months anyway?" he asked, his tone growing a little colder now. "Do you know how much money you've cost me?"

"I don't owe you anything," said Ignac.

"Just because you've found your own tricks doesn't mean—"

"I haven't turned any. Not in months. I don't do that anymore."

The man frowned. "Who told you that?" he asked.

"What?"

"That you don't do that anymore. You make it sound as if it's a decision you can make for yourself."

"It is," said Ignac, and Damir burst into a beatific smile. Anyone passing us on the street might have thought we were the best of friends. "I paid you for everything that I did. I want to stop now."

"And I want a house in the Bahamas and Bo Derek on my arm," said Damir with a shrug. "And instead I have a grotty flat near Erasmuspark and a woman who only makes me hard when the lights are off and I don't have to look at her ugly face. You still work for me, Ignac. I say when that's over."

"It's over now," I said, and his smile faded as he turned back to me.

"And you can shut the fuck up, faggot," he said, poking me hard in the shoulder with one of his fat fingers. "This is between me and my—"

"Whatever he did for you," I said, raising my voice and feeling my heart start to pound in my chest. "I'm sure you got your money's worth. He doesn't want to do it anymore, all right? There must be plenty of other boys you can exploit instead." I paused and softened my tone, hoping to appeal to his good nature, if he had one. "Can't you just leave him be? He wants a different life, that's all."

"There are hundreds of other boys," said the man, reaching down and running a finger across Ignac's cheek. "But none quite as pretty as this one. Well, you must understand that, Cyril. You've been fucking him for three months, after all. So you owe me . . ." He looked toward the canal and his lips moved silently as if he was trying to calculate. "I'd need a paper and pen to be accurate," he said. "I've never been very good at mental arithmetic. But I tell you what, I'll work out a figure and send it your way. I don't want to overcharge you."

"There's nothing like that between us," said Ignac. "I just live at his place, that's all."

"And you expect me to believe that, do you?" asked Damir, laughing. "Let's not play each other for fools. Tell me, do you like living with this man?"

"Yes," said Ignac.

"And you want to continue doing so?"

"Yes," he repeated.

"All right then. That's not a problem at all. I have no objections to such a happy arrangement. But he will have to pay for the privilege. You belong to me, after all. Not to him. And you, Cyril Avery," he said, turning back to me, "you have a debt toward me. And all debts must be settled. Such is the nature of capitalism."

"I'm not giving you any money," I said.

"Of course you will. Ask Ignac what I do to people who don't pay me what they owe. It's not pleasant. Now." He glanced at his watch and shook his head. "I'm afraid I have another appointment. But I'll be in touch. Goodbye, Cyril. And you, Ignac. Stay out of trouble!"

And with that he pushed between us and kept on his way. We watched as he disappeared around a corner and Ignac turned to me with a terrified expression on his face.

"I knew it couldn't last," he said. "Nothing ever does."

"If you mean living with me and Bastiaan," I said, "then trust me, Ignac, that's not going to change."

"Yes, it will. He won't stop until he's taken every penny from you. And even when you're broke, he'll still ask for more. He'll never leave me alone."

"How many boys does he have on his payroll?" I asked.

"A couple of dozen. Maybe more. The number changes all the time."

"Then he'll be busy with other people. He'll forget about you. He's just angry with you for walking out on him, that's all. I doubt we'll ever hear from him again. Anyway, he doesn't even know where to find you."

"Amsterdam is a small city," said Ignac. "And you gave him your name."

"You've got nothing to worry about," I said, not believing a word of this.

Two Towers and a Ship Sailing
Between Them

It was growing dark as Bastiaan and I made our way to MacIntrye's a fortnight later. The woman whom Smoot had described as his best friend was visiting him from Dublin, and a plan had been made for us all to go for a late dinner together, an idea that made me a little nervous. I wasn't sure that I wanted to hear stories about how the city had either changed or stayed the same, even if it was from a stranger. She'd hired a car for a day's expedition outside the city but was due back to her hotel shortly, from where we were planning on collecting her. Turning the corner onto Herengracht, however, I noticed a figure walking unsteadily from the other direction.

"That's him," I said, feeling my heart sink as I tugged on Bastiaan's sleeve.

"Who?" he asked.

"Ignac's pimp. The one I told you about."

Bastiaan said nothing, but I could feel him increasing our pace slightly and within a minute or two we were all standing outside the pub. The doors were closed and locked, which meant that Smoot and Ignac were probably upstairs, lodging the day's takings in the safe.

"My old friend Cyril," said Damir as he recognized me, the stench of whiskey so strong on his breath that I took a step back. "They told me I might find you here."

"Who did?" I asked.

"The very kind people at the Anne Frank House. It wasn't difficult to track you down. The Irish fag with his teenage boy. All your friends at the museum know about him, don't they? You must be very much in love if you talk about him so much."

"Why don't you just fuck off?" said Bastiaan quietly.

"And who's this?" asked Damir, glancing at him, and I could tell that he felt a little more intimidated by my boyfriend than he did by me.

"It doesn't matter who I am," he replied. "Just fuck off, OK? Ignac's not going anywhere with you."

Damir shrugged and lit a cigarette. "Calm down, the pair of you," he said. "I haven't come to cause any trouble. In fact, I come with good news. In my generosity, I've decided not to charge you for all the time you kept Ignac away from me, even though it left me seriously out of pocket. But I'm good-natured that way, so I've decided to let you off. However, I have a client who has met with Ignac before and has some very specific and, I must say, imaginative plans for him. There's a lot of money in it for me. And so he simply has to come with me. He's had his holiday, but that's over now. He works in here, doesn't he?" he added, nodding toward the bar. "That's what I've been told anyway."

"No," I said.

"Of course he does," he said, rolling his eyes. "There's no point lying. I'm a well-informed man." He reached out now and tried to open the door but to no avail. "Open it," he said.

"We don't have a key," said Bastiaan. "It's not our bar."

Damir ignored him and banged on the door a few times, calling out for someone on the inside, and I looked up and saw Smoot pulling the curtains back in the flat above and glancing down, probably expecting to see a group of late-night drinkers and instead finding two familiar faces and a stranger.

"There's rooms up there, isn't there?" asked Damir, looking up now. "Is that where the bar owner lives?"

"You must have many boys," said Bastiaan. "Why can't you just leave Ignac alone? He wants a different life."

"Because he doesn't get to make that choice."

"Why not?"

"Ten years," he said. "In ten years' time he won't look like he does now and then he can do whatever he likes with his time. I won't stand in his way. But right now . . . right now he must do as I say."

"But why?" insisted Bastiaan.

"Because that's what sons do for their fathers," said Damir.

I felt my head grow a little dizzy at the words and glanced at Bastiaan, who was frowning as he took them in. Of course, now that I thought of it the man might have borne no physical similarity to Ignac but their accents were similar.

"You've pimped out your own son?" I asked, appalled.

"I left him with his mother," he said. "But the stupid woman died and my lazy bitch of a mother wouldn't take care of him. So I paid for him to come here instead. I took him from a troubled homeland to a safe city."

"There's nothing safe about what you make him do," said Bastiaan. "How can you do this to your own son?"

Before he could answer, however, the door opened and a girl named Anna, one of the waitresses, came outside as she left for the night. She recognized us, of course, but not our companion, who pushed past her and marched inside, leaving us standing on the street, uncertain what to do next.

"We're closed!" shouted Anna after him.

"Where's Ignac?" asked the man.

"Go home," said Bastiaan to the girl. "We'll sort this out."

She shrugged her shoulders and continued on her way, and we followed Damir inside to find him marching around the empty bar.

"He must have left already," I said, hoping he might believe me, but Damir shook his head and looked toward the staircase behind the bar that led upstairs to Smoot's flat and marched toward it.

"I'll call the police," I called after him.

"Call whoever the fuck you like!" he roared back, disappearing out of sight.

"Shit," said Bastiaan, running after him.

We ran up after him to find the man ineffectively rattling the door handle to the flat. When it didn't open immediately, he took a step back and kicked it so hard that it flew open, slamming against the wall and causing a shelf of books to fall to the floor. The living room was empty but even as he stumbled inside with me and Bastiaan in pursuit, the sound of anxious voices could be heard from the kitchen beyond. I had been up here a few times before. There was a safe in one of the cupboards and Smoot locked his takings in there each night before bringing them to the bank the next day.

"Get out here, Ignac!" roared the man. "I'm a patient man but even I have my limits. It's time to come with me now."

He lifted his hand and brought it down solidly against the table a few times as Smoot and Ignac appeared in the doorway. The boy looked terrified, but it was Smoot's expression that most concerned me. He looked angry and upset but also strangely calm, as if he knew what to do.

"Leave," I said, reaching for the man's sleeve, but he pushed me away violently and I tripped on a rug and fell backward against the floor, landing on my elbow.

"I'm not going with you!" shouted Ignac, looking young and sounding terrified as Smoot disappeared back into the kitchen behind him. His father just laughed and reached one arm out, grabbing him by the scruff of the neck and slapping him hard across the face, knocking him off his feet, before picking him back up and slapping him again.

"You'll do what I tell you," he said, dragging the boy through the living area, and when Bastiaan tried to pull him away, he simply swatted him away with his free hand. In the corner of the room I saw a hurley stick, a red and white sticker affixed to it showing two towers and a ship sailing between them, an unexpected reminder of home that Smoot must have brought with him when he left Ireland. I grabbed it and ran for Damir now, holding the hurley in a lock position, and as he turned to me, his teeth were bared like an animal and he pushed his son to the ground. "Come on then," he said, beckoning me forward. "Hit me with it if you dare."

I raised it, doing my best to appear threatening as I struck an ineffective blow across his arm, but he lunged at me, pushing me to the floor and grabbing the stick, snapping it easily across his knee and tossing it across the room. For the first time, I began to panic that he would take out his anger not just on Ignac but on the rest of us too. Even though he was outnumbered, he was so big that I wasn't convinced we could fight him off. But I could not allow Ignac to be taken either. As he turned around, Bastiaan was standing before him, his hands clenched into fists.

"Don't," I cried, for as strong as Bastiaan was I did not rate his chances against this giant. The man barely hesitated, rushing at him with such force that Bastiaan toppled backward and when Damir kicked him on the ground I could hear what was obviously the sound of ribs cracking. I called out his name, but before he could answer Damir had dragged him to his feet and thrown him back down the stairs toward the bar.

"Enough!" he cried, when he turned around. "Ignac, you're coming with me. Do you understand?"

The boy looked across at me but nodded sadly. "All right," he said. "I'll come. Just don't hurt anyone else."

Damir walked toward me and looked down to where I lay on the floor. "That's the end of this," he said quietly. "If you come near my boy again, I will cut your head off and throw it in the canal, do you understand me?"

I swallowed, too frightened to say anything, but the way in which his expression suddenly changed baffled me. The anger was gone, as was his threat, replaced by pain and disbelief. I stared at him and then toward Ignac, who was holding both hands across his face in fear. Damir reached his arms around his body, trying to grab at something and then his legs went from under him as he slipped, trying to catch hold of the living room table but instead falling to the floor next to me, groaning. I staggered away, crawled to my feet, and looked at him. He was lying facedown with a knife in his back. When I turned to my right, I saw Smoot standing over him.

"Go," he said calmly.

"Jack!" I cried. "What have you done?"

"Go, the pair of you. Get out of here."

I made my way toward the door and looked down the staircase toward Bastiaan, who was struggling to his feet and rubbing the back of his head. Ignac reached down and looked at his father's face. The man's eyes were wide open and staring. One firm stab had been all it took; he was dead.

"I couldn't let it happen again," said Smoot quietly, and I turned to him in confusion.

"Let what happen again?" I asked. "Jesus Christ, you killed him. What will we do?"

Smoot looked around and, to my astonishment, seemed to be perfectly calm. He was even smiling. "I know exactly what to do," he said. "And I don't need any of you here to do it. Just go, all right? Here's the keys of the bar. Lock the door behind you and throw the keys back through the letter box."

"We can't just—"

"Go!" he roared, turning on me, spittle flying from his lips. "I know what I'm doing."

I could think of no alternative and so I nodded and took Ignac by the arm and led him downstairs. Bastiaan was sitting on a chair, wheezing.

"What happened?" he asked me. "What's going on up there?"

"I'll tell you afterward," I said. "Come on, we need to get out of here."

"But—"

"Now," insisted Ignac, turning to him and helping to lift him. "If we don't leave here now, we never will."

And so we left. We went out on the street and did as Jack Smoot had instructed us, locking the door behind us and throwing the keys back inside. We were home within twenty minutes and sat up half the night, torn between guilt, hysteria and confusion. When Bastiaan and Ignac had gone to bed, I found myself unable to sleep and so I made my way back across the river and bridges and toward the canal, where I watched as a car pulled up outside MacIntyre's, a rental car from the ads on its side, and in the moonlight I watched a dark-cloaked figure stepping out of it and opening the boot before knocking three times on the bar door. When it opened, Smoot gestured the person inside and, a few minutes later, they reappeared on the street carrying what seemed to be a heavy rolled-up carpet obviously containing the body of Ignac's father for they struggled to hold him. They threw it in the boot before slamming it shut and both climbed into the front seats.

Before they drove away, however, the moonlight caught the face of the driver. It was too quick for me to be absolutely certain, but in that moment I was certain that Smoot's accomplice in the disposal of the body was a woman.

1987 Patient 741

Patient 497

Every Wednesday morning at eleven o'clock, I left our apartment on West 55th Street and made my way toward Columbus Circle, where I took the B train forty-one blocks north to walk across Central Park in the direction of Mount Sinai Hospital. After a quick coffee, I would take the elevator to the seventh floor and check in with Shaniqua Hoynes, the supremely dedicated and authoritative nurse in charge of the volunteer program who frankly terrified me. On my first day there, having skipped lunch out of an almost overwhelming feeling of anxiety, she'd caught me stealing a candy bar from her desk and given me a severe dressing-down before deciding forever that I was an untrustworthy person.

Shaniqua, who was part of a growing team reporting to Bastiaan, always began by asking me the same question—"You sure you're ready for this today?"—and when I confirmed that I was she would reach over to a never-decreasing pile of patient folders, remove a list from the top and run her finger along a page before calling out two numbers: the number of the patient I was seeing that day and the number of their room. Occasionally, she might offer some particulars about how advanced his or her condition was, but more often than not she'd simply turn her back on me, shooing me out of her office. Typically, many of the patients on the seventh floor had no visitors at all—in those days, even some of the hospital workers were terrified to go near them and the unions were already asking questions about whether or not medical personnel should be put in danger's way—but in moments of depression or extreme isolation they had put their names to the list of people hoping for an hour's company with a volunteer. One never knew, however, what to expect; sometimes they could be grateful, wanting to tell you their life stories, but occasionally, in lieu of family members, they were simply looking for someone at whom they might lash out.

Patient 497/Room 706 was one of the older people I had visited so far, a sixty-something man with plump, exaggerated lips. He glanced over warily as I entered the room and let out an exhausted sigh before turning back to stare out the window in the direction of the North Meadow. Two intravenous drips were standing next to his bed, their bags filled with a fluid that seeped hungrily through the feeding tubes into his veins, while a heart monitor, its wires disappearing like thirsty leeches beneath his gown, beeped quietly in the background. He was pale but his skin remained unblemished, as far as I could see.

"I'm Cyril Avery," I told him, standing next to the window for a few moments before pulling a chair out from the wall and sitting down. I reached out to pat his hand in a pathetic attempt at making some form of physical connection between us but he pulled away. Although I had been thoroughly educated by Bastiaan on the various ways in which the virus could be spread, I still felt nervous whenever I entered rooms like this and perhaps it showed, despite all my attempts to appear brave. "I'm a volunteer here at Mount Sinai."

"And you came to see me?"

"I did."

"You're very kind. You're English?" he asked, looking me up and down, apparently judging my fairly nondescript clothing.

"No, Irish."

"Even worse," he said, waving this away. "My aunt married an Irish man. A total bastard and a walking cliché. Always drunk, always beating her up. The poor woman had nine children by him over eight years. There's something animalistic about that kind of behavior, don't you think?"

"Well, we're not all like that," I said.

"I never liked the Irish," he said, shaking his head, and I looked away when I saw a snail's trail of spittle seeping down his chin. "A degenerate race. No one talks about sex and yet it's all they ever think about. There's not a nation on the face of the planet more obsessed with it, if you ask me." His accent was pure New York—Brooklyn— and I wished he'd mentioned his racial prejudices to Shaniqua when placing his visitor request. It might have saved us both a great deal of trouble.

"Have you ever been there?" I asked.

"Oh for Christ's sake, I've been everywhere," he said. "I've been all over the world. I know the side streets and hidden bars in cities you've never even heard of. And now I'm here."

"How are you feeling? Is there anything I can get you?"

"How do you think I'm feeling? Like I'm already dead but my heart keeps pumping blood around my body just to torment me. Get me some water, will you?"

I glanced around and reached for the jug that sat on the bedside table—"There! Over there!" he snapped—holding it close to his mouth as he sipped on the straw. Those enormous lips were flecked with white and I could see how deeply his yellow teeth were sunk inside his mouth. As he dragged the water through the thin plastic tube, an act that required enormous amounts of effort on his part, he stared directly at me with pure hatred in his eyes.

"You're shaking," he said, when he pushed the jug away.

"I'm not."

"Yes, you are. You're frightened of me. You're right to be frightened of me." He laughed a little, but there was no lightness in his tone. "You a fag?" he asked eventually.

"No," I said. "But I'm gay if that's what you're asking."

"I knew it. There's something about the way you're looking at me. As if you're afraid you're having a vision of your own future. What did you say your name was, Cecil, was it?"

"Cyril."

"That's a fag name if ever I heard one. You sound like a character from a Christopher Isherwood novel."

"But I'm not a fag," I repeated. "I told you, I'm gay."

"Is there a difference?"

"There is, yes."

"Well, let me tell you something, Cyril," he said, trying to sit up a little in the bed but failing. "I never had any problems with fags. I worked in the theater, after all. Everyone there thought there was something wrong with me because I liked pussy. But now they all think I'm a fag too because of this disease. They think I was hiding it all these years, but I never hid a goddamn thing. I don't know what bothers me more, the fact that they think I'm a fag or that they think I didn't have the balls to be honest about it from the start. Believe me, if

I'd been a fag I would have told them and I'd have been the best god-damn fag out there. I would never have lied."

"Does it matter what people think?" I asked him, already tired of his aggression but determined not to allow him to drive me away. That was what he wanted, after all: for me to leave so he could feel abandoned again.

"It does when you're lying in a hospital bed feeling the life seep out of you," he said. "And the only people who walk through the door are doctors, nurses and do-gooders who you've never laid eyes on in your life before."

"What about your family?" I asked. "Do you have—"

"Oh fuck off."

"All right," I said quietly.

"I have a wife," he told me after a moment. "I haven't seen her in two years. And four boys. Each one more selfish prick than the last. Although I guess I can blame myself for how they turned out. I wasn't much of a father. But show me a successful man who's given his family everything they ever demanded of him who can say differently."

"And they don't visit you?"

He shook his head. "I'm already dead to them," he said. "Once my diagnosis came through, that was it. They told their friends that I had a heart attack while I was on a cruise around the Mediterranean and that I'd been buried at sea. You have to admire their creativity." He shook his head and smiled. "Not that it matters," he said quietly. "They're right to be ashamed of me."

"No, they're not," I said.

"You know the funny thing is I've fucked about a thousand women over the last forty years," he said. "And not once in all that time did I ever get any kind of disease. Nothing. Not even when I was in the Navy when, you know, most guys were fifty percent penicillin by the time they got discharged. So I guess it was inevitable that when I fi-nally caught something it was gonna be something big. You people have a lot to answer for."

I bit my lip. This was another familiar trope: a heterosexual patient lashing out at homosexuals for what he saw as their responsibility for the spread of both the virus and the disease that sprang from it, and I knew from experience that there was no point arguing with any of them. They couldn't see beyond their own suffering. And why, I supposed, should they?

"What did you do in the theater?" I asked him, eager to change the subject.

"I was a choreographer," he said with a shrug. "I know, I know. The one straight choreographer in New York City, right? But it's the truth. I worked with all the greats. Richard Rodgers, Stephen Sondheim, Bob Fosse. Bob came in to see me a few weeks ago, actually; he was the only one who did. That was kind of him. Most of the others haven't bothered. All those pretty young dancers. They'd do anything for a part in the chorus line and I was happy to oblige. Not that I ever did any of that casting-couch crap. I didn't have to. You wouldn't think it to look at me now but I was a good-looking guy in my day. The girls, they all came running. I had my pick of them. But where are they now? They're afraid to come near me. Maybe they think I'm dead too. My sons have done a better job of killing me off than AIDS has done so far. At least they were quick about it."

"I don't go to the theater much," I said.

"Then you're a philistine. I bet you go to the movies, though, don't you?"

"Yes," I admitted. "Quite a lot."

"You got a boyfriend?"

I nodded. I didn't mention that my boyfriend was the Head of Communicable Diseases at the hospital, had probably met him dozens of times and was the doctor in charge of his treatment. Bastiaan had made it clear to me from the start that I should reveal nothing about our personal relationship to the patients.

"You fuck around on him?" he asked.

"No," I said. "Never."

"Sure you do."

"I really don't."

"What kind of fag doesn't fuck around? It's the 1980s, for Christ's sake."

"I told you," I said. "I'm not a fag."

"So you keep saying," he replied, waving this distinction away. "If you don't fuck around, then my advice is for you to stay that way and hope that he doesn't fuck around on you either. Then you'll probably both be safe. But if you're not doing it, then he probably is. There's no chance the only two monogamous fags in New York City found each other."

"He's not like that," I insisted.

"Everyone's like that. Some are just better at hiding it than others."

He started to cough and instinctively I reared back in my seat, reaching for the mask that was hanging around my neck and placed it across my face. "You little shit," he said, looking across at me contemptuously when he'd recovered his breath.

"I'm sorry," I said, taking it off and feeling my face redden a little in shame.

"I'm kidding. I'd do the same if I was you. Actually, I wouldn't even be here if I was you. Why *are* you here anyway? Why do you do this? You don't know me; why do you want to come inside this room?"

"I wanted to do something to help," I said.

"Maybe you want to watch someone die. You get your kicks from that, is that it?"

"No," I said. "That's not it."

"Have you ever seen anyone die?"

I thought about it. I'd seen several people die, of course: the priest who'd fallen out of the confession box on Pearse Street; my first fiancée, Mary-Margaret Muffet; and Ignac's father, of course, on that terrible night in Amsterdam before we'd decided to leave Holland for good. But I'd never seen anyone die of AIDS. Not yet anyway.

"No," I said.

"Well, stick around for the show, buddy, because I don't have much time left. None of us do. The way I see it, this is the beginning of the end of the world. And it's *you* people who *my* people have to thank for it."

Three Types of Lies

The restaurant was located on 23rd Street, near the Flatiron Building, and from where we were seated I could see couples making their way through Madison Square Park, where, only a few weeks earlier, an old woman had spat in my face when Bastiaan, in a spontaneous moment, had put his arm around my shoulder and kissed my cheek.

"Fuck you," the woman, who was old enough to remember the Great Depression, had snarled at us, and there was so much invective in her voice that the other people walking nearby had turned around and stared. "Fucking AIDS carriers."

I would have happily avoided the area for a while, but Bastiaan's friend Alex, one of the doctors who worked under him at Mount Sinai, had made the booking not knowing what had taken place there.

I tried to put the memory from my mind now as Alex's wife Courteney, a journalist, drowned her sorrows, having been passed over for promotion earlier that day. The dinner had been intended as a celebration—both she and Alex had been certain that the job would be hers—but it had turned instead into something of a wake.

"I think I should quit," she said, looking downcast as she swept her fork ineffectively through her food, taking only the occasional bite. "Do something useful with my life. Become a brain surgeon or a garbage collector. My whole career has been building toward becoming lead White House correspondent and for what? I've put so much time into getting to know all the people there. And instead that bastard gives the job to some guy who hasn't even been at the paper for a year and probably couldn't name the Secretary of Agriculture without looking it up. It's just fucked up is what it is."

"I couldn't name the Secretary of Agriculture," said Alex.

"Yes, but you don't *need* to name him," she said. "You're not a political reporter. And it's Richard Lyng," she added under her breath, as I knew she would.

"Did you talk to him about it?" I asked.

"Of course I did. Well, it was less of a conversation and more of an argument. Voices raised, name-calling, the whole nine yards. And I may have thrown something."

"What?"

"A plant. At the wall. Which just gave him the ammunition to say that he didn't think I had the right temperament for such a responsible position."

"What could have given him that idea?" asked Bastiaan, taking his life in his hands with his sarcasm.

"It's not funny," said Courteney, looking across at him angrily. "He couldn't even give me a good reason why I didn't get it. Well, he *could*, but he chose not to. But the truth is I know exactly what happened. The White House put pressure on him not to appoint me. They don't like me over there. Reagan's people think I'm trouble. I just can't believe that he caved, that's all. Whatever happened to journalistic integrity?"

"Sometimes, if you can't believe something," said Alex, "it's because it's not true."

"But it *is* true," insisted Courteney. "I know it's true. I said as much to him and he didn't deny it. He couldn't even look me in the eye, the little prick. He muttered something about the paper having to maintain important relationships with powerful people, but when I challenged him on this he just clammed up."

"What's he like anyway?" asked Bastiaan, who was far more interested in these matters than I was. He even read a newspaper every day, which was something I almost never did. "Is he as stupid as people say he is?"

"He's not stupid at all," said Courteney, shaking her head. "No one gets to be President of the United States if they're stupid. He might be marginally less intelligent than anyone who has ever held the office before him, but stupid? No. Actually, I think he's quite smart in some ways. He knows exactly what he's doing. He uses his charm to get himself out of difficult situations. And people love him for it. They'll forgive him anything."

"I can't even imagine having a run-in with Reagan," I said. "The closest I ever got to something like that was being punched in the face by a Press Officer in the Irish parliament. The woman who ran the tearoom had to pull him off me."

"So what did you do to Reagan that was so wrong?" asked Bastiaan, who had heard that story before.

"Maybe we shouldn't get into all of this right now," she said, lowering her voice. "You and Alex don't want to talk work tonight. I'm just venting."

"Work?" he said. "Why, what has it got to do with our work?"

"She challenged him about his response to the AIDS crisis during a press conference," said Alex. "And reporters are under strict instructions never to bring that word up with the President."

"And what did he say?"

"Nothing. He pretended that he hadn't heard me."

"Maybe he hadn't," I suggested. "You know, he's a very old man. I think he's like eighty or something."

"He heard me just fine."

"Did he have his hearing aid in?"

"He heard me *just fine!*"

"Did it have its batteries in?"

"Cyril!"

"So he just ignored you?" asked Bastiaan.

"He stared down at me and gave me that little smile of his that he uses whenever his mind is drifting away and you just know he'd rather be riding his horse over the prairie in Wyoming than standing in front of a bunch of reporters, and then he just pointed at someone from the *Washington Post*, who asked some boring question about the Iran-Contra affair. No, what I was asking about was something far more controversial. Something that *hasn't* been written about enough yet."

"Look, Reagan's never going to do anything to help us in this fight," said Alex. "Eighteen months from now we'll have another election and Dukakis or Jesse Jackson or Gary Hart or one of those guys will be in the White House, guaranteed. After that, there's a lot more chance of our voices being heard. Reagan can't stand gays; everyone knows that. He doesn't even like to acknowledge that they exist."

"*Society can't condone that lifestyle and neither can I,*" I said, quoting the President in what I thought was a pretty good impression, and for the first time I noticed a table of four sitting at the table next to ours staring over at us with utter disdain on their faces.

"Fuck society," said Courteney. "What has society done for any of us lately?"

"Margaret Thatcher says there's no such thing as society," I said.

"That there are only individual men and women, and there are families."

"Fuck her too," said Courteney.

"The strange thing is," said Bastiaan, "Reagan worked in movies and television for years before he went into politics. He must have been surrounded by homosexuals."

"Yeah, but he probably never even realized that any of them were gay," said Alex. "You ever hear the story of how Charlton Heston didn't know that Gore Vidal was writing a love story for Ben-Hur and Messala? He thought they were just old pals from the Jerusalem kindergarten. Reagan was probably just as clueless. It's not as if anyone would have ever made a pass at him, is it?"

I had the misfortune of taking a drink from my wine glass as he said this and it was all that I could do not to spit it all over the table. Once again, I noticed the table next to us and a woman seated there, shaking her head in contempt.

"A truly great American," I heard her husband say in a loud, aggressive voice.

"Well, what about Rock Hudson?" asked Bastiaan, who was oblivious to our neighbors. "They were friends, weren't they?"

"When Rock Hudson died, Reagan said absolutely nothing despite decades of friendship," said Alex. "Look, as far as the President is concerned this is a gay disease wiping out gay people and that, by its very nature, is not the worst thing that he can think of. It's been six years since the first case was identified in America and in all that time the man has said absolutely nothing. He hasn't even uttered the words HIV or AIDS once in public."

"Anyway, I went to see the Chief of Staff afterward," continued Courteney, "and he made it clear that the subject wasn't even on the President's agenda. Off the record he told me that the government would never put any substantial funding into research for a disease which was seen by the majority of the population as something that primarily killed homosexuals. *Normal people don't like fags*, he said, grinning at me as if he couldn't understand what I was getting so worked up about. *So what does that mean?* I asked him. *That they should all die because they're not popular? The majority of members of the House of*

*Representatives aren't popular either, but no one's suggesting that they should
all be killed off."*

"And what did he say to that?"

"He basically shrugged his shoulders as if he didn't care. But later
that same day I was coming out of the press room and making my way
toward the West Wing to check a quote about something else entirely
when Reagan just happened to pass me in the corridor and I pigeon-
holed him. I guess he'd forgotten me from earlier in the day, 'cause I
got him to stick around by throwing a few softballs at him to get his
attention, and once I had him hooked I asked him whether he was
aware that since he had first come into office over twenty-eight thousand cases of AIDS had been reported in the U.S. and that of those
twenty-eight thousand people almost twenty-five thousand had died.
More than eighty-nine percent. *I don't know if that's entirely accurate,* he
said"—and here she did an even better Reagan impression than I had
done—"*and you know what they say about statistics, don't you?*"

"What do they say about statistics?" I asked.

"I interrupted him, which you're not supposed to do with a President,
and asked him whether he thought the administration should be responding in a more serious way to a pandemic of such enormous pro-
portions and one that showed no sign of slowing down anytime soon."

"There are three types of lies," said Alex, looking at me. "Lies,
damn lies, and statistics."

"And did he give you an answer?" asked Bastiaan.

"Of course not," said Courteney. "He just grunted a little and smiled
and his head twitched a bit and then he said, *Well, you gals in the press
room know all the gossip, don't you?* And then he asked me whether I'd
seen *Radio Days* yet and what I thought of Woody Allen. *He's a leading
man?* he asked me, scratching his chin. *In my day he would have been
working in the mailroom.* Basically, he just ignored my question and before I could drag him back to it, the Press Secretary came running
down the corridor and told the President he was needed in the Oval
Office. Once Reagan had gone, he gave me the mother of all dressings-
down and threatened to take my press pass away."

"And you think he spoke to your editor about your promotion?"
asked Bastiaan. "You think he was punishing you for that?"

"Him or someone else in the administration. The fact is they don't want anyone asking questions on this subject. Especially not someone so closely connected to it, someone who just happens to be married to an AIDS doctor and has the inside scoop on what's actually happening on the ground."

"Please don't call me that," said Alex, grimacing. "I hate that phrase. It's so reductive."

"Well, it's what you are, isn't it? Essentially? It's what you both are. There's no point in sugar-coating it."

"The fact is, until the heterosexual community accepts that this affects them too," said Bastiaan, putting his knife and fork down, "nothing is ever going to get any better. There's a patient in Mount Sinai at the moment, Patient 741. You know him, Alex, right?" Alex nodded. "Have you volunteered with him?" he asked, turning to me.

"No," I said, for I had a pretty good memory for patient numbers, they seemed to tattoo themselves into my brain, and I hadn't encountered anyone in the seven hundreds yet.

"He was first referred to me last year by a doctor at the Whitman-Walker clinic in Washington. This guy had been getting terrible headaches for a few weeks and then he developed a cough that he couldn't shake. He'd tried antibiotics but they hadn't done any good. His local doctor ran some tests and she had her suspicions about what it might be, so she sent him to me for a consultation. I knew when I saw him that she was right, I could tell just by looking at him, but I didn't want to alarm the poor guy unnecessarily by saying anything until I was absolutely certain, so of course I ran the usual tests."

"How old is he?" asked Courteney.

"Around our age. No wife, no children, but not gay. He had that sense of entitlement and arrogance that goes with really good-looking straight guys. He told me how he'd spent a lot of his life globetrotting and was worried that he'd picked up a bug along the way, malaria or something, and I asked him whether he was sexually active. *Of course I am*, he said, laughing as if the question was ridiculous. *I've been sexually active since I was a teenager.* I asked him whether he'd had many partners and he shrugged and said that he'd lost count. *A couple of hundred at least*, he told me. Any men, I asked him and he shook his head and looked at me as if I was crazy. *Do I look like I have sex with men?* he asked, and I didn't bother answering him. When he came back in for his results a week later, I sat him down and told him that I was very sorry but that I'd identified the HIV virus in his bloodstream and although he had yet to develop full-blown AIDS and we might be successful in warding it off for some time, there was a distinct probability that the virus would mutate into the full-blown disease within a few months and of course, as he probably knew, there was no cure at the moment."

"You know how many people I've had that conversation with this year alone?" asked Alex. "Seventeen. And it's only April."

I had a sudden flashback to a moment I hadn't thought about in years. Sitting in a coffee shop in Ranelagh on the morning of my wedding and somehow finding myself looking after a nine-year-old boy, the son of the woman who ran the tearoom in Dáil Éireann, while she tried to phone Aer Lingus to book a flight to Amsterdam. *You're a bit of an oddball, Jonathan,* I'd said to him. *Has anyone ever told you that?* / *Nineteen people this year alone,* he'd told me. *And it's only May.*

"So how did Patient 741 take it?" asked Courteney. "You know, I feel like I'm in a science-fiction movie calling him by a number. Can't you just tell us his name?"

"No, of course not," said Bastiaan. "And he didn't take it well. He looked at me as if I was playing some crazy practical joke on him, then he started shaking, visibly shaking, and asked me for some water. I went out to get some and when I came back he'd taken his file off my desk and was reading through it like a madman. Not that he would have been able to understand a word of it, of course, he wasn't a doctor, but it was as if he wanted to prove to me that I was wrong. I took the file back and handed him his water but his hands were trembling so badly that he spilled it all over himself when he tried to drink it. When I finally calmed him down, he told me that there was no way I could be right in my diagnosis and he wanted a second opinion. *You can have one, of course,* I told him, *but it's not going to change anything. There are very specific tests in place today for how we identify the virus and there's simply no doubt about it whatsoever. I'm very sorry.*"

I shook my head in sympathy and as I glanced around I noticed that the people at the table next to ours were watching us with disgusted expressions on their faces. I caught the eyes of one of the men—he was well into his fifties, bald and obese with an enormous steak bleeding onto the plate before him—and he simply stared back at me with utter loathing before turning back to his friends.

"Despite all this," continued Bastiaan, "Patient 741 was still not willing to accept the truth. He wanted to know who the best doctor in the field was, where was the best hospital; he insisted that someone must be able to help him. That someone would be able to prove me wrong. *But Doctor,* he said leaning forward and taking me by the shoulders as if he wanted to shake some sense into me, *I can't possibly have that disease. Do I look like a queer? I'm normal, for Christ's sake!*"

"You see?" said Courteney, sitting back and throwing her hands in the air. "No education. No understanding at all."

"And did he come to terms with it in time?" I asked.

"Well, he had to," said Bastiaan, reaching across and taking my hand for a moment and squeezing it. Despite how close we were with Alex and Courteney, there was still a moment where I noticed how their eyes glanced toward our hands and they seemed a little embarrassed by our physical affection. "He had no choice. When I told him that he would have to contact all the women he'd been intimate with and tell them that they needed to get tested too, he said that he didn't even know the names of half the women he'd slept with in the last year, let alone their phone numbers. Then he said he wanted a blood transfusion. *Take all my blood out and replace it with good blood,* he said, but I told him that was ridiculous, that it didn't work like that. *But I'm not fucking gay!* he kept insisting."

"And where is he now?" I asked.

"At Mount Sinai," said Bastiaan. "He doesn't have long left. He was admitted a few weeks ago and it's only a matter of time at this point. In the end I had to call security. He started to lose his mind. Came around to my side of the desk, pinned me up against the wall—"

"He did *what*?" I asked.

"He pinned me up against the wall. He said he knew that I was a dirty faggot too and that I shouldn't be allowed anywhere near patients, that I was probably infecting them one by one."

"Oh for God's sake," said Courteney.

"Did he hurt you?" I asked.

"No. Look, this was a year ago anyway. And I was bigger than him.

And stronger. I could have taken him down if I'd needed to, but I was able to control the situation, to calm him down, to make him realize that his anger would not help. Finally, he backed off and that's when he just crumbled and started to cry. *Jesus Christ*, he said. *What will they say at home? What will they think of me?"*

"Where was home?" asked Courteney.

Bastiaan hesitated for a moment and turned to me. "Well, that's the thing," he said. "He was Irish."

"You're kidding me," I said. "I haven't even kept up with what's going on over there. Do people have AIDS in Ireland too?"

"People have it everywhere, Cyril," said Alex. "Probably on a much smaller scale, but there's bound to be a few cases."

"So why didn't he go home to die?" I asked. "Why stay in America?"

"He said he didn't want his family to know. That he'd rather die alone here than tell them the truth."

"You see?" I said. "That country never fucking changes. Better to cover it all up than to face up to the realities of life."

I looked up as the waiter came over to the table and stood before us, smiling nervously. He had enormous bouffant hair and was wearing a leather waistcoat with no shirt underneath, revealing a hirsute chest, and looked as if he belonged on stage with the rest of Bon Jovi.

"How was your dinner?" he asked, and before we could reply his expression grew noticeably anxious. "I'll just leave this here for you for whenever you're ready," he said, laying a small silver tray on the table and turning around to walk away.

"What's that for?" asked Alex, summoning him back. "No one asked for the check."

"I'm afraid we need this table," said the waiter, glancing toward our neighbors for a moment. "We didn't expect you to stay this long."

"We haven't even been here an hour," I said.

"And we haven't had dessert or coffee yet," said Courteney.

"I can give you some coffee to go if you like?"

"We don't want coffee to go!" she snapped. "Jesus Christ!"

"Just take the check back and we'll order something else when we're ready," said Bastiaan.

"I can't do that, sir," said the waiter, looking around for reinforcements, and I noticed a couple of his colleagues gathered near the bar area watching what was going on. "This table is reserved for another party."

"Well, where are they?" I asked, looking around.

"They're not here yet. But they're on their way."

"I can count at least four empty tables," said Courteney. "Seat them at one of those."

"They specifically requested this table," said the waiter.

"Then it's hard luck," said Alex. "Because we were here first."

"Please," said the waiter, looking at our neighbors again, who were watching with smiles on their faces. "Don't make a scene. We have the other diners to think about."

"What's going on here exactly?" said Bastiaan, throwing his napkin down on the table and growing angry now. "Are you throwing us out, is that what's going on here? Why? What have we done?"

"We've had some complaints," said the waiter.

"About what?" I asked, completely baffled.

"Why don't you just do what the man says and get the hell out of here," came a voice from the next table, and we looked over at the man with the steak who was staring at us in disgust. "We're trying to have a nice dinner and all we can hear from you people is a lot of talk about that queer disease. If one of you has it, then you shouldn't be in a restaurant anyway."

"None of us has it, you moron," said Courteney, turning on him. "These two are doctors. They treat victims of AIDS."

"I think you misunderstand the meaning of the word *victim*," said one of the women. "You're not a victim if you're asking for it in the first place."

"What the fuck?" I said, looking around, half-amused and half-shocked by what I was hearing.

"Waiter, you need to throw away all their plates and cutlery," said the man. "No one else should have to eat off them after these people. And wear gloves, I advise you."

It took just a moment for Bastiaan to be on his feet and marching over to their table. The waiter stepped back in fright and Alex jumped up, as did I, uncertain what to do at a moment like this.

"Let's just leave," said Courteney, grabbing Bastiaan by the arm as he passed her. "But don't think we'll be paying the bill," she added to the waiter. "You can stick that where the sun don't shine."

"What's the matter with you?" asked Bastiaan of the fat man, pushing him with both hands against the chest as he stood too, and his Dutch accent became more pronounced the more furious he got. This was something that happened whenever he grew really angry; I called it "the tone" and dreaded its rare appearance. "You think you know what you're talking about? You don't understand anything of what you're saying. Develop a little humanity, why don't you?"

"Get the fuck out of here before I call the police," said the man, not even slightly intimidated despite the fact that Bastiaan was younger, fitter and taller than him. "Why don't you and your friends go down to the West Village. They'll be happy to serve all you perverts whatever you want down there."

I could see Bastiaan trembling as he summoned all his self-control to stop himself from picking the man up and throwing him through the windows, but finally, controlling his temper, he turned around and walked away. We made our way to the doors and left, the eyes of everyone in the restaurant on us as we marched back out on to 23rd Street, where the lights from the corner offices of the Flatiron shone down on us.

"Fuckers," said Bastiaan, leading us down the street toward a bar where we had every intention of getting riotously drunk. "Bunch of fucking fuckers. They'd have a bit more decency if one of them came down with it. I wish they would. I wish they all would."

"You don't mean that," I said, wrapping my arms around him and pulling him close to me.

"No," he whispered with a sigh as his head rested on my shoulder. "No, I suppose I don't."

Patient 563

The curtains were drawn in Room 711 and in a husky voice that sounded as if it had not been used in sometime, the young man asked me not to open them. Enough light was seeping through, however, to allow me to make out the figure in the bed. He was around twenty years old but probably weighed no more than a hundred pounds. His arms, which were lying on top of the sheets, were stick-thin, his long fingers skeletal, the elbow joints inflamed beneath the hospital gown. His face was gaunt, the skin stretched taut against the skull beneath in an anatomical miscreation that summoned images of Mary Shelley's monster to my mind. Lesions on his neck and above his right eye—dark black bruises that melted into the skin—appeared to pulsate as if they had a life of their own.

Shaniqua had told me that if I ever felt uncomfortable then I should leave, that it wasn't fair for a patient to witness my discomfort, but I had never done such a thing yet. Today she had insisted that I wear a gown and mask, and I had followed her instructions even though the boy's bed was covered in a white plastic tarpaulin that reminded me of the scene at the end of *E.T.* when Elliott's house is quarantined by the government and the alien appears close to death. I told him my name and explained why I was there and he nodded, his eyes opening a little wider as if he was trying to physically draw some more life into his body, and when he tried to speak again the words came out as a sequel to a prolonged bout of coughing.

"It's good of you to come," he said. "I don't get many visitors. I haven't had one in weeks, other than the chaplain. He comes every day. I've told him I'm not religious, but he comes anyway."

"Do you want him to stop?" I asked. "Because if you do—"

"No," he said quickly. "No, I don't want him to stop."

"All right then," I said. "How are you feeling today?"

"Like the end is nigh," he said, laughing a little, which turned into another series of coughs that lasted for more than a minute and brought me out in a cold sweat. *Relax, you can't catch it*, I told myself. *You can't catch it just by standing here.*

"Do you want to tell me your name?" I asked. "You don't have to if you don't want to. They just identified you as Patient 563 to me."

"It's Philip," he said. "Philip Danley."

"It's nice to meet you, Philip," I said. "Are they making you comfortable at least? I'm so sorry that this has happened to you."

He closed his eyes and I thought for a moment that he was falling asleep but then he opened them again and turned to look at me, breathing in so deeply that I could see his chest rise and fall beneath the blanket. I imagined how pronounced his ribcage would look beneath his skin.

"Are you from New York?" I asked.

"Baltimore. Have you ever been there?"

"I haven't been anywhere in the States outside of Manhattan," I said.

"I used to think there was no point in going anywhere else. I only ever wanted to come here. From the time I was a kid."

"And when did you first arrive?"

"Two years ago. I came to study Literature at CCNY."

"Oh," I said, surprised. "I know someone who's studying Literature there."

"Who?" he asked.

"His name's Ignac Križ. He's probably a couple of years older than you, though, so you may not—"

"I know Ignac," he said, smiling at me. "Czech guy, right?"

"Slovene."

"Oh yeah. So how do you know him?"

"I'm one of his guardians," I said. "Not in a strictly legal sense, but it's how things have been for seven years. Not that he needs a guardian now, of course. He's twenty-two years old. Anyway, he lives with my boyfriend and me."

"I think he's going to be a famous writer someday," he said.

"Perhaps," I said. "I'm not sure fame is what he's after, though."

"No, I didn't mean that. Only that I think he's going to be very successful. He's a lovely guy. And I've read a few of his stories. Everyone thinks he's very talented."

"Did you enjoy studying there?" I asked, biting my lip when I realized that I'd used the past tense, as if that part of his life was entirely over. Which, of course, it was.

"I loved it," he said. "It was my first time outside Maryland. I'm still enrolled there, I guess. Or maybe they struck me off their books, I don't know. It doesn't matter anymore, I suppose. My parents didn't want me to come here at all. They said I'd get mugged my first time out in the city."

"And were they right?"

"In a manner of speaking. What do you do anyway?" he asked. "Do you work at the hospital?"

"No," I told him. "I just volunteer."

"And what do you do when you're not volunteering?"

"Not much. I think I'm turning into a 1950s housewife. I don't have an employment visa, so I can't legally do anything, although I work a few nights a week at a bar near where we live. My boyfriend earns enough to keep us both, so I guess I'm scrounging off him. Anyway, that's why I volunteer. I wanted to do something positive with my days."

"You're gay then?" he asked me.

"Yes. And you?"

"Yes," he said. "How do you think I got in this spot?"

"Well, not because you're gay," I said. "You can't think that's the reason."

"But it is the reason," he said.

"No, it isn't. There are plenty of straight patients on this floor."

"It's the reason," he insisted.

I came closer to him now and sat down on a chair. Despite the trauma that the disease had done to his face and body, I could tell that, when he had been healthy, he would have been a good-looking boy. His dark hair, which was cropped close to his skull now, complemented his eyes, which were bright blue and could not be dulled by the worst efforts of the disease.

"Do you remember when we were kids," he said eventually, turning to me again, "the time we took the sleigh up to Ratchet Hill on Christmas morning? You said that if we held on to the sides as tightly as we could, then we'd be OK? But you fell off and sprained your ankle and Mom blamed me for it and I was grounded for a week?"

"I don't think that was me," I said gently. "Was that your brother, Philip? Are you thinking about your brother?"

He turned his head and stared at me for a moment and frowned. "Oh yes," he said, turning away again. "I thought you were James. You're not James, are you?"

"No, I'm Cyril," I said.

"Does your ankle still get sore in cold weather?"

"No," I told him. "No, it healed. It's fine now."

"Good."

A nurse came in and ignored us both as she took a reading from one of the monitors, then changed his IV bag before leaving again. As she did so, I glanced toward the bedside table where copies of *The Sound and the Fury* and *Catch-22* were piled one on top of the other.

"You're a reader," I said.

"Of course," he replied. "I told you, I study Literature."

"Did you want to write? Like Ignac?"

"No, I wanted to teach. I still do."

"Anne Tyler's from Baltimore, isn't she?" I asked, and he nodded. "I've read a few of her books. I liked them very much."

"I met her once," he said. "I worked part-time in a bookshop when I was in high school. She came in to buy some Christmas presents and I went bright red I was so in awe of her."

I smiled and then, to my horror, I saw tears beginning to stream down his face.

"I'm sorry," he said. "You should go. You don't want to see me making a fool of myself."

"It's fine," I told him. "And you're not making a fool of yourself. I can't begin to imagine what you're going through. Can you . . ." I hesitated, uncertain whether I should even ask. "Do you want to tell me what brought you here?"

"It's ironic really," he said. "They say that you're most at risk of catching AIDS if you're promiscuous. Guess how many people I've had sex with?"

"I have no idea," I said.

"One."

"Christ," I said.

"One, and even then it was only once. I've had sex one single time in my entire life and that's what brought me here."

I said nothing. What was there to say?

"I was still a virgin when I came to New York," he continued. "I was such a shy kid. Back in high school I had crushes on practically every guy I knew, but I never acted on any of them and never told anyone that I was gay. They would have beaten me up if they'd known. They would have killed me. That's why I wanted to study here. I thought that maybe I could find a new life for myself. But it wasn't easy. For the first six months, I stayed in my dorm room, jerking off, frightened to go to any clubs or bars. And then one night I did. I just decided, *Fuck it*. And it felt so good once I was inside. I felt like I belonged somewhere for the first time in my life. I'll never forget that sensation. How difficult it was to walk through the doors and how easy it felt once I was inside. Like I was where I was supposed to be. And then some guy took me home, the first guy who talked to me. He wasn't even hot. Jesus, he was *old*. Old enough to be my father. I wasn't even attracted to him. But I was so desperate to get laid, to lose it, you know? And frightened of staying in a club where I didn't even understand the rules. So I went home with him and we had sex. It lasted about twenty minutes. And then I threw my clothes back on and ran back home. I didn't even know his name. And that was it. That's how I got it." He took a long breath and shook his head. "Isn't that just the worst thing you ever heard?"

"I'm sorry," I said, reaching out and putting my hand under the tarpaulin to take his in mine. His skin felt paper-thin and I feared that if I squeezed too hard I would hear his fingers break beneath the pressure. "The universe is a fucked-up place."

"Will you tell Mom I'm sorry when you see her?" he asked. "Tell her that if I could go back I'd never have done it?"

"I'm not James," I said quietly, squeezing his hand. "I'm Cyril."

"Do you promise you'll tell her?"

"I promise."

"Good."

I took my hand back and he shifted a little in the bed. "Are you tired?" I asked.

"I am," he said. "I think I'll get some sleep. Will you come back and see me again?"

"I will," I told him. "I can come in tomorrow if you like?"

"I have classes in the morning," he said, his eyes starting to close now. "Let's catch up on Saturday."

"I'll come back to see you tomorrow," I said, standing up and watching over him for a few minutes as he drifted off to sleep.

Emily

The noises emerging from Ignac's room told me that he and Emily were at home and my heart sank deeper than the *Titanic* on the floor of the Atlantic Ocean. I made sure to close the front door with as much force as I could and coughed a few times to give them notice that I was back, and my reward was a series of giggles followed by a hushed silence as I made my way into the kitchen.

Five minutes later, sitting at the table with a cup of coffee and flicking through a copy of *Rolling Stone* that Bastiaan had left there, I glanced up as Emily came in, barefoot and wearing one of Ignac's shirts open halfway down her chest, revealing a little more of her breasts than I really needed to see. Her denim shorts were cut off high up the thigh and the top button was noticeably open while her hair, which she normally wore up on her head in a messy bird's nest, was hanging loose around her shoulders.

"Hey, Mr. Avery," she said in a sing-song voice, wandering over to open the fridge.

"Please, call me Cyril," I told her.

"I can't say that name," she said, waving her hand in the air and pulling a face as if I'd made some perverted request of her. "It's a weird name. Every time I hear it I think Cyril the Squirrel."

I turned around with a jolt, recalling how Bridget Simpson had insisted on calling me by that very name some twenty-eight years earlier in the Palace Bar on Westmoreland Street. Bridget, Mary-Margaret and Behan were all dead now, of course, and Julian? Well, I had no idea where Julian was.

"What?" she asked, turning around. "You look like you've seen a ghost. You're not having some type of stroke, are you? It's not uncommon in men your age."

"Don't be ridiculous," I said. "Just stop calling me Mr. Avery, all right? It makes me feel like your father. Which would be very strange considering I'm only ten years older than you."

"Well, that is quite a big difference, you know," she said. "And I don't want to be disrespectful by being too familiar."

"It's exactly the same age difference as the one between you and Ignac," I pointed out. "And he doesn't call you Miss Mitchell, does he?"

She took a carton of yogurt from the fridge, peeled the lid off and looked at me with barely concealed amusement as she ran her tongue across the inside, some of the strawberry sticking to her lips. "He does when I tell him to," she said. "And anyway, I'm not ten years older than Ignac, Mr. Avery. I'm only nine years older than him. And how old was Ignac again when you took him in?"

Before I could say another word, Ignac himself appeared and I had no choice but to let it go. He wasn't ignorant as to how I felt about Emily and I knew that he didn't like it when we sniped at each other. She had timed her remark perfectly.

"Hey, Cyril," he said, turning the kettle on. "I didn't hear you come in."

"Yes, you did," I muttered.

"You were otherwise engaged, hon," said Emily without looking up.

"How was school today?" I asked, turning around and wishing that Emily would either go into the other room and get dressed or leave. Or perhaps go to the fridge again, trip over on a piece of loose linoleum and fall out the window into the middle of 55th Street.

"Pretty good. I got an A on my Lewis Carroll paper. And another for my Yeats essay."

"Good for you!" I liked the fact that Ignac had taken an interest in Irish literature, much more than he ever had in Dutch or Slovene. He was working his way through most of the big Irish novels, although for some reason he'd chosen to avoid Maude's work for now. I'd thought about buying him some copies from the Strand Bookstore— they had some first editions in there that were quite reasonably priced—but I didn't want him to feel obliged to read her and was uncertain how I'd feel if he didn't happen to like them. "Good for you," I repeated. "I'd love to take a look at the Yeats piece."

"It's very analytical," said Emily, as if I was a complete illiterate. "It's not really for the layman."

"I'm pretty good with big words," I told her. "And if I get stuck, I can always look them up in the dictionary."

"That's not really what analytical means," she said. "But hey, knock yourself out."

"What is it you teach again?" I asked her. "Remind me. Women's Studies, is it?"

"No, Russian History. Although there's a module on Russian women, if that's what you're thinking of."

"Interesting place, Russia," I said. "The Tsars, the Bolsheviks, the Winter Palace and what have you. You've been there many times, I presume?"

"No," she said, shaking her head. "No, I've never been. Not yet anyway."

"You're kidding me."

"Why would I lie?"

"No, I'm surprised, that's all. I would have thought that if you were so interested in a country and its past, then you'd actually want to go there and experience it in person. I find that very odd."

"Well, what can I tell you? I'm an enigma."

"But you speak the language, of course?"

"No. Why, do you?"

"No, of course not. But then I don't teach Russian at university level."

"Neither do I. I teach Russian History."

"Still, that's very strange."

"It's not that unusual when you think about it. Ignac is interested in Irish literature," she pointed out. "And he's never been to Ireland. Nor does he speak Irish."

"Well, of course, most Irish literature is written in English," I pointed out.

"Does your country suppress its native writers?"

"No," I said.

"So no one writes in the Irish language?"

"Well, I'm sure they do," I said, growing flustered now. "But those books are not very well known."

"You mean they don't sell well," she said. "I didn't realize you were such a populist. Actually, I read one of your mother's books last year. They sell very well, don't they?"

"My adoptive mother," I said.

"Same thing."

"It's not, really. Particularly if she wasn't exactly a maternal presence."

"Have you read *Like to the Lark*?"

"Of course I have."

"It's quite good, isn't it?"

"I think it's a little better than *quite* good."

"The child in the book is such a monster, though. One of the greatest liars and sneaks in literature. It's no wonder the mother wants to kill him. Was it autobiographical at all?"

"Do you know there's a poster of Maude in the Literature department at CCNY?" asked Ignac, interrupting us, and I turned to him in surprise.

"Is there?" I said.

"Yes, it's one of four posters hanging outside the administration office. Virginia Woolf, Henry James, F. Scott Fitzgerald and Maude Avery. They're all looking away from the camera, except for your mother—"

"My adoptive mother."

"Who's looking directly into the lens. She looks absolutely furious."

"That sounds like her," I said.

"She's sitting by a desk in front of a lattice window with a cigarette in her hand. There's an ashtray on the table behind her and it's overflowing with butt ends."

"That was her study," I said. "In Dartmouth Square. A smoky place at the best of times. She didn't like to open the windows. Of course, that's the house that I grew up in. She'd be horrified if she knew that her picture was hanging up in your university, though, even if it is next to writers of that caliber. She wasn't even published in the States during her lifetime, you know."

"Some people only achieve success after they're dead," said Emily. "And their lives on earth are utter failures. Are you bartending tonight, Mr. Avery?"

"No," I said, rolling my eyes. "Not until the weekend."

"I only ask because Ignac and I were thinking of staying in."

"Well, you could always go to a movie, I suppose. Ignac can get into the over-eighteen shows now so you'll have some company. You could try *Fatal Attraction*."

"Come on, Cyril," said Ignac quietly.

"I'm kidding," I said, disappointed by how quickly he defended her honor over mine.

"We should go sometime," he said after a moment.

"What, to *Fatal Attraction*?"

"No, to Dublin. I'd like to see where you grew up. And maybe we could go to that house and I could take a picture of you in that same study."

"The house isn't in the family anymore," I said, looking away.

"What happened to it?"

"My adoptive father sold it. He had to when he was put in jail for tax evasion. His solicitor bought it from him afterward. At a knock-down price."

"That's ironic," said Emily.

"It's not ironic at all, actually," I said. "That's not really what ironic means."

"That's a pity," said Ignac. "But maybe whoever lives there now would let you back in to see it? It'd be pretty cool to see your childhood home again, wouldn't it? There must be so many memories there."

"It would be if any of them were good," I told him. "But so few of them actually were. Anyway, I don't think I'd be particularly welcome in Dartmouth Square now." Other than the basic facts of my brief marriage, I had never gotten around to telling Ignac the complete stories of Julian, Alice and I. The things that had taken place between us were all so long ago, after all, and they seemed quite irrelevant to my life now. Still, for the first time in years I wondered about that house and whether Alice, perhaps, might still live there with whoever she had married after me. I hoped that she had a houseful of children populating the rooms and a husband who lusted after her still. Or maybe Julian had taken it over. It was always possible, if unlikely, that Julian had settled down and started a family himself.

"How long has it been since you were in Dublin, Mr. Avery?" asked Emily.

"Fourteen years, Miss Mitchell. And I don't have any plans to go back."

"But why not? Don't you miss it?"

"He never talks about it," said Ignac. "I think he likes to keep it a secret. It's all his old boyfriends, I guess. He doesn't want them coming after him. He probably left a trail of broken hearts behind him when he moved to Amsterdam."

"I was in a lot of places between Dublin and Amsterdam," I pointed out. "And I don't have any old boyfriends in Ireland anyway. Bastiaan is the only boyfriend I've ever had. You know that."

"Yeah, so you say. But I don't believe you."

"Believe what you like," I said.

"Well, perhaps when we're over there we can go take a look at that house," said Emily, turning to Ignac and reaching for his hand, playing with his fingers as if he was a child. "And then you can always send a picture to Mr. Avery to remind him of it."

It took a few moments for her words to sink in. "When *who* is over *where*?" I asked. She stood up now and strode over to the counter to take an apple from a bowl and then stood with one foot against the wall behind her, chomping into it.

"When Ignac and I are in Dublin," she said with a shrug of her shoulders.

"And why would you and Ignac be in Dublin?" I asked.

"Emily," said Ignac quietly, and I turned to look at him, catching the expression on his face which was telling her that this was not the time to raise the subject.

"Ignac?" I asked. "What's going on?"

He sighed and his face flushed a little as he looked at me.

"Oh I'm sorry," said Emily, putting the half-eaten apple on the table and sitting down again. "Was I not supposed to say anything?"

"It's nothing really," said Ignac. "It might not even happen."

"What might not happen?"

"There's a Master's degree at Trinity College," he said, looking down and scratching at a mark on the table. "In Irish Literature. I'm thinking about applying for it for next year. I haven't fully decided yet. I'd need a scholarship for one thing. It's just something I'm thinking about, that's all."

"All right," I said quietly, trying to process this unexpected piece of information. "Well, I suppose that would be an interesting thing to do. But you're not thinking of going too, are you, Emily? What has Russian History got to do with Ireland?"

"They do have a History department," she said with a sigh, as if she was trying to explain the theory of relativity to an imbecile. "I could apply for a job there."

"I think they'd take a much dimmer view of faculty dating students back in Ireland," I said. "You'd be fired for taking advantage of your position. Or arrested on suspicion of having an unhealthy interest in children."

"I'm not worried about any of that. I can look after myself. Anyway, I'd be closer to Russia too if I was in Dublin, so perhaps I could finally visit. After all, as you pointed out, I really should go there."

I said nothing. I didn't particularly want Emily going anywhere with Ignac but for the moment I was more concerned with the idea of him leaving New York. On one hand it seemed like an idea that had come out of nowhere, but on the other it made a certain amount of sense. We were close, the two of us. The three of us, in fact, for it had been Bastiaan who had been the prime mover in instigating our unusual family seven years before in Amsterdam, but since then Ignac had shown a lot more interest in my heritage than in Bastiaan's or even his own. Coupled with his passion for writing, it made some sense that Irish Literature should be a specialty to which he might be drawn.

"Have you talked to Bastiaan about this?" I asked Ignac, and he nodded.

"A little," he said. "Not too much. It's still a year away, after all."

I frowned, feeling hurt that no one had thought to mention it to me before now and especially irritated that Emily knew before I did. It was obvious that she was happy to get one over on me.

"Well, we'll talk about it again," I said. "Another evening, when Bastiaan's at home."

"We're pretty sure," said Emily. "There's nothing for you to worry about. I've done a little research into the university and—"

"I think it's really something for Bastiaan, Ignac and I to talk about together," I said, turning around and glaring at her. "As a family."

"As a family?" she asked, raising an eyebrow.

"Yes, as a family. Which is what we are."

"Of course," she said with a half-smile. "Hey, it's 1987, right? No judgments." She stood up and made her way out of the kitchen, walking back in the direction of the bedroom but making sure to ruffle

Ignac's hair with her hand as she passed. She might as well have pissed on him to mark her territory.

"Jesus," I said under my breath when she was gone.

"What?" asked Ignac.

"*No judgments*," I repeated. "What do you think she meant by that?"

"She didn't mean anything, Cyril," he said.

"Of course she did," I said. "You just don't want to see it."

"Why don't you like her?" he asked, his eyes filled with unhappiness, for he couldn't bear confrontation or negativity. He was a relentlessly kind person.

"Because she's old enough to be your mother, that's why."

"She's nowhere *near* old enough to be my mother."

"Well, a much older sister then. Or a youthful aunt. Not to mention the fact that she's your teacher."

"She's not my teacher! She works in a completely different department."

"I don't care. It's unprofessional."

"She makes me happy."

"She mothers you."

"So do you."

"Well, I have a right to," I said. "I'm *in loco parentis*."

He smiled and shook his head. "There's a side to her that you don't see."

"The side that doesn't go around seducing her students?"

"I told you, I'm not one of her students," he protested. "How many times?"

I dismissed this with a wave of my hand. That was all semantics as far as I was concerned. I knew what I wanted to say but was unsure whether I could express it correctly. I didn't want him to get angry with me.

"You haven't noticed the way that she looks at me and Bastiaan?" I said. "The way she speaks to us?"

"Not particularly," he replied. "Why, what has she said?"

"It's not something specific," I began.

"So she hasn't said anything then? You're just imagining things?"

"She doesn't respect what we have here," I told him. "What the three of us have."

"Of course she does," said Ignac. "She knows how much you've both done for me. And she respects it."

"She thinks there's something untoward about how we took you in."

"No, she doesn't."

"She practically said as much to me! How much does she know anyway?" I asked. "About your history, I mean."

He shrugged. "She knows everything," he told me.

"Not *everything*?" I said, leaning closer to him and feeling my heart skip a beat.

"No, of course not," he said, shaking his head. "Not about . . . that." The things that had happened toward the end of our stay in Amsterdam were never discussed between any of us. They were part of our past, something that perhaps we all thought about privately from time to time but never discussed aloud.

"But she knows about me," he said. "What I was. The things I did. I'm not ashamed of any of it."

"And nor should you be. But you should be careful who you talk to about those times. When people know too much about your life, they can use it against you."

"I don't like to keep secrets," he said.

"It's not about keeping secrets," I insisted. "It's about holding some of yourself back. It's about privacy."

"But what's the point? If I'm going to be close to someone, Cyril, then they can ask about my life and those days are part of my life. If they're bothered by it, then they can move on, I don't care. But I will never lie about who I am or what I've done."

He wasn't trying to be cruel, I knew that. He knew very little about my own past and the lies that I had told over the years of my youth, not to mention the damage that I had inflicted on so many people. And I wanted it to stay that way.

"If you really want to go to Dublin," I said. "If you want to see Trinity and find out whether it would be a good fit, then perhaps I could take you there." The idea slightly terrified me, but I said it nonetheless. "The three of us could go together."

"You, me and Emily?"

"No, you, me and Bastiaan."

"Well, maybe," he said, looking away. "I don't know. At the moment, it's just an idea, that's all. It might come to nothing. I might end up staying on in the States. I don't have to make any decisions for a while yet."

"All right," I said, not wanting to push him. "But just make the decision yourself, OK? Without anyone pressuring you."

"And will you try to get on better with Emily in the meantime?" he asked.

"I can try," I said doubtfully. "But she has to stop calling me Mr. Avery. It's driving me fucking crazy."

Patient 630

The patient who I enjoyed spending time with the most was a lady in her eighties named Eleanor DeWitt who had spent most of her life flitting between the island of Manhattan and the parlors of political salons in Washington, D.C., while summering in Monte Carlo or on the Amalfi Coast. A lifelong hemophiliac, she found herself infected with the disease after a careless transfusion delivered corrupted blood into her body. She had taken her misfortune steadfastly, however, never complaining, and claiming that if it hadn't been AIDS that had taken her down, it would have been cancer or a stroke or a brain tumor, which might have been true, of course, but I'm not sure that many people would have shared her stoicism. When she was a girl, her father had run unsuccessfully for governor of New York—twice—and in between political campaigns he'd made a fortune in construction. She'd been a debutante in the 1920s and had mixed, she told me, with a fast and witty crowd: writers, artists, dancers, painters and actors.

"Of course, most of them were fairies, just like you, darling," she told me one day while I sat feeding grapes to her, as if she was Elizabeth Taylor in *Cleopatra* and I was her Richard Burton. She was lying in her hospital bed, her skin unnaturally thin, almost transparent, the contaminated blood visible as it coursed through her veins. She wore an enormous blonde wig to hide the sores and wounds that lay beneath, many of which were replicated around her body. "I should know," she added. "I married three of them."

I started laughing, even though I'd been there myself. She was one of those flamboyant old doyennes one didn't expect to meet outside of a movie theater and the idea of her walking down an aisle in a wedding dress while a terrified homosexual husband waited for her—three times—was priceless.

"The first time," she told me, throwing her head back against the pillows, "why, I was just a girl. Seventeen years old. But such a beautiful girl, Cyril! If you saw pictures of me then, I promise you'd fall over in a faint. People said I was the most beautiful girl in New York. My father, who was in concrete, wanted an alliance with the O'Malley family—the steel O'Malleys, that is, not the textile O'Malleys—and so he basically sold me like a piece of chattel to a friend of his who had an idiot son going begging. Lance O'Malley III was his name. Seventeen years old, just like me. Irish blood in him, just like you. The poor child could barely read and had feathers in his head where his brain should have been. But he was a looker, I'll give him that. All the girls were crazy for him as long as he didn't open his mouth. Most of his conversation revolved around whether there might be aliens living in outer space. They don't need to live there, I told him. There's enough of them already here on earth, but he was too dim to understand what I meant. On the wedding night, after the reception, I took him to bed and I don't mind admitting I was quite looking forward to what was going to happen next, but the poor boy started to cry when I took my panties off. I didn't know what I'd done wrong and so I started crying too. And so there we sat, the pair of us, all night long, weeping into our pillows. The next morning, I waited until he was fast asleep and I carefully pulled his drawers down and climbed on top of him, but he woke up and got such a fright that he punched me in the face and I fell off the bed. Of course, Lance was distraught—he hadn't a violent bone in his body—and when we came down to breakfast both our families tried to ignore the fact that I had a black eye. They must have thought we'd been up to wild games in the night! No such luck. Anyway, Lance and I stayed married for a year and he never touched me once during all that time and then one day I confided in my father that the marriage had never been consummated because, the truth is, I was close to killing myself with anxiety and that was the end of that. The whole thing was annulled and I never saw Lance O'Malley III again. The last

I heard, he'd become a merchant sailor. That may or may not be true, however, so don't spread it around."

"But he didn't put you off marriage?" I asked.

"Well of course not! That's what people did in those days. If one husband didn't work out, then you took another. It didn't matter whose. You just kept going till you found a match. I'm sure there's a card game that works along those lines if I could only remember what it's called, but this damn disease is playing fast and loose with my memory. Now, my second marriage was by far my happiest. Henry liked boys as well as girls and he told me all about this before we went down the aisle and so we made an agreement that he could have a little fun on the side if I could too. We even shared a young man from time to time. Oh, don't look so shocked, Cyril. It was the 1930s, people were a lot more evolved then than they are today. Henry and I might have rubbed along pretty well together forever, but the problem was that he was quite mad and threw himself off the Chrysler Building on his thirtieth birthday because he thought the best was all behind him. His hair had started to thin, poor dear, and he couldn't stand the idea of what other indignities middle age might throw at him. Such drama! I could have lived without it. Although when I look in the mirror now, I wonder whether he might have had the right idea."

"And the third time?" I asked.

She turned her head slowly to look out the window and her body suddenly began to pulsate with a spasm of pain. When she looked back at me, her expression had darkened and I could see that she wasn't entirely sure who I was.

"Eleanor," I said. "Are you all right?"

"Who are you?" she asked.

"It's me, Cyril," I said.

"I don't know you," she replied, waving me away. "Where's George?"

"There's no George here," I told her.

"Get George!" she screamed, and then began to cause such a commotion that one of the nurses had to come in to settle her. Finally, she calmed down and I was considering whether I should leave for the day but she turned back to me with a cheerful smile as if nothing untoward had happened.

"The third time was no good either," she continued. "It lasted only a few months. I married a famous Hollywood actor in secret on a beach in Mustique. I was rather besotted with him, to be honest, but I think that was because I was so accustomed to seeing him up there on the silver screen. He was pretty good in the sack, but he got bored with me after a few days and went back to his boys. The studio wanted to keep me on salary, but I had too much self-respect for that and we ended up getting divorced too. It never even came out that we'd been married."

"Who was it?" I asked. "Someone famous?"

"Someone very famous," she said, beckoning me forward. "Come here and I'll whisper his name to you."

I leaned forward, but perhaps I moved too slow for she quickly pushed me away.

"Oh, you're just like everyone else, aren't you?" she snapped. "You say you've come to help but you're just as frightened of me as the rest of them. What a shame! Oh, you've let me down terribly!"

"I'm sorry," I said. "I didn't mean to—"

I leaned forward again but she lifted her scarred hands and held them in front of her face. "Just go," she said. "Just go. Just go. Leave me to suffer alone."

I stood up to leave, certain that when I returned a few days later she would have forgotten the incident entirely, and made my way back toward the reception area, where Shaniqua eyed me suspiciously and moved her purse into the top drawer, locking it carefully. I phoned up to Bastiaan's office to see whether he was able to leave early for the day and he told me that he'd be another hour yet, but could I wait for him?

"Of course," I said. "I'll see you at reception."

Hanging up, I did my best to make small talk with Shaniqua, but she was having none of it.

"Isn't there anything useful you can do?" she asked. "Other than sitting around here bothering me?"

"I'm waiting for Dr. Van den Bergh," I said. "I have time to kill. Tell me about yourself, Shaniqua. Where are you from?"

"What the hell do you care where I'm from?"

"I'm just making conversation, that's all. Why do you always wear yellow?"

"Does it offend you in some way?"

"No, not at all. As a matter of fact, I happen to be wearing yellow boxer shorts today."

"I didn't care to know that."

"Shaniqua," I said, sounding out the syllables on my tongue. "It's an unusual name."

"Says Cyril."

"Point taken. Is there anything around here to eat?"

She spun around in the chair and gave me her death-stare. "Ever been thrown out of a hospital by security?" she asked.

"No."

"Wanna keep it that way?"

"Yes."

"Then go back to Patient 630. I'm sure she'd appreciate some more of your company. I know I find it totally stimulating."

I shook my head. "She's a little antsy today," I said. "I think it's best if I steer clear. Maybe I'll go visit Philip Danley. He's a nice kid."

"We don't use names here," she said. "You should know that by now."

"But he told me his name," I said. "He said I could call him by it."

"I don't care. Anyone could be passing by. Reporters are always looking for families to embarrass by—"

"Fine," I said, standing up. "I'll go see Patient 563."

"No, you won't," she said. "He died on Tuesday."

I sat down again, astonished by how she'd broken the news to me. I'd lost patients before, of course, but I'd visited Philip many times and liked him. I understood that she had to keep a distance from the emotion of her job or be unable to survive it but there was such a thing as compassion.

"Was anyone there?" I asked, trying to keep the anger out of my tone. "When he passed away, I mean?"

"I was there."

"Any of his family?"

She shook her head. "No. And they wouldn't take the body either. It went to the city crematorium. Well, to the AIDS section. You know they don't even want the dead bodies of AIDS victims to mix with the dead bodies of other people now?"

"For fuck's sake," I said. "That's ridiculous. What the hell can they do to the dead? And how could the boy's family stay away when he needed them the most?"

"You think that's the first time that's happened?"

"No, I guess not, but it's just so fucking heartless."

We said nothing for a few minutes and then she reached for a file from her desk and flicked through it. "You want to go see someone else or not?"

"Sure," I said. "I might as well."

"Patient 741," she said. "Room 703."

A bell rang in my head. Patient 741. The patient that Bastiaan had told us about that night in the restaurant on 23rd Street. Heterosexual, angry and Irish. Not necessarily a combination I wanted to deal with at that moment.

"Isn't there someone else I could visit?" I asked. "I've heard he's quite aggressive."

"No," she said. "You don't get to pick and choose. Patient 741, Room 703. Take it or leave it. What the hell's the matter with you, Cyril? The man's dying. Show a little compassion."

I rolled my eyes and gave in, leaving the office to make my way slowly down the corridor. For a moment, I wondered whether I could skip out of this visit entirely and just go down to the cafeteria and wait for Bastiaan there but Shaniqua knew everything that took place on the seventh floor and the chances were she'd never let me back in again if I disappointed her.

I paused outside Room 703 for a few moments, taking a deep breath like I always did when I met a new patient for the first time. I never knew how badly the disease might have affected him or her; they could look frail but unscarred or their appearance could be devastating. And I never wanted my reaction to be too cruelly revealed in my expression. I opened the door slowly and peered inside. The curtains were closed and as evening was drawing in the room was quite dark but I could just about make out the man lying in the bed and hear his heavy and labored breathing.

"Hello?" I said quietly. "Are you awake?"

"Yes," he murmured after a short pause. "Come in."

I stepped inside and closed the door behind me. "I don't mean to disturb you," I said. "I'm one of the hospital volunteers. I understand you've been on your own and wondered whether you might like a visitor?"

He said nothing for a few moments and then, in an anxious tone, said, "You're Irish?"

"A long time ago I was," I said. "I haven't been back in years, though. You're Irish too, I'm told?"

"Your voice . . ." he said as he tried to lift his head a little in the bed, but the effort proved too much for him and he collapsed back with a groan.

"Don't disturb yourself," I told him. "Can I open the curtains, though, to let in a little light? Would you mind?"

"Your voice," he repeated, and I wondered whether the disease had eaten into his brain too much and I would get little sense out of him. Still, I had resolved to sit and talk with him and that is what I would do. He neither offered permission nor withheld it regarding the curtains, so I stepped over to the window and pulled them apart, glancing down onto the New York streets below. The yellow cabs were driving up and down honking their horns and the view between the skyscrapers held me for a minute. I had never fallen in love with this city—even after almost seven years my head was still in Amsterdam and my heart was still in Dublin—but there were moments, like this one, when I understood why others did.

Turning back, I looked toward the patient and our eyes met in a moment of recognition that sent a shiver through my body so deeply that I was forced to reach a hand out to the windowsill to steady myself. He was no older than me but almost completely bald, a few wisps of hair clinging pathetically to the top of his head. His cheeks were sunken, as were his eyes, and a dark oval of purple-red sent a hideous bruise along his chin and down his neckline. A line came into my mind, something that Hannah Arendt had once said about the poet Auden: that life had manifested the heart's invisible furies on his face.

He looked a hundred years old.

He looked like a man who had died several months earlier.

He looked like a soul in pure torment.

But still I knew him. All the changes that the disease had made to his once-beautiful face and body and still I would have known him anywhere.

"Julian," I said.

Who's Liam?

I left a message with Shaniqua, asking her to let Bastiaan know that I'd see him at home later, and made a quick escape from the hospital without even stopping to take my coat, running westward in a daze and somehow ending up seated on a bench near Central Park Lake. It was cold and I could tell that people were staring at me, thinking I was crazy to be dressed for summer on such a cold day, but I couldn't go back yet. There had only been time for me to utter his name in astonishment, and for him to whisper mine in reply, before I found myself running from the room and charging along the corridor, certain that if I didn't get outside into the fresh air quickly I would pass out. It had been fourteen years since he realized that our friendship was based on a simple deceit on my part, and this was to be the cruel circumstances of our reunion. In New York City. In a hospital room. Where my oldest friend was dying of AIDS.

I remembered now how careless he had been from the start with his sexual health. It was true that things had been very different in the 1960s and '70s than they were by 1987, but it seemed to me that Julian had been particularly cavalier throughout his youth, as if he believed himself to be invincible. How he had never gotten a girl pregnant was a mystery to me but then, I realized, perhaps he had and I had simply never found out. He could have a gang of children for all I knew. Still, I had never even imagined that he would one day contract a disease that would not only threaten his life but bring it to a premature end. Not that I could condemn him, of course, without facing up to my own hypocrisy. After all, I had been so promiscuous as a younger man that I was lucky never to have come down with something myself. Had I been twenty years younger and in my sexual prime when the AIDS crisis was beginning, I had little doubt that I would have been putting myself in harm's way with the number of hazardous situations in which I found myself with strangers. How had we reached this point, I wondered? We were middle-aged, both of us, but we had been cheerful teenagers once, who had gone on to waste so much of our lives. I had squandered my twenties in a cowardly attempt to present a deceitful facade to the world and now Julian had thrown away what might have been another forty years of life through his own carelessness.

Staring into the water now, I could feel tears forming behind my eyes and remembered how Bastiaan had told us over dinner how Patient 741 didn't want his family to know what he was going through because of the extra stigma that would come with the disease in Ireland. So Alice, I realized, who had adored her older brother, knew nothing of his illness.

A woman came over to ask whether I was all right, an unusual occurrence in New York, where weeping strangers are usually left to fend for themselves, but I had no ability to converse and simply stood up and walked away. I wasn't sure where I was going but my feet somehow led me back toward 96th Street, back to Mount Sinai Hospital, and when I exited the elevator on the seventh floor, I felt grateful for small mercies when I saw that Shaniqua was not at her desk, giving me the freedom to return to Room 703 without having to answer any questions.

This time, I didn't hesitate or knock but walked straight in, closing the door behind me. The curtains were still open, just as I had left them, and Julian's head was turned away from me to catch whatever view he could see from where he was lying. He moved a little in the bed to see who had entered the room and when he saw me an expression crossed his face that combined anxiety, shame and relief. I took a chair and sat next to him, my back to the window, saying nothing for a long time as I looked down at the floor, hoping that he would speak first.

"I wondered whether you'd come back," he whispered eventually, his voice croaky from lack of use. "I figured you would. You never could stay away from me for long."

"That was a long time ago now," I replied.

"I hope I haven't lost any of my appeal," he said, and the half-smile on his face forced a small laugh from my mouth.

"I'm sorry I ran off like that," I told him. "It was a shock, that's all. To see you again after so many years. And here, of all places. I should have stayed."

"Well, you have a history of disappearing without a word, don't you?"

I nodded. Of course, this was a subject that would inevitably come up but I wasn't ready for it, not yet.

"I needed some fresh air," I told him. "I went for a walk."

"On 96th Street?" he asked. "To where?"

"I went over to Central Park. You don't mind that I've come back?"

"Why would I?" he asked, shrugging as best as he could, and as his lips parted I could see how his teeth, which had once been spectacularly white, had grown yellow and uneven. There was at least one missing from the lower set and his gums were a whitish shade of pink. "The truth is, I was as shocked to see you as you were to see me. I was glad of a little time to process it. Only I can't make a break for it as easily as you can."

"Oh, Julian," I said, giving in to my emotions now as I buried my face in my hands to stop him from seeing the grief on my face. "What happened to you? How did you end up here?"

"What can I tell you?" he said calmly. "You always knew what I was like. I fucked around. I made a career of it. Stuck it in one too many places, I suppose, and my degenerate ways eventually caught up with me."

"I thought I was the degenerate."

"Yeah, whatever."

I had thought of him many times over the last decade and a half, sometimes with love and sometimes with anger, but the truth was that since I had met Bastiaan he had started to fade from my memory, a thing that I had never previously imagined could happen. I had grown to realize that although I had once loved him—and I *had* loved him—it was nothing like the love I had experienced with Bastiaan. I had allowed a crush to become an obsession. I'd been infatuated with the idea of his friendship, with the awareness of his beauty, and by his unique ability to transfix all those around him. But Julian had never loved me in return. He may have liked me, he may have cared about me like a brother, but he had never loved me romantically.

"So you live in New York?" he said finally, breaking the silence.

"Yes," I said. "For about seven years now."

"I never would have imagined you here. For some reason, I always thought of you living in some sleepy English village. A schoolteacher or something."

"You thought of me then? Over the years?"

"Of course I did. I could hardly have forgotten you. Are you a doctor, is that it? That's quite a life change."

"No, nothing like that," I said, shaking my head. "I'm just a volunteer. Although my boyfriend is. He works here at Mount Sinai. When we first met, his specialty was communicable diseases and I suppose he was the right man in the right place at the right time because once this thing broke, his services were in demand. But of course we know a lot of gay people here in the city and it started to affect me when we lost friends. I developed an interest in what was going on, in what I could do to help. And I found out that a lot of victims have been abandoned by their families because they're so ashamed of what's happened to them. That's where I come in."

"You've become a do-gooder," he said. "Strange, considering how selfish you always were."

"It's nothing to do with that," I said sharply. "You'd never hear of a cancer sufferer being cast aside by their family, but it happens all the time with AIDS victims. And so I come here a couple of times a week to visit patients and talk to them, and sometimes I go to the library and bring them books if that's what they want. It gives me a sense of purpose."

"And your boyfriend," he said, the word catching a little in his throat as he said it, and I knew that if he had more energy he would have lifted his hands and made quotation marks in the air with his fingers. "You found a boyfriend in the end then?"

"Of course I did. It turns out I wasn't so unlovable after all."

"No one ever said that you were. If I remember correctly, you were very much loved when you left Dublin. By a lot of people, myself included."

"Yeah," I said. "I'm not so sure about that."

"I am. So how long have you been together anyway? You and your boyfriend."

"Twelve years," I told him.

"That's impressive. I don't think I've ever stayed with the same girl for even twelve weeks. How can you stand it?"

"It's not difficult," I said, "since I love him. And he loves me."

"But don't you get bored with him?"

"No. Is that such a strange concept for you?"

"It is, to be honest." He stared at me for a moment as if he was trying to understand how that would feel and finally he just sighed, as if he was giving in. "What's his name anyway?" he asked.

"Bastiaan," I said. "He's Dutch. I lived in Amsterdam for a while and that's where we met."

"And are you happy?"

"Yes," I said. "Very happy."

"Well, good for you," he said bitterly, and I could see how his expression darkened as he said the words. He glanced over toward the top of the locker where a plastic bottle of water stood, sealed with a straw through the top. "I'm thirsty," he said. "Pass me that, will you?"

I reached over and held the bottle to his lips, and he used all his strength to draw the water through the straw into his mouth. Watching the amount of effort it took saddened me. Two or three mouthfuls and he collapsed back on his pillow in exhaustion, breathing heavily.

"Julian," I said, putting the bottle back and reaching for his hand, but he pulled it away quickly.

"I'm not gay, you know," he said before I could say anything else. "I didn't get this from a man."

"I know you're not," I said, amazed that even at this moment it was so important for him to assert his heterosexuality. "I probably know that better than anyone. But what does it matter anymore?"

"I mean it," he insisted. "If this ever gets out, I don't want anyone thinking that I went around fucking men on the side. It's bad enough that I've got your disease—"

"*My* disease?"

"You know what I mean."

"I don't, actually."

"If people back home knew what I caught, they'd never think about me the same way again."

"What do you care what people think about you? You never used to."

"This is different," he said. "I never cared what people did before. They could go out and fuck a hedgehog for all the difference it made to me. Because it didn't affect me. Until now."

"Look, it's an epidemic," I said. "It's going to affect people around the world. If they don't find a cure soon, I don't know what's going to happen."

"Well, I won't be around to find out," he said.

"Don't say that."

"Look at me, for Christ's sake, Cyril. I don't have much time left. I can feel the life leaving my body hour after hour. The doctors have told me as much anyway. I've got a week at most. Probably less."

I felt myself starting to cry again but took a few deep breaths. I didn't want to appear pathetic before him and somehow felt that he would grow angry with me if I showed too much emotion.

"They don't know everything," I said. "Sometimes people last a lot longer—"

"I guess you've known quite a few then," he said.

"Quite a few what?"

"People with this . . . thing."

"Quite a few, yes," I admitted. "This entire floor of the hospital is devoted to AIDS patients."

He flinched a little when I said the word.

"I'm surprised you don't have the Village People playing over the speakers all day long. Make everyone feel at home."

"Oh fuck off, Julian," I said, surprising myself with a burst of laughter, and he glanced at me anxiously, as if he was worried that I might walk out again, but said nothing. "Sorry," I said eventually. "But you really can't talk like that. Not in here."

"I can talk any way I like," he said. "I'm in a hospital full of queers dying of a queer disease and someone forgot to tell God that I'm straight."

"I don't remember you having much time for God when we were younger. And stop saying queers. I know you don't mean it, really."

"That's the problem having a best friend who knows me so well. I can't even be bitter without you calling me on it. Still, New York isn't the worst place to call it a day. Rather here than Dublin."

"I miss Dublin," I said, the words out of my mouth before I had the chance even to consider whether I meant them or not.

"So what are you doing here then? What brought you to the States anyway?"

"Bastiaan's job," I said.

"I would have thought you'd prefer Miami. Or San Francisco. That's where all the fags hang out, isn't it? Or so I hear."

"You can keep on insulting me if you think it will make you feel better," I said quietly. "But I don't think it will do you much good in the end."

"Fuck off," he said, without a lot of passion behind the words. "And can you please stop patronizing me, you little shit?"

"I'm not."

"Look, there's nothing you can do to help me anyway. What have you done with the other people you visit? Helped them to find inner peace before they met their maker? Put your arm around them, taken their hand in yours and sung a little lullaby to them as they drifted off into unconsciousness? Well, take my hand then if you want to. Help me feel better. What's stopping you?"

I looked down at his left hand, which was lying on the bed next to me. An intravenous drip was going into the central vein, covered by a large white dressing. The skin around the bandage was gray and, at the place where his thumb met his index finger, a bright-red scar stood out as if he had been scalded. His nails were bitten down to the quick and what was left of them was blackened. I reached down nevertheless but as my skin touched his own, he pulled his hand away.

"Don't," he said. "I wouldn't wish this on my worst enemies. Which includes you."

"For God's sake, Julian, I can't catch it by holding your hand."

"Just don't."

"And we're enemies now, are we?" I asked.

"We're not friends, that's for sure."

"We used to be."

He looked at me and narrowed his eyes, and I could see that it was getting more difficult for him to talk. His anger was exhausting him.

"We weren't, though, were we?" he said. "Not really. Everything about our friendship was a lie."

"No, it wasn't," I protested.

"It was. You were my best friend, Cyril. I thought we were going to be friends for life. I looked up to you so much."

"That's not true," I said, surprised by his words. "It was me who looked up to you. You were everything I wanted to be."

"So were you," he said. "You were kind and thoughtful and decent. You were my friend. At least that's what I thought. I didn't hang out with you for fourteen years because I wanted someone following me around like a puppy. It was because I liked being around you."

"My friendship was genuine," I said. "I couldn't help how I felt. If I had told you—"

"That day in the church, when you tried to jump me—"

"I didn't try to jump you," I said.

"Sure you did. And you said that you'd been in love with me ever since we were children."

"I didn't know what I was talking about," I said. "Look, I was young, I was inexperienced. And I was frightened at what I was getting myself into."

"So you're saying that you made it all up?" he asked. "That you didn't have those feelings for me at all?"

"No, of course not. I did have those feelings for you. I still do. But that wasn't why I was friends with you. I was friends with you because you made me feel happy."

"And because you wanted to fuck me. Well, I bet you don't want to fuck me anymore, do you?"

I winced at the bitter way he said it and, more so, because of course it was true. How many times during my teenage years and beyond had I fantasized about him, imagined what it would be like if somehow the two of us could be together, if I could lure him back to my flat, get him drunk and hope that he might reach for me in a moment of weakness when there was no girl around to satisfy his needs. Hundreds, probably. Thousands. I could hardly deny that a large part of our friendship was, for me at least, based on a lie.

"I couldn't help how I felt," I repeated.

"You could have talked to me about it," he said. "Much earlier. I would have understood."

"But you wouldn't have," I said. "I know you wouldn't have. Nobody did back then. Not in Ireland. Even today it's still illegal, for Christ's sake, to be gay in Ireland, do you realize that? And it's 1987 now, not 1940. You *wouldn't* have. You say that now but that's *because* it's now. You *wouldn't* have," I insisted.

"I went to one of your groups, you know," he said, raising a hand to silence me. "When I was first diagnosed with HIV. I went to a group in Brooklyn run by some priest and there were eight or nine guys in the room, all of them at different stages of the disease, and each one looked closer to death than the one next to him, and they were holding hands and sharing stories about fucking strangers in bathhouses and saunas and cruising and all that shit, and I looked around and do you know something, it made me absolutely *sick* to realize that I was even there, to think that I had anything in common with any of those degenerates."

"What makes you so different?" I asked. "You fucked any girl that moved."

"It's completely different."

"How? Explain it to me."

"Because that's *normal*."

"Oh fuck *normal*," I said. "I thought you had a bit more originality than that. Weren't you supposed to be the rebellious one?"

"I never claimed to be," he said, trying to sit up. "I just liked girls, that's all. You wouldn't understand."

"You fucked a lot of girls. I fucked a lot of guys. So what?"

"It's different," he insisted, practically spitting out the words.

"Calm down," I said, glancing up at one of the monitors attached to his body. "Your blood pressure is getting too high."

"Fuck my blood pressure," he said. "Maybe it can kill me before this disease does. The point is, I sat there in Brooklyn while this priest poured out his platitudes and told us all that we had to make peace with the world and with God while we were still alive, and I looked around at the other people in the group and do you know something, it was as if they were happy to be dying. There they were, grinning away at each other and showing their scars and bruises and discolorations and talking about boys they'd screwed in the toilets at some queer club, and all I wanted to do was push them up against the wall, one by one, and smash their fucking faces in. Put them out of their misery forever. I never went back. I felt like planting a fucking bomb at the place. You see the irony of this, don't you?" he said finally after a lengthy pause when he seemed to struggle to get some control over his emotions again.

"What?" I asked. "What's the irony?"

"Well, by rights it should be the other way round, shouldn't it?" he asked. "You should be lying in this bed rotting away from the inside out and I should be sitting over there, looking down at you with puppy-dog eyes and wondering where I'm going for dinner when I can eventually get the fuck out of this room."

"That's not what I'm thinking," I said.

"Sure you are."

"No, I'm not," I insisted.

"Then what are you thinking? Because I know for sure that's what I'd be thinking if I was in your place."

"That I wish we could go back in time, both of us, and do things better or differently. We've both been fucked over by our natures, can't you see that? Seriously, Julian, sometimes I wished I was a fucking eunuch. It would have made life a lot easier. And if you don't want me here, well what about having someone you love come over? Where's your family? Why don't you tell them?"

"Because I don't want them to know. There's hardly anyone left anyway. My mother's long gone. Max died a few years ago."

"No! How?"

"Heart attack. And other than that there was only Alice and Liam, and I don't want my sister knowing anything about this."

"I wondered when her name would come up," I said tentatively. "Can we talk about her?"

He gave a bitter smile. "We can," he said. "But be careful what you say. I may be lying in this hospital bed, but there's still no one on this planet whom I love more than her."

"What I did all those years ago," I said, "It was terrible. You don't have to tell me. It's something that I've had to live with. I hate myself for it."

"No, you don't. That's just a thing that people say."

"I do."

"Well, at least you apologized," he said. "When you wrote to her afterward, I mean, and threw yourself on her mercy and begged her forgiveness for humiliating her in front of three hundred people, including the President of Ireland, not to mention ruining her entire life. The *second* guy who had done that in a couple of years. Oh no, wait, I'm wrong, amn't I? Because you never wrote to her at all. You just left her there. You weren't even man enough to say sorry. And you *knew* what she'd been through before when she'd been stood up at the altar by that fucker Fergus. You knew all about that. Only this time she got as far as the altar but not out the other side of the reception. Jesus Christ, how could you have done it? Do you have no decency, Cyril?"

"You *made* me do it," I said.

"No, I didn't! What are you talking about?"

"That day. In the sacristy when I . . . when I told you how I felt. You made me go through with it. I could have stopped it right then—*we* could have—but you forced me—"

"So you're saying it's *my* fault? Are you fucking kidding me?"

"No, it's mine. I know that. I should have never let things get that far in the first place. I should never have started anything with Alice. But I did and I can't change that." I took a long breath, recalling the person I had been at that time. "I thought about writing," I said, starting to tremble at the memory. "I did, honestly. But I was in a terrible place. I was close to suicide, Julian. You have to understand, I needed to get away, to leave everyone and everything behind me. To start afresh. The idea of even communicating with Alice . . . I just couldn't have done it."

"That's because you're a fucking coward, Cyril," he said. "And a liar. You always were and I bet you still are."

"No," I insisted. "I'm not anymore. I don't have to be now. Because I don't live in Ireland. I can be exactly who I want to be now that I'm not part of that country anymore."

"Just get out," he said, turning away from me now. "Can't you leave me to die in peace? You won, all right? You get to live and I get to die."

"I didn't win anything."

"You won," he repeated quietly. "So stop gloating."

"How is she?" I asked, refusing to go. "Alice, I mean. Was she all right afterward? Is she happy now?"

"What do you think?" he said. "She was never the same. She loved you, Cyril; do you actually understand that? You who seem to set so much store by the concept. And she thought that you loved her too. I mean, marrying her kind of gave her that impression."

"It's all so long ago now," I said, shaking my head. "I never even think about those days anymore. And she's probably forgotten all about me, so what's the point of opening old wounds?"

Julian stared at me with an expression that suggested he wished he could rise from the bed and throttle the life out of me. "How could she ever have forgotten you?" he asked. "I told you, you completely ruined her life."

I pulled a face; yes, it must have been difficult and embarrassing for her back then. Of course, I accepted that. But time had passed. I wasn't that much of a catch; she had surely got over it by now. And if she hadn't, then she should have. She was a grown woman, after all. I would take responsibility for hurting her but not for ruining her entire life.

"Did she not marry again?" I asked. "I presumed she would. She was young and pretty and—"

"How could she marry again?" he said. "She was married to you; do you not remember? You didn't leave her at the altar, Cyril, you left her at the fucking reception in the middle of the Shelbourne Hotel! The vows had already been exchanged."

"Yes, but surely she had it annulled," I said, feeling a sense of anxiety building inside me. "Once it was clear that I wasn't coming back, she must have done that?"

"She didn't get it annulled," he said quietly.

"But why not?" I said. "What, did she want to play Miss Havisham for the rest of her life, was that it? Look, Julian, I'll hold my hands up and admit my part in this. I did a terrible thing to Alice and she certainly didn't deserve any of it. I was the guilty party. A coward. A total shit. But like you said, I left during the reception; we hadn't even made it to the bridal suite. She'd have easily been able to get the marriage annulled if she'd wanted to. And if she didn't, then I can't be held responsible for that. That was her decision."

He looked at me as if I was quite mad and opened his mouth to say something but then closed it again.

"What?" I said.

"Nothing," he replied.

"What?" I insisted, looking at him, certain that there was something he wasn't telling me.

"Look, Cyril," he said. "Why don't you stop with the bullshit, all right? You might not have made it to the bridal suite, but you found some place to have sex with her before you got married, didn't you?"

I thought about it, confused by what he was saying. And then I remembered that night, a couple of weeks before the wedding. *I think you should come over, Cyril. Come for dinner, we'll drink a couple of Max's best wines and, you know, go to bed together.* A night I hadn't even thought about since it had happened. It took an effort on my part even to recall it now.

A thought struck me and I felt a chill run through my body.

"Who's Liam?" I asked.

"What?" asked Julian, who had turned away from me now and was staring out the window toward a sky that was growing overcast as the evening drew in.

"You said there wasn't much of your family left," I told him. "That your father had died and there was only Alice and Liam left. Who's Liam?"

"Liam," said Julian quietly, "is the reason why Alice couldn't get the marriage annulled. The reason why she had to stay married to you and wasn't able to meet someone else. Why she couldn't find happiness with a husband who was a real man. Liam is her son, my nephew. Liam was your parting gift to her. And I suppose you'll tell me now that you never even thought such a thing was possible?"

I stood up slowly, feeling my legs weaken beneath me. I wanted to call him a liar, to tell him that I didn't believe a word of it, but what was the point when the truth was that I believed every word he said because what possible reason would he have for lying? I'd left Alice pregnant. She'd been desperate to talk at the reception, she'd kept insisting that she needed to speak to me in private, but I wouldn't hear her out. She must have known already, or guessed, and wanted to tell me. But then I'd disappeared off to Europe and never contacted anyone from my past afterward. And so she'd borne the shame of it in Ireland in 1973, when an unmarried pregnant girl was considered little better than a whore and was treated by everyone accordingly. I'd always assumed that my own mother, my birth mother, had been unwed and given me up because of how difficult it would have been to rear a child alone in the forties. But things hadn't changed that much since then. Had I done to Alice what my own father had done to my mother?

But of course she wasn't unmarried and perhaps that was even worse, because without a ring on her finger she might have yet met a man, someone who wouldn't have cared and would have brought up the child as his own. But with the ring, there was no chance. Not then. Not in those days. Not in Ireland.

"I didn't know a thing about it," I told him. "I swear, I never even thought about it for a moment."

"Well, you know now," he said, his temper abating. "I probably shouldn't have said anything. My mind is gone, that's the problem. Just leave it alone, Cyril, all right? They're fine without you. They've been fine without you all these years. They don't need you now. It's too late for you to involve yourself in their lives."

I stared at him, unsure what to say. I had a son. He would be fourteen years old by now. I stood up and slowly made my way toward the door but before I could go through it I heard my old friend's voice once more, quieter now, frightened, scared at the end that his life was taking.

"Cyril," he said. "Please don't go—"

"If she'd wanted to let me know," I said, interrupting him and considering the matter carefully, "she would have been able to. There are ways that she could have found me."

"So it's her own fault, is that what you're saying?"

"No, I just mean—"

"You know what, just get the fuck out of here, OK?" he said, his mood changing dramatically in a moment. "You treated her like shit and you spent a lifetime lying to me. I don't even know why I'm giving you the time of day when I have such little time left. Get out."

"Julian—"

"I said *get out!*" he shouted. "Get the fuck out of here!"

The Last Night

There was a thunderstorm on the night of May 11, 1987, and the rain pounded on the window of our apartment as I sat in my favorite arm-chair reading an article in the *New York Times* on Klaus Barbie, the Butcher of Lyon, whose trial had just begun in Europe. Across from me on the sofa Emily was doing everything in her power to make me feel uncomfortable as she gave Ignac a foot rub and occasionally leaned across to nibble on the poor boy's ear while he reread "Araby," his fa-vorite story from *Dubliners*. How he could stand the way she pawed him I didn't know; she was like a hungry mouse working her way through a block of cheese.

"I don't know why anyone is interested in that stuff anymore," she said as I made some comment about the lawyer who had been hired to defend the former Gestapo captain. "It's all so long ago."

"It's not *that* long ago," I said. "And you're supposed to be the histo-rian, aren't you? How can you not find it interesting?"

"Maybe if I'd been alive during the war, like you, then I would. But I wasn't. So I don't."

"I wasn't alive during the war," I said, rolling my eyes. "As you very well know, I wasn't born until August 1945."

"Well, close enough then. What did this guy do anyway? He's an old man now, right?"

"Yes, but that's no reason why he shouldn't be held accountable for the things he did in the past. And are you actually trying to tell me that you don't know what he did?"

"I mean, I think I've heard the *name* . . ."

"He dragged forty-four Jewish children out of an orphanage in Izieu, for one thing," said Ignac, not looking up from his book. "And had them deported to Auschwitz. Where, you know, they died. Most intelligent people would know that."

"OK," said Emily, unwilling to argue with him as she would have with me. I was glad to hear a note of discontent in his voice. "Let me have a look at that paper."

"No," I said. "I'm still reading it."

She let out a deep sigh, as if I had been put on this earth for no other reason than to torment her. "Anyway, Mr. Avery," she said after a moment. "Has Ignac told you our news yet?"

"What news?" I asked, putting the paper down and looking across at him.

"Another time," said Ignac quickly, throwing her a look. "When Bastiaan is home."

"What news?" I repeated, praying that they weren't getting married or having a baby or doing anything that would connect him to this awful woman for the rest of his life.

"Ignac's been accepted," she said.

"For what?"

"For a place at Trinity College. We're moving to Dublin in the fall."

"Oh," I said, feeling an unexpected surge of both excitement and anxiety at the mention of my hometown's name. To my great surprise, my first thought was *Does that mean I can go home at last too?* "I didn't think you'd made your mind up about whether or not to apply."

"Well, I wasn't sure," he said. "But I wrote them a letter and they got back to me and we had a few phone calls and they've said there's a place for me in October if I want to take it up. I haven't decided for certain yet. I wanted to talk to you and Bastiaan about it. Privately."

"We have decided," said Emily, slapping him on the knee. "It's what we both want, remember?"

"I don't want to rush into anything that I might regret."

"Have you spoken to them about scholarships?" I asked.

"Oh don't worry," snapped Emily, perhaps sensing the same annoyance from her boyfriend toward her that I was and taking it out on me. "No one's asking you for money."

"That's not what I meant," I said.

"Of course it's not," said Ignac. "And, yes, I have. It looks like there's a few different funds that I can apply for."

"Well, that's good news," I said. "If you're sure that it's what you want."

"It's what we both want," said Emily. "And anyway, Ignac's not a child anymore. It would be better for him to be living with people his own age."

"So he won't be living with you then?" I asked.

"Someone closer to his own age," she said with a half-smile.

"I would have preferred to tell Cyril and Bastiaan together," said Ignac quietly. "And when we were alone. As a family."

"Well, they had to find out at some point," said Emily. "And Dr. Van den Bergh is almost never here, is he? He's always at the hospital."

"He's not *always* at the hospital," I said. "He's back here every night. You saw him only this morning."

"No, I didn't."

"Emily, we all had breakfast together."

"Oh, I'm no good in the mornings. I'd barely notice either of you at that time of the day."

"You need more sleep then," I said. "That's what happens when you get older."

The phone rang and Ignac leaped off the seat, happy to walk away from our sparring. He almost never joined in when Emily and I argued, and I liked to think that it was because he was not fully on her side. A moment later, he returned and poked his head around the door. "It's Bastiaan," he said. "For you."

I stood up and walked into the hallway, taking the receiver from the stand.

"I'm glad you called," I said. "You're not going to believe what I've just been told."

"Cyril," said Bastiaan, and the serious tone in his voice sent a wave of dread through my body.

"What is it?" I said. "What's happened?"

"I think you should get in here."

"Is it Julian?"

"He's taken a turn for the worse. He doesn't have long. If you want to see him, you should leave now."

I sat down on the chair by the telephone table before my legs could give way beneath me. Of course I had told Bastiaan about my relationship with Patient 741 and he remembered me telling him about Julian more than a decade earlier when we had first met. But I hadn't spoken about him since, so he'd failed to make the connection when he first began treating him.

"I'm on my way," I said. "Stay with him, will you? Until I get there?"

I hung up the phone and reached for my jacket as Ignac appeared in the doorway. "What is it?" he asked. "Is it your friend?"

I nodded. "Bastiaan says he's near the end. I need to see him before he dies."

"Do you want me to come with you?"

I thought about it for a moment and appreciated the gesture but shook my head. "There's no point," I said. "You'll only be left waiting outside with nothing to do. And besides, Bastiaan will be there for me. You stay here with Emily. Or, you know, tell her to go home and stay here on your own."

I made my way toward the door and he followed me quickly. "Nothing's decided, you know," he said. "About Dublin, I mean. The offer's there, that's all. Emily wants to go, but I haven't made up my mind yet."

"We can talk about this later," I said. "I've got to go."

He nodded and I ran downstairs, hailing a cab on the street, and within about fifteen minutes found myself stepping out of the elevator on the seventh floor to find Bastiaan waiting for me.

"Hey," I said as he looked up. "How is he?"

He nodded toward the seats in the waiting room and we sat down. "He's dying," he said, reaching out and placing a hand on top of my own. "His CD4 count is as low as I've ever seen. He's got pneumonia and his internal organs are failing. We've made him as comfortable as we can but there's really nothing more that we can do for him now. It's only a matter of time. I wasn't sure he'd even make it till you got here."

I felt a great burst of grief building inside myself and struggled to contain my emotions. I had known this was coming over the last few days, of course, but had had little time to prepare myself.

"Can I call Alice?" I asked. "Bring the phone to him?"

"No," he said. "I've asked him and he doesn't want it."

"But maybe if he hears her voice—"

"Cyril, no. It's his life. It's his death. It's his choice."

"All right," I said. "Is there anyone in there with him now?"

"Shaniqua," he said. "She said she'd stay with him till you got here."

I made my way toward Room 703 and tapped quickly on the door before pushing it open. Julian was lying on his back in the bed, his breathing heavy, and when Shaniqua saw me she stood up.

"He drifts in and out," she said quietly. "You want me to stay here with you until it's over?"

"No," I said. "I'd prefer if you left us alone. But thanks."

She nodded and left, closing the door quietly behind her, and I sat down on the chair next to the bed, watching him as his breath came in short bursts. He was so skinny that he was almost frightening to look at but somewhere beneath that scarred face lay the boy that I had once known, the boy that I had loved, the boy in the ornamental chair in Dartmouth Square, the boy whose friendship I had betrayed. I reached out to him, taking his hand in mine, and the sensation of his paper-thin skin, clammy and tender against my palm, unsettled me. He mumbled something and, after a moment, he opened his eyes and smiled.

"Cyril," he said. "Did you forget something?"

"What do you mean?"

"You were just here. You just left."

I shook my head. "That was a few days ago, Julian. I've come back to see you."

"Oh. I thought it was earlier. Did you see Behan?"

"Who?"

"Brendan Behan. He's over there by the bar. We should get him a pint in."

I looked away for a moment and waited until I had full control of my emotions.

"We're not in the Palace Bar anymore," I said quietly. "We're not in Dublin. We're in New York. You're in hospital."

"That's right" he said, as if he was simply humoring me.

"Is there anything I can do for you, Julian? Anything I can do to help you?"

He blinked a few times and looked back at me with a little more awareness in his eyes. "What was I just saying?" he asked me. "Was I talking nonsense?"

"You're confused, that's all."

"I seem to have moments of clarity and moments when I don't know what's happening. It's a strange thing to know that you're living your last hour on earth."

"Don't say that—"

"It's true, though. I can feel it. And Dr. Van den Bergh said as much to me earlier. He's the one, isn't he? Your boyfriend?"

I nodded, glad that he didn't sound as if he was putting quotation marks around the word this time. "That's him," I said. "Bastiaan. He's outside if you need him."

"I don't need him," he said. "He's done all he can. He seems like a good man."

"He is."

"Too good for you."

"Probably."

He tried to laugh but the effort caused him a lot of pain and I saw a terrible expression of suffering cross his face.

"Take it easy," I said. "Just relax."

"I've been lying in this bed for weeks," he said. "How much more relaxed can I get?"

"Maybe you shouldn't talk."

"All I have left is talk. If I don't speak, then I might as well give up. I'm glad you came, really I am. Did I insult you last time you were here?"

"I deserved it," I told him.

"Probably. But I'm glad you came back. There is something you can do for me. After I'm gone, I mean."

"Of course," I said. "Anything you want."

"I need you to tell Alice."

I closed my eyes, my heart sinking in my chest. This was one thing I really didn't want to do.

"There's still time," I said. "Time for you to talk to her."

"I don't want that. I want you to tell her. After I'm gone."

"Are you sure I'm the right person for that?" I asked him. "It's been fourteen years, after all. I don't think the first time I speak to her since our wedding day should be to call to tell her that . . . to tell her . . ."

"Someone has to do it," he insisted. "That's your penance. Tell her that I didn't want her to see me like this, but that you were by my side at the end and I was thinking of her. There's a diary in the locker drawer next to you. You'll find her number in there."

"I don't know if I can," I said, feeling the tears starting to roll down my cheeks.

"If it's not you, then it will be some anonymous Garda knocking on her door," he said. "And that's not what I want. And that's not what you want. He won't be able to tell her how it ended, how I felt about her, but you will. I need you to tell her that she was the best person I ever knew. And to tell Liam that my life would have been a lot emptier without his presence in it. That I loved them both and that I'm sorry for all of this. Will you do that for me, Cyril? Please, I've never asked you for anything but I'm asking you for this. And you can't deny a dying man his last wish."

"All right," I said. "If it's what you want."

"It is."

"Then I promise I'll do it."

We sat in silence for a long time, punctuated only by the occasional expression of pain from Julian as he twisted uncomfortably in the bed.

"Will you tell me about him?" I asked finally.

"About who?"

"About Liam. About my son."

"He's not your son," he said, shaking his head. "Biologically, yes. But that's the only way."

"What's he like?"

"He's like his mother. Although everyone says he looks like me. But his personality is very different. He's shy. He's quiet. He's more like you in that way."

"Were you close to him?"

"He's the closest thing I ever had to a son," he said, starting to cry. "Which is ironic, really."

"Is he happy?" I asked. "Does he have adventures like we had?"

"We had some, didn't we?" he said, smiling.

"We did," I replied.

"Remember when you got kidnapped by the IRA?" he said. "That was some afternoon."

I shook my head. "No, Julian," I said. "That wasn't me, that was you."

"Me?"

"Yes."

"I got kidnapped?"

"Yes."

"Why? What had I done to them?"

"Nothing," I told him. "They hated your father. They wanted him to pay a ransom."

"And did he pay it?"

"No."

"Typical Max. They cut off my ear," he said, reaching a hand up to his face, but the effort was too much and he put it back above the sheets.

"They did," I told him. "Fucking animals."

"I remember now," he said. "They were very nice to me most of the time. Except when they were cutting bits of me off. I told them I liked Mars Bars and one of them went out and got me a whole box of them. He put them in the fridge to keep them cold. I grew friendly with him, I think. I can't remember his name."

"You visited him in prison," I said. "I thought you were crazy."

"Did I ever tell you that they nearly cut my dick off?"

"No," I said, uncertain whether this was something that had really happened or something he was misremembering in his delirium.

"It's true," he said. "The night before the Gardaí found me. They said that I had a choice. That they'd either pop one of my eyes out or cut my dick off. They told me I could choose which."

"Jesus," I said.

"I mean I would have said my eye, of course. Probably the one on the other side to the missing ear, just to balance things out. But can you imagine if they *had* cut my dick off? I wouldn't be lying here right now, would I? None of this would have happened."

"That's one way of looking at it," I said.

"They would have saved my life."

"Maybe."

"No, you're right. I'd be dead already because I'd probably have killed myself if they'd cut my dick off. There's no way I would have gone through my life dickless. It's amazing, isn't it, how one small part of our anatomy completely controls our lives?"

"Small?" I said, raising an eyebrow. "Speak for yourself."

He laughed and nodded. "That first day we met," he said. "You took me up to your bedroom and asked to look at mine. Remember that? I should have known then. I should have guessed your dirty little secret."

"I didn't," I insisted. "All these years you've been saying that but it never happened. It was *you* who wanted to look at *mine*."

"No," he said. "I can't imagine that. I wouldn't have been interested."

"You were obsessed with sex right from the start."

"Well, that's true. I used to fancy your mother, you know."

"You never knew my mother. Neither did I."

"Of course I did. Maude."

"She was my adoptive mother."

"Oh that's right," he said, waving the distinction away. "You always insisted on that."

"It was them who insisted on it. From the day they brought me home. And you didn't really fancy her, did you? She was old enough to be your adoptive mother too."

"I did. Older women were never really my thing, but Maude was something else. And she fancied me too. She once told me that I was the most beautiful boy she'd ever seen in her life."

"She did not. That doesn't even sound like her."

"Believe what you like."

"You were *seven*."

"That's what she told me."

"Jesus," I said, shaking my head. "Sometimes I think my life would have been a lot better if I had never felt any sexual desire at all."

"You can't live like a eunuch. No one can. If the IRA had cut my dick off, I'd have put a bullet in my head. Do you think this is a punishment for all the things I've done?"

"Not for a moment," I said.

"I was watching the news," he said. "There were people on, congressmen, saying that people who developed AIDS were—"

"Don't even pay attention to those fuckers," I said. "They know nothing. They're despicable human beings. You were unlucky, that's all. Everyone who passes through this floor has been unlucky. There's nothing more to it than that."

"I suppose," he said with a sigh, before letting out a cry of pain.

"Julian!" I said, leaping to my feet.

"I'm OK," he said.

But then, before he could relax again, he let out another cry and I jumped up, making for the door to get Bastiaan.

"Don't," he said. "Don't leave me, Cyril, please."

"But if I call a doctor—"

"Don't leave me. There's nothing they can do."

I nodded and came back around to the chair, sitting down and taking his hand in mine again.

"I'm sorry," I said. "For everything I ever did to you and Alice that you thought was deceitful. I'm truly sorry. If I could go back, if I could be the man I am now but be young again—"

"It's in the past," he said, his eyes starting to close. "And what would it have helped Alice to have spent her life married to you? At least she's got laid occasionally over the years."

I smiled.

"I'm going," he whispered after a moment. "Cyril, I'm going. I can feel myself going."

It was on the tip of my tongue to say *Don't*, to say *Fight it*, to say *Stay*, but I said nothing. The disease was finally winning.

"I loved you," I said, leaning in to him. "You were my best friend."

"I loved you too," he whispered and then, a startled expression on his face, he said, "I can't see you."

"I'm here."

"I can't see you. It's just darkness."

"I'm here, Julian. I'm here. Can you hear me?"

"I hear you. But I can't see you. Will you hold me?"

I was already holding his hand and squeezed it a little to make sure he knew that I was there.

"No," he said. "Hold me. I want to be held again. Just one more time."

I hesitated, uncertain what he meant, and then released his hand and walked around to the other side of the bed, lying down next to him, my arms wrapping themselves around his thin, trembling frame. How many times throughout my youth had I dreamed of such a moment and now all I could do was bury my face in his back and weep.

"Cyril . . ." whispered Julian.

"Just let go," I whispered back.

"Alice . . ." he said as his body relaxed into my embrace, and I held him for what felt like a very long time, even though it was probably no more than a couple of minutes, as his breathing began to slow down and eventually fade away. I held him until Bastiaan came in and checked the monitor and told me that it was over, that Julian was gone, and I continued to hold him for a few more minutes until it was time to stand up and let the nurses do their job. And then we took the elevator down to the ground floor, left the hospital and Bastiaan raised a hand to hail a cab, and in that moment I made the biggest mistake of my life.

"No," I said. "The rain has stopped. Let's walk. I need some fresh air."

And so we started to walk home.

Central Park

We walked in silence across the avenues and into Central Park.

"I forgot his address book," I said, stopping in the middle of one of the tree-lined pathways. "I left it in his bedside locker."

"Do you need it?" asked Bastiaan.

"I promised I'd phone Alice. His sister. I have to tell her."

"You can get it tomorrow. His personal items will be collected."

"No," I said, shaking my head. "No, I have to tell her tonight. We have to go back."

"It's late," said Bastiaan. "And you're upset. Wait until tomorrow."

I started to shake with the cold and before I knew it I was weeping uncontrollable tears.

"Hey," said Bastiaan, pulling me to him and wrapping his arms around me. "Don't cry. I'm here for you. I'll always be here for you. I love you."

And then a voice called out: "Hey, faggots!"

And I turned around to see three men running toward us.

But I don't remember anything else after that.

PART III
PEACE

1994 Fathers and Sons

One of Them

During the early 1950s, when my adoptive father Charles had first spent time as a guest of the Irish government in Mountjoy Prison, I had never been allowed to visit. Of course, I was just a child at the time and Maude had no interest in the three of us undertaking any embarrassing or cathartic reunion behind bars, but the idea of entering a prison had intrigued me ever since a seven-year-old Julian had revealed to me how Max had permitted him to sit in with him while he conferred with a client who'd murdered his wife. To the best of my knowledge, Maude never visited either, despite weekly visiting orders coming her way. Rather than discarding them, she made a point of keeping each one, creating a neat pile on the telephone stand by the front door of our small apartment, and when I once asked her whether she was ever going to use one of those precious tickets for their intended purpose, she responded by slowly removing the cigarette from her mouth and extinguishing it in the center of the pile.

"Does that answer your question?" she asked, turning to me with a half-smile.

"Well, perhaps *I* could visit," I suggested, and she frowned as she opened her cigarette case to remove her sixty-fourth smoke of the day.

"What a strange thing to say," she replied. "Why on earth would you want to do something so perverse?"

"Because Charles is my father. And he might welcome the company."

"Charles is not your father," she insisted. "He's your adoptive father. We've told you that time and again. You mustn't get ideas, Cyril."

"Still, a friendly face—"

"I don't think you *do* have a friendly face, though. To be honest, I've always thought you have a rather sour countenance. It's something you might want to work on."

"Someone he knows then."

"I'm sure he's getting to know plenty of people," she said, lighting up. "From what I understand, there's a great sense of community in prisons. A man like Charles will probably do very well for himself in there. He's never had any difficulty ingratiating himself with strangers in the past. No, it's out of the question, I'm afraid. I simply couldn't allow it."

And so I had never gone. But this time, during Charles's second experience behind bars, I was a grown man, almost fifty years of age, and needed no one's permission. So when the visiting order arrived, I felt quite excited by the prospect of seeing how the criminal classes were treated.

It was a fine Dublin morning and, although I was no longer able to undertake very long walks because of my leg, I decided that a few kilometers would be all right and took my crutch from where it hung next to the front door before making my way down Pearse Street to cross the Liffey over O'Connell Street Bridge, remaining on the left-hand side of the street as I always did in order to avoid the area near Clerys department store where I had once inadvertently caused the deaths of both Mary-Margaret Muffet and a hard-working, if homophobic, member of An Garda Síochána. Nelson's Pillar was long gone, of course. After the IRA had toppled the admiral from his pedestal, the remaining structure had been taken down in a controlled explosion that had been so ineptly planned that it had blown out half the windows of the shops on O'Connell Street, causing thousands of pounds' worth of damage. But the memories remained and I didn't care to relive them.

At the top of the street, I passed the Irish Writers' Center, where only a few weeks earlier I had attended the launch party for Ignac's fourth children's book, the latest in his hugely popular series about a time-traveling Slovenian boy that had captured the imagination of children (and many adults) around the world. All the Dublin writers were there, of course, and when word got around the room as to the identity of my adoptive mother, several came over to introduce themselves, asking questions about her novels that I had no way of answering. A publisher inquired as to whether I might like to write the foreword to an anniversary edition of *Like to the Lark*, but I declined, even when he told me there was two hundred pounds in it for me if I did a good job. A journalist whom I had seen several times on *The Late Late Show* informed me that Maude was Ireland's most overrated writer, that women could never be trusted with the novel form, and proceeded to spend ten minutes explaining why until Rebecca, Ignac's wife, came over and rescued me, for which I was eternally grateful.

Along Dorset Street then and left toward the Mater Hospital, and even as I approached the jail I felt in uncommonly good spirits, for it was one of those fine mornings where one just feels happy to be alive. Seven years had passed since that terrible night in New York when I had lost the only two men I had ever loved within an hour of each other, six years since the trial, five since I had left the States forever after half a dozen operations on my leg, four since I had returned to mainland Europe, three since I'd come back to Dublin, two since Charles's arrest for fraud and tax evasion and one since he found himself back in jail and had finally reached out to me in the hope of a little filial assistance.

At first, I had been deeply unsure about returning to Ireland. Throughout my years of exile, I had often longed to explore the streets of my childhood once again, but it had seemed like an impossible dream.

However, as things turned out, I felt immeasurably happy to be back and somehow glad that my years of travel were behind me. And I even found work in one of my old haunts, in the library of Dáil Éireann on Kildare Street, a quiet study area rarely frequented by the TDs themselves but more often populated by parliamentary assistants and civil servants searching for answers to questions that their ministers might be asked later that day in the chamber.

It was in Dáil Éireann, in fact, that I encountered a figure from my past, Miss Anna Ambrosia from the Department of Education, alongside whom I had worked for a brief period during the mid sixties. Miss Ambrosia, it turned out, had gone on to marry her Jewish boyfriend with the non-Jewish name, Peadar O'Múrchú, and produced half a dozen daughters, each of whom, she told me, was harder to control than the last. Her career had prospered in the intervening years and at the age of fifty-three she found herself the senior civil servant in the department, a post once held by Miss Joyce. We recognized each other immediately on the morning she called into the library and arranged to meet again during my lunch break, when we went upstairs to the tearoom to catch up.

"Guess how many ministers I've had to contend with in my years at the department?" she asked.

"I don't know," I said. "Eight? Nine?"

"Seventeen. A bunch of thickos, every one. Half of them are completely illiterate and the other half can't do long division. There seems to be some irony to the fact that the least intelligent member of the government always seems to end up running Education. And you know who has to make them look good, don't you? Muggins, that's who. Who was the minister when you worked here, do you remember?"

I mentioned the man's name and she rolled her eyes. "That lunatic," she said. "He lost his seat at the next election. Didn't he punch you in the face when he got caught with his pants down?"

"No, that was the Press Officer," I said. "Happy memories."

"I don't know why I've spent so long there, I really don't," she said wistfully. "Maybe I should have traveled like you did. You must have had a great time of it all the same."

"Good days and bad days," I told her. "You never thought about leaving then?"

"I thought about it," she said. "But you know what it's like, Cyril, with the civil service. You get your foot on the ladder and you're set for life. And when they changed the rules to allow married women to stay on, I felt like doing it just to prove a point. Anyway, with six children, Peadar and I needed the money. I'm not complaining, I've been happy here for the most part. Except when I've been completely fucking miserable."

Out of the corner of my eye I could see a young waitress running into the room and looking up at the clock in a panic—she was red-faced and late for work, I assumed—and as she made her way behind the counter, another familiar face from the old days, the manageress of the tearoom, emerged from the kitchen area to give her a scolding.

"I'm sorry, Mrs. Goggin," said the girl. "It was the buses, they're always so unreliable and—"

"If that's the case, Jacinta, then you might be a bus yourself," came the reply. "Because your unreliability is on a par with that of the number 16."

Miss Ambrosia—Anna—watched the ensuing dressing-down and grimaced. "That woman is not to be crossed," she said. "She rules this place with a rod of iron. Even Charlie Haughey was frightened of her. She threw him out one day when he put his hand on a waitress's backside."

"He came into the library the other day," I said. "I'd never seen him in there before. He looked around in amazement and said, *I think I must have taken a wrong turn somewhere.*"

"Somebody should save that line," said Anna. "They could put it on his gravestone."

"Mrs. Goggin must have been here for donkey's years, all the same," I said. "I remember seeing her here when I was just a boy."

"She's retiring soon," said Anna. "Or so I've been told. It's her sixty-fifth birthday coming up in a few weeks. Anyway, tell me all your news. Is it right what I heard about you? That you ran out on your wedding day before you could say *I do?*"

"Where did you hear that?" I asked.

"Oh, I don't remember. Gossip spreads quickly in this place, you know that."

"Well, it's half true," I admitted. "I got through the *I do* part. I waited until the reception to make a run for it."

"Jesus, Mary and Joseph," she said, shaking her head and trying not to laugh. "You're some bollix."

"So I've been told."

"Why did you do that?"

"It's a long story."

"And did you never marry again?"

"No. But tell me," I said quickly. "Whatever happened to the other pair we worked with, Miss Joyce and Mr. Denby-Denby? Do you stay in touch with them?"

She put her cup down and leaned forward. "Well, therein lies a tale," she said. "Miss Joyce lost her job after she had an affair with the Minister for Defense."

"No!" I said in surprise. "She always seemed so straight-laced!"

"Oh they're the worst ones. Anyway, she was mad as a hatter for the man but of course he was married and when she got a bit clingy and wanted more than he was willing to offer he saw to it that she was paid off and kicked out of the service. She wasn't a bit happy about it, I don't mind telling you, but what could she do? The ministers had it all their own way back then. They still do for the most part. She tried to sell her story to the papers but they didn't want to upset the poor man on account of him having a family. The Archbishop intervened with the editor of the *Irish Press*."

"And what happened to Miss Joyce afterward?"

"Last I heard she'd moved down to Enniscorthy to open a bookshop. And then I heard she wrote a song that almost made it to the Eurovision Song Contest. After that, I heard nothing more."

"And Mr. Denby-Denby?" I asked. "What about him? I presume he's retired by now?"

"Well, that was a very sad story," she said, lowering her eyes, her smile fading.

"Why, what happened?" I asked.

"I suppose you didn't keep up with the Irish papers when you were away, no?"

"Not very often," I admitted. "Why?"

"Oh it was a terrible business," she said, shuddering a little as she shook her head. "He only went and got himself murdered."

"*Murdered?*" I said, and perhaps my voice rose a little high, for I noticed Mrs. Goggin glancing over at me, although when our eyes met she looked away.

"That's right, murdered," repeated Anna. "Of course, you know he was one of them, don't you?"

"One of who?" I asked innocently.

"One of *them*."

"Them being . . . ?"

"A gay fella."

"Oh right," I said. "Yes, well, I always assumed that he was despite his constant references to the legendary Mrs. Denby-Denby and all the little Denby-Denbys. Was he making them up?"

"Oh no, they existed all right," she said. "But then the country was littered with Mrs. Denby-Denbys back in those days who had no idea what their husbands were getting up to behind their backs. Well, you know that better than anyone, I suppose. Would I be right in thinking that you're one of them too?"

"I am," I admitted.

"I always thought so. I remember when we worked together you never seemed at all interested in me and one day I said to Miss Joyce that I thought you must be one of them but she said, no, you were far too nice to be one of them."

"I'm sure there's a compliment in there somewhere," I said.

"It's very popular now, isn't it?"

"What is?"

"Being one of them."

"I don't know," I said. "Is it?"

"Oh it is," she said. "There's Boy George and David Norris. And half of this place, of course, although they keep it to themselves. The woman who lives next door to me, her youngest son is one of them." She shrugged and sniffed the air. "It's a shame for her, of course, but I don't say anything. I've never been judgmental in that way. And there are two women who run a flower shop near where I live and they share the upstairs flat and Peadar says they're one of them—"

"Two of them, surely?"

"Yes, two of them. I never even knew that a woman could be one of them. You don't mind it so much in a man but in a woman it's just peculiar, don't you think?"

"I've never really given it much thought," I said. "But I imagine there's not a lot of difference."

"Oh you've gone very modern, Cyril. That's what living abroad will do for you, I suppose. My second-to-eldest girl, Louise, she wants to go to America on a J-1 visa with her friends and I'm doing everything I can to stop her because they're fierce modern over there. I just know that if she goes to America she'll end up being raped by a black man and having an abortion."

"Jesus Christ," I said, spitting out my tea. "For God's sake, Anna, you can't say things like that."

"Why not? It's true."

"It's not true at all. And you sound very small-minded saying it."

"I'm not racist if that's what you're implying. Remember, my husband is Jewish."

"Still and all," I said, wondering whether I could just leave before she opened her mouth again.

"Louise says she's going, no matter what her father or I say. *On your own head be it*, I've told her but will she listen? She will not. Do you think we were like that when we were that age? Did you give your parents that level of grief?"

"Well, I had a rather unconventional upbringing," I said.

"Oh that's right. I remember you telling me something about that back then. Who's your mother, Edna O'Brien or someone, isn't it?"

"Maude Avery," I said. "Adoptive mother."

"That's right, Maude Avery. You'd think she was bloody Tolstoy the way people carry on about her—"

"Mr. Denby-Denby," I said, interrupting her before she could get lost on this road. "You were telling me about how he was murdered."

"It was a terrible business," she said, leaning in and lowering her voice. "So it turned out that Mr. Denby-Denby rented some cheap flat on Gardiner Street that his wife knew nothing about and every so often he'd go down to the canals to pick up some young lad and bring him back there for a bit of you-know-what. This had been going on for years apparently. Well, it all must have got out of hand on one of those nights because the neighbors reported a terrible smell coming from his apartment and he was discovered there, two weeks later, one hand chained to a radiator, half an orange in his mouth and his trousers wrapped around his ankles."

"Jesus," I said, shuddering at the image. "And did they ever catch the boy?"

"They did. Eventually. He got life."

"Poor Mr. Denby-Denby," I said. "That's a terrible way to go."

"I suppose you knew all about it back then, did you?"

"About what?" I asked.

"About Mr. Denby-Denby. Did you and him ever . . . ?"

"Of course not," I said, appalled by the notion. "He was old enough to be my father."

Anna looked at me as if she wasn't entirely convinced. "You have to be very careful of those boys, Cyril," she said. "The rent boys down the canals, I mean. Think of the diseases they carry for one thing. They all have AIDS. And they'd kill you as quick as look at you. I hope you don't go in for anything like that."

I didn't know whether to laugh or be offended. The truth was that I hadn't so much as kissed another man in seven years and had no interest in ever doing so again. The last thing I was going to do was cruise along the Grand Canal in the middle of the night looking for cheap trade.

"Would you like another pot of tea?" asked the waitress, Jacinta, approaching us now, and before I could reply Anna shook her head.

"I can't," she said. "I need to get back to the office. Those windows won't stare out themselves all afternoon. But it was good to see you, Cyril," she added, standing up. "I'll probably run into you again in the library downstairs, will I? Are you there every day?"

"Every day except Friday," I said. "And only when the Dáil is in session."

"Grand," she said. "Sure we'll catch up again another time. Don't forget what I've said now and stay away from trouble. I don't want another Mr. Denby-Denby on my conscience."

I nodded and as she left I turned to the waitress and said that I'd have another pot of tea, and when it arrived a few minutes later it was Mrs. Goggin who was carrying it.

"Do you mind if I join you for a moment?" she asked. "It's Mr. Avery, isn't it?"

"That's right," I said. "Cyril. Please, sit down."

"I'm Catherine Goggin. I don't know if you remember me but—"

"I do, of course. It's nice to see you again."

"And you're back working in the Dáil again?"

"I am, for my sins. In the library. It's only been a couple of weeks but I'm enjoying it."

"This place sucks you in, doesn't it?" she asked, smiling. "You can never get out of it. But I'm glad to see you back again anyway. Did I hear that you were in the States in the meantime?"

"For a time, yes. And in Europe."

"And your leg," she asked, nodding toward my crutch. "Did you hurt it recently?"

"No, that goes back seven years," I told her. "From when I was living in New York. My friend and I were walking through Central Park one night and were assaulted."

"Oh dear God," she said. "That's terrible. And what about your friend, was he all right?"

"No, he died," I said. "Very quickly. Before the ambulance even arrived."

"Well, I'm very sorry to hear it," she said. "I suppose I shouldn't even have asked. It's none of my business."

"I don't mind."

"It's just that I remember you, from when you were here before. You always reminded me of someone I knew years ago. You have the look of him."

"Someone you were close to?" I asked.

"Not really," she said, looking away. "An uncle of mine, that's all. A long time ago."

"I remember your son," I said. "How is he these days?"

"My son?" she asked, looking up sharply with a frown. "What do you mean?"

"You have a son, don't you?" I asked. "I met you both in a coffee shop once, more than twenty years ago now. You probably won't remember. It was the morning I was getting married, so it's burned into my memory. I can't remember his name, though, and—"

"Jonathan."

"Oh, yes. He was a precocious little fellow, as I recall."

She smiled. "He's a doctor now. A psychiatrist. He got married himself only a few weeks ago to a lovely girl, Melanie. They've known each other since they were children."

"Do you have others?" I asked.

"Other what?"

"Other children?"

She paused for a moment and shook her head. "No," she said. "And how about you?"

"I have a son," I told her. "Liam. He's twenty."

"Well, that must be nice for you."

I shrugged a little, uncertain why I was confiding in her. "We're not very close," I said. "I wasn't there for him when he was growing up and he resents me for it. It's fair enough but I don't seem to be able to bridge the divide between us, no matter how hard I try."

"Then you must try harder," she said. "Make sure to keep him in your life, that's what's important. Don't ever lose sight of him."

The doors opened and a group of TDs came in, their voices loud and arrogant, and she stood up with a sigh.

"Well," she said. "I better get back to it. I'm sure I'll see you in here regularly now that you're back with us."

"You will," I said, watching her as she walked away, and for some reason our conversation lingered in my mind now as I arrived at the gates of Mountjoy Prison. I showed my passport and my visiting order to the officer on duty, and he read it carefully before telling me to take off my jacket and shoes and walk through a metal detector, but all the time I was thinking of Mrs. Goggin and the way she had looked at me, and I felt a strange urge to continue the conversation with her at another time.

The 'Joy

As it turns out, a prison waiting room can be a great leveler of people, with relatives and friends of inmates from every social class gathered together in varying degrees of outrage, shame and bravado. I took a seat toward the rear on a white plastic chair nailed to the floor and tried to ignore the smell of antiseptic in the air. A carving on the right arm of my seat informed me that "Deano" was "a dead man" while the left added that the same Deano "sux cock." On the wall facing me, a poster displayed an image of a cheerful police officer, a jovial young man and an almost hysterical older woman standing next to each other under the slogan *We Can All Get Through This Together!* in what I could only assume was an ironic statement on the prison experience.

Glancing around, I noticed a young woman in a shell suit struggling with a small child whose hair was cut into a Mohawk with green frosting at the tips to complement the series of avocado-colored hoops that pierced his left earlobe. Unable to control him, she turned her attentions to a baby who was mewling like a possessed cat in the pram next to her.

"You have your hands full there," I remarked, giving her a sympathetic look as the older boy ran over the empty seats and stopped before various people, turning himself into a human rifle and letting rip at his unsuspecting victims, a trick he had presumably learned from his incarcerated father.

"Fuck off, ya ol' pedo," said the woman casually.

I took the hint that she and I were not going to bond and moved to a different part of the room, next to a lady around my own age who looked absolutely terrified to be in such an awful place. She held her handbag tightly in her lap and her eyes scanned the room back and forth as if she had never seen such awful specimens of humanity in her life.

"Your first time here?" I asked, and she nodded.

"Of course," she said. "I'm from Blackrock." She looked at me meaningfully. "There's been a terrible misunderstanding, you see," she continued after a few moments. "A miscarriage of justice. I shouldn't be here at all and nor should my Anthony."

"None of us want to be here," I said.

"No, I said I *shouldn't* be here. They have my son locked up but he didn't do anything at all. He's always been a very decent young man."

"Do you mind if I ask what he's been charged with?"

"Murder."

"Murder?"

"Yes, but he didn't do it, so don't look so shocked."

"Who is he supposed to have murdered?"

"His wife. But there was no real evidence, other than fingerprints, DNA and an eyewitness. Also, for what it's worth, my daughter-in-law was a horrible girl and had it coming to her, if you ask me. I'm not a bit sorry she's gone. She wasn't from Blackrock and I told Anthony that he should marry locally."

"Right," I said, wondering whether I should move again. "Is he on remand then?"

"No, he's serving life. The trial was a few months ago. I'm going to speak to my TD about it and see what can be done. I'm sure if I just explain things they'll realize their error and let him out. What about you? What brings you here?"

"My adoptive father is in for tax evasion," I told her.

"That's a disgrace," she said, sitting up straight and sounding positively appalled. She clutched her handbag closer as if there was a risk that I was going to steal it. "Sure we all have to pay our taxes, do you not know that? You should be ashamed of yourself."

"Why?" I protested. "It's got nothing to do with me. I pay mine."

"And what do you want, a medal? If you ask me, prison is too good for tax evaders. They should be strung up."

"And what about murderers?" I asked. "What should happen to them?"

She shook her head in annoyance and turned away from me, and I was relieved when a handsome young prison guard came into the room carrying a clipboard and called our names one by one, directing us along a corridor toward an open-plan room where we all took our seats behind small white tables with numbers inscribed across the top. A few minutes later, a door opened at the front of the room and a group of men in woolen jumpers and gray slacks trotted in, their eyes scanning the room for people they knew. I was a little surprised to see Charles waving at me with unbound enthusiasm and when he approached me and I stood up to shake his hand I was even more shocked to find him pulling me into his arms in a tight hug.

"Sit down, Avery," said an older officer, marching toward us and bringing an unappealing stench of four-day-old sweat with him. "No physical contact allowed."

"But this man is my son!" cried Charles, appalled. "What kind of country has this become if a man cannot embrace his only child in public? Was it for this that Robert Emmet died? And James Connolly? And Pádhraic Pearse?"

"Take a seat or go back to your cell," said the officer, who was clearly in no mood for a debate. "It's your choice."

"Fine, I'll sit," grumbled Charles, giving in as I took my place opposite him. "Honestly, Cyril, I'm treated like some sort of criminal in here. It's beyond the beyonds."

He'd grown old since I'd last seen him—he was well into his mid seventies by now—but he wore the years well. He'd always been a handsome man, of course, and his good looks had stayed with him into old age, as they so often do with undeserving men. The only surprise was the gray stubble that lined his cheeks and chin. As long as I had known him, he'd been scrupulous about shaving, condemning men with beards or mustaches as socialists, hippies or reporters, and I was a little surprised to find that he was not sticking to his morning routines in prison. Also, he smelled a little and his teeth looked more yellow than I remembered them.

"How are you anyway?" he asked, smiling at me. "It's good to see you at last."

"I'm fine, Charles," I said. "I would have come before if you'd invited me."

"No need to apologize," he said. "I don't get too many visiting orders and when I do I tend to send them to old friends and young women. But they all seem to be dying off now. The old friends, that is; the young women just don't show up. And then one day your name popped into my head and I thought, *Why not?*"

"I'm touched," I said. I'd only seen him a couple of times since my return to Dublin three years earlier, so we weren't exactly close. Once was when I'd run into him in Brown Thomas on Grafton Street and when I went over to say hello he mistook me for a shop assistant and asked me did I know where the handkerchiefs were kept. I pointed him in the right direction and he went on his way. The second time was at his trial, when he asked me to bring some shoe polish and a Cornetto in to him in his remand cell the next morning.

"So how's prison life?" I asked. "Everything going all right in here?"

"Well, I haven't been raped by a gang of multi-ethnic bank robbers, if that's what you mean."

"It wasn't what I meant at all," I said.

"I suppose it's not too bad, all things considered," he said. "It's not like I haven't been in here before, and things have improved a lot since the last time. I have my own television set, which is wonderful, as I've grown quite addicted to Australian soap operas and wouldn't want to fall behind."

"I'm glad to hear that you're spending your time usefully," I said.

"Actually, I think I might go to Melbourne when I get out of here. It looks like a nice place. Full of drama, beautiful beaches and pretty girls. Do you watch *Neighbors*, Cyril?"

"Well, I've seen it," I admitted. "Although I wouldn't go so far as to say I watch it."

"You should. It's magnificent. Shakespearean in its characterization."

"Anyway, I'm not sure if Australia allows convicted criminals in," I told him.

"If I have to, I can always give the immigration people a little back-hander," he said with a wink. "Everyone has a price. I'm sick of this country. Time to start again somewhere fresh."

I shook my head in disbelief. "So it looks as if you didn't learn any-thing from the first time you were in here," I said. "And you're learn-ing nothing this time either."

"What are you talking about?" he asked. "What should I have learned?"

"That we have a little thing called income tax in this country. And that you have to pay it. Or they lock you up."

"Well, as it happens," he said dismissively, "I know all about the tax laws and on this occasion I don't believe that I did anything wrong. Last time around I admit they had every right to put me behind bars. I was earning a lot of money in the forties and fifties and squirreling most of it away without paying a single penny to the government. Bloody fascists, all of them anyway, feathering their own fascist nests. Although if you ask me, a case could be made that Max Woodbead was the real culprit back then. He was the one who thought of all the an-gles and gave me such bad advice. How is old Max anyway, I wonder. Do you ever hear from him? I sent him a visiting order a few weeks ago but I've heard nothing back yet. Do you think he still holds a grudge against me for all that business with Elizabeth?"

"I doubt it," I said. "Max has been dead for almost ten years now, so I imagine he's past caring. Didn't you know that?"

He scratched his head and looked a little confused. I wondered whether his mind was starting to play tricks on him. "Oh, yes," he said finally. "Now that you mention it, I think I did hear something about him dying. Poor Max. He wasn't a bad sort, really. He married up, which every intelligent man should do. I married up several times. And then across once or twice. And then beneath me. I never quite found the right level somehow. Perhaps I should have married diagonally or in a slightly curved direction. But Elizabeth was a great beauty, that's for sure. She had it all: class, money, breeding and a fine pair of legs."

"I remember," I said, for it was certainly from his mother's side of the family that Julian had got his looks. "You had an affair with her."

"We didn't have an *affair*," he said, the word emerging like something crude on his tongue. "We just had sex a few times, that's all. An affair implies that there are emotions at play and there were none. Not on my part anyway. I can't speak for her. I suppose she's dead too, is she?"

"Yes," I said.

"Everyone's dead," he said with a sigh, before sitting back in his seat and staring up at the ceiling. "Poor Max," he repeated. "It's a shame that he died before he got a chance to apologize to me. I'm sure he would have liked to."

"For what?"

"For landing me in here first time around. And for punching me in the face when I was in the middle of bribing a jury. That really didn't help my case. If I remember right, his son was one of your lot, wasn't he?"

"My lot?" I asked, frowning. "What lot are my lot?"

"A gay."

"Julian?" I said, almost laughing at the absurdity of the idea. "No, he wasn't at all. He was one hundred percent straight."

"That's not what I heard. Didn't he get . . . you know . . ." He leaned forward and whispered. "The AIDS."

"It's just called AIDS," I said. "Not *the* AIDS. And you don't have to say *a* gay either."

"Well, whatever it's called, that's what he died of, isn't it?"

"Yes," I said.

"So I was right," he said, sitting back and smiling. "He was a gay."

"He wasn't," I insisted, thinking how furious Julian would be if he could overhear this conversation. "Anyone can get AIDS, regardless of their sexual persuasion. Not that it matters anymore anyway. He's gone too."

"There are two chaps in here with the HIV," said Charles, looking around as he lowered his voice again. "They're kept away in solitary confinement, of course, although once in a while they're allowed out for a game of table tennis with each other while the rest of us are in lockdown. The guards wash down the bats with disinfectant afterward. Say nothing to no one."

"I won't breathe a word," I said. "But we were talking about tax, remember? And your inability to pay it."

"I do think it's very unfair what they've done to me," he said, frowning. "After all, this time it was an honest mistake."

"I heard it was two million honest mistakes," I said.

"Yes, something around that number. But correct me if I'm wrong, there's a little thing called the Artists' Exemption in this country. Writers are not required to pay tax on their earnings. Thank you, Mr. Haughey, you generous patron of the arts."

"That's true," I said, for it was a law that had been of great benefit to Ignac since his novels had become successful. "But here's the thing, Charles. You're not actually a writer."

"No, but most of my income comes from artistic earnings. Do you know how many books Maude has sold around the world now?"

"Last time I heard it was around twenty million."

"Twenty-two million," he said triumphantly. "No, don't congratulate me! And she's still shifting around a million every year, God bless her."

"But just because her estate was left to you doesn't mean that you can claim the tax exemption for yourself. That was explained to you at the trial, although I would have thought that it would have been obvious in the first place."

"But that's grossly unfair, don't you think? The Man from the Revenue has always resented my success."

"But it wasn't your success," I insisted. "It was Maude's. And to be fair, you had an excellent income as it was without having to cheat the system."

He shrugged. "Oh well," he said. "It doesn't matter too much, I suppose. I paid back what I owed and I still have a fortune in the bank and it just keeps flooding in. Maybe I'll pay a little next year. I'll see how I feel. Thank God for universities, am I right? Every single one of them seems to teach her books. Except the Canadians. What's that about, do you think? Why don't the Canadians like Maude's work?"

"I couldn't tell you," I said.

"Funny people. Try to find out, would you? You still work at the Department of Education, don't you? There must be some sort of cross-cultural group or . . . or . . ." He trailed off, apparently uncertain how to finish the sentence.

"Charles, I haven't worked in the civil service in nearly thirty years," I said, growing a little concerned for him now.

"Haven't you? That's a very good job, you know. Pensionable. I'm sure if you went back they'd give you a second chance. What did you do wrong anyway? Hand in the cookie jar? A little slap-and-tickle with your secretary when the office door was closed?"

I sighed and glanced out the window into the courtyard, where a group of men were playing football together while others stood around the perimeter, smoking and making small talk. I watched, expecting a fight to break out as it always did in films, but nothing untoward happened. Instead, everyone seemed to be just enjoying the good weather. Very disappointing.

"How long more have you got?" I asked eventually, turning back to him.

"Only six months," he said. "It's not so bad in here really, you know. The food is actually pretty good. And my cellmate, Denzel, is a decent fellow. Held up three different post offices around the country but you should hear some of his stories!" He laughed as he recalled them. "You could put them in one of your books only he'd probably sue you for stealing his intellectual property. You know what these cons are like. All taking law degrees in their spare time."

"I don't write books, Charles," I said. "I work in the Dáil library."

"Of course you write books. You write those children's books about the time-traveling Croatian boy, don't you?"

"He's a Slovenian boy," I said. "And no, that's not me. That's Ignac."

"Who's Ignac?"

"He's . . . well, he's sort of a son to me. Sort of."

"I thought your son's name was Colm?"

"No, that's Liam."

"And he writes the books?"

"No," I said, sighing. "Ignac writes books, Liam's a student."

"Did he write that one about the woman who hated her husband so much that she visited his grave every day and pissed on the headstone?"

"No, that was Maude," I said, recalling one of the more melodramatic scenes from *Like to the Lark*.

"Oh, yes, Maude." He thought about this. "Good old Maude. She would have hated to see how popular she's grown."

"She would," I said. "But she's been gone a long time now. She never had to suffer the indignity."

"What was it she called it?" he asked. "The vulgarity of popularity?"

"That's right."

"It's a blessing then that she's gone," he said. "Although I still rather miss her sometimes. We never got along very well but, still, she wasn't a bad sort. Smoked like a chimney, of course, and I never much cared for that in a woman. She wasn't your real mother, you know. Oh wait, did you know that? Perhaps I shouldn't have said anything."

"No, I knew," I said. "I never had any confusion on that score."

"Oh good. Because you're not a real Avery, don't forget."

"Yes, I knew that too," I said, smiling.

"But I'm glad we adopted you," he added. "You're a good boy. A kind boy. You always were."

I felt a curious sensation inside myself and was unable to identify it until, on further examination, I realized that I was a little moved. This was probably the nicest thing he had ever said to me in the forty-nine years that we'd known each other.

"And you weren't a bad father," I lied. "All things considered."

"Oh I think we both know that's not true," he said, shaking his head. "I was terrible. I showed no interest in you at all. But that's just who I was. I couldn't help it. I put a roof over your head all the same, and that's something. Some men don't even do that for their children. Do you still live there, Colm?"

"It's Cyril," I said, correcting him. "And no, if you mean in the house on Dartmouth Square, then no. You lost that after you went to prison the first time, remember? Max bought it."

"Oh yes, that's right. I suppose that boy of his lives there now with his—" He made quotation marks in the air. "*Partner.*"

"No, Julian doesn't live there," I said. "I told you, Julian is dead."

"No!" he cried. "That's terrible! Wait, I remember now. He got attacked, didn't he? By a gang of some sort. They beat him up and left him for dead."

I sat up straight and closed my eyes, wondering how much more of this I would have to endure. "No," I said. "That wasn't Julian. That was Bastiaan."

"Max told me that he was dead before he even got to the hospital."

"Max didn't tell you that," I said. "I did. And anyway, that wasn't Julian," I repeated. "That was Bastiaan."

"Who's Bastiaan?"

"It doesn't matter," I said, shaking my head, even though it did matter. It mattered a great deal. "Look, Charles, I'm getting a little worried about you. Have you seen a doctor?"

"Not lately, no. Why do you ask?"

"You seem a little . . . confused, that's all."

"I'm not dementia, if that's what you mean," he said.

"You don't *have* dementia," I said. "Is that what you're trying to say?"

"I'm not dementia," he insisted, wagging a finger in my face.

"All right," I said. "You're not dementia. But look, I don't think it would do any harm for a doctor to take a look at you."

"Only if I can go to him," he said. "Or her. I hear there are some wonderful lady doctors these days. Whatever's next?" he added, laughing. "They'll be driving buses and allowed to vote if someone doesn't do something to stop them!"

"The prison isn't going to allow you out on day release to see a doctor," I said. "They'll insist that one comes here instead. Unless you need tests. And you might, you know. You might need tests."

"Well, you do whatever you think is best," he said. "The only thing that's really important to me is that when I get out of here, I can go home."

"Where are you living now anyway?" I asked, for the truth was that I didn't have any idea. Ever since his most recent divorce—his third, if my calculations were accurate, following his fifth marriage—he'd lived a rather nomadic existence.

"Where do you think?" he asked. "Dartmouth Square. The same place I've always lived. I love that house. They'll carry me out of there in a box."

"They probably won't," I told him. "Since you don't live there any-more. It's been decades since you sold it."

"Just because I don't live there," he said, "doesn't mean that I can't die there. Use your imagination, why don't you? What kind of writer are you anyway?"

"One who doesn't write," I told him.

"I refuse to die in prison like Oscar Wilde or Lester Piggott."

"Neither of whom died in prison."

"They would have if the fascists had had their way."

"Look, leave it with me, all right?" I said. "I'll figure it out. We've got six months after all."

"Unless I get out early for good behavior."

"Do me a favor, Charles," I said. "Try not to be too good, all right? Serve out your time. It'll make things a lot easier for me if you do."

"All right," he said. "I don't mind. I'll kick up a fuss over breakfast one day and that'll keep me here till the bitter end."

"Thanks," I said. "I appreciate that."

"No problem. Now, where shall we go today?"

"You'll probably stay here," I said. "Don't you have art classes on a Tuesday afternoon?"

"I stopped doing them," he said, pulling a disgusted face. "We were doing life drawing and this three-hundred-pound, morbidly obese passport forger with tattoos all over his body was posing in the nip for us. He even had the word *Mother* tattooed on his penis, which Freud would have had a field day with. It made me want to tear the eyes from my head. You'd probably have loved it, though. Or Max's son, Julian. He would have been all over that."

"Well, go back to your cell then," I said. "And maybe have a nap. You might feel better when you wake up."

"I will. I didn't sleep at all well last night. What are you going to do?"

"I don't know. I thought I might go to see a film. I was supposed to be meeting Liam but he canceled on me. Again."

"Who's Liam?"

"My son."

"I thought your son's name was Inky or something?"

"You're thinking of Ignac. He's a different son."

"Gosh, you really love the ladies, don't you?" he asked, grinning in delight. "A real chip off the old block! How many children do you have by how many different women now?"

I smiled and stood up, reaching out to shake his hand. He took it, but his grip was nowhere near as firm as it had once been.

"I'm not dementia," he told me again, quieter this time, and there was a pleading expression on his face as he said it. "I just get a little confused sometimes, that's all. It's old age. It comes to us all. It'll come to you too, you mark my words."

I said nothing, just walked away thinking how wrong he really was. Old age hadn't come for Maude. Or for Julian. Or for Bastiaan. Or for the hundreds of young men and women I'd counseled in New York at the height of the plague years. Old age didn't necessarily come for everyone at all. And I still didn't know whether it would come for me.

Two Bars

The television was broken in my apartment, so I made my way along Baggot Street toward Doheny & Nesbitt's to watch the match. There was great excitement over it, of course; once again the country was losing its collective mind and the same English players that were vilified on a Saturday afternoon when they played for Arsenal or Liverpool were now being worshipped because they found themselves in an Ireland jersey, thanks to their grandparents having got out of the country fifty years before.

The bar was as busy as I had expected it to be but after I ordered a pint I discovered a table in the corner with a good view of the screen. I leaned my crutch against the wall and, with a bit of time to kill until kick-off, took Ignac's latest Floriak Ansen novel from my pocket and picked up where I'd left off the night before. In this one, our time-traveling hero had gone back to the Ice Age and was causing mayhem among the Eskimos, who were teaching him how to drill holes in the ice to catch fish, which was no good to him at all, as he was a strict vegetarian. I was only a few pages in when the volume went up and every head in the place turned to the massive screen hanging from the ceiling. The teams were coming out onto the pitch. As the anthems played, you could see the players squinting in the sunshine of Giants Stadium and the commentator made a few remarks about the heat and how it would surely be more advantageous to the Italians than it was to the Irish, who were not accustomed to such luxuries.

Glancing over toward the bar, I noticed a couple of young lads paying for their pints and turning around in search of somewhere to park themselves for the next couple of hours. As they looked in my direction, I caught the eye of one, and he caught mine in return, and I had no choice but to point out the empty seats at my table. He glanced at his friend for a moment before whispering something in his ear and a moment later they came over and sat down.

"This is a surprise," I said, doing my best to sound friendly. "I didn't expect to run into you here."

"Me neither," said Liam. "I didn't think you'd be interested in football."

"Sure everyone is interested in it right now, aren't they?" I said. "You're considered a traitor if you go into work and can't discuss every tackle that you saw on TV the night before."

He took a sip from his pint as he looked up at the screen. "Jimmy, this is Cyril," he said after a moment to his friend, who was about the same age as him—twenty—but larger, a big bear of a lad who I could imagine charging down the rugby field at Donnybrook with a look of pure determination on his face and sinking ten pints of Guinness in Kielys afterward without blinking an eye. "He's my . . ." He seemed to struggle for the word even though there was only one legitimate way to finish the sentence. "He's my father," he conceded finally.

"Your oul' lad?" said Jimmy, clinking his glass against mine and looking at me with genuine delight on his face. "Nice to meet you, Mr. Woodbead."

"Actually, it's Avery," I said. "Although please call me Cyril. No one calls me Mr. Avery."

"Cyril?" he said. "You don't meet many of them anymore. That's one of the old names, is it?"

"I suppose so," I said. "I'm ancient."

"How old are you?"

"Forty-nine."

"Jesus, that's mad."

"Tell me about it."

"I can't even imagine being that old. Is that why you have the crutch? Have the oul' knees gone?"

"Shut up, Jimmy," said Liam.

"Here, Liam," said Jimmy, giving his friend a dig in the ribs. "Your da's the same age as my ma. Are you married, Cyril, or are you on the market? My oul' wan broke up with her fella about a month ago and she's been a fuckin' nightmare to live with ever since. Any interest in taking her out for a night on the town? An oul' pizza and a few beers, something like that? She doesn't take much lookin' after."

"Probably not," I said.

"Why not?" he asked, looking offended. "She's still a good-lookin' woman, you know. For an oul' wan."

"I'm sure she is, but I don't think we'd be right for each other."

"Do you just go for the young ones, is that it? Fair fucks to you if you can still manage to pull them."

"He's not interested in women," said Liam.

"How can he not be interested in women?" he asked. "He's still alive, isn't he? He's got a pulse? The oul' knees might be gone, but the oul' jackanory still works, doesn't it?"

"He's not interested in women," repeated Liam. "*Any* women. Think about it."

He thought about it.

"You don't mean he's a queer, do you?" He looked across at me and held his hands in the air. "No offense meant, Cyril," he added.

"None taken."

"I have no problem with the gay lads. Let them all be gay, that's what I say. All the more moths for me."

I laughed and took a drink from my pint. Even Liam turned around with a half-smile on his face, which was about all I ever got from him.

"There's a fella lives three doors down from me," continued Jimmy. "He's one of your lot. Alan Delaney's his name. Do you know him?"

"I don't," I said.

"Tall fella. Dark hair. Has a gammy eye."

"No, doesn't ring a bell," I said. "But we don't all gather together for conventions, you know."

"Why not? Would that not be a good way to meet someone?"

I thought about it; it wasn't the stupidest idea I'd ever heard.

"Nice fella, this Alan lad," he continued. "A bit of a player too. You never know who you're gonna see coming in and out of his front door in the morning. What sort of fellas do you like, if you don't mind me asking?"

"I'm not really looking for anyone at the moment," I told him. "I'm happy in my own company."

"Ah that can't be right. You're old but you're not that old. Would you like me to introduce you to Alan?"

I looked across at Liam, hoping for a little support, but he seemed amused by both the exchange and my discomfort and happy for it to continue.

"Give us your number, Cyril," said Jimmy. "Write it down on a beer mat there and I'll make sure he gets it."

"There's really no—"

"Give us your number," he insisted. "I'm good at this sort of thing. Matchmaking and the like."

I took a beer mat and wrote a random number on it and handed it across; it seemed the easiest way to end this.

"Now, if you end up getting the oul' shift off Alan Delaney, you have me to thank, Cyril," he said, putting it in his pocket. "And you can stand me a pint another time."

"I will so," I said.

"So has it always been fellas for you?" he asked.

"Jesus Christ," said Liam, shaking his head. "Is this going to go on all night?"

"I'm only asking," said Jimmy. "I have a deep interest in human sexuality."

"You do on your hole."

"Yes," I said. "It's always been fellas."

"Still and all, you must have been into the women once. To produce this fine figure of masculinity, I mean."

"Just leave it, will you?" said Liam. "Watch the match."

"It hasn't started yet."

"Then watch the ads and shut up."

"Ads are for talking through, everyone knows that." He took a breather for a minute or two, then came back with this: "So was Liam's mother the only woman you ever did it with?"

I noticed Liam glance over, as if he was interested in the answer to this question himself.

"Yes," I said, uncertain why I was revealing so much of myself to a perfect stranger, other than the fact that his questions seemed entirely guileless. "The only one."

"Fuck me," said Jimmy. "I can't imagine that. I'm nearly at double digits."

"Five is not nearly double digits," said Liam.

"Fuck you!" roared Jimmy. "It's six."

"Blowjobs don't count."

"They fuckin' do. Anyway, five is still two better than you, ya skinny fuck."

I looked away; I wanted to know more about my son but not necessarily this much.

"So how come you two don't have the same surname?" asked Jimmy after a pause when I managed to catch the barman's eye and three more pints arrived at our table.

"What's that?" I said.

"You and Liam. He's a Woodbead and you're an Avery. I don't get it."

"Oh right. Well, Liam uses his mother's surname," I explained.

"My uncle's, actually," added Liam. "My Uncle Julian was like a father to me growing up."

I took the blow with the force with which it was intended and said nothing as Jimmy glanced back and forth between the pair of us with a wide smile, as if he couldn't understand whether this was some form of teasing that we enjoyed or if it was something more serious.

"Was this Julian lad your brother?" asked Jimmy, looking at me.

"No," I said. "He was Liam's mother's older brother. He died some years ago now."

"Oh right," he said, lowering his voice a little. "I'm sorry to hear that."

"I loved him very much," said Liam, in an uncharacteristic show of emotion on his part that was clearly directed more at me than his friend.

"Kick-off," said Jimmy, nodding toward the screen, where the ball was now in play and both sides were moving around the pitch, starting tentatively enough. A few of the customers at the bar were roaring encouragement at the players but it seemed a little early for anyone to be getting too dramatic and after a few minutes they quieted down.

"So how do you pair know each other?" I asked, and Liam shook his head as if he couldn't be bothered to reply to such a tedious question, leaving Jimmy to answer.

"We're in Trinity together," he said.

"Are you studying History of Art too?"

"Jesus, no. I'm studying Business. Some of us want to make money, Cyril. I want a big house, a fast car and a Jacuzzi full of revolting birds."

"Do you mean revolving?" I asked.

"Oh, yeah. That. Do you wanna know what my big goal in life is?"

"Wait till you hear this," said Liam.

"Go on so."

"I want to buy a house on Vico Road next to Bono."

"Why?" I asked.

"Why not? Can you imagine the parties we'd be having? I'd be looking over the fence and saying, *Here, Bono, ya ponce, why don't you and Madonna and Bruce and Kylie come over here and we'll all jump in the Jacuzzi and have an oul' laugh?* And Bono will be like, *Give us five minutes, Jimmy, and we'll all be over.* Do you know Salman Rushdie used to live in the shed at the end of Bono's garden?"

"I didn't," I said. "Is that true?"

"That's what I heard. During the . . . what do you call it?"

"The fatwa?"

"That's the one. Oul' Salman was down in the shed with the lawnmower writing his books and oul' Bono was up in the house cleaning his sunglasses, and I suppose they got together once in a while for a game of chess or whatever."

The Italians got a shot on target and the place erupted in dismay and then relief when it cleared the top of the goal. Watching the two boys react in the exact same way that everyone else in the pub did, I wondered whether they might have more in common than I realized, for in the short space of our acquaintance they seemed completely different types to me.

"I wouldn't have thought there'd be too much fraternization between the business lads and the arts lads," I said finally.

"Why not?" asked Liam, looking at me as if he could scarcely imagine a more idiotic remark.

"Different types of people, I suppose."

"I don't see why."

"We're only friends because your son here stole a girlfriend from me and then some wanker from Sociology stole her off him," said Jimmy. "And we bonded, as they say, over our mutual indignation."

"Fair enough," I said, laughing.

"Sociology students are the worst," he continued. "Bunch of fuckin' knobs. What kind of plank wants to become a sociologist anyway? It doesn't even mean anything. What the fuck are you supposed to do with a Sociology degree?"

"He didn't steal her off me," said Liam grumpily. "And I didn't steal her off you. She's a twenty-year-old woman, not a piece of chattel."

"She's a slutbag is what she is," said Jimmy, shaking his head. "A dirty little slutbag who's working her way through the lads in Trinity like shit through a goose." He seemed more incensed over the break-up than Liam did and I wondered whether this was typical of my son's approach to girls. I didn't want him to be as useless with relationships as I had been at the same age but nor did I want him to be as cavalier as his uncle. As role models, I felt that both Julian and I had failed him.

Liam and I hadn't met in the immediate wake of Julian's death, which probably should have been how we entered each other's lives. And although I could hardly be held accountable under the circumstances, I regretted that I hadn't been able to fulfill his uncle's last wish of me—that I would be the one to call Alice and tell her that her brother had died. I would have done it as soon as Bastiaan and I had got back to our apartment that night but of course we never made it there, and around the time that I was being rushed into surgery, a nervous Garda was arriving at the house on Dartmouth Square to deliver the news himself. When I emerged from my coma a few weeks later to find Ignac sitting by my bed ready to deliver bad news of his own—that Bastiaan was not only dead but that his body had been returned to Holland, where Arjan and Edda had given him a private burial without me—I could scarcely give any thought to my promise, so consumed was I by depression and grief. Ironically, around the same time, Ignac broke up with Emily, whose lack of compassion in the face of a family tragedy had been enough to turn him off her once and for all. Every cloud, as they say.

In the end, I waited several years, until I had recuperated, until the trial had come to an end, until I had returned to Dublin, to contact Alice, writing her a long letter to explain how sorry I was for the way that I had treated her all those years before. I told her how circumstances had found me in the same place as Julian in New York during the last week of his life and how I had been with him when he died. I wasn't sure if this would provide any comfort to her but I hoped that it would. And then, finally, I mentioned that, perhaps without meaning to, Julian had let slip to me that our one night of intimacy had resulted in a child. I understood why she'd never told me, I said, but I would like to meet our son if she agreed.

Not surprisingly, it took her several weeks to reply. The letter I eventually received sounded as if it had been written and rewritten many times before she'd committed to a final draft, and the tone in which she wrote was one of utter detachment, as if it had taken a great effort on her part even to remember who I was, which was, of course, impossible considering we were technically still married and had a child together. She told me that Liam had asked about me over the years, that he'd shown a natural interest in the identity of his father, and that she'd told him the truth: that I had left her on our wedding day, humiliating her in front of all her friends and family, but that she had said nothing to him about what she called my "tendencies." *I didn't want to inflict that on him,* she wrote. *It was hard enough for him growing up without a father without his having to deal with that too.*

She added that she was uncertain about my meeting him and would prefer to discuss the matter in person, and so one Wednesday evening after work, anxious and uncertain how the encounter might go, I met my wife of nearly twenty years in the Duke public house, laying eyes on her for the first time since our wedding day.

"There you are at last," she said when she walked in, fifteen minutes late, and found me sitting in the corner with a pint of lager and a copy of that day's *Irish Times.* "I thought you said you'd be back down in a few minutes?"

I smiled; it was a good line. She looked incredibly beautiful, her long dark hair now shoulder-length and her eyes glowing with as much intelligence and wit as they ever had.

"Sorry, I got a little sidetracked," I told her. "Can I get you a drink, Alice?"

"A glass of white wine. Large."

"Any particular kind?"

"The most expensive that they have."

I nodded and made my way to the bar. When I brought it back to the table, she had taken my seat by the wall, giving her a view of the room and demoting me to the stool opposite her. My drink and newspaper had been moved too.

"Your hair's a lot thinner than it used to be," she said, taking a sip from her drink and ignoring my attempt to clink glasses. "You've not exactly gone to seed but you could stand to lose a few pounds. Do you exercise much?"

"It's not that easy," I said, nodding toward my crutch, which she must have overlooked, and she had the good grace to look a little abashed.

"We should have gone to the Horseshoe Bar really, shouldn't we?" she said. "Picked up where we left off? The last time I saw you was in there. You were working the room and looked as happy as I'd ever seen you."

"Did I?" I asked, doubting this. "Really?"

"Yes, you did."

"OK."

"And then I never saw you again."

A long silence.

"Well, at least I made it up the aisle that day," she continued finally. "The previous time I didn't even get that far. It was what I liked to think of as *progress*. My hope is that next time around I'll get to the end of the honeymoon."

"I don't know what to say to you, Alice," I said, unable to meet her eye. "I really don't. I'm extremely ashamed of what I did to you. It was cowardly and cruel and heartless."

"That's putting it mildly."

"The man you're talking to," I replied, choosing my words carefully. "The man you're talking to is not the man who walked out of the Shelbourne all those years ago."

"Isn't he? Because he sure as hell looks like him. Only less attractive. And you didn't walk, you ran."

"I can't excuse my actions," I continued. "And nor can I atone for what I did to you, but I am able to look back now, all these years later, and see how my life was always going to reach a moment where I would have to face up to who I was. Who I am. Of course, I should have done it long before, and I certainly should never have dragged you into my problems, but I didn't have the courage or maturity to be honest with myself, let alone with anyone else. But on the other hand, my life is my life. And I am who I am because of what I went through back then. I couldn't have behaved any differently, even if I'd wanted to."

"Do you know," she said, her tone hardening now, "I never thought I'd lay eyes on you again, Cyril. I really didn't. And if I'm honest, I hoped that I never would."

"I'm assuming that there's nothing I can say to make any of it better?"

"You assume correctly."

"You have to understand that—"

"Just stop," she said, putting her glass down loudly on the table. "Just stop, all right? I'm not here to rehash the past. I've put it behind me. That's not what we're here to talk about."

"Well, you started it," I said irritably.

"Can you blame me? I think I have the right to a little anger."

"I'm just trying to explain, that's all. If you knew what it was like growing up gay in Ireland in the fifties and sixties—"

"I'm not interested in any of that," said Alice, waving this away. "I'm not a political person."

"It's not politics," I said. "It's about society and bigotry and—"

"You think you had a terrible time of it, don't you?"

"Yes. I do."

"And yet if you'd only been honest with everyone from the start—with Julian, with me—then all of this trouble and heartbreak could have been avoided. Not just mine, but yours too. I don't doubt that you had difficult times, Cyril. I don't doubt that you suffered the unfairness of your condition—"

"It's not a condition—"

"But my brother was your best friend. And isn't that what best friends are for? Confiding in?"

"He wouldn't have understood," I said.

"He would have if you'd told him."

"I *did* tell him."

"You told him five minutes before you were due to marry me!" she said, laughing out loud. "That wasn't telling him. That was trying to sabotage the marriage so he'd give you permission to walk away. Which you still could have done then, by the way. You could have simply made a run for it, like Fergus did."

"How could I have done that?" I said lamely. "It would have been history repeating itself."

"Do you think what you did was any better?"

"No, of course not."

"It was worse by far. Look, I hated Fergus for what he did to me but at least he had the guts not to go through with something that he didn't think was right for him. You couldn't even do that."

"So I'm worse than he is?" I asked, surprised by the comparison, for in my arrogance I had always believed that he had behaved badly while I had my reasons for what I had done.

"Yes. You are. Because I gave you an out."

"What?" I asked, frowning at her.

"You must remember. We were out for a drink and I knew there was something wrong, I just didn't know what. I was too naïve to guess. Nowadays it would be obvious, I suppose. *Whatever it is, just tell me*—that's what I said to you. *I promise that it will be all right.* If you had told me—"

"I tried to tell you," I said quickly. "Several times. The first night we met, as adults I mean, I thought I could tell you."

"What?" she asked, dumbfounded by this. "When?"

"The night Julian was going off traveling with those Finnish twins. I was about to tell you and—"

"What are you talking about?" she cried. "That was before we even started dating!"

"I was about to tell you," I repeated. "Only we got interrupted by your brother. And then another time, over dinner, the words nearly came out but something inside me wouldn't let them. And even a few weeks before the wedding, we were in a bar together and a man came over to ask for your phone number. I was about to tell you but suddenly he was standing there, talking to you, and when he'd gone the moment seemed to have passed and—"

"Christ, you're such a shit, do you know that?" said Alice. "You were a shit back then and I can see that you're a total shit still. A selfish, arrogant, conceited shit who thinks the world has done you such a bad turn that you can do whatever you like to get back at it. No matter who you hurt. And you wonder why I didn't tell you about Liam?"

"If it's any consolation, my life after I left you wasn't easy. It got better for a while but eventually—"

"Cyril," she said, interrupting me. "I'm sorry, but I really don't care. I have no problem with your way of life, I really don't. As it happens, I have several gay friends."

"Well, good for you," I said petulantly.

"The point is that this has got nothing to do with your being gay," she said, leaning forward and looking me directly in the eye. "It has to do with you being dishonest. Can't you see that? Anyway, I have absolutely no interest whatsoever in discussing this with you, do you understand me? I don't want to know what you've been through since you left Dublin or whom you've been with or what your life has been like. I don't want to know anything at all. I just want to know what you want from me."

"I don't want anything from you," I said, keeping my voice low in order to show her that I was not looking for an argument. "But now that you mention it, I suppose I'm a little surprised that you had a child by me and never bothered to let me know."

"It's not like I didn't try," she said. "That afternoon, when we were in the Shelbourne, I told you over and over that I needed to talk to you in private. I even phoned you when you were upstairs in the room and told you to wait there for me."

"How was I to know that's what you wanted to talk about? No, once I was gone you could have—"

"And how would I have contacted you, even if I'd wanted to?" she asked. "I don't remember you leaving a forwarding address with the concierge as you ran screaming out of the hotel."

"All right," I said. "But there were plenty of people who probably could have tracked me down if you'd really wanted to. Charles, for example."

She softened a little at his name. "Dear Charles," she said, her expression filling with warmth.

"I'm sorry?"

"Charles was very good to me. Afterward, I mean."

"No, I meant my adoptive father, Charles," I said. "Why, who are you talking about?"

"That's who I'm talking about."

"*Charles* was very good to you? Charles Avery? Are you kidding me?"

"No," she said. "The poor man was absolutely mortified by what you'd done. He kept apologizing to people on your behalf and telling me over and over how you weren't a real Avery, not that I cared much about that at the time, but even afterward, over the weeks and months ahead, he stayed in touch, making sure that I never wanted for anything."

"I'm astonished," I said after a lengthy pause as I tried to digest this. "I don't have any major issues with the man, but he's never shown a moment's compassion or consideration toward me in my lifetime."

"And did you ever show any toward him?" she asked.

"I was just a child," I told her. "And he and Maude barely noticed me."

She laughed bitterly and shook her head. "You'll forgive me if I find that rather hard to believe," she said. "Anyway, I was sorry to read in the papers that he's back in prison. It's been years since I've spoken to him, but if you're in touch please pass on my good wishes. I'll always be grateful to him for how he behaved in the couple of years after you did your disappearing act."

"As it happens, I saw him not so long ago," I told her. "He's only got a few months left in Mountjoy. He'll be out soon enough to cheat The Man from the Revenue yet again."

"He's too old to be in there," she said. "They should let him out on compassionate grounds. A man with that much kindness inside him deserves better."

I said nothing but ordered a couple more drinks from a passing bar boy, finding it almost impossible to reconcile the Charles in whose house I had grown up with the Charles that she described.

"I suppose you're right, though," she said eventually. "I could have found you if I'd wanted to. But what would have been the point? Julian told me what happened in the sacristy that morning. He told me who you were, all the things that you'd done, all the men that you'd been with. What would have been the point of me going looking for you? To have some type of sham marriage with a homosexual? I'd like to think I'm worth more than that."

"Of course you are. I don't know what else I can say."

"If you had just *told* me. If you had just been *honest*—"

"I was very young, Alice. I didn't know what I was doing."

"We were all young," she said. "But we're not so young anymore though, are we? You're on a crutch, for God's sake. What's that about?"

I shook my head, not wanting to get into it with her. "I had an accident," I said. "My leg never healed. Anyway, did you meet anyone else? I hope you did."

"Oh that's very good of you."

"I mean it."

"Of course I met other people," she said. "I'm not a nun. Do you think I was sitting at home every night mooning over you?"

"Well, I'm glad to hear it."

"I wouldn't get too excited if I was you. Nothing ever came of any of them. How could it have? I was a married woman with a child and a missing husband. And it's not as if I could get a divorce in this god-forsaken backwater of a country. And so no man would ever stay with me. Why should he when I couldn't give him a family of his own? You stole that whole part of life from me, Cyril, I hope you realize that."

"I do," I said. "I do. And if I could go back in time and change things, I would."

"Let's stop talking about this," she said. "We both know where we stand on it. I need to know something else." She hesitated now and I could see her expression grow more anxious than angry. "When

Julian was dying," she said, "why didn't you get in touch? Why didn't you tell me? I would have been out to New York in a heartbeat if I'd known."

I looked down at the table and picked up a beer mat, trying to balance it on one corner as I thought of an answer. "To begin with, there was very little time," I told her. "I only found out that he was in the hospital a few days before he died. That was the first time I saw him. And the second time was the night he passed away."

"But that doesn't make sense. What were you even doing there?"

"My partner was a doctor in Mount Sinai. He was treating Julian. I was a volunteer. I visited patients with no families."

"Julian *had* a family."

"I mean patients who, for whatever reason, had no family present. Some had been disowned by their families. And some didn't want their families there. Julian was in the latter group."

"But why? Why didn't he want me with him? And Liam? They were so close."

"Because he was ashamed," I said. "He had no reason to be, but he was ashamed of the disease that he'd developed."

"Of AIDS?"

"Yes, of AIDS. For someone like Julian, who had practically been defined by his heterosexuality, it was an insult to mind and body. It's not how he wanted you or Liam to remember him."

"You said in your letter that you were with him on that last night."

"I was, yes."

"Was he in pain?"

I shook my head. "Not by then," I said. "He was drifting away, that was all. He was on a lot of morphine. I don't think he suffered at the end. I held him as he died."

She looked across at me, startled, and put a hand to her mouth.

"He said your name, Alice. Your name was the last word he spoke."

"I loved him so much," she said quietly, looking away. "From the time we were children, he always looked out for me. He was the best friend I ever had. And I don't say this to be cruel, Cyril, but he was so good with Liam. Our son couldn't have wished for a better father figure. He's still not over it, you know. Well, neither am I, really. I never will be. But Liam is suffering very badly."

"Can we . . ." I began, unsure what was the best way to phrase this. "Can we talk about Liam?"

"I suppose we have to. That's why we're here after all."

"Not the only reason," I said.

"No."

"Do you have a picture of him?"

She thought about it for a moment and reached into her handbag, taking a photograph from one of the side pockets and handing it across to me.

"He looks like him, doesn't he?" she asked quietly, and I nodded.

"He looks like how he looked when we were teenagers. They're very alike. But there's someone else there too."

"Who?"

I frowned, shaking my head. "I'm not sure," I said. "There's something in his expression that reminds me of someone, but for the life of me I can't think who."

"He isn't like Julian in temperament, though. Liam is much more quiet. More reserved. Almost shy."

"Do you think he'd be interested in meeting me? Would you allow it?"

"No," she said firmly. "At least, not until he's eighteen. And I'd ask you to respect my wishes. He has his exams coming up and I don't want anymore trauma in his life right now. He'll be eighteen in a year's time and you can see him then."

"But—"

"Please don't argue with me, Cyril."

"But I want to see him."

"And you can. When he's eighteen. But not a day before. Tell me you won't go behind my back on this. You owe me that much at least."

I took a deep breath. She was right, of course. "All right," I said.

"And there's one other thing," she said.

"Go on."

"When you meet him, from the first day that the two of you talk, you have to be completely honest with him. No lies. You have to tell him who you are. You have to tell him everything about yourself."

Which is what I did. One year later, ten days after his eighteenth birthday, when Alice introduced us for the first time and we went for a walk along Dun Laoghaire pier together and I told him the story of my life from the day that I had come downstairs in the house on Dartmouth Square, the house in which he now lived, to find his Uncle Julian sitting in the hallway, through to the world that had slowly unfolded for me and the realizations I had had about myself. I talked to him about why I had married his mother, why I had left her and how badly I felt about what I had done. I talked about my life in Amsterdam and New York, about Ignac and Bastiaan. About how he had been killed by a group of thugs who had seen us embracing in Central Park and how nothing had ever seemed quite as bright for me since. And through it all he listened and barely spoke and seemed shocked at times, embarrassed at others, and finally, when we parted, I went to shake his hand, but he refused it and walked off to catch the DART back into town.

In the two years between then and now he had thawed a little toward me and we saw each other occasionally, but there was still nothing like the affection or love that I imagined should exist between a father and son, and while he didn't seem to want me to leave his life—he never picked a fight, for example, or attacked me for not being a part of his childhood—he seemed unwilling at the same time to allow me to involve myself in it either, appearing distrustful of me on the occasions that we met, which were few and far between.

But then this, I told myself, was the bed that I had made for myself. There was no one else that I could blame.

"Goal!" roared Jimmy and Liam together in the eleventh minute as Ray Houghton hit a shot past the head of Pagliuca and the ball landed in the top right corner of the net. The whole of Doheny & Nesbitt's exploded in cheers, pints were knocked over left, right and center and there was much hugging and dancing around. The two boys embraced each other, jumping up and down in delight, but I stayed where I was, smiling and applauding, feeling unable to rise to my feet and behave as others were doing and not just because I would have looked ridiculous with my crutch.

"We're going to win this," said Jimmy, practically hovering off the stool in delight. "The Italians are too cocky by half."

"Will you be going on celebrating somewhere if we do?" I asked, and Liam turned to look at me.

"We will," he said. "But you can't come with us. We'll be out with our uni friends."

"I never asked to come with you," I said. "I was only asking, that's all."

"And I was only saying."

"All right."

And we left it at that and turned our attention back to the screen. The players were coming to the sidelines now and asking for bottles of water. The heat was too much for them. There was war on the pitch, Jack Charlton running on and complaining to the referee, substitutes pacing up and down in frustration. It looked as if the thing was going to end badly for everyone.

Date Night

I had given no thought to romance since Bastiaan's death and so it came as something of a surprise to me when I got asked out on a date. The man in question—fifteen years younger than me and quite attractive, which did my ego no harm whatsoever—was a TD in Dáil Éireann and a regular user of the library, unlike most of his colleagues, who generally sent their assistants down to do their donkey work for them. He'd always been quite talkative and friendly but I had put this down to an affable temperament on his part until the afternoon when he inquired whether I was doing anything that Thursday night.

"Nothing that I know of," I said. "Why, do you need to use the library late?"

"Oh Christ, no," he said, shaking his head and looking at me as if I was half mad. "Nothing like that. I just wondered whether I could tempt you out for a drink, that's all."

"A drink?" I asked, unsure whether I had heard him correctly. "How do you mean?"

"You know. Two people sitting down in a bar. Having a couple of pints and a chat. You do drink, don't you?"

"I do, yes," I said. "I mean, not to excess but—"

"So how about it?"

"Do you mean just the two of us?"

"Jesus, Cyril. I feel like I'm negotiating an EEC treaty here. Yes, just the two of us."

"Oh. All right then. Where were you thinking of?"

"Somewhere discreet," he said.

"What does that mean?" I asked, and perhaps that should have been my first clue that our night out together would not end well.

"Do you know the Yellow House in Rathfarnham?" he asked.

"I do," I said. "I haven't been there in years. Would somewhere in the city center not be easier?"

"Let's go to the Yellow House," he said. "Thursday night. Eight o'clock."

"No, that's the night of Mrs. Goggin's retirement party."

"Who?" he asked.

"Mrs. Goggin from the tearoom. She's retiring after almost fifty years here."

He looked a little blank. "So what?" he said. "You're not planning on going along, are you?"

"Of course I am."

"Why?"

"Because, like I just told you, she's retiring after almost—"

"Yeah, yeah." He thought about it. "Do you think I should go too?"

"How do you mean?"

"Well, would it mean a lot to her if I showed my face?"

I stared at him, trying to decipher his meaning. "Because you're a TD?" I asked. "Is that what you're getting at?"

"Yes."

I shook my head. "I honestly don't think she'll care one way or the other."

"I'd say she would," he said, looking half-offended.

"Well, I'm going anyway, so Thursday's out."

"*Fine,*" he said with a dramatic sigh, as if he was a frustrated teenager and not a grown man. "Friday night then. No, wait, I can't do Friday night. Constituency dinner. And weekends are out for obvious reasons. How's Monday?"

"Monday's good," I said, unsure what the obvious reasons were. "Will we just go from here? When I lock up the library?"

"No. Let's meet there."

"What, at the Yellow House?"

"Yes."

"But if we're both going to be in the Dáil, wouldn't it be easier if we—"

"I don't know what Monday might have in store," he said. "It'll be easier if we just meet there."

"All right."

In the intervening days, I gave a lot of thought to what I might wear. The truth was that I had no real idea what I was letting myself in for. I had long guessed that the man was gay but he was so much younger than me that I couldn't quite believe that he would be interested in someone my age. At the retirement party, I confided my dilemma to Mrs. Goggin, who seemed delighted by my quandary.

"Good for you," she said. "I'm delighted for you, Cyril. You're far too young to be giving up on meeting someone new."

"I don't really see it like that," I told her. "And I'm not lonely. I know that's what lonely people generally say but I'm really not. I'm happy with my life just the way it is."

"Who was it anyway?" she asked. "Which TD?"

I told her his name.

"Oh," she said, her face falling a little.

"What?"

"Nothing."

"No, go on, tell me."

"I don't want to put you off him."

"I'm not particularly *on* him. It's just a date."

"Well, he just seems like a sneaky sort to me," she said. "He strolls in here as if he owns the place and tries to sit at the tables with the ministers without going through me first. The swagger on him and him only in the place a wet weekend! I've thought about putting him out a few times. I learned long ago from Mrs. Hennessy—she was the woman who hired me back in the forties—that if I didn't put my foot down with the TDs from the start, they'd use their country boots to walk all over me. And I've put that advice to good use ever since."

"You ran a tight ship here, that's for sure."

"I had to. You'd see less bad behavior in a kindergarten."

"So you don't think I should go?"

"I didn't say that. Just be careful of him, that's my advice to you. I remember you told me that you lost your . . . your friend some years ago."

"I did, yes," I said. "Bastiaan. And to be honest, in the seven years since then I've never had any great longing for sex or a partner. Sorry, you don't mind me being so blunt, do you?"

"Go ahead," she said. "Remember, I brought tea up to Charlie Haughey's office for thirty years, so I've seen and heard a lot worse."

"I suppose I've felt for a long time that that side of my life is over," I said.

"And do you want it to be?"

I had to think about it. "I don't know," I said. "It's never brought me anything but torment. Well, at least until I met Bastiaan anyway. I don't think I can start over with someone new. But maybe there's a little fire still inside me somewhere. Which is why I'm fretting about the whole thing. But anyway, I shouldn't be talking about this tonight. It's *your* night. You have a great turnout all the same."

Our heads turned in unison to look around the room. Practically everyone who worked in the Dáil had shown up and the Taoiseach, Albert Reynolds, had given a good speech earlier. My TD friend had popped his head in for twenty minutes but, despite standing quite close to me at one point, had completely ignored me, even when I said hello.

"I do," she said, sounding pleased. "I'll miss the place. Would you believe I haven't had a single sick day in forty-nine years?"

"Albert said that earlier. I thought he was making it up."

"It's as true as I'm sitting here."

"So what will you do?" I asked. "Is there a Mr. Goggin somewhere who'll be happy to have you at home for a change?"

She shook her head. "There isn't," she said. "There was never a Mr. Goggin. A long time ago, a priest stood on the altar of a church in West Cork and told me that I'd never find a husband. I thought he was just being a sanctimonious old prig, but as it turns out he was right. Sure I even had to pretend that I was a widow to get the job here."

"Why?" I asked.

"Different times," she said. She took a deep breath and looked around to make sure we weren't being overheard. "I was about to have a baby, you see. So I said my husband had been killed in the war.

Mrs. Hennessy knew the truth but if anyone else had found out I'd have been out the door in a flash."

"Bunch of charmers, aren't they?" I said. "The priests."

"I've never set any store by them," she told me. "Not since that day. Anyway, I've done well enough all these years without a husband."

"And your son?" I asked. "How is he doing?"

"My son?" she asked, her smile fading a little.

"Jonathan, isn't it?"

"Oh Jonathan. Sorry, I . . . Yes, he's grand. Well, he was a little sick over the last year or so, but he's better now. He has a couple of kids of his own, so I'll be able to help out a little more there now that my time will be my own. I'm looking forward to that at least."

Before she could say anymore, one of the girls from the tearoom came over and interrupted us, asking Mrs. Goggin whether she would come over and join them all for a photograph.

"Oh, I take a terrible photograph," she said. "I always end up looking angry in them."

"We need one for the wall," insisted the girl. "After all your years of service. Come on, Mrs. Goggin, we'll all be in it with you."

She sighed and stood up, nodding her head. "All right," she said. "One last duty before I'm set free. And look, you should go on that date, Cyril," she added, turning back to me. "But just be careful of that fella. That's all I'm saying."

"I will," I said. "And good luck to you in your retirement if I don't see you later."

To my surprise, she reached down and kissed me on the cheek and gave me a curious look before the young girl dragged her away.

A few days later, I arrived as planned in the Yellow House and found my date sitting in a corner with his back to the room as if he didn't want anyone to notice him.

"Andrew," I said, taking the seat opposite him with a full view of the room. "I almost missed you there. It's like you're hiding away from the world."

"Not at all," he replied, laughing and ordering me a drink from one of the lads passing by. "How are you, Cyril? How was work today?"

"Grand," I said, which led to the usual exchange of pleasantries for twenty minutes or so before I decided to get to the heart of things.

"Can I just ask?" I said. "And forgive me if this sounds ridiculous, but I was a little surprised when you invited me out in the first place. Is this just a friendship thing or is it something else?"

"It can be anything we want it to be," he replied with a shrug. "We're grown men, after all. And we've always got along, haven't we?"

"That's true," I said. "You do know that I'm gay, right?"

"Of course I do," he said. "I wouldn't have asked you out otherwise."

"Oh right," I said. "So you're gay too then? I wasn't sure. I assumed but—"

"Here's the thing, Cyril," he said, leaning in a little. "I'm not really comfortable with labels, you know? They're so defining."

"Well, yes," I agreed. "I mean, that is what labels do, by their nature. They define things."

"Exactly. And it's 1994, not the fifties. I feel like we should be past all that type of thing by now."

"I suppose," I said. "Sorry, what do you mean? What type of thing?"

"Labels."

"Oh right. OK."

"Anyway, tell me about you," he said. "Are you married or anything?"

"No," I said, deciding not to get into the technicalities of the completely honest answer. "Why would I be married? I just told you, I'm gay."

"Well, that doesn't mean anything. You work in the Dáil, for Christ's sake. Throw a stick, as they say."

"I suppose I've heard the odd rumor," I admitted.

"So if you're not married, are you seeing anyone right now?"

"No one special."

"Anyone who isn't special?"

"Actually, no," I said, shaking my head. "I'm not seeing anyone at all. And I haven't in a long time. I was with someone for many years, but he died in 1987."

"Oh right," he said, pulling back a little. "I'm sorry to hear that. Do you mind if I ask how he died?"

"We were both attacked in Central Park," I explained. "I survived. He didn't. The crutch is what I was left with."

"I'm sorry," he repeated, and now he leaned back in, a gesture whose meaning was all too obvious to me.

"It's all right," I said. "I miss him, of course. A great deal. We should have had a long future together yet and that was stolen from us. But I've come to terms with it. Life happens and death happens. Do you know something?" I added, a thought coming into my head. "I've just realized that I'm forty-nine years old and yet this is the first time I've ever gone on a date in Ireland with another man."

He frowned a little and took a long drink from his beer. "You're in your fifties?" he asked. "I thought you were younger than that."

I stared at him, wondering whether he was a little hard of hearing. "No," I said. "I'm forty-nine. I just said."

"Yes, but you don't mean that you're *really* forty-nine, do you?"

"What else would I mean?"

"Jesus, you've been off the dating scene quite a while, haven't you? The thing is, most men looking for other men claim to be younger than they really are. Especially older men. If you meet a man from a personal ad and he says he's in his late thirties, that means he's pushing fifty and thinks he can get away with thirty-nine. Delusional, most of them, but you know. Whatever. When you said you're forty-nine, I assumed that meant you were mid to late fifties in real life."

"No," I said, shaking my head. "I really am forty-nine. I was born a few months after the war ended."

"Which war?"

"The Second World War."

"Oh, that one."

"Well, not the First."

"No. Obviously not. You'd be, like, a hundred then."

"Well, not quite."

"Close enough."

"Do you meet a lot of people from personal ads?" I asked, wondering how he had done in history at school.

"From time to time," he said. "I met a lad a couple of weeks ago, he said he was nineteen but when he showed up he was almost my own age. He was wearing a Blondie T-shirt, for Christ's sake."

"I used to have one of those," I said. "But why would you want to meet someone who you thought was nineteen anyway?"

"Why wouldn't I?" he said, laughing. "I'm not too old for a nineteen-year-old."

"Well, I suppose that's a matter of opinion. But what would you have in common with a boy that age?"

"We don't need to have anything in common. It wasn't his conversational skills that I was after."

I nodded, feeling a little uncomfortable. "Anyway, it just seems surprising to me, that's all," I said. "If you're attracted to younger men, then why did you ask me out?"

"Because I'm attracted to you too. I'm attracted to lots of people."

"OK," I said, trying to process this and wishing for all the world that Bastiaan was sitting across from me drinking a beer and not this tosser.

"So how old are you?" I asked finally.

"Thirty-four."

"So does that mean you're really thirty-four?"

"It does. But I'm twenty-eight when I meet people."

"You're meeting me right now."

"Yes, but that's different. You're older. So I can be my own age."

"Right. And have you had many relationships?"

"Relationships? No," he said, with a shrug. "That's not really where my focus has been over the last ten years or so."

"Where has your focus been?"

"Look, I'm a normal guy, Cyril. I like getting laid."

"Fair enough."

"Don't you like getting laid?"

"Of course. I mean I did. Once."

"When was the last time?"

"Seven years ago."

He put his pint down and stared at me, his eyes opening wide. "Are you fucking kidding me?" he asked.

"I told you, that's when Bastiaan died."

"Yeah but . . . you're telling me that you haven't had sex since then?"

"Is that so strange?"

"It's fucking weird is what it is."

I said nothing; I wondered whether he realized how rude he was being.

"You must be fucking *gagging* for it," he said, his voice rising a little, and I noticed a couple at the next table looking at us in disdain. Some things didn't change.

"I'm not really," I said quietly.

"Yeah, you are."

"No, I'm not."

"If you really are forty-nine, then you're way too young to be closing up shop."

"I *am* forty-nine," I insisted. "And funnily enough you're the second person to say something along those lines to me over the last few days."

"Who was the first?"

"Mrs. Goggin."

"Who's Mrs. Goggin?"

I rolled my eyes. "I told you before. The lady from the tearoom."

"What tearoom?"

"In Dáil Éireann!"

"Oh, yes, you said something about her before. She was retiring, wasn't she?"

"Yes. You were there!"

"Oh that's right. I remember now. I think it made her night when I showed up but I couldn't stay."

"I said hello to you and you ignored me."

"Didn't see you. Did she do it anyway?"

"Did she do what?"

"Retire."

"Yes, of course she did. Why else would she have a retirement party?"

"I don't know," he said. "Lots of people say they're retiring but they never do. Look at Frank Sinatra."

"Well, she has," I told him, growing exhausted now by the conversation. "Anyway. I suppose you're single, are you?"

"What makes you think that?"

"The fact that you asked me out."

"Oh yeah," he said. "Well, sort of."

"What does that mean?"

"It means I'm open to offers," he replied, grinning at me. "If anyone was to make one."

"I'll be back in a minute," I said, taking the opportunity to go to the bathroom for a few moments to myself. When I came back, there were two more beers on the table and I reconciled myself to the fact that I would have to stay a little longer.

"I'd say it's a lot different now," I said, sitting down and hoping to start a sensible conversation with him. "Being gay in Ireland, I mean. When I was younger, it was near impossible. We had a terrible time of it, to be honest. It's easier these days, I imagine."

"It's not, actually," he said quickly. "The laws are still against us; you still can't walk down the street holding a man's hand without risking getting your head caved in. There's a few more bars, I suppose, it's not just the George anymore, and things aren't quite as underground as they once were but no, I don't think it's any easier. Maybe it's not so hard to meet people, though. You find a few things online sometimes. The odd chat room or dating page."

"On what?" I asked.

"Online."

"What does that mean? On what line?"

"The World Wide Web. Have you not heard of it?"

"A little bit," I said.

"It's the future," he told me. "One day we'll all be online."

"Doing what?"

"I don't know. Looking stuff up."

"Sounds great," I said. "Can't wait."

"My point is that it's not much better than it used to be but maybe it'll get there. We need some serious changes to the law but that'll take time."

"If only we knew somebody who worked in politics," I said. "Someone who could make a stand and get the ball rolling."

"I hope you're not thinking of me. That's a vote loser. I wouldn't touch something like that with a barge pole. Anyway, kids these days are a lot more comfortable in their own skin. They actually come out to people, which is a very nineties thing to do, if you ask me. Did you ever come out to your parents?"

"I never knew them," I told him. "I was adopted."

"Well, your adoptive parents then?"

"My adoptive mother died when I was just a child," I said. "I never actually told my adoptive father that I was gay but, due to a set of circumstances which I won't bore you with right now, he found out when I was twenty-eight. He never really cared, to be honest. He's an odd fish in many ways but he doesn't have a bigoted bone in his body. What about you?"

"My mother's dead too," he said. "And my father has Alzheimer's, so there's no point."

"Right," I said. "And what about your brothers and sisters? Have you told them?"

"No," he said. "I don't think they'd understand."

"Are they older or younger than you?"

"Older brother, younger sister."

"But that generation, your generation, they don't care so much about these things, do they? Why don't you just tell them?"

He shrugged. "It's complicated," he said. "I'd rather not get into it."

"All right."

"Shall we have another drink?"

"Go on so."

While he was at the bar, I watched him, unable to decide whether my being here was a good or bad idea. I found him slightly obnoxious but I also couldn't deny the fact that I found him physically attractive and, as I started to realize, that spark inside me hadn't quite died away yet, as much as I'd tried to extinguish the flame. The fact that he'd been interested enough to ask me out in the first place had been flattering me. He'd only been elected to the Dáil at the most recent election but there was a lot of talk about him being a potential future minister. He'd made some good speeches, impressed his party's leadership and was a regular on the current affairs shows. At the next reshuffle, he was almost guaranteed a junior ministry at least. And that would be a first, I realized. A gay man rising through the ranks of Irish politics. De Valera would turn in his grave. And still, with all of that ahead of him, he'd asked me out.

"Why did you choose the Yellow House?" I asked, when he sat down again. "You live over on the Northside, don't you?"

"I do," he said.

"So why over here?"

"I thought it would be more convenient for you."

"Sure I live on Pembroke Road," I said. "We could have gone to the Waterloo or somewhere."

"I don't like drinking in my own constituency," he said, changing his answer. "People come up to me all the time over there and ask me about potholes and electricity charges and will I come to their kids' sports day at school to hand out the medals, and you know, I really couldn't give a fuck about any of that stuff."

"But isn't that the job of a TD?"

"It's part of it," he admitted. "But not the part I'm interested in."

"So what part are you interested in?"

"Climbing the ladder. Reaching the highest rung that I can."

"And doing what?"

"What do you mean?"

"I mean when you get to the top of the ladder, what's it all for? You can't just want to have power for its own sake, surely?"

"Why not? In the end, I want to be Taoiseach. And I'm pretty sure that I can go all the way. I have the brains. I have the ability. And the party's behind me."

"But *why*?" I asked. "What do you actually want to achieve in politics?"

He shook his head. "Look, Cyril," he said. "Don't get me wrong. I want to do right by my constituents and by the country. I mean that would be, you know, great, I suppose. But can you think of any other profession where you would ask such a question? If I was starting off as a teacher in a school and I said I'd like to be principal one day, you'd say *Good for you*. If I was a postman and said I'd like to run An Post, you'd say that you admired my ambition. Why can't it be the same with politics? Why can't I just seek advancement and try to get to the top and then, when I'm there, if I can do something positive with it, then that's great, and if I can't, sure I'll just enjoy being the top man."

I thought about it. On one hand his argument sounded ridiculous but on the other, it was difficult to identify its flaws.

"You realize it'll be difficult, though, don't you?" I said. "Being gay, I mean. I don't know whether Ireland is even ready for a gay minister yet, let alone a gay Taoiseach."

"Like I said, I don't put labels on myself. And of course there are ways around these things."

I nodded, uncertain whether I really wanted to stay in his company much longer when a thought popped into my mind. It was like a light-bulb moment. "Can I ask you a question?" I said.

"Sure."

"You don't have a girlfriend, by any chance, do you?"

He sat back and seemed surprised by what I'd asked. "Of course I do," he said. "Why wouldn't I? I'm a good-looking man with a great job in the prime of my life."

I shook my head. "You have a girlfriend," I said, more of a statement than anything else. "So I presume she doesn't care about your lack of labels either?"

"How do you mean?"

"Does she think you're straight?"

"That's kind of a personal question, don't you think?"

"Well, you asked me out, Andrew. And we're here on a date. So I don't think it's unreasonable of me to ask."

He thought about it for a moment and shrugged his shoulders. "Well, she's never asked any questions," he said. "And sure what she doesn't know won't hurt her."

"Oh for God's sake," I said.

"What?"

"Next thing you'll be telling me that you're getting married."

"We *are* getting married as it happens," he said. "Next July. I think I can get Albert and Kathleen to come to the reception if I play my cards right."

I started laughing. "You're some chancer," I said. "Why on earth are you marrying this poor girl if you're gay?"

"I told you, I'm—"

"Not into labels, I know. But let's use one just for a moment. Why are you marrying her if you're gay?"

"Because I need a wife," he said unapologetically. "My constituents expect that of me. The party expects that of me. There's no way that I'm going anywhere unless I have a wife and children."

"And what about her?" I asked, aware of the hypocrisy in my outrage but, in fairness, it had been twenty-one years since my own wedding day and I hadn't deceived a single person about my sexuality since then.

"What about her? What do you mean?"

"You're going to ruin some poor girl's life because you don't have the guts to tell the truth about yourself."

"How will I be ruining her life?" he asked, looking genuinely baffled. "If I go all the way, we'll be on state visits to Buckingham Palace and the White House and all sorts of places. Are you saying that's a wasted life?"

"It is if the person you're with doesn't love you."

"But I do love her. She's a terrific person. And she loves me too."

"Right," I said. "I'll take your word for it."

"I don't know what you're so worried about," he said. "No one's asking you to marry her."

"True," I said. "Look, to each their own. Do whatever makes you happy. Shall we finish these up anyway and get out of here?"

He smiled and nodded. "Fair enough," he said. "We can't go back to mine, though. You live alone, though, right?"

"Yes," I said. "Why?"

"Will we go there?"

"Why would we go there?"

"Why do you think?"

I stared at him. "You're not actually expecting us to spend the night together, are you?" I asked.

"No, of course not," he said. "Not the full night anyway. A couple of hours, that's all."

"No, thanks," I said, shaking my head.

"Are you kidding me?" he asked, looking utterly confused now.

"No, not at all."

"But why not?"

"Firstly, because we barely know each other—"

"Oh, like that's a big deal."

"No, maybe not. But you have a girlfriend. Sorry, you have a fiancée."

"Who doesn't need to know anything about this."

"I don't do that, Andrew," I said. "Not anymore."

"Do what?"

"I'm not interested in being part of a deception. I spent enough of my life lying to people and hiding away. I'm not going down that road again."

"Cyril," he said, smiling in such a way that made me know he believed his charm would always work. "Not to put too fine a point on it but you're supposedly forty-nine years old, I'm only thirty-four and I'm offering it to you on a plate. Are you really telling me that you're going to turn this opportunity down?"

"Afraid so," I said. "Sorry."

There was a long pause while he took this in and then he simply shook his head and laughed. "All right," he said, standing up. "I'll leave you to it so. What a complete waste of an evening. You blew it big time, my friend, that's all I'm saying. And for what it's worth, I have a massive cock."

"I'm delighted for you."

"You sure you don't want to change your mind?"

"Believe me, I'm completely sure."

"Your loss. But look"—he leaned over now and looked me directly in the eye—"if you ever tell anyone about this conversation, not only will I deny everything but I'll sue you for libel."

"A libel is written down," I told him. "If I tell someone, then it would be a slander. Although it wouldn't be anyway since it would be the truth."

"Fuck you," he said. "Don't mess with me, all right? Remember, I know some pretty powerful people. That job of yours could be taken away from you without much difficulty."

"Just go if you're going," I said wearily. "I have no intention of talking to anyone about this. The whole thing is just embarrassing. You don't have to worry."

"Right," he said, putting on his coat. "Well, you've been warned."

"Go," I said.

And he went.

I ordered another drink and sat quietly in the corner of the bar watching the couples and the groups of friends enjoying their evenings. And *nothing changes*, I thought. *Nothing ever changes. Not in Ireland.*

A Real Avery

A month before he was due to finish his sentence, Charles was diagnosed with an inoperable brain tumor and released from prison early on compassionate grounds. With no desire to return to his solitary penthouse apartment in Ballsbridge, he begged me to allow him to spend his final weeks in the house on Dartmouth Square where, he claimed somewhat improbably, he had spent the happiest days of his life. I explained that I hadn't lived there in forty years, but he seemed to think that I was just being difficult and so I found myself phoning Alice to explain the predicament. Three years after our testy reunion in the Duke, we were on slightly better terms and to my delight she agreed immediately, finding a wonderful opportunity to remind me how good Charles had been to her after I had walked out on our reception, humiliated her in front of all her friends and family, left her alone to bring up our child and generally ruined her life.

"I'm glad you don't hold a grudge," I told her.

"Shut up, Cyril."

"No, really. You're a very easy-going person. How some man didn't snap you up years ago is beyond me."

"Is that supposed to be a joke?" she asked.

"It was," I admitted. "As I heard the words coming out of my mouth, they sounded less amusing than I thought they would."

"Some people just shouldn't try to be funny."

"Well, joking aside, I do appreciate it."

"I think it's the least my family owes him," she said. "Max bought the house for far below market value when Charles was incarcerated the first time around. And let's face it, it was partly Max's fault that he got locked up at all. But the house will be Liam's eventually and he's Charles's grandson as much as he was Max's. There's just one thing that you should be aware of. Has Liam told you that I've made a few changes to my living situation?"

"No," I said. "He's not answering my calls at the moment."

"Why not?"

"I have no idea. He seems to hate me again."

"Why? What did you do?"

"Nothing, as far as I'm aware. It's possible that he took a remark I made about his girlfriend the wrong way."

"What did you say? And which girlfriend?"

"The Julia one. I asked whether it was trendy for girls not to shave their legs or armpits anymore."

"Oh, Cyril! Although you're right. She's like a gorilla. So what did he say?"

"He said that only old people used the word *trendy*."

"Well, that's true too. The correct term is *with-it*."

"Do you know, I really don't think it is."

"Cyril, I'm a university lecturer. I'm around young people all day, every day. I think I know the lingo."

"Still," I said doubtfully. "*With-it* does not sound anymore with-it than *trendy*. And I don't think people say *lingo* anymore either. Anyway, for whatever reason, Liam seemed to take offense at what I'd said. I don't know why; I wasn't trying to be rude."

"Oh I wouldn't worry about it. He'll get over it. He takes offense at everything these days. I asked him what he wanted for his birthday last week and he just sneered and said a new teddy bear."

"Get him a really hairy one. He's obviously into that."

"I don't think he was serious."

"He might have been. Lots of grown men have a teddy bear. I know a fellow who carries a Pooh Bear with him everywhere he goes and dresses him up in appropriate clothing on national holidays. It's a comfort thing."

"Trust me, he didn't mean it. He was just being snarky."

"You said that you'd made some changes to your living arrangements," I said, trying to get things back on track. "What sort of changes?"

"Oh yes. Well, the thing is, I've moved someone in," she said. "A man."

"What sort of a man?"

"What do you mean *what sort of a man*? What kind of question is that?"

"Are you saying that you've moved a boyfriend in?"

"I am, yes. Problem?"

"Need I remind you that you're still married to me?"

"Is that another one of your jokes?"

"It is," I said. "Well, I'm very happy for you, Alice. It's about time you shacked up with someone. What's this fellow's name and are his intentions honorable toward you?"

"You promise you won't laugh?"

"Why would I laugh?" I asked.

"His name's Cyril."

I couldn't help myself. I laughed.

"You've got to be kidding me," I said. "The only two men in Dublin named Cyril and you end up with both of them."

"I didn't end up with you, Cyril," she pointed out. "I barely got to the starting line, remember? And look, it's just a rather awful coincidence, so please don't make a fuss about it. It's embarrassing enough as it is. All my friends already think he's a homosexual."

"It's not the *name* that's gay, you know."

"No, they think Cyril is you and that we've got back together."

"Would you like that, Alice?"

"I'd rather bore a hole to the center of the earth with my tongue. Why, would you?"

"Very much. I miss your body."

"Oh, shut up. But if Charles moves in here, you are not allowed to make fun of Cyril."

"I'll probably have to," I said. "It's too good an opportunity to pass up. So what does he do, Cyril II?"

"Don't call him that. And he plays violin with the RTÉ Symphony Orchestra."

"Very posh. Is he age appropriate?"

"Not really. He's only just turned forty."

"Seven years younger," I said. "Good work. And how long has he been living in our marital home, cuckolding me?"

"It's not our marital home. It might have been if you hadn't run off to Dublin Airport screaming like a girl. And he's been here slightly over two months."

"Does Liam like him?"

"He does, actually."

"Has he actually said that or are you just saying it to annoy me?"

"A little of both."

"Well, I have to say I'm surprised, because as far as I can tell, Liam doesn't like anyone."

"Well, he likes Cyril."

"Good for Cyril. I can't wait to meet him."

"I don't think there'll be any need for that."

"Will he mind your father-in-law moving in? A cuckoo in the nest, so to speak."

"It's not a nest; it's a house. And don't call Charles my father-in-law; it's irritating. And, no, Cyril won't mind. He's very easy-going. For a violinist."

And so a few days later my adoptive father returned to the first-floor room that had been his when I was a child, although now, instead of being out in the city carousing with women until the small hours of the morning, he kept to his bed and began fulfilling his last major ambition in life: to work his way through all of Maude's novels in chronological order.

"I only ever read one when she was alive," he told me one afternoon during one of his more lucid moments, which seemed to come and go with alarming frequency. "And I remember at the time thinking that it was terribly good. I told her that it was the sort of book that could get made into a film if it found its way into the hands of a David Lean or a George Cukor and she replied that if I ever said anything that crass about her work again she would put arsenic in my tea. Not that I ever knew that much about literature, you understand, but I could tell that she had something."

"Most people seem to think so," I said.

"I've made a very good living from her, I have to admit. That will all be yours soon."

I looked at him in surprise. "What did you say?" I asked.

"Well, you're my next of kin, aren't you? Legally speaking. I've left everything to you, including the rights to Maude's books."

"You haven't?! But that's millions!"

"I can change it if you like. There's still time. I could give it to one of those homeless charities. Or leave it to Bono, because I'm sure he'd know what to do with it."

"No, no," I said quickly. "Don't do anything hasty. I'll take care of the homeless charities myself when the time comes. And Bono can probably take care of himself."

"Good old Maude," he said, smiling. "Who knew that a writer could actually make such a good living? And they say that the world is full of philistines. Your wife wrote her thesis on her, didn't she?"

"She did," I admitted. "She even turned it into a book. But it's probably best not to call Alice my wife. She really doesn't care for it."

"I must have a chat with her about the novels, because reading them now, one by one, I can finally see what all the fuss is about. The only thing I'd tell Maude, if she was here, is that she runs the risk of sounding a little anti-man at times, don't you agree? All the husbands in her novels are stupid, insensitive, faithless individuals with murky pasts, empty heads, micro-penises and questionable morals. But I suppose she had a good imagination, as all writers must, and she was simply making things up. I seem to recall that she didn't have a very good relationship with her father. Perhaps that's come into play in her work a little bit."

"That must be it," I told him. "I can't think where else she might have got such ideas."

"Did your wife mention that in her biography?"

"A little bit, yes."

"Did she mention *me* in her biography?"

"Of course."

"How did I come out of it?"

"Not well," I said. "But perhaps a little better than expected."

"All right. How about you? Were you in it?"

"Yes."

"How did you come out of it?"

"Not well," I said. "Perhaps a little worse than expected."

"Such is life. By the way," he said. "I don't mean to sound indelicate but I'm finding it a little hard to sleep with the constant sounds of love-making coming from your bedroom. Last night I woke up to hear your wife screaming your name out in rapturous pleasure with all the passion of a young nymphomaniac let loose in the dressing room of an under-seventeen boys' football team. Good for you, my boy, especially after all these years. I admire your ardor! But if you could keep it down a little, I'd appreciate it. I'm a dying man and I need my sleep."

"Actually, I don't think it was my name she was calling," I said.

"Oh it was, it certainly was," he insisted. "I heard it over and over again. *Oh God, Cyril! Yes, Cyril! Right there, Cyril! Don't worry, that happens to everyone sometimes, Cyril!*"

"That's not me," I told him. "That's Cyril II. The boyfriend. I haven't actually met him yet but I'm assuming that you have."

"Tall, miserable-looking streak of piss?"

"I don't know, but let's assume so."

"Yes, I've met him. He looks in on me every so often and shouts at me as if I'm deaf, the way English people do with foreigners because they think it'll make them understand them better. He told me that he was playing Pugni's *La Esmeralda* all week in the National Concert Hall and I just shook his hand and said *Good for you.*"

A nurse came to visit every second morning to check up on him, and most afternoons Alice would take him for a walk around Dartmouth Square. As it became clear that he was reaching the end, however, I asked Alice whether I might move in too so that I could be with him when he departed this life for the next.

"What?" she said, looking at me with an expression on her face that suggested she was astonished that I would even ask such a thing.

"The thing is," I explained, "if he were to take a turn for the worse, you'd have to phone me and by the time I got here he might already be gone. But if I was already here, that wouldn't happen and there's the added advantage that I could help you with his care. You've done so much for him as it is. You must get exhausted. What with your job and looking after Liam and having raucous sex with Cyril II."

She stared out the window as if she was trying to think of a good reason to say no. "But where would I put you?" she asked.

"Well, it's not as if it's a small house," I said. "I could take the room at the top, the one that was mine when I was a boy."

"Oh no," she said. "I haven't been up there in so long. It's probably very dusty. I consider that part of the house to be closed."

"Well, I could reopen it. And I'd be happy to clean it up myself. Look, if you'd rather I didn't, then that's fine. If you don't want Charles to spend his last moments on earth with his son—"

"Adoptive son."

"Then I can't blame you. It would be totally understandable. But if not, then I really would like to."

"And what about Cyril?" she asked.

"I am Cyril. You don't have a brain tumor too, do you?"

"*My* Cyril."

"I thought I *was* your Cyril."

"You see, this is why it will never work."

"Cyril II, that's who you're talking about, is it?"

"Stop calling him that."

"Well, he'd have to be incredibly insecure to be threatened by me," I said. "I am, as has been clearly established by this stage, not exactly a ladies' man. Look, I know it would be an unconventional arrangement but it wouldn't be for very long. I won't cause any trouble, I promise."

"Of course you will," she said. "You always cause trouble. That's your role in life. And I don't know what Liam would say."

"He'd probably be very happy to have his mummy and daddy together under the same roof at last."

"You see? I haven't even said yes yet and you're already causing trouble. With your little jokes."

"I just want to be with him," I said quietly. "Charles, I mean. I've made a mess of most of my relationships and it's been a strange one between the two of us but I'd like it to end well if possible."

"Fine," she said, throwing her hands in the air. "But this won't be a long-term arrangement, as long as you understand that. When he's gone, you're gone too."

"I'll take a lift from the undertaker as he carries the box out the door," I said. "Promise."

That night, when Liam returned home, he seemed startled to find both his parents eating dinner together in front of *Coronation Street*.

"What's this?" he asked, stopping in the center of the kitchen and staring at us both. "What's going on?"

"Everything's changed," I told him. "We're getting back together. We're even thinking of having another child. You'd like a little brother or sister, wouldn't you?"

"Shut up, Cyril," said Alice. "Don't worry, Liam. Your father is just teasing."

"Don't call him that," said Liam.

"Cyril is just teasing you then. He's moving in while your grandfather is still with us."

"Oh, all right," he said. "But why?"

"To help out."

"I can help out," he said.

"You can," said Alice. "But you don't."

"It won't be for long," I told him. "And he is my father after all."

"Adoptive father," said Liam.

"Well, yes," I said. "But still, the only father I've ever known."

"And what about Cyril?" he asked.

"What about me?"

"No, the other Cyril."

"Cyril II."

"Stop calling him that," said Alice. "Cyril is fine with it. He'll be home soon and I'll make the introductions then."

Liam shook his head and walked over to the fridge and began building a mountainous sandwich. "I don't know what to think," he remarked. "For years, it was just the two of us. And now the house is full of men."

"Full of Cyrils," I said.

"It's hardly *full* of men," said Alice. "There's just two of them."

"Three," said Liam. "You're forgetting Charles."

"Oh, yes. Sorry."

"Four if you include yourself," I pointed out to him. "The number just keeps growing, doesn't it?"

"You're not to go anywhere near my room, is that understood?" he said, glaring at me.

"I'll try to resist the overwhelming urge," I replied.

A couple of hours later, Cyril II arrived home and we shook hands as Alice stood between us, looking extremely flustered. He was a pleasant enough fellow, I thought, if a little dull. Within five minutes he asked me whether I had a favorite symphony and, if I did, would I like him to play it as an anthem of welcome to Dartmouth Square. I told him that I didn't but thanked him for the thought. That was him for the night, other than to ask me whether I knew a good cure for bunions.

A week later, as I made my way upstairs to my bedroom with a mug of hot milk close to midnight, I heard crying coming from Charles's room and I listened at the door for a few moments before tapping quietly and walking in. He was sitting up in bed with Maude's final novel by his side, wiping his eyes.

"Are you all right?" I asked.

"I'm feeling very sad," he said, nodding toward the book. "That's the last one, you see. I've read them all now, so I think I'll probably be gone soon. There's nothing left. I wish I'd realized at the time how much talent she had. I wish I'd praised her more. And been a better husband to her. She was so tired of life by the end. And tired of me. I treated her poorly. You didn't know her in the thirties, of course, but when she was a young woman, she was full of fun. *Spirited* is the word people used back then. The type who would jump over streams and not think anything of it. The type who carried a hip flask in her hand-bag and took it out for a swig if the Sunday sermon went on too long."

I smiled. I found it hard to imagine Maude doing anything of the sort.

"You know she assaulted The Man from the Revenue after you went to prison the first time?" I said.

"Did she? Why?"

"She said that he'd worked so hard to prosecute you that her name was in all the papers and the result was that *Amongst Angels* had reached number four on the bestseller charts. She slapped him in the middle of the Four Courts."

"That was a blow to her all right," he said, nodding. "I remember her being very upset about it. She wrote me a letter afterward and it wasn't pleasant, although it was incredibly well written. Is she up-stairs, Cyril? Why not ask her to come down and I'll try to make amends to her before I go to sleep."

"No, Charles," I said, shaking my head. "No, she's not upstairs."

"She is. She must be. Please send her down. I want to tell her that I'm sorry."

I reached out and brushed a strand of long white hair from his fore-head back across his head. The skin was cold and clammy to the touch. He lay back down and closed his eyes, and I waited with him until he was asleep before going to bed myself, lying in that single bed looking through the skylight at the stars above, the same stars that I had stared at more than forty years earlier, dreaming about Julian Woodbead and the things I wanted to do to him, and I understood at last why Charles had wanted to come back here. For the first time in my life, I started to think about my own mortality. Should I fall or have a heart attack, I could lie on the kitchen floor decomposing for weeks before anyone thought to come looking for me. I didn't even have a cat to eat me.

Charles lasted another four days and, with impeccable timing, passed away when Alice, Liam, Cyril II and I all happened to be at home. He'd been rambling all day and it was clear that he didn't have long left, although we didn't think it would be just yet. Alice and I were downstairs preparing dinner when we heard Liam calling us from the floor above.

"Mum! Cyril! Come quick!"

All three of us ran upstairs and into the bedroom where Charles was lying with his eyes closed, his breathing slowing down. We could hear the effort it took for him to make every sound.

"What's happening?" asked Liam, and it astonished me to see that my son, who had shown almost no emotion whatsoever in the time that I had known him, was close to tears, particularly since he hadn't even met his grandfather until a few weeks earlier.

"He's going," I said, sitting down and taking one of his hands while Alice took the other. From the hallway outside, I heard the sound of a maudlin violin tune being played and rolled my eyes.

"Does he have to do that?" I asked.

"Shut up, Cyril," said Alice. "He's only trying to help."

"Then couldn't he at least play something more cheerful? A jig or something?"

"Tell her it wasn't my fault," muttered Charles, and I bent my head down closer to his mouth.

"What wasn't your fault?" I asked, but he shook his head.

"Cyril," he said.

"What?"

"Come closer."

"I can't come any closer. We're practically kissing as it is."

He pulled himself up a little in the bed and looked around the room with a horrified expression on his pale face before grabbing me by the back of the head and pulling my face close to him. "You were never a real Avery," he hissed. "You know that, don't you?"

"I do," I said.

"But Christ on a bike, you came close. You came damned close."

And with that he released me and fell back on his pillow, said nothing more and we all watched as his breath slowed down until, finally, he was breathing no more. Somehow, I felt entirely removed from the scene at that moment, as if my own soul was ascending from my body toward the heavens. Looking down from above I could see myself, my wife and son sitting in the room over the remains of my adoptive father and I thought what a strange family I had grown up in and what a peculiar one I would leave behind one day.

Two days later we buried him in the church graveyard at Ranelagh and when we returned to Dartmouth Square Alice sat me down and said that she was happy that I'd been there toward the end and pleased that she'd been able to help but that was it, she didn't want any misunderstandings between us, and I would have to go home now.

"But I don't even own a cat," I said.

"What has that got to do with anything?"

"Nothing," I said. "And of course I must go. You've been very kind to me, you and Cyril II."

"Don't—"

"Sorry."

I slept there one final night and early the following morning packed the few personal items and clothes that I had brought with me and left the house for good, while my son, my wife and her lover were still asleep, depositing my key on the small table by the front door, opposite the chair where Julian had sat as a seven-year-old boy, and making my way outside into a cold autumn morning to find that a gray fog had descended on Dartmouth Square, making the path to the main road practically invisible.

2001 The Phantom Pain

Maribor

In the summer of 2001, shortly after my fifty-sixth birthday, Ignac invited me to accompany him to Ljubljana for a literary festival. Usually his wife, Rebecca, went with him on publicity tours but having given birth to twin girls only a few months earlier—their second set of twins following a pair of boys born only fourteen months before—she didn't want to leave Dublin and so he asked me along instead.

"He's very anxious about it," Rebecca told me when she wheeled the enormous two-level buggy into Dáil Éireann one morning, appearing a little dazed to see sunlight again. Collapsing into a chair opposite me, she looked as if she could fall asleep for weeks if given the chance. "I think he regrets having accepted the invitation at all." One of the babies on the upper level promptly threw up all over one of the babies on the lower, leaving a parliamentary secretary glaring over at us with disapproval as a round of raucous crying ensued, mostly from Rebecca herself.

"Why would he be anxious?" I asked her when they were cleaned up again. "He's attended hundreds of book festivals over the years. He must be comfortable with them at this stage."

"Yes, but it'll be his first time back in Slovenia since he left."

"Since he was sent away, you mean."

"Do I?"

"Well, that's what happened, isn't it?"

She shrugged her shoulders and looked away. "It's complicated," she said.

I frowned, uncertain what she meant. Ignac had always said that his grandmother had dispatched him to his father in Amsterdam immediately after his mother's death, saying that she had no interest in raising another child. And that, as far as I understood it, was what had happened.

"I'm worried that he'll find it upsetting," she continued. "He's quieter than he normally is. And he's not sleeping."

"Are any of you sleeping?" I asked, glancing down at the babies.

"Well, no. Now that you mention it, I think I last had a full night's sleep in March. I'm hoping to have one again next year at some point if I'm lucky. I just think it might be a difficult trip, that's all. He's so famous over there."

"He's famous everywhere."

"I know, but—"

"Look, why don't *I* take care of the kids for a few days?" I suggested. "And you go to Slovenia with Ignac?"

"Seriously?" she said. "You want to take care of four babies for five days?"

"Well, not really, no. But I'll do it. How difficult can it be?"

She laughed and shook her head. "Oh, not difficult at all! It's a total breeze!"

"Come on, I can do it! And you look like you could do with a break anyway."

"Why?" she asked, her eyes opening wide in dismay. "Do I look awful? I do, don't I? I must look like one of those women. You know those women? Who look awful all the time? Do I look like one of them?"

"You look as gorgeous as ever," I told her, which was true, because despite how tired she might have felt, and regardless of how many babies she popped out, Rebecca always looked amazing.

"I feel like that old woman from *Titanic*," she said, resting her head on her hands. "Only less fuckable. The way my body looks right now, Mother Teresa would beat me in a swimsuit competition."

"I'm sure Ignac doesn't think that," I said, trying to dismiss this image from my mind.

"I hope he does," she said. "If he comes near me with that thing again, I'll cut it off with scissors. Four babies in a year and a half is enough. Anyway, no, as much as I'd like to just run away and leave you to it, it wouldn't be possible."

"Why not?" I asked.

"Because I think I might be better at breastfeeding than you."

"Oh yes," I said. "All right. Good point."

And so it was settled and I boarded a plane, finding myself swept up in the chaos of Slovenia's best-known expatriate returning to the country of his birth for the first time in more than two decades. To my astonishment, photographers were gathered at the airport in anticipation of his arrival, along with television news crews, each of whom thrust microphones into Ignac's face as they roared incomprehensible questions at him once we appeared through the Arrivals door. The hordes of children waiting were so deep and noisy that we might have been a boy-band coming to town. By now, of course, the eighth volume of the Floriak Ansen series had been published, so the enthusiasm was understandable, and Ignac, to his credit, spent more than an hour at the airport signing books while I sat with a cup of coffee before we traveled by limousine to the city center for a champagne-fueled meeting with his publisher in advance of a sold-out evening event at a local theater.

Throughout her entire writing career Maude had given a public reading on only one occasion, and although that disastrous night is well documented in Alice's biography,* she wasn't actually present to witness it, but I was. It had taken place in a bookshop in the center of Dublin to a packed audience of literally tens of people and as a culture journalist from the *Sunday Press* introduced Maude, listing the titles of her various novels to date, my adoptive mother sat quietly in a corner, dressed entirely in black, lighting one cigarette after another and rolling her eyes at every supposed compliment he paid her. (*She would give any male writer a run for his money*, was one of his choice lines. Along with: *She writes wonderful sentences but has even better legs*. Not to mention: *How she manages to write her novels while taking care of a husband and child is a mystery to me. I hope she's not neglecting her duties!*) When he was finished, she stood up, marched over to the microphone and with absolutely no preamble began reading from Chapter One of *Amongst Angels*, which had been published to universal indifference a few months earlier. Perhaps she had never attended a literary event before

---

* *Hymns at Heaven's Gate: A Life of Maude Avery* by Alice Woodbead, pp. 102–4 (Faber & Faber, 1986).

or perhaps she simply misunderstood the nature of public readings, for having completed the first chapter, which seemed to take an interminable forty minutes, the audience burst into applause and she glared out at them and told them to *Shut up, for Christ's sake, I'm not finished*, before launching into the second. And then the third. Only when the last audience member shuffled out of the bookshop more than two hours later did she stop reading, slam the book shut and, taking me by the hand, storm out, hailing a taxi for Dartmouth Square.

"What a complete waste of my time," she complained as we drove through the traffic for home. "If they didn't like my work, why on earth did they come along to hear me?"

"I think they expected you to read for only a few minutes," I told her. "And then perhaps to answer some of their questions."

"The novel is four hundred and thirty-four pages long," she replied, shaking her head. "If they want to understand it, then they must hear the entire thing. Or, preferably, *read* the entire thing. How can they possibly get a sense of it from a mere ten minutes? The time it takes to smoke three cigarettes! Philistines! Barbarians! Boors! Never again, Cyril, I promise you that. Never again." And on this matter, she was as good as her word.

Ignac, of course, made no such errors of judgment in Ljubljana. By now he was experienced on stages, knew exactly how long an audience was prepared to listen and had a good sense of how to charm them with a few well-chosen and self-deprecating quips during the interview that followed. His publisher had lined up an enormous amount of newspaper, radio and television interviews and by the third afternoon, when his writerly responsibilities came to an end, he suggested a trip to Maribor in the northeast of the country for the following day.

"What's in Maribor?" I asked, consulting the guidebook that I had clung to over the previous few days as tightly as Lucy Honeychurch had to her *Baedeker*.

"It's where I was born," he told me. "Where my family comes from."

"Really?" I said, surprised, for I had never heard him mention the town before. "And you're sure you want to go back there?"

"Not entirely," he said with a shrug. "But I think it might be good for me."

"Why?" I asked.

He took a long time to answer. "It's not as if this will be my only trip back to Slovenia," he said. "I'll come again but probably not for a long time. Not until the children are old enough to see it. And when that day comes, I don't want to be still dealing with the past. I think I should see Maribor now, with you, and then lay it to rest forever."

And so we went, renting a car and driving north, eventually finding ourselves on the cold, run-down streets where he had spent his childhood and adolescence. He was quiet as he led me through the town, shortcuts and alleyways coming back to him without any hesitation, recalling shops and the houses of friends from his childhood. We passed a school that was boarded up, its facade covered in indecipherable graffiti, and another that had been built more recently but looked as if a strong wind might take it down. We ate lunch in a restaurant where the locals stared, recognizing their most famous son from newspaper articles and television reports, but seemed wary of approaching him, as if uncertain what his response might be. Only one person, a nine-year-old boy who had been sitting with his father reading a Floriak Ansen novel, came over, and when the pair spoke, before Ignac signed his book, it was in Slovene and I didn't understand a word of it and asked no questions afterward. Finally, he took me down a cobblestoned lane that led to a tiny abandoned hut with boarded-up windows, a roof that was falling off, and he placed his hand flat on the front door, closing his eyes and breathing deeply, as if he was either trying to control his temper or prevent tears from falling.

"What is it?" I asked. "Where are we?"

"This is the one," he said. "The house where I was born. Where I grew up."

I stared at it. It was so small that I could scarcely imagine a single person living inside, let alone two adults and a child.

"There were just a couple of rooms," he said, guessing what was going through my mind. "As a child, I slept in the bed with my parents. Then, after my father left, my mother made a nest for me on the floor. There was a toilet out the back. Nowhere to wash."

I looked at him, uncertain of what to say. We had never spoken of his father since that night in Amsterdam twenty-one years earlier when Jack Smoot had stabbed him in the back.

"Do you want to go inside?" I asked. "If we pulled off some of these wooden beams—"

"No," he said quickly. "No, I don't want that. I just wanted to see it, that's all."

"What about your neighbors?" I asked, looking around. "Do you remember them?"

"Some. A lot will be dead by now."

"And your friends?"

"I didn't have many. I won't be knocking on any doors."

"Then let's leave. You've seen it, let's move on."

"All right," he said. "Do you want to go back to the hotel?"

"No, let's go for a beer," I said. "I feel like we should get drunk, don't you?"

He smiled. "That's exactly how I feel," he said.

We wandered down the road and I suggested heading back into the center of the town where I had noticed some decent-looking pubs earlier but he said no, that there was a bar close by that he wanted to visit. When we reached it, I was surprised that it was nothing special, just a couple of tables placed on the street outside a delicatessen, but we sat down and ordered a couple of Slovenian lagers, and he seemed happy to be there. There was a strange atmosphere in the air between us, however, and I felt uncertain whether he wanted to be left in peace with his thoughts or would prefer to talk.

"Do you remember the first night that we met?" I asked him finally, recalling the evening that Bastiaan and I had discovered him lying on the street outside our apartment on Weesperplein, his dark hair bleached blond and a bruise discoloring the skin beneath his eye as a line of blood ran from his lip to his chin. "When we reached down to help you, it felt like picking up a frightened puppy who doesn't know whether you're going to feed it or beat it."

"You know I was planning on robbing you?" he asked, smiling a little.

"You weren't just planning it," I reminded him. "You actually did it. You took my wallet the next morning, remember?"

"Oh that's right," he said. "I'd forgotten that."

"Any chance I'll ever see any of that money again?"

"Probably not," he said, smiling. "But I'll buy you dinner later if you like."

"I was afraid you'd come in and kill us as we slept."

"I would never have done that," he said, looking a little offended. "But I thought that if I could sell some of your things then I might be able to get off the streets. Get away from my father. It was only after I ran away the next morning that I came up with a better plan. I brought your wallet back, hoping that you might let me stay."

"You have Bastiaan to thank for that," I told him, taking a sip from my beer and feeling the ache that built inside me whenever I recalled happy times between the two of us, times that seemed so long ago now. He had been dead for fourteen years by now; it was hard to believe it. "I thought he was crazy when he suggested it."

"But still, you said yes."

"He persuaded me."

"I'm glad he did. I don't know what would have become of me if he hadn't."

"Don't underestimate your own strength," I told him. "I think you would have been fine in the end."

"Maybe," he said.

"I wish he was here," I said after a pause.

"I do too," said Ignac. "The world is a fucked-up place."

"It is."

"Don't you ever miss having someone in your life, though?" he asked.

"Of course I do."

"No, I don't mean Bastiaan. I mean someone else."

I shook my head. "No," I said. "I'm part of that generation of gay men who were lucky if they met someone once. I don't have any interest in starting something new. For me, it was Bastiaan or no one."

"Not even Julian?"

"Julian was different," I said. "Julian was always an impossibility. But Bastiaan was reality. Bastiaan was the love of my life, not Julian. Julian was just an obsession, although I did love him and I still miss him. We had some resolution at the end but not enough." I shook my head and sighed. "Honestly, Ignac, I look back at my life and I don't understand very much of it. It seems like it would have been so simple now to have been honest with everyone, especially Julian. But it didn't feel like that at the time. Everything was different then, of course."

"Liam says that Julian felt the same way. That he didn't know why you didn't tell him how you felt when you were teenagers."

I turned to him in surprise. "You've talked to Liam about us?" I asked.

"The subject has come up," he said carefully. "You don't mind, do you?"

"No," I said. "I suppose not. I'm glad you two are friends."

"Of course we're friends," he said. "He's my brother."

"The two things don't always follow."

"They do in our case."

"Well, I'm glad," I said. Liam was, in fact, godfather to Ignac and Rebecca's first set of twins, but there was a part of me that sometimes felt envious of their relationship. They were the older and younger brother that both had always sought, connected by a father of sorts who had been there for one and not for the other.

"And if someone showed up now?" he asked.

"Someone . . . ?"

"Someone to love."

I shook my head. "I don't know," I said. "Maybe? Probably not."

"OK."

"Can I ask you something?" I said, ready to broach a subject that we had never, in more than twenty years, discussed.

"Of course."

"It's just because we're here," I said. "In Slovenia. And it makes me realize that we've never talked about Amsterdam, have we? Not about the city. But about what happened there."

"No," he said. "No, we haven't."

"Sometimes I think there's something wrong with me," I said, lowering my voice even though there was no one sitting outside to overhear us. "Because I feel no remorse at all. No guilt."

"Why would you?"

"Because I killed a man."

"You didn't kill him," he said, shaking his head. "Jack Smoot did."

"No, we all did it," I said. "We were all there. And I was a part of it as much as anyone."

"My father got everything that was coming to him," insisted Ignac. "If Jack Smoot hadn't stabbed him, then God only knows what would have happened. Remember, I knew him. You didn't. He would have never let me go. Never."

"I know that," I said. "And I don't regret any of it."

"Do you think about it a lot?"

"Not a lot, no. But sometimes. Why, don't you?"

"No, never."

"OK."

"I'm not sorry, if that's what you're asking."

"I'm not sorry either," I said. "He'd never have left you in peace, that much was obvious. But I must admit, I often wondered what Smoot did with the body. I've spent twenty years wondering whether the police might catch up with us."

"They won't. The body is long gone."

"How can you be sure?"

"I just am."

I looked across at him in surprise. "Do you know what happened to it?" I asked.

"Yes."

"How?"

"Smoot told me."

"I didn't realize you were still in touch," I said.

"Only occasionally."

"I was always nervous about contacting him. I thought I should keep as much distance between us as possible just in case. But as it happens I heard from him after Bastiaan died. He wrote me a letter. I always wondered how he knew. I thought perhaps Arjan or Edda had come into the bar and told him."

"And did you write back?"

"I did," I said. "But that was the end of it. Maybe I should write again sometime. Assuming he's still alive."

"Oh he's still alive all right," said Ignac. "I saw him the last time that I was in Amsterdam."

"You went to MacIntyre's?" I asked in surprise.

"Of course I did. I go whenever I'm there, which is pretty often, because my Dutch publisher brings me over for every book. Nothing's changed. He's older, of course. But the bar is still making money. And he seems happy enough. The last time I was there I even met the woman from the photograph."

"What photograph?"

"Remember the picture on the wall next to your favorite seat? Where you and Bastiaan always used to sit?"

"The one of Smoot and his boyfriend from all those years ago?"

"Yes, but there was a young woman standing next to them, half cut off by the frame."

"Oh yes," I said, recalling it. "It was taken on Chatham Street."

"We were supposed to meet her that night, remember? She was on holiday in Amsterdam. Turns out that she helped dispose of the body. So we have her to thank too."

I thought about it, recalling Smoot putting the body in the trunk of a rental car before stepping into the passenger seat next to a woman and driving away. His visitor from Dublin. His old friend. The woman who'd saved his life when his lover was killed.

"And did you talk about it?" I asked, hoping that they hadn't. Years might have gone by but I still thought it was foolish to discuss the events of that night with strangers.

"No," he said. "Not a word. Smoot told me later, that's all."

"So what did he do?" I asked again. "How did he get rid of it?"

He smiled and shook his head. "Like I said. You don't want to know."

"I do."

He sighed and shrugged his shoulders. "All right," he said. "You remember how the people of Amsterdam, during the seventeenth century, would tie millstones around the necks of convicted homosexuals before throwing them into the canals and leaving them to drown?"

"Yes."

"Well, that's what he did. He would have sunk right to the bottom and never resurfaced."

"Jesus," I said, feeling a shiver run through me. "I don't know what to say."

"It feels like justice to me. It feels like—"

He stopped suddenly in mid speech and I watched as his face grew a little pale in the afternoon sunlight. Following the direction of his eyes, I noticed an elderly woman making her way along the road, dragging a shopping trolley behind her, followed by a dark-gray dog of no specific breed. The woman was so small, with a face so deeply lined that a portrait photographer would have had a field day with her. Ignac put his glass down on the table beside him and when she reached the bar she stopped by the side door and called out something in a language I didn't understand. A moment later, the waiter came out and handed her a glass of beer, placing a bowl of water on the ground for the dog, and as she sat down, she looked around and her eyes landed on us for a moment before she turned away and gave a deep sigh, as if the weight of the world was on her shoulders.

"The famous writer," she said, her English underpinned with a thick Slovene accent.

"I suppose so," said Ignac.

"I saw your picture in the newspaper. I wondered when you'd show up here."

Ignac said nothing but the expression on his face was one that I had never seen before, a mixture of distress, contempt and fear.

"And who are you?" she asked, leaning over to look me up and down derisively.

"I'm his father," I said, an answer that I had given people before when it seemed easier than the technical truth.

"You're not his father," she said, shaking her head, and when she laughed at my presumption I could see how many teeth were missing from her mouth. "Why would you say that?"

"His adoptive father then," I said, a phrase I never used in relation to Ignac, whom I thought of as my son, more so than I did even my own son.

"You're not his father," she repeated.

"And how would you know that?" I asked irritably.

"Because his father was my son. And I would know my own son if he was seated next to me."

Ignac closed his eyes and I could see his hands trembling as he reached for his drink. I looked back and forth between the pair and although there was no family resemblance that I could decipher I assumed from Ignac's lack of protest that she was telling the truth.

"You had a dog just like him when I was a boy," he said, nodding toward the mutt who was lying on the ground now, having a snooze.

"It's his pup," she said. "Or his pup's pup. I can't remember anymore."

"Ignac," I said. "Do you want me to leave you alone? If you want to talk."

"No," he said quickly, turning to me with a panicked look on his face. *How strange*, I thought; *he's in his mid thirties, married with four children, a successful man, and yet he's still frightened to be left alone with this old woman.*

"I'll stay then," I said quietly.

"So you took him on?" said the woman, looking at me as she drank her beer.

"I did," I said.

"Poor you."

"I'm glad I did."

"But he's so disgusting," she said, spitting on the ground. "So dirty."

Ignac turned and glared at her and she looked back at him, reaching out a hand to touch his face, but he pulled away, as if she was holding a flame to his skin.

"All that money and he never sends a penny to his grandmother," she said now, putting her head in her hands and beginning to cry so suddenly that it seemed to be a completely fake and futile gesture.

"The grandmother who sent him away, you mean?" I asked.

Ignac shook his head and reached into his back pocket, removed his wallet and emptied it of all its notes—about twenty or thirty thousand tolars—before handing them across. She snatched the cash from him as if it was her right and secreted the bundle beneath her coat.

"All that money," she said. "And this is all I get."

And with that she stood up, the dog leaped immediately to his feet, and she continued on her way, dragging the shopping trolley behind her, my eyes on her all the way as Ignac looked in the opposite direction.

"Well, that was unexpected," I said finally. "Are you all right?"

"I'm fine," he said.

"Did you know you'd run into her?"

"I thought I might. She's a woman of routine. She passes by here every day. She always did anyway." He paused for a moment. "I never told you why I left Slovenia, did I?" he asked.

"You said that after your mother died, your grandmother didn't want to look after you."

"That was only partly true. My grandmother kept me with her for a few months."

"So why didn't you stay?"

"Because she was just like my father. She wanted to make money off me."

"How?"

"The same way. There were a lot of men here, bored of their wives and looking for something different. My grandmother found out. She walked in on me with one of them one afternoon. I was just a kid at the time, and when she saw what was going on she closed the door and went back to the kitchen, banging pots and pans around, and that was the extent of her anger. That's what she did to save me. Afterward, she whipped me and told me that I was disgusting, a worthless piece of shit. But maybe she saw what an asset I could be. I was a good-looking boy. I was pretty. And she told me that if I was going to let men do that to me, then she would be in charge of it from then on. And the money would be hers."

"Jesus," I said, putting my glass down.

"It wasn't just me. There were others too. One of my friends from school, she rented him out too, but he ran away and drowned himself in the Drava. His body was brought back and at the funeral all the men who had fucked us sat in the church and wept for his lost soul, making their way to the front row at the end of the service to offer their sympathies to his mother as if they held no responsibility for any of it. It wasn't long after that that I decided to run away too, only I knew I was not going to throw myself in the river. Instead, I stole enough money for a train ticket. It got me as far as Prague and from there I did the only thing I knew how to do in order to survive. But at least then the money was mine. After a while, I moved on to Amsterdam. I wasn't even planning on stopping there. I had no ultimate

destination in mind. But I knew my father lived in the city and somehow I thought that he might take care of me. That he'd turn my life
around. But he was no different from my grandmother. Then all I
wanted was to keep moving, to keep traveling, to get as far away from
Maribor as I could. And I did in the end. I left it all behind. And look at
me now. That's all thanks to you and Bastiaan."

We sat there for a long time, saying nothing, drinking, and finally
we stood up and made our way back to Ljubljana and the plane for
Dublin.

The Planes

Back in Dublin a month later, a Fianna Fáil TD approached me in the
tearoom at the Dáil one afternoon while I was eating lunch. A rather
inconsequential public servant, she had never spoken to me before and
took me by surprise, sitting down with a wide smile on her face as if
we were old friends and placing her pager on the table, glancing at it
occasionally in the desperate hope that it might buzz and make her
feel important.

"How are you, Cecil?" she asked.

"It's Cyril," I said.

"I thought your name was Cecil?"

"No," I said.

"You're not just being difficult, are you?"

"I can show you my ID badge if you like."

"No, you're all right. I believe you," she said, waving my offer away.
"Cyril then, if you prefer. What's that you're reading?"

I turned the book over to reveal a copy of Colm Toibín's *The Story of
the Night*. I'd owned it for years but had never got around to reading it
until now.

"Now, I haven't read that one," she said, picking it up and reading
the back. "Is it any good?"

"It is," I said.

"Should I read it?"

"Well, that's up to you, really."

"Maybe I'll give it a go. Have you ever read Jeffrey Archer?"

"I haven't," I admitted.

"Oh, he's wonderful," she said. "He tells a story, and that's what I like. Does this fella tell a story? He doesn't spend twenty pages describing the color of the sky?"

"He hasn't so far."

"Good. Jeffrey Archer never talks about the color of the sky and I like that in a writer. I'd say Jeffrey Archer has never even looked up at the sky in his entire life."

"Especially now that he's in prison," I suggested.

"The sky is blue," she declared. "And there it is."

"Well, it's not always blue," I said.

"It is," she said. "Don't be silly."

"It's not blue at night."

"Stop it now."

"All right," I said. I was beginning to think that she thought I was someone else entirely: one of her junior party colleagues perhaps. If she started to talk about votes or internal coups, I'd have to set her straight.

"Now, Cyril," she said. "Put the book down like a good man while I'm talking to you. I'm glad I caught up with you. I have good news for you: this is your lucky day."

"It is?" I said. "How so?"

"Would you like me to change your life for the better?"

I sat back and folded my arms, wondering whether she was going to ask whether I had accepted Jesus Christ as my personal savior.

"My life isn't all that bad as it is," I said.

"But it could be better, couldn't it? All our lives could be better. Mine could be better. I could be less of a workaholic than I am! I could care less about my constituents!"

"I suppose my hair could stop receding," I told her. "That'd be something. And I never used to need reading glasses until a couple of years ago."

"I can't do anything about either of those things. Have you spoken to the Minister for Health?"

"No," I said. "I was only joking, to be honest."

"Well, that's more his department than mine. No, I'm thinking about something a bit more intimate."

And *Oh Christ*, I thought. *She's making a pass at me.*

"When you say intimate," I said, "I hope you don't mean—"

"Hold on there now, like a good man," she said, turning around and looking for one of the waitresses. "I'm only gasping." When no one appeared immediately, she started clicking her fingers in the air and I looked around as the TDs from different parties stared at us in contempt.

"You really shouldn't do that," I said. "It's terribly rude."

"It's the only way to get their attention," she said. "Ever since Mrs. Goggin retired this place has gone to the dogs."

A few moments later, one of the waitresses walked over with a world-weary expression on her face.

"Is there a problem with your fingers?" she asked. "They seem to be making a terrible racket."

"I'm so sorry," I said to the woman, whose name tag said *Jacinta*.

"Be a dear," said my companion, touching her on the arm, "and get us two teas, would you? Nice and hot, there's a good girl."

"You can get your own tea," replied Jacinta. "You know where it's kept. Are you new to the place?"

"I am not," said the TD, appalled. "I'm on my second term."

"Then you should know how things work. And what are you doing sitting over here anyway? Who put you here?"

"What do you mean who put me here?" she asked, sounding half-outraged and half-insulted. "Sure don't I have the right to sit where I want?"

"You sit where you're told. Get back to the Fianna Fáil seats and don't be making a show of yourself."

"I will not, you rude little pup. Mrs. Goggin would never let you speak to me like this if she was here."

"I *am* Mrs. Goggin," said Jacinta. "Or the new Mrs. Goggin anyway. So you can help yourself to tea over there if you like. And if not, don't expect any to be brought to you. And next time, sit where you're supposed to sit or don't come in at all."

And with that she marched off, leaving my new TD friend looking shocked.

"Well, I never did!" she said. "Such rudeness! And I've been on my feet all day trying to provide a better life for the working classes like her. Did you see the speech I gave earlier?"

"You can't see a speech," I said. "You can only hear one."

"Oh, don't be so pedantic, you know what I mean."

I sighed. "Was there something I could help you with?" I asked. "Is it a library issue? If so, I'll be back there at two o'clock. In the meantime." I picked up the Toibín again, hoping that I could get back to it. I was at a good, dirty bit and didn't want to abandon the mood.

"You can, Cecil," she said.

"Cyril."

"Cyril," she said, shaking her head quickly. "I'll have to get that straight in my head. Cyril. Cyril the Squirrel."

I rolled my eyes. "Please don't say that," I said.

"Am I right in thinking that you're a widower?" she asked, grinning like the Cheshire cat.

"No, you're wrong," I said. "Actually, I'm divorced."

"Oh," she replied, looking a little disappointed. "I had hoped that your wife might be dead."

"I'm sorry to disappoint you," I told her. "But no, Alice is alive and well and living in Dartmouth Square."

"She's not dead?"

"Not the last time I checked. I had lunch with her on Sunday and she was in fine fettle. Full of insults."

"You did what?"

"I had lunch with her on Sunday."

"Why did you do that?"

I stared at her, wondering where on earth this conversation was going. "We often meet for lunch on a Sunday," I said. "It's a pleasant thing to do."

"Oh right," she said. "Just the two of you, was it?"

"No, her and her husband, Cyril II. And me."

"Cyril II?"

"Sorry, I mean Cyril."

"You met your ex-wife for lunch with her new husband, who has the same name as you, is that what you're telling me?"

"I think you have it now."

"Well, if you ask me, that's just peculiar."

"Is it? I don't see why."

"Do you mind if I ask when you got divorced?"

"I don't mind at all."

"So when was it?" she asked.

"Oh, a few years ago now. When the legislation first came in. Alice couldn't get rid of me quick enough, to be honest. As far as I understand, we were one of the first couples to take advantage of the new law."

"That's not a good sign," she said. "You must have had a very unhappy marriage."

"Not particularly."

"So why did you get divorced?"

"Do you know, I don't think that's any of your business."

"Oh don't be so defensive, we're all friends here."

"We're not though, are we?"

"We will be when I change your life."

"Maybe this conversation was a bad idea," I said.

"No, it wasn't," she replied. "Don't be worrying, Cecil. Cyril. Look, you're divorced. I won't hold it against you."

"That's very kind of you."

"Do you mind if I ask if you're seeing anyone at the moment?"

"I don't mind at all."

"So are you?" she asked.

"Am I what?"

"Seeing anybody?"

"In a romantic sense?"

"Yes."

"Why, do you have a crush on me?"

"Would you get away with yourself!" she said, bursting out laughing. "Sure amn't I a Fianna Fáil TD and you're just a librarian! Plus, I have a husband at home and three children who are training to be doctors, lawyers and PE teachers. Well, one of each, if you get my meaning."

"I do," I said.

"So are you?"

"Am I what?"

"Seeing anybody?"

"No," I replied.

"I didn't think so."

"Any particular reason?"

"Any particular reason what?"

"Any particular reason why you didn't think I would be seeing anyone?"

"Well, I never see you with anyone, do I?"

"No," I said. "But there again, this is a workplace. I'm not likely to be bringing someone into the book stacks for a little afternoon delight, am I?"

"Would you get away, you," she said, laughing as if I'd made the funniest joke ever. "You're an awful man!"

"We're all friends here," I said.

"We are. Now listen to me, Cecil."

"Cyril."

"I'll tell you why I'm asking. I have a sister. A lovely woman."

"How could she not be?"

"Her husband was knocked down and killed by a bus a few years ago."

"Right," I said. "I'm sorry to hear that."

"No," she said, shaking her head quickly. "Don't get me wrong. Not a regular CIÉ bus. A private bus."

"Of course."

"He was killed instantly."

"The poor man."

"Well, he'd always been complaining about his health and none of us ever took a bit of notice of him. It just goes to show, doesn't it?"

"It does."

"Anyway, after the funeral, we went to the Shelbourne."

"I got married in the Shelbourne."

"Let's not talk about that. Your past is your own business."

"I'm glad you're not prying," I said.

"So my sister is a widow and she's on the lookout for a nice man. She can't bear life on her own. She was in here to see me a couple of weeks ago and she caught sight of you in the library and she thought you were terribly handsome. She came over to me and *Angela*, she said, *Angela, who's that terribly handsome man over there?*"

I gave her a skeptical look. "Really?" I said. "I don't hear that very often these days. I'm fifty-six years old, you know. Are you sure she wasn't talking about someone else?"

"Oh no, it was definitely you, because I looked over and I couldn't believe she was talking about you either so I made her point you out. But it really was you."

"I'm flattered," I said.

"Don't let it go to your head. My sister would be any man's fancy. And I told her all about you and I think you're a perfect match."

"I'm not so sure," I said.

"Cyril. Cecil. Cyril. Let me lay my cards on the table."

"Go for it," I said.

"When Peter died—that was my brother-in-law—he left my sister very well looked after. She has her own house in Blackrock and there's no mortgage on it. And she has an apartment in Florence that she visits every few months and rents out the rest of the time."

"Lucky her," I said.

"And I know all about you."

"What do you know?" I asked. "Because something tells me that you really don't."

"I know that you're a multi-millionaire."

"Ah," I said.

"You're Maude Avery's son, aren't you?"

"Adoptive son."

"But you inherited all her estate? And her royalties."

"I did," I admitted. "I suppose that's common knowledge."

"So you're rich. You don't have to work. And yet you come in here every day and work anyway."

"I do."

"Do you mind if I ask why?"

"I don't mind at all."

"So why do you?" she asked.

"Because I enjoy it," I said. "It gets me out of the house. I don't want to sit at home, staring at the four walls every day, watching daytime television."

"But that's my point," she said. "You're a hard worker. You don't need money. You certainly don't need *her* money. That's why I think you'd be a perfect match."

"I'm not sure we would be," I repeated.

"Now hold on, there's a good man, don't say another thing until you've seen her picture." She reached into her handbag and took out a photo of a woman who looked just like her and I took to be her sister. I wondered whether they might even be twins, they looked that alike. "That's Brenda," she told me. "Isn't she beautiful?"

"Stunning," I agreed.

"So will I give you her number?"

"I don't think so," I said.

"Why not?" she asked, sitting back, preparing to be insulted. "Amn't I after telling you that you'd be perfect for each other?"

"I'm sure your sister is very nice," I said. "But to be honest with you, I'm not looking for a girlfriend at the moment. Or, in fact, at any moment."

"Oh," she said. "Are you still hung up on your ex-wife, is that it?"

"No," I said. "Definitely not."

"Your ex-wife has moved on to a different Cecil."

"Cyril," I said. "And I'm happy for her. We're good friends, the three of us."

"But you're trying to win her back?"

"I'm really not."

"So what is it then? You can't be telling me that you don't find Brenda attractive?"

"I don't," I said. "Sorry. She's just not my type."

At that moment, I heard a shout from one of the Fine Gael tables and looked over to see a small group of TDs who had previously been chatting over their cream buns and coffees, turning their heads to look at the television that hung on the wall in the corner of the tea-room. The sound was muted but I turned to look at it too and the more that people looked that way, the more the conversation in the room quieted down.

"Turn that up, would you?" called one of the men, and Jacinta, the waitress who had replaced Mrs. Goggin as manageress, reached for the remote control and turned up the volume as we watched a plane disappear into the heart of the World Trade Center over and over again, on what seemed like an endless repeat.

"Jesus, Mary and Joseph," said the TD. "What's going on there, do you suppose?"

"That's New York," I said.

"It is not."

"It is. It's the World Trade Center. The Twin Towers."

I stood up and walked slowly over toward the television as the TDs around us did the same thing, and when the coverage moved back to a live feed and another plane flew toward the second tower, burying itself inside it, we let out a groan of horror and stared at each other, not quite understanding what was going on.

"I better get back to my office," she said, picking up her silent pager. "The Taoiseach might need me."

"I doubt that he will."

"I'll come back to you about Brenda another time. Remember, you're perfect for each other."

"Right," I said, barely listening to her. The people on Sky News were talking about a terrible accident but then one of the guests asked how it could be an accident when it had happened twice. It must be hijackers, someone said. Or terrorists. From outside the tearoom, I could see the TDs running back and forth, going back to their offices or in search of a television set. It wasn't long before the room was half full.

"I've never been on a plane in my life," said Jacinta, coming over to stand next to me. "And I never will either."

I turned to her in surprise. "Are you frightened of them?" I asked.

"Wouldn't you be? After seeing that?"

I looked back at the screen. Reports were starting to come in that a third plane had crashed into the Pentagon in Washington and somehow there were already cameras on the streets of the capital, from the White House to the Senate Office Buildings, from the Mall to the Lincoln Memorial. A few minutes later, there was a live feed from the streets of New York, where I could see people running down the streets of Manhattan like something out of a cheesy Hollywood disaster movie.

Another switch and now a different reporter was standing in Central Park at exactly the same location where Bastiaan and I had been walking fourteen years earlier and suffered our attack. An involuntary cry came from my mouth as I saw it—I hadn't been there or seen it since that terrible night—and Jacinta touched my shoulder.

"Are you all right?" she asked.

"It's that place," I said, pointing at the screen. "I know it. My . . . my best friend was murdered right there."

"Stop watching it," she said, pulling me away. "Why don't you take a cup of tea with you and go back downstairs to the library and drink it in peace. There'll be no one in there for the rest of the day, I daresay. They'll all be watching this."

I nodded and turned back to the counter as she made the tea. I was moved that she was being so kind to me. She had learned well, I thought, from Mrs. Goggin.

"It's not easy losing someone," she said. "It never goes away, does it?"

"The Phantom Pain, they call it," I said. "Like amputees get when they can still feel their missing limbs."

"I expect so," she said, and then she gasped and I turned to look back at the television, where a series of black dots seemed to be falling from the windows of the buildings. The pictures quickly cut back to the studio, where both reporters looked shocked.

"Was that what I think it was?" I asked, turning back to her. "Were there people jumping from the windows?"

"I'm going to turn it off," she called out to the people gathered beneath the set, watching it.

"No!" they cried, gobbling up the drama.

"I'm the manageress," she insisted. "And what I say in this tearoom goes. I'm turning it off and if you want to keep watching you can find another television set somewhere in the building." And with that she reached for the remote, pressed the red button in the top right-hand corner and the screen went black. There was a roar of annoyance from the crowd, but they quickly scattered back to their offices or the local pubs, leaving us in silence.

"Ghouls," she said as she watched their departing backs. "The types that slow down when they see an accident on the motorway. I won't have people using this room to stare at someone else's misfortune."

I agreed with her but still wanted to get back to a television myself. I wondered how long would be respectable to stand there before I could leave.

"Go on then," she said finally, looking at me with disappointment in her eyes. "I know you're only itching to get out of here."

The Unspeakables

Christmas morning. The roads into town were practically empty and the snow that we'd been promised hadn't materialized. The taxi driver, surprisingly cheerful considering he was sitting behind the wheel of his car rather than at home opening presents and knocking back the Baileys with his family, was flicking between radio stations.

"Nothing serious, I hope?" he asked me, and I caught his eye in the rearview mirror.

"What's that?"

"Whoever you're visiting in hospital. Nothing serious, is it?"

I shook my head. "No, it's good news," I told him. "My son and his wife are having a baby."

"Ah that's great news. Their first, is it?"

"Second. They have a three-year-old boy, George."

I glanced out the window as we stopped at a red light. A little girl was cycling a brand-new bicycle with a broad smile on her face and wearing a shiny blue helmet as her father trotted along beside her, shouting words of encouragement. She wobbled a little but managed to steer in a relatively straight line and the pride on the man's face was something to behold. I might have been a good father. I might have been a positive force in Liam's life. But at least I had the grandchildren, Ignac's four and Liam's one. And now there was another on the way.

"They should call the child Jesus," said the taxi driver.

"What's that?"

"Your son and his wife," he said. "They should call the child Jesus. On account of the day that he's born."

"Yeah," I said "Probably not."

"I've got ten grandchildren myself," he continued. "And three of them are in the 'Joy. Best place for them. Vicious little bastards, each one. I blame the parents."

I looked down at my shoes, hoping to discourage him from further conversation, and soon enough the hospital loomed into sight. I reached into my pocket for a ten-euro note, handing it over as he pulled up outside, and wished him a happy Christmas. In the lobby I looked around, hoping to see someone I recognized, and when I didn't I took my phone from my pocket and rang Alice.

"Are you in the hospital?" I asked when she answered.

"I am," she said. "Where are you?"

"I'm in the lobby. Would you do me a favor and come down and get me?"

"Have you lost the use of your legs?"

"No, but I'll get lost in this place if I try to find you. I have no idea where I'm going."

A few minutes later, the doors of the elevator opened and Alice, looking elegant in her Christmas outfit, stepped out and beckoned me over. I leaned in to kiss her cheek, inhaling a breath of perfume, lavender and rose, that brought me instantly back in time to dates, engagement parties and weddings of the past. "You're not going to run out of the hospital before the baby's born, are you?" she asked.

"Hilarious," I said. "That joke never gets tired, does it?"

"Not to me, it doesn't."

"How's it going anyway? Is there any news?"

"Not yet. We're waiting."

"Who's up there?"

"Just Laura's parents," she said.

"Where's Liam?"

"He's in with Laura, of course," she said as the doors opened and we stepped out onto the corridor. A sound to my left made me turn around and I noticed a middle-aged woman embracing two small children, locked in grief with tears streaming down her face. Our eyes met for a moment before I turned away.

"Poor woman," I said. "Has she lost her husband, do you think?"

"What makes you think that?"

"I don't know. It seems like the natural thing to assume."

"I suppose so."

"On Christmas Day too. How awful."

"Don't stare," said Alice.

"I'm not staring."

"You are. Come on, they're down this way."

We turned a corner and made our way down a corridor that was almost deserted except for a middle-aged couple sitting in the waiting area. They stood up as we approached them and I extended a hand when Alice introduced us.

"Cyril, you remember Peter and Ruth, don't you?" she said.

"Of course," I replied. "Happy Christmas. Nice to see you both again."

"Happy Christmas to you," said Peter, an enormous man bursting out of an extra-large shirt. "And may the blessings of Jesus Christ, our Lord and Savior, be with you on this momentous day."

"Fair enough," I said. "Hello, Ruth."

"Hello, Cyril. Long time no see. Alice was just talking about you."

"All bad things, I imagine."

"Oh no, she was being very complimentary."

"Don't mind them," said Alice. "I haven't said much about you at all. And if I did, I'm sure it wasn't very nice."

"Well, this is a great way to spend Christmas morning," I said, smiling as we all sat down. "I was hoping to be at home with the mince pies."

"I can't eat mince pies," said Peter. "They give me terrible gas."

"That's a shame."

"Although I must admit I ate four before I left the house earlier."

"Right," I said, sitting back from him a little.

"I keep the mince pies locked away," said Ruth, smiling at me. "But he always manages to track them down. He's like a truffling pig!"

"Maybe you just shouldn't buy any," I suggested. "Then he wouldn't be able to find them."

"Oh no, that wouldn't be fair to Peter," she said.

"Right," I said, glancing at my watch.

"If you need Mass," said Peter, "they have one in the chapel here at eleven."

"No, I'm grand."

"They do a lovely Mass here. They really put the effort in since it'll be the last one for a lot of the patients."

"We got Mass last night," said Ruth. "So there's that to be grateful for at least. I couldn't face it later."

"I'm not really the Mass-going type, to be honest," I said. "No offense."

"Oh," she said, sitting back a little and pursing her lips.

"To be honest, I haven't been inside a church since Alice and I got married."

"Well, don't brag about it," said Peter. "That's nothing to be proud of."

"I wasn't bragging. I was just saying."

"If you'd known it was your last time in a church, you would have made the most of it, wouldn't you, Cyril?" said Alice, smiling at me, and I smiled back.

"Maybe," I said.

"Where did you get married?" asked Ruth.

"Ranelagh," said Alice.

"Was it a lovely day?"

"It was a lovely morning," said Alice. "It seemed to go downhill a bit after that."

"Well, the ceremony's the important part. And where did you have your reception?"

"The Shelbourne. You?"

"The Gresham."

"Nice."

"Let's not talk religion," I said. "Or weddings."

"All right," said Ruth. "What will we talk about then?"

"Anything you like," I suggested.

"I can't think of anything," she said, looking distressed.

"Do you think I should get my rash looked at while I'm here?" asked Peter.

"What's that?" I asked.

"I have a terrible rash on my unspeakable," said Peter. "This place is full of doctors. Maybe I should get one of them to look at it."

"Not today," said Ruth.

"It's getting worse, though."

"Not today!" she snapped. "Peter and his unspeakable! He's a martyr to it."

"The snow never came," I said, desperately trying to change the subject.

"I wouldn't believe the weather forecasters. They're all in it for whatever they can get for themselves."

"Right," I said.

"Did it take you long to get over here?" asked Ruth, looking at me.

"Not long, no. The roads were empty. You don't get too many people out on a Christmas morning. Has there been any news at all anyway?"

"Not for a while. She's been in labor for a few hours, though, so I expect we'll hear something soon enough. It's exciting, isn't it? Another grandchild."

"It is," I said. "I'm looking forward to it. How many do you have now?"

"Eleven," said Ruth.

"That's a lot," I said.

"Well, we do have six children. Peter here would have had more if I'd let him," she continued. "But I said no. Six was enough. I closed up shop after Diarmaid."

"She did," agreed Peter. "The shutters came down and they haven't been lifted since."

"Stop it, Peter."

"She might as well have put a sign on her unspeakable saying, *Gone to lunch. Won't be coming back ever.*"

"Peter!"

"Isn't the paint on the walls a funny color?" asked Alice, looking around her.

"Who sang that song 'Unchained Melody'?" I asked.

"Cyril and I might try France this summer," said Alice.

"I have an ongoing pain in my left knee that doesn't seem to be shifting," I said.

"I always wanted a big family," said Peter with a shrug, ignoring our desperate attempts to stop talking about their private parts.

"Six was plenty," insisted Ruth.

"Six is more than plenty," said Alice. "I thought one was difficult enough."

"Well, of course, there were the two of us to look after them," said Peter. "You didn't have the same luxury, Alice, did you?"

"No," she said after a brief hesitation, perhaps wondering whether she should defend me in front of outsiders. "Although Liam's uncle was very involved. He helped me a lot in the early years."

I threw her a look; we liked to tease each other, but our jokes rarely if ever involved Julian.

"You and Liam are very close, aren't you?" said Ruth, looking at me.

"Well, we're doing well, yes."

"The poor boy needed a strong father figure, from what I hear."

"How do you mean?"

"Well, after what his real father did. Alice was lucky that she met a real man in the end."

"Ah," I said.

"I prefer a masculine man, don't you, Alice?"

"I do," said Alice.

"Me too," I said.

"It takes a big man to take on another man's child," said Peter, slapping a hand down on his knee. "Especially the son of a gay homosexual. No offense, Alice. I meant your ex-husband. No, I admire you, Cyril. I really do. I don't think I could have done what you did."

"No offense taken," said Alice, beaming from ear to ear.

"All I can say is that it's a good job Liam didn't turn out like his father," continued Peter. "Do you think that sort of thing runs in families?"

"Ginger hair can," said Ruth. "So it's a possibility."

"Will you tell them or will I?" I asked, looking at Alice.

"Oh I don't think either of us should," she said. "Let's hear what else they have to say. I'm enjoying this."

"What's that?" asked Ruth.

"Alice tells us that you're a wonderful violinist," said Peter. "I play the ukulele myself. Have you ever played the ukulele?"

"I haven't," I admitted. "Nor have I ever played the violin."

"Oh I thought that's what you said he played, Alice," said Ruth. "Is it the cello?"

"No, it's the violin," said Alice. "But you're thinking of my husband, Cyril, who plays in the RTÉ Symphony Orchestra. This isn't him. This is my ex-husband, Cyril. Don't you remember meeting him before? I thought you realized. It's been a few years, I suppose."

"Cyril I," I said, to clarify things. "Where is Cyril II anyway?" I asked, turning to Alice.

"Don't call him that. And he's at home putting the dinner on."

"Woman's work," I said. "I prefer a masculine man."

"Shut up, Cyril."

"Am I still invited?"

"If you promise not to run away before we serve the meal."

"Hold on there," said Peter, looking back and forth between the pair of us. "This is your ex-husband, is that right?"

"Correct," I said. "The gay homosexual."

"Oh but you should have told us!" said Ruth. "We never would have said such things if we'd known that *you* were the gay homosexual. We thought you were Alice's second husband. You're quite alike, the pair of you, aren't you?"

"They're nothing alike!" cried Alice. "Cyril II is a lot younger for one thing and much better looking."

"And a straight heterosexual," I added.

"Well, we can only apologize. We'd never say such things to a person's face, would we, Peter?"

"No," said Peter. "No hard feelings. It's all forgotten."

"All right," I said.

"Of course, I should have realized," said Ruth, laughing. "Now that I look at that jumper you're wearing, I suppose I should have guessed."

"Thank you," I said, glancing down at myself, uncertain what my jumper had to do with my sexuality. "It's like Christmas morning here with all the compliments. Oh wait, it *is* Christmas morning."

"Am I right in thinking that you work in the Dáil?" asked Ruth.

"That's right," I said. "In the library."

"Now, that must be very interesting. Do you get to see any of the TDs or the ministers?"

"Yes, of course," I said. "I mean that's where they work, after all. I see them most days wandering around the place in search of drinking companions."

"What about Bertie? Do you ever get to see Bertie?"

"Yes, quite often," I said.

"What's he like?"

"Well, I don't really know him," I said. "Other than to say hello, that is. He seems friendly enough, though. I've had a drink with him in the bar a few times and he's always full of chat."

"I love Bertie," said Ruth, putting a hand to her chest as if she needed to control her palpitations.

"Do you?"

"I do. I don't mind at all that he's divorced."

"That's good of you."

"I always say that he's a fine figure of a man. I always say that, don't I, Peter?"

"Ad nauseam," said her husband, reaching down and picking up a book that he had left on the table between us, the latest John Grisham. I wondered whether he was going to start back into it now. "You should hear her, Cyril. All day long it's Bertie this and Bertie that. She'd run off with Bertie if she could. Whenever she sees him on the television, it's like watching a teenage girl at a Boyzone concert."

"Oh, don't be ridiculous," said Ruth. "Bertie's a lot better looking than any of those lads. The thing is, Cyril, Peter doesn't like politicians. Fianna Fáil. Fine Gael. Labor. They're all the same as far as Peter's concerned. Crooks."

"Scumbags," said Peter.

"That might be going a bit far," I said.

"It's not going far enough," he said, raising his voice. "I'd string them all up if I could. Do you never get the urge to take a machine gun in to work and just blow all those politicians away?"

I stared at him, wondering whether he was joking or not. "No," I said. "No, I don't. The idea's never crossed my mind, to be honest."

"Well, you should think about it," he said. "That's what I'd do if I worked there."

"Cyril will be putting the turkey in the oven around now," said Alice.

"Cyril II," I said, clarifying things for Peter and Ruth.

"Don't call him that."

"We're going to our eldest boy's for dinner," said Ruth. "Joseph. He works for an animation company, if you can believe it. We don't mind. It takes all sorts. He makes lovely roast potatoes, though, doesn't he, Peter? He hasn't taken a wife yet even though he's thirty-five. I think he's very particular."

Her husband looked at her and frowned, as if this was a matter that needed deep thought. "His roast potatoes," he said finally, "would stand comparison with those of a Michelin-starred chef. I don't know what his secret is. He didn't get it from me, that's for sure."

"Goose fat," said Alice. "That's the trick."

"Peter couldn't boil an egg," said Ruth.

"I never needed to," he protested. "I had you for that."

Ruth rolled her eyes at Alice as if to say *Men!* But Alice refused complicity and glanced at her watch instead. It was just coming up to noon.

"Your daughter is a credit to you," I said, changing the subject. "She's a wonderful mother to young George."

"Well, we brought her up properly."

A door to our right opened and a nurse walked out and we all turned our heads in anticipation, but she walked away from us toward the nurses' station, where she gave an almighty yawn before leaning down to peruse a copy of the *RTÉ Guide*.

"I wonder what would make a man want to be a gynecologist," said Peter in a thoughtful voice, and Ruth threw him a look of warning.

"Be quiet, Peter," she said.

"I'm only saying. Laura's gynecologist is a man and I think it's a funny job. Looking at unspeakables all day. A fourteen-year-old boy might think it was fun, but I couldn't be up to it. I was never a big fan of looking at women's unspeakables."

"Am I right in thinking that you're a psychiatrist, Alice?" asked Ruth, and my ex-wife shook her head.

"No," she said. "I'm nothing of the sort. What made you think that?"

"But you're a doctor, that's right, isn't it?"

"Well, yes. A Doctor of Letters. I teach Literature in Trinity College. I'm not a medical doctor."

"Oh, I thought you were a psychiatrist."

"No," said Alice, shaking her head.

"I actually considered cardiology for a while myself," said Peter. "As my specialty, I mean."

"Oh, are you a doctor?" I asked, turning to him.

"No," he said, frowning. "I work in construction. Why would you think that?"

I stared at him. I had no answer.

"Peter and I actually met in a hospital," said Ruth. "Not the most romantic place in the world, I suppose. He was a porter and I was in to have my appendix out."

"I wheeled her down to the operating theater," said Peter. "And I thought there was something very attractive about her as she lay there under the sheet. After they put her under, I stayed to watch the operation. When they took the sheet off her, I took a look at her body and said to myself, *That's the woman I'm going to marry.*"

"Right," I said, telling myself not to look at Alice in case her expression would make me laugh.

"And how about you two?" asked Ruth, and now we did exchange a look. "How did you two meet?"

"We'd known each other since we were children," I said.

"Well, not quite," said Alice. "We *met* when we were children. Once. When I ran screaming out of Cyril's house. And we didn't even meet then, to be honest. Cyril just saw me, that's all."

"Why did you do that?" asked Peter. "Did he do something to upset you?"

"No, his mother frightened me. It was the only time I ever met her, which is unfortunate because she ended up being my particular field of study. Cyril's mother was a brilliant novelist, you see."

"Adoptive mother," I said.

"But anyway, we met again when we were a little older."

"Alice's brother was a friend of mine," I said carefully.

"Is this the brother who helped out with Liam?" she asked.

"Yes," said Alice. "I only had one."

"This'd be the lad who died over there in America, would it?" asked Peter, and Alice turned to him and gave a brisk nod. He'd obviously heard the full story.

"Christ, you haven't had an easy time of it either, have you?" he asked, laughing a little. "You got it on both sides."

"Got what?" asked Alice coldly.

"Well, you know, your brother and your . . ." He nodded toward me. "Your husband here. Your ex-husband, I mean."

"Got what though?" she repeated. "I don't understand what you're talking about."

"Don't mind Peter," said Ruth, reaching across and placing her hand on Alice's, somewhere between a caress and a slap. "He thinks before he speaks."

"I'm in trouble again," said Peter, looking at me with a grin, and I began to wonder whether he was trying to be offensive or was simply an idiot. There was another extended silence and I glanced down at his book.

"What's that like?" I asked, nodding at the John Grisham.

"It's not bad," he said. "Your people read a lot, don't they?"

"My people?"

"Your people."

"Irish people, do you mean? Sorry, I thought you were Irish too."

"I am," he said blankly.

"Oh right," I said. "Did you mean gay homosexuals?"

"Isn't it awful how that word has been co-opted to pursue the liberal agenda?" asked Ruth. "I blame Boy George."

"Yes," said Peter. "That's what I meant."

"Right," I said. "Well, I suppose some do. And some don't. Like anyone else."

"Here," said Peter, leaning forward and grinning at me. "Bertie or John Major? Which one would you rather have as your boyfriend? Or would it be Clinton? I bet it would be Clinton! I'm right, amn't I?"

"I'm not really looking for a boyfriend," I said. "And if I was, it wouldn't be one of them."

"It always makes me laugh when fellas use that word," said Ruth, and true to her word she started laughing. "*Boyfriend!*"

"It'll be something new for you, all the same," said Peter. "A baby, I mean."

"It will," I agreed.

"The traditional family."

"Whatever that is," I said.

"Ah, you know what it is," said Peter. "A mammy and a daddy and a few kids. Look, Cyril, don't get me wrong, I don't have anything against your lot. I'm not prejudiced at all."

"He's not," agreed Ruth. "He's never been prejudiced. Sure he had a whole load of darkies working for him back in the eighties before it was even fashionable. And he paid them almost as much as he paid the Irish workers. We even had one in the house once." She leaned forward and lowered her voice. "*For dinner,*" she added. "I didn't mind."

"True enough," said Peter proudly. "I'm a friend to every man, black, white or yellow, gay, straight or homosexual. Live and let live, that's my motto. Although I have to admit that lads like you baffle me."

"Why is that?" I asked.

"It's hard to explain. I just never understood how you can do the things you do. I couldn't do it."

"I don't suppose anyone would want you to," I said.

"Oh I wouldn't say that," said Alice, poking me in the ribs. "Peter's a good-looking man for his age. I'd say they'd be lining up. You have the look of Bertie Ahern, if you ask me."

"He looks nothing like Bertie," said Ruth wistfully.

"Thank you, Alice," said Peter, pleased by the compliment.

"You don't have any gay children yourselves then?" I asked, and they sat bolt upright in shock, the pair of them, as if I'd taken out a stick and started to beat one or the other of them senseless with it.

"We do not," they said together.

"We wouldn't be the sort," added Ruth.

"What sort is that?" I asked.

"It's just not the way I was brought up. Or the way Peter was brought up," she said.

"But your son Joseph makes lovely roast potatoes, is that right?"

"What has that got to do with anything?"

"Nothing. I was just saying. I'm getting hungry, that's all."

"Can I ask you," said Ruth leaning forward. "Do you have a . . . what do you call it . . . a partner?"

I shook my head. "No," I said. "No, I don't."

"Have you always been alone?"

"No," I said. "There was someone. Once. A long time ago. But he died."

"Do you mind if I ask you, was it AIDS?"

I rolled my eyes. "No," I said. "He was murdered."

"Murdered?" asked Peter.

"Yes. By a group of thugs."

"Sure that's even worse."

"Is it?" asked Alice. "How so?"

"Well, maybe not worse, but no one asks to be murdered, do they?"

"No one asks to get AIDS," I said.

"Well, maybe no one specifically asks for it, but if you're going to ride your bicycle on the wrong side of the street, you can expect to get knocked over, am I right?"

"No, you're completely wrong," snapped Alice. "And if you don't mind me saying so, that's a very ignorant thing to say."

"I don't mind at all, Alice," said Peter. "Speak as you find and I'll do the same. That way we'll stay friends."

"It's attitudes like that that cause so much trouble in the world," she said.

"We could always eat in the hospital canteen, I suppose," said Ruth, interrupting her.

"What?"

"If we get hungry, I mean. We could eat in the canteen."

"Sure the food there is even worse than the rubbish they serve the patients," said Peter. "Would we not be better going over to Joseph's and having our dinner with him there and coming back when we get the call? We should eat his roast potatoes while they're fresh. And you know he wanted us all to watch *The Sound of Music* in the afternoon. It's Steven's favorite film."

"Who's Steven?" I asked.

"His flatmate," said Peter. "They're great pals. They've been sharing for years."

"Right," I said.

"No, we would not," said Ruth. "You won't be able to drive for one thing."

"Why wouldn't I?"

"Because I know what you're like, Peter Richmond. You'll get started on the red wine and that'll be the end of it. I won't get a word of sense out of you and there'll be no taxi drivers on the street later.

They'll all be at home with their families." She paused for a moment and put a finger to her lip. "It must be terrible to be murdered," she said, turning back to me. "I'd hate it."

The door opened again and now Liam appeared, wearing similar blue scrubs to those that the nurse had worn earlier. Turning and seeing us all waiting, we stood up and he grinned, holding his arms out wide.

"I'm a dad," he said. "Again!"

We all cheered and embraced him. I was touched that when he threw his arms around me he seemed to squeeze me extra-tight and when he pulled away he looked directly into my eyes and smiled.

"And how's Laura?" asked Ruth anxiously. "Is she all right?"

"Not a bother on her. They'll be bringing her up to her room in about half an hour and you can see her then."

"And the baby?" asked Alice.

"A little boy," he replied.

"You'll have to try for a girl next time," said Ruth.

"Steady on," said Liam. "Give us a chance."

"Can I see him?" I asked finally. "I'd love to hold my grandson."

Liam looked up and his face broke into a smile of pure happiness as he nodded. "Of course you can, Dad," he said. "Of course you can."

Julian II

Laura's parents left first, looking forward to Joseph's roast potatoes and Steven's rapturous appreciation of *The Sound of Music*. Alice left shortly afterward, but I told her that I was going to stay with Liam for a little while longer and that I'd take a taxi to Dartmouth Square and be there before Cyril II was ready to carve the turkey.

"You're not going to *not* show up, are you?" she asked, looking me directly in the eye with all the coolness of a trained assassin.

"Why wouldn't I?" I asked.

"You do have form in this area, Cyril."

"Not fair. I always show up. I just don't always stay until the end."

"Cyril—"

"Alice, I'll be there. I promise."

"You better. Because if you don't, Ignac, Rebecca and the children will be very disappointed. And so will I. It's Christmas Day, after all. I don't want you hiding out in Ballsbridge on your own. The whole family should be together. And I've bought a massive box of Quality Street."

"Well, that seals the deal."

"And every flavor of Pringles."

"I hate Pringles."

"And I'm planning a game of *Who Wants to Be a Millionaire?* later. I even bought a book."

"Even so. I'll still come. As long as I can be the question master."

"No, Cyril II wants to be the question master."

"Don't call him that."

"Oh shut up, Cyril."

"I just feel like spending a little more time with Liam, that's all. And it would be nice for you and your young man to have an hour together before I arrive. You can kiss and do all sorts of man and woman dirty things with each other."

"Oh for God's sake."

"You can wax his strings."

"Cyril!"

"Tighten his bow."

"I'll swing for you in a minute."

"By the way, I was planning on getting completely sloshed tonight and staying over. I assume that's all right."

"If you don't mind sleeping in your childhood bedroom and hearing your ex-wife have sex with a man five years younger than you while five infants scream their heads off, then it's fine with me."

"Sounds delightful. I'll be there by four. Promise."

And so I spent another half hour with my son and his wife, and before I left I brought Liam down to the hospital café, where we bought two bottles of beer and toasted the latest addition to our unconventional family.

"It was very kind of you," I told him, feeling a little emotional now, partly because I was a grandfather again, partly because it was Christmas Day and partly because I was looking forward to the evening ahead. "To invite me in to meet the baby first, I mean. I'm not sure that I've earned that right. I would have thought your mother or Laura's parents—"

"I don't care about all that stuff anymore," he said quickly. "I've put all that behind me."

"That's good to hear. But still."

"Look," he said, putting his bottle down. "Cyril. Dad. It doesn't matter, OK? I know I wasn't the easiest person to get along with when we first found each other but things are different now. You've done nothing since we first met but make me like you. Despite my best efforts. And it's quite annoying, actually, because I was determined to hate you."

"And I was equally determined to love you," I said.

"You know I had to do it, don't you?" he said eventually.

"Do what?"

"His name. My son's name."

"I guessed that you might," I said. "I hoped that you would."

"It's not a slight against you."

"I never thought for a moment that it was. You and your uncle had a close bond and you loved each other. I respect that. And my relationship with him was just as deep as yours, only different. I loved him very much. Our relationship was a complicated one and I didn't come out of it covered with glory, but then again neither did he. Still, we were together from the start, we went through a lot together, and we were by each other's side at the end."

To my surprise, Liam buried his face in his hands and started crying.

"What is it?" I asked, reaching out and taking his hand. "What's wrong?"

"I still miss him so much," he said. "I wish he was here."

I nodded. And the lesser part of my character allowed myself to feel envious, knowing that my son would never love me as much as he had loved Julian.

"Did he talk about me?" he asked. "When he was dying, I mean? Did he mention my name?"

I felt the tears form in my eyes now too. "Are you kidding me?" I asked. "Liam, you were the son he never had. He talked about you all the time at the end. He wanted you there but he didn't want you to see him as he was. He loved you so much. You were the most important person in his life."

He lifted his bottle. "To Julian," he said, smiling.

It took me a moment, but I lifted my bottle too. "To Julian," I said quietly.

And to this day, I don't know which Julian we were each toasting, Liam's beloved uncle or his newly born son.

A Little Hunchbacked
Redemptorist Nun

As I made my way back toward the ground floor, my phone rang and I glanced at the screen, knowing exactly what it would say: *Alice.*

"You have one hour," she said without any preamble when I answered.

"I'm leaving now."

"One hour and then I lock the doors."

"I'm literally walking out of the hospital as we speak."

"The twins are asking where you are."

"Which twins?"

"Both sets."

"Impossible," I said. "One set are only babies. They can't even speak, let alone question my whereabouts."

"Just be here," said Alice. "And stop annoying me."

"How's Cyril II? Is he cracking under the pressure of cooking for so many people?"

"Fifty-eight minutes and counting."

"I'm on my way."

I hung up and made my way toward the exit but the sound of weeping coming from behind a set of doors to my left gave me pause. I glanced over to where the doors to the chapel were ajar. The room inside seemed so different from the rest of the hospital—the clinical white walls replaced by something warmer and far more inviting— that I found myself moved to take a closer look.

There was only one person inside, an elderly lady seated at the end of a pew halfway toward the altar. Classical music was playing softly, a piece I half recognized, and the door to one of the confessionals was open. I watched the woman for a few moments, uncertain whether I should walk away and leave her to her sorrow or see whether she needed some help. Eventually, my feet made the decision for me but as I stepped closer, my eyes opened wide in surprise at who she was.

"Mrs. Goggin," I said. "It's Mrs. Goggin, isn't it?"

She looked across at me as if woken from a dream and stared at me for a few moments, her face pale. "Kenneth?" she said.

"No, it's Cyril Avery, Mrs. Goggin," I said. "From the Dáil library."

"Oh, Cyril," she said, nodding her head and putting her hand to her chest as if she was afraid she might be having a heart attack. "Of course. I'm sorry; I took you for someone else. How are you, dear?"

"I'm fine," I said. "It must be years since I saw you last."

"Is it that long?"

"Yes, it was at your retirement party."

"Oh yes," she said quietly.

"But what's wrong?" I asked. "Are you all right?"

"I'm not, no," she replied. "Not really."

"Is there something I can do for you?"

She shrugged. "I don't think so," she said. "But thank you anyway."

I glanced around, hoping that one of her family members might be nearby and come in to help but the chapel was silent and the doors had closed shut behind me.

"Do you mind if I sit down for a few minutes?"

She took a long time to decide but finally nodded her head, moving over a little in the pew to let me join her.

"What's happened, Mrs. Goggin?" I asked. "What has you so upset?"

"My son is dead," she said quietly.

"Oh no. Jonathan?"

"A couple of hours ago now. I've been sitting here ever since."

"Mrs. Goggin, I'm so sorry."

"We knew it was coming," she told me with a sigh. "But that doesn't make it any easier."

"Had he been ill for long?" I asked, reaching across and taking her hand in mine. Her skin felt paper-thin and there were dark-blue veins running toward her knuckles.

"On and off," she said. "He had cancer, you see. He first developed it about fifteen years ago, but he managed to beat it then. Unfortunately, it came back late last year. Six months ago, the doctors told us there was nothing more that they could do for him. And today was the day."

"I hope he didn't suffer too much."

"He did," she said. "But he was very stoical about it. It's those of us who are left behind who'll have to suffer now."

"Would you like me to leave you on your own or is there someone I can call for you?"

She thought about it and dabbed the corners of her eyes with her handkerchief. "No," she said. "Can you stay a little while? If you don't mind?"

"I don't mind at all," I told her.

"You don't have anywhere to be?"

"I do. But it won't matter if I'm a few minutes late. But is there anyone from your family here to take care of you? You're not all alone, surely?"

"I don't need taking care of," she said defiantly. "I might be old, but you have no idea the strength that's left in this body."

"I don't doubt it," I said. "But you're not going home to an empty house, are you?"

"No. My daughter-in-law was here earlier with my grandchildren. They've gone home now. I'll follow shortly."

"All right," I said, remembering the woman and the two little girls whom I'd seen wrapped in each other's embrace earlier when I'd first arrived at the hospital. "I think I noticed them in the corridor upstairs a couple of hours ago."

"You might have done. They were here all night. Well, we all were. A terrible way for children to spend Christmas Eve. They should be waiting for Santa Claus, not watching their daddy die."

"I don't know what to say to you," I said, looking toward the front of the church where a large wooden cross holding the crucified Christ stood on a wall, looking down at us in all his pity. "Are you religious?" I asked. "Do you find some peace in here at least?"

"I'm not really," she said. "I have some sort of relationship with God, I suppose, but I had a bad time with the Church when I was a girl. Why, are you?"

I shook my head. "Not even slightly."

"I don't even know why I came in here, to be honest. I was just passing, that was all, and it looked quiet. I needed somewhere to sit, that's all. The Church was never a friend to me. I've always felt that the Catholic Church has the same relationship to God as a fish has to a bicycle."

I smiled. "I feel the same way," I said.

"I don't even come into churches very often. Except for weddings and christenings and funerals. More than fifty years ago, a priest picked me up by the hair and threw me out of my parish church and I haven't had much time for it since. But I should have asked you why you're here," she added, turning to look at me. "Something must be wrong if you're in a hospital on Christmas Day."

"No, it's not nothing like that. My son and his wife had a baby boy earlier today. I came in to see him, that's all."

"Oh, well that's good news at least," she said, forcing a smile. "Do they have a name for him yet?"

"They do. Julian."

"That's unusual," she said, considering it. "You don't get many Julians these days. It makes me think of Roman emperors. Or the Famous Five. One of them was a Julian, wasn't he?"

"I think so," I said. "It's been a long time since I read those books."

"And how are things in the Dáil?"

"Oh you don't want to worry about that, today of all days."

"I do," she said. "Just for a moment; it will take my mind off things."

"Well, they're much the same as ever," I said. "Your successor is running the tearoom with an iron fist."

"Good for her," she said, smiling. "I trained her well so."

"You did."

"If you don't keep those TDs in line, they'll walk all over you."

"Do you miss it?" I asked.

"I do and I don't. I miss the routine. I miss getting up every morning and having a place to go and people to talk to. But it's not as if I ever particularly enjoyed the job itself. It was a living, that was all. Something to put food on the table."

"I suppose I feel the same way," I said. "I don't need to work but I do it anyway. I don't look forward to retirement."

"That's a long way off for you yet."

I shrugged my shoulders. "Less than a decade," I said. "The time will fly. But look, let's not talk about me. Will you be all right, Mrs. Goggin?" I asked.

"I will, in time," she said carefully. "I've lost people before. I've known violence, I've known bigotry, I've known shame and I've known love. And somehow, I always survive. And I still have Melanie and the girls. We're all quite close. I'm seventy-two years old, Cyril. If there is a heaven, then I suppose it won't be long before I see Jonathan again too. But it's hard to lose a child. It's an unnatural thing."

"It is."

"An unnatural thing," she repeated.

"And he was your only one?"

"No. I lost another son a long time ago."

"Oh Christ. I'm sorry. I didn't realize."

"It was completely different," she said, shaking her head. "He didn't die. I gave him up. I was pregnant, you see. And just a girl. Different times, of course. That's why the priest threw me out of the church," she added with a bitter smile.

"They have no compassion, do they?" I asked. "They talk about Christianity and yet it's just a concept to them, not a way of life at all."

"I heard afterward that he had fathered two children himself by two different women, one in Drimoleague and one in Clonakilty. The old hypocrite."

"He wasn't the one who . . . ?"

"Oh my Lord, no!" she said. "That was someone else entirely."

"And what about the child?" I asked. "Have you never been tempted to find him?"

She shook her head. "I've watched the news," she said. "I've seen the documentaries and films. I daresay he would blame me for whatever went wrong in his life and I haven't the energy for that. I did what I thought was right at the time and I stand by my decision. No, a little hunchbacked Redemptorist nun took him away from me and I knew that day that I would never see him again and I've made my peace with that over the years. I just hope he was happy, that's all."

"All right," I said, squeezing her hand, and she looked at me and smiled.

"Our paths seem to cross every so often, don't they?" she said.

"Dublin is a small city," I told her.

"It is."

"Is there anything I can do for you?" I asked.

"No. I'll go back to Melanie's now. And what about you, Cyril? Where are you going for your Christmas dinner?"

"To my ex-wife's house," I said. "And her new husband. They take in all the waifs and strays."

She smiled and nodded. "It's good that you can all be friends," she said.

"I don't like to leave you here on your own," I told her. "Would you like me to stay with you a little longer?"

"Do you know," she said quietly, "I think I'd prefer to have some time to myself. After a while, I'll get up and go. I can get a taxi outside. But you were very good, Cyril, to come in and say hello to me."

I nodded and stood up. "I'm very sorry for your loss, Mrs. Goggin," I said.

"And I'm glad to hear that you have a new grandchild. It was nice to see you again, Cyril."

I reached down and gave her a kiss on the cheek, the first time I had done such an intimate thing with her, and turned back down the aisle, making for the door. As I left, I looked back and saw her sitting upright on the seat, staring at the crucifix, and it struck me that here was a strong woman, a good woman, and what kind of God was it who would allow her to lose one son, let alone two?

I was out in the corridor again before a sentence that she had spoken came back to me, bursting through my brain like a shot of electricity. *A little hunchbacked Redemptorist nun took him away from me and I knew that day that I would never see him again.* I stopped still and reached out to the wall for support, leaning heavily on my crutch with the other arm. Swallowing hard, I turned around and looked back at the doors of the chapel.

"Mrs. Goggin," I said, walking through them again and calling out to her. She spun around in surprise and stared at me.

"What is it, Cyril?" she asked.

"Do you remember the date?"

"What date?"

"The date your son was born."

"Of course I do," she said, frowning. "It was in June 1964. The seventeenth. It was a—"

"No," I said, interrupting her. "Not Jonathan. I mean your first son. The one you gave up."

She said nothing for a moment, simply stared at me, perhaps wondering why on earth I was asking her such a question. But then she told me. She remembered it quite clearly, of course.

2008 The Silver Surfer

Aquabatics with Alejandro

Arriving at Heuston Station, I glanced up toward the Departures board but had to squint to make out the platform from which our train was scheduled to leave. For weeks, I had been feeling both excited and apprehensive about the trip ahead, a journey that I'd never imagined either of us taking, and now that the day was finally here I was nervous about the emotions that it might stir up in us both. Looking around, I saw my seventy-nine-year-old mother marching through the front doors, apparently full of energy as she wheeled a suitcase behind her, and I made my way over to take it from her, reaching down to give her a kiss.

"Get away," she said, dismissing my offer of help. "I'm not giving my bag to a man with a crutch."

"You are indeed," I said, wrestling it off her.

She gave in and when she looked up at the Departures board I could tell that her eyesight was better than mine. "On time, I see," she said. "What's seldom is wonderful."

It was a constant source of amazement to me that she was so sprightly. She didn't even have a regular doctor, insisting that she didn't need one because she never got sick.

"Will we board?" I asked. "And try to get a good seat?"

"Lead the way," she said, following me down the platform, and I walked toward the most distant carriage, the one that had the least chance of being crowded. There were groups of young people and parents with small children climbing into the nearer ones and I wanted to be as far from them and their noise as possible.

"You're like an old man, Cyril," said my mother when I made this observation to her.

"I *am* an old man," I said. "I'm sixty-three."

"Yes, but you don't have to act like one. I'm seventy-nine and I went to a disco last night."

"You did not!"

"I did so. Well, a dinner-dance anyway. With some friends."

When I finally found a carriage that suited me, we climbed on board and sat down at a table facing each other, windows next to both of us for the view.

"It's good to get off my feet," she said with a sigh. "I've been up since six."

"Why so early?" I asked.

"I went to the gym first thing."

"I'm sorry?"

"I went to the gym," she repeated.

I blinked, uncertain whether I was understanding her right. "You go to a gym?" I asked.

"I do, of course," she said. "Why, don't you?"

"No."

"No," she said, glancing at my stomach. "Well, you should try it, Cyril. Losing a few pounds wouldn't kill you."

"Since when have you been going to the gym?" I asked, ignoring this.

"Oh, for about four years now," she said. "Did I never tell you about it?"

"No," I said.

"Melanie signed me up for my birthday when I turned seventy-five. I go three times a week now. One for a spin class, one for cardio, and one for aquabatics with Alejandro."

"What on earth is aquabatics?" I asked.

"It's a bunch of old ladies in the pool shaking their booties to pop music."

"What's a booty? And who's Alejandro?"

"He's a twenty-four-year-old Brazilian trainer. Oh, Cyril, he's lovely! When we all behave ourselves, he gives us a treat and takes his shirt off. It's a good job we're all in the pool, as we'd need to cool off."

"Jesus," I said, shaking my head in a mixture of bewilderment and amusement.

"There's life in the old dog yet," she said, winking at me.

"I don't think I want to know."

"Actually, I think Alejandro might be a gay too," she said. "Like you," she added, as if I'd forgotten that I was one. "I could introduce you if you like."

"That would be great," I said. "I'm sure he'd like nothing more than to be introduced to a man old enough to be his grandfather."

"Perhaps you're right. He probably has a fella anyway. Well, you could always just come along to aquabatics and perv over him like the rest of us do. It's open to anyone over sixty."

"Please don't use that word, Mum," I said. "It sounds really creepy coming out of your mouth."

She smiled and looked out the window as the train began to move. We had a couple of hours' journey ahead of us to Cork City, followed by a bus to Bantry, and then I planned on hiring a taxi for Goleen from there.

"So anyway," she said. "Have you any news for me at all?"

"Not much. I bought a new vase for the front room."

"And you're only telling me now?"

I smiled. "It's a nice one," I said.

"And did you go on that date?"

"I did," I said.

"What was his name again?"

"Brian."

"And how did it go?"

"Not well."

"Why not?"

I shrugged. I'd spent the previous Thursday evening in the Front Lounge with a man in his fifties who had only come out of the closet after thirty-four years of marriage a few weeks earlier. None of his children were talking to him and he'd spent the entire evening bemoaning this fact before I found an excuse to leave. I hadn't the energy for any of that.

"You need to get out more," said my mother. "Go on more dates."

"I do occasionally," I said.

"Once a year."

"Once a year is enough for me. Anyway, I'm happy as I am."

"Do you go into the chat rooms at all?"

"Excuse me?"

"The chat rooms," she repeated.

"What chat rooms?"

"The ones where gay men meet other gay men. You send pictures to each other and say the age and type of man you're looking for and if you're lucky—"

"Is this a joke?" I asked.

"No, it's very popular among the gays," she said. "I'm surprised you haven't heard of it."

I shook my head. "I think I'll stick to the old-fashioned way," I said. "How do you know so much about this stuff anyway?"

"I'm a Silver Surfer," she said.

"A what?"

"A Silver Surfer," she repeated. "Oh, I'm very with-it, you know. I take computer classes in the ILAC Center every Wednesday afternoon with Christopher."

"Does he take his shirt off for you too?"

"Oh no," said my mother, shaking her head and grimacing. "And I wouldn't want him to either. He's a bit of a minger."

"You've been hanging out with your grandchildren too much," I said.

"Now that you mention them, did I tell you that Julia has a boyfriend now?" she asked, referring to her eldest granddaughter.

"Does she indeed?"

"She does. I caught them shifting each other in the living room last weekend. I said nothing to her mother but I sat her down later and told her to be very careful and keep a hold of her ha'penny. One fallen woman in the family is enough."

"What's shifting?" I asked.

"Oh come on," she said, rolling her eyes. "Are you alive at all, Cyril? Are you living in the twenty-first century?"

"I am," I protested. "I imagine it's some form of . . ." I hesitated with the words. "Some form of sexual activity, is it?"

"No, it's just kissing," she said. "But I suppose it can lead places. Young people can lose the run of themselves and she's only fifteen. Although he seems like a nice lad, from what I can tell. Very polite. He looks like he could be one of those Westlife fellas. If I was only sixty years younger, I'd have a go myself!" she added with a laugh. "Anyway. How's work? Am I missing much in the Dáil?"

"Not much, no. It's fairly quiet. I'll be ready for my retirement when it comes."

"You can't retire," she said, shaking her head. "I won't allow it. I'm not old enough to have a retired son."

"I've only got two more years," I said. "And then that's it."

"Do you know what you'll do then?" she asked me.

I shrugged. "I might do a little bit of traveling," I said. "If I have the energy. I'd quite like to see Australia, but I don't know if I'd be up for the journey at my age."

"A friend of mine from the Silver Surfers went to Australia last year," she said. "He has a daughter in Perth."

"Did he have a good time?"

"No, he had a heart attack on the plane and had to be shipped back from Dubai in a coffin."

"Great story," I said. "Encouraging."

"Ah well, he should never have gone. He'd had four heart attacks already. He was an accident waiting to happen. He was very good with spreadsheets, though. And email. I think you should go. And take me with you."

"Really?" I said. "You'd be interested in seeing Australia?"

"I would if you're paying," she said with a wink.

"It's an awful long way to go."

"They say First Class is very comfortable."

I smiled. "I'll think about it," I said.

"We could see the Opera House."

"We could."

"And climb the Sydney Harbor Bridge."

"You can. I don't like heights. And they wouldn't let me up with a crutch anyway."

"You're old before your time, Cyril, did anyone ever tell you that?"

The train pulled into Limerick Station and a young couple got on and sat in the two seats across the aisle from us. They looked as if they were in the middle of an argument and were sitting on it for the time being so as not to be overheard by an audience. She was clearly fuming and he was sitting with his eyes closed, his hands clenched into fists. An inspector walked past, checked their tickets, and when he moved on to the next car the man, who was about thirty, reached into his backpack and pulled out a can of Carlsberg. Holding the can with thumb and third finger he popped the ring-pull and a spit of foam flecked up onto his girlfriend's face.

"Do you have to?" she asked.

"Why shouldn't I?" he said, picking up the can and taking a long slug from it.

"Because it would be nice if, just for once, you weren't drunk by six o'clock."

"You'd be drunk every day too," he said, "if you had to put up with you."

I looked away and caught my mother's eye, who was biting her lip and trying not to laugh.

"And you can't smoke on here," said the woman, glaring at him when he took a pouch of tobacco from his bag and a packet of Rizlas. "It's a train."

"Is it?" he asked. "I thought it was a plane and I wondered why we were still on the ground."

"Fuck off," she said.

"You fuck off," he replied.

"You can't smoke in here," she repeated, raising her voice now.

"I'm not smoking," he insisted. "I'm just rolling them for later." He shook his head and looked across at me before glancing at my mother. "Have you had fifty years of this?" he asked me and I stared back at him. Did he think my mother was my wife? I didn't know what to say, so simply shook my head and turned back to look out the window.

"The trains are very comfortable these days, aren't they?" said my mother, pretending that none of that had happened at all.

"They are," I said.

"Not like in my day."

"No?"

"Of course, it's years since I was on a train. And when I left Goleen first, I took the bus, not the train. It was all I could afford."

"That was where you first met Jack Smoot, wasn't it?" I asked.

"No, it's where I met Seán MacIntyre. Jack was waiting for us at the other end." She sighed a little and closed her eyes for a moment as she traveled back in time.

"Have you spoken to Jack lately?" I asked.

"About a month ago. I'm planning my next trip over."

I nodded. We'd told each other almost every detail of our lives but had always avoided mentioning one particular night in Amsterdam almost thirty years earlier; it seemed easier not to talk of it even though we both knew that we'd been there.

"Can I ask you a question?" I said.

"Of course," she said. "What is it?"

"Why did you never go back?" I asked. "To West Cork, I mean. To Goleen. Back to your family?"

"Sure I couldn't have, Cyril. They threw me out."

"No, I know that. I mean later on. When tempers had softened."

She raised her hands in an uncertain gesture.

"I honestly don't think anything would have been different even if I had," she told me. "My father was not a man to change his mind on anything. My mother wanted nothing to do with me. I wrote to her a few times but she never replied. And my brothers, except perhaps for Eddie, were always going to side with Daddy because they each wanted the farm when he was gone and didn't want to get on the wrong side of him. And of course, Father Monroe would have chased me out of town on the back of a donkey if I'd dared to show my face. And your father . . . well your father was certainly never going to help me."

"No," I said, looking down at the table and scratching away at a mark there in a nervous gesture, one that took me back in time to the Dáil tearoom many years ago with Julian Woodbead. "No, I suppose not."

"And the second reason," she continued, "was an even more basic one. Money. It wasn't easy to travel in those days, Cyril, and what little I had I was saving in order to be able to survive. If I wanted a holiday, I took a couple of days in Bray, or if I was feeling adventurous, maybe I went as far south as Gorey or Arklow. And then, in time, I started going to Amsterdam every few years. The truth is, Cyril, that I never gave it much thought. Once I was gone, I mean. I never thought about going back. I never wanted to. I put it all behind me. Until today."

"Fair enough," I said.

Another noise from across the aisle and I stared at the young couple who, without my noticing, had moved seats so they were sitting next to each other. He had his arm around her now and she was leaning into his shoulder, her eyes half shut in tiredness as he reached down and kissed the crown of her head. At that moment, they looked like a picture postcard. Give it an hour, I thought, give it one shake of the train on the tracks and they'll be at each other's throats again.

"Young love," I said, smiling at my mother as I nodded my head in their direction.

"Been there," she said with a shrug and a roll of her eyes. "Done that. Bought the T-shirt."

Kenneth

We'd waited a few weeks to meet again after that day in the hospital chapel. It was possible, of course, that it had been pure coincidence, that the use of that phrase *a little hunchbacked Redemptorist nun* was just chance. Could it have been hers at first and somehow been adopted by Charles and Maude as if it had traveled across the city along with my small body? Or had Charles just thought the same thing and these had been the obvious words to use? And even the date of birth could have been happenstance. How many children, after all, were born in Dublin on the same day each year? And yet somehow I knew immediately that this was no coincidence; that we had been in each other's lives all these years without ever realizing who the other one was.

But, of course, our timing was terrible. My mother had just lost one son; she wasn't ready to deal with the implications of potentially finding another only a few hours later. She grew terribly upset when I sat down and told her what I suspected, and finally I had no choice but to call her daughter-in-law, whose number the hospital gave me, and dispatch her in a taxi for home. Afterward, I waited a couple of weeks to write to her—I didn't attend Jonathan's funeral, as much as I wanted to—making it clear that I needed nothing from her and that I was not one of those unfortunate souls seeking retribution for my abandonment many decades earlier. I simply wanted to talk to her, that was all, and for us to get to know each other in a way that we hadn't to date.

And in time, she replied.

Let's meet, she said. *Let's meet and talk.*

And so we met in Buswells Hotel, across the road from Dáil Éireann, one Thursday evening after work. I could barely keep still all day, so anxious was I about what lay ahead, but once I crossed the road I began to feel strangely at peace. The bar was fairly empty, save for the Minister of Finance sitting in a corner of the room with his head in his hands, apparently weeping into his Guinness, and I turned away from him, not wanting to get involved with whatever madness was going on over there. I looked around and saw Mrs. Goggin, as I still thought of her, sitting on the other side of the room, and gave her a wave as I approached and she smiled back nervously. She had a cup of tea in front of her that was almost empty and I asked her whether she wanted another.

"What will you be having?" she asked. "Will you be having a drink?"

"I might have a pint," I said. "I have a thirst on me after the day's work."

"Then perhaps you'd be good enough to get me one too."

"A pint?" I asked, surprised. "Of lager?"

"Of Guinness," she said. "If you don't mind. I might need it."

Somehow it made me happy that we were both going to be drinking; it would take the edge off, I decided.

"Sláinte," I said when I returned, lifting my pint, and she lifted hers too and we clinked glasses, failing to look each other in the eye as one is supposed to do at such moments. I didn't know what we were expected to do next and for a while we sat quietly, making small talk about the weather and the condition of the soft furnishings.

"Well now," she said at last.

"Well now," I repeated. "How have you been?"

"As well as can be expected."

"It's a terrible loss that you've suffered."

"Yes."

"And your daughter-in-law and the girls?"

She shrugged. "They're remarkably strong, all of them," she said. "It's the thing I most admire about Melanie. But I hear her at night, crying in her bedroom. She and Jonathan loved each other very much.

Of course, they were together since they were just teenagers, the pair of them, and he should have had many decades ahead of him yet. But then, you know what it is to lose someone too young, don't you?"

"I do," I said. I had told her about Bastiaan many years earlier when she was still employed in the tearoom.

"Does it ever get any easier?" she asked.

I nodded. "It does," I said. "You reach a point where you realize that your life must go on regardless. You choose to live or you choose to die. But then there are moments, things that you see, something funny on the street or a good joke that you hear, a television program that you want to share, and it makes you miss the person who's gone terribly and then it's not grief at all, it's more a sort of bitterness at the world for taking them away from you. I think of Bastiaan every day, of course. But I've grown accustomed to his absence. In some ways it was more difficult to get used to his presence once we started going out."

"Why is that?" she asked.

"Because it was new to me," I said, considering it. "I messed up everything when I was young. So when I finally found myself in a normal, healthy relationship I wasn't sure how to deal with it. Other people learn those tricks so much younger."

"He left them very well provided for all the same," she said. "Jonathan, I mean. So there's that to be grateful for. And Melanie is a wonderful mother. I've been living there since Christmas. But it's time I went back to my own place. I'm going back next week, in fact."

"You keep talking about your daughter-in-law," I said. "But how are *you*? How are *you* coping?"

"Well, I'll never get over it," she said with a shrug. "A parent never could. And somehow I have to find a way to cope with that."

"And Jonathan's father?" I asked, for I had never heard her mention him.

"Oh he's long gone," she said. "He was just a man I met. I can barely remember what he even looked like. The thing is, Cyril, I wanted a child, a child that I could keep, and I needed a man's help to make the baby. He wandered in and out of my life over the course of one night and that was as much as I ever knew of him or wanted to. Does that make me sound like a terribly wanton woman?"

"It makes you sound like someone who wanted to be in charge of her own destiny. Who didn't want anyone telling her what to do ever again."

"Perhaps," she said, considering this. "Anyway, the thing is, Jonathan was all that I needed from then on. He was a good son. And I think I was a good mother."

"I'm sure you were."

"Does that make you angry?"

I frowned. "Why would it?" I asked.

"Because I wasn't a good mother to you."

"I have no interest in blaming you for anything," I told her. "I said as much in my letter. I'm looking for no argument nor do I want any unpleasantness. I'm too old for that. We both are."

She nodded and looked on the verge of tears. "Are you sure about that?" she asked. "You're not just saying it?"

"I really am. There doesn't have to be any drama here. None at all."

"You must have had very loving parents to feel that way."

I thought about it. "Actually, they were very *strange* parents," I told her. "Neither of them were what you might call conventional people. And they had an extremely peculiar approach to parenting. Sometimes I felt as if I was little more than a tenant in their house, as if they weren't entirely sure what I was even doing there. But they never mistreated me, nor did they ever do anything to hurt me. And perhaps they loved me in their own way. The concept itself might have been slightly alien to them."

"And did you love them?"

"Yes, I did," I said without hesitation. "I loved them both very much. Despite everything. But then children usually do. They look for safety and security, and one way or another Charles and Maude provided that. I'm not a bitter person, Mrs. Goggin," I added. "I have no bitterness inside me at all."

"Tell me about them," she said.

I shrugged. "It's hard to know where to start," I told her. "Charles was a banker. He was quite rich, but he was always cheating on his taxes. He went to prison a few times for it. And when he was younger he always had a string of women on the side. But he was good fun. He was always telling me that I wasn't a real Avery, though. I think I could have done without that."

"That sounds quite mean on his part."

"I honestly don't think that he was trying to be cruel. It was more a matter of fact. Anyway, he's dead now. They both are. And I was with him when he went. I miss him still."

"And your mother?"

"Adoptive mother," I said.

"No," she said, shaking her head. "She was your mother. Don't be unkind."

Something about the way she asserted that brought tears to my eyes. Because of course she was right. If anyone had been my mother, it was Maude.

"Maude was a writer," I said. "You know that, don't you?"

"I do," she said. "I've read most of her books."

"Do you like them?"

"Very, very much. Her work has great compassion. She must have been a very caring woman."

I laughed, despite myself. "She really wasn't," I said. "She was a lot colder than Charles. She spent most of her time in her study, writing and smoking, emerging only occasionally in a fog to terrorize any visiting children. I think she just about tolerated my presence in the house. Sometimes she saw me as an ally and sometimes as an irritation. She's been dead a long time now, though. Almost fifty years. I think about her a lot, though, because one way or another she's become so much part of the Irish consciousness. The books, the films. The fact that everyone seems to know her. You know she's on the tea towel now?"

"The tea towel?" she asked. "What do you mean?"

"It's a writers' thing," I explained. "Do you know that picture, eight old men who were supposed to be the best of the best? Yeats, O'Casey, Oliver St. John Gogarty, the lot of them. The same picture is on posters and mugs and table settings and coasters. Maude always said they'd never let a woman on the tea towel. And for years, she was right. But then they did. Because she's right at the center of it now."

"It's not much of a legacy," she said doubtfully.

"No, probably not."

"And you had no brothers or sisters?"

"No," I said.

"Did you want any?"

"It might have been nice," I said. "I've told you about Julian in the past, of course. I suppose he was like a brother of sorts. Until I realized that I was in love with him. I only wish that I'd got to know Jonathan."

"I think you'd have liked him."

"I'm sure I would have. I liked him on that one occasion that we met. It seems quite cruel that you and I have only made this connection between us as a result of his death."

"Well, Cyril," she said, leaning forward and surprising me by her choice of words. "If there's one thing I've learned in more than seven decades of life, it's that the world is a completely fucked-up place. You never know what's around the corner and it's often something unpleasant."

"That's quite a cynical view of the world, Mrs. Goggin," I suggested.

"I'm not sure it is," she said. "And I think we might have to move past Mrs. Goggin now, don't you?"

I nodded. "I'm not quite sure what I should call you," I said.

"How about Catherine?"

"Catherine, then," I said.

"I never let anyone call me that in the Dáil," she said. "I needed to have authority in there. I remember once when Jack Lynch called me by my first name and I looked him right in the eye and I said, *Taoiseach, if you ever call me by that name again you'll be banned from the tearoom for a month*. The next day, I received a bunch of flowers and an apology note addressed to Mrs. Goggin. Nice man," she added. "Of course, he was from Cork too. Like me. But I didn't hold it against him."

"I never would have dreamed of calling you by your first name," I said. "I was terrified of you. Everyone was."

"Me?" she asked, smiling. "Sure I'm a sweetheart. I can remember you when you were a little boy," she added. "Do you remember that day you came in with your pal and pretended to be old enough to drink and I had to run you out of the place?"

"I do," I said, laughing as I remembered the joy that Julian could offer in those days with his mischief and his cheek. "But you took down one of the priests while you were at it."

"Did I?"

"You certainly did. I don't think anyone had ever spoken to him like that before. Let alone a woman. I think that was the thing that infuriated him the most."

"And good for me," she added.

"Good for you."

"He was the boy who was kidnapped, wasn't he?" she asked.

"That's right. Not long after that, actually."

"That was such a big story back in the day. They cut off one of his ears, didn't they?"

"One of them," I said. "And a finger. And a toe."

"Terrible," she said, shaking her head. "The papers were so cruel about him when they found out how he died."

"It was disgusting," I said, feeling the anger grow inside me. I had said that I felt no bitterness but whenever I remembered this I found that dangerous emotion lurking deep within my soul. "No one had spoken about him in years and they took such pleasure in telling the country what had happened to him. I remember a woman calling in to a radio show to say that she had felt such sympathy for him when he was a child but now she only felt disgust. It would be better for everyone, she said, if all the gays were rounded up and shot before they could spread their disease."

"But he wasn't gay, was he?" she asked.

"No, he wasn't."

"Poor boy," she said. "But then that's Ireland for you. Do you think the place will ever change?"

"Not in our lifetime," I said.

To my surprise, a moment later she placed her head in her hands just like the Minister for Finance on the other side of the room, and I reached across to her, worried that I had said something to upset her. "Mrs. Goggin," I said. "Catherine, are you all right?"

"I'm grand," she said, taking her hands away and offering me a half-smile. "Look, Cyril, there must be things you want to know. Why don't you just ask me?"

"I don't want to know anything that you don't want to tell me," I said. "Like I said, I'm not looking to cause you any trouble or pain. We can talk about the past or we can simply forget about it and look toward the future. Whatever you prefer."

"The thing is, I never *have* talked about it," she said. "Not to anyone. Not to Seán or to Jack. Not even to Jonathan. He knew nothing about you or what had taken place in Goleen in 1945. That's a regret now. I don't know why I never told him. I should have. He wouldn't have cared; I know he wouldn't. And he would have wanted to find you."

"I must admit," I said tentatively, "I am interested. I'd like to know what led you from there to here."

"Of course you would," she said. "There'd be something wrong with you if you didn't." She took a long pause and another sip from her pint. "I suppose," she said finally. "I suppose I should start with my Uncle Kenneth."

"All right."

"And now this is going back a long way, so you'll have to bear with me. I was brought up in a small village in West Cork called Goleen. Born in 1929, so I was only sixteen when these events took place. And I had a family, of course. I had a mammy and daddy like everyone has. And a gaggle of brothers, each one more feather-brained than the last except for the youngest one, Eddie, who was a nice fella but probably a bit too timid for his own good."

"I've never even heard of Goleen," I said.

"No one has," she told me. "Except those of us who come from there or lived there. Like me. And my family. And my Uncle Kenneth."

"Were you close with him?" I asked.

"I was," she said. "He was barely ten years older than me and always took a special interest in me because we had similar senses of humor and I was just crazy about him. Oh, he was so handsome, Cyril! He was the only man I ever truly fell in love with. Now, you must understand, he wasn't actually my blood uncle. He was married to my Auntie Jean, who was my mammy's sister. Kenneth himself was from Tipperary, if I remember right, but of course we didn't mind. Everyone loved him, you see. He was tall and funny; he looked a bit like Errol Flynn. And he could tell jokes and do wonderful impressions. He was a demon on the piano accordion and when he sang one of the old songs there was never a dry eye in the place. And I was only a

child at the time, really. Sixteen years old, just a silly girl with notions
in my head. I was mad for him and I saw to it that he was mad for
me too."

"How?" I asked.

"Well, I led him on, I suppose," she told me. "I flirted with him constantly and sought any opportunity to get him on his own. I didn't
even really know what I was doing but it felt good, I knew that much.
I would cycle my bike up to his farm and talk to him over the fence,
my skirt hiked up shamelessly. And I was pretty, do you see, Cyril? I
was a very pretty girl at that age. Half the lads in the village were always trying to get me to go to dances with them. But I only had eyes
for Kenneth. There was a lake on the outskirts of the village and I saw
him there one time with my Auntie Jean. It was late at night and they'd
gone for a dip. And the pair of them without a stitch on them. It was
an awakening for me. I saw the way he held her and the things he did
to her. And I wanted him to hold me like that, to do those things to me
too."

"And did you tell him?"

"Not for a while. You see, Kenneth and my Auntie Jean were a great
match, everyone said so. They walked around the village hand in
hand, which in those days was considered a bit brazen, even for a married couple. I think Father Monroe had a word with them about it. He
said it promoted immorality in the young, that if they weren't careful,
young boys and girls would be following their example and getting up
to all sorts. I remember Kenneth saying this to me and laughing his
head off. *Can you imagine, Catherine*, he said. *Jean and I holding each other's hands and suddenly Goleen turns into Sodom and Gomorrah!*

"And what did I do, only slip my hand inside his own and say that
maybe he should hold my hand instead for a while, and I can see the
look on his face even to this day. The shock and the desire. Oh, I loved
the power I had over him! The power I could sense in myself! You
won't understand this but it's something that every girl realizes at
some point in her life, usually when she's around fifteen or sixteen.
Maybe it's even younger now. That she has more power than every
man in the room combined, because men are weak and governed by
their desires and their desperate need for women but women are
strong. I've always believed that if women could only collectively

harness the power that they have then they'd rule the world. But they don't. I don't know why. And for all their weakness and stupidity, men are smart enough to know that being in charge counts for a lot. They have that over us at least."

"It's hard for me to relate to," I said. "I never had any power at all. I was always the wanter, not the wanted. I was always the one filled with desire, but in my whole life I think Bastiaan was the only man who ever desired me in return. All those boys when I was young, it wasn't me they wanted. It was just a body, it was just someone to touch and to hold. I might have been anyone to them, but Bastiaan was different."

"Because he loved you."

"Because he loved me."

"Well, you might have been better off. Girls can cause a lot of trouble and other men will forgive them for it if they have a chance themselves. I certainly didn't understand the trouble that I was causing. But, as I said, I liked how it made me feel and so I kept at it, making that man want me more than he'd ever wanted anyone before, and when I'd just about driven him to distraction and he could take no more he came up to me one day when I was on his farm and grabbed me to him, pressing his lips against mine, and of course I kissed him back. I kissed him like I'd never kissed anyone before or since. And then one thing led to another and before I knew it we were in the middle of what I suppose people would call an affair. I would call over to the farm after school and he would take me to the hayshed and off we'd go, rolling around, a pair of mad things."

"So he was the one?" I asked. "My father?"

"Yes. And the poor man was tortured about the whole thing," she said. "Because the truth is, he loved my Auntie Jean and felt terrible about the things he'd done. Every time we finished, he started to cry, and sometimes I felt bad for him and sometimes I just thought he was trying to have his cake and eat it. The only time I got frightened was when he said he'd leave Jean and we could run off together."

"You didn't want that?"

"No, that was too much for me. I wanted what we had and I knew full well that even if we did, he'd be bored with me within a month. It was the start of me feeling guilty about what I'd done."

"Yes, but you were still a child," I said. "He was a grown man. How old was he, twenty-five? Twenty-six?"

"Twenty-six."

"Then he was responsible for his own actions."

"He was, of course. But I don't think it would ever have crossed his mind to start something with me if I hadn't pushed and pushed and pushed. He wasn't the type. He was a good man; I believe that now. And eventually, once the excitement of what we were doing began to calm down, he broke it off with me and begged me not to tell a soul, and of course, young as I was and foolish as I was, I took the greatest umbrage and said I was having none of it, that I was not going to be dropped by him, not after he'd had his fun. But he was adamant and one day he just started crying in front of me again, saying that the person he was turning into was not the person he had ever wanted to be. He said that he'd taken advantage of me, of my youth, because he was weak and he wished that he could go back and change it all. He begged me to forget everything, wanting everything to go back to the way it had been before, and I don't know, but something about his upset told me that I had done a terrible thing. And I cried too and we hugged each other and we parted as friends and we swore that we would never speak of what had taken place between us and that it would never happen again. It was over, that was what we agreed. And I think, if events hadn't conspired against us, then we both would have stood by that. It would have ended. And in time, it would all have been forgotten. Just a terrible mistake that we'd made years ago."

"So what happened?" I asked.

"Well, you happened, of course," she said. "I found that I was going to have a child. And back then, in the country, there was no greater disgrace than this. I didn't know what to do or who to confide in and in the end my mother found out and she told my father and he told the priest and the next day that bastard stood on the pulpit of the Church of Our Lady, Star of the Sea, and denounced me to my family and all our neighbors as a whore."

"He used that word?"

"He did, of course. Sure the priests ran the country back then and they hated women. Oh my God, they *hated* women and anything that had to do with women and anything to do with women's bodies or ideas or desires, and any chance that they had to humiliate a woman or bring her down, they would take full advantage of it. I think it was because they all *wanted* women so badly and they couldn't have one. Except when they did, of course, on the quiet. Which was going on too. Oh, Cyril, he said some terrible things about me that morning! And he hurt me. If he could have, he would have kicked me to death, I believe that. And he made me leave the church in front of the whole parish and he threw me out and disgraced me, and me only sixteen years of age and not a penny piece in my pocket."

"And Kenneth?" I asked. "Did he not help you out?"

"He tried, in his way," she said. "He came out of the church and tried to give me money and I ripped it up in his face. I should have taken it! And in my childishness I blamed him for what had happened, but it wasn't all his fault, I see that now. I have my share of blame to take. Poor Kenneth was terrified that someone would find out that he was the father and of course he would have been ruined if anyone had. The scandal would have killed him. Anyway, I took the bus to Dublin that same day and found myself living with Seán and Jack until the night when Seán's father came up to kill the pair of them and he nearly managed it too. How Jack Smoot survived I will never know. And that was the night that you were born. Seán was lying in the living room, his body growing cold, and Jack was lying next to me in a pool of his blood that intermingled with my own as you came screaming into the world. But I had a plan, you see. I'd arranged the plan months in advance with the little hunchbacked Redemptorist nun who helped girls like me. Fallen girls. The plan was that she was going to take the baby away from me when it was born and give it to a family who wanted a child of their own but for whatever reason couldn't have one."

I looked down at the table and closed my eyes. That was my birth. That was how I had come to Dartmouth Square, to Charles and Maude.

"The truth is," she continued, "I was just a child myself. I could never have taken care of a baby. We wouldn't have survived, either of us, if I'd held on to you. And so I did what I thought was right. And I still think I was right. So I suppose if we're going to have any future together, Cyril, you and I, then that's what I have to ask you. Do you believe that I did the right thing?"

Goleen

The Church of Our Lady, Star of the Sea, was bathed in sunlight that afternoon as we arrived. We walked slowly and silently up the path together, making our way toward the graveyard, and I stood back as she began to walk around the stones, reading the names of the dead.

"William Hobbs," she said, stopping at one and shaking her head. "I remember him. He was in school with me in the early forties. He was always trying to put his hands up girls' skirts. The master used to beat him black and blue for it. Look, it says he died in 1970. I wonder what happened to him?" She stepped away and looked at a few others. "And this is my cousin Tadhg," she said. "And what must have been his wife, Eileen. I knew an Eileen Ní Breathnach back in the day. I wonder did he marry her?" And then, stopping at a particularly ornate stone, she stopped and put a hand to her mouth in fright. "Oh Good Lord," she said. "It's Father Monroe! Father Monroe is buried here too!"

I came over and looked down at the inscription on the marble. *Father James Monroe*, it said. *1890–1968. Beloved parish priest. A kind and saintly man.*

"No mention of his children on the headstone, of course," she said, shaking her head. "I bet the parishioners denounced the women who bore them as they lowered him down. The women are always the whores; the priests are always the good men who were led astray."

To my surprise, she knelt down by the side of the grave. "Do you remember me, Father Monroe?" she asked quietly. "Catherine Goggin. You threw me out of the parish in 1945 because I was going to have a child. You tried to destroy me but you didn't. You were a terrible monster of a man and wherever you are you should feel shame for the way you lived your life."

She looked as if she wanted to rip the stone out of the ground with her bare hands and break it over her knee but finally, breathing heavily, she stood up and moved on. I couldn't help but wonder what might have happened to her if the priest had shown her compassion instead of cruelty, had he intervened with my grandfather and helped him realize that we all make mistakes. If the parish had rallied behind my mother instead of casting her out.

I wandered off and looked around the gravestones myself and stopped short when I saw one for Kenneth O'Ríafa. There was no particular reason that I should have noticed it except for the fact that beneath his name were the words: *And his wife Jean*. I checked the dates. He was born in 1919, which would have been exactly right. And dead in 1994, the same year I had sat by Charles's bed as he passed away. Who, I wondered, had sat by Kenneth's? Not Jean, for she had passed five years earlier in 1989.

"Well now," said my mother, appearing before me and looking down at the inscription. "There he is. But do you see what they did?"

"What?" I asked.

"Auntie Jean died first," she said. "She would have had her own gravestone. *Jean O'Ríafa*, it would have said. *1921–1989*. But when he died they must have taken her stone away and made it all about him. *Kenneth O'Ríafa. And his wife Jean*. The afterthought. The men just get it all, don't they? It must be great for them all the same."

"No children on the headstone," I said.

"I see that."

"And that's my father," I added, more to myself than anyone else, the words low and quiet. I didn't know how to feel. I didn't know how I was supposed to feel. I had never known the man. But the way my mother told it, he wasn't necessarily the villain of the piece. Maybe there were no villains in my mother's story at all. Just men and women, trying to do their best by each other. And failing.

"All these people," she said sorrowfully. "And all of that trouble. And look, they're all dead now. So what did it all matter in the end?"

When I looked around, Catherine was gone. I turned my head toward the doors of the church and caught sight of her as she disappeared inside. I didn't follow for a while but continued to wander around the graves, reading the names and the dates, thinking about the children who had passed away at such young ages and wondering what had happened to them. I found myself lost in thought for a long time and then finally I turned around and stared up at the mountains that surrounded me, at the village that I could see down the road. This was Goleen. This was where my mother and father were from. My grandparents. This was where I had been conceived and where, in a different world, I might have grown up.

"You're praying," I said a few minutes later as I entered the church to find my mother on her knees on the padded rest before one of the pews, her head bowed to the back of the seat in front of her.

"I'm not praying," she said. "I'm remembering. Sometimes the two things look alike, that's all. This was it, Cyril, you see. This was where I was sitting."

"When?" I asked.

"The day I was sent away. We'd come to Mass together, all of us, and Father Monroe dragged me up onto the altar. I was sitting right here in this very seat. The rest of my family were lined up next to me. It's so long ago and yet I can see them, Cyril. I can see them all as if it was yesterday. Still alive. Still sitting here. Still looking at me with humiliation and disgust in their eyes. Why did they abandon me? Why do we abandon each other? Why did I abandon you?"

A sound from the side of the altar startled us, and a young man of about thirty appeared from the sacristy door. A priest. He turned to us and smiled, leaving something on the altar itself before walking over.

"Hello," he said.

"Hello, Father," I said, as my mother stayed silent.

"Are you just visiting?" he asked. "It's a beautiful day for it."

"Visiting and returning," said Catherine. "It's a long time since I last set foot inside this church. Sixty-three years, if you can believe it. I wanted to see it one last time."

"Are your people from here?" he asked.

"They are," she said. "The Goggins. Do you know them?"

He frowned, thought about it and shook his head. "Goggin," he said. "It rings a bell. I think I've heard some parishioners mention a Goggin family from back in the old days. But as far as I know now, there's none left here. They scattered, I suppose. To the winds and to America."

"Most likely," said my mother. "I'm not looking for any of them anyway."

"And will you be staying with us for long?" he asked.

"No," I said. "We go back to Cork City tonight. And then the train back to Dublin in the morning."

"Well, enjoy," he said, smiling as he turned away. "We welcome everyone in the parish of Goleen. It's a wonderful place."

My mother snorted a little and shook her head. And as the priest returned to the altar, she stood up, turned her back on him and walked out of the church for the last time, her head held high.

EPILOGUE

2015 Beyond the Harbor on the High Seas

Dartmouth Square

I woke to the sound of Pugni's *La Esmerelda* rising through the old bones of the house on Dartmouth Square and settling, somewhat muffled, in the top-floor bedroom where I had spent the night before. Looking through the skylight to the blue sky above me, I closed my eyes and tried to recall how it had felt to wake in this same bed, seven decades earlier, a lonely and attention-starved child. The memories, which had always been such a part of my being, had dimmed slightly over the last twelve months. It saddened me that no strong emotions came back to me now. I tried to recall the name of the housekeeper who had worked for Charles and Maude and been something of a friend to me throughout my youth, but everything about her was gone. I searched for the face of Max Woodbead, but it was a blur. And as for why I was even there? That took a moment too, but then it came back to me. A happy day, at last; a day that I thought would never come.

I hadn't slept well: a combination of anxiety, the temozolomide tablets that I had been taking daily at bedtime for the last five weeks and the sporadic fits of insomnia that they in turn caused. My doctor had told me that they might also result in decreased urination but, quite the contrary, I had gone to the bathroom four times during the night. On the third occasion, I'd continued downstairs in search of a snack only to find my seventeen-year-old grandson, George, lying on the sofa in a T-shirt and boxer shorts, stuffing his face full of crisps while watching a superhero movie on the enormous television that dominated a wall of the living room.

"Shouldn't you be in bed?" I asked, opening the fridge and looking inside in the vain hope that there might be a sandwich waiting in there for me.

"It's only one o'clock," said George, turning around and dragging the hair out of his eyes as he held the open crisp packet in my direction. I tried a few: awful.

"Is that a beer you're drinking?" I asked.

"It might be," he said.

"Should you be drinking that?"

"Probably not. You won't tell anyone, will you?"

"Not if you get one for me too."

He grinned and jumped up, and a minute later we were sitting next to each other, watching as grown men in capes leaped from building to building looking manly and utterly furious with the world.

"Do you like this kind of thing?" I asked, confused by the sweeping action that was taking place before me.

"It's a whole universe," he said. "You have to watch all the films to understand them."

"Seems like a lot of work to me."

"It's worth it," he replied, and we continued to watch silently until the credits rolled and he muted the television and turned to me in delight. "Told you," he said. "Wasn't it great?"

"No, it was terrible."

"I'll give you a box set. If you watch them all, you'll appreciate them. Trust me."

I nodded. I'd take it if he gave it to me. And I'd probably watch them, just so I could tell him that I had.

"So," he said. "Are you excited about tomorrow?"

"I suppose so," I said. "I'm more nervous than anything else. I just want everything to go well, that's all."

"No reason why it shouldn't. Do you know that this will be the first wedding I've ever been to?"

"Really?" I said, surprised.

"Yeah. I suppose you've been to lots."

"Actually, no. Not as many as you might think. My own wedding day to your grandmother rather put me off them."

He sniggered. "I wish I'd been there," he said, because of course he'd heard the story many times. Alice liked to wheel it out whenever she felt like annoying me. "It sounds like it was hilarious."

"It really wasn't," I said, smiling despite myself.

"Oh come on. You must be able to see the funny side of it now, though, right? It was more than forty years ago."

"Don't say that in front of your grandmother," I warned him. "Or she'll beat you with a stick."

"I think even she thinks that it's funny."

"I'm not so sure that she does. Even if she pretends to."

He thought about this and shrugged. "You know I have a new suit?" he said.

"I heard."

"It's my first one. I look the business in it."

I smiled. Of all my grandchildren, George was the one with whom I connected best. I'd never been particularly good with children in general—I'd never really known any—but somehow we seemed to amuse each other and I enjoyed his company. How thin he was, I thought, looking at him now, his long pale legs so skinny as they stretched out before him. And how fat I had grown. When had that happened? The body going to flab. My mother had been hounding me about it for years, encouraging me to go to a gym, but there was something comforting to me about it. I was an elderly man, after all, with the kind of girth one expected from an elderly man. It was strange, though, since I wasn't much of an eater, wasn't much of a drinker and yet was still going to seed. Not that it mattered now anyway. What would be the point of losing weight when I had only a few months left to live?

Dragging myself from the bed now, I put my dressing gown on and went downstairs to find Liam, Laura and the three children busying themselves with breakfast.

"How did you sleep?" asked Liam, looking across at me.

"Fine," I said. "Do you know, I haven't slept in this house since the night my father was buried."

"Your adoptive father," he replied.

"I suppose. When was that anyway? Twenty-one years ago? Doesn't feel that long."

Laura came over and put a mug of coffee in my hands. "How's the speech coming along?" she asked.

"It's getting there."

"You haven't finished it yet?"

"I have. Almost. It was too short at first. And then it was too long. But I think I have it now. I'll give it another run-through before we leave."

"Do you want me to have a read of it?" asked Julian, looking up from his book. "I could put in some dirty jokes."

"Good of you," I said. "But, no. I'll wait and surprise you with it."

"Now, showers," said Laura, all business. "There's six of us, so five minutes for everyone or the tank will run cold, OK?"

"I need more time than that to wash my hair," said Grace, my youngest grandchild, twelve years old and already obsessed with her appearance.

"I'm going first," said George, charging from the room and up the stairs with a speed that nearly knocked me off my feet.

"I'll go back to my room," I said, taking my tea with me. "I'll have one when George is finished."

It was difficult at times to believe that this was the same house in which I had grown up. After Alice and Cyril II moved into their own apartment and Liam and Laura took it over, they did so much remodeling that it was like a different place. The ground floor had been gutted entirely so the living area and kitchen blended into one enormous living space. The first floor, which had once belonged to Charles, held the master bedroom and George's room. The second floor, where Maude's office had once been and where she had written her nine novels, contained two bedrooms, one each for Julian and Grace, while the study itself was long gone. The top floor was the guest room, my room, and this had remained largely unaltered. It both felt like home and didn't feel like home. If I looked around, the house was alien to me, but if I closed my eyes and walked up the stairs, inhaling the scent of the place and feeling the presence of the ghosts of the past, then I might have been a child again, longing for Julian to come over and ring the doorbell.

Half an hour later, when I returned downstairs, I was taken aback to see a boy in the hallway, looking at some of the family photographs that decorated the wall. He was standing in the exact spot that had once held the chair where Julian had been sitting when I first laid eyes on him sixty-three years earlier. As he turned to look at me, the way the light was coming through the glass above the door recalled him to me instantly, with his messy blond hair, good looks and clear complexion. It was a deeply unsettling moment, and I had to reach out to the bannister for a moment to prevent myself from falling over.

"Julian?" I said.

"Hello, Cyril."

"It is you, isn't it?"

"Of course it is. Who else would it be?"

"But you're dead."

"Yes, I know."

I shook my head. This wasn't the first time I had seen him recently. He'd been coming to see me more and more over recent months and always at the most unexpected moments.

"Of course, you're not really here," I said.

"Then why are we having this conversation?"

"Because I'm ill. Because I'm dying."

"You have a few months yet."

"Do I?"

"Yes," he said. "You die three nights after Halloween."

"Oh. Is it painful?"

"No, don't worry. You go in your sleep."

"Well, that's something, I suppose. What's it like anyway, being dead?"

He frowned and thought about it for a few moments. "It's hard to say," he said eventually. "I'm getting even more action than I ever did before, so that's something."

"It's not as if you were ever short of it in the past."

"No, but now that I'm dead I get to have sex with women from all periods of history. I did it with Elizabeth Taylor last week. She looks like she did in *Father of the Bride*, so, you know, she's not short of offers. But she chose me."

"Lucky you."

"Lucky her," he said, grinning. "And Rock Hudson made a pass at me."

"What did you do?"

"Told him I wasn't into dirty queers."

I burst out laughing. "Of course you did," I said.

"No, I'm only kidding. I let him down gently. Although Elizabeth wouldn't speak to me again afterward."

"Will there be someone up there for me?" I asked hopefully.

"One person," he said.

"Where is he?" I asked. "I never see him."

"He doesn't visit you?"

"He hasn't so far."

"Be patient."

"Sir?"

I shook my head and looked back at him but he'd changed now, he was no longer Julian but a young boy, a boy of about seventeen. I took another step down so I could see him without the sunlight blinding my vision.

"Yes?" I said.

"Are you all right?"

"I'm fine. Who are you?"

"I'm Marcus," he said.

"Oh yes," I said, feeling as if I could just sit down on the lowest step and never stand up again. "The famous Marcus."

"You must be Mr. Avery? George's grandfather?"

"I'm his grandfather all right. But please don't call me that. Call me Cyril."

"Oh, I couldn't do that."

"Why not?"

"Because you're . . . you know . . ."

"An old man?"

"Well, yes. I suppose."

"I don't care," I said, shaking my head. "I hate it when people call me Mr. Avery. If you don't call me Cyril, I won't call you Marcus."

"But what else would you call me?"

"I'll call you Doris," I said. "See how you like that."

"OK, I'll call you Cyril," he said, smiling as he extended his hand. "It's nice to meet you."

"Why are you standing out here all on your own anyway?" I asked. "Is no one looking after you?"

"George let me in," he said. "Then he went up to his room because he looked in the mirror and found an eyebrow out of place. And I didn't want to go in there alone," he added, nodding toward the kitchen, from where I could hear the sounds of the rest of the family gathered together.

"I wouldn't worry if I was you," I said. "They're very friendly. They don't bite."

"I know," he said. "I've met them all before. But I just feel nervous going in on my own."

"Well, I'll wait with you," I said.

"You don't have to."

"I don't mind," I said. "You look very smart."

"Thank you," said Marcus. "I bought a new suit."

"So did George."

"I know. We bought them together. We had to be careful that we went for completely different styles and colors. We didn't want to look like, you know, Jedward or something."

I smiled. "I actually know who they are," I said. "Believe it or not. Despite my advanced years."

"Are you excited about today?" asked Marcus.

"People keep asking me that," I said.

"It's a big day."

"It is, yes. I never expected to see it, if I'm honest."

"And yet here it is."

"Indeed," I said.

We sat in silence for a few moments and then he turned to me enthusiastically. "Is it true that Maude Avery was your mother?" he asked. "Your other mother, I mean?"

"She was," I said.

"We study two of her books in school. I really like her work."

"Do you see that room up there?" I said, pointing up through the staircase toward a door on the second floor. "That's where she wrote them."

"Not all of them," said Maude, stepping out of the front room and leaning up against the wall, lighting a cigarette.

"No?"

"No. Before you came to live with us, when it was just me and Charles in the house alone, I used to write downstairs. After he'd gone to work, I mean. The light was better, frankly. And I had more chance of catching people in the gardens."

"You always hated them," I said.

"They had no business being there. It's private property."

"It's really not."

"It *is*, Cyril. Please don't contradict me. I find it so tiresome."

"Sorry," I said.

"Anyway, after you showed up, I moved upstairs. I needed space. And privacy. And as it turned out, I was better off up there. I produced some of my best work in that study."

"You know you're on the tea towel?" I said.

"I've heard," she replied, rolling her eyes. "It's disgusting. The idea of people wiping their dirty coffee cups on my face. How on earth do people think that's a compliment?"

"It's immortality," I said. "Isn't that what every writer craves? To have their work read long after they're dead?"

"Well, it's not as if anyone reads it when they're alive."

"Your books have lived on. Doesn't that make you happy?"

"Not in the slightest," she said. "What does it matter? I should have done a Kafka. Had everything burned after I died."

"Kafka has a museum in his honor."

"Yes, but he told me how much he hates it. I'm not sure whether he means it, of course. That man could moan for Czechoslovakia."

"It's the Czech Republic now," I said.

"Oh don't be difficult, Cyril. It's such an unattractive trait."

"I can't believe you're friends with Kafka," I said.

"*Friends* might be overstating it a little," she said with a shrug. "*Acquaintances* would be a better word. You know, Emily Dickinson is here too. All she does is write poems about life all the time. The irony! She keeps asking me to read them. I refuse, of course. The days are long enough as it is."

"Mr. Avery?"

"What?" I glanced to my left, to Marcus.

"I said, I can't believe I'm in the same house where Maude Avery wrote her books."

I nodded and said nothing for a few moments and was glad to see George bounding down the stairs with the enthusiasm of a puppy.

"How are my eyebrows?" he asked, looking from one of us to the other.

"Perfect," I said. "But I'll keep a close eye on them as the day goes on, just in case."

"Would you? That would be great."

"Should we go inside?" asked Marcus.

"I thought you were already in there," said George.

"No," said Marcus. "I was waiting for you."

"Granddad," said George, frowning at me. "You haven't been perving over Marcus, have you?"

"Shut up, George," I said. "Don't be so ridiculous."

"I'm only joking."

"Well don't. It's not funny."

"I don't mind. I perv over him all the time. But then I'm allowed."

I shook my head. "I'm going inside," I said. "I heard the sound of a champagne cork being popped."

I led the way into the kitchen, where Liam and Laura were dressed in their finery, glasses before them, while Julian continued with his book and Grace listened to her iPod.

"Hi, Marcus," said Laura.

"Hello, Mrs. Woodbead," he replied politely, and I noticed that neither she nor Liam invited him to call them by their first names. My son made some remark about a football match that had taken place the night before and within a minute the two were engaged in a lively conversation about it. From what I understood, the team that Liam supported had beaten the team that Marcus supported and the young lad was raging about it.

"You look very smart, Cyril," said Laura, reaching over and giving me a kiss on the cheek.

"Thank you," I said. "As do you. If I was forty years younger, of a different sexual orientation and my son wasn't married to you, I'd be after you in a heartbeat."

"I'm sure there's a compliment in there somewhere," she said, pouring me a glass.

"Isn't this just fucking great?" said George, raising his voice now, and we all turned to see him beaming in delight as he held his glass aloft.

"Watch the language," said Liam.

"I'm just saying," said George. "To find love when you're . . . you know . . . so ancient. It's fantastic. And then to be able to stand up before the world and declare it out loud. It's fucking *brilliant*."

I smiled and nodded. It was, I supposed.

"It's probably more unexpected than anything else," I said.

"No, he's right," said Laura, raising her glass. "It's fantastic."

"*Fucking* fantastic," insisted George, pulling Marcus close to him and giving him a quick peck on the lips. I couldn't help but notice how both his parents looked away instinctively, while his younger brother and sister stared and giggled, but it felt very good to watch the moment as he pulled away and they looked into each other's eyes, a couple of teenagers who had found each other—and would surely lose each other again for someone else soon but were happy right at that moment. It was something that never could have happened when I was that age. And yet for all my happiness at seeing my grandson happy and secure in who he was, there was something terribly painful about it too. What I would not have given to be that young at this time and to be able to experience such unashamed honesty.

"We should start to make a move," said Laura a moment later, glancing at the clock. "Shouldn't the car be here by now?"

As if by magic, the doorbell rang and everyone jumped. "Right," said Liam. "Has everyone got everything they need? Dad, you have your speech?"

"It's right here," I said, touching my breast pocket.

"All right. Let's go then," he said, marching down the hallway and opening the front door, where two silver Mercedes were waiting to bring us into the city center.

Yes or No

"They haven't taken all the signs down, I see," said Charles as we drove along.

"What's that?" I asked, turning to look at him, surprised to see how neatly he'd fit into the seats opposite me, next to Liam, George and Marcus.

"The signs," he said. "On the telephone poles. There's still quite a few up. The referendum was months ago now."

"People are lazy," I said. "There'll be a storm sooner or later and they'll blow the rest down."

"I'm bloody glad it's over," he said, shaking his head.

"Me too."

"I knew it would bring out the worst in people."

"Well, you were right."

"It brought out the worst in you too," said Charles.

"What do you mean?" I asked, offended.

"You know what I'm talking about," he said. "Engaging with all those morons on your phone. Arguing with complete strangers."

"It was impossible not to," I said. "I spent long enough staying silent. There was a chance to speak up at last and I took it. And I'm glad I did."

"Well, you won, so you don't have to worry about it anymore."

"But all it did was remind me how unkind people can be. And how ugly."

"And you weren't part of that ugliness?"

"I don't think I was," I said.

"All right," said Charles, taking an iPhone from his inside pocket. "Let's take a look, shall we?" He pressed a few buttons and scrolled down. *"Why are you so afraid of people being happy?"* he read. *"Why can't you just live and let live?* Now, who wrote that . . . oh let me see . . . oh yes! @cyrilavery!"

"That was that awful Mandy woman," I said. "Every day, tweeting about how her relationship was more valid than anyone else's. Just a vile human being."

"And this one," said Charles. *"If your relationship was a successful one, then you wouldn't care what other people did in their own private lives.* Also @cyrilavery."

"An awful married couple," I said. "Tweeting all day long, every day, to practically no followers. They must just have sat on their phones from morning to night. They deserved all the abuse they got."

"And how about this one?" he asked. *"You must be filled with self-loathing to be behaving the way you are."*

"I know that one!" I said. "That was to that gay guy who was voting No."

"Well, didn't he have the right?"

"No!" I shouted. "No, he didn't! He was just looking for attention, that's all. Fuck him! He was betraying his own people."

"Oh, Cyril," said Charles. "Don't be a moron. And as for that radio debate—"

"They asked me on!" I said.

"You should have just ignored them all," said Charles with a smile. "It's the best thing to do with your enemies. And anyway, they lost, didn't they? By a landslide. Their day is over. They're the past. They're history. Just a bunch of bigots screaming into the void, desperate to have their voices heard. They were always going to lose. And you know what? The world didn't fall off its axis when it happened. So stop being so angry. It's over. You won, they lost."

"But *I* didn't win, did I?" I said.

"How do you mean?"

I shook my head and looked out the window. "When the vote was passed," I said, "I was watching the news reports on the television. And there was David Norris. *It's a little bit late for me,* he said, once he knew that it was a Yes and that the country had changed forever. *I've spent so much time pushing the boat out that I forgot to jump on and now it's out beyond the harbor on the high seas, but it's very nice to look at.* And that's how I feel. Standing on the shore, looking out at the boat. Why couldn't Ireland have been like this when I was a boy?"

"That, I can't answer," said Charles quietly.

"Look," said George, pointing out the window, and I turned around to him in a daze.

"What?" I asked.

"We're here," he said. "There's Ignac."

The car pulled over to the side of the road, and I saw Ignac, Rebecca and the children standing outside, talking to Jack Smoot, who was in a wheelchair but had shown up as he had promised.

"I can't believe it," said Marcus. "I've read all of his books three times. He's my favorite writer ever."

"I'll introduce you to him," said George proudly. "Ignac and I are big pals."

I smiled. It was nice to hear.

"Right," I said, opening the door. "Let's do this."

"Wait!" cried George. "Does anyone have a mirror?"

"You're only gorgeous," said Marcus. "Stop looking at yourself."

"Shut up."

"You shut up."

"Both of you shut up," said Liam.

We got out of the car into the sunlight, and I felt a slight pain in my head and remembered that I had forgotten to take my morning pill. It didn't matter too much; we'd be passing by the house later on the way to the reception and I could stop in for a moment and take it then. The doctors had told me that I had six months but if Julian was to be believed, it was more likely to be just over two. Three days after Halloween.

"Just like me," said Charles, waving goodbye to me as I stepped out onto the street. "A brain tumor. Turns out you're a real Avery after all."

I laughed, then turned to look at the registry office before me. Death was coming for me, I knew that. But I didn't want to think about it today.

The New Ireland

As I entered the registry office, I saw Tom hovering near the front, looking handsome in his wedding suit, his daughter, son-in-law and grandchildren standing next to him with wide smiles on all their faces. When he saw me, he raised a hand in the air and I walked over, my arms open wide to embrace him.

"Didn't we get great weather for it all the same?" said Jane, leaning over and giving me a kiss on the cheek.

"We did," I said. "Somebody up there is in our corner."

"And why wouldn't they be?" said Tom, smiling. "When you look back, Cyril, did you ever think a day like this would happen?"

"Honestly?" I said, shaking my head. "No."

"Do you have your speech ready?"

"Everyone is very concerned about this speech," I said. "It's written. It's the right length, there's a few good jokes in it and I think we'll all be happy."

"Good man."

"We weren't sure we were even going to make it," said Jane.

"Why?" I asked, frowning.

"Don't," said Tom.

"His arthritis," she said, lowering her voice a little. "He's been having a terrible time of it."

"But it's fine today," said Tom. "There's not a bother on me."

"Sure none of us are as we were," I said. "We'll all get through the day anyway."

"It'll be very strange to have a son who's only a few years younger than me," he said.

"I won't be calling you Dad, if that's what you're expecting," I said, smiling. He was a nice man, Tom. I didn't know him very well, but from what I'd seen, I liked him. An architect by career, he'd been retired for thirteen years and had a nice bungalow in Howth with a great view over Ireland's Eye. I'd been out there a couple of times already and he'd always made me feel very welcome.

My mother and he had met on Tinder.

A hand touched my arm and I turned around to see Ignac standing behind me. "They're here," he said.

"They're here," I repeated, turning back to Tom, my voice rising like an excited child, and we took our leave of each other, he going to the front of the registry office, me going to the back, while everyone else took their seats. As the guests sat down, I said a quick hello to Jack Smoot, who shook my hand and told me that there was nothing that would ever have brought him back to Ireland except for this.

"And I'm getting the fuck out of the place first thing tomorrow morning," he added.

The doors opened and that's when I saw her. Standing at the end of the aisle, eighty-six years old without a care in the world and looking as happy as any bride on her wedding day. Next to her, my ex-wife Alice and Cyril II—she'd stayed with them the night before—who surrendered her to me.

"I want to see you at the reception," said Alice, as she kissed me. "All the way to the end, do you hear me?"

"You don't need to worry," I said, smiling.

"Because if you disappear, I'll do a Liam Neeson, do you hear me? I have a very particular set of skills and I'll hunt you down, I'll find you and I'll kill you."

"Alice," I said. "I give you my solemn oath. I'll be the last one to bed tonight."

"Right," she said, smiling and looking at me with something approaching love in her eyes. "You've been warned."

They took their seats, leaving my mother and me together.

"You look wonderful," I said.

"You're not just saying that, are you?" she asked nervously. "I'm not making a fool of myself?"

"How could you be?" I asked.

"Because I'm eighty-six years old," she said. "And eighty-six-year-old women don't get married. Especially not to seventy-nine-year-old men. I'm a cougar."

"Sure everyone can get married now," I said. "It's the new Ireland. Did you not hear?"

"Cyril," said a voice behind me, and I turned around.

"You're busy today," I said. "I thought I wouldn't see you for another few days yet."

"You can come over later tonight if you want," he said.

"No," I replied, shaking my head. "You said Halloween. Actually, you said a few days after Halloween."

"All right," said Julian. "I was just checking. We'll have a bit of a laugh when you do get here, though. There's a couple of girls I want us to double-date with."

I rolled my eyes. "You don't change, do you?" I asked.

"Just be my wing-man, that's all," he said. "You don't have to actually *do* anything."

"Halloween," I said. "A couple of days after."

"*Fine*," he said.

"Are we set then?" asked my mother.

"I am if you are."

"Is he here? He didn't change his mind?"

"Oh he's here all right. You're going to be very happy, the two of you. I know you are."

She nodded and swallowed a little as she smiled at me. "I feel that too," she said. "He was wrong, wasn't he?"

"Who?" I asked.

"Father Monroe. He said I'd never have a wedding day. He said that no man would ever want me. But here that day is. He was wrong."

"Of course he was wrong," I told her. "They were all wrong. They were wrong about everything."

I smiled and leaned forward to give her a kiss on the cheek. I knew this might be one of the last things I got to do in this world, leaving my mother in the hands of someone who would take care of her, and I felt great relief to know that there was a family, a big family, who would look after her when I was gone. She needed that. She'd missed out on it all these years. But now here it was.

"Walk slowly," said a voice from behind me, and I turned around and felt my heart jump in delight. "Remember, you're on a crutch and she's an old lady."

"You came!" I said.

"I heard you were looking for me. Julian told me."

"I didn't think I'd see you. Not till, you know, till it was my turn."

"I couldn't wait," he said.

"You look exactly the same as you did on that last day. In Central Park."

"Actually, I'm a few pounds lighter," he said. "I've been on a fitness drive."

"Good for you." I stared at him and felt the tears forming in my eyes. "Do you know how much I've missed you?" I asked him. "It's been almost thirty years. I shouldn't have had to spend all that time on my own."

"I know, but it's nearly over. And you haven't done a bad job of it at the same time, given the mess you made of the first thirty. The years apart will feel like nothing compared to what we have before us."

"The music's started," said my mother, clutching me to her.

"I have to go, Bastiaan," I said. "Will I see you later?"

"No. But I'll be there in November when you arrive."

"All right." I took a deep breath. "I love you."

"I love you too," said my mother. "Shall we go?"

I nodded and stepped forward, and slowly we made our way down the aisle, passing the faces of our friends and family, and I delivered her into the arms of a kind man who swore to love her and take care of her for the rest of her life.

And at the end, when the entire congregation broke into applause, I realized that I was finally happy.

Acknowledgments

With thanks, as ever, to Bill Scott-Kerr, Larry Finlay, Patsy Irwin and Simon Trewin.

A Reader's Guide for
The Heart's Invisible Furies

By John Boyne

In order to provide reading groups with the most informed and thought-provoking questions possible, it is necessary to reveal important aspects of the plot of this novel. If you have not finished reading *The Heart's Invisible Furies*, we respectfully suggest that you wait before reviewing this guide.

1. In the opening pages of *The Heart's Invisible Furies*, the unmarried and pregnant sixteen-year-old Catherine Goggin is denounced as a whore and ostracized by the parish priest of Goleen. Pages later, Sean MacIntyre is beaten to death by his father in the Chatham Street flat he shared with Catherine and his lover, Jack Smoot. How did these early scenes frame the influence of the Catholic Church and the patriarchal state of 1940s Ireland? What did they reveal about societal regard for women and intolerance for homosexuality at the time? How did they prefigure themes that were to develop throughout the novel?

2. In accordance with her "Great Plan" for her son, Catherine sacrifices her place in his upbringing so that he may have a better life than she could provide. Keeping in mind the social attitudes toward single mothers in 1950s Ireland, in what ways do you think Cyril did or did not have a better childhood with his adoptive parents?

3. During her lifetime, Maude Avery winces at what she refers to as "the vulgarity of popularity." Considering that

Maude specifically endeavours to write as a woman, do you think her negative perception of popularity had something to do with patriarchal strongholds in Ireland? Might she have taken a different regard for literary acclaim if more female voices populated culture and politics? Further, could her posthumous fame suggest that she had been a precursor of shifts in Irish consciousness?

4. *The Heart's Invisible Furies* charts many of Dublin's haunts and landmarks, from the Gresham Hotel on upper O'Connell Street to the Shelbourne on the other side of the Ha'penny Bridge, or from the Palace Bar on Fleet Street to Bewley's and Switzer's on Grafton Street. How do you think the experience of reading the novel differs depending on one's familiarity with the city? You might refer to your own connections, or lack thereof, to Dublin or Ireland.

5. Were you ever taken aback by the violent incidents scattered throughout Cyril's lifetime? Did you find comic relief in some of the novel's darker moments?

6. What did you think of the representation of Irish political figures, such as Éamon de Valera and Charles Haughey? Can fiction, such as *The Heart's Invisible Furies,* be used to critique historical narratives dominated by "great men"? Might fiction also provide a site to acknowledge those who were written out of popular history? Who might these be?

7. Cyril's early twenties were defined by the dangers of being gay in the 1960s and his intense longing for intimacy. Do you think his numerous sexual encounters with other men exacerbated his frustration and loneliness during this time of his life? Why or why not?

8. The climax of Cyril's discontent in Ireland, to put it mildly, can be seen in the hours after he marries Alice, when he considers committing suicide by jumping, naked, from a balcony of the Shelbourne Hotel. Instead, he chooses life and flees to Amsterdam. How did you interpret this scene?

For instance, could his flight indicate a form of rebirth for Cyril or the death of a particular version of himself? Were you angered by his actions and the pain they caused for Alice and Julian?

9. Cyril learns to differentiate between the feelings he had for Julian in his youth and the mutual exchange of romantic love he experiences with Bastiaan. Do you think that the young Cyril was more enthralled by the idea than the reality of Julian? In your view, what makes a healthy and stable relationship?

10. Edda Van den Bergh's suggestion that Cyril abandoned Ireland causes him to feel "unexpected stirrings of patriotism in a soul that I had always thought devoid of such parochial bullshit." What are the features of patriotism or nationalism with which Cyril would not identify?

11. It is in Amsterdam that Cyril and Bastiaan first meet Ignac, who they will later think of as their son. Did the moment in which Ignac's biological father, Damir, is killed remind you of Sean McIntyre's death and Cyril's birth on Chatham Street, thirty-five years previously? How might it be significant that Jack Smoot stabs and kills Damir?

12. Do you think that Cyril's exposure to homophobia in Part II: Exile prompts a revision to the idea that Ireland was a uniquely bigoted or "backwards" place? You could refer to the stigma that is attached to AIDS in New York City as well as Ireland, or the hate crime in Central Park in which Bastiaan is tragically killed.

13. Upon his return to Ireland in the 1990s, how had Cyril's relationship with himself changed and what effects did this have on his capacity to relate to others? Can you list some of the ways Ireland itself had changed? Thinking of the country's continued progression into the twenty-first century, what remnants of "old Ireland" might be identified in the expressions of some characters in later years?

14. As readers, academics and writers, do you think some characters used literature to grapple with their pasts? Do you see writing as an act in which "the heart's invisible furies" find expression or healing? In a similar vein, do you think that John Boyne's novel attempts to reconcile Ireland's history with its present?

15. How did you react when Catherine and Cyril revisit Goleen in County Cork? Were you surprised by how forgiving Catherine was of Kenneth, Cyril's biological father?

16. For decades, Cyril was continually reminded that he was not a "real Avery" by his adoptive father, Charles. How does Cyril's relationship with his own sons compare to Charles's approach to fatherhood? By the novel's end, how might the non-nuclear dynamics of the house on Dartmouth Square challenge traditional definitions of a "real" family?

17. In the summer of 2015, Ireland became the first country to legalize same-sex marriage by popular vote. Consider the reference that Cyril makes to David Norris, an Irish politician and patron of LGBT rights:

    It's a little bit late for me, he said, once he knew that it was a yes and that the country had changed forever. *I've spent so much time pushing the boat out that I forgot to jump on and now it's out beyond the harbor on the high seas, but it's very nice to look at.* And that's how I feel. Standing on the shore, looking out at the boat. Why couldn't Ireland have been like this when I was a boy?

    Do these bittersweet words suggest that pain and suffering are necessary components in the push for positive change? What issues from Cyril's youth might remain in this "changed" Ireland, and what new battles are his grandchildren tasked with that previous generations might not have faced? Seeing the drastically different social climates of the novel's beginning and its end, does *The Heart's Invisible Furies* galvanize optimism for tackling even the most difficult challenges of today?

About the Author

John Boyne was born in Ireland in 1971. He is the author of eleven novels for adults, five for younger readers, and a collection of short stories. His 2006 novel *The Boy in the Striped Pajamas* sold nine million copies worldwide and has been adapted for cinema, theater, ballet, and opera. John has won three Irish Book Awards and many other international literary awards, and his novels are published in over fifty languages. He lives in Dublin.

johnboyne.com
@john_boyne

Also by John Boyne